"Even though Christopher Conlon's *The Unspoken* is the author's coming-of-age novel, it is written with a mastery of style that a writer twice his age might envy. He has painted his characters, especially Robin Withers and Heather Seabright, with such luminous strokes that we are drawn to them as they move through the riveting twists and turns of this fascinating story. Conlon, a writer in full command of his craft, has a lyrical style that illuminates these characters and makes them come alive. Christopher Conlon is an extraordinary talent and a storyteller of enviable perception and sensitivity. There is little doubt we'll have many more fine novels from this exceptionally gifted writer."

—Aldo P. Magi, Editor Emeritus, *The Thomas Wolfe Review* (1995)

THE UNSPOKEN

The Lost Novel

Christopher Conlon

Mango Biscuit Press
2015

Copyright © 1992, 2015 by Christopher Conlon
All rights reserved.

Mango Biscuit Press
Silver Spring MD
ISBN: 1503183378
ISBN 13: 9781503183377

They talked of this and that, their little superficial ideas about themselves, and of their circumstances and tastes, and always there was something, something that was with them unspoken, unacknowledged, which made all these things unreal and insincere.

H.G. Wells: *Love and Mr. Lewisham*

CONTENTS

Introduction: Speaking *The Unspoken*		xi
Acknowledgments		xvii
THE UNSPOKEN		
One	Strange Islands	1
Two	Waiting For Morning	111
Three	All The Beautiful Demons	236
Four	The Song Of The Earth	359
Five	A Dark And Vicious Place	565
Six	Where The Shore Meets The Sea	665
About The Author		757

THE UNSPOKEN

The Lost Novel

INTRODUCTION

Speaking *The Unspoken*

"This is a very long novel and I am ashamed to make it longer by writing a preface to it," an apologetic W. Somerset Maugham stated in the Introduction to his great *bildungsroman, Of Human Bondage*. I know how he felt. *The Unspoken* is also a very long novel, and yet a few words about it seem necessary at the outset.

I began writing what would become *The Unspoken* in 1987, while still a student at Humboldt State University in Arcata, California. "Drowning," which appears in the text as a novel-within-the-novel being written by the protagonist, Robin Withers, was the first section completed. After graduation I joined the Peace Corps, where I served from the middle of 1988 to the end of 1990 as an English teacher in Botswana; it was there, in a little village in the middle of the Kalahari Desert called Tsabong, that roughly the first half of the main narrative was finished. Much of this was written in the pre-dawn hours, by the light of an oil lamp, on a small Sears portable typewriter. I remember that in the winter months it would be so cold—of course the house had no heat or electricity—that I would sit pecking away at the keys with my hands ensconced in fingerless wool gloves and blankets from my bed wrapped over my shoulders. Only endless mugs of hot tea kept me going.

At the end of my service I traveled for a while, as many volunteers do. Finding myself in Ecuador for a couple of months, I enjoyed the luxury of a mid-priced hotel in downtown Quito and worked on the first forty or fifty pages of Chapter Four, "The Song of the Earth."

Then it was time to go home. A relative in Shepherdstown, West Virginia offered me free lodging for a time while I got my life sorted out. That time stretched to six months, feverishly productive months which concluded in July of 1991 when, at last, I typed the words "The End" on the last page of the manuscript. I can clearly recall that moment, and the odd feeling I had walking around little Shepherdstown's streets later that day—part melancholy, part euphoria.

Of course what I'd finished was only the first draft. I had a solid year's revision work still ahead of me. I got a job teaching English as a Second Language in the DC Public School system and moved to a basement apartment on Washington's Rhode Island Avenue; it was there that, in the summer of 1992, I finally, once and for all, completed *The Unspoken*.

Though I was still a mostly unpublished writer, I secured an agent for the book quickly enough—actually two agents, a husband-and-wife team. Their enthusiasm for the project seemed boundless, at least initially; they were convinced they were representing a "major new American novel" by a "major new American novelist." But they were quickly disabused of those notions when they began trying to submit the manuscript to publishers. Most refused outright to even read it, citing its extraordinary length and utterly uncommercial subject matter—the story of a sensitive, artistic, middle-class boy's coming of age? And the young man's dream is to be a *writer?* These fields were already, to put it mildly, well-plowed.

But the rejections that came from the houses brave enough to give *The Unspoken* a look were interesting. In discussing the manuscript with my agents more than one editor used the word "brilliant" (I remember "gorgeously written" too), but when it came to the prospect of actually publishing the thing, all of them demurred. The husband-half of my agenting team wrote to me, "We have to find an editor who will fall in love with this book and fight for it." But we never found that editor, and after a year or so of trying, the agency released the novel back to me.

I made my own efforts, this time with smaller houses—independents, university presses. There were nibbles, but no bites. One nibble from a university press seemed, at least briefly, serious enough that I contacted a friend who had read the novel for a "blurb" that might be used on the book's cover. That friend, Aldo Magi of *The Thomas Wolfe Review*, wrote a lovely paragraph of praise; but as it turned out there was no occasion to use it. The press's final decision was negative. Another agent tried with the novel for another year. Again nothing. And so the saga of *The Unspoken* seemed to be at an end.

The experience was devastating. For some years I wrote relatively little, confining myself to the occasional short story or poem. My confidence was broken. My mood toward my writing career was black.

Eventually, though, I managed to move on, and after a few more years I was getting books of poems and stories published. I edited several anthologies. I even became a novelist at last—*Midnight on Mourn Street* appeared in 2008, followed by *A Matrix of Angels*, *Lullaby for the Rain Girl*, and *Savaging the Dark*. These books sold modestly but were critically well-received. A couple of them got significant award nominations. As a novelist, I had arrived.

But *The Unspoken* was never far from my mind. I knew it was one of the strongest pieces I'd ever written—and certainly the most ambitious. I didn't think of it as a "trunk novel"; to me it was still vivid and alive, even if nothing happened on it for a decade at a time. Themes, settings, and narrative strategies from the book found their way into later works of mine (especially *Lullaby for the Rain Girl*). Now and then friends would ask to read this unpublished early work, and reactions were always extremely encouraging. I wondered again and again if there might not be some way of bringing my "lost" novel into the light at last.

That way has now appeared, and you hold in your hands the result.

I've resisted the temptation, twenty years on, to rewrite parts of the book; to begin doing so would be to initiate a process that might never, I fear, quite end. It's true that I wouldn't write the novel the same way today. But as Conor McPherson has remarked, "As you grow older…you may gain a little wisdom. But you lose your recklessness." He was discussing being a playwright in mid-career, but the same holds true for novelists. Many of the elements of *The Unspoken* that I would excise now—the long serpentine sentences, the often unconventional punctuation, the extended lyrical metaphors—are, I think, the very elements that give this youthful novel its vitality, its pleasing recklessness. *The Unspoken* is a young man's book. Now in middle age, I refuse to mute that young writer's passionate voice. All these years later, it's finally time for him to have his say.

That young man's influences are fairly obvious at times. Reading the book now, I hear quite clear echoes of Tennessee Williams, Thomas Wolfe, James Baldwin, Carson McCullers, William Styron, Truman Capote; I was enthralled with the rolling, musical cadences of their work. Somerset Maugham is also present—the early Maugham who wrote *Of Human Bondage*. The "camera eye" section early in "Strange Islands" apes, perhaps a little too obviously, Christopher Isherwood. Structurally the novel is indebted to Proust, whose *Remembrance of Things Past* (as it was titled in English then) I read and loved on many a long, blazing-white Kalahari afternoon. And yet it seems to me that this young writer's voice, if a tad derivative at times, is mostly his own—that he's found a way to absorb and transform those influences into something uniquely his.

A final note. Whenever a writer publishes a novel about a young writer, especially a young writer of the novelist's own age, race, and gender, the question invariably arises: Is it autobiographical? In his "To the Reader" note for his own classic *bildungsroman*, *Look Homeward Angel*, Thomas Wolfe asserted, "Fiction is not fact, but fiction is fact selected and understood, fiction is fact arranged and charged with purpose." So yes, the novel is autobiographical; but no, it's not autobiographical at all. Nothing depicted in *The Unspoken* actually happened. And all of it is true.

C.C.

ACKNOWLEDGMENTS

The original pages of *The Unspoken*, produced on a manual typewriter, were first retyped to a Mac-format set of computer discs in the early 1990s by a personable young woman hired for the task named Katie; alas, her last name and whereabouts today are unknown, at least by me. Around the year 2000 my friend Steve Schlich converted the old Mac-format discs to IBM discs. In 2014 another friend, Norman Maynard, was able to take the old IBM discs and convert them to Word files usable on my 21st century HP computer. My gratitude to Katie, Steve, and Norman is deep.

   I also wish to thank my old friend Aldo Magi for his early support of this novel, and in particular for the wonderful blurb. It took twenty years, but that blurb is finally in print.

CHAPTER 1
STRANGE ISLANDS

Didst thou ever see a lark in a cage? Such is the soul in the body....

John Webster:
The Duchess of Malfi

1

Yesterday I came home. It was midmorning; a heavy mist, not quite rain, filled the sky. I turned the lock of the familiar front door and stepped into a foyer that younger versions of myself had crossed many thousands of times: and although I knew it had not been occupied for the better part of a decade, the house was dim and my fingers instinctively flipped up the light switch. Nothing, of course, happened. So I went to the front window and pulled open the drapes, securing them with the same sashes I recalled from my youth.

The furniture had been covered with great sheets of plastic shortly after my father passed away (brain cancer, an appalling, torturous death) and they were there still, submerged now under a layer of thick gray dust. There was a comfortable feeling of familiarity within me as I looked in at the covered form of the sofa in the living room and saw also the draped coffee tables and bookcase. But commingled with this contentment was the uneasy sensation of being in the presence not just of something dead, but of a thing murdered by a tribe of cannibals. Moving around the downstairs, through the dining room and into the kitchen, I had forgotten how many items financial reality had forced me to strip from the house when I had moved to the east, belatedly resuming my college career—the television, the dining table and chairs, even the refrigerator. Adding to the skeletal impression was the fact that I had long ago removed all the hanging pictures and stored them in the basement, leaving the walls a stark and staring white-turned-gray.

After opening all the downstairs curtains, which managed to achieve a sort of hazy, half-lit effect, I found a flashlight stored under the kitchen sink and discovered to my surprise that its batteries were still capable of producing a feeble glow. Duly armed, I made my way up the stairs. I stood in the dark hall staring at the door to my old room and the other doors up the corridor and suddenly had a peculiar sensation of—what to call it? Proportionlessness? The doorways seemed not to be the dimensions they had been. The hallway seemed shorter and narrower than I remembered. The ceiling was too close to my head. It was the same sensation I have heard described by adults who revisit their old grammar schools and view with astonishment the low drinking fountains and tiny desks; but where they might feel amusement, I felt only discomfort.

I pulled open the curtains of the hall window slowly, watching the gray light beam into the corridor illuminating the thousands of tiny dust-dabs suspended in the still air. When I moved my hand through the beam the dabs swirled gracefully like colorless blossoms, sparkled like gems. I stepped into my old room and opened the curtains there. The view was obscured, as it had always been, by the limbs of the huge pepper tree growing in the yard. I opened the window, the fragile branches making soft scratching sounds against the glass panes, and turned to look at the room itself. I moved past the plastic-cocooned bed and opened the closet door: there were all the old things, unmoved, untouched except by dust, of no possible significance to anyone but myself. Clothes in styles fifteen years out of date. Childhood board games. Boxes of long-forgotten school papers. Old books.

I moved then through the connecting door to the bathroom. Perhaps it was my memory of ever-glistening porcelain, but the bathroom seemed to have an especially dirty and abandoned look. Filth covered everything: the sink, the countertop, the bathtub; the toilet, dry for years, was covered with layer upon layer of unidentifiable grime. My footprints left sharp outlines as I moved across the tile floor to the sink. The mirror above it was covered with gray; taking up an old rag, I cut a swath gently through the dust and revealed a reflection of myself.

I was for a moment shocked by what I saw.

I am a man in my late thirties, with a receding hairline and streaks of silver around my temples, a thin, somewhat pale face, and glasses which encircle a pair of deep blue eyes. All of these familiar features stared back at me from the mirror, and so it took me a moment to comprehend my reaction. It was a question of context. The face which I now found more-or-less satisfactory in my daily life, which was comfortable to me, was very different from the ones which used to stare back at me from this mirror, in this bathroom, years ago; and as I had wiped the dust away from the glass, something in me had expected to see one of those earlier selves. Something in me had assumed that when it looked at itself here, in this place, it would see a small boy with long butter-colored hair; or perhaps a teenager with smooth young skin and bright eyes. Certainly it had not expected the gaunt stranger it had seen, who—in appearance at least—was little more than a specter of those boys.

A few minutes later I was downstairs again, tossing the big dust-covers out onto the grass. All things considered, it did not seem an impossible proposition to make the house livable again:

I would need to get the electricity and water and telephone reconnected, buy a few things, give the rooms—those I intended to occupy—a thorough cleaning. I knew I would find various creaking doors and frozen faucets, but these did not concern me overmuch. At any rate, I was not taking up permanent residence.

I could not be certain, however, just how long I *would* be here. At first I had thought of coming only for a day or two, to have a look around and retrieve some diaries and photo albums. But as I made the drive from New York, as the days passed and the miles rolled by on the odometer, it occurred to me that I might stay longer. I had no pressing business waiting for me. I knew of several friends eager to sublet my apartment if my visit were to become extended. And perhaps, I thought, I might at last arrive at a decision on the house: for years I had dallied about, unsure what to do. I had thought of selling, but had not been able to bring myself to it. I might have rented it, but something disturbed me about the idea of unknown bodies and lives passing through these doorways. I had never seriously considered living in it again. And so it just sat; I had paid my property taxes on it and hired a man to care for the lawn. Other than that I did nothing at all.

I should tell you that I am a writer. However, since in looking over my last paragraph I see I have dropped in a casual reference to New York, I had best disabuse you of certain notions before they have a chance to form. I do not mean to suggest that I am a well-known writer hobnobbing in elite Manhattan literary circles. I have published two books, the first travel essays, the second poetry, which have received generally good notices and sold almost no copies. But in certain respects I am lucky. My agent, a man with the alliterative name of S. Simon Stillman, is one of an exceedingly rare breed: a literary agent who is a true practicing idealist. He runs a small agency, only a handful of clients, which makes its bread and butter from cookbooks which frequently manage to crawl onto the bestseller lists—but his real interest is in "literary" writing, and his really quite tireless efforts have seen through the publication of several books, including mine, which otherwise might not have been published at all.

Two weeks ago, on the kind of not-quite-sweltering afternoon one gets in New York in late spring, the kind of afternoon in which pedestrians' eyes seem to glaze over in a unique variety of panic at the now-irrefutable evidence of an imminent summer's inferno, Simon and I had lunch. I would ask you to visualize in your mind not the cool elegant interiors of the Four Seasons or "21" but rather what is called a "family restaurant," with counter seating and booths, paper place mats, and huge plastic-embossed menus with color photographs of veal cutlets and Salisbury steak platters. Simon was wearing a pale suit which accentuated his already sallow, pinkish complexion; he is thin to the point of illness, with unevenly-cut white hair and a pair of hopeless, rather lovesick eyes. He gives one the impression he might fall over dead at any moment.

I described to him my idea for a book, an autobiography of my youth written in the form of a novel.

"It's been done," he said in his weak, husky voice. "Henry Adams. Isherwood."

"Not the way I want to do it," I said. I told him my ideas: that while staying to the basic truths involved and never actually lying, I would feel free to utilize all the equipment of fiction—motif, metaphor, stream of consciousness—and by so doing arrive at an account more real, more vivid than any straightforward recitation of facts.

I will not bore you with the details of the conversation. It is enough to say that at the end of it I asked Simon if he thought he would be able to get an advance from somebody for the book.

"I can try," he said in his perpetually-regretful tone, wiping ice cream from his lips. "Do a proposal for me. And make it sound commercial. Publishers want proof that Robin Withers can write something that will actually sell copies. Lie if you have to."

I smiled. "I'll need to go back home," I said. "At least for a day or two. To get some old papers—letters, stuff like that. Photo albums."

He nodded and his sad eyes looked at me. "That's all the way across the country, isn't it?"

"Mm-hm. I'll drive it. I'll take a week each way."

"What about your classes?"

"School's out. I've got two months free, unless I decide not to renew my contract. Then I'd have all eternity."

He smiled wistfully. "I'll see what I can do, Robin," he said. "Meanwhile, go ahead. Do your go at it."

Do your go is one of Simon Stillman's trademark expressions. Before I could do, however, my go, I had to have my car serviced; arrange for my landlady, a beautiful little woman in her eighties named Mrs. McKay, to feed my cat Marcel; and finish out some paperwork at school (did I suspect all along that I would decide not to return? that I had had my fill of five-paragraph freshman compositions and fluffy young girls' poems about shuddering autumn leaves?). These things took several days, longer than I had intended, but at last, ten days ago, I made my exit.

No one who has failed to travel across the country at a leisurely pace can possibly understand the United States. I have felt this for years, probably since my first such journey—with a young woman who will feature prominently in this narrative—when I was nineteen; and I was reminded again of the fact as I made my way across its awesome vastness. This was not a pleasure trip; I rarely stopped for sightseeing; still, I was moved by the seemingly endless succession of cities and towns and cultures, by the flowing beauty of the Kansas wheat fields and Mississippi River: a majestic continent unsurpassed by any I have toured. I made a slight detour in Colorado to visit my cousin Priscilla and her friend Koofie, neither of whom I had seen in several years, and give them the possibly unsettling information that I was writing a book in which they would both appear. I must say they took it well. Priscilla laughed and asked if I would use their real names.

"No, I'll change the names," I said. "To protect the guilty." Which I have done.

And so it was that yesterday I came home. "Home" in my case, where I spent the first two decades of my life and where I sit at this moment—typing at a makeshift table in the kitchen as a rain-filled night descends outside—is located in a town called Wind Point, a tiny village on the southern Oregon coast: so named because it is situated at the very tip of a sort of terrestrial outgrowth, a point, which juts several miles into the Pacific Ocean. The reference to wind is apt too, for it is often whippingly fierce here; but in fact the town was named after its founder, a prospector of the mid-eighteen hundreds with the unlikely name of Jedediah Hopeweller Wind (the Third, no less).

One reaches Wind Point by means of the old Scully Road, a poorly-paved one-lane affair with deep cracks and chuckholes and a broken-down, rusty guardrail. More than once, drivers from Greyfield or Hollowstone—towns Wind Point residents call "the mainland"—have, if they have had a bit to drink, perhaps, run clean off the road, sailed through a hole in the safety rail, and splashed straight into the Pacific. Some have lived to tell of it; others have been fished out later, sometimes days later. Although the road itself is not difficult to negotiate, the constant fog and rain make it nonetheless hazardous. Windows mist; tires slip; visibility, especially at night, can be no more than a few feet. Headlights switched to low display nearly nothing; those on high illuminate only the boiling white clouds like formless sea-monsters before them. Indeed, to reach the town, one journeys almost as to another planet: at night, at least, the fog rolls in and surrounds everything so that the traveler, as he makes his way along the old Scully Road, thinks himself cut off entirely from familiar shapes and warm lights. Before him, the fog—behind him, out of the glare of beaming eyes, nothing but flat starless dark. It seems a long, uneasy journey in the night; it is in fact less than five miles.

Then, materializing out of the void, a lighted sign: *Wind Point, pop. 1550, elev. 10. Where the Shore Meets the Sea.* It is an attractively painted sign, or was once: the legend, however, is misleading, for there is no shore at Wind Point, only craggy colorless rocks, a harbor, and a sea-softened pier. Other lights, now, follow upon the first—dim, flickering, isolated and lonely in appearance. A single naked bulb brightens the grime-veined door of Riley's Salvage; the salvage itself can just be glimpsed, out beyond the main building, as an aimless conglomeration of twisted, silent shadows. Farther along, just as Riley's bulb is swallowed into the receding dark, a small cluster: a cafe, closed for the night, announcing *Great Burgers and Shakes*; and, across the street from it, a line of shops including a hardware store, beauty parlor, and bakery.

A stop sign now; on the right, past the cross-street, can be seen the glow of the Wind Point Shopping Center, where sits a mist-shrouded grocery, liquor store, five-and-dime, savings and loan, and children's clothing shop; past this, on the left, is the Town Center Cinema, the marquee still blazingly lit though the last show exited hours ago. Then a long stretch of blackness, broken only by the quiet, moody glow of the Public Library, a huge old Victorian structure rising forbiddingly out of the night like a dark sentinel.

The road curves. On the left, set in among grass silver in the darkness, are the city's government offices; past these, a primary school and non-denominational church. On the right, just beyond an almost sheer drop-off only yards from the road (protected by a firm-looking, much newer guardrail, and warned of by several *Caution* and *Curve Ahead* signs nearby), is the glistening, oily sea; and the harbor, a set of blurred sea-shadows. The road traces the path of the rocky land's end for some distance until at last it curves away, back in the direction from which it came, and arrives at the residential district of Wind Point.

A right turn brings the traveler into a set of narrow crisscrossing streets with parked cars on either side. The houses, most of them, are old, and big: Victorians from the early part of the century, built when the town held promise (never fulfilled) as a major fishing port. There are clusters of more modern dwellings, especially on some of the narrower side-streets, but their bland housing-tract appearance seems incongruent among the aged attic windows and front porches. Most of the cars on the streets are ten years old or more; even the newer ones give the appearance of age, for the damp salt air blisters and rusts them prematurely. Trees, especially huge pepper trees that loom like drooping specters over the street, obscure many of the houses; their tiny, slender leaves are a constant soft covering over the lawns and autos. Rain-faded bicycles lie on the lawns along with baseball bats, rubber tires, sprawled water hoses. The effect would be one of almost absurd Americana were it not for the night mist blurring everything like a ghostly cloak; and the rain, just now beginning to patter the windows and bicycles, bringing with it a gusty wind that rattles glass and creaks boards but somehow nonetheless fails to dispel the omnipresent fog.

At the end of a particular street, then, in the belly of a particular cul-de-sac, is the Withers residence. It is not unlike most of the other houses in the block: a nice two-story affair, paint reasonably fresh, lawn nicely mowed, bushy pepper tree obscuring much of its northern end; it has its problems, as all houses of this vintage do—sagging steps, a porch that leaks annoyingly; but the overall effect is one of a fine residence, solid, beautiful in its way. Its exterior appearance has altered little over the past thirty years. A photograph from decades before reveals that the tree was smaller once, the steps were solid flat planes, boyhood toys littered the lawn; but the differences are so slight that this fog-filled night might be now or years ago. It might be now or years ago that a light is switched out in a second story window, leaving the house in darkness; now or years ago that the window is opened narrowly and gossamer curtains can be seen to billow in the breeze.

We may approach this window. The curtains make a smooth, sighing sound as we near them, as we float like a camera-eye through the pepper tree's elastic limbs, feel the soft and mist-covered leaves on our face. The wind, whipping up now through the tree's upper branches, makes a foreboding sound, vaguely threatening, like distant thunder; tiny rain droplets drizzle down the branches and run from the leaves, stretching like momentary spiderwebs before they snap and tumble earthward.

When we reach the window, hover next to the open crack and flowing curtain, we hear breathing. For a long moment it is even, deep, growing deeper: sleep overtaking the room's occupant. But then there is a sudden intake, nearly a gasp, and the rustle of bed sheets.

Soon the room is quiet again.

We pass beyond the curtain, slip into the room itself, and study it from a high vantage point. It could be a boy's room or a girl's. The basketball and sports magazines in one corner suggest the former; but the orderly array of books, record albums, hand-drawn pictures, and pop-star photographs give the room a feminine feel. The dresser is old-fashioned, polished oak with a big mirror on top. A simply-patterned throw-rug covers the floor. The bed is brass, quite large, with a lacy spread; its color is impossible to discern in the darkness but it is light-toned; perhaps lavender.

The occupant of the bed, now: again, veiled as the figure is by darkness, it might be male or female. A child, at any rate. Its face is turned on its side and we can see that the hair is even lighter than the bedspread; blonde, anyway, if not actually silver or white, collar length, covering the ears in a not-unappealing disarray of sleepiness. One arm is uncovered, or rather covered only by a pajama sleeve, and the hand, slender and delicate, twitches. Moving a bit nearer we can make out that we are looking at a boy—though one with remarkably unmasculine features. His cheeks, round, finely boned, appear to have the softness of ripe peaches but not their color: even in the dimness, the complexion is obviously pale. The lips, through which breath enters and escapes in quiet sighs, are perhaps too large for the face, giving them a somewhat exaggerated, painted-on appearance. The nose is tiny and upturned, almost elfin. The eyes we cannot see, but the closed lids suggest they are exceptionally large; the lashes are lightly graceful, wands through which small tremors pass.

His age is difficult to judge; he might be only eight or nine. If that is his age, and if his name is Robin Withers, we can make certain assumptions about what is crossing his mental landscape just now: distant images of the San Francisco Giants at Candlestick Park, the sound of bats snapping at balls, the crowd roaring like a seashell held to the ear; spooks and walking corpses in the awful night, courtesy Lovecraft and Blackwood and Edgar Allan Poe; Sonya Skyler, an extraordinarily blonde angel of light who sits in front of him in English and homeroom and who once actually and truly spoke to him, two magnificent, unexpected words soaring across the space of a hallway: *Hi, Robin!*; snatches of music; his father in the shadows of the upstairs hallway, the heavy clump-clump of his boots passing the boy's room (an unpleasant image, curiously mixed in his mind with the phantom grotesques of Poe); and his mother, her hair a curtain of dark curled silk spilling onto the shoulders of her white robe, her face, nearly round as the moon, pale as his own, Siamese-shaped eyes like bits of sky; her hands, small, short-fingered, scooping into bowls of sugar-sticky cookie batter; his head in her lap, she humming an aimless and beautiful melody behind the softly flickering TV downstairs; pre-dawn doughnuts and warm white bags from the bakery....

But if we look more closely at the face, we see it has a certain development, a kind of maturity, which suggests greater age. The boy turns onto his back and we see the face fully, the mouth half-open. His child's teeth are gone; this is an older boy. His eyelids twitch, he sighs suddenly; then his breathing becomes steady again.

If we glance at the room now, we see it has changed: once the room of an eight- or nine-year-old, it now has many more books, the sports materials are gone, and there in the desk drawer, were we to peak under the stacks of school papers and pencils and protractors, we would discover a magazine with pictures of naked women. Records and papers are strewn about in boy-confusion. Above the desk, taped to the wall, a group of cards: one with a grinning dinosaur on the front is inscribed: *Happy 13th Robin from Aunt Margaret, Uncle Otto, and Everybody. Looking Forward to Seeing You Soon!*

He is placed, then, this boy, this figure in the bed: for now, at least, he has just turned thirteen. And he is still, to the outside observer, recognizably *Robin*; though his emotional readings are quite different from those of the younger boy. His *I* is in the process of becoming infinitely more complex: voices, shadows, yearnings are changing him, his body is changing him, his world is an old-fashioned dark lantern slowly being opened, the dizzying bar of light growing ever wider.

Let us pass beyond the gently-breathing face, then, the open lips, the hair that is almost albino in tone. Inside the skull, within the brain, we journey into a dark cavern filled with shadowy workmen scurrying about. These workmen control the basic mechanisms of the organism, sending messages as if by telegraph to all the distant posts, keeping heart beating, lungs pumping, blood flowing. They are a remarkably efficient bunch; indeed, watching them, it is amazing that so much can be kept in such perfect working order. But then the basic system is sound—perfected after many hundreds of ancestral generations—and this particular organism in which the workmen are housed is one of the most perfect possible, a healthy pubescent boy. Of course the age of the organism creates certain demands, and sometimes it is difficult to keep everything in precise ticktock order: a bit too much of this enzyme might be released, or a mite too little of that; at such times the organism feels uneasy, confused, and waves of agitation flow through—but that, after all, is another department. These workmen are only responsible for keeping the mechanisms running smoothly on a purely physical, animal level. They have no other concern.

But if we pass them by, journey further into the glistening caves, we find other workmen. Running about here and there, pushing packed wheelbarrows, driving filled fork-lifts or overflowing pickup trucks, they haul their cargo to their necessary destinations: the various sections of the cortex, the hypothalamus.

Their cargo?

His father, passing clump-clump by the open door at night; a dream-fantasy of a wished-for little sister, her arms around his waist and squealing in terrified delight as they soar down a wild hill on his bicycle; the wet damp palm of Sonya Skyler, a girl he one held hands with years ago; vivid bits of a sex film once glimpsed; his mother's voice in the bedroom, behind the closed door and strangely slurred, muttering *Honey, don't*; and literally hundreds of thousands of other bits, fragments, pieces of dreams, remembered rooms. A request comes in—hundreds of them a minute—and someone rushes to the file (which contains millions upon millions of such pieces, many requested over and over, some all but thrown away for lack of use), finds the request, hurls it onto the nearest transport. Sometimes the arrival-time is instantaneous, particularly with the oft-requested items. Other times it takes a few seconds. On rare occasions it might take days; or the file may have been completely lost, and the request lies unfulfilled—although someone will remain on the job for days, even months, searching. On the whole, though, their efficiency, their perfect synchronicity in the midst of such apparent chaos, is staggering.

And if we travel even a bit further, far into the dark depths, we come across a tiny room with a number of men busily hunched over papers and charts and calculations. They receive requests too; not the same kind, not with the same frequency or specificity, but just as important: these men are the bridgers, the connectors, the ones who take the raw-memory files and develop them, interpret them, connect ones to others, create patterns and metaphors and meanings. They pool the files, tack them all together, and paste a large horizontal *I*-bar over the conglomeration; and it lasts, for a while; but all along they continue their work, because they know that otherwise the patchwork mass will ultimately warp and distort into unrecognizability. They do not have as certain a goal as those in physical maintenance or memory-filing and retrieval. For those others, success or failure is easily measured; for the I-workers, however, there is no true measure of success, only constant work to keep the I-montage from folding and bending too extremely, by constantly adding chosen bits, frequently pulling things away for disposal or refiling in the memory section.

This, at least metaphorically, is what we are seeing as we study the breathing boy upon the bed. He is hardly dormant, though to the untrained eye he appears to be. In fact, everything—body, mind, brain—is busily occupied. The boy himself is not aware of it, of course. All of this busyness, all these levels of activity inside him, are to him manifested only in a single plane, like a glass ocean streaming past—his consciousness. All the activity within him contributes towards the creation of this, giving him the illusion of uncluttered, perfect continuity, when in fact it is made up of millions of separate, fragmentary elements.

And so somewhere else in the boy's mind—perhaps we must take an elevator to some dark, mysterious floor—we find this sea of glass. At first it may appear somewhat intimidating, a river of melted crystal roaring and crashing past: for in it are bits of everything, all the memories, all the sensations and impressions, surfacing and sinking again, surfacing and sinking. And sounds, too, flow from the river, a cacophony of recalled voices and musics and cries; and odors, bread, sweet things, one rushing past another. Intimidating, even terrifying, this mad charge of collected experience, these rapids of memory: but again, there is order here, like a smoothly-traveled freeway. There are no accidents in this river, no screams of sudden twisted metal; only new sensations, ever-changing impressions and remembrances rising and disappearing, rising and disappearing, like islands ripped loose from their sea-floor, sent sailing into the flowing glass. This river, these loose islands, are what Robin thinks of as *I*.

Let us now step into this river. To discover this *I*, to find out just what it is, we must ride these rapids; and search out his unmoored islands.

2

He hears his mother stumble. *Oops*, she mutters under her breath; then her bare feet continue unsteadily up the stairs. When she reaches the top she bumps the wall, and he can hear her nightgown swishing against his door as she passes.

It plays again: the stumble, the muttering: and he shifts in the bed, vaguely trying to whisk the vision away. He is somewhere between consciousness and sleep, things surfacing and sinking. He sees his math teacher Mr. Kropp, a huge black-bearded man who despises him: *Mr. Withers*, he demands, *What is the answer to number nine?* And Robin leaps up, crying, *I don't know, you bearded bastard, and I don't want to know, and you can go to Hell for all I care!* And he stalks out triumphantly, the other kids gaping in open-mouthed admiration.

The Unspoken

He is riding down an enormously steep hill on his bike, a girl's arms wrapped around him tightly and her squealing girl-voice crying *Not so fast!* but obviously delighted anyway. His sister: a pretty little girl he could take on bike rides and walks to town: he would show her how to tie her shoes and scold her when he caught her in Mom's bathroom smearing lipstick on her face. But the scolding would be good-natured, he would take Kleenexes and wipe her clean, she would giggle, he would say, *You're so lucky, Star-eyes*—that would be his nickname for her, her eyes bright as stars—*you're so lucky I showed up first and not Mom or Dad.* She would giggle again, knowing it, knowing that he would never really punish her for anything, and very well-behaved on the whole, because she would be a good, bright child, just sometimes a little mischievous. He pictures himself braiding her hair on her first day at school, holding her that morning as they prepare to leave her and she is suddenly scared: *Don't leave me Big Brother!* And well he should know: he remembers his own first day at school, clinging desperately to his mother's dress—*Come with me! Come with me, Mom!*—but his mother firm, terrifyingly so, No, Robin, it's time for you to grow up, honey, look at all the other children, you don't see them hanging onto Mommy's dress now do you? But he didn't care about them, only about himself, and her; it was like being ripped apart, an actual physical convulsion: he'd had to throw up twice after she'd gone. An embarrassing, shameful memory...And yet he can remember enough of who he was then, at five years old, to understand it. He hardly recalls even stepping out of the house at that age: everything was so wrapped up in her, focused toward her, their life together: it was perfect, really, except for that clump-footed Other, the shadow-man who made his appearances in the dark night; but even he hadn't been enough to spoil the perfect coloring book and lemonade bliss that he hadn't even known, then, *was* bliss; for it had always been that way, as long as he could remember; until that awful day when she took him in the station wagon across town and said, *Now honey, I'll be back for your at...* The terror, he remembers the stark terror: and that is why he would be so comforting to little Star-eyes as her blonde pigtails bobbed up and down and she tearfully told him she couldn't, she couldn't. But she would; and that afternoon she would come back beaming, telling him of all the friends she had made and how nice the teacher was and look I drew this just for you Big Brother...

The vision blurs, darkens. He is standing next to Melissa Rosselli, the tall, unutterably beautiful Italian girl in homeroom: she turns to him, her sultry black eyes like rings of moonlit darkness, warm with love; he sees himself on an amazing white horse that glows as if its heart were sun, a huge flashing sword in his hand, battering and chopping down Huns, Indians, Nazis, Russians, all of them with hideous evil faces like Mr. Kropp's, he dashes on his sun-horse toward the burning castle where she is crying to be rescued, he leaps from the horse and dashes up the burning stairways, finds her fainted in a fantastic bedroom of singeing lace and smoking velvet; he takes her in his arms easily, feels her soft vein-pulsing warmth next to him; then back down the staircase, great fiery beams exploding to the shattered floor, and at last escaping; and the entire castle collapsing in a wild flight of fire as they charge away on the sun-horse, her arms wrapped around him now, her cheek against his back, her tears dampening his skin.

The castle and the horse melt, fade: he finds himself in a black dungeon, with Melissa his prisoner: wrapped in chains, half-starved, naked, she pleads with him for food, for mercy; he simply walks up to her and kisses her long, deeply. She does not resist. The smell of her sweat is incredibly enticing and he presses himself against her. He can taste the salt in the kiss. Not just sweat, now: tears, and they excite him, make him press himself against her nakedness even harder.

Suddenly there is a noise and he whirls around. Behind him his mother has stumbled on the stairs, muttered *Oops*; and he takes a step forward but before him is only a black maw of emptiness—

His eyes snap open.

He is sweating. He feels the warmly wet patina on his forehead and chest as he lies there, his breath slowly calming.

He pushes back the covers and numbly opens his pajama top, feeling the breeze from the open window flow across him.

He closes his eyes again.

If his mother were to come in just now, he realizes, she would close the window, she would sit on the bed buttoning his top and whisper, *Honey, you'll catch your death*; but then he corrects himself. No, she would not do that. An earlier woman he remembers from another time would have, and stroked his chest with her palm and kissed him goodnight on his cheek. Now, though, she would most likely stumble past his room with her grotesquely ungraceful gait, perhaps stopping for a moment at his door and peering in, slurring *G'night, baby*, but saying it wrong, not just slurred but actually wrong, the whole quality and timber of the voice belonging to some other woman, not his mother. Or, worse, she *would* come in: and go to the window, slap it shut too loudly, nearly fall onto the bed and fumble at his pajama buttons while he pretended to be asleep.

Later, after she had gone, he would straighten the buttons she had misaligned.

But she is not home. He knows because they have not waked him with their late-night entrance downstairs. Not that they are loud, not usually; but his mind is somehow super-tuned to their nightly arrivals, so that when the key rattles in the lock and the door creaks open he is wide awake, listening to their muttered monosyllabic conversation, the refrigerator opening and closing, sometimes the TV being flipped on or a newspaper rattling. They seem even later than usual tonight. He listens, noticing for the first time the spattering of rain on the roof and the wind rustling the tree at the window. He hears the foghorn, mournful, lonely. Images blur into focus: out in the black sea, a single lonely ship, a man in a yellow raincoat guiding her, rain streaming down his stubbly face, his body shivering with the salt cold. The ship tossing and heaving in the stormy ocean. But there: he cups his hand to his ear, thinks he hears something in the dark distance: yes...

He sighs and his mind floats back to Melissa Rosselli.

He often finds his mind floating back to Melissa Rosselli. In fact it's an everyday, sometimes every-hour or every-minute occurrence. She dominates his mind at odd moments—in class; reading; watching TV. But especially in class. Mr. Kropp might be standing at the front pontificating (a word Robin has recently discovered) on some algebraic gibberish, and though Robin might be in a state of terror over the likelihood of being called on, nonetheless Melissa Rosselli floats into his mind like some gossamer ghost, the mathematics class sputters into nonexistence like a candle in darkness, and only she is there, her smell, her voice.

He cannot imagine that anyone else in the world feels as he does. No: utterly impossible. Things simply couldn't function if everyone wandered around in his brand of all-consuming passion. But then he is quite aware of his sickness. His dangerous mental imbalance. It shows itself with alarming regularity now, and though he hates to think of it, he knows he must. The fantasy in the dungeon, for instance. Sheer sickness. And yet he has it all the time: she is walking along the street when he suddenly comes up from behind and grabs her, presses a chloroform rag to her face and carries her inert form back to his oily lair where he straps her down naked and keeps her there, all his own. He feels a terrible shame as he thinks of it. Always, now, he tries to control his thoughts: to mentally discipline himself, to keep himself clean, not to allow such disturbed fantasies to dirty his mind; and yet it comes back, this fantasy, again and again, to have absolute, perfect control.

What he would do with her if he had such control...that is another question. He thinks of his mother and father in the bedroom down the hall. He used to get up in the darkness and pad into the bathroom and listen at the far wall. They did not know that he could hear them, that he was listening; and it shamed him, too, to listen, and he would find himself quivering with emotion as he listened, but he could not help himself. The bed creaking. Quiet close voices, mostly hers: *It's all right. Go ahead.* Then signs, rhythmic squeakings, sometimes a moan, hers, and as he listened sometimes he would touch himself, knowing he was filthy and depraved yet unable to control his thoughts or body. An animal.

Lately he has taken to praying for salvation. Lying in the bed, he will press his hands together and think, *Please, I don't want to be a monster.* But thus far his prayers have gone unanswered. Perhaps, he thinks, he isn't praying correctly. He has tried different positions, different times of day, but they haven't helped. Of course, he realizes grimly, his knowledge of the Bible is limited to the children's stories his first-grade teacher, a fat English woman named Mrs. Balfour-Ritchie-Ritchie, had read to them. How clearly he recalls them: not the stories so much, but the way Mrs. Balfour-Ritchie-Ritchie read them, her deep English accent winding through Adam and Eve and Noah's Ark and Jonah and the Whale. For some time after first grade Robin had thought himself deeply religious, and believed firmly in God. But somewhere something had happened—he had noticed first Sonya Skyler and then Michele Henry and now, most glorious and awful of all, Melissa Rosselli, and somehow God, like his math class, had sputtered into oblivion....

But of course there are other things. His body, for instance. Mysterious events are occurring, hair now grows where none had been before and sometimes he wakes up with terrible shooting pains running through his legs and, even stranger, he is subject to awful mood swings: sometimes he feels euphoric, nearly ready to jump out of his seat, and then just a moment later he will sink into despair. Formless despair: a free-floating sensation of...what? Approaching doom?

Melissa, he thinks. Melissa, Melissa.

And then there is his hideous ignorance to consider. Just last month little Lisa Robinson, a dull-looking girl with carrot-colored hair who sat behind him in Social Studies, had dropped out of school—rumor had it she was pregnant. Pregnant! Lisa Robinson! It was almost unimaginable. How could she have sat behind him day after day, working the same problems and writing the same essays and listening to the same lectures, and yet possessing such incredible *knowledge?* Such experience...for he has none whatsoever. Until very recently, in fact, he had had only the vaguest idea of how girls even became pregnant. (And, when he is very honest with himself, he will admit that even now things are rather blurry.) He tries to imagine Lisa Robinson nude. Stark naked, lying on her back on a bed in a dim room, waiting, legs open, for a shadowy figure coming toward her. He tries to picture himself as the shadowy figure. He looks at her body, but somehow the image is hazy, indistinct; it will not hold. He switches the girl to Melissa Rosselli. He is able to hold it then. He approaches her, stares hungrily at her small breasts and brown nipples and that mysterious dark place between her legs—does she have hair there?—and then leans toward her, smells her musky Italian girl-smell.

But then, abruptly, they are back in the dungeon again. He quickly whisks the image away.

He is ashamed of himself. Not just because of his filthy thoughts, but because of his ignorance. The depth of Lisa Robinson's knowledge, her understanding, fills him with speechless awe. He is quite sure he will never possess such incredible awareness, for girls have never shown interest in him, not the way they do in John Hubbard or Mike Grossi, two beefy football-playing boys in his class. In comparison, Robin is a nonentity.

Thunder rumbles; distant, growing closer.

He opens his eyes again and becomes aware of a soreness between his legs. His body is straining against his shorts. Sighing, he tosses back the covers and walks across the rug onto the cool wood floor and finds his way into the bathroom. He does not turn on the light. He pulls down his pajama bottoms and stares at nothing as he feels himself soften and relax. He hears his father's voice: *Don't pull your pants down like that. Kids will laugh at you.*

Unpleasantly, the man drifts onto his mind-stage. He thinks of the times his father used to force him to take weekend trips in the boat, the wet fog soaking him, the salt water cold and terrifying, the fish that they reeled in that would slap and flop against the side of the plastic garbage can.

And another memory—long unrecalled, this one—of how once they had gone out and there had been no fish biting and they were about to leave when, finally, something tugged at Robin's line. He had prayed that it wasn't a fish, but it was: and his father had grown suddenly excited, pressing in close behind him and shouting, *You've got one! You've got one!* Robin had imagined the fish down in the liquid darkness trying to fight, not understanding, each tug simply sinking the hook farther into the roof of its mouth, its eyes bulging, its head crushed with the sudden deadly changes in pressure. Then the fish had burst forth into the light, spraying Robin's face with icy sea water, his father shoving the net under it and hurling it into the garbage can where it gasped and flopped.

Later, as they were heading back and his father was taken up with running the boat, Robin had stared at the lone fish in the can. A big bubble of milky white skin filled its mouth. It had stopped gasping and was very still. He had leaned over, touched the slime-scaly surface of its body; then, after glancing back at his father, he had—he didn't know why—picked up the fish and dropped it back into the sea. It floated there, rocking gently in the boat's wake, until the fog swarmed over it and it disappeared.

Robin flushes the toilet and makes his way back to the bed. How old had he been? Eight? Nine? He can still picture his father's face when they had pulled into the harbor: *What the hell happened to the fish?*

I guess it got away, Robin had answered.

He smiles as he slips between the sheets again. They have grown cold in his absence and tingles rush up his body as he settles back into bed. He thinks of the fog, out there in the boat: it had a somber, grainy look that reminded him of a silent movie he'd seen once, about a vampire: as the sun had set there had been pictures of a castle looming darkly against a flickering black-and-white dusk. Out there in the ocean, in the boat, the fog always seemed to him exactly like that aged movie twilight…But it was not always the same, the fog. Years ago he and his mother had walked on the pier and he remembers her in her white gown and bare feet, brushing her dark hair back with her hand, her other hand in his, and smiling down at him: *Oh Robin,* she would say, *it's a real diamond day.* And, pointing, she would tell him to look at the sky. It wasn't just flat, dull gray, she told him; no, if you looked at it closely enough, really stared, it would break up, become hundreds of little bits of sparkle, pieces of suspended rain; and they looked like diamonds, those pieces, a sky packed with them. She used to talk dreamily about what they would do if there really were diamonds there, that they could reach up and take: *We could wrap them around ourselves,* she would say, *and we would float right up to the moon.*

But that was before the change had come and some other woman, or perhaps a devilish spirit, had taken her away and left someone reminiscent but wrong.

It had not happened at any particular, identifiable moment; rather, it was a slowly-growing malignance, a cancer whose presence Robin became aware of only gradually. He remembers a few years ago, when his realization was just dawning, imagining that he literally had two mothers: one the woman he knew, the other a parasitic impostor that periodically stole his real mother and locked her away somewhere deep underground and then invaded the household, haunted him with her slurred sloppy nightmare presence. And dreams, not unlike those with Melissa Rosselli now, would pour liquidlike through his mind: unmasking the evil one, stripping away its mask like snakeskin to reveal the awful black creature beneath, destroying its screaming repugnance with his magnificent flashing sword and rushing to his mother's rescue, releasing her from her inky dungeon prison and riding the fantastic sun-horse into the gem-dazzled light....

There is a sound. The dream visions vanish abruptly.

He listens.

A key is finding its way into the lock downstairs. After a moment he hears it slip into place, turn, and the door opens. Carpeted footsteps; the door closing; an indistinct muttering and the click of the light in the foyer. He listens for any conversation between them, but there is none. He wishes there was: although the words he remembers are largely evil ones, shouted ones, they somehow seem oddly comforting compared to the tense, sentient silence that hovers between the two of them now.

I'm sorry! I'm sorry! she would cry, when they did not know he was listening. *I'm sorry!*

Minutes pass and he lies in the darkness listening to the familiar sounds. The refrigerator; the sink; the TV turned low, his father sitting in the brown leather reclining chair, the newspaper rattling. His mother in the kitchen, dishes. She drops one and it breaks. Once, he would have jumped at the sound—now it blends unobtrusively into the soundscape. The broom comes out of the closet, the dustpan, broken tinklings sift into the trash can, doors are closed. Finally he hears her voice. He does not hear a response from the man in the chair.

As her footsteps come up the stairs he realizes suddenly that his body is tense. Tight. He makes himself relax. He listens. Uneven, the footsteps, but perhaps not entirely chaotic; he hears her reach the top without incident and then the hall light is switched on. The bright yellow bar shines in under his door. For several moments there is silence. Then she clears her throat and continues up the hall toward his room.

He finds himself strangely torn. In one way he prays she will just continue on, not even consider trying his door; calmness then, peace, and in a while his father will turn off the TV and go to bed too and silence, blissful, safe, will fill the house. But then he also, against logic, hopes she will stop. He doesn't know why. He hates the woman in the corridor, hates her for stealing his mother, hiding her, killing her; hates her boozy odor and ungainly footsteps; yet he hopes she will stop in his room, perhaps only to close his window—to say nothing, not touch him, not come close to him, just close the window and go. But to be there, for a moment.

His body has grown tense again. He relaxes.

The footsteps have stopped outside his door. He tries to will them to keep going, keep moving down the hall to bed and silence; but she turns the door handle softly. Light, very bright, pours across the floor and the corner of the bed as she puts her head into the room. With the light coming from behind she is a dark shadow, a shape of night.

"Baby?" she whispers. "You asleep?"

He does not respond. He studies her through half-closed eyes as she steps in, leaving the door open a crack so that a thin rod of light cuts the room in two.

"You asleep, baby?"

Silence. The TV downstairs.

"Sure keep it cold in here, don't you," she says finally, moving toward the open window and closing it. He watches her at the window, the lights from the street below framing her silhouette against the tree branches and spatters of rain drizzling down the glass.

Stay, he thinks. Then: *Leave. Get out of here!*

He relaxes his body again.

She stands at the window for a long time and he can hear her breathing. He cannot quite decide on her condition. It is possible that she is not very bad; but the appearance can be deceiving: sometimes, when she is far, far gone, she gives this sort of comforting impression—at first.

He needs to scratch in a dozen places but keeps himself from moving...He sees her in warm apricot light, folding his clothes and putting them in the drawers. *Can we go to the record store tomorrow?* he asks her from the bed. She turns to him and touches his forehead, checking for signs of fever. She smiles. *You're taking advantage of your old mother,* she says. *Just because you've been sick.* Nuh-uh, he grins. Uh-huh, she answers: *You think Mom'll just do anything for sick little Robin, don't you?* She tussles his hair. *You little monster!*

Thunder returns him to the room and the breathing form at the window. She moves toward him in the darkness and he closes his eyes, feels her weight press down onto the bed. He is tense again and the need to scratch is unbearable. Finally, as she grasps his pajama top, he moves slightly and emits a tiny moan.

"Baby?" she whispers.

"Mm," he mumbles mock-sleepily, scratching himself. He opens his eyes part way.

She smiles down at him. "Hi."

She is wearing a black dress with white lilies on it, cut low in front, with a pearl necklace. Her voice is not bad but her eyes are unfocused and dull: he is immediately on his guard. He wants to draw away from the hands at his shirt but he stays still. He notices the ring on her finger as she pulls at the buttons, a little diamond that seems in the dimness to be made up of a dozen tiny, dark mirrors with splinters of both of them flickering inside it. She finishes with the shirt, which she has managed to do correctly.

"What, Mom?" he says.

She touches his hair and lets out a small belch. For a moment the air is full of whiskey.

She shakes her head. A dark curl falls in front of her eyes and she pushes it back.

"Looking forward to seeing your aunt and uncle?" she asks.

The trip—he had nearly forgotten about it. But she is correct: in a few days he is to ride a bus down to California to visit his Uncle Otto and Aunt Margaret and their kids. How could it have escaped his mind? But then, the way it was planned, or, perhaps, unplanned: a sudden announcement two weeks ago, that he was to go away until the end of August.

Why?

Your father and I...honey, we just have to work some things out. That's all.

Are you getting a divorce?

No, Robin, of course not. We just have to work some things out.

But the lie was unconvincing. He is quite sure he knows what is happening. He tries to picture himself and the woman sitting on the bed living together by themselves, without the clump-footed Other, the grimly dark shadow-man. Years ago, perhaps: now, however, it strikes a deep foreboding in him. He sees her stumbling on the stairs and dropping dishes and screaming: no: his mother, yes, but this intruder, this snake-masked monster—impossible. He would run away, yes, he would go somewhere; maybe he would get on the bus on Saturday and never come back. He has heard of places. Malibu. Santa Barbara. Venice Beach. Places where the sun beats down and the sand is white and soft and the skies are blindingly blue and clear. Oh, he has heard of places. Not like this rain-blurred nowhere. That is one thing he has learned, at least: that there are no diamonds suspended in the mist, not here; no floating gems; only damp and salt and cold. Nothing.

"What's going to happen when I come back?" he asks her in the darkness.

"Why, what do you mean?"

He shifts uneasily. He hears the dish break and the soft tinkling tumbling into the garbage can.

"...I don't know," he mutters.

She looks at him but really seems to be looking somewhere else, somewhere beyond him, and it gives him an eerie feeling, like a kind of death. She is still beautiful, he knows. Heavier, perhaps, than she once was; but her round, pale face is still much the same, her hair that spills onto her shoulders like a dark ocean wave, the sky-colored cat's eyes which are such a mirror of his own: here, in the darkness of after midnight, he can almost believe that there has never been any change at all: but when he looks into her eyes they are the eyes of someone he does not know, will never know.

"Baby...are you still worried about all that? What we talked about?"

"I don't know..."

"I told you, baby, there's nothing to worry about. Not a thing." She hiccups and touches her chest. Then she emits a long sigh. "Okay?"

"Okay."

"Everything's going to be fine."

"Okay."

This is the worst of all possible times: when the invader has taken over, but is not acting like the invader. No: she appears normal, or very close to it, and the illusion is so tempting, to think of this woman above him as his mother; but he knows she is not, knows it from years of making such suppositions; knows that at any moment she might change, alter suddenly like an unstable acid. Sometimes he imagines his mother and the invader at war with each other, at times like this: battling to gain ascendancy: but no, its is only an illusion. The snake-mask is firmly in control.

And suddenly, as the woman stands, something seems to grab hold of Robin, something from some distant, secret place, and catch his breath abruptly in his throat. He wants to reach to the woman, grasp her hand, bring her back; his hand moves tentatively toward her: but she fails to see.

A moment later his hand is on his chest again and she is moving toward the door.

"G'night, baby," she says.

She closes the door and the bar of light is extinguished. She goes down the stairs again.

He listens.

He asleep? his father says, his voice distant, faint.

She mutters a reply. He hears the refrigerator open and close again. Then nothing but the TV and an occasional rustle. He can picture them perfectly: his father in his brown leather reclining chair staring dully at the flickering screen; his mother in the kitchen with a cup of booze-laced coffee, looking out the window at the empty dark. As if they were both waiting, he thinks, for some mysterious thing that never quite seemed to arrive.

They had not always been so silent; he feels shame returning as he remembers listening at the bathroom wall. Even a year ago, there had not been such silence. But now it covers everything: like a dull, gemless blanket.

Hang on, Star-eyes!

Wind rushes against the house and thunder rolls like the ocean swooshing onto the shore.

Hang on! Hang on!

The Unspoken

His breathing slows. The tightness begins to seep from him. *Clump. Clump.*

He is instantly aware again and tense. Minutes have passed. The TV has been turned off and his father's footsteps thud toward him on the stairs. The floor creaks as the footsteps pass and move up the hall. A door closes. He hears water running, a toilet flushing. Then silence.

He listens.

A slight sound. She is still downstairs; still staring, he knows, out the kitchen window. He remembers going down once and studying her from a hidden vantage point on the stairs. From there he could see past the living room into the kitchen. He remembers watching her take a pot of stew from the refrigerator and spoon some of its fat-congealed contents into a bowl and sit at the kitchen table and eat it. How long ago had it been? It is extraordinarily vivid, this vision of her sitting at the kitchen table in a pool of light with her cold stew and cup of whiskey-laced coffee. He had been able to smell the coffee and whiskey from where he sat. It had affected him, this vision, stayed with him the brilliant clarity of a dream....

Things blur, melt, fade: indistinct murmurs of memory, recalled shadows: he drifts: at last she stirs, and he listens again. He wonders vaguely how much time has gone by. He hears her rinsing out the cup in the sink and then turning off the water and moving toward the stairs. Lamps are switched out; only the light in the hall remains.

The footsteps are slower now, wobbly. He tries not to listen but his mind is super-tuned to the sound. Each step is somehow like a knocking on some strange door to the future: and as he listens he thinks of disasters, wars, the end of the world: for, he knows, it *is* the end of the world: soon he will be on the bus to California and maybe, he thinks, he will not come back, but keep going, into the sun, to Malibu or Santa Barbara or Venice

Beach, forever. And even if he were to come back it would not be the same, for they would be alone, he and the woman on the stairs, completely alone. They tell him differently but he knows the truth. He knows how the two of them do not speak to each other, how silence hangs between them like a kind of darkness, how they play-act for his benefit: and how it makes him want to cry, or scream, watching their absurd parodies of affection, their drunken kissing and saying of love words, but, as soon as he leaves the room, separation; and a return to the dark silence. He knows. Sometimes he feels he knows everything there is to know in the world. Sometimes he thinks he is God, looking down on all the ignorant pathetic lost souls of the world. Sometimes he pictures himself as God and the commands he would make, the way he would run the universe. Certainly he would do better, he thinks: at times he suspects that there isn't even anyone up there, that the world is like a car sailing down the road at ninety miles an hour with no one driving…And yet he knows that such thoughts are only further proof of his sickness, his blasphemous, poisoned-mind madness.

He clasps his hands before him. *I'm sorry. I'm sick. I don't mean any of it. I'm sorry.*

There is a thick *thud*.

He listens. The footsteps have stopped.

Though the window is closed he feels a cold blast of air suddenly slapping him in the face. He listens.

Silence.

Finally, after a long time, he stands, almost as if he were no longer himself but rather someone else looking down on him. He goes to the bedroom door. He opens it.

His mind is free of thought: free of emotion: he feels nothing but a flat dead blankness, as if he does not even truly exist, as if he were unreal. She is lying in the hallway near the stairs. Next to her open mouth is a thick trickle of some viscous substance.

He watches himself as, without thought, he walks to the bathroom, wets a washcloth, and walks back to her.

"Mom?" he hears himself saying from a remote place. "It's okay, Mom."

He touches the cloth to her forehead, to her closed eyes.

She does not respond. He watches himself as he wipes the fluid next to her mouth away.

Then he, or rather someone named Robin he watches from a distance, goes back to the bathroom and rinses the cloth and tosses it into the hamper. After a moment he returns to the hall and stares at her. He can feel his heartbeat inside his chest.

She does not stir. He hears her breathing, heavy, even.

He goes to the hall closet, opens it; pulls down a blue blanket from the shelf. He walks over to her still form, stands over it as he unfolds the blanket and places it gently across her body, methodically tucking it under her arms and feet. Then he takes a pillow from the closet and crouches down and pushes it softly under her dark hair. Then he goes to the closet again and shuts the door. Finally he walks to the light switch and drops the hallway into darkness.

He goes back to his room then, closing the door quietly.

He gets into bed. His mind is utterly empty. No images, no echoes, no cries. Nothing.

Then, after a long time, a formless desire begins to grow in him: a raw, nameless thing, almost a wound, aching at him between his legs but also in his head, in his chest, as if some grotesque weight had been placed on him. He touches himself. There is no pleasure in it. It is like the salving of pain. He forces his mind to remain cold, barren. No thoughts must trespass. He reaches under the mattress for a crusty sock he keeps there for this purpose. Lightning begins to flash outside, he sees himself in the electric blue; so he closes his eyes, listening to the booming thunder and the rain pouring onto the roof, and keeps his mind a frozen landscape. He uses himself harshly until, at the end, emotion finally rises in him, sickly, like bile. Hate. Hate, a seething scattered hate for himself, for the world, for everything, everyone, blind rage, insane anger, disgust. Hate! Hate!

Finally the hate bursts; and flows from him.

He lies there for a long time after, thinking of nothing.

He knows he should pray; but he cannot bring himself to form the words in his mind. He feels hollow and cold. He watches the lightning behind his eyes and listens to the falling rain.

At last he begins to grow sleepy with the lateness of the hour. He puts the sock away and rolls onto his side, pulls the covers to his neck.

...The person they call Robin floats over a sun-streaked sea, the brilliant light dazing and warm, and he feels a sudden enormous peace, as if he had been cut free of everything, died, become a spirit. The fog and the rain he has left far behind in some other, only dimly remembered world. Here there is only sun and warmth and the sensation of things flowing over him caressingly.

Finally, as he drifts over the vast expanse of glittering blue, he sees in the distance a tiny island. It is strangely beautiful, there in the sunlit distance; and he wants to approach it. He hears voices, far away.

Hang on, Star-eyes.
Don't worry about a thing, honey.
He asleep?
Don't worry. Don't worry.

But they fade, he forgets them as he floats over the sea toward the sandy little island. After a time he realizes that there is someone on the island, standing at the edge of the shore. He cannot discern who it is, even whether it's a man or a woman; but as soon as he sees the figure he is drawn to it passionately, with an aching need. The voices are gone; he hears only wind whipping in his ears; and he tries to reach the faraway figure on the shore, for he realizes suddenly that he is in love with the figure, wants the two of them to be together forever; but the vision begins to dim, to grow soft and waver like a mirage, until finally he feels himself dropping away into a place of nothingness. He calls to the vision, but it is gone. And then he is, as well; vanished, for a few hours at least, forgotten.

3

The bus is largely empty. Robin sits near the back, gazing out the window at Wind Point as it recedes into the past, down the old Scully Road. He listens to the great grinding motor as the driver, a large man with a butch haircut and square head, shifts gears. There is something beautiful in the sound. He rides the school bus down this same road to Hollowstone every day, but it is a smaller bus, crowded with noisy children; and it is not the same, it gives Robin none of the same mysterious, almost mystical feeling that he has as he sits here in the big hulk of a vehicle, wiping mist from the window, watching rain smear the glass and glancing around to see only a few other silent heads on board. And no one he knows. He is on his own, he realizes suddenly, truly independent: just him and his luggage, the small bag next to him and the big case stowed away. He had left his mother in front of the bus depot only minutes before, and yet already he has a glorious feeling of being mature, grown-up, free.

As the bus rumbles along the old Scully Road toward the mainland, Robin sees that the fog is dissipating; the rain, disappearing; and this happens every day too, as he goes to school: as soon as they get away from the point, the weather clears. But this time! This time is different! As he sees the skies turning a sudden magic blue he feels he will never go back there again, that he has burst through to a whole new plane of existence and has no more need of Wind Point or the big white house in the cul-de-sac. Or anything that happens within it. As he thinks of the man and the woman in the house they seem somehow faraway, people he once knew but whom he knows no longer; and he realizes that this is a brand-new feeling, a heady euphoric feeling, that he is finally escaping, bursting free like a bird from a cage.

Strange: he had not felt this way only minutes before, standing before the hardware store with his mother. There everything seemed gray and terrible and the bus, as it approached, seemed more like a malevolent gray slug than his agent of freedom. Images flew through his mind of kindergarten, clinging to her dress; and for a wild moment he wanted to do the same as he had years before, suddenly turn and throw his arms around her and scream, *Come with me!* But of course that was impossible. And so as the bus pulled up with a mighty hissing he pretended—they pretended—that there was nothing wrong, that everything was perfectly all right.

You'll call when you get there, won't you, honey?

Mm-hm. Yeah.

Okay. Have a good time. She handed him his bag and kissed him on the forehead. *And don't worry, okay?*

He tries to reconstruct the scene in his mind. He can remember her words; but her voice is harder to recollect. As he ponders the matter it occurs to him that he cannot even picture what she was wearing. How did her hair look? Her face? Had he in fact even *seen* her? Did he ever see her, anymore?

The thought makes him uneasy and he stops thinking about it.

But then (the thought reappears instantly) does he ever truly see anyone? Can he picture his father's face in his mind? Or Uncle Otto's? Aunt Margaret's? Mr. Kropp's? It seems to him that he can visualize only pieces: his father's long drooping nose, Mr. Kropp's beard: but the reality of their appearances is lost. Even Melissa Rosselli, he realizes with a strangely vertiginous sensation, he pictures more as a soft focus dream-fantasy than as she really is. It is, oddly enough, fantasy figures that are the most real to him. His little sister, for instance. He can picture her perfectly. Fantasies, and people he knew only long ago—they are vivid too. He thinks of another uncle, Uncle Jasper, now dead, whose creviced face and sawmill voice are imprinted on his mind like a brand. He can hear the man's voice in his mind just as if they were sitting together right here, right now; and yet he cannot do the same with his own parents. Their voices are lost in some enormous sea, a dark fog of unreality.

Jasper Wills: not a blood relative but one of his aunt's husbands, on his father's side: he can visualize the old man perfectly even now, years after his death. His burlap-hanging skin, his cataract-cloudy eyes; the big red heart-surgery scar running all the way down his chest. He remembers sitting in their dark parlor, the curtains drawn, the room smelling of old people, eating fancy chocolates that his aunt got from her work at the factory and watching baseball games with Uncle Jasper on TV. He would sit there, it had always seemed to Robin, like some great mound of mashed potatoes, stripped to the waist, his body covered with strange dents and lumps; and looking suddenly toward Robin he would shout, *The fool can't hit!* or *We got 'em now!*

They had not visited Uncle Jasper often but each time is bright as day in Robin's mind. He and his mother would take the car to the mainland, then up the coast through a long winding drive filled with great green trees and sunlight glistening through them like light on water. Their house was hidden away in a canyon far enough from the sea that when he stood in the front yard and looked about at the great pines surrounding them Robin could hardly imagine it at all. The air was filled with earth smells: intoxicating grass and soil and pine; and the sea was gone, in some other land. And even though his mother would be there, and she would drink too much and get drunk and sometimes there would be bad scenes, it somehow was never too bad with Uncle Jasper and the baseball games on television.

But there had been one time, he suddenly remembers, when his mother had been in their kitchen, drunk, laughing too loudly, and suddenly she said: "Oh yes, I forgot to tell you—my little Robin's in love!"

He blushes as he thinks of it, and of their reaction—the open mouths, the *Isn't that cute* comments—but it was true: he was head-over-heels, madly in love. Sonya! Perfectly seven years old, blonde hair reaching to her waist, deep lavender eyes, soft peach-blushed skin…Yes, it had been very true that he was in love—and feeling it every moment of every day, just as now…but he wonders. Wonders if Melissa Rosselli is truly as strong a love as Sonya had been, then. Melissa is an all-consuming passion, a moment-to-moment siren in his mind; but Sonya, Sonya had been a brilliant sun, a blinding angel of light, overwhelming, unreal. And so when his mother announced so nakedly that he was in love it had shamed him, for it somehow made his feelings cheap, funny, little-boy things….

It had been like a fever in the days before his mother finally discovered his dreadful secret. He couldn't think straight; couldn't concentrate to do his homework assignments; could think only of the girl who sat in front of him in class, her bobbing brilliant hair, the indescribable girl-smell he could detect if he leaned forward just slightly. He had wanted to tell her, his mother, about Sonya, but even then she had begun to split in two and sometimes Robin did not know who she was. And so he had stayed terribly silent, even when she sat on his bed and asked him, "Honey, is anything wrong? You're acting so strange these days…."

He shook his head. He could not tell anyone. But one afternoon downstairs he had been in front of the television, doodling absently on the back of an old advertisement, when she came up behind him and whispered suddenly: "*Ohhhhh.*"

His head darted up. "What?"

She grinned down at him; and when he looked at the paper he saw he had been writing the name *Sonya* over and over again, in girlish curly-cue script like that Sonya herself used.

"Why, honey," his mother exclaimed delightedly, "you're in love!"

But at Uncle Jasper's house, weeks later, her voice was altered: it held not delight but mockery; the words were the same, but the meaning, he knew, was completely different.

Still, Uncle Jasper had taken him aside later in the evening. He led him back to his study, a dark cornucopia of strange old things (a Japanese Samurai sword, a Confederate flag, Indian medicines in clay jars, comic books, odd-shaped candles with exotic scents) and they sat together in the quiet darkness, the voices of the women like distant sighs, Jasper studying him levelly.

"So," he said. "You got yourself a woman."

Robin fidgeted. "I don't exactly *have* her, Uncle Jasper."

"Are you *going* to have her?"

He giggled. "I don't know."

"Tell you what you do," Jasper said, leaning back in his chair and reaching toward something on a nearby shelf. "You give her this."

He tossed a small object Robin's way. Robin caught it and looked at it.

"Just a paperweight," his uncle said. "Just junk. But it's pretty. She'll like it."

The paperweight, it seemed to Robin, was more than pretty. It was a tiny glass ball, domed on top and flat on the bottom, inside of which was a delicate pink and white cherry blossom frozen as if for all time.

"But Uncle Jasper," he started to say, "I can't..."

"G'wan, take it," he interrupted. "Have your mother wrap it up pretty and you give it to her. See what happens." He grinned, displaying the spaces between his teeth. He leaned forward, leering, and in a husky stage whisper said: "This kind of shit gets 'em every time!"

And so it was done: and so, from his mother's drunken announcement, the matter was pursued. Valentine's Day approached: and his mother found crinkly red paper for the cherry blossom; it was wrapped and, after nights and days of hopeless terror, nightmare fantasies that Sonya would laugh or throw it back at him or think it ridiculous, he had approached her, she had looked up from her desk quizzically, he had put the shiny package before her....

There follows in his mind a long haziness. Somehow he had been invited to have dinner with her family at their home. He found himself in an almost never-worn suit and tie, being delivered by his mother to the household of his goddess on earth—trembling with fear, with anticipation, with anticipation of fear.

The meal he recalls only vaguely. It is what happened afterward that is vivid as a gem in his mind: they had gone to her room, to Sonya's room, just the two of them, and at a small table there they had played checkers. Oh, game of games! He cannot remember the room itself, anything about it; only the small cloth-covered table and red-and-black checkerboard and her presence, the tension he felt between them like an electric charge, her face pensive in concentration, and his astonished realization that she was wearing a sweet perfume. And when she had shifted in her seat, their knees suddenly touched under the table: hers were bare, for she was wearing a short white dress, and yet she had not moved them, she had left her knees where they were, and for minutes afterward they had sat there, this subterranean connection between them, Robin's heart beating wildly. Then when it came time to go home she had ridden in the back seat of her parents' station wagon with him, the darkness like a sentient being between them, and when they came close to Robin's house she suddenly took his hand in hers and he felt her cool, damp palm in his and the slight tremors that ran through it. They said nothing to each other; had, in fact, hardly spoken all evening. But the memory makes his breath come short.

She had moved away two weeks later.

Uncle Jasper, when Robin saw him, seemed filled with the pride of accomplishment: "Boy!" he would shout. "You *owe* me one!" But slowly, over the course of several months, his grinding voice became weaker; and there came a time when Jasper showed off not only his huge chest scar but also a thick coffee-brown one on his throat; and his voice was reduced to a thin whisper. Soon he was little more than an all-but-mute ghost covered to his chin in bed sheets. Robin can remember sitting in the bedroom, dust motes orbiting slowly in the twilight, and his uncle's voice whispering a mysterious phrase: "*I can remember all the old things.*" Later there was a funeral and another man, a still waxed-fruit replacement, lay with closed eyes in a garish coffin.

Go ahead, he can hear his mother whispering. *Kiss your uncle goodbye.*

Wide-eyed, horrified, he had leaned forward, closing his eyes. The skin, its texture, its softness, was exactly like a ripe nectarine he might take from the bowl on the kitchen counter. He had a sudden vision of rotten fruit, soft pulpy masses of black; and he had whirled away, heart crashing wildly, mind dark with terror.

When the bus arrives at Greyfield it turns south and eventually reaches the freeway. It is midmorning now, and the sky, crystalline in its clarity, seems to Robin almost unnaturally bright: without haze, without clouds, there is something very nearly indecent about it, naked. And yet a thrill of anticipation courses through him as he watches the great flowing mountains of redwood and pine roll past his window, as the bus's great grinding motor rumbles on like a grand, unstoppable freight train. There is something magical, it seems to him, in its motion; in the earth rushing past under his feet; he has felt it before, this magic, but never, with the California border drawing near, so intensely.

He thinks of these relatives of his, his Aunt Margaret and Uncle Otto, the Wilder family. His mother's sister and her husband and four or five children...how long since he has seen them? he wonders. Five years? His memories are, at best, vague; he pictures Aunt Margaret as a large, loud woman with an amazingly wide mouth and brassy, snake-coiled hair; Uncle Otto as a thin, emaciated ghost of a man with gray skin and a thin beard. The children he recalls hardly at all. Most, he remembers, are older than himself; one, a girl named Priscilla, is his age, and he recalls her more clearly than the rest—if only because he recalls despising her so completely. He wonders why; but the memory is lost.

And so he does not expect, really, so much out of this so-called vacation; but it is irrelevant, because he has every intention to light out within a few days of his arrival. He will stock up on food at his relatives' house and then move on, sneak out in the middle of the night and find a way—hitchhike, maybe—to get farther south, to those sun-soaked beaches where he can live on someone's roof somewhere and be a free man, really and truly, for the first time in his life. Of course there will be problems—money, most significantly. But it seems to him he can find a way to pick some up, perhaps as a busboy or a clerk. It will not be easy, he knows, but it is the life he feels he must lead, one of adventure and surprise and...freedom, always freedom.

Escape! Flight! The words flutter in his brain like bright butterflies. He wants to leave himself, the self he remembers being back in the house in the cul-de-sac, far behind, in a dimly recalled distant past. The woman with the dully unfocused eyes, the man rattling his newspaper in the big chair late at night: phantoms, receding ghosts, to be utterly and finally forgotten while a shiny new life rises before him as clean and pure as the sky outside the window.

And Melissa Rosselli: he will write to her from his beach-roof in southern California, he will compose a beautiful irresistible love letter to her telling her of his crazy, bohemian life and long hair and inviting her to be with him. Oh, she would reject him now, if he were to write such a letter today—he is sure of it; but once he had built his new, liberated life for himself, how could she say no?

And after all, he could write such a letter. He knows that he is a very good writer. He always receives high marks from his English teacher, a rotund woman named Mrs. Peterson, although the marks are frequently accompanied by comments such as, "Excellent—but not quite what I asked for," or, "Stick to the assignment, Robin!" It is difficult, though, to stay to such dull tasks—nearly all of his free time is spent reading, and the books—H.P. Lovecraft, Ray Bradbury, Mark Twain, and most especially Poe—excite him, make him want to do different things, not stupid eighth-grade assignments. Once he had written an entire book report in verse, after "Annabel Lee":

...And then a book came up,
Chilling and killing our ROBIN WITHERS;
For the author he had to read
Just blathers and blathers;
While Robin snores, the author bores,
And blithers and blithers and blithers.

Mrs. Peterson had given him an "A," adding: "VERY FUNNY. Write a real book report next time."

He likes Mrs. Peterson, though—and he will miss her when he goes to high school (that is, he would, if he were going). But he knows he will have to grow accustomed to the idea of leaving people, for, very soon now, they will all be gone from him forever, dissolved like smoke in wind. All but Melissa. Mr. Thorndyke, the History teacher with a lisp; Mrs. Bent, given to hysterical outbursts; the horrifying Mr. Kropp; and others too: he thinks of the town librarian, a gentle old European lady named Mrs. Klibo, who let him check out adult books way back when he was eleven. Yes, he would miss her, and her library, that big Victorian structure that was once a home for families but was now a home only for books, thousands of books. He remembers spending dozens of rain-filled afternoons there in the fat comfortable chairs, his mind filled with wandering corpses and rocket ships and happy, adventurous boys as the cold rain fell outside and the radiator across the room hissed and hummed....

He feels a wave of melancholy pass over him. He wishes there were a way to bring along just a few things from his old life—to carry them into the new; but that, of course, is impossible. It must be a total break, or nothing.

And yet...

He stares out the window. It suddenly seems too confusing. After a time he brings out a paperback, *Great Supernatural Stories*, and tries to read; but he feels uneasy somehow, jumpy, uncertain. He senses within himself a sudden hole, a kind of void. Strange: he had never thought of himself as having lacked anything before. The idea had never even occurred to him. But now, with visions of everything he has ever known receding into the mist of the past, he has a terrible sense of loss, waste. He wants to go—knows that he must go—knows that there is nothing remaining in that old life to hold him back. And yet he still senses loss. Even when he remembers that, after all, in bed at night he often spends his time fantasizing what it might be like to live in some other world, like the ones he sees on TV shows—those simple, happy families who live their lives to constant laugh-track accompaniment and resolve all their conflicts in the neat space of thirty minutes each week. The thought embarrasses him now, but he recalls wishing—even praying, blasphemously!—that he could become one of those people, the people in the TV shows, that he could live that sort of life forever and ever. Stupid kid stuff, he now thinks contemptuously; but oh, how he had wished for it!

He feels a vague dissatisfaction with himself. He does not like feeling sorry for himself. His father's voice: *Stop moping around all the time.* And he would stop; but that, somehow, never seemed to alter his inner landscape. For his father's benefit he might make an effort to smile, to not let on anything was wrong—for he would realize that he had no right to such feelings. And yet his interior life would remain unaltered, and he would still be aware—too aware—that something was wrong, or rather many things, even if he could not always identify or define them, even if the sentient silence between the three in the house in the cul-de-sac would not allow any of them to speak.

But in a new, different family, things would be changed. Not in this one: for this one it is too late. It is all too deeply ingrained. But with a brand-new family, with a second chance, life would be brightly altered...he doesn't know just how, but he knows there would be great profound changes....

It is, he realizes, impossible; and so he tries to stop thinking of it, tries to return to the book in his lap. But his mind wanders.

He sees after a while the big blue *Welcome to California* sign rising ahead. Oddly, his earlier elation seems to have abated to a large degree and he feels nothing in particular as the sign comes closer and closer and finally passes by. California...freedom, yes...but—

He stares blankly at the vista of rolling green outside the window and the roadside flowers waving gently in the late-summer breeze. He begins to feel unaccountably frightened. As he shifts in the warm bus seat he can sense tremors passing through him: his body is a taut wire: he is afraid, and yet there is nothing to be afraid of. He had left the fear far behind, he thought; and yet it has followed him, and he wonders how it could have found him again so quickly, why it couldn't have just stayed back there in the unreal place, the fog-filled cul-de-sac. For that is how he has thought of it, the fear: the tight tension he feels when his mother sits on his bed at night or when his father's footsteps pass heavily by: as a free-floating thing, something not connected to him but rather to the room, the house, something that comes like a parasite and latches onto him. Because it seems to him that *he* is not a frightened *person*; but rather that other things, outside things, make him frightened—and so the fright itself, the night terror, he has viewed all along as something else, something outside. And yet it has followed him. He thinks to himself: There's nothing to be afraid of. And yet that does not help ease the tension or calm the tremors. And as minutes pass the fear grows to sheer terror: he wants to crash through the window of the bus and run, run...Where? Where is there to run to? His mind is blank. He is in California. He is free. This is what he has wanted. And yet he pushes himself up against the window and wishes that somehow, for just a moment, he could stop living, cease to exist, be gone. It is nearly unbearable, this sensation, this parasite of horror, and he tells it to go away, stop, get out! Yet it stays. It stays. His inner pleas are no more effective than his prayers to God when he asks for the other woman, the snake-mask, to be taken away, to disappear, and leave only the woman he remembers from...when? Eons ago. When he had been a different person, a dimly-remembered shadow. But even then the terror had found him, late at night, when he woke up screaming from dreams in which he looked on helplessly as she cried out to him, flames licking at her dress and turning her skin to black ashes and her cries like something from beneath the earth, some prehistoric dying thing: *Robin! Robin!* And now the terror has returned, and it is the same terror, just in a different form, but the same, and he wants to cry out to someone but there is no one, he wants someone to grab his hand and pull him away into some new world, leave the demon, all the demons, far behind but there is no one; he wants to be cut free, to become disembodied, a floating spirit, but he is paralyzed and there is no one. He can do nothing but try to fill his mind with words, any words, to keep the terror from crawling in and taking over completely, forever. He can feel it trying to. He can feel it as a huge mass of darkness impinging on the edges of his consciousness, a great pool of void, like malignantly spreading ink. He tries, tries to fight it.

God. God. God. God. God. God.

And still it remains. But weakened, now. He keeps the word flowing in his mind.

God. God. God.

And finally he feels the blackness begin to recede. God, God. He imagines it crawling reluctantly back, seeping backward. God. Knowing that it will not succeed, not this time. God, God.

It recedes... (*God*)

Recedes... (*God, God*)

It disappears.

Sighing shakily, the tension passing from him like a suddenly-relieved pressure valve, he imagines a light, a bright light, shining down upon him. The light is warm and it soaks his face in its radiance and he looks up at it and smiles; for his worries, they are gone; there is nothing more to worry about ever. The light shines down and he closes his eyes. He is warm; and vaguely, distantly, he can hear the steady soothing rumble of the bus engine and everything is all right. The darkness is gone. Vanquished. His victory is complete, at least for now. Only the light remains, the peaceful and warm white light....

Time passes: and his eyes snap open suddenly as the bus bumps and hisses to a slow stop. He looks out the window and realizes with some astonishment that they have arrived. He looks at his watch: three hours have gone by. It is early afternoon. The morning, his mother kissing his forehead and saying goodbye, seems far away; he sees now only the bright walls of the Runningwater bus station, and, across the street, a line of pleasant-looking shops in the sunlight—a restaurant; a book shop; a grocery store. People ride by on bicycles and the small children wave at the arriving bus. It gives him a warm feeling, this vision of a California small town, rather like an old movie or a painting from the *Saturday Evening Post*: and it rejuvenates him, makes him feel alive again, so much so that, as he stands and presses his bag close to his stomach, he is almost euphoric: California!—Malibu! Santa Barbara! Venice Beach! They are far away still; but as he climbs down the bus steps and feels the golden glow of the sun wash over his face, they seem close. Obtainable. Possible....

4

The dinner had been awkward and not at all promising. It had seemed to Robin that they must have known, Margaret and Otto, of the real reasons for his being there: for while there had been a great initial gush of emotion toward him at the bus station ("Why honey, look how you've grown! You're nearly as big as your uncle! And it's so *wonderful* to have you here!"), he had thought all evening that he could detect them surreptitiously glancing at each other, and a vague, intangible unease between them. Not that they were less than cordial. They had arrived, complete with three of the four kids (David, Damien, and Donald, all older and obviously not much interested in him), minutes after the bus had pulled in, and, after the expected ceremonial shows of affection, had taken him for a hamburger and ice cream at the restaurant across the street. Uncle

Otto had not changed, except that he was perhaps even more of an ashen ghost than before; he had a benign, oval face with sagging skin and he walked with a stoop. Aunt Margaret, too, was the same, her hair coiled like a nest of golden cobras ready to strike, and her voice, emanating from a mouth so wide as to appear to be pasted on, covering the proceedings in a sort of indeterminate hum: "Why, I just can't get over how much our little Robin has grown! Otto, isn't it something? How long has it been since we've seen you? It can't have been very long, and yet you've sprouted up like a weed! Five years? No! Has it been all of five years? Still and all, honey, to have sprouted like this in just five years…!"

Nor had the sons been of any interest. He was reintroduced to each of them but quickly forgot which was which, for they seemed so basically interchangeable. They all had short blonde hair, cashmere pullover sweaters, and, incredibly, all wore identical horn-rimmed glasses.

When they spoke, it was as if one person had been split into three:

"It's so nice to have you here," one would say.

"In Runningwater," added another.

"All the way from Wind Point." The third.

"It's a long trip, isn't it?" One.

"From Wind Point." Two.

"All the way to Runningwater." Three.

"We made that trip once."

"To Wind Point."

"From Runningwater."

"It was a very long trip."

"He means from Runningwater."

"To Wind Point."

Inside his mind Robin ceased making any distinction at all and simply thought of them as D^3.

But, he muses, the drive out had been pretty: they lived not in the town proper but a few miles outside it, past long stretches of grass field dotted occasionally with old houses. All around them were big mountains, some of them powdered at their peaks with tiny puffs of snow; and when they had at last pulled into the driveway Robin had been shocked at the sheer size of the place. It was not old but new, composed of soft slopes and angles, brilliantly white in color, and when he stepped into the cool interior he saw that the layout was positively labyrinthian: doors leading to more doors, to unseen rooms, mysterious passageways. In the backyard—immaculately green and trimmed—there was a glittering blue swimming pool and, as one-third of D^3 pointed out to him, over the back fence and perhaps fifty yards down a sloping valley was a river: the Molopo, he called it: it was hardly raging, being more like a sparkling ribbon imbedded in the landscape; but the effect was undeniably breathtaking, for the valley was filled with wild grass and a carpet of butter-yellow flowers that stretched nearly as far as he could see. Big willow trees dotted the vista, and he could hear the long grass murmuring in the breeze.

California, he thought. I'm in California.

But by dinner the ceremonial business had ended and he sat near the end of a big dining-room table eating roast chicken covered with a strangely sweet glaze. Uncle Otto sat at the head, near Robin, and across at the other side of the table was Aunt Margaret. D^3 was spread out randomly between them: and next to Margaret's seat was the girl, Priscilla.

"You'll have to excuse Cissy for not meeting you at the bus station," Aunt Margaret explained through her vacant smile. "She wasn't feeling well. Were you, darling?"

"No," the girl replied sharply, looking straight at Robin.

Priscilla was not what Robin would have called pretty. Her head was oddly shaped, rather like a block, her chin too flat and wide for the face; her short black hair was oddly, unevenly cut; and her small eyes seemed too close together, making her appear pinched and intense. And yet, for all that, there was something appealing about her—her scrubby jeans and T-shirts; her surprisingly low, husky voice; her bare feet. He didn't know quite what it was, except perhaps that she so clearly did not fit in with this group of false smiles and forced gaiety and cashmere sweaters...He was very surprised that they even let her sit at the table, looking as she did. When he had thought of her earlier he had imagined a bright, girlish dress and makeup; for that is what he had supposed her parents would have forced her into; but there she sat, quite out of place and obviously wanting to leave.

"My poor darling," Aunt Margaret continued airily, "has had a terrible chest cold all week, and it's been making her cough and wheeze and it's frightened me half to death. But the doctor didn't say it was anything to worry about, did he, honey?"

"No," Priscilla repeated, again staring straight at Robin. He felt as if she could see clear through him to the wall behind.

But even the considerable conversational abilities with which God had endowed Aunt Margaret had not been enough to keep silence from descending upon the table before long. Uncle Otto, quiet as death—as usual—said nothing. Aunt Margaret glanced at him now and again, and it seemed to Robin that the glance was intended to convey some sort of message regarding himself, but he could not guess what it might be. Priscilla stared at her plate and ate sullenly. The various elements comprising D^3 glanced at each other occasionally and looked bored.

And so the dinner had been uneasy; attempts at talk had sputtered into silence; yet at the end, when the activity of clearing away the dishes had begun, things seemed to return to their usual animated state. Aunt Margaret began chittering again. D^3 talked among itself, and even Uncle Otto allowed a few hoarsely whispered words to escape his lips. Priscilla did not stay for the clearing of the table, instead disappearing somewhere into the dark halls of the house.

Eventually they had gone to the living room—they called it the "TV room," for apparently there was another room called the living room—and, while situation comedies played across the screen (and Robin remembered but tried to forget his youthful prayers of deliverance to the lands of the TV families), D^3 gradually made its exit so that he was left only with Margaret and Otto. Of course Robin noticed that there had been none but the most perfunctory inquiries after his parents; beyond that it was almost as if they didn't exist at all, as if Wind Point itself had vanished in the mist. Which, he supposed, was fine with him. But it was the secrecy he found odd: if the man and the woman in the house in the cul-de-sac had actually ceased to be, if Wind Point was in fact only a mirage, shouldn't they simply have told him? But then he was used to charged silences floating between others and himself. At times he pictured the silence in the house in the cul-de-sac as a black cloud hovering ominously in the air of the rooms: but whereas a cloud was composed only of puffs of air, the black cloud in the house was different: it was actually alive: and it could stretch from room to room, could seep under doors and through windows and sometimes it could even occupy every room at once, so that the house was completely filled with the threatening darkness, the living silence...

And so the evening had passed. Finally Aunt Margaret showed him to his room—opulent as the rest of the house, a big room with a four-poster bed and a view of the huge backyard, a color television, a stereo.

"Have a good sleep, dear," she said.

"Okay. Thanks, Aunt Margaret."

She stared out the window for a moment. "And then," she began, "tomorrow..."

The Unspoken

But she fell silent, and for a long moment said nothing. Finally she looked back at him and smiled strangely.

"Funny," she said. "I forgot what I was going to say. Goodnight, honey—"

It is, he has to admit as he looks around the room, quite a set-up. The room is practically its own apartment: but for a kitchen, it has everything anyone could need. He can even lock his door, something which has always been impossible in the house in the cul-de-sac. He walks to the door and turns the lock and feels a sudden rush of exhilaration. Control, he thinks: privacy. Yes, the relatives are peculiar, the silences are uncomfortable, but with a room like this one...He goes to the window and looks out at the pool, glittering blue in the darkness. As he watches, someone switches on the light and the water appears suddenly alive and depthless, a bright oasis in a swamp of night. Yes, he thinks; after the initial difficult months in Malibu or Santa Barbara or Venice Beach, this is the kind of place he will acquire for himself.

Impulsively he fishes his swimming trunks out of his bag and begins to change into them, his sudden nudity giving him a wild feeling of liberty—the door is locked, after all, no one can see in. Usually he feels ashamed of his nakedness and rushes to hide it when he steps from the shower or changes out of his gym shorts at school, but now the sensation is quite different: and he stands there looking out at the pool for some minutes.

He cannot recall ever standing in a room unclothed for any length of time. He can feel the cool breeze of the air conditioning flowing over his body and he is suddenly overcome by a wave of sensuousness—not sex, but rather the sensation of his body as millions of nerve endings, delicate sensors. He feels astonishingly alive. He wonders how a mere doffing of clothes can make him feel so totally different; but there it is: and he thinks again of his new-found freedom, or at least approaching freedom. He can almost touch it.

Finally, after some minutes, he hears movement in the house and the lights being switched off. Soon there is silence. He remains standing at the window, staring out at the sparkling gem-like waters and sensing a remarkable awareness of himself as a living thing, a breathing organism of sinews and synapses and nerve fibers. For a moment he wonders if, in fact, he is actually any more than that; or if he is simply a physical unit with no other purpose or meaning to his existence. But, he knows, he is *alive*. Remarkably so, standing at the window staring out at the waters. Intensely alive.

At last he pulls himself from the window and slips into his trunks. He finds a towel in the bathroom and opens his sanctuary door quietly, glancing up and down the hall in the silent darkness. He doubts that he is supposed to be doing this, but soon, he knows—very soon!—he will be free, his own man in sun-soaked California, and then no one will tell him what to do.

He moves to the sliding glass door which leads to the rear patio.

When he is outside, the cool night breeze touching him, the feeling of sensuousness returns: and when he crawls into the pool—wonderfully well-heated—and paddles out into the middle, he looks up at the dazzling night sky above him and feels. . .*connected*. As if he is part of all this: the water, the air, the stars overhead: that he is not utterly separate from them, not alone and lost in a dark void, but integrally a part of it all, a participant, an essential spoke in the vast wheel. He is aware of his body again, its vivid aliveness, and as he looks around he imagines, or perhaps perceives, that everything else shares in his aliveness. The water, the air, the stars, he is not isolated from them, not cut-off and distant, but a part of them, as they are a part of him.

He closes his eyes. It is too complicated for words. He wants, now, only to float on the living waves, to think of nothing. *I am alive.* This had never really occurred to him before; intellectually, perhaps, but the emotional reality of it had always eluded him, until now, until he found himself floating....

He feels ripples on the water and slowly, without opening his eyes, realizes that he is not alone in the pool. For a moment he remains drifting, eyes shut, uninterested; but finally he looks toward the other end of the pool.

It is Priscilla. She is sitting on the edge of the pool kicking gently at the water. She is wearing a dark one-piece bathing suit and she is not, Robin supposes, entirely ugly; her body seems too big for her somehow, as if someone had connected the wrong head to the wrong torso, and yet the effect is not one of unpleasantness but rather an almost pleasing strangeness.

"Hi," he says.

She does not respond, only glances at him and then looks down pensively at her feet in the water.

Robin waits a moment and then, inwardly shrugging, closes his eyes again and tries to regain the mystical sensation of connectedness he had had before...but though he floats on the water for some minutes he cannot find it again. He is too aware of the girl at the other end of the pool. He opens his eyes and glances towards her; she simply kicks her feet in the water, first one, then the other, methodically.

Robin paddles closer to her.

"Going to swim?" he asks.

"I dunno," she answers, glancing at him and then looking into the water again.

"Maybe..." he begins, trying to think of something to say, "maybe you shouldn't, if you've been sick."

"Maybe."

"I mean, it might make your mom mad or something."

The girl looks at him for a moment and then suddenly laughs. The sound is hoarse, somehow rude. "That's a fat one!" she says. She stares at her feet in the water. "I can do *anything*."

"Anything?"

"Anything. She doesn't care. Well…she cares. But I mean she doesn't *do* anything."

Robin watches her as he floats in the warm blue.

"I wasn't sick, anyway," she says.

There is a long silence; only the sound of the water lapping on the girl's legs.

"You weren't?" Robin asks finally.

"Nah. She just made that up. She does that when…." She pauses momentarily, glances at Robin and grins quickly. "…When I'm a brat."

"Oh." He wishes he could think of something brighter to say, but he finds within himself a growing nervousness, a tension running through his arms and legs.

"Mm-hm. She just makes up stories. It's really funny. Nobody ever says anything about them. I mean even though everybody knows they're just lies."

He looks at her. "Why does she…lie?"

Her quick grin surfaces again, then disappears. "She has to. I'm abnormal."

"What do you mean?"

She shrugs. "Just abnormal. I do weird things sometimes. Or people say they're weird."

By this time Robin has floated to within a yard of her feet and he leans his arms up onto the side of the pool. He is listening closely. "Like what?" he asks.

"I dunno. Weird stuff. Like once when I was a kid I took all my dolls outside in the backyard and burned them up. Weird stuff."

"Why did you do that?"

She doesn't answer for a moment. "I dunno," she says finally. "I just did it."

Robin stares at her legs moving in the fluid depths. He becomes fascinated with how the water makes her legs change shape, bend and shrink and quiver. Her voice is unlike any girl's he has ever heard: oddly low, and with a curious drag that almost makes it sound like a record played at too slow a speed. And yet she herself is quick: he watches as she notices a mosquito flying near her. Suddenly her hands dart up and smash it.

"Got him!" she says, looking at her palms. She leans forward and runs her hands through the water.

They are silent for a moment.

"Do your parents let you do anything?" she asks.

He shakes his head.

"See, you're normal."

Robin frowns slightly. *Normal* is the last word he would ever use to describe himself: images, shadows play across his mind of blasphemous prayers, his dirty touchings of himself: but he says nothing. Instead he asks her again if she is going to swim.

"I guess so," she sighs, and stands up. He watches as she takes a deep breath and then dives head-first into the water. She begins swimming laps powerfully. She is an expert swimmer. Robin watches her for some minutes as she chops through the water in the same way, it seems to him, a warrior would chop through enemies. He sees himself on a blazing white sun-horse....

At last he paddles to the shallow end and sits on one of the submerged steps. He enjoys the feeling of weightlessness as he watches her, though somehow she makes him nervous and he can feel his heart thumping quickly in his chest. He begins to think that she will never stop, but will just go on chopping through the water until morning; at last, however, she stops at the deep end, leans her arms over the edge, and breathes heavily. After a minute she paddles slowly back toward Robin.

"How was that?" she asks breathily, sitting on the lowest step in the pool so that she is submerged over her chest. She faces away from him and he can see her powerful shoulders rising and falling as she catches her breath. "Do you want to race?"

"I can't swim like that," he admits.

She glances back at him. "Sure you can. You live right on the ocean. You must swim all the time."

"But it's cold in Wind Point. Nobody ever swims. There's not even any beach."

"Oh. Still...A guy should be a better swimmer than any girl."

He feels vaguely embarrassed and remains silent. She turns in the water and looks at him. Her small, close-set eyes study him rather as one would study a specimen in a butterfly collection.

"I hurt your feelings," she says suddenly in her too-slow voice. "I'm sorry. I didn't mean to hurt your feelings."

"No," Robin says, and smiles slightly. "I'm fine."

"No you're not. I'm a pig."

He laughs. "You're not a pig."

"I am. That's what my brothers call me, a pig. They're the pigs though. I've seen them when they…" She looks at him. "You know what they do? Damien and Donald grab me when my parents aren't home and they hold me down and then David comes up and farts in my face."

He laughs again, loudly. "You're kidding!"

"I am not. And it's not funny. And they call *me* the pig."

Chuckles continue to rifle through him for a moment. He says again, "You're not a pig."

"You're right. I'm no fluckin' pig." She puts her hands behind her head as a model would. "I'm a bootiful goil," she says.

Robin grins and chuckles.

"Why are you laughing?" she says, puckering her lips and looking down her nose at him. "Don't you think I'm bootiful?"

"Is that different than beautiful?"

"Sure it is. Don't you know anything? 'Bootiful' means you only look good in boots. Ha! I made that up myself."

"You're not wearing boots, though. So I can't know if you're bootiful."

"Hey, you're right." She glances at her bare feet under the water, then looks suddenly toward the sliding glass door. "Too bad they're asleep already. My dad has some old cowboy boots. You'd see how bootiful I am."

"I thought you said they'd let you do anything, though."

She glances sharply at him; then smiles. "Smart guy," she says.

Robin grins again and shrugs.

"Oh no!" she cries suddenly, staring at him with wide eyes.

"What?"

"It's...I can't tell you!"

"What, what?"

"It's...it's a *water fight!*" And she chops her hand through the water, drenching him. He laughs wildly and shoves water back at her: keeping his eyes half-shut he can see only the glittering liquid as it splashes to and fro crazily. He can hear her laughter and his own as they soak each other; then somehow they touch one another and her strong arms grab him: they struggle for a long moment, giggling, Robin closely aware of her wet skin, her muscles. She is much stronger than he is and she quickly locks him in a half-nelson.

"Okay!" Robin shouts, laughing. "I give!"

Instead of letting go, she dunks his head under the water. Then she pulls it back up.

"Priscilla, okay, okay!" he gasps through giggles. "I give up already! You win!"

But she dunks him again. She holds him down longer this time and Robin suddenly finds his heart pounding and a sensation of sheer terror coursing through him. Then she pulls him up.

"*Priscilla...!*"

She slams his head into the water again: he struggles frantically to free himself but his arms flail uselessly at her. Her grip is vicelike. He is helpless. He tries to kick at her but the water makes his feet too heavy, too slow. His vision seems to blur under the water. He cannot breathe. He tries to cry out but only water fills his throat.

...Then, just as suddenly, she pulls him up and pushes him away.

Coughing, shaking, he staggers to the pool's edge and crawls weakly out of the water. He coughs up the bitter chlorinated liquid and tries to keep his body from shaking so uncontrollably. But it is hopeless. He lays at the side of the pool coughing and quivering, his head burning hot, his body freezing.

Finally he looks toward her. She is standing waist-deep in the water with her hands on her hips, grinning.

"I could of killed you," she says.

He tries to breathe. "Why..." He breaks off as he hacks up water. "Priscilla—why..."

But then he has to cough again and he closes his eyes. When, after a full minute, his body at last calms, he opens them again and looks toward the girl. She is gone.

5

Over the next several days Robin plans his escape. He has money in his pocket: and yet he must be careful. It would be disastrous to be caught before disappearing into the sun-drenched anonymity of Southern California. He feels a bit like a criminal, scheming this way without giving his relatives the slightest inkling of his plans—but he can see no alternative. To say anything would be suicide....

Strangely, after a few days the incident at the pool seems to take on the haziness of an only partly-remembered dream, or rather nightmare; and indeed, at times he finds himself wondering if it really happened. Priscilla he hardly sees except at meals where she sits in sullen silence, offering him only the same occasional piercing glances she had given him the first dinner.

Instead he is forced to spend his time with various combinations of D^3. These are awkward encounters, for they are too many years older, and it is too obvious that their parents have told them to "entertain" him. Thus, long dull evenings in town at hamburger restaurants and movies when really he would rather just stay in his room reading and enjoying the luxury....

And planning. Though, honestly, it is a difficult thing to plan; there are so many variables, and who knew where he would actually end up? Or what he would do when he got there? Still, plan or no plan, he would go soon, he would disappear into his new life. On that he was certain, unbendable.

But at times it seems an impossible thing. At times he thinks of the man and the woman in the cul-de-sac and it seems to him that they are eternal, that things will always be the way they have been; he will always be there, with them. He can see their hands extended hugely, stretching across the states to smother him...and yet at other times it all seems so easy, so possible. He cannot imagine anything simpler than just hopping on a bus and disappearing forever. Who would stop him? Who, really, would *care*? He was free. His own man. He would make his own decisions. Still, he is, he feels, realistic; he is only thirteen, and surely that fact will cause difficulties. What jobs were there for thirteen-year-olds? Anyway, it is questionable if anyone would even believe that he really is that age—when he looks in the mirror at his long, pale hair and nearly cream-colored skin, he thinks of someone much younger. And he is short for his age. And...but there is no sense, he supposes, in going through the whole rigmarole of his shortcomings. The subject is too depressing.

Days and nights, a bright haze of them, pass in this fashion. Just as he thinks that *this* might be the day, some other doubt seizes him and makes him delay. The terrible thing is his inability to confide in anyone; and he feels dirty, plotting his subterfuge in the middle of everyone's hospitality. He is consumed with guilt over it. And yet what else is there to do? For surely they would stop him if they knew—he is "only a child," after all, and he knows that his aunt and uncle would feel it their duty to force him back to the house in the cul-de-sac, the one place he is sure he never needs to see again. So it is like being a kind of spy, leading a double life: the simple straightforward boy everyone sees; and then the dark underlife hidden away, about to burst into the light....

As time passes in the house Robin begins to feel more and more isolated from the rest of them. There are fewer and fewer excursions with D^3. He spends less time in the family room with the television. Eventually he takes to spending nearly all his time in his room just, he realizes, as he did in Wind Point: he reads; he writes in a diary he has begun keeping; often he simply listens, but increasingly there is silence in this part of the house, increasingly footsteps do not approach his room. They leave him alone.

But finally there comes a time one evening when he hears the dull thudding of bare feet on carpet approaching the room. He puts down his book of Poe and, without knocking, Priscilla steps into the room.

"Hi," she says, closing the door behind her.

"Hi," he says, surprised, for he has hardly seen her in days. She wears a tattered black T-shirt and dirty jeans.

As he watches, she walks over to the window—where he had stood nude, he remembers—and stares outside pensively.

"How come you never come out of here?" she asks. "Mom and Dad think you don't like this place."

He feels his heart accelerating slightly as he recalls the pool. His hand twitches. "I come out," he says.

"Not very much."

"For breakfast and stuff. And I went shopping with Aunt Margaret just this morning."

She glances at him with her small eyes. "Yeah, but they still talk about you."

Robin looks away. "What do they say?"

"I dunno. Things."

"Like what?"

She turns from the window and leans against the wall with her hands behind her back.

"Just things," she says.

There is a pause.

"What do you do in here?" she asks.

He glances at her and shrugs. "Read, mostly."

"*Read.*" She spits the word out. "I hate reading. It's stupid."

"What do you like to do?"

"Nothing."

"Nothing at all?"

"I hate everything," she says, looking blankly at the opposite wall.

"Why?"

She shrugs. "I just do. You don't like it here, do you?"

"No. I like it. Really. It's just…" And for a wild moment he wants to tell her everything, all his plans: but then he sees himself underwater again, held down, trapped.

Priscilla wanders over to the television and switches it on, the volume very low. "Just what?" she asks.

"I don't know. Nothing."

"And," she continues, flipping the dial aimlessly before the picture has faded in, "I don't have anybody to do anything with. I'm always by myself."

He is not sure how to react. He swallows. "I—well, I didn't know were were…friends. I mean…"

She glances sharply at him. "Friends? Who said we weren't friends? I thought we should have been…Oh, *that*," she says suddenly. "You mean when I tried to kill you? Oh, that wasn't anything." Her eyes return to the blank TV screen. "I wouldn't really of killed you."

"Still..."

"You're right, it wasn't very nice." She takes a half-eaten Baby Ruth bar out of her pocket, unwraps it, and breaks what there is in two. "Here," she says, tossing a piece to him.

They chew for a moment and then, through a full mouth, she says: "Did you really think I would of killed you?"

He grins. The conversation seems rather silly. "I don't know."

"Because I wouldn't of. I was just being mean. I'm a pig anyway. That's what my brothers call me. I told you that, didn't I?"

"Yes."

"Yeah. So who knows what a human pig might do." She stares at the television. "I wouldn't of killed you, though."

He smiles again. "That's nice to know."

Priscilla laughs suddenly, a hoarse, low laugh, and looks at him. "Don't you *get* it?"

He looks at her and shakes his head.

An odd expression comes to her face and she stares at a spot on the wall behind him. In her slow voice she says, "I just...do things sometimes." She sighs. "Things. Just things, I dunno. I'm sorry. I'm sorry I tried to kill you."

Robin giggles. "It's okay."

"It's not nice, trying to kill somebody."

"No," he grins, "you're right."

"I'll never try to kill you again."

"That's good to know, Priscilla."

She stands suddenly and falls onto her stomach on the bed. "You call me *Priscilla*," she says. "That's funny. Everybody calls me *Cissy*."

"Should I call you Cissy?"

"No! I hate that name. I'm no fluckin' sissy. *Cissy. Cissy Wilder.*" She minces the words. "That should be my mom's name, *Cissy*. Why didn't they give me a real name? Like *Alex*. That's a good name. It can be a girl's name too."

"Alexandra. Mm-hm."

"No. Just Alex. That's the name I'd like. Not stupid fluckin' *Cissy*. The boys used to make so much fun of me at school! 'Till I whipped them. I beat the tar out of two of them at once, one time. Now everybody leaves me alone. I like it that way."

"But you have friends?"

"Nah. I don't need friends. Who needs a bunch of silly girls or stupid boys hanging around? I just go my own way. But you should hang around," she says. "You're all right. For a guy."

He thinks of his willowy reflection in the mirror, how it seems to him more like a girl's: the hair, too fine; the face, too pale, too soft; the eyes, too round and big; the lashes, too long. *Why I'd give anything to have your eyelashes, honey,* he hears one of his mother's friends telling him inside the steamy, sweet-smelling beauty parlor in Wind Point. He remembers how his face would grow hot with embarrassment as the ladies swarmed over him: *Oh baby,* they would say, *are you a shy one, hm?* And yet he liked it too, when they ran their fingers through his hair and spoke to him in silly voices and kissed him. Years before, his mother had taken him there every Wednesday afternoon and when they came in all the women would stop doing what they were doing and rush over to him and offer him cookies, comic books: yes, it was embarrassing; yes, at school he had been made fun of; but the feeling he had upon entering that parlor, the feeling of glory, or of being glorified, transcended any reservations he had. He liked it.

And of course when he thinks of his fantasies, when he reflects on what he spends his time dreaming of, he realizes that they are most often dreams of fame: as an actor, an athlete, a dancer, an author: he dreams of crowds on their feet in appreciation, calling out his name. At the same time, he is too aware of his sickness, and how the sickness would always render any such fame impossible. He would, of course, be found out. Discovered. Unmasked. The unspeakable thing—worse than touching himself, worse even than his blasphemous prayers—would be shoved rudely into the harsh white light. And that would be unbearable, like a dream he often has in which he is standing on a huge empty stage, a crowd of people cheering him, when suddenly he looks down and realizes he is wearing no clothes. The applause suddenly dies; and he stares back at them all, horrified, panic-stricken, helpless.

He looks at Priscilla, lying crossways on the bed.

"Well—okay." he says. He smiles slightly. "I'll hang around."

She rolls over and faces him, swallowing the last of the chocolate. "Good. I'm so bored I could puke. We'll find something to do."

"Burning dolls, maybe?"

As soon as he speaks he realizes it is a mistake. She looks at him with obvious annoyance.

"It's not nice to make fun of people."

"I wasn't making fun. I'm sorry—"

"I tell you something and then you just laugh at me." She sighs and stares at the ceiling. "You think I'm a freak, just like everybody else does."

"I don't think you're a freak. Really."

"No? Everybody does. Maybe you're the freak, then."

"Maybe I am."

"Oh, fluck it. I like being a freak. People leave you alone. Let's watch a dirty movie on TV." She jumps up and switches the station. "Mom and Dad don't think I know that after ten o'clock this one station runs dirty movies. They're not really dirty, though. They're just naked people and stuff. I mean nobody *does* anything."

The creakings, the moans: his ear at the wall.

She finds the station and sits back on the bed. "Here it is. Watch. It won't take more than five minutes for some chick to take off her shirt. Some of them have the biggest boobies I've ever seen. I'm glad I don't have big tumors like that on *me*."

The Unspoken

Oh, unspeakable thoughts: unsurfaced yearnings: and he stares at the screen, knowing how silent he must remain about it all, the true sickness, the true pathology, how he cannot allow even the thought of it to enter his mind, for it is a disease, something from Hell, and he knows his mind must be purged of if somehow, and he prays, but the thoughts come back to him, he cannot stop them: and this, he knows, is a sign of his weakness. His lack of moral strength. He closes his eyes briefly, tries to keep his mind silent.

"*Ha!*" Priscilla's hoarse laugh snaps his eyes open. "What'd I tell you?"

Sure enough, there on the screen are two women, one white, one Oriental, dancing to loud music in someone's apartment with their tops off.

"Look at those suckers bounce," Priscilla says, staring raptly at the screen. "Jesus."

But Robin does not want to look, for this is part of the illness, it reminds him too much of it. Sometimes he can nearly forget about it, but other times, like now, it swarms over him. He cannot bring himself to formulate the actual idea in his mind. It is too bizarre. He tries to keep a note, a single musical note, droning through his brain; but the note keeps falling away and he is left with the awful rising visions. He feels the terror creeping upon him again. He breathes very slowly. *God*, he thinks. *God. God.*

Priscilla is still speaking but Robin does not hear. He tries to keep the note in his mind; failing that, he thinks of God, whom he cannot see, has never seen, but who, he knows, must exist, must, because if he does not...but then even that thought is too horrifying and he feels the black ink of the terror encroaching upon his awareness, his mind. He clamps his teeth together tightly. *Don't think of it. Think of anything. Not it.*

Pictures run crazily through his brain, in mad jumble: Melissa in the cellar; the staircase at night; creakings, moans; fat-congealed stew slopping into a bowl. He lets them play, fills his mind with them. For at least then the terror cannot enter, cannot find its way to him through the dark subterranean corridors. It seems to him that he can hear a phone ringing somewhere; but he cannot be sure; and yet it seems incredibly near, loud, someone must pick it up or he is sure the terrible ring will soar straight through his heart like a poisoned arrow, and dimly, only dimly, does he see the bright flashes of the women's breasts on the television screen, dimly, only dimly does he hear Priscilla's slow voice speaking, but he cannot make out the words: they are too far away: and he sits there unmoving for what seems an endless time: he notices a watch on Priscilla's wrist and sees a clock stretching like licorice down a dark hall: the hands of the clock like spider's legs: the numbers on the distorted face blur grotesquely as if underwater: and then he is underwater again with the clock ticking madly in his ears, with his lungs drowned, his scream muffled to silence, the only sound the stark slamming of each second passing on the mad clock, and the ringing, the ringing which has stopped but which he can still hear like the knocking on a strange door: he cannot answer, cannot answer: footsteps: they approach: he can hear them approaching: Priscilla looks toward the door: someone is fondling the Oriental woman's breasts: putting his mouth to them: the clock stretches, flips inside out, each second like a hammer in his ears: he cannot breathe: knocking, knocking: as to wake the dead: he sees his own corpse in the water: huge-nippled breasts quivering in sunlight: *crash* goes the door, *crash*, and it begins to open: he is sure the crashing clock will come tumbling in or some snake-masked monster: oh deep dark helpless: he knows: he knows: she need say nothing: but her mouth opens: the woman at the door opens her mouth: Robin, honey (knockings, knockings) could you come into the other (*crash!*) room, something terrible (*crash! crash!*) has happened, something has happened, honey, something terrible has happened—

6

Reflecting on it later, Robin would wonder how it was that it never seemed strange or mystical that he already knew what they were going to say before they opened their mouths: that the information, the essential aspect of it, some secret vein of himself had already received; but it did not, at the time, seem strange at all. She had led him into Otto's study where they had sat down together on a small sofa, Otto at his desk facing them. Both of their faces were ghastly, horror-stricken. Margaret had fidgeted; Otto had stared at his shoes; Robin sat watching both of them.

"I...don't know how to start," Margaret said, her eyes appealing to Otto for help.

Otto cleared his throat. "I—Robin, we...received a telephone call a few minutes ago. Something—something has happened. Very bad. Your—"

Say it, say it, he thought to himself, knowing in some instinctive unspeakable way what was the matter. And as they stutteringly told him he had hardly listened, instead hearing the single musical note droning inside his head. Only snatches of their words permeated his consciousness: "*Terrible accident... hospital...*" Words suspended in air, sailing around in circles in the dark, jumbled and meaningless. He began to think he could actually see the words coming from their mouths, pouring out like the words of characters in a comic strip, and then they themselves were like that, their outlines ink-black, their faces two-dimensional and exaggerated and mad. The words swooped and dived in the air like bumper cars in an amusement park, rolling together, colliding, bursting apart: *gone* and *Robin* and *honey* and *hospital* careened into each other, the letters flying asunder in the dark sky that was no longer the air of the room but rather a crystalline night vista, the letters bright and glowing, flying here and there and then bursting and tumbling like falling stars when they collided and fell earthward.

The facts were so simple as to be absurd, and he hardly heard them. What use were they? What possible use? He kept the note driving through his mind as other words stabbed inward: *tonight* and *home* and *sorry* and *tomorrow*. What they said had no meaning, but they could not realize that. They could not know. And even when Aunt Margaret put her arms around him and sobbed, that had no meaning. He was watching himself from a distant place, staring as he awkwardly returned the embrace and wondered what in the world all the fuss was about. It was simply a collection of facts, nothing to be concerned about. Nothing at all. And soon the voices died in the room and there were no more words flying about in the night sky: nothing but Aunt Margaret's sobbing, Uncle Otto's manly squeeze of his shoulder. But they were the shattered ones, not he. For Robin it was as simple as one and one: merely facts....

And later, after a long time, she had led him back to his bedroom—Priscilla was gone—and helped him to undress and helped him into bed, and stroked his forehead tenderly, and really she was very nice, but it was all totally unnecessary. She had even asked if he wanted her to stay with him that night.

"I'm all right," he answered.

And yet she had remained with him a long time, holding his hand. It was understood that they were all to go to Wind Point tomorrow morning, it was too late tonight, Robin was to try to sleep, there was nothing that could be done. Try to sleep, she said to him, try to sleep. But she hardly had to encourage him, for he felt sleep pouring over him like balm, a thick, dark sleep, dreamless and void. He wondered what everyone was so excited about. Really, it was just another thing that had happened, and what reason was there to get excited over finished things, foregone conclusions? She was dead. Simple as that. There were details; but those details could never alter the basic truth, and so he did not hear them. Dead. *Dead.* It was simple, it was complete, not at all difficult to understand, even rather mundane really, not something that needed to be discussed or argued over, finished. And so not worth thinking about anymore.

He slept for hours, dreamlessly.

When he awoke it was still dark. For long moments he did not know where he was. Then he knew where he was but neglected to think of the new facts which had been revealed to him. Then he remembered those too.

But he did not think about them very much. Rather, as he lay there staring at the ceiling, his plans returned to him. They were to take him away in a matter of hours…California would be gone. All his plans gone. Everything gone. There seemed little he could do about it; and yet his mind rebelled against the notion. Wind Point! How could he go back? How? When he had been so close? When it had been a matter of days until he would have lighted out once and for all? How? What would he be going back to? It was impossible. He tried to imagine the house in the cul-de-sac with just the shadow-man and himself in it. Tried to imagine the clumping footsteps on their own in the darkness, nothing preceding them, nothing following. The sound of coffee percolating late at night, gone. The muttered late-night conversation between them, gone. And the weight on his bed: the creakings as she sat down heavily next to him and buttoned his pajama top, the little diamond in her ring reflecting the two of them like tiny mirrors. Gone, smoke in wind. He tried to imagine these things, but the visions would not come. He tried to imagine sitting at home by himself when the shadow-man came through the door and it would be the two of them alone in the house together. He could not envision it. He could not envision any of it. Clearly, obviously, it was impossible. It simply was not in the realm of possibility. This all seemed quite logical to him, self-evident; and yet what was there to do about it? In this state of marvelous mental clarity he also realized that, envisioned or not, these things would happen upon his return to Wind Point: these unimaginable events: and how could he knock on the strange door to the future without being able to imagine what lay on the other side? Before, all had been perfectly clear; now...

He was suddenly aware of the fact that he was alone in the room. Aunt Margaret had gone; the house was silent; though he was sure that people were lying awake in their beds, listening. For what? He thought about Aunt Margaret and Uncle Otto. He thought about Priscilla in her room. He thought of the Oriental woman's breasts on the TV screen and wondered vaguely if he were to turn on the television if she would still be there.

Finally he stepped from bed and stood at the window overlooking the pool. It was dark; but the light from the moon made the water glitter. He looked beyond the pool, at the darkness past the fence. He tried to picture what the tiny ribbon of river looked like in the darkness. He thought he could feel a breeze touching his face, but the window was closed; there was no breeze. And yet he could feel it: he was sure of it.

He watched himself as he put on his clothes and slipped a sweater over his head. He watched himself as he opened the door to his room. He watched himself in the dark hallway, and heard the quiet sliding of the glass door as he stepped outside. Later he heard the sound of his legs passing through the long wet grass toward the river in the valley below.

7

Her voice comes to him out of the darkness.

"Psst! Hey!"

He is not sure how long he has been sitting at the edge of the river: perhaps hours: as he turns to look toward her it seems that she is pulling him from some deathly sort of deep sleep from which he might never have emerged. And yet he has not been asleep.

"Hi," she says, her legs swishing through the grass and crushing twigs underfoot. It is still night, but the moon is nearly full; he can see her clearly as she moves through the silver-lit grass.

"Hi, Priscilla."

"What're you doing?" she says, coming closer to him.

He shakes his head. "Just sitting."

"In the middle of the night? Out here?"

She comes up next to him and looks at him a moment before sitting. She has on jeans, sandals, a gold Mickey Mouse sweater several sizes too large; she stares piercingly at him.

"Are you going to run away?" she says.

He glances at her. "Who says that?"

"Nobody."

They are silent for a moment.

"I wasn't going to run away," he says finally. "I was just sitting here."

She shrugs.

They stare at the tiny trickle of river. The water splashing over the rocks makes a gentle, comforting sound; a slight breeze in the flowers and grass behind them is like a long sigh. He looks up at the moon.

"I heard about what happened," she says.

He does not respond.

"Mom and Dad brought us all together and told us. I guess we're all going to Wind Point in the morning."

"Guess so," he answers quietly.

She stares at him. "Are you crying?"

"No."

"Have you?"

"No."

"Are you going to?"

"No."

"Good," she says. "Crying is stupid. Anyway, I wouldn't know what to do if you all of a sudden started bawling."

Robin smiles vaguely.

"Maybe you should come back into the house," she says. "I mean if you're not going to run away or anything."

"I was going to run away."

After a moment she nods. "See, I knew it. Where were you going to go?"

"Where *am* I going to go." He glances at her. "I'm still going."

"Where?"

"South. Malibu. Someplace like that."

She scowls and picks up some pebbles in front of her, tosses them into the water. "What're you going to do there?"

"I don't know. Get a job, maybe. Live on the beach."

She chuckles deeply and says in her slow voice: "They'll arrest you. They got laws about people sleeping on beaches."

For a moment he does not answer.

"Still," he says finally.

They stare into the river for a time.

"You're definitely going," she says.

"Mm-hm."

"You should start out, then. It'll get light in a couple of hours."

"You're right." And he stands suddenly, his muscles complaining after the long rest. He stretches and looks down the river, imagining that it must run forever, beyond the stars on the distant horizon. It suddenly seems so easy. His worry is gone; his anxiety vanquished; it is as easy as putting one foot in front of another.

"What're you going to eat?" she asks.

He does not look at her. "I don't know. I've got some money. I'll just buy things."

"Look here," she says. When he looks toward her she shows him a yellow plastic bag he had not noticed when she arrived. She opens it and looks inside. "Cookies. Cheese. Crackers. All sorts of junk." She grins up at him.

He smiles. "Why'd you bring all that?"

She shrugs and looks down; and acts, amazingly, a bit shy. "I thought maybe...I could come along," she says finally.

"You? Why?"

She shrugs, does not look at him.

It seems several minutes before either of them say anything. Robin looks at the sky and at the glittering water. Priscilla scowls and fiddles with the handle of the plastic bag.

"You really hate it here," Robin says at last. "Don't you?"

Priscilla nods.

"I hate it too...I mean Wind Point. I hate everything about it..." Briefly the facts come back into his mind: his father's footsteps, alone: never again a weight pressing down upon his bed: he tries to visualize these things: cannot: he knows, abstractly, that they are facts, or soon will be, but his vision remains dark. He wonders how it is that simple facts can seem so unreal. Why can his mind not envision them? It would be he and his father alone in the house, were he to go back: alone forever: and so his mind should be able to conjure up pictures of what that life would be; but it cannot. He can only think of it distantly, in words, not in pictures or sounds.

Robin abruptly finds himself walking along the dark river. He has traveled perhaps fifty yards from where he had been and Priscilla is following along behind him.

"So?" she says. "Robin? Is it okay if I come along?"

He stops for a moment, looks back at her. She has the bag in one hand and is staring at the ground as she makes her way to him. Her short stringy hair bounces in the moonlight.

"Sure, I guess," Robin answers. "If you want."

She glances at him and nods seriously, looking down again. They walk on, Priscilla beside him now, walking along the water's edge.

"Where does the river go?" Robin asks.

"I dunno. It just goes. For a long time."

"I was thinking of just following it. It's going south. So maybe just follow it for a few days and then cut over to the coast."

She nods again. Robin feels rather pleased with himself: he realizes that he has managed to sound almost authoritative. Actually he is only half-sure the river is actually flowing south; as for "cutting over to the coast," well, he hasn't the slightest idea of how or when or where to do it. Nonetheless, as they stroll along through the low glistening grass at the edge of the river, it somehow does not seem to make very much difference: to keep one foot in front of the other, that is the trick, to keep moving, not to lie down and die. For that is what he would be doing if he were to return to the house in the cul-de-sac—suffocation, death: he sees himself underwater again: and glances at Priscilla.

"How old are you?" he asks.

"Twelve," she says. "Almost thirteen. How old are you?"

"Thirteen. Only just."

She giggles huskily. "So you're an *older man*," she says. "That's what Damien's girlfriend calls him, an older man. Because he's like six months older than her or something."

"Mm."

"Yeah. And then Donald has a girlfriend too. Her name's Eva. She's like Polish or something. Talks really funny. But she's nice. I like her. Sometimes she gets Donald to take all three of us to a movie or something. Except we haven't done that now for a long time. See, at the beginning it was okay. But then they got to where they always had to smooch whenever they saw each other. So we would go to the movie but they'd sit there and smooch in the theater. All these *wet, smacking* sounds—yuk! It was gross. So finally they stopped taking me. That was okay."

"What about—" he mentally sifts through the components of D^3—"David?"

"I dunno about David. He doesn't have a girlfriend. I think maybe he's a fairy."

Robin's face grows hot. The unspeakable thing invades his mind again: but he does not let it remain. He forces it away, the unmentionable thought, pushes it out and feels only a slight tremor pass through him. Then he is all right again and the thing is gone, or at least hovering far enough away that he can try to forget about it. And he knows that he must keep it that way, must allow no disgusting depravity to soil his mind: he thinks of the single note, humming...and of God, the invisible One he always looks to. *God. God.* But then sometimes, of course, he says blasphemous prayers, he prays that he might escape into some different world, the world of a television family, and he prays for awful things, for...No: none of these things must enter his mind: this night, he thinks, is the beginning of a new, clean self, pure, unsoiled, a rebirth. Everything, he thinks, starts over now. From the beginning. Erase what went before like a bad dream; everything is fresh again, shiny, bright, new.

And he believes it, looking up at the glittering sky. The air is cool, crisp. The grass is fresh. The water is clean. He knows—he *knows*—that this is the new beginning he has longed for all this time. It must be. As he walks along in the dew-sparkled grass he stares up at the cold sky and again feels the sensation of connectedness: of being part of it all: not separate: and it is exhilarating, this sensation, this togetherness, this communion with the universe. He is part of it all, he knows. He belongs. He glances at Priscilla and for a wild moment wants to tell her these things: but how can he? It would sound silly and crazy, because it is something beyond words, and yet words would be all he could use. But it fills him still with such an exquisite and indefinable joy that it threatens to burst from him in some way: he does not know how. He thinks of floating on the waters, staring up at the night sky:

the feeling, which he had thought forever lost and unobtainable, has returned, just as it was before.

"What're you laughing about?" Priscilla asks suddenly.

"Hm? I—I don't know."

"Seems like a weird time to be laughing."

"I don't know. It's like—" And he is nearly breathless as he thinks of what it truly is like: and yet he knows he cannot communicate it, not any of it, or rather such a tiny, infinitesimal fragment that it would be all but meaningless. "It's just—" And he stops again. Finally he says: "It's like…being free. That's all. Free."

She nods. They walk in silence for a time, and Robin notices that the river is slowly growing wider—what had been a mere trickle is now quite a considerable small stream. He looks to the east and it seems to him that he can detect, very faintly, the beginnings of sunrise: a vague glow at the edge of the horizon, so dim yet as to be colorless; but soon, he knows, to burst into fiery brilliance. He has always loved sunrises. Sometimes when he was younger he would get up in the darkness—long before the rest of the house was awake—and walk down the cold hall to a window which faced the light directly. At these times he would take a straight-backed chair and stare at the budding light and often he would think of stories he had read about madmen who would stare at the sun until they were blinded. The idea held some sort of appeal for him: he could imagine sitting there (how long would it take? minutes? hours?) until the sun was bright and warm in the hallway, but dim to him, growing black; and then his mother's footsteps, her bare feet coming toward him in the hall: *Honey, what are you doing?* And it would be like the end of King Oedipus, a story Mrs. Peterson had read to them in homeroom: he would look toward her but see nothing, and she would scream in fright to see his glassy, sightless eyes.…From then on he would be a cripple, and he is unsure that that would be the worst of fates: he would be waited upon, his every need catered to, he would be different, special, a celebrity. Everyone would have to do whatever he said, because after all he would be a poor helpless invalid, and so he could tell people anything, he could ask his mother to—

Then he remembers the new facts he has to consider. They seem very distant and he still cannot visualize them: as he thinks of going back to Wind Point (if he were to go, which is no longer a possibility) he suddenly realizes that he has been picturing both of them there, his mother and the shadow-dark Other, there greeting him at the door, leading him inside to the living room, whose curtains are drawn, whose suffused light is soft and hazy, where there is a casket: and it seems to him vaguely odd, that after all he is attending his mother's funeral and yet she is at the door to greet him: but then as he steps near the coffin (*Kiss your uncle goodbye, honey*) he sees that it is not her within it but himself—but he is not afraid; he does not scream or run away: he simply stares at the body the way he might stare at a difficult algebra problem assigned him by Mr. Kropp; a logical difficulty, to be alive and dead simultaneously—something to be worked out. He looks closely at the satin pillow under his own head and the narrow dimensions of the box itself. It seems to him that there has been an attempt to make him comfortable (the vision changes, it is no longer himself in the coffin but Jasper, Uncle Jasper), to make it look as if he is simply sleeping, not dead, "at rest," and yet it does not look comfortable, not like his big bed with the lavender spread: here there is no room to spread out, and anyway a lid would soon be slammed down on the thing forever, and who could rest in such awful darkness, such black claustrophobia? And satin: he pictures his own cotton sheets back home, so much more comfortable and warm: and the ridiculous outfit Uncle Jasper has on, a dark suit and tie; totally unlike the sandals and shirtless suspenders he had worn when watching baseball with Robin. Who are they trying to fool? This is not Uncle Jasper: this is waxed fruit in a bowl: pretty, but not alive.

Kiss your uncle goodbye. . . ..

And yet Robin is alive! Remarkably, vividly alive! He can feel his heart beating inside his chest; can feel, as he looks up at the incandescent stars, a drive—a force of life!—coursing through him. Strangely, the more he thinks of death and dead things the more alive he feels: the more aware: the more connected. Just now it is very intense, amazingly so...And as they continue down the river the intensity grows, becomes an almost animate thing, breathless and fantastic....

They walk for perhaps three hours in the morning sun: they leave Runningwater far behind and see from then on no signs of human habitation anywhere save an occasional farmhouse set off on a distant hill. The terrain is sometimes difficult, thick bramble bush driving thorns into their shoes and pulling at their clothes; but they keep on. The river grows deeper and wider. They say little—and yet Robin has the sensation that they are very much together, the two of them; he glances at her walking beside him, and though they exchange no words he feels oddly close to her.

By now, he realizes, their disappearance has been discovered. He can imagine the panic coursing like blood through the halls: Aunt Margaret in her bathrobe, her early-morning cobra's nest wild and ready to strike, calling shrilly throughout the house: *Cissy? Robin?* And Uncle Otto, knocking grimly from door-to-door, asking if anyone has seen them. And D3, no doubt dispatched in their cars to search the town. He smiles. It gives him a feeling of tremendous power. And, of course, once they had been gone long enough, a call would have to be made to Wind Point: *I don't know where they are,* he can hear her crying, *they've disappeared!* But oh, little would she know that her darling daughter and nephew were well and safe and starting brand-new lives away from them and from houses smelling of secrets and silence. New lives, sun-drenched ones, where they would sleep on the beach and eat fresh fruit and watch the light glittering gloriously on the waters.

He notices dimly the terrain beginning to clear, the thorn bushes becoming thinner, and gold-tinted grass stretching forward as far as he can see: and willow trees, great drooping ones: as they walk along the river grows still wider, until it is perhaps thirty feet across and probably knee-deep. He glances up at the sun; the day is growing warm, though it is still early and the grass is still damp with the night dew.

"Oh look!" Priscilla cries, pointing. "Robin, look!"

He looks. There, on the other side of the river, perhaps fifty yards from them, is a young doe standing in the long strands of green and gold. It stares back at them with soft black eyes that glisten in the sun. If he were a painter, he thinks: the glistening of the eyes, the moistness on the grass…and if he could paint the sounds, the light crunching of twigs under the animal's feet and the wind-sigh in the grass….

"Isn't it pretty?" Priscilla whispers. "Robin, wouldn't you like to be one?"

"A deer?"

"Uh-huh. Just to be there in the grass and run free—"

Just then the doe turns and begins to trot lightly away. As they watch it disappears behind the long grass and trees.

Priscilla stares for a long time at where the doe had stood, a strange smile on her face. He has seen her smile so rarely that he is fascinated by it. Finally she glances at him and looks down.

"Let's stay here," she says. "For a while. Do you think we should?"

Robin considers. "Sure. They don't have any idea where we are. We're safe."

Priscilla leads them under a large old willow and they sit cross-legged in the shaded grass, facing the river.

"Look," she says. "I got something in here."

She fishes through the bag for a long moment. Finally she brings out a small object and says, "Know what this is?"

He stares at it. "No."

She chuckles. "It's a *joint*, stupid. Marijuana."

He takes it out of her hand and gazes at it, fascinated and a bit horrified. "Where did you get it?"

"From Damien. He's scared I'll tell Mom and Dad that he uses it. They don't know. They would *crap*. So I make him give me some sometimes."

"That's blackmail," he says, staring at the small handmade cigarette.

"Uh-huh," she answers proudly. "You want some?"

He glances at her embarrassedly. "I—I've never..."

"Oh, it's easy," she says. "Except it's hard the first time. It'll make you cough."

"What's it like?" he asks, sniffing at it.

She giggles. "I dunno. It's hard to describe. It's good, that's all. C'mon, let's have some."

He passes it back to her, his eyes wide. He realizes that this is an early test of his new freedom: his new life without rules. It is utterly unimaginable to him, to be smoking marijuana: as impossible to visualize as the two of them behind the closed door when he listens at the bathroom wall (listened, he corrects himself, listened; never again will there be anything to listen to, never): and so, breathless, exhilarated, terrified, he says, "Okay, I'll try it."

She grins at him, obviously pleased with his answer. She looks through the plastic bag and brings out some matches, lights the small cigarette. She takes a deep drag on it and holds it for a long moment. Finally she exhales and the sweet smoke fills the air. "There," she says. "See how I did that? You suck it in, then hold it as long as you can. You gotta hold it or it won't be as good. Except you haven't done it before, so here." She hands him the joint. "Just try to breathe in a little bit at first. Get used to how it feels."

He hesitates; can feel his nerves jumping inside his skin.

"Go ahead," she encourages him.

"You'll laugh. I'll start coughing."

"I won't laugh, I promise. I told you, just try a little at first. It's good for you. Helps Build Strong Bodies Twelve Ways."

He laughs giddily. Finally he raises the thing to his lips. For a moment he does not dare to inhale. Then he does, lightly: the hot smoke hits his lungs and he gasps.

"See? Told you you'd cough. So did I at first. But it's not that bad, is it?"

"It's terrible!" Robin chokes.

"Aw, no it's not. Here." She takes it back and drags on it again. After exhaling she says: "Now you again."

"I've had enough."

"Come *on*. You didn't hold it at all. It won't do anything."

He looks at her again, takes it reluctantly. The second one is not quite so bad; by the third he is able to hold it at least a moment before coughing it out.

"There!" she says cheerily, wetting two fingers and using them to butt out the joint. "Now wait. We'll be bootiful."

He swallows. "What's going to happen?"

"It's already happening. Don't you feel it?"

He does, but he had been hoping he was mistaken. "It's like I'm kind of light-headed," he says.

"Mm-hm." Suddenly she lies back in the grass. "Relax. Let it do its thing."

He lies next to her: the grass between them obscures her and he can see clearly only the bent knee of her leg. He stares up through the thickly matted willow branches to the patches of sky beyond.

"How do you feel?" she asks, after minutes have passed.

"Good," he says. "Like everything's...okay."

"It is," Priscilla says. "It always will be."

"Mm-hm."

"You know what? The teacher told us once in class that there are big nuclear bombs that could blow us up anytime."

"Mm-hm..."

"It used to scare me. She said they would take twenty minutes to get here—twenty minutes and everything would be blown to smithereens. Everybody dead. But now even that seems okay."

He sees the pictures in his mind: slow houses dissolving, people fading gently to x-rays of themselves: and it does seem peaceful, calm, unworrisome.

"I know," Robin says. "I heard that once too."

"But it doesn't make any difference."

"No."

"Want some more?"

He giggles. "Sure, why not?"

She sits up, also giggling, and lights the joint again. They both take drags on it. He had been afraid he would somehow lose control, make an idiot of himself; but that is not the sensation at all. Instead he feels calm, serene, rather as if he were floating on waves of air. Everything around him—grass, trees, sky—seems somehow intensified, super-real, like a vivid dream.

"You like it?" she asks, propped on one elbow and looking at him.

He nods, grinning.

"Everything back there—" she tips her head back slightly toward the town—"it all seems so far away now."

"Mm-hm."

"And we're someplace where nobody can ever catch us."

"Mm-hm."

"Aren't we?"

"Mm-hm."

She looks closely at him, a faintly sleepy smile on her face. The breeze picks up strands of her thin hair and she brushes them back with her hand.

"Look," she says. "I got something else."

She reaches into the pocket of her blue jeans and brings out a small, clear gem: a diamond, or a copy of one, attached to a gold chain.

"What's that for?" he asks.

"To hypnotize you with."

"Hypnotize? Me?"

"Sure," she says, waving the jewel lightly before him. It catches the light in a dozen places, flashing and flashing. "I read a book about it."

"Are you going to make me bark like a dog or something?"

She laughs. "No! That's not what it's for."

"Why, then?"

"I dunno. It's supposed to put you in a weird place."

He looks around at the vibrant grass, the vivid trees. "I'm already in a weird place."

She laughs again. "C'mon, let me hypnotize you."

"Why?"

"'Cause I want to." She wafts the gem before his eyes.

"Uh-uh," he says, closing his eyes. "I'm weird enough now."

"Oh, don't be a poop."

"I'm not being a poop."

She sighs. "Okay, then. What do you want to do?"

He shakes his head. "Why do we have to do anything?"

"'Cause it's fun. When you're high." Robin opens his eyes again and sees that she is looking toward the river. "I wonder how the water is?" she says.

He giggles again. "Why don't you find out?"

"I think I will."

She jumps up and runs to the water's edge; squats down, and puts her hand in.

"Oooh, it's *cold!*"

Robin laughs, propping himself up on his elbows and watching her. The sparkling of the water seems incredibly intense, alive. "Are you going swimming?"

She stands and looks toward him. "Do you think we should?"

"Not we," he laughs. "I said you!"

"I will if you will!"

He smiles and shrugs. "Didn't bring any swimming trunks," he says. Which, in fact, is true. He had left them at the house along with everything else—he had packed nothing.

"So?"

The word flies across the space between them and hits him square between the eyes with the force of a freight train, one rushing full-tilt downhill without brakes. Over a cliff.

"*What?*" he calls to her.

"Don't you like to skinny-dip?" she asks; and giggles.

He considers for a moment; realizes that his heart has suddenly begun beating wildly.

"I will if you will!" he shouts back to her.

She looks toward him; considers; then calls, "Deal!" And to his complete open-mouthed astonishment, she suddenly pulls the Mickey Mouse sweater over her head and exposes a tanned, boyish chest.

"Well?" she shouts as she slips off her sandals. "Is it a deal or not?"

His face is burning hot; his pulse has gone wild. He wonders vaguely what happened to the state he had been in just moments before, floating on the air-puffs...He stares at her shirtless body and wonders that his jaw does not simply fall from his face and land with a loud *crash* in his lap. Her chest is flat, it looks nothing like the women in the magazine he keeps in his drawer in his room, nothing like the women on TV the night before, she is not beautiful, and yet the effect of her presence on him is like a sheer jolt of electricity, more exciting than anything he has ever seen. He cannot believe it.

"Robin?" she says. "Is it a deal?"

He stands up.

"*Yeah!*" he shouts back to her.

He begins taking off his shirt, but is hardly aware of what he is doing; for his universe is filled only with the vision of Priscilla unbuttoning, and then unzipping, and then slipping off her blue jeans, leaving on lacy white panties; then, turning away, she slips those off as well, rushes into the water and dunks herself.

"*Ohhh!*" she cries. "Holy fluckin' shit, it's *cold!* Robin, get in here! A deal's a deal! Ohhh, I'm gonna *die!*"

He sits to take off his shoes; then slips out of his pants.

But as he takes off his shorts, he realizes suddenly, sinkingly, that he cannot do it. He cannot appear before her. His face burns with shame, but he knows it is impossible. He has never been naked in front of anyone: the shame of it, the embarrassment, would be too much to bear. His body is hideous. He hates it. And to display it before Priscilla…

"*Robin!*" she calls to him.

But it is as if he is frozen to the spot, paralyzed. He cannot speak or move, even to cover himself, though his shorts are halfway down his legs. He feels his heart charging wildly but cannot stand. He clenches his eyes shut, wishes suddenly that he were somewhere else, anywhere else, away from this unimaginable horror.

After a long moment he hears the swishing thump of bare feet coming toward him through the grass but still he is frozen, terrified.

She stands before him, her body blocking out the morning sun. She stares at him for a long moment. But he cannot bear to look at her.

"Hey, Robin," she says suddenly, pointing. "You've got a hard-on!"

Oh, unspeakable things—

She laughs. "Is that why you wouldn't come into the water?"

Oh deep dark—

"Here." She crouches down next to him, dazzlingly naked, and droplets from her wet hair splash onto his chest. He covers himself with his hand and she leans close to his face.

"Know what I've seen?" she whispers.

He cannot look at her. "What?"

She giggles again. "Sometimes Donald and his girlfriend—in that room you're in—when they think nobody's home…"

She looks at him. "You want me to?"

His body shakes. "To what?"

"Look."

She suddenly pushes his hand away and takes hold of him. She shifts so that she is sitting next to him and her hand begins to move.

"I know what happens," she whispers. "Stuff comes out of it. Like you're peeing, only different."

He gazes at her, at her body: at the light patina of hair between her legs: at the boyish nipples: at the glistening water dripping from her body onto him: he can smell her skin, her hair. She looks at him and their eyes meet. His body is shaking uncontrollably. He feels wild excitement pouring through him but the terror, the terror is suddenly clutching at him. He tries to control it, tries to sound the musical note, tries to think of God, but the ink is too thick in his mind, he feels himself plunging into the terror's black miasma: oh deep dark helpless: he cannot control it: he sees her naked body before him waveringly, he reaches out to touch her hip: he is suffocating, sinking—

"*Stop! Stop! Stop!*"

"Robin?"

"*Stop it!*"

Limbs fumbling into unbuttoned pants: legs swishing through grass: he runs, runs until he is breathless: the terror, he must outdistance the terror: finally he stumbles, feels something tear at his leg: he falls. Something bubbles up within him and at first he thinks he is going to cry. But he does not cry. The thing bubbles and boils within him, then pours forth as he leans over and vomits, his stomach wrenching, his mouth gasping for air, his eyes wide. He vomits again and then coughs weakly, manages to step a few yards away and collapses. The world pulsates before his eyes, its colors madly intense; his heart thunders terribly in his ears. The sound is just the same as when he was trapped underwater. And the feeling is the same too. He cannot breathe. He lies gasping in the grass.

He floats: and time passes. The sun rises in the sky, its fiery light darkly red to his eyes. He wants to stare at it until he is blinded forever. Then he would never have to see anything again, ever. A world of cool and perfect darkness. Oh, a fine wish: but when he tries, the brightness is too much and he looks away, bright white singes flashing inside his head when he blinks.

For a time he very nearly forgets where he is. He floats interminably on waves of nothingness. And he does not care. He is only vaguely aware of the earth beneath him, the grass, the wind sounds: he is disconnected, set free, an unmoored island swaying in the sea. He is part of nothing: an entity unto himself, adrift in nowhere: and it occurs to him distantly that this isolation, this aloneness, should frighten him; but it does not. He wants only to stay where he is forever, unbothered, silent; it is all very clear to him; he sees it with absolute clarity.

Her voice, from another world: "What are you doing?"
His: "Nothing."
Hers: "Shouldn't we get going?"

To move: the idea is nearly inconceivable. But he opens his eyes and looks at her, feels himself re-entering his body as if he had been a spirit, the way in old times people thought their spirits left them and dwelled at night in dreams: and slowly he begins to wake, though he had not been asleep.

She is standing over him, dressed again in her jeans and Mickey Mouse shirt. He hair is dry; he wonders how long they have been here. The sun, he notices abruptly, is very hot above them.

"Here," she says in her slow voice, handing him a warm bottle of Orange Crush.

He sits up, still feeling somehow uncentered, as if part of him were looking on at all this. He is wearing his jeans, but is shirtless and shoeless.

"Thanks," he says, taking the bottle.

She sighs and sits next to him suddenly, heavily. "I'm a pig," she mutters.

"You're not a pig."

"I am too. That's what my brothers call me."

They sit in silence. She takes the bottle and drinks from it, hands it back to him.

"What…happened?" she asks.

He does not look at her; is not sure what she is talking about. But then it materializes before him again.

"I don't know…it doesn't matter."

"Yes it does. I'm a pig. I started it."

He shakes his head. "I don't…know."

She scowls and stares at the ground. "I never did that before," she says.

He glances at her.

"I guess you hated it though, huh. I mean…"

"No," he says. "It wasn't that. It wasn't *you*. It was…" He shakes his head helplessly, knowing he can never explain the terror. "I…I don't know, I don't know…"

She takes the bottle of Orange Crush and puts it to her lips but before she drinks she suddenly starts to cry. She clenches her eyes shut and big round tears rush down her face and when she tries to put the bottle down again it spills. Robin picks it up and stares at her.

"Priscilla, why are you crying?"

"Because—" she wipes her eyes, speaks chokingly—"oh, fluckin' shit…I dunno."

He stares dumbly at her.

After a moment she begins to calm. She sniffs loudly. "Now you must think I'm really stupid," she says haltingly.

"No, I don't."

"You should. What wrong with me, anyway…?"

"Nothing's wrong with you."

"Everybody hates me."

"I don't hate you."

She glances at him. "Then you're stupid."

"Why?"

"Because I'm a…" She smiles quickly and wipes her eyes. "A pig."

They are silent for a long time. They drink from the Orange Crush bottle.

"Has anybody," she begins to ask, "has anybody…ever—you know, done that before? To you?"

"No."

It is a moment before she speaks again. "Maybe you were just…"

"Yeah."

"Because I thought…maybe I was so gross that…"

"No," Robin says emphatically. "No."

She stares into the grass, her eyes empty; as if something has vanished within them and left only blankness.

"It's just that…" he begins.

There is a silence. "Just that what?" she finally asks.

No: no, no.

He shakes his head. "Nothing."

She sighs heavily and looks away from him. "I wonder if they're looking for us."

"Sure they are."

"They won't find us, though, will they?"

"No."

"They can't. They can't find us."

He watches as she brings out the gem again and twirls it in the sunlight. Her eyes seem distant.

"I'm not high anymore," she says. "Are you?"

"No."

"Did you like it, though? When you were?"

He nods. In fact, he finds it hard to remember: the entire day seems to have receded in a mad dash into the past. He is disconnected from time; nothing exists but the present. Yet he knows it is an illusion; and there arrive echoes in his mind, of sitting on the riverbank the night before, and Margaret and Otto in the room with him before, and the footsteps in the house in the cul-de-sac, nothing preceding them, nothing following. He thinks of Priscilla, years before, when he had first known her. She had been fat, he'd thought, obnoxious: but now she is different: or maybe, he realizes, he is.

"Know why I tried to kill you?" she asks.

"Why?"

"'Cause I was jealous."

He stares at her. "Why?"

"I'm jealous of everybody. But especially you. Or I was."

"Why were you jealous of me?"

She sighs. "'Cause you're so *normal*. You're not weird like me."

"I'm not so sure about that."

She glances at him. "I know. That's what I've been thinking. That maybe you're not as normal as I thought. It's just that you *seem* so normal."

He considers. "I…hide things."

She swings the gem before him. "Let me hypnotize you," she says.

He grins. "You'll make me do something stupid."

"I will not. Look. Just look at the diamond."

He looks at it, spinning before his eyes. He imagines himself stepping into its sun-dazed brightness and losing himself forever in its chambers of darkness and light…he hears her voice, softer now, telling him to look at the diamond, look at it. He looks. He is not hypnotized, he knows, not even after she has been talking for minutes; but nonetheless he is fascinated by the spinning sunlit gem; and when she asks him a question he finds that he feels disconnected from his own voice, as if, again, his spirit has stepped out and now watches him from some nearby place.

"Can you hear me?" she says.

"Sure I can hear you."

"Look at the diamond."

"I'm looking."

"Don't talk. Just look. Look at how it's spinning. Look at the light."

Look at the light; look at the light, she repeats, and he does. He knows that he could look away at any moment, but he does not. He looks at the light, imagining himself infinitesimally small and wandering in the chambers of the jewel, like the dark mirrors on his mother's finger…And he sees people there: there, behind the darkness, he sees the shadow of a man: hears his footsteps: there, a woman in a gown: the sound of the ocean: and before his eyes float sparkles of mist, themselves like gems, and he hears her voice: *We'll wrap them around ourselves*, she says, her skylike eyes filled with light; *and we'll float right up to the moon.* And her face is the moon, round like that, and he sees her hair blowing back from her face, the smell of the sea thickly around them: her bare feet on the wet wood (never again, a voice whispers): the gown whipping in the wind of an approaching storm: her hands on his face: her lips on his: her voice talking of diamonds in the descending dark, the light of the moon making the gown glow ethereally, her eyes shining in the pearl light: never again, a voice whispers.

"How do you feel?" she asks.

I don't, he says.

"What?"

I don't feel. I've stopped. I don't feel anything. I'm not going to feel anything ever again.

"Why?"

...Because I might die.

"Do you want to die?"

...I don't know...

From somewhere in the sky he looks down on them, two children in a bright field: he sees them with perfect clarity: and yet he is a part of them, he knows. Somehow. And he hears his terrestrial twin saying the unspeakable thing at last: the thing that could never be said to anyone: he hears it coming forth in a tense gasp, that she is not the freak, he is the freak, the mad one, the demented animal—unnatural, perverted. Why? she asks him. Because, he says, because I have terrible thoughts, sick thoughts... Like what? she asks him. Like...like...He hears himself saying it at last, irrevocably: Like praying to God for awful things...(What awful things? What?) Awful things like. . .*like not wanting to be a boy anymore*—

He sees himself in a mirror, or rather a hundred mirrors, diamond ones, his soft features reflected sickly back at him—and he hates them, all of them: he sees himself stabbing at his face with a gleaming blade, blood spurting from the slashes, chopping at the chest, between the legs, destroying and obliterating everything: finishing it, ending it: and it is agony but also joy, ecstasy, this blood-soaked climax, and he laughs: blood pours from his mouth, choking him delightfully: he would complete it, oh, he would complete it, once and for all!

Priscilla's voice rudely shatters the mirrors. "Oh, *shit!*"

He leaps up, terrified, whirls around: the sight, in the dazingly bright light, of Aunt Margaret running toward them: and he backs away, shaking his head, holding out his hands like a blind man to keep her away: *Robin, run!* He backs toward the river: the scorching sunlight crashes down on him like an atomic blast: and there, he sees, there across the river is the doe in the grass, looking toward him with glistening, uncomprehending eyes as grass-softened footsteps rush toward him; and then everything, doe, field, sky, Priscilla, is lost in the nuclear light as he tumbles toward the soft grass, and then through it: into a yawning and endless black abyss.

8

At first he does not know where he is. As he fades slowly into consciousness, he hears no clue: only silence: and when his eyes flutter open he finds himself looking at a white ceiling he cannot identify. The room is cool and the light dim, softly diffused. It does not occur to him to feel concerned about his disorientation; he simply lies there, trying, sleepily, to think.

Then he looks toward the closed door and the memories pour over him thickly and suddenly. He recognizes with abrupt clarity the room, the curtains, the silence. He looks at the lavender bedspread: at the soft light of the room: at the curtains: at the familiar things on the walls—and it comes to him in a sinking, vertiginous sensation. He has returned. Or rather, has been returned.

He listens. He hears distant sounds somewhere; he is not alone in the house. He stirs, touches his hair, rubs his eyes. They have put him, or perhaps he has put himself, into his thickest cotton pajamas. He unbuttons the top. He wonders how long he has been here…Wonders, in fact, how he got here at all. As he concentrates, small bits of it seem to come back to him: but he cannot be sure which parts are real, which dream. He sees Priscilla and himself in the long grass field: yes, that had happened; he sees them smoking the marijuana; and then later, nude together (had that happened?): then his running and vomiting, and Priscilla crying, and the spinning sunlit gem…his aunt's voice…

There follows a long haziness. He remembers, or thinks he remembers, being in their house; Aunt Margaret putting a wet cloth to his head, saying, *Poor dear, it was the heat*; and he even hears his own voice answering her, though he cannot make out the words. He sees Priscilla standing in the doorway. *How is he?* she asks. Aunt Margaret tells her that he will be fine, just overextended, Cissy, how *could* you have talked him into such a thing? At a time like this?

And then the long drive north: but much quicker now, in a car instead of a bus; only pieces of it still survive in his mind, hazy fragments of towns, glimpsed faces. The sky, he recalls, had been hugely blue, limitless: utterly empty but for a few wispy clouds like bits of frozen smoke in the sky: enormous, clear, free. But when he had seen that sky? In the field, with Priscilla? In the car later? Or some other, now-forgotten moment? Time itself seems to have stretched, turned back on itself, overlapped endlessly—ancient memories of fishing in salty gray awful mornings seem remarkably recent and vivid; his knees touching the girl's under the table; the woman's hands covered with cookie batter: all old now, but vivid and real like a long mirage.

The Unspoken

He sees a clock in an endless hall, its face distorted grotesquely, an infinity of mirrored reflections stretching as far as he can see; hears the second-to-second thumping, like a hard metronomic heartbeat. He hears the number *twenty* in his mind and sees houses dissolving to x-rays and disappearing in a blinding silent whiteness.

"At a time like this": for long moments the phrase conveys no meaning to him. He cannot think of what particular time this might be, or why Aunt Margaret had said such a thing. Then, very slowly, like a faraway light approaching through thick fog, he remembers. He recalls the facts that had been told him about accidents and hospitals, but it seems to him that they must have been talking about some stranger; for he is sure that at any moment he will hear her unsteady footsteps on the stairs, will watch through half-closed eyes as she enters the room and sits heavily on his bed and buttons his pajama top. He almost thinks he can hear her coming now: or if not now, then surely soon. He glances at the window again and wonders abstractly—like an academic exercise—whether the soft light is a result of the sun rising, or setting. He has no idea what time it is, or what day; whether morning has arrived, or night.

At last he hears footsteps on the stairs. He feels immediately comforted. They had, in fact, been talking of someone else; she is coming now. Her step is steady, as usual in the morning: no snake-masked monster has yet made its appearance; and yet as the footsteps approach he feels the familiar tension rising within him. He wants to see her; he does not want to.

Finally the door opens but the woman standing there is not the one he had anticipated.

"Honey?" Aunt Margaret says.

Oh, reality: perhaps they had not, after all, been making up stories, talking about strangers; perhaps, after all, what his mind was telling him was impossible, unimaginable, had actually happened.

She stands there like a slight, comic version of the woman he had expected. He stirs in the bed.

"How are you feeling?" she asks, coming into the room.

"I'm okay."

"You gave us quite a fright yesterday."

Yesterday! Could it possibly have been only one day ago? He had thought weeks, months...

"No...I'm okay. Where's..." And he is about to ask about her, but catches himself: "...my dad?"

"He's up, poor dear. I imagine he'll come in to talk to you soon."

The idea strikes an almost hilarious terror into his mind, but he says nothing. His father? This has always been Robin's own sanctuary, where the shadow-man never dared enter. He is not welcome here. Robin can picture the man's face in his mind only blurrily, can hear his voice only distantly; perhaps, it occurs to him, it is the shadow-man who is the ghost, not...But then he stops thinking.

Aunt Margaret asks him if he needs anything; no, he is fine, he'll get up soon (for it is, he has deduced, morning); and after kissing him on his forehead, she leaves the room.

The house's silence seems fantastically large and awesome now. It seems as if there could never be anything bigger in the entire world. But after a long time it is broken by footsteps coming from the other end of the hall. They clump along flatly and stop at his door.

He has closed his eyes. His heart is pumping rapidly and tremors are racing through his body, jumping, it seems to him, across his skin. He can feel the man looking at him, though he has not come into the room. He can feel the two eyes on him from the doorway. He vaguely imagines an insect under a magnifying glass.

"Wake up," the man says.

Robin does not respond for a long moment. Then he begins to twist and writhe in the bed, to stretch.

"How are you feeling?"

Robin opens his eyes. The man is standing in the hall, only half-visible to him; his face is turned away and all Robin can see are the man's clean faded blue jeans and yellow shirt; and the man's hand, he can see that—gnarled, ropy; the hand, it seems to him, of some sea monster, a creature of the swamps; and part of the back of his head, the thin, stringy hair that, in the last few years, has turned slowly gray.

"I'm okay, Dad," he says.

The figure in the doorway nods. Then it hesitates, as if it wants to say something more; but it turns and quickly moves down the stairs.

An idea comes to Robin in that moment which has never occurred to him before—and it is, he knows, absurd; impossible to imagine. But it nonetheless plays in his mind: that, incredibly, the figure in the doorway, the shadow-man, the Other, may actually be afraid of him.

He lets the idea tumble about in his mind. The shadow-man? Afraid? Of what? And yet some secret vein seems to whisper it to him....

After a long time he gets up. Silence has descended again in the house; he goes to the door, which is ajar, and stares down the hallway toward the stairs. Between his door and the stairwell is the window at which he used to watch the brightly glowing sunrises. He imagines himself there now, sitting in the straight-backed chair and musing upon what it might be like to go blind. The sunlit glow, just now, is warmly gorgeous: the shaft of apricot light some heavenly benediction on that spot of golden wood: it makes him want to run to it, feel the love and warmth soak into his body, his soul...but he knows that it is only his imagination, that it is just a sunrise like other sunrises. A strictly predictable astronomical phenomenon. Still, it is beautiful and enticing—but he knows he cannot do it now; can, in fact, never do it again in his life, if, at least, the stories they have told him are true.

After he showers and puts on clothes—which *she* folded, he realizes, not wanting to unfold them, feeling as if pieces of her were dying with each bit of clothing removed from the place she had put it—he goes downstairs.

Sounds: people talking: things being moved about. And when he enters the family room, he surveys the scene with dumb-struck horror.

All around the room are her belongings. Stacks of books. Piles of papers. Shoes. Dresses slung over chairs like collapsed mannequins. And, all around the floor, boxes: letters, cosmetics, jewelry. His father stands there in the midst of it all with Aunt Margaret and two others he does not recognize and they talk about her things quietly, moving an item here or there. "How about this?" one of them will ask, and the shadow-man will look at it—tiredly, Robin thinks, resignedly—and say to put it in this box, or that one, or throw it away.

Robin has the feeling of being torn apart, ripped to pieces.

He goes to the kitchen; notices, vaguely, Uncle Otto and D^3 and Priscilla out in the front yard, getting ready to go someplace in their station wagon.

He opens the refrigerator. There in the door are familiar bottles of ketchup, mayonnaise, steak sauce: cans of cola; a bowl of tuna, a nearly-empty bag of carrots. He reaches toward one container and lifts the lid. Beef stew. She must have made it, he realizes, sometime while he was gone; and yet here it is, intact, as if nothing had happened at all.

His first impulse is to toss the stew down the sink. He reaches to the bowl, takes off the lid. But then he looks inside again. *Beef stew. Her beef stew.* Of which, he thinks, there will never be another—although the idea is silly and impossible. They have always been here, in the refrigerator. Always.

He stares at the potatoes and vegetables and bits of beef floating in the thick brown broth and again he wants to put it away; but he does not. For a long moment he does not move. Then he puts the container into the refrigerator again and closes the door softly.

He looks in the cupboards. Flour; sugar; baking things; apples, bananas; oatmeal; old unfinished boxes of cold cereal that have been there for months. All of which *she* bought, he realizes wonderingly. All of which she picked off the shelves with her own hands and put in the grocery cart, and paid for, and brought home, and placed here, just here, where they are now. How can these things still be here?

Later, he watches from the window of his room as his father and Aunt Margaret and the others he does not recognize begin taking her boxes of things out of the house and loading them into a big van. Robin wants to stop them: wants to say, *Wait, wait.* But no one waits.

Aunt Margaret visits him in his room every hour or so. Robin simply sits at his window looking blankly at the procession of boxes making their way away.

"Honey?" she says. She sits next to him at the window sill. "Why don't you and I go for some ice cream?"

"I'm okay, Aunt Margaret."

"Come on," she says affectionately. "It'll do you good. You shouldn't sit up here all day."

"No, really, I'm okay." It occurs to him that Aunt Margaret should not be here: it should be the shadow-man. But the shadow-man continues to load things in boxes downstairs.

"Come on, honey," she says, gently tugging at him. "Let's go. Maybe we can even go to a movie on the mainland. Do you want Cissy to come along?"

Priscilla: oh, it seems a hundred years ago, the field, the river. And yet the mere suggestion of it raises Aunt Margaret in his estimation. He knows that under different circumstances he and Priscilla might not have been allowed to see each other at all: that would have been his father's proclamation. Finally he agrees, though he does not really want to; he knows that she is only trying to keep his mind off the subject and will not stop until he acquiesces. Though really, his mind is not particularly preoccupied with it, except at isolated intervals. He watches them loading boxes the way he would watch men at the harbor loading ocean gear. It is meaningless, something which has no connection whatsoever to him.

So they go, he, Aunt Margaret, and Priscilla: they have ice cream: people in town see him, some express condolences, others, incredibly, are unaware of what has happened, and Aunt Margaret must gently inform them and then the looks of shock on their faces are nearly hilarious: and he and Priscilla glance at each other, silently sharing the humor. On the ride to the mainland they sit together in back and Priscilla puts her hand in his, and it reminds him so much of another hand, years earlier, and the knees touching under the table, and the purity of it all, the cleanliness, the simplicity, before the world came to contain death and pain and disgust. *Not so fast!* Little pony-tailed Star-eyes cries delightedly, her arms around him as they soar down a wild hill; but somehow it is his voice too: he hears it sounding through his mind: *Not so fast! Not so fast…!*

It would be a week after the funeral that Aunt Margaret would manage to sit down next to him in the living room one evening and tell him the details—at least some of them. Even then, Robin had to fill in certain things of his own. But by then,

The Unspoken

by a week afterward, all her things had vanished and there remained very nearly no trace at all of her ever having lived there, ever having existed at all: everything had been neatly whisked away, so that anything that had been uniquely hers was now quite gone.

But not quite everything. Each time Robin would open the refrigerator, each time he would see the container of beef stew, he would think of throwing it away: and yet he would not. Finally, one day, he poured some into a pan and heated it and then sat at the kitchen table and ate it. And then the next day he had another bowlful, this one rather smaller. The next day, another. But after three days the level of the container became very low and for two days Robin did not touch it. Then, finally, he poured the remaining broth into the pan and heated it, but when he touched the spoon to his lips he realized the stew had gone off. He tossed it into the sink.

The folded clothes, now: these, he knew, some of them, could stay in his drawers for months untouched. Particularly his winter things at the bottom of the stacks. Sweaters, thick wool socks. There was no reason to touch them, and he realized that they could stay just so for a very long time. And yet he was not sure that he wanted them to stay that way. He often considered reaching into the drawers and pulling out everything, crumpling them up, refolding, replacing. But one day after school he came home to find that his father had re-washed and rearranged everything in the drawers.

The details swam in his mind like bits of dreams: and yet, he knew, Aunt Margaret would not tell him the whole truth about it: but she told him enough of the thing, the accident. They had been walking back home at dusk (*from the bar,* Robin had to add, mentally) when she went to cross the street (*they were fighting,* he amended) and a car (*they didn't see it, they were drunk*) suddenly came from nowhere: and an ambulance was called: and she went to the hospital: but in a few minutes it was over, finished, forever.

For months afterward he would have dream of dim headlights coming at him from out of the dark. Of sudden dull *thump*ings and cries. Of blood spattered on the sidewalk...And Robin even came to know exactly where it had happened, and sometimes he would stand at that very spot for long periods, reconstructing in his mind what had happened, the two of them, the vehicle, the darkness. It seemed completely absurd. How could anyone die that way? Abruptly? Randomly? If she had stepped out a few seconds earlier or later...or if they had left the bar a minute sooner... or the driver of the car had...There were a thousand mad variables. And where had God been, then?

There was a court case Robin was only dimly aware of, one he did not attend. Aunt Margaret looked after them for some weeks; he even saw Priscilla now and then, but they had little to say to each other. He had little, really, to say to anyone. Even when he returned to school and saw Melissa Rosselli in her pink shirts and tight blue jeans, he felt only numbness. When he looked at Melissa Rosselli he could think only of things long past, old ghosts.

But this would be later. For now there are only the boxes carried from the house, the bits of her scattering like evanescent vapor into space. Which is literally true: for the decision is made to cremate, and her ashes, he is told, are scattered across the sea. He can picture it: imagines himself as a bit of her floating, floating down from the silent sky to the glittering blue below, imagines himself plashing gently onto the surface of the sea, and floating, floating there for minutes, perhaps hours, rocked gently into the warm curtain of blue, and then sinking, descending, through the endless echoing depths, the fluid silence, down, down forever, never touching bottom, always softly sinking, wafting into eternity....

Nights pass, days: Aunt Margaret cooks meals for them and they sit silently at the table eating. One day they dress in fine clothes and go to a church and listen to someone who had never known her speak of what kind of woman she was, and also of other things: of salvation, eternal life. Robin sits on the hard bench next to the shadow-man and cannot believe any of it. *God, he thinks, you are not in this place.* He looks at the high windows of pretty colored glass and the cross behind the minister and his voice intoning verses from the Bible: no, not here: this is not God: not the God he knows, or thinks he knows, the one he whispers to. But if God is not here, he wonders, then where?

He thinks again of her bits of her floating down through the depthless blue....

And then it is over. It is over. They go home. Aunt Margaret and the rest of them prepare to leave; and when the morning arrives, Priscilla stops him in the hallway.

"G'bye, Robin," she says quietly.

"Goodbye," he says numbly. He has vague memories of them in the field, nakedness, marijuana, sharing an Orange Crush, but it all seems like fantasy now, unreality, things that never happened. Or rather, that happened; but a hundred, a thousand years ago.

"I'll write you a letter," she says in her slow deep voice.

"Sure."

"Will you answer it?"

"Sure."

As he stares blankly at her, he sees again the mad, multi-reflected clock stretching like taffy down an endless hall: hears the harsh hammering of the seconds as they pass, one after another, in infinite procession, unstoppably. He sees the clock twist and writhe as it stretches down the hall and each second bangs in his mind like a mallet to an anvil.

Priscilla nods. "Okay. I guess we're gonna go now."

Robins speaks from a distant place, the visions fading out slowly.

"Sure."

And they are gone, the six of them: their car pulls from the driveway and the sound of its engine fades slowly away. He stands next to the shadow-man, watching them go. The shadow-man touches his shoulder. Robin does not move.

⛤

And then nights, many of them, pass, with only furtive moments of sleep to take him from the silent darkness. And one night a thought occurs to him—or rather almost occurs, because he feels his mind suppressing it, not allowing it to surface. It is not the terror. It is not his dreams of long flowing hair and soft lace panties. All of that is far away: things left over from his childhood. No, this is a new thought, a new terror; he feels the tremors jumping across his skin; but no, it does not surface.

Nights pass with dreams of her dress catching fire, her body dissolving to ashes: Robin! Robin! And then the ashes descending into the blue sea: scenes of fatty beef stew slopping into a bowl, the pungent odor of whiskey-laced coffee: diamond days (distant, distant, thousands of years ago) and floating to the moon: and then dim, moonlike headlights, her foot slipping from the curb, her head whirling suddenly, a horn, a cry, an awful dull thud: it plays, it plays, endlessly, night after night, and he wakes up gasping, sweating, shaking uncontrollably.

But not, he knows, because of the visions, awful though they are; he gasps because of the thought, the idea, the new terror which one night, through a mind seared with fear, surfaces, surfaces for all time: what, he thinks breathlessly, what if it wasn't an accident? What if the foot stepping from the curb did it deliberately? What if the snake-masked monster had been in control, firmly in control, and had watched her die? What then? What was left to his life then? And why had he been in Runningwater, stupidly watching tv, when it happened? Why had he not been here?

Why had he not saved her?

Useless sun-horses dead in brown fields. Silence. Ash-colored dusk. Emptiness.

9

He lies sharply awake in the darkness. The house is awesomely silent: its other occupant had gone to bed hours ago: and Robin lies in his bed, listening.

After a long time—minutes, perhaps hours—he hears footsteps on the stairs. They are immediately familiar and he feels tension tightening his body. His hands are clenched into fists and he unclenches them. He listens.

The footsteps arrive at the door; hesitate; and then the door opens softly.

"Honey?"

He feels his heart beating. He does not respond. She comes into the room. She wears a white gown that seems to glow in the moonlight. Her feet are bare. Her hair, brushed back and spilling onto her shoulders, is like an ocean wave.

She hesitates before coming near him; turns instead and closes the window.

He looks at her for a long time as finally she walks to the bed and sets her familiar weight upon it. He can smell her skin as she looks down at him, smiles, and begins buttoning his pajama top. Then she touches his forehead; her hand is cool.

"Hi, Mom," he says.

She says nothing; just looks at him, her Siamese eyes bright in the darkness. They are silent for a long time. Robin enjoys the weight on his bed, the slight creaking of the bedsprings.

"I thought you were…"

She puts her fingers to his lips.

He stops trying to talk. Instead they stay there together without speaking. His eyes fall onto the little diamond on her finger, the deep reflecting chambers within it. This is how it was, he remembers, before.

Before...Islands begin to surface in the stream, remarkably vivid and alive, one tumbling after another: her unsteady footsteps and stumbling; the shadow-man's muted queries (*He asleep?*). The sound of the refrigerator opening and closing and the squeaks of the big chair the man would sit in. The crash of a breaking dish, the tinkling of it sifting into the garbage can. And then others, so many others: his knees touching the girl's under the table; black-bearded Mr. Kropp's accusing voice; Uncle Jasper crying, *We got 'em now!*; the bus breaking away from the clouds of Wind Point into the brilliant blue; the warmly hissing radiator in the library, and Mrs. Klibo smiling toward him; Melissa Rosselli, the dark fantasy in the dungeon; his awful toyings with himself and the dark listenings at the bathroom wall; a fish exploding into the gray air, *You got one! You got one!*; praying for deliverance, praying to be taken away, to disappear; clinging to her dress, *Come with me! Come with me, Mom!*; holding the crinkly white bag next to his stomach and the sugar flakes tumbling onto his plate; the gray sky filled with suspended gems, and riding them, riding them into dark space, toward the glowing moon: these things pour over him: and he looks at her: she is beautiful.

"Mom," he whispers finally, "look. Your feet are dirty."

And they are: covered with mud. Robin realizes dimly that it is raining outside. He hears the foghorn in the distance, lonely and low, subdued by the rain.

She leans close to him.

"I've come a long way, honey," she whispers. "And I'll come back someday."

Her fingers touch his eyelids: and he tries to stay awake, tries to stay with her, but feels himself dropping into a peaceful dark. Come with me, he wants to cry: but his body is heavy: he touches the sleeve of her gown: Not so fast, he wants to say, not so fast: but he drops: he is a tiny thing in an enormously blue sea: he drops: the blue is depthless, it stretches forever: like the clock he sees, waveringly stretching beside him, and the muffled bang of the seconds as they pass: he drops: and soon he sees a light. Soon he comes to a new place. The sea, he reaches the bottom of the sea, but it has no bottom: he passes through into another sky above another ocean: and the air is clean and breezy and warm: and there, below him, he sees an island: and as he floats closer he sees a figure on the island, unidentifiable, and yet someone he loves: someone: he cannot tell anything of the figure, he is too far away: but he feels an overwhelming, nearly crushing love: and he yearns toward the figure: tries to reach toward it: but the island begins to disappear, to be lost in the depthless blue, and he tries to call to it, but he has no voice, no voice, the seconds pulse, he drops, he drops, into an infinity of blue that is neither sky nor sea but simply void, silence, non-being....

He is walking in hazy sunshine among Wind Point's tombstones. None of them are hers: there is no monument to her whatsoever, it is simply as if she had never existed at all. Cherry trees outside the fence frame the yard in green and deep red. He stares at the stone markers, some of them ancient, some fresh; but most old; most from the nineteen-thirties, nineteen-forties. He is fascinated. He stares at the dates of birth and the dates of death and the Biblical inscriptions carved into the stones. After crouching down and peering at one stone he stands up again, and realizes that there, across the yellow haze of sun and fog, on the other side of the graveyard, is his father.

He is wearing a denim jacket and blue jeans and is standing completely still with his hands in his pockets, looking toward Robin. But through the brightness and mist Robin does not know if his father can see him at all. It is strange, very strange: for although there is such distance between them, Robin can see his father with remarkable clarity: can see the man's face as, it seems to him, he has never seen it before—starkly real: the domed hairless forehead; the large, milky blue eyes that seem set into the head too deeply; the hooked hawk nose; the ruddy, pockmarked skin; the deep crevices around the mouth; the sagging, paunchy flesh under the chin; he sees all of it as if for the first time.

As he stares bewildered at this mystically clear vision, his father's eyes suddenly meet his own.

Neither of them move.

They stare at each other, eyes locked together as if in some speechless contest of wills.

The man's glowing eyes seem as far away as ashes in a blue sea; and yet the eyes are also a mirror: Robin seems in an untranslatable way to be looking at himself; and he hears knockings on a strange door, or is it the seconds, the awful slice of time, the warped clock? And he knows suddenly that he will always remember this instant of time, that for the rest of his life it will always be brilliantly clear in his memory, sharp as a freshly-printed photograph, motionless in the hazy sun....

And this is where we shall leave him, our Robin: as he stares frozenly toward his father across the distance of the graveyard, the older man soft and bright in the morning mist, incredibly clear yet distant as remembered love; and as the boy's heart bangs wildly in his chest like some fantastic bird, one trying to crash through the bars of its cage to the imagined blissful freedom of the sunlight beyond the clouds.

CHAPTER 2
WAITING FOR MORNING

In school the winding river of time and dullness
    Slithers sluggishly on, though boredom and bewilderment.
    O loneliness. O time, disillusionist.

    Rilke: "Childhood"

1

I finished "Strange Islands" last night; it has been seven weeks since I first sat down at the kitchen table in this house and typed the words "Yesterday I came home." In the time that has passed I have managed to turn the house from a dark, dusty husk to a fairly livable habitat. It took the better part of a week of mops, buckets, and dust-rags, but finally I was able to make the foyer, living room, and kitchen more or less presentable; on the second floor I limited my efforts to my old bedroom and the bathroom. I have lights now, and water, and a telephone. Perhaps most important, a week's constant airing managed to dispel the stale and omnipresent odor of dust.

Not that the house is in any way fully functioning. I replaced the missing refrigerator with a tiny unit found at a garage sale; it sits now beside the sink, rather incongruous in its brown weather-beaten appearance next to the now-gleaming tile and porcelain. But it is adequate to my needs. I have not replaced the dining room set, so the space where the old one had been remains an empty vacuum. And I have not touched the other rooms upstairs. The "guest room," so-called, does not seem worth the bother; and my parents' room creates a psychic difficulty. For several days after arriving here, I did not set foot inside it; and when I did I found myself acutely uncomfortable there. I tried to reason with myself, thinking that after all, it is no one's bedroom now (except, legally, mine); I could even sleep in it if I wished. I pulled the dust cover from the big bed and lay down on it, trying to will myself into feeling that this was completely natural and normal. But I could not fool the young boy inside me, the one whom I have spent the last several weeks writing about. It felt not only unnatural but actually dirty. This had been, once, a room into which I never stepped: from which strange sounds emanated, sounds of mysterious adult rites I had thought I would never understand. And although the mystery of those rites has long since been dispelled, I still had no business being there. It was an illogical feeling I could not control. Within a minute of setting myself on the bed I left it again, covered it, and stepped out of the room. I closed the door and have not opened it again.

Thus I have slept in my old room, though that too was difficult at first. I kept having nightmares: one in particular I remember had a monster crawling up the pepper tree outside toward my open window while I was strapped down to the bed, unable to move or scream. For a while I considered sleeping on a cot downstairs, but finally decided I was being silly; after a few nights the dreams ceased and I feel no particular discomfort in the room now, nor in the bed. They are mine, after all.

And Wind Point—is it "mine" too? After all these years of absence? I am unable to decide. The town itself has not changed a great deal: different faces abound, of course, but also some familiar ones; the old Scully Road has been improved somewhat. It is an accident of geography, I suspect, that Wind Point has been denied (spared?) the explosive development which has struck

Greyfield and Hollowstone, which are practically unrecognizable from the medium-sized villages I recall from my youth: covered over now with the glowing plastic banners of fast-food restaurants, and with new glittering shopping malls where once stood only wind-stroked grass, they seem almost entirely unconnected to anything I ever knew. Even Hollowstone High School, my alma mater, can hardly be glimpsed through a thicket of new trailers and buildings on its campus which seem to have crawled up out of the earth like prefabricated crabgrass. It is all part of a northern migration that has been going on for a decade, a migration that has largely excluded little Wind Point. It is not quite true that there has been no development at all: I have seen several new shops, and a number of unfamiliar houses: but certainly the town has missed out on the economic boom times enjoyed, or endured, by the villages on the mainland. My own reaction to this is mixed. There is something exceedingly comforting in being able to walk into the cool, dim interior of the old library and hear the radiator hissing just as it did all those years ago (although Mrs. Klibo, of course, has long since vanished); but there is an element of the macabre in it too. Nearly a decade has passed since I have last been here, a decade in which I went to college in New York and traveled in Europe and South America and Africa, published books; and to come back here, to find things so substantially the same, is in a way bizarre. And so I do not know what my relationship is to this town now. I have no family here and the faces I do recognize are only those of casual acquaintances, neighbors and shopkeepers. I am a stranger.

The pier and harbor are unchanged; and yesterday I took a walk out toward those familiar sea-structures. I wandered for a time amongst the boats, thinking of the vessel my father had owned and how I had hated those salt-filled early morning journeys with their worms and slippery gasping fish. They did not seem far away, those journeys, not as I walked among the boats and breathed the salt air and listened to the ocean smashing itself against the rocks. The foghorn blew then and I found myself looking into the sky...For what, I did not know. I had another life, I told myself, a good one, in New York: with friends and students and occasional writing assignments (including the words you are now reading: S. Simon Stillman came through). But it all seemed far away just then. I stepped toward the pier, walked up the steps to it, and stood looking out at the creaking wet wood that all but vanished in the mist beyond. For some reason I hesitated to make the walk out to its end. I felt, absurdly, as if there were something dangerous waiting for me in the fog. I realized that I was likely only a victim of too much autobiography: probably all I needed was a few days' break, a pleasant drive to Portland or San Francisco. But I could not shake the feeling. And as I stood there staring into the motionless mist, I remembered other walks on that pier. Early ones, with my hand wrapped within my mother's. And later ones, alone.

I would like to ask you now to visualize again our young Robin. Imagine him walking slowly along the Wind Point pier on a particularly wet and fog-drenched morning with his hands in the pockets of a thick blue jacket. Now as he walks along the pier, picture if you can something else. Imagine his face growing older. Study the pale feminine features as they begin to thin and elongate, to change from the face of a thirteen-year-old to that of a late teen—say seventeen. Consider how the eyes seem to become set more deeply in the head, how the ears stretch, how shaving shadows appear on his jaws. The hair on his head grows longer and darker. Tiny lines become visible around his mouth. The forehead becomes more pronounced. Round wire glasses appear over his eyes. Picture him as he walks along the pier, his legs growing longer, his stride becoming more graceful and manly. (Of course we shall have to assume that his clothes grow with him, lest I be left with a naked hero by the time he reaches the end of the pier.) Imagine his face and body undergoing these alterations as he moves along the wet wood, a bit like Lon Chaney Jr. in *The Wolf Man*.

Of course if Robin's tale were to be made into a film (not, one assumes, starring Lon Chaney Jr.), we could handle this stretch of narrative with considerable ease-Robin would grow older as you watched effortlessly from your seat in the theater, or before the television, thanks to the Special Effects Department. Here, however, things are not so easy, and so I must ask you to participate, to be a co-conspirator in this creation of an individual who is supposed to be myself as a young man but who truly, of course, is no more than black specks on a sheet of paper (or computer monitor) given life by the reader's own imagination.

Submitted for your approval, then, one Robin Withers. Seventeen years old, fair hair reaching past his collar, blue eyes, glasses, delicate features. Thinner than he was at thirteen, less girlish now. There is something in the narrowness of his face which suggests the ascetic, the intellectual, even the severe. He stands at the edge of the pier in the misty morning, arms folded atop the wooden safety rail, staring out at the sea. He listens to the water lap against the wood and looks out to his left where some thirty yards off is the harbor: twenty or thirty boats, most of them fishing boats, nestled into their cubbyholes, bumping gently against the wood. The more distant of them are largely lost in the haze of sky. He is not thinking of anything in particular; he often comes here just to stand and look, or to talk to the occasional fisherman he sees dangling a line from the pier. Today, however, there is no one, and so he stands thinking of nothing as he gradually becomes aware of a sound behind him: hasty footsteps.

"Robin!"

As if suddenly wakened, he starts; then he looks behind him and sees little Davy Carp walking quickly toward him. Robin thinks of him as "little" not because of his age, which is the same as Robin's, but because of his sticklike physique and shortness. Robin himself is one of the tallest boys in school, a fact that never ceases to surprise him. He remembers too well his fey shortness when he was younger. He stares toward Davy Carp as the boy comes toward him hurriedly, a paper in his hand. Davy is wearing jeans and a crisscross design shirt over which is a light gray wind breaker.

He is breathing hard as he comes up to Robin. "Hey," he says.

"Hey."

"Why aren't you in school, man?"

Robin shakes his head. "No classes until eleven."

"Oh yeah, me neither. I stopped at your house but you weren't there. Thought you might be here."

"Here I am."

"Yeah. Did you see this...this *stuff?*" Davy is always hesitant to use profanity. He holds the paper up for Robin to see: the *Hollowstone High Courier.*

"No. What's in it?"

"Ha. Wait'll you see." His face twitching slightly in a characteristic nervous tic, Davy flips through the pages of the typewritten-and-stapled thing until he comes to a page near the back. "Check this out," he says, handing it to Robin.

Under the "Letters to the Editor," a girl both of them know and purport not to like has written a response to an editorial of Robin's—he is, pompously enough, the paper's "Cultural Editor," a title he dreamed up himself—the subject of which had been the lack of culture of people in the United States today, and most especially, of the students of Hollowstone High. How delightedly, with what glee he had written that article! "Why is it," he had written, "that the average American—not excluding the average student in this venerable institution—knows not a whit about anything besides football scores and the schedule for their favorite TV comedy? Why does he or she not know the difference between Holst and Hindemith, Goya and Gaugin, Wells H.G. and Welles Orson? The answer is simple. This country has the most anti-art, anti-intellectual viewpoint of any civilized country in the history of the world."

Robin does not consider himself one for the indefinite statement.

He reads the girl's reply. It is predictable enough: rather indignant, a bit shrill, badly written. Robin smirks contemptuously and hands the paper back to Davy.

"Well, that's nothing much to worry about," he says.

"Nah, you're right," says Davy, who almost always agrees with Robin about everything. "She's nothin'."

This dialogue between them is as it must be, because the girl in question has reached number four on their list of *Personas Non Gratas*. Now, secretly, Robin sometimes admits to himself that, really, this girl is not so bad, and, really, she is even fairly attractive. However, her cultural politics are highly suspect, for last semester it was she who argued the Drama teacher out of a production of *Jane Eyre* and into something called *Hey, Everybody! Let's Sing*! The fact that this latter play became a huge success in the community was only a tribute, so Robin and Davy had reasoned, to the cultural ignorance of the local people.

"Anything else in there?" Robin asks, motioning at the paper.

"Nah. Club meetings. Song dedications. An article about 4-H raising money. Dull."

Robin nods. "As usual."

"What're you going to do now?"

"I dunno. Maybe go to Bernie's."

Robin sighs. Whenever boredom hits, which is more or less all the time, they go to Bernie's, a bakery and sandwich shop in Greyfield.

"All right," Robin says. "We've got an hour and a half. We might as well."

"Sure. I mean why not."

Davy does not own a car, so they walk back along the pier to where Robin's nondescript old four-door, "The Brown Bomber," sits. As they pull through Wind Point and find their way onto the old Scully Road, Robin turns on the heater and thinks about the article he had written. While it had delighted him, thoroughly pleased him in every respect—for he knew quite well with what indignation it would be received—there were nonetheless some gnawing worries and uncertainties in his mind. "Holst and Hindemith": his knowledge of the former extended as far as *The Planets,* and the latter to one listening to a radio broadcast of the Symphony in E-flat. "Goya and Gaugin": thumbing through reproductions in the school library, reading encyclopedia entries. "Wells, H.G.": *The Time Machine,* the movie of *War of the Worlds.* "Welles, Orson": appearances on TV talk shows. Sometimes he must admit to himself that he is a bit of a fake.

And yet! Oh, if only he could translate, as he tries to in his editorials (which he knows are rather stuffy and pretentious), the joy, the sheer wonder and mystery of music, art, literature, drama! It is a source of constant bewilderment to him that others do not see the breathing life in a Renoir portrait (known to him thus far only through books) or the awesome profundity of a Mahler symphony (heard on records). Words fail him: he cannot communicate it. And so his articles tend toward the windy, the empty, and when he tries to talk of these things, the words he uses are not the right ones: he sounds haughty, callous, arrogant. He knows it, and hates the sounds of the words even as they come from his mouth;

but he cannot find another language, a new, secret language, to speak of it.

But in his own mind it is dazingly clear. He cannot remember just when it started. Perhaps it had always been with him, ever since Poe and late-night movies and his mother's melodic humming. Or perhaps he had caught it at some particular point, a holy and benevolent disease. But whatever it was, however it had gotten hold of him, it was there, this visceral sense, this knowledge of the secret life, the buried life, treasures unexplored, senses unexpressed. And pieces of it, glitteringly translucent like ice crystals tumbling from a clear sky, he could find in writing, in pictures, in music: when he read "The Hollow Men," or looked at reproductions of Monet, or—most especially—when he listened to Mahler, it was as if private and lovely ghosts were sitting next to him, whispering the secrets of the universe, secrets he could not yet fully comprehend, only bits of which he could grasp: but that process of realization, of taking hold of the eternal mysteries, he could never express in syllables. The nakedness of language betrayed, made stupid and false. The mysteries, the questions themselves, could be phrased in words: What are we? What is this place? What is existence? Time? God? But the answers: that was where language utterly failed, where reason and rationality burned to cinders, where logic fractured like a shattered picture puzzle. Where analysis melted and warped to nothingness. For the ghosts did not speak in language. He could never explain it in words, for they did not use words. And yet he understood them—felt he understood them, at least partially, at least in the tiny ice-crystal fragments.

"But really, man," Davy says suddenly. "Shouldn't we do something about that girl?"

"Hm? What girl?"

"Crossman. The letter-writer."

"Like what?"

"I dunno. But something. I mean, maybe we should make a re-evaluation of our *Personas Non Gratas*."

Robin winces. This list Davy refers to they had invented when they first knew each other as freshmen; and yet it embarrasses him now. He likes to think that he has moved beyond such juvenilia, but Davy has persisted with the game. As he has with other things, things that make Robin feel as if Davy were in a case of permanently arrested development; and that being around him is arresting Robin's own development too. "Personas Non Gratas"! It had begun one afternoon in Study Hall, as a simple catalog of despised personalities: but had since grown to epic proportions, at times including over thirty names, each carefully ranked and cataloged according to seriousness of crime and perceived paucity of thought. Typical entries might read:

1. Mr. Moore. Principal of school. Cut drama funding. Makes condescending attempts at conversation with W & S (Withers and Carp). Has stupid wife. Contemptible.
4. Crossman, Bobette. Senior. Pretentious, pseudo-sophisticated. Prefers light comedies to serious dramatic work. Has committed grievous crimes against Art. Worthless to an astonishing degree.
9. Feeley, Jeff. Senior. On football team. Not worth discussion. Idiot.

"But," Robin says, "I thought we just re-evaluated it."

"We did. But that was before this letter. This is serious, man. I mean I think she might just hit Top of the Pops for this one."

"Oh, you're taking it too seriously. It was exactly what we expected, anyway."

Davy continues talking. Robin stops listening. He wonders why he keeps on with such ridiculous, childish things. He often finds himself wondering at the irony of being the student who holds himself up as the ultimate example of cultural sophistication, while behind the scenes he is still making up grade school hate-lists with his best friend; and yet, he has to admit, he sometimes enjoys them. Something about the blowing off of steam, the sheer trivial joy of it, attracts him.

He turns on the windshield wipers to clear away the mist on the glass. Soon they arrive at the mainland, where the fog has not yet burned off for the day: the skies are still cold and thickly overcast. Within a few minutes they are at Bernie's. They each order donuts, milk, and coffee, and sit in a booth near the corner. The place is empty.

It is quite amazing to Robin when he considers that after all, he will be graduating within a few months. He wishes that he could feel some exhilaration, some excitement at the prospect, but it leaves him numb and unfeeling. He has no idea what he will do after graduation. College, he supposes; but the idea is very unreal to him. In many ways he would prefer to do nothing, or to simply pack a bag and *go*. He doesn't know where: but somewhere, far away. And when he thinks of this he remembers years ago, glimpses his thirteen-year-old self in the open field. He wonders if he has changed at all since then, if he has matured or even altered in any significant way: he still has largely the same feelings. And yet, in another way, he knows he has, that he is hardly recognizable as the same boy—externally or internally.

"Do you have to work tonight?" Davy asks him.

"Mm-hm." Robin works as a busboy at a restaurant in Wind Point.

"Too bad. I was hoping we could get to a movie or something."

"I might be off early enough. Let's wait and see."

Davy nods and they continue with their donuts in silence. They remain there for an hour, talking of trivial things: assignments, the *Hollowstone Courier*, movies. Robin becomes increasingly bored and dissatisfied, feeling on the one hand that he has moved beyond these childish things, but realizing, on the other, that he still enjoys them: and a long conversation about the *Personas Non Gratas* list commences. Davy argues for placing Bobette Crossman in the top position, knocking off Mr. Moore who has been there for months on end; Robin thinks she should remain where she is. They compromise by moving her up to number two.

At this point a boy named Michael Lyon comes into the bakery. Michael Lyon is one of those students who never ceases to amaze Robin: not only good-looking, athletic, and popular, but also, to all indications, fairly intelligent. He is also one of the few truly popular boys who seems to even be aware of the existences of Withers and Carp, the southern Oregon coast's cultural policemen.

"Hey, Robin," he says, bringing his donuts toward their table. "Hey, David. Didn't see you guys here. Mind if I sit down?"

He sits. Glancing at him, Robin wonders what it might be like to be Michael Lyon. The windblown blonde hair, the winning smile, the physique, the friends. It occurs to Robin in a shamefaced instant that Michael Lyon could not possibly be a virgin.

"I see you're in some hot water over at the *Courier*," Michael Lyon says to Robin.

This is just like him, Robin thinks. Michael Lyon is unquestionably coming to a great career in politics, because of his extraordinary ability to know and at least appear to care about the affairs of even the most insignificant of his fellow beings.

"Oh, it's no big deal," Davy interposes.

"Yeah, well, you're right about what you said in that editorial, you know, Robin. I mean people don't like to hear things like that, but you're right. I remember when my family went to the San Francisco Symphony I couldn't believe it when people started applauding between the movements of Tchaikovsky's Fourth. They don't know *what's* going on. I'm sure you've seen that happen yourself."

"Sure. All the time," Robin says. Which is a boldfaced lie, but this is typical of the position Michael Lyon unwittingly puts him in. Just as Robin thinks he has perfected his image as cultural arbiter, someone like Michael Lyon comes along to remind him what a true fake he is. Now Robin is absolutely positive that serious music means nothing to Michael Lyon. He is positive that Michael Lyon knows nothing of the lovely ghosts, has never heard one whispering to him about the mysteries, the secrets. But Michael Lyon has learned enough, just enough, to appear confident in conversation: just as he would have confidence in a discussion about Russian literature, pre-Raphaelite art, or Greek drama: not that he actually gives a damn about them, but it is important to a future politician like this one (and Michael Lyon is perfectly open about his ambitions: his father, after all, is a state assemblyman, and he himself is already class president as well as captain of the basketball team and the class's star debater) to be able to appear interested in anything his constituency—or future constituency—might be interested in. So he attends a few concerts, reads a few novels and poems, goes to a museum or two, sees a couple of plays, and he is assured of never looking stupid in any conversation about "culture."

And the thing that drives Robin mad is the fact that it works. Robin does not know how many times he has been discussing art or drama with one of his teachers, expressing his usual strong opinions, when the teacher has gently "set him right," given him new information that showed up his view to be ignorant and pretentious. This never happens to Michael Lyon, although Robin knows full well the boy doesn't know one one-hundredth what he himself knows about these subjects. Robin has analyzed it and come to the conclusion that it is because Michael Lyon has such a strong and likable personality, and that he so naturally and easily dominates any conversation that he is in, that he simply manages to nimbly step away from such controversies.

Robin looks over at him again. The skin is baby-soft, smooth, tanned. The profile is that of a Greek sculpture. The eyes are not brilliant, but sharp and intelligent and lively; the lips, full and attractive without being gaudy. Robin can see the campaign posters already. *Put a Lyon in Your Corner—Vote Mike Lyon!* Robin is absolutely certain of the boy's future—as certain, he supposes, as Michael Lyon himself is. Most faces, it occurs to him, are at this age question marks: still in the process of formation, not yet solidly set, the eyes tentative, the angle of the head uncertain; but Michael Lyon's is set as in stone. His future is preordained.

He wonders what it might be like to have such a certain vision of tomorrow. To be so supremely—yet unarrogantly—confident of absolutely everything. To be attractive, loved, to come from a "good family." The boy sitting next to him seems to crystallize so perfectly exactly what Robin is not, and never will be: no, no confusions in that magnificent carriage: no uncertainties: nothing but a smooth plane of success to be manifested in ever-more grand political appointments, a beautiful wife and beautiful children, vacations in Acapulco, speedboats, charming fund-raising barbeques, a healthy and happy passage into an athletic middle age, a life handed to him on a silver platter free of charge and with compliments of the chef. In some ways, certainly, Robin despises him; but in another Michael Lyon is so strange, so utterly foreign to his experience, that he feels more like he is looking at some strange beast in a zoo.

There follows a long discussion of school trivialities: the *Courier*, the Drama Club, teachers, classes. Michael Lyon is as engaging and charming as always; but it occurs to Robin that it is not like him to spend so much time alone with obscurities like himself and Davy Carp.

"Fact is," Michael Lyon says, "I've never been here in my life. I'm waiting for Kathy. We're supposed to meet here, since she lives so far out, you know. But she's late."

"Women," Davy interjects.

"Sure. But it's no problem." He smiles. "I'm used to it with Kathy."

Kathy Collins: another name bleeding of future success and opulence. In fact, she might well end up as Michael Lyon's wife. Kathy Collins: Volleyball, Pep Squad, Journalism, School Treasurer. Robin knows the resume well. She and Michael Lyon were of course voted Best Couple at the Homecoming dance (which neither Robin nor Davy attended). He does not believe that Kathy Collins has ever spoken a word to him.

"So what have you heard from UCLA, Mike?" Robin asks him. It is well known that Michael Lyon has been applying to the top schools.

"Well," he answers casually, "they took me, no sweat. But I'm thinking that maybe I should go back east for awhile instead. I don't know if UCLA really has the kind of atmosphere I'm looking for. I could go to Boston, or to NYU..."

Robin smiles at the casual tossing about of names: he can do it so effortlessly. If Robin were to have said the exact same words, he knows, they would have sounded arrogantly superior.

"So what are you going to do, Robin?" Michael Lyon asks him. "I haven't heard much about your plans."

Robin shakes his head. He would like to tell the truth, that he hasn't a plan in the world: that the future appears to him like a bottomless abyss he is about to tumble unwillingly into. There are only months left, and yet it is as if he has some mental block as to the future: he can hear the knocking on the door but cannot answer: and he has been paralyzed about it for months on end. He cannot see a future for himself, cannot imagine what might happen after the routine of high school draws to a close. He often fantasizes about simply packing a bag and leaving, taking off to somewhere...and yet that does not seem possible. College is expected of him; however uncertain he himself might be, however drifting and aimless he feels, his father talks of it. College! He has the grades, but not for the kind of institutions Michael Lyon so casually rattles off. A smaller, lesser-known campus somewhere; but what on earth would he study? The only thing that interests him anymore are the lovely ghosts, about which he cannot speak, for others do not know their language.

"I don't know," he admits, smiling sheepishly. "It's hard to decide. Maybe I should give it all up and get a job in a gas station somewhere."

Michael Lyon laughs. "You? Your only problem is finding a way to make a living while you write your articles and things. Isn't that it?"

On target, Robin thinks, as usual. "Yeah: that's it, all right."

"You should go overseas. London. Paris. Venice. That's your kind of atmosphere—it would be. When we were there last July, we went to the..." And he is off again on the magnificent stallion of his conversation: enragingly charming about dull London, exciting Paris, quaint Venice. Places that exist in books; but to Robin it is utterly unimaginable that he could actually go to them. Wind Point, he thinks, is not a place, but a state of mind—an abyss—

"Of course," Michael Lyon is saying, wiping his mouth, "I know money is a problem. But you know what? I've got a suggestion for you. It'll sound crazy, I know, but hear me out. *Join the service.* No kidding. How else will you be able to see the world and have your expenses paid at the same time, without a college degree? It would get you out this place, it would...open your eyes, you know? Seems to me that that's what you need for your articles. A world view. Think of Hemingway. Think of the people you'd meet, the places you'd see. Try the Navy, or get an overseas posting on an Army base. Look into it, Robin. I've got a very good friend, really my dad's friend, who's a recruiter." He scribbles a telephone number on a fresh napkin. "Give him a call. He's not a hard-sell guy, he'll give you the real story. Now if you'll excuse me—" he hands Robin the paper, glances out the window—"I believe that's my lady's vehicle pulling up now." He stands. "I mean it, Robin, give it some serious thought, okay? See you. See you, David. Nice talking to both of you."

And he moves with absurd grace to the door, where Kathy Collins, tall, blonde, less than real, greets him with flawless smile and embrace.

"See?" Davy says, after the couple has moved out of sight. "All your problems solved in one fell swoop. Why worry? Join the Army, man."

"Jesus," Robin mutters. The idea is of course completely ridiculous, but it takes Robin minutes to formulate in his mind exactly why. He feels like a clumsy flesh-and-gristle gnome trailing stupidly behind golden, ethereal Michael Lyon. He thinks of his own personality; of his solitary habits; of the lovely ghosts; and the ridiculousness of it comes clear, articulate. As for Hemingway, he is now ready to counter: the Bronte sisters, Emily Dickinson! But of course it is too late. The boy is long gone, having left them in his sunny wake.

"Hey, we better head out," Davy says, looking at his watch.

"Yeah." Robin finishes his milk.

"Hey." Davy adds, bringing out the sheets of paper, "don't you think we oughta adjust that guy?"

"Hm?"

"Lyon."

"Oh." Robin feels a formless shame. "Where is he now?"

"Sixteen."

Robin is silent for a moment, not thinking of it, or of anything except the gray mist outside, the silence. "Yeah," he says finally, not hearing himself. "Yeah. Let's put him in the Top Ten."

2

The house is dangerous at night. When Robin is not working at the restaurant, he finds ways to avoid it: goes to study at Davy's house, goes to movies, drives to a late-night coffee shop on the mainland. Where he goes is not important, as long as he does *go*. He does not think about it consciously; does not think: *It's getting dark, I'd better find someplace to go.* It is simply a reflex, as natural as eating or sleeping: as natural, and as necessary.

The house is dangerous at night, and so he spends long hours in Davy's room studying or, more often, talking about anything that comes to mind. On nights he feels less social, he goes to the Wind Point Cinema; or he may drive as far as the mainland to see more recent releases. He has seen virtually every film that has played locally for the past year and a half, since he got his driver's license. Comedies. Action films. Kung-fu epics. And occasionally, something that whispers to him, something that gives him a glimpse of the lovely ghosts…But for the most part it does not really matter, because he does not really watch them. They are something to pass time, to keep him for a few hours from thinking of the abyss of the future. Up to last year, he had not thought so much of it, and had even had a certain amount of fun getting involved with school drama. He was a poor actor but had had one triumph: in an adaptation of a Chekhov story he had played an arrogant, intellectual young man; and though he had done little more than stand in the right place and remember his lines, he had been extremely effective. His role was not large, but the local papers had singled him out for praise. Following fast upon this, Robin immediately had dreams of becoming an actor. He went so far as to write to the Royal Academy, the Actor's Studio, the Old Vic: here, he thought, was the proper direction, the blaze of glory he had always sought! Ambition quickly outstepping ability (he realized later), he wrote an original play and, in defiance of the Drama Department ("The

Broadway of the West Coast," he had derisively labeled it), raised money and staged it himself. He was halfway through rehearsals before he came to the realization that his highly symbolic, pseudo-Greek drama was not only unplayable, it was practically unreadable. Opening night became closing night, and so closed Robin's theatrical ambitions. The derision heaped upon him by other students was nearly unbearable (the guest Drama critic for the school paper—the Crossman girl—had gloated: "It seems our ambitious young actor/writer/director has more talk than talent"); and from then he had abandoned any interest in the school whatever. He went to his classes, he left.

But the house is dangerous at night, and so he is unable to stay there, unable to stay anywhere near until late. Thus, he finds ways of filling his time.

Some nights he sits in the late-night cafe writing English papers for Marylou Kirk. Marylou! he thinks. His object of passion, his vessel of desperation! Marylou! Jet-black hair in pigtails, pixieish face, tiny lithe body: Girl's Track Team, Tennis Team: and completely hopeless in the subject of English. When he thinks about it objectively, which he rarely does, he supposes he has never met anyone quite so downright *dumb* as Marylou Kirk; but, O! the vision of her in a skimpy track suit on a clear, cool afternoon!

It had begun innocently enough. She had approached him after class once for some help on an assignment. They made an appointment to meet in the library, he helped her, and that was that; but a week later she approached him again—rather more friendly, it seemed to him, this time. And then again. And again. He had begun by helping her write better sentences, to organize her thoughts more clearly; but soon Robin was basically writing the papers for her, merely asking for her approval on a point now and then. In this writing of papers he became an expert. He disguised his own style perfectly, and made enough errors in the text that the teacher didn't have the slightest doubt that Marylou had simply begun to improve her work.

For these efforts the girl seemed appreciative.

"Oh Robin," she would gush, her voice rather comically high and childish, "you've *saved* me, you know. How can I ever repay you?"

But the situation, it seems to him, had quickly deteriorated. Marylou soon stopped bothering to show up at the library and simply let him write the papers himself; finally she wouldn't even bother to pick them up. He had to drive to her house to make the weekly delivery.

"Oh Robin," she would squeak each time, "how can I ever repay you?"

Once, after this had been going on for some months, he had answered: "Well, Marylou, I could get into a lot of trouble for this, you know. I mean I could get suspended from school if they found out. We both could."

"I *know*." She gazed up at him, her dream-vision emerald eyes filled with deathless devotion. "And it means so *much* to me that you would *risk* yourself that way for little me."

Marylou Kirk, he would remember ironically, was widely known around school as "Miss Goody Two-Shoes." Nice to everyone—too nice—too polite: too damned *perfect*. Freshman boys had been known to do mincing imitations of her; in fact, Davy Carp could do a rather good one himself. But her attractiveness was undeniable. She inspired doglike devotion; she certainly had, at least, with Robin. Though sometimes he wondered just exactly what *he* was getting out of the deal. A certain perverse amusement, yes, in discovering that Miss Two Shoes was hardly the infallible wonder everyone thought she was; but that amusement had worn thin quickly. And yet he continued with his dark toil.

And for only one reason.

The reason had arisen on a certain spring afternoon. He had been sitting in Marylou's living room as she glanced over the newest essay (she always looked them over and tried to understand them, in case the teacher asked her something: Marylou was dumb, but not stupid) and he had at last said: "You know, Marylou, I've been doing these things for you for over half a year now."

"I *know*," she said, "and you're *so* sweet."

"Well, I—" he looked at her gorgeous love-filled eyes and nearly stopped, but forced himself to continue: "Marylou, it's getting too dangerous. I could blow everything if I get caught."

She cocked her head inquiringly. "What are you saying, Robin?"

"I'm saying—" he cleared his throat—"I think we'd better not do this anymore."

She stared up at him with the expression of a small child who has been surprised by something but hasn't yet made up her mind whether it is good or bad. "But Robin," she said, "how could I get along without you?"

He looked at her. She was wearing a short pink and blue dress that would have been more appropriate to a twelve-year-old, but which somehow only increased her attractiveness, her downright sexiness. "I—I don't know. But you don't seem to understand how dangerous this is."

"But I *do* understand." After a moment she stood and came to him, sat next to him on the sofa. "Don't you know that I *do* understand?"

"I—well, you don't seem to. Sometimes."

"Robin, haven't I thanked you? Don't I thank you *every* time?"

"Sure, but…"

"Haven't I told you over and over what it *means* to me?"

"Yeah, sure you have, but…"

"Poor Robin," she said. And to his astonishment, her hand suddenly moved to his face and gently brushed back his hair. "You're feeling unappreciated, aren't you?"

"I...well..."

She had tucked her feet up under her and was leaning very close to him now. Robin stared straight forward in fast-growing, hilarious terror. "But don't you know," she said, her voice fading to a whisper, "that I *do* appreciate you."

"Yeah, well, sure..."

"And that I'm *not* the kind of awful person you think I am."

"I didn't say..."

Her hand was on his arm. "...And that I *show* my appreciation."

Robin's heart stopped beating for a moment.

"You—?"

"Listen," she whispered. Her mouth was next to his ear. "Robin, it's *only* a few more itty-bitty months."

"I know..."

"And if you could write just a *few* more itty-bitty papers for me..."

"Uh-huh..."

"If you could be patient with me just a *little* longer..."

"Yeah..."

"...I'll *show* you how much I appreciate it."

Silence descended in the room.

"How...?" he tried to ask.

A whisper. "How do you think?"

"I...don't know..."

"*Any way you like.*"

Her hand on his knee. Her lips, good glorious God, on his earlobe...

"*When is the next paper due?*" he gasped.

Afterward! Oh, the feeling of power and coming glory! To have not only extracted such a promise, but from *her*: Two Shoes herself! The little innocent! Not only did she have him doing her English papers for her little guiltless self, but now *this*....

Of course there was one slight problem, a single minor anxiety. He would think of it, grieve over it on long rainy evenings: he would devise mad plots that involved trips to San Francisco's red-light lowlife to solve it; but for all his dreamy plotting, it was still there, as it had always been: the cold dry jail cell of his virginity. It was his secret shame, his private apocalyptic humiliation. To know *nothing*. Seventeen years old, at his physical peak, and in matters of this nature to have nothing imprinted on his brain but a huge turdlike zero. He had not so much as gone out on a real date, let alone gotten involved with anything else. (Those things that Michael Lyon no doubt got involved with so easily and naturally: in his worst moments he imagines Michael Lyon and Kathy Collins steaming up the windows of Kathy's little Fiat: but no, they would never be so crass as that. They would drive down the coast for the day, to the house that Michael Lyon's father owns on the beach there. Easy. There they would have their steamy sex... their steamy *responsible* sex, for, Robin is sure, Michael Lyon would hardly be so stupid as to let his passions run away with him and thereby jeopardize the golden road to glory that has been so carefully mapped out for him.) In the afternoons, when the house was empty and safe, Robin would sometimes doff his clothes and study himself in the full-length mirror in his bedroom. His body did not seem to have any obvious hideous defects. The face: not handsome, exactly, but hardly ugly—attractive long hair, piercing blue eyes; his body: very thin, sorely lacking musculature, but decently formed, smooth, hairless. The chest desperately needed some building up, but the stomach was very fine, the hips thin and shapely. As to the other, obvious feature of interest (the one hair-filled area in an otherwise pristine geography), he wondered.

What was it supposed to look like, at this age? Was his a pitifully underdeveloped seedling where should stand a mighty vine? He had occasionally tried to compare in the locker room after P.E., but he had never had the courage to so much as take a shower there: a hurried change of clothes and he would be gone. Any real analysis had been impossible. Nor did he feel that he would ever be able to bring himself to wandering around casually naked before the boys of the school: the unhappy fate of Rodney Baker is never far from his mind. Rodney was a shy, painfully introverted freshman who had once been seen in the shower sporting an inadvertent erection. He had been known forever after as "Rodney the Rod."

Robin's enforced virginity lent him enough shame. He hardly needed to become Robin the Rod.

And there were other disturbing considerations. At times, when he glanced at the undressed boys in the locker room, images came to his mind: images he quickly buried but which surfaced sometimes at night when he was lying in bed. He would try never to think of them. But they reappeared at unexpected moments, bobbing up out of the sea—boys....

And so he would focus his mind only on the sensuous vision of Marylou Kirk, the seventeen-year-old in her little-girl party dress, and imagine what secret delights were under that dress. What kind of savage sexual animal was concealed beneath that cool, prim exterior. And he would focus on the breathless, nearly-impossible-to-believe promise she had whispered into his ear....

So he would study himself in the mirror, searching for any obvious malformations that might account for the fact that women seemed to have no interest whatever in him. He really could find none. He seemed to himself a reasonably acceptable package. Running his palms down his sides, he would think: I'm here. Look at me. Of course, at these times he would also sometimes think of earlier days, old dreams: he would muse on what his body might look like were it a girl's, if the seedling were to shrink and vanish and the face soften, become rounder, if the breasts were to enlarge. It was an interesting vision. But usually such thoughts would not last long, for he would remember Michael Lyon and Davy Carp and Marylou Kirk and they would bring him abruptly back to reality.

And if darkness was falling, if the room was growing dusky and cool, his internal censor would interrupt his reveries: would remind him that it was time to go, it would soon be time to go. Because he knew that the house would be dangerous at night, he would begin formulating his evening plans: Davy Carp, the movies, the cafe. The restaurant, if he were working that night. Whatever it was, as long as it was a plan.

Robin knew the house would be dangerous at night because he was not alone there. Although sometimes, many times, he liked to imagine that he had the entire place to himself, that illusion could not hold at night when his father made his dark appearance. He arrived punctually, always within an hour of nightfall, having left his job at the office in Greyfield and stopped somewhere to drink for awhile. He would not come home staggeringly drunk. That he left to the auspices of the booze in the house. In the liquor cabinet in the kitchen he kept many multi-colored bottles for this purpose; bottles containing things Robin found unswallowable. It was not that the man made scenes while drunk. It was, in fact, quite the opposite. Often there were no scenes. No screaming accusations. It was the silence itself that was deadly, dangerous. The way Robin ceased to exist when the man arrived: the way he would not be looked at, spoken to, as if he had simply disappeared, become mist. He could wander the house at will; sometimes he felt he could break up the dishes, light the kitchen on fire, and there still would be no reaction: for, if he was a ghost (as it seemed to him he was, after dark), how could he do any damage? He was mist, smoke, vapor, air.

In earlier days, before he had learned of the dangers in the house at night, he had acted as if he were still alive, as if he were flesh-and-blood and a beating heart. He would come downstairs and sit with the man while he watched television. Or he would try to ask him about a difficult Algebra problem. But, although the man would answer, or try to—depending on the lateness of the hour—it soon became clear to Robin that the man was speaking to an irrelevance, an unreality. The words were perfunctory; their eyes never met. And thus the house is dangerous at night, for it threatens his life, his existence, his very being.

For years he had studied the man as if one them were film: illusory, not essentially there. Or, perhaps, Robin was more of a film camera, passionlessly recording how the man moved, how he spoke, how he behaved. He could remember long scenes almost verbatim: where they had been, what they had said, the sounds, the light. The quality of the man's voice (low, rumbling, but with drink rising to an unnaturally high pitch). Paranoid shoutings. Yes, he could remember scenes; but when he thought of them, he realized that there were remarkably few to remember. They spoke few words to each other. Even day-to-day necessities were largely taken care of by a hired woman who cooked and cleaned the house several days a week. Few words: but he could remember them vividly—especially the ones that had been spoken long ago, after the disaster. More recent words were not as clear. Although he had noticed this: the further time went on, the clearer they would become, as if a certain distance were required between himself and the words before he could recall them well. But then the recollection was perfect, crystalline. He could remember, for instance—years later—scenes that, when he was fourteen or fifteen, he had had no memory of whatever. He could remember, after having long since forgotten, his father coming into his room, sitting down on the side of the bed: the only light coming from the hall: and the man's nervousness, his obvious unease, at invading

Robin's private sphere. And he could remember his own shock, his own feeling of violation, as the man, grotesquely out of place in the room, set his heavy bulk on the bed and for long moments said nothing. His face was in shadow: but perfectly profiled, the prominent brow ridge, the hawk nose, the thin uncertain lips. *How are you doing?* the man had asked. Robin whispered an answer; the man said *What?* Robin repeated himself, louder this time. It always seemed that the man wanted him to speak louder, as if Robin's voice registered on some difficult frequency the man could not hear. A long silence passed between them. Robin could hear the wind rising in the pepper tree outside. *Good*, the man finally said. *The important thing...*and he paused, as if briefly forgetting what the important thing was—*...the important thing is to—to not let it get you down. Know what I mean?* I know, Robin answered. I'm not. *Yes, well, Robin, you tend to—I don't know—brood, and I just want you to know that that's a...a bad way of...*I know, Robin said again. I get it, Dad. His father had sputtered into silence then, like a fizzling fourth-of-July rocket: and they had sat in the tense silence together for a minute or more. Finally his father said: *Yes, well, that's what I came to tell you.* Mm-hm, Robin answered. Thanks, Dad. The man nodded and stood and, finally, disappeared from the room.

Robin had not thought of the incident since it happened; but it reappeared in his mind abruptly one evening. As if it had been there all along, a submerged island that had suddenly, inexplicably surfaced. What frightened him was that he never knew when these new, remembered memories would appear. It could happen at any moment: in bed, driving to school, talking to Davy Carp, anywhere. And wherever he was at the time, he would suddenly be transported to that other, former place: it would appear brightly before him, a glittering gem that obscured what had been there before. He would lose track of what he had been doing, lose the thread of a conversation, when suddenly he found himself again in the house, years before, in a scene between his father and himself, or his mother: they were there, suddenly, mysteriously more real than real life. His father, in a strange way, far more vivid and tangible in the bright memory than in the times Robin would actually see him in the house. He was, somehow, a man more real in remembrance than reality.

And when he thought of her—which he did not often do—he found that he could often not quite visualize her face: as if Renoir had worked at it, blurred the outline, made it dreamy and uncertain. The room he would see perfectly; his father would be brilliantly clear; the sounds, vivid: but her face, it would blur, change, transform itself into shifting clouds. He found that he could recall photographs of her brilliantly; but the living, breathing image, her expressions and the movement of her eyes and rhythms of her voice, had begun to disappear. At times he could still put her image together in his mind. At times she would be there for him again, real, tangible in the chambers of his brain. But more often he felt he was somehow leaving her behind, that she was lost in a particular place, unmoving in one spot in his mental plane while the psychic distance between them only grew and grew with each passing moment. As if she were disappearing, irrevocably, forever. And at these times, when he was trying to conjure as an illusionist does a woman's image from nothing, and when he found that she could not be found except in the vaguest, blurriest outlines, he would want to shout: *Come with me!* But that she did not do; and so she receded ever further into the vast maw of the past, becoming a smaller and smaller figure on the horizon, alone there, while Robin was hurled ever-faster toward the strange door, toward the abyss.

But the house is dangerous at night, and so Robin does not spend time there dwelling on such things; they are thoughts only for very late, when the house is silent again and asleep, and he is able to come in out of the darkness to the darkness of the rooms, and on very good nights he will be so tired that no thoughts will interfere with his smooth passage into unconsciousness. On good nights he will be tired enough that, next morning, he will recall no more than a minute or so of consciousness after getting into bed; then, nothingness. On other nights, however, it will take him longer, as he turns over and over in the bed, a storm of people and remembrances whirling in his head. At that time he often will bring the sock or the towel from under his bed, left there for nights like these: and in his barren, frozen mental landscape he will become an automaton, making automatic gestures and motions until he relaxes again. And then he will sink, almost invariably, into the nothingness he desires. He will sink, for he must sink; for the memories, so often like a tape recorder on an endless loop, may otherwise draw him in forever, turn him from the strange door. And so he knows he must quiet them, ease them into motionlessness. The memories are dangerous, he knows. They are a whirlpool into which he must keep from losing himself. He must keep the strange door before him: for still, still he wants to go to it, to open it, to discover what awaits him on the other side. An abyss it may be; but he must see it, feel it; even if the only sensation is that of his own body freefalling into darkness. He must know. He must reach the strange door and knock on it. Someone, he knows, will answer.

3

Thus time winds its course for Robin. Days turn to night and again to day; but he is not very much aware of the process. He keeps it from invading his mind, for when it does he is suddenly filled with tingling, formless fear that freezes up his mind, makes everyday living impossible. One day he goes to the Academic Counseling Office and looks aimlessly through a number of college catalogs. Almost at random he chooses three to apply to; he takes their addresses and writes to them. But it is an unreal thing.

The Unspoken

It is unimaginable, the idea of going away from Wind Point, from the house in the cul-de-sac: and yet he knows that unimaginable things do occur, that disasters do take place.

Sometimes, on weekends, he and his father have discussions about it. It is at these times, with gold sunlight filtering through the drawn morning curtains, that Robin notices most clearly how much the man has aged in the past few years: how what once were light, gentle lines, almost as if they had been artificially applied with makeup, have become crevices, like dry river beds crisscrossing his face; how the eyes, once (very long ago, in an almost unremembered time) bright and lustrously blue, have faded to a pale, hazy milkiness. Not that his father has become a lifeless husk. He still works every day in Greyfield at the insurance office (*I Can Insure Your Future*, the sign reads); he plays an occasional game of tennis on a good Sunday morning. When Robin thinks of his father, these are the times he likes to recall. When they drive to the high school courts together, the wind breezing through the open windows and through their hair, the tension seems, for an hour or so at least, to dissolve: and they play a relaxed, leisurely game. Afterwards they use the high school locker room (deserted now, on the weekend: Robin showers in a separate stall) to change; and often his father will take him then to a cafe or restaurant. The tension will still be gone, and they will sit together with iced tea on an open terrace on a warm spring afternoon as if the skies had always been this clear, this crystalline. They will not always talk, for talking is something that even the idyllic mood of such days cannot make easy. But they can be together, comfortably, without words. On clear gemlike afternoons like these the swarming memories will be far away, in another land. For they discuss—when they do talk—nothing of the past. In fact, when Robin thinks of it, he realizes that within a few days—weeks, at most—of the disaster, she had disappeared from their conversation utterly. A curtain of silence had been tacitly drawn; and she had ceased to exist. There was no monument or plaque to serve as a reminder; there was nothing at all. She had misted into nothingness, sunk into the sea. Except at night, of course, late, when she would reappear inside his mind, her voice and her manner increasingly difficult to recollect, but still there sometimes, alive, real, free. It was when his mind was at its most relaxed, the images flowing freely across it, that she would live again, move, breathe: never at any other time. He remembers that for a long time he had tried to draw her out of his memory through constant prayer. He had prayed a great deal in the years after the disaster; but, although he had tried, he never felt that his mind-words were going anywhere beyond the four walls of his room. When he was fifteen he had undertaken to join a church. He sought out all he could find in Wind Point and the mainland. He loved Mass: the dark sanctuary of the cavernous church, the candles, the priest's voice intoning *This is the word of God* and holding up the book as if it were concrete proof of the fact. He learned to genuflect; and for a few months he loved nothing more than to sit in the silent church after the service, staring up at the huge and golden crosses that decorated the pulpit and listening to the silence, filled here and there with faint echoes, while he tried to imagine that this was God's place, God was here with him. But the illusion would not hold. He enjoyed the quiet solitude, but ultimately that was all it was: he could detect no other, grander presence in the room. Nor, when it came down to it, did he much care for the idea of eating the god incarnate's body and drinking his blood. Rather barbaric, it seemed to him; and they tasted only like ordinary biscuit and wine. Once he had been roaming around the empty church after services and had found a giant cardboard box filled with the little golden biscuits: exactly as they would appear, he thought, in any supermarket stockroom. No, that church held nothing for him.

And so he had begun to visit a Baptist group in Greyfield. He had enjoyed them a great deal at first. Unlike the Catholics, there was no solemnity here, no moody melancholy silences. The preacher's arms waved wildly and his voice exploded across the room: *And we shall be saved, yes! And we shall be saved, yes!* and the congregation had shouted back *Yes! Yes!* It was quite a lot of fun; they sang upbeat, nearly rock 'n' roll style hymns, and Robin was much fussed over. But finally he decided that the minister was too interested in talking about sinners who were en route to Hell. This was a great sticking point between Robin and the God who was spoken of in these churches. Try as he might, he could never reconcile the loving, merciful God that the preachers talked of with the one who allowed his own children to sink into eternal damnation. That God did not, certainly, seem like the ideal Father. Then he had visited a Mormon church; but he had gotten out of there fast. He could never for a moment believe the careful mapping-out they had for the various levels of Heaven—it seemed patently absurd—and, after reading a bit of the church's history, he grew suspicious of the elders' habit for revelation—usually arrived at around the same time the church had run into trouble about some point or other.

In some ways, of all the churches he attended he preferred the simple, nondenominational one just down the street in Wind Point. There were no mystical rituals here, no talk of burning in Hell, no road maps to salvation. The minister was straightforward and, Robin thought, rather eloquent: he talked of loving oneself, cooperation, helping others; and here there was no sense of competition. In the other churches members seemed terribly concerned that Robin join *their church* because he would find that *those other churches* were not *the right churches*. It all seemed to him not unlike a group of football teams trying to recruit a new linebacker. In the small, simple Wind Point church, there was none of this...but neither was there any feeling of revelation. The preacher was pleasant and interesting; but it certainly seemed to Robin that there must be more to God and Eternity than this little church, the minister's little words. It was adequate as entertainment, but for Robin it was certainly not Holy Truth.

And so at seventeen he is spiritually adrift. The churches hold no answers for him. But he wonders if churches are the only possible solutions, the only path toward truth or Truth. When he lies back on his bed, stereo headphones over his ears, and listens to a symphony of Mahler, it seems to him then that he is finding something closer to it than any preacher has shown him. When he looks through books of Van Gogh in the school library, he thinks again: *Maybe this is God.* For these things fill him with the same sensation he has heard religious people talk of: a tingling, an inner light, some inexpressible connection to something warm and eternal, like a golden shaft of light to the stars. But Mahler, Van Gogh, all the rest, were only human, not supernatural beings: and thus he wonders what that says about Truth, the Eternal. He begins to consider the idea of Man as his own God, his own absolute maker and maintainer of life, time, reality. But he cannot puzzle it all out: it remains in his mind an inchoate jumble of half-realized ideas, unfinished concepts.

Once the nondenominational preacher had talked of *the sacred pact of marriage* and this had interested Robin a great deal. It set him wondering whether love had something to do with this final Truth: whether it could not be reached except by this strange, magical bond, this connection and completion of oneself. But it was a depressing line of inquiry, since he had come nowhere near to finding such a bond himself. He likes the idea, however, in theory: that he is somehow incomplete, and will grow complete only when he finds that magic someone who will become part of him: like two halves of an apple. It is nice to ponder: but of course it strikes him as far less than likely, or even possible, that he will find his missing half. There are clearly no prospects on the horizon. Given his reputation for arrogance, remoteness, intellectualism, he rarely meets anyone new; really, he suspects that he frightens others away. The psychology of it, he realizes, is simple enough: bad early experiences leading to construction of emotional wall through which he will allow no one, and assumption of superior manner to mask deeper feelings of inadequacy. Easy. But being aware of it does not change it. This is why the breezy affability of a Michael Lyon is such a source of continual wonder to him: to be so completely comfortable around others!

But *completion*. That is an idea which quite appeals to him. The notion that there is a wandering, lost soul out there somewhere waiting for him and only him to come and give it life, joy. That somewhere there is someone on a magnificent collision course with him. Who knows what that lost soul might be doing at any given moment? It must go about on its lonely daily routines much as Robin does. It must take out the garbage, make sandwiches... it is fascinating to think of. Perhaps, sooner or later, he will be in a long grocery line—or at a film, or a party—and he will see, for the first time, the lost soul that is his own, his other apple-half. It reminds him of the dream he used to have when he was younger: when he would be floating high above a great green-blue ocean and there, in the distance, an island would come into view. On the island he would see a figure: but it was distant, and turned away from him, and so he could never make out who it was. But he always knew, immediately, that he was in love with the figure. He would try to reach toward it; to swim through the streaming air; to get closer; but the dream, no, it never allowed him to: he would always find himself sinking back into consciousness, the island and the figure on it dissolving to mist and echoes. He has not had the dream in years, and yet he remembers it with perfect clarity. The aching, the longing, being that close to his beloved and yet not able to breach the gulf: it is sharp, vivid, real in his memory.

And yet, of course, he always comes back to the realization that there are no prospects whatever for such a union. It fills him with sore loneliness and thus he tries to keep from thinking of it: tries, at moments like these, to think of *lust* instead. There is a definite prospect for the satisfaction of *that*: and he finds it quite delightful to think about. For the school year is nearing its end and Marylou Kirk's promise, her whispered vow, nears its consummation as surely as crystalline water flies over a waterfall. Oh, to be through with the dread disease, once and for all! To be able to stand as an equal in any conversation about such worldly matters! To free himself from his burning solitary confinement! But, at the same time, he worries about this innocence of his. Just how experienced *is* this girl? Obviously she is not the cutesy-tootsy virginal Mary Poppins she makes out to be; what, then, if she had *expectations*? Could he, utterly inexperienced as he is, satisfy them? What if the entire thing became only black humiliation? He would visualize awful scenes that could take place: *Oh, he can hear her saying, is that all you have?* Or *My God, don't you know anything at all?* What if he panicked and wasn't able to… What if…No! He has to stop thinking of it! What will happen, will happen. He will be a smooth pond of placidity.

But it doesn't last; and when the whirlpool of fear rages again in him he starts thinking of other, darker, more vicious things. He thinks of death, of time. He listens to the tiny alarm clock on the table next to his bed and tries not to hear its small sharp ticking. The sound terrifies him. And, if he does not reach to put the clock under a blanket or pillow, the sound will grow in his mind: the tiny ticking grow to a hammering: each tick, he realizes, representing a moment in time gone, never to return in the entire history of the universe, another second dead, and others following, domino-like, an endless procession of them: each tick another second which is behind him, in his past, not in his future: a steel-gray sky ever-filling with these used and wasted seconds, while his storehouse of future time dwindles ever more precariously each second, each second. If only he could peer into that storehouse, to espy the number of ticks left! Perhaps it is full, overflowing, with years and decades worth, virtually endless; or maybe he will go to cross the street tomorrow and he will hear a sudden rush of sound and he will look up to see the strange door flying open and all his future time stored there: but there will be nothing, the room will be empty, only a blank abyss awaiting him....

Stop.

He breathes.

After a moment he takes the clock and puts it under his pillow. It is silenced then. It is all right then.

He chuckles slightly. It is just like him, he thinks, to turn the coming reality of Marylou Kirk into an excuse for death-fantasies. Of course he is sick—he knows that—but at times his sickness seems to take on such grotesque proportions that it becomes more like comedy, black and acidic. Humiliation! Death! Abyss!

When will you stop feeling sorry for yourself? His father's voice. But not harsh, not accusing. Gentle, in fact. In the seafood restaurant, after their Sunday tennis.

But Dad, if I don't, who will? No, he hadn't said it. But he had wanted to. His father, across the table, studying him. His blue eyes searching, mirrors of Robin's own. Robin uncomfortable under the stare. He hadn't replied at all. What could he say? How could he explain the terror? How could he make the man understand? There seemed not to be a way. Robin saw himself a prisoner inside his own mind, his own mask, a cell for which the key had been irrevocably lost; and as for the rest of the world, were they all together, as one, or were they each locked inside their own masks as well? He didn't know, looking down at his plate under the man's hard stare. He doesn't know now. He thinks again of his missing apple-half, somewhere out in the dark distance beyond the clouds, the rain, the thunder. Is it possible? he wonders. Possible that even now, at this instant, this very tick of time, that someone, his destiny, his completion, is out there, on a magnificent collision course with him? Someone who will save him? Who will retrieve the key to the mask? Who will soften the ticking, even stop it? Will he ever see the face of the figure on the island? When? When, when?

4

On the mainland the weather is slowly, like a flowering bud, beginning to open: it is mid-May, and the fog and mist burn off quite early, before nine o'clock, leaving brilliantly bright and cool skies so light in color as to be nearly white at the horizon. Wind Point, of course, is unchanged, the mist like a curtain of steel overhanging everything. But Robin spends his days in Hollowstone, and so can live through the mornings and afternoons under clear, free skies.

One morning he and Davy Carp are heading toward Social Studies (the teacher, a Mr. Benny Bates, is currently number twelve in the *Personas Non Gratas* catalog), when Robin hears the blessed voice of coming bliss behind him.

"Oh, *Robin*..."

He turns and there is Marylou, sweet succulent Miss Goody Two Shoes, scampering up to him. She wears a white dress and her dark hair is done up in little-girl pigtails. His vision immediately blurs and he is with her in some other time, close to her, reaching around and undoing the pigtails, watching the hair spill like black gold onto her shoulders—

"Hi, Marylou."

"Hidee-hi, you two. Robin, could I talk to you for just a teeny little minute?"

His heart beats. "Sure," he says. "Davy, I'll check you in Bates' class, okay?"

Robin notices, though he only glances at the boy, that Davy Carp has an odd, annoyed expression on his face. "Yeah," Davy says, turning away. "Sure."

Robin turns back to the girl. "What is it, Marylou?"

She drops her voice to a stage whisper. "Oh, stupid me has a teeny little problem, I'm afraid. C'mere." She leads him around a corner where they cannot be seen. The sky is cold and clear above them.

"See," she says, bringing a paper out of her notebook, "sometimes I'm a little scatterbrained. Look at this handout from Mrs. Holgate. That paper about William Faulkner? Look, it's due tomorrow!"

He looks over the assignment sheet. Marylou is in an optional Comparative Literature class Robin does not attend. "Mm-hm," he says. "I remember, you told me about this. But you said it was due in a couple of weeks."

"I *know*." Her bottom lip sticks out slightly in an absurdly cute pout. She looks plaintively at him. "I didn't read it right. I'm sorry."

"Well, Marylou," he says, "it'll have to be late. This is supposed to be a five-page paper about imagery in Faulkner. I can't knock that out in one evening. I've got my own homework to do—"

"I know. The things you go through for little me."

"So maybe I can get it to you by Friday."

"Well, Robin," she says, stepping close to him and touching his chest gently, "you know how Mrs. Holgate is about late papers. One full letter grade."

"I know. But Marylou, be reasonable."

She smiles shyly up at him. "I'm not reasonable. If I was reasonable I wouldn't ask you to do the kinds of things I ask you to do."

There is a brief pause.

"Now Marylou," Robin begins, "come on…"

The smile covers her face, lights up her innocently helpless eyes. "Please?"

"Marylou, I can't possibly write a paper that long in one—"

"Robin, it's the next-to-the-last. Only *one* more."

"I know—"

"And you've been *so* wonderful to me."

"Yeah—"

"And we're *so* close to being finished, now…"

"Yeah, but Marylou, when am I supposed to do my own homework? There's a test in Social Studies tomorrow, I'm behind in my Math assignments…"

She looks down. "It's horrible of me to ask, I know."

He sighs. "It's not that. It's just that, you know, I have my own homework—I spend a lot of time doing things for you, you know—"

"I *know*."

"And I must say that I get mighty little appreciation for it." He knows he is treading on dangerous ground, but he cannot stop the sudden flow of words. "*Mighty* little appreciation. I think you've just grown used to me and used to my doing all your English for you. I haven't really minded. But come on, Marylou, this is…"

She looks at the assignment paper in Robin's hand sadly and takes it from him. "I know," she sighs quietly. "You're right. Never mind." She begins to fold the paper into her notebook again.

He looks at her for a moment. "Now—look, I said I'd have it by Fri—"

"No, Robin, you're right." She looks at him the way girls look at boys when they are calling relationships to an end. "It's time for me to do my own work. I'm just taking advantage of you. I know it. Never mind. I'll do it myself." And, with a witheringly saddened expression, she turns away.

"Marylou—" Suddenly his entire sexual future seems to be melting like wax, turning to hot liquid sludge in his hands. "Marylou, wait. Wait!"

"Why?" She looks back at him, sad-wistful. "I don't think there's anything more to discuss."

"There is!" He comes close to her. "Now—it's just that…" He looks at her. She gazes up at him, her deep, green crystal eyes innocently questioning. Oh my God, he thinks, what am I doing? "It's just that—I didn't say...I wouldn't do it. I was just saying that—that I wouldn't be able to do anything like this *again*. I mean on such short notice."

"Are you sure?" she asks hesitantly.

"Sure...sure I'm sure. That's—that's all I meant." God damn it! he thinks.

"Because I *do* put you out, I know. I'm awful, aren't I?"

"You're not awful," he says, grinning sheepishly. "You're... you're Marylou." Now, he wonders, what the hell did *that* mean?

The smile that could launch a thousand ships returns to her face. She fishes out the assignment paper. "You're such a darling," she says. "You really are."

"Sure I am. I'm okay."

"You're more than okay."

He feels his heart beating again as he stares at the sheet. "Well, we *are* close to the end now."

"Mm-hm. We are!"

"And—well—" How to broach this one? he wonders. It had not been discussed but that one time, in her house. "And—Marylou, well, you haven't...forgotten? Have you?"

"About what?"

"Well—" he feels his face flush—"we talked about something, once..."

A brief pause. "What?"

"In your—house," he says lamely.

"What did we talk about?"

"Marylou, you know. About...appreciation. And...things."

"I *do* appreciate you."

"I know. But we talked about a kind of...a sort of...way of...you know...showing—appreciation."

"What way was that?"

He stares at her, unable to speak.

"Oh," she says finally, "I remember what you mean. Of course." Her voice is oddly flat. "So, when can I have the paper? Tomorrow morning, before class, let's say?"

Should have gotten a fucking legal contract, he thinks. *The undersigned agree that Robin Withers will provide a damn near endless supply of English papers and that in return Marylou Kirk will—* Oh, God. *Of course*, she'd said; and immediately changed the subject. Was it possible that she had no intention of living up to the bargain? What, then, could he do? What recourse did he have? He could threaten to expose the whole sordid deal, perhaps; but of course he was as guilty as she was. He was trapped! It was Faustus and Helen all over again, devilish dealings, sold souls! And all for the sake of—it was a nightmare. It wasn't Faustus. No, it was "The Pit and the Pendulum," with Robin strapped down to the hard iron bed of his virginity while the swooping blade of eternal ignorance swept closer, ever closer....

He glances up and realizes that he has long passed Benny Bates' classroom and is stalking blindly into the school parking lot. He stops.

Where am I going? he wonders. His car isn't even parked around here. He stares forward for a moment; then turns quickly, wildly. A girl who had been coming up behind him starts.

"Oh!" she says, pausing for a moment. "I'm sorry. You scared me." Blonde, cute. Robin doesn't know her name.

He glares at her. He tries to think of something to say but can only hear his heart pounding inside his chest and his heavy, ragged breathing.

The girl looks at him. "Excuse me," she says, a tentative, rather frightened look on her face. "Are you...are you *all right?*"

He supposes that at any moment fire might blaze forth from his nose or mouth, like Godzilla, but he forces himself to breath calmly.

"Mm-hm. Just fine!" he says too loudly, attempting a smile but uncertain of its success.

The girl nods and, with the querulous, strained expression with which one takes leave of criminals or mental defectives, she walks off to her car.

He stands there chewing violently on his lower lip and trying to clear his thoughts. He had been worried, before, about black humiliation...little had he known that the humiliation might occur long before any bedroom scene! Long before he had gotten so much as a glance at those firm little peach breasts, the smooth curves of that amazing little behind, that secret pocket of love between her legs. Long, long before! He feels himself straining against his shorts. Oh, God. He swallows, feels faint. Dully he staggers to the nearest car and sets his body against it.

An instant later a blasting *whoop whoop whoop* like an ambulance or police siren fills the air. Robin jumps away from the malevolent, alarm-wired vehicle. Glancing around wildly, he suddenly runs for the cover of the toilets at the end of the lot. As he runs he can see the headline: *Virgin Tries to Steal Car, Becomes Laughing Stock.* He begins to giggle. By the time he locks himself in the sanctuary of the toilet he is laughing crazily, uncontrollably, nearly drowning out the mocking *whoop whoop* of the vehicle, the hilarious derision of the universe....

Until night falls, he works on the paper in his bedroom. Faulkner. Imagery. He has the required texts before him—"Barn Burning,"

"A Rose for Emily," *As I Lay Dying*. Every word is painful; he sits at his typewriter feebly pecking, mechanically watching the words appear on the white sheet. Later Marylou will take the beautifully typed script and recopy it in her girlish, curly-cue handwriting for submission to Mrs. Holgate. He doesn't even like Faulkner. But he sits and pecks. It is a triple melancholy. Not only is it for Marylou Kirk, in whom his confidence has suddenly shattered like glass; not only is it dull, aimless work when he could be studying for his own test tomorrow; beyond those pains, he realizes—with every stab of a key on the machine—how he is wasting his time: how he should simply rip the paper from the machine and insert a fresh piece and begin, finally, his *real* writing, his stories, his poems, his bid for communion with the lovely ghosts. For he is sure of his genius. Sure that, if he were only to do it, he could make fly from his old Royal portable the greatest of novels, plays, poems. He can feel them inside him, churning, boiling, inchoate. But there. He *must* have genius, it seems to him: how else could he know the lovely ghosts so well, feel the peculiar oneness with them? How could he understand them as he does, in that mysterious way that is beyond language, words?

On impulse, he takes Faulkner out of the typewriter and winds in a new, blank sheet. He stares at it for several minutes, his mind as blank as the paper he stares at. What is it, he wonders, that he wants to write? What does he have to say? Surely, he thinks, he has the necessary experience. His mother. His father. Great things had been written from lesser raw materials. But then Marylou Kirk invades his mind again. Oh, he has experience all right! He has never once kissed a girl. He has seen exactly one naked female form, and that a twelve year old, years ago in another time, another country. He can hardly remember it at all; can picture nothing of what she looked like, how her voice sounded, nothing. He wonders. Whatever happened to Priscilla, or to any of them? They dissolved after the disaster like figures of air or vapor, never to be seen again. She would be sixteen now. Unreal thought: for, he suddenly realizes, while people age in life, they do not in memory: to him she is still a blurrily recalled twelve-year-old. No doubt he would not even recognize her now, nor she him.

But is it true that she was the only unclothed female he had ever seen? Something tickles his memory, a thing long forgotten. He can remember when he was very young—no more than six or seven—hearing the sound of the faucet running the water for his mother's bath in the evening. In the bathroom next to his room, just a few steps away even now. She liked the water tremendously hot: the steam would seep under the door and fog Robin's windowpanes. He could hear, as he lay in his bed in the darkness, the sound of the water being turned off and her body stepping lightly into the tub. He could hear her hands passing through the water and the hard thump of the wet soap being placed in the porcelain dish. Sometimes she would hum. This was long before the slurred words and misaligned pajama buttons and awful downstairs silences. Long, long before. She would hum in the bathtub and many times it would send Robin off to sleep, the sound of the humming and the sound of the water: as if he were floating gently into an ethereal, night place with her. He would drift. He would picture her face, its moon-shape, the Siamese eyes, the long curtain of hair damp on her shoulders. But once something had happened. Once he had had a nightmare—floating in that celestial blue, he had suddenly dropped screaming into a depthless black void—and he had awakened with a gasp. In the darkness of the room, it had seemed to him that the air itself was black liquid, threatening, suffocating. He trembled, holding himself for long moments, staring panicked into the darkness. Then he had jumped up and knocked rapidly on the bathroom door.

Mom...?

What is it, honey?

I...I had a dream. I'm afraid....
What? Did you have a nightmare?
Yes....
Oh, Robin. Come in here. The door's not locked.
Is it...okay—?
Of course it's okay. Come in, honey.

He opened the door softly, cautiously, looking down at the floor.

Honey, it's all right. Come here.

Then, looking up through the thick steam, he saw her there in the tub. He was astonished at her breasts, her nipples. Her entire body glistened with the water and he went and sat at the side of the tub and she put her arms around him. *There, there. It's okay. Mom's here.*

Robin stares at the blank sheet of paper in the typewriter.

Odd. He had completely forgotten about it. Hadn't thought of it in...what? Years. And the fact that she had gotten up then, stood up in the bath right before him, leaned over and taken a gray terrycloth robe and wrapped it around herself and said, *Honey, let's get you back to bed, okay?* He had gazed at her narrow hips, the shock of wet black hair between her legs. The vision, so long unremembered, burns now in his mind. He can recollect it all perfectly. She had taken him back to bed, tucked him in; she had hummed and stroked his forehead until he fell into a calm, dreamless nothing.

Into a glittering blue sea, sinking, descending...

He stares at the paper, letting the images flow across his consciousness.

After several more minutes have passed, he slowly types:

when I come home

He looks at it. Wonders why he didn't capitalize "when." Stares at it for some moments longer.

from somewhere

Time passes.
The room is silent.
she is there
A pause. Time; images.
waiting for me.
He sits back and looks at the line he has written. *when I come home from somewhere she is there waiting for me.* It exists. What comes after, or what came before, he cannot imagine. But he gazes at the single line for several minutes.

The intensity, however, has vanished; and he knows nothing else of it.

After some minutes he slowly pulls the sheet out of the typewriter and puts it aside. Then, mechanically, he reinserts Faulkner and begins pecking again.

Later, before the darkness falls, he puts his papers into his car and makes the drive out to the mainland to sit in the late-night cafe. Working now in longhand, he sits with a cup of lemon tea finishing with Faulkner. It is exhausting work. He had begun at three in the afternoon; when at last he puts the final period to the final sentence, it is past ten. Wearily, he looks through the paper. It is too good, he realizes; and so, grimly, he begins to scratch out some of the more complex syntax, the more creative points, until, forty-five minutes later, he is left with a perfectly acceptable medium-quality Marylou Kirk English paper. He sighs, pays his bill, and leaves.

When he reaches Wind Point again he turns onto a side street, impulsively deciding to see if Davy Carp is still up. Davy lives with only his mother; she works a late-night shift at the telephone company—so Davy is often to be found staring at the television into the early hours of the morning. Davy loves old movies as much as Robin; it was what had brought them together in the first place, when they were freshmen. Robin had found much to his delight that there was someone else in the world willing to forgo sleep to see *Dead of Night* at one in the morning; someone else in the world who had seen virtually every episode of *Alfred Hitchcock Presents* and *The Twilight Zone*. The first two years of their friendship they had been all but inseparable. Sometime in the third year, however, something had begun to happen: they were together as much as before, but Robin began to lose interest. He loved old movies as much as before; but it seemed to him that he was moving uncertainly into emotional regions where Davy was not willing to follow. Although the same age as Robin, Davy had changed little since they had first met. He was still perfectly satisfied to watch his movies and memorize his trivia and keep the *Personas Non Gratas* catalog up-to-date. He didn't even seem terribly concerned about what he was going to do after graduation: "Stay with my mom, I guess," he would say. "Maybe go to junior college." And Davy, of course, knew nothing of the lovely ghosts....

Robin sees a dim light in the window of Davy's little single-story, two-room house and he pulls up in the driveway. It was odd, he would often think: in many ways Davy had had as troubled an upbringing as Robin himself. Davy's father had disappeared when he was ten, never to be heard from again. He had had a brother once, a long time ago; he had died. His mother was a peculiarly somber, mousy little woman who seemed to have no abiding interest in anything. And yet none of this seemed to have affected Davy much. Or perhaps it had; but he would express nothing of it. Sometimes, long ago, Robin would try to talk to Davy about his own worries, his own fears: but, though Davy listened, he was able to offer Robin nothing. And so such talk had ceased.

The Unspoken

He knocks, and in a moment Davy answers.

"Hey, man."

"Hey, Davy."

"C'mon in."

Viewed objectively, Robin supposes, Davy Carp is quite remarkably unattractive. His dull mud-colored eyes are too big for his head, giving the face an almost comical look of perpetual shock; his hair is greasy and unkempt. Davy is, he realizes, something of an object of scorn in the school. But then, so is Robin. It binds them together.

They step through the narrow foyer into the flickering darkness of the TV room, where Davy sleeps. Robin sits on the fold-out sofa which is Davy's bed.

"What's on?" he asks.

"*Outer Limits*, in just a minute."

"Mm." Robin never watches such things anymore, but he still enjoys them when he is with Davy.

"What've you been doin', man?" Davy asks.

"Just school stuff. Went to the cafe."

"Should've taken me. I wasn't doin' anything around here."

"Well, I had a lot of work to do."

"Social Studies?"

"Yeah." Oh sure, he thinks. He can see the "D" flying toward him even as they speak.

"Hey," Davy says, flipping past used-car advertisements, news reporters, an old police drama, "what's with you and Marylou Kirk, anyway? I've never seen you guys hanging out together."

"Oh," he says, rather uncomfortably, "it's nothing." Actually, he had forgotten that Davy had seen him with her. They had been careful not to be seen together too frequently.

"Got somethin' *goin'*, man?" he asks, kiddingly.

"Ha. I wish." He also wishes Davy would change the subject.

"Yeah, well, I dunno if that's exactly the chick to get involved with, man."

"What do you mean?" It is quite unlike Davy to comment on girls.

Davy simply shrugs. "Here. *Outer Limits.* I hope it's one from the first season. The second season sucked."

Robin listens as the disembodied announcer calmly informs them that for the next hour *they* will be in complete control. It's fine by Robin. He sits in the darkness of the room, not paying any particular attention to the monster-laden science fiction story with the kooky music. Instead he wonders about Davy's cryptic comment regarding Marylou Kirk.

At the commercial break Robin says: "What did you mean about Marylou?"

"Hm?" Davy is distracted by a frozen pie advertisement. "Oh. Well. I just hope you're not...I dunno."

"Not what? Why are you being so mysterious?"

"I'm not."

"I don't get you."

"Look, it's just that there are some stories floating around about her. Just rumors. I dunno."

"Rumors about what?" Robin leans forward.

"Well—" Davy at last moves his eyes from the television to Robin—"just that she...You're not, like, doin' anything for her, are you? Writing papers or something?"

"No."

"Oh. Good."

"Why?"

"'Cause, well—it appears that Miss Goody Two Shoes sort of *borrows* people now and then to do her work for her. And then she promises to pay them back somehow but she never does."

"How do you know this?"

"Bill Flynn. Know him?"

"Sure. Math brain."

"Yeah. I heard him talking once, in the locker room. Said he'd done all her homework assignments for her and at the end she just said 'Thank you' and left him high and dry. I don't know what the deal was, but she welched on it."

Robin hears his heartbeat inside his ears.

"Why—" he clears his throat—"why didn't Flynn go to the teacher? Or Moore?"

"He was over a barrel, man. She would've just said it was all his idea. You know that face of hers and that little pouty expression she gets. No male teacher is gonna get her in trouble for much."

"I can't...I can hardly believe it. I mean, Marylou Kirk. Of all people."

"Yeah, it's somethin', isn't it?" His eyes turn back to the screen, where the monster story has resumed.

Robin grows silent. It's the worst-case scenario, he realizes. This is it. The jig is up. Finished. He's been had, utterly and completely. Not only does she have no intention of keeping her part of the bargain, she's doing the exact same thing to other guys too! His heart is beating heavily. To have been taken in so goddamned completely by that innocent little face. He thinks of the Faulkner paper out in his car, a murderous rage growing inside him. And the even bigger paper, the final paper, due in two weeks.

The final paper...

A few minutes later, at the next commercial, Robin asks: "Davy, are you sure? I mean about this thing with Marylou?"

"Sure as shit, man."

They stare at the television screen.

"In fact..." Davy begins.

"What?"

For a moment Davy says nothing. "Well," he finally mutters, "if you want to know the truth, last year I did a couple of Biology assignments for her."

Robin's heart is pounding behind his eyes now. "Are you kidding?"

"Nah. At least I wasn't involved in it very long. See, it was Bill Flynn and me talking in the locker room. She was supposed to pay me for my labors but..." His voice fades off, embarrassed.

"Well, Jesus," Robin says, "couldn't you and Flynn have gotten together and gone to the principal—"

"Yeah. I guess we could've. But there was still the problem that we were willing to do it. I just decided to forget it."

"Well, it seems as if there should be something—"

"You're doin' her English papers for her, aren't you, man?"

Robin's face flushes deeply. There is a pause in the room.

"Yeah," Robin finally admits. He begins to giggle.

Davy giggles with him. "I knew it. As soon as I saw her come up to you, I knew it. The nerve of that chick, right in front of me!"

"How many guys do you think are...helping her?"

"I dunno. Flynn was pretty sure that Willy Delmont was doing some of her Social Studies."

"Jesus Christ," Robin whispers. "She's like some sort of corporation."

Davy laughs. "Anyway," he says, noticing that *Outer Limits* has come on again, "you oughta forget about that chick. Tell her to write her own papers."

It is a long moment before Robin replies. "Yeah," he finally mutters. "Yeah, I sure will."

He turns it over and over again in his mind on the drive back to the house in the cul-de-sac. It is now well past midnight and a fog-shrouded moon stares down on him like a hazy eye. He shivers slightly inside his jacket: while the mainland has begun to see spring, it will still be another month or even two before Wind Point enjoys its brief foray into blue skies. They open, if they do open, in June or July: then there will be six or seven weeks of mistless air and T-shirt temperatures. But then the steel curtain will draw closed once again, and the jackets will return, the heavy wool shirts, the cold beads of dampness on the face.

Had, he thinks. He has been utterly, totally, all-encompassingly had. If someone were to write a book about the most stupid things men have ever done for women, certainly this would merit at least a footnote. All the work. All the anxiety. All the driving over to her house every weekend to deliver papers. All the lost time from his own schoolwork. All the *anticipation*. Gone, gone, smoke up the flue! His sexual future lies in a burned, blackened post-apocalyptic pile of rubble.

Lost in such reveries, Robin pulls up in front of the house. He does not stop to think about whether the house is safe; it is long past the hours of danger. All should be quiet now. He walks up the drive and unlocks the door, steps into the foyer.

He hears a sound like quiet hissing; it takes him a moment to recognize its source. He steps toward the living room and there, with an empty glass fallen to the floor next to him, is his father: his head fallen to one side, mouth agape, gently snoring. The room is dark but for the television, turned low, displaying only snowlike static. Robin stands at the entrance to the living room for several moments, listening to the TV's hissing and the rhythmic gasps of the man in the big leather chair. Finally he goes softly to the television set and switches it off.

"*What?*" the voice from the chair suddenly shouts. Robin flinches and says nothing in the new, luminous darkness of the room. The screen still emits its dim, strangely glowing light; as it will, Robin knows, for several more minutes, fading slowly, very slowly, to nothingness.

He can see the figure in the chair only very dimly. It adjusts itself again, emits a slight moaning sound, and is silent.

Robin stands next to the television for a long time, listening. The heavy, labored breathing resumes again. He listens as it fills the room, the air.

He is suddenly struck with an absurd image. His face burns with embarrassment even as he thinks of it, in this dark: but it nonetheless floats there, inescapable, like a leering ghost. He sees himself moving toward the man in the chair and crouching before him on his knees. He sees himself reaching up to the sleeping face, the closed eyes, the forehead made prominent by middle-aged hair loss, the large, elongated ears, the skin that hangs loosely from the man's neck: sees himself searching the face in the strange living darkness of the dimly fading television screen: sees himself, at last, leaning forward, actually leaning forward and kissing the man's broad cheek, his forehead, his eyes.

Robin squeezes his eyes shut and, flushed with shame, moves hurriedly past the man in the chair to the dark steps, to the other darknesses waiting for him upstairs.

5

"Oh, *Rob*in. . ."

He has hardly stepped out of his car, on his way to the anticipated D of his Social Studies test, and already she is descending on him, drawn like a magnet; or a bee to honey.

Robin smiles inwardly. The plan, when it had emerged from the subterranean cooking-pot of his brain the night before, arrived fully conceived: every detail, every nuance: and the perfection of it is awe-inspiring. Clean, flawless, hermetically sealed. There is no possible way for it to go wrong. His worries, his anxieties, his terrors have all dissolved like smoke in wind, because his perfect plan puts him in complete control. He grins again, inside himself. Marylou Kirk…the name rolls through his mind, all anxiety vanquished. All he has to do is have patience, patience.

"Hi, Marylou."

"Hidee-hi, Robin," she says, the big innocent emerald eyes meeting his own as she comes up to him, pigtails bobbing. "How are you?"

"I have it here." He takes Faulkner from his notebook.

"Oh, wonderful. And I have one free period to recopy it. That's *just* enough time!" The smile becomes a fluffy grin, displaying rows of perfectly even, pearl-colored teeth. "Thank you, Robin. You're so sweet."

He looks down at her. "Do you have the assignment for the final paper?"

"Mm-hm."

"Better give it to me. I'll need to get it done early so I have time for my own stuff."

"Oh, of *course*," she says agreeably. She flips through her own notebook until she finds the mimeographed sheet: an essay, eight pages minimum, comparing "The Treatment of War in Crane and Hemingway."

"I'm afraid," she says sympathetically, "this will be a *lot* of work for you."

"Oh, no," he answers, coolly slipping the sheet into a book. "This is no problem. Easy. Piece of cake."

"You're *such* a darling. What would I do without you?"

"I don't know," he smiles. "Anyway, I'll have it for you by the end of the week."

"So soon!" she gushes.

"Mm-hm," he says; a calm, a perfect placidity has swept over him. "And I'll drop it by…shall we say Saturday?"

"Oh, that would be just perfect!" The teeth, the eyes, the dark pigtailed hair...

Mine, Robin thinks. All mine.

———

Time passes that week; and so school winds slowly to its close. The morning skies in Hollowstone are dazzlingly bright and clear: soon the jackets and sweaters are being abandoned for shirt sleeves and even, in the afternoon, shorts. Ever more sorely, Robin sees Wind Point as a gray and lifeless prison cell to which morning never comes. But at least it is all finishing, at last.

In the mail one day arrives an acceptance from a school in northern California, a small university located amongst the redwoods; since it is the first such reply he has received, he decides—for no special reason—to plan on attending. He and his father discuss financing. It is agreed that he will stay in the school dormitories and perhaps get a part-time job; his father will send him a monthly allowance. These details swim by his mind: it seems to him that they are deciding someone else's future, not his own. He fills out forms, mails them. He does not think about it much.

Instead, his mind is filled completely with the plan. The revenge. The payoff. He need have only patience, O Patience!—and to write this final paper of hers; and all will be his. At times he feels giddy with excitement about it; but more often he is calm, unperturbed, even limpid. There is no need for excitement. He will be as calm as an unexploded bomb. As calm as Humphrey Bogart telling off Mary Astor at the end of *The Maltese Falcon*. Perfectly controlled.

Of course, at night his thoughts inevitably run away with him: scenes sweep across his mind: but he relaxes himself with a liberal use of his hidden sock. As Saturday approaches, though, he forces himself to stop. He must be well-stored, fully-stocked....

And when he does think about the university in California, it is with an odd lack of emotion: as if it does not really matter. But it is *California*—and he remembers, for the first time in ages, the kind of mystique that name used to hold for him, years ago. He remembers: his plans for Malibu, Santa Barbara, Venice Beach! Little had he known, then. Little had he known that at seventeen he would still have not seen those places: would still have not escaped the steel-dark solitude of Wind Point. But his university is in the north, not the south; a world away from those dream-soaked beaches and sunlight. He wonders vaguely if Priscilla ever thinks about California, or about the time they spent together all those years ago. Wonders, really, what has become of her—and of the rest of them: cobra-coiled Aunt Margaret, deathlike Uncle Otto, the three interchangeable D's. He has occasionally seen Aunt Margaret's flowery signature on Christmas cards; but that is all.

Oddly, when he thinks of them, he rarely thinks of the disaster. He would have supposed that his mind would inevitably associate the two, but it does not. He thinks of the disaster only at isolated times: when he hears his father passing by in the hall at night, when he goes by the corner where the event occurred. Once, passing by that corner had been a strange, unreal experience, for he could not keep his mind from picturing the darkness, the drunken shouting, the unnoticed vehicle, the foot stepping from the curb. Every time, the event would replay in his mind. Then the other details would arise: waking up in Wind Point, the slow ripping-apart of her as the boxes left the house, the funeral, the hearing he was told about in which the driver—Robin never learned his name—was acquitted of what was deemed an *unavoidable accident*. Strange thought: having no information, it could well be that Robin had seen this driver at some point. Perhaps one day they passed each other on the road. Perhaps their eyes met. He does not know; realizes with an odd, rather giddy sensation that he will never know. But he is not very interested at this point. Today he can pass by the corner without even a thought about it. The road has since been re-paved; and businesses that had been there at the time have since closed, and others have opened. Even in Wind Point, Robin realizes, time passes: and the corner is hard now to recognize as the same one where, years ago, his mother had stepped off the curb in the darkness to hear, only for an instant, the oncoming *whoosh* of the end—

But he never cries about it. Never had, in fact. Not once. He feels somewhat guilty about this. His own father he had seen, a full four or five months after, suddenly rush from the room with one hand covering his face. But Robin, never. He wonders why. He remembers, years before, lying on his bed and trying to *will* tears into existence: this, he felt, he owed her, this he had to offer to her. But they would not come. Sometimes he regrets the lack of any sort of monument, any place to center his feelings: as it is, he can only walk to the end of the pier and stare out into the gray-blue of the shadowy sea, thinking of the blackened bits of her sinking, sinking, breaking up, dissolving: he thinks of her then, but does not weep. He has long since given up trying to weep for her. The tears are not there. The tears are not there, really, for anything: he has not cried since he was small…Maybe, he thinks, people are right when they think him cold, arrogant, intellectual. Perhaps he simply has no capacity for feeling. Perhaps he was born without it. And yet he remembers the lovely ghosts: and his emotions when he listens to Mahler, or reads *Lear*: he does not cry, but his mind and emotions are stirred into a hot, terrible soup, he is wrung out like a towel…Surely, then, he is not without emotion. But it is always this other, less real world (but more real, to him) to which he reacts so strongly. In what others call the real world, he is cold: hyperborean, he likes to think, using a word he has found in Joyce. Existing somewhere in strange, remote icy regions. But is he really? He is not sure. Perhaps he is deluding himself. But there is one thing of which he is quite sure: he never mourned for her. Thought of her, yes; regretted the loss; sifted through memories; but never mourned. Never felt any catharsis. No light ever dawned on that darkness. It was a fact, and would be a fact for all time: that she was no more: and he accepted it. He did not mourn. It helped, really, that he and his father had never discussed her. That had allowed her to vanish all the more completely, disappear utterly: no lingering words floated around the rooms keeping her there with them. It was finished.

But another project, now, that is just begun....

He had completed the paper the night before, on Friday—eight-and-a-half pages of Hemingway and Crane—and now he stands before his bedroom mirror. Tremors of excitement course through him but he has them under control. He puts on his best jeans, a nice pink open-neck shirt; he sits on his bed and slips on his tennis shoes. He wonders how Humphrey Bogart would feel at such a moment. He wishes he had a 1940's style suit and hat, and a cigarette he could smoke in that special Bogart manner: maybe a gat hidden in a holster under his arm. *Vengeance is mine, saith the Lord.* He grins. Feels himself straining against his shorts. *Down, boy. Down. All in good time.* Everything comes to those who wait... and plan.

The drive to the mainland seems to take forever, though Robin breaks the speed limit. Halfway there, the skies come out of the gray cocoon and bloom blue above him: a perfect day, he thinks. For...everything. His heart flutters inside his chest. He breathes deeply and slowly to calm it. Relaxation is the key. Would Bogart be nervous? Silly. And so he must be totally, perfectly placid, like a still and windless lake.

At last he pulls up in front of her family's Hollowstone house. It is a tract house, fairly nondescript: though the lawn, of course, is impeccable, and the shrubbery is carved into perfect little rectangles like green television screens. There is a car in the drive, a yellow sedan no doubt driven by old man Kirk; Marylou's pink convertible is across the street. Hail, hail, he thinks, the gang's all here.

He steps from the car, notices the cool breeze on his face. He walks to the door and rings the bell.

In a moment Marylou answers it. She wears white slacks and a pink halter top and no shoes and has a magazine in her hand. "Oh, Robin!" she says brightly, the rows of pearl gleaming in the morning light. "How nice of you to come! Come in!"

Bogart steps over the threshold, an icy frown covering his face.

"Mom and Dad are out back in the garden," she says, more quietly now. "Do you have the—"

"I have it," he says, frost in his voice.

They stand there in the hall for a moment, looking at each other.

"Where—" she giggles slightly—"where is it?"

"In the car."

She stares at him blankly.

"In the car?" she says finally.

"You and I have something to discuss before you get that paper."

"What?"

"You know what."

The innocent emeralds on him. "Robin, I don't know what you're talking about."

"I think you do."

"Robin—"

He advances on her. She steps back. "We had a deal, Marylou."

"What deal? Listen, my parents are out back, Robin…"

"I know they are." He advances on her again and she retreats. "Think of that paper, Marylou. One-third of your final grade."

"I—"

"You're only carrying a weak B as it is. I wasn't able to write anything better for you because Mrs. Holgate would never have believed you could have done it. Looks to me like you could slip down to a D real easily if you don't turn in that paper. Maybe an F."

"Robin," she says, grinning, "you're playing a joke on me. Stop being silly." But she steps back again.

"That's right," he says. "I'm playing a joke. A very funny joke." He backs her against the wall and stands very close to her. Bogart is in full-flight now. "I'm playing a joke on you just like you tried to play one on me. Just like you played one on Davy Carp. And Bill Flynn. And Willy Delmont. All hilarious jokes." Her eyes are wide, her mouth open in shock. "But guess what, Marylou. Now the joke's on you. *You're taking the fall.*"

"Robin, you don't mean it!" she cries.

"You bet I mean it."

"But...but Robin," she says, suddenly soothing, touching his chest, "what makes you think I wasn't going to live up to our little arrangement? Of course I was. You don't think I'm such an awful person as all that, do you?"

"Yes."

She stares at him, eyes wide. "Robin, I don't know what's come over you. We've had such a wonderful friendship."

"Yeah, friendship. I work and you recopy."

"But that's what we agreed to."

"Only for the payoff that was supposed to come at the end."

"Shhh!" She glances down at the other end of the house. Then she looks at him again, toys with the buttons of his shirt. "Robin, I was going to live up to the deal. I wouldn't welch on you."

"Then why did you welch on all the other guys?"

"I didn't welch on them. We had misunderstandings."

"Funny. You seem to have a history of misunderstandings with guys who do your schoolwork for you."

"But not with you."

"I'll believe it when I see it."

"Oh, Robin," she says plaintively, "don't be so cross with me. Please. Really. I *swear* I'll live up to the bargain."

"When?"

"Shall we say sometime next week? After school is closed?"

"I think we should say sooner than that."

"But Robin, I'm *so* busy..."

"Busy enough to lose one-third of your grade?"

She looks at him. For the first time he detects some annoyance in those sea-emerald eyes. "Okay," she says. "Let's say... Wednesday."

"The year-end pep rally is on Wednesday. You won't be here."

She looks away. "Oh yes...I'd forgotten. Well, look: why don't you just give me the paper now and when we both have time next week—"

"Ho, ho," Robin interrupts. "No dice."

"Why?"

"You get the last paper *after* you live up to the deal."

She stares at him, putting her best little-girl-lost expression into her eyes. "Robin," she whispers, "why are you being this way?"

"The deal," Bogart answers. "Then the paper."

And suddenly, fantastically, two big round tears well up and spill from Marylou Kirk's eyes. They run down her cheeks and splash onto her pink halter top.

"I can't bear to think," she says quaveringly, "that you believe I'm some kind of...some kind of..." Her voice breaks off momentarily and she sobs. Finally she touches his shirt again. "Look," she smiles up at him, mouth quivering, "we're both wearing pink today."

For a moment he wavers. For a moment the vision of that lovely tear-streaked face almost makes him say, *Oh, you're right, I'm being stupid, here's the paper, you're wonderful.*

But only for a moment.

"No dice," he says again.

And, as if by magic, the tears disappear almost as quickly as they had arrived.

"All right," she says coldly.

"When?"

"Tomorrow. Morning. No one will be here. Come around eight. And bring the paper."

"And the payoff?"

She nods sourly. "Tomorrow morning. Is that good enough for you?"

Very nice, he thinks. Even when she's beaten, she'll damn well make me feel guilty about it.

She looks at the floor, her voice soft again: one last try. "You've disappointed me so, Robin..."

He smirks. "Sorry. But business is business." Bogart backs away from her and moves to the door. "Take my advice," he says. "Never mix business and pleasure. It's a very volatile combination."

And, satisfied with his exit line, Bogart turns and stalks out the door.

6

He finds himself on an infinitely high diving board, nothing around him but a depthless dark: naked, shivering, he looks down at the black pool below him, infinitely distant: yet it is a dive he knows he must make: and, sucking in his breath, he jumps. But as he approaches he realizes it is not a pool. It is not a pool but an enormous vagina that is open and ready to receive him. The sides of it are two giant, open legs, and he descends faster and faster, joyfully ready to dive into the warm dark, it comes toward him, gigantic, all-encompassing…And when he passes through this gate he finds himself in a suspended plane of space, soundless, lightless. But on his left, something white and shining flies toward him: a huge, mountain-sized breast, its nipple aimed right at his head. As it picks up speed he begins to feel fear but as it nears him it dissolves to nothingness. Then another breast, from the right. A pair of buttocks that separate and whiz past him just as they are about to collide into his freefloating body. Then a rain of furry, quivering vaginas: he reaches out and one lands in his hand like a dark snowflake. It is alive and he feels it nestling against his palm. His pet! Others land on him, on his face, on his shoulders, and he can hear them purring, feel them vibrating against his skin like tiny kittens. He sees the giant open legs again and suddenly he is plunged within them, his body pumping wildly; he hears echoing sighs, unearthly moans, tremulous gasps: and then a white rain explodes from his body, drenching the giant legs, the snowflake vaginas, soaking space itself, rain, rain, streaming from him, gushing and glistening—!

He wakes suddenly.

His heart is hammering against his chest. He is panting.

His hand falls on a wet spot on the bed and he hastily pulls it away, wipes it. He sits up.

Just dandy, he thinks. It's all he needs, to have sheets to wash in the morning. It has been a long time since he has done this, he realizes, staring in the semi-darkness at the wet stain. One would think there couldn't be so much of it in the entire world! But he had done it before: when he was quite young, in fact. Eleven or twelve. *Honey, did you wet the bed, hm?* He had been ashamed, there in the partial light of early morning. She had heard him cry out, she said. Had he had a nightmare? But he didn't know what had happened; all he knew was that he was frightened. *There, there. It's okay. You go to the bathroom and put on some fresh clothes, okay?* Then, later, her voice in the hall: *You'd*

The Unspoken

better talk to Robin. There had even been a slight tone of amusement in her voice. *He's growing up.*

But it remained a source of mystery and shame, that evening his body had suddenly burst while he'd been asleep. The shadow-man had not talked to him.

He needs no explanation now, however. He sighs, pulls his glowing clock out from under the sweater he muffles it in: three in the morning.

He hopes he hasn't just wasted himself for the rendezvous, the golden beacon of womanhood waiting for him in a few hours. He thinks of her again, pictures himself undoing those pigtails, slipping the pink halter top off her breasts and watching as they poke up into the warm morning light, unbuttoning her slacks—or would it be reaching up under her little girl's dress, pulling the lacy panties down, feeling the warm dampness between her legs? Feeling her tongue intertwined with his own. Breathing the delicious odor of her sweat as she moaned and gasped under him…

He looks down at himself: realizes that he is hardly wasted, that there is plenty more where that came from. He is an ocean of it. His supply is endless. The fact quite delights him; he slips under the covers again, rolling his body away from the damp remains, and falls into a deep, dreamless sleep.

"Okay," she says, opening the door. "Come in."

She is wearing a powder-blue dress with white sandals and her hair is pulled into the usual dual pigtails. Robin is nearly trembling. He had been serene upon waking; calm, placid as a morning lake as he showered, applied cologne, dressed; only a few flutters of nervousness had crossed his mental landscape as he made the drive to Hollowstone. But when the actual house came into view, and when he saw that were no vehicles before it but Marylou's own—oh, then panic set in! He nearly threw the paper out the window and drove away. As he rang the doorbell, he thought of calling the whole thing off: *Oh, never mind*, he could have said. *You don't owe me anything. I did it because we're friends.* But when she opened the door, his voice was frozen into silence; and so he finds himself standing in the foyer of the house.

"Do you have the paper?" she asks.

He swallows. "In the car." His voice is a thin gasp.

"Okay." She is not smiling today. No gushy words of everlasting friendship. Pure business. "Come in here, then."

She leads him down the hallway and into her bedroom. It is the first time he has seen it, the first time he has been allowed into the sanctuary: and it is much as he had imagined it. A big double bed covered in heaven-cloud pink. Fat, fluffy white pillows. A mahogany dresser with an oval mirror; makeup things. A desk with schoolbooks—most, he imagines, unopened for months. Thick pink shag carpet. On the walls, cutesy animal posters: horses, mostly, along with hamsters, koalas, a bulldog in a chef's apron. A few academic awards in frames. He wonders who did the work to get them. Soft, diffused light glows through a big, pink-curtained window over the desk.

Marylou locks the bedroom door behind them and goes to the window. She opens it, allowing in a pleasant morning breeze, and shuts the gossamer curtain. She turns to him. "We only have a little while," she says, her voice flat, emotionless. "My parents went to early services. I told them I didn't feel well."

Robin nods, looks around nervously.

"So?" she says.

"So," he answers, smiling lamely.

"This is what you want, is it?"

His face burns. He manages to nod.

"All right." She crosses to the door at the side of the room. "Get yourself ready. I'll be ready when I come out." She closes the door behind her.

Robin stands helplessly in the middle of the room. His mind seems incapable of thinking. He reaches to his shirt, pulls it out of his trousers; but then he stops. Is that what she wanted? For him to take off his clothes? He isn't sure. *Get yourself ready*, she'd said. He sits on the bed; jumps off it immediately, as if it were on fire. Sighs shakily. Sits down again. He slips off his shoes and socks; takes a quick olfactory check. No stink there. The silence in the room is overwhelming. He starts to unbutton his shirt, hesitates again. Feels the breeze billowing the curtains and touching his face. He hears an indefinable noise in the bathroom. He pictures how she will look when she comes out: will she be in sexy black underwear? A nightgown? Or totally nude? He feels the blood racing in his body. Time seems to pass, a great deal of time, eternity; finally he slips out of his shirt, hesitantly.

At last Marylou comes out of the bathroom. She is still fully dressed.

"Well, aren't you ready yet?" she says.

"I..."

"Come on, already. I told you, we don't have that much time." She sits on the other side of the bed and slips off her shoes. He supposes she is about to undress further, but she lies back on the bed.

"Come on," she says.

She watches with no apparent emotion in her eyes as Robin slips out of his pants; then, turning away from her, his underpants. He is quivering. Much to his surprise, however, he finds his organ, his partner in crime, quite ready to roll.

He turns and faces the girl.

"Okay," she says. "Where's your thing?"

Robin's mouth opens, then closes again. He glances down helplessly at himself.

"Not *that*," she says impatiently, "your *thing*. Don't tell me you didn't bring your *thing*."

Utterly befuddled, Robin stammers, "I...I..."

"Oh, Jesus!" She suddenly jumps from the bed. "Wait a minute, I have some. You didn't really think I was going to let you do this without a thing, did you?"

She rummages in a drawer in her desk and brings out a small, soft plastic case. She tosses it to him. "Here," she says. "Put this on."

King's Haven, it reads. *When It's Time For Closeness.*

He swallows. He has never seen one in his life. With shaking fingers, he tears clumsily into the plastic wrapper and brings out the cold slimy—yes, he thinks, *thing*. Marylou reclines again on the bed, watching him. She crosses her legs and puts her hands behind her head.

He steps close to the bed; then sits, facing away from her, and slips the plastic monstrosity onto himself. It feels as if he is encased in cold, greasy stone. He looks at Marylou.

"Okay?" he says, his voice a breaking whisper.

She nods. "Okay. Come on."

He stares at her. "Aren't you going to...take off...anything?"

"I *took* my underwear off."

"I...I'd like you to..."

"Robin, come on already. Do you want to do this or not?"

"...Yes."

"Then come on. Here I am."

He smiles sickly, and crawls toward her on the bed. She opens her legs narrowly.

"Careful of my dress," she says.

He nods. He is shaking. He moves on top of her. She is staring somewhere above him, at the ceiling.

"Could you—could you lift your dress out of the way?" he asks huskily.

She sighs and moves her dress slightly.

He feels his heart fluttering wildly as he leans toward her.

"Could you...Marylou, could you—?"

She sighs again, impatiently. "It's right *there*, Robin. No, lower. Lower. Lower. There. Now hurry up, okay?"

He has to take her at her word that he has found what he is looking for. He cannot feel anything. He moves slightly. His naked hips rustle against her dress. There is no sensation whatever. He glances at her emerald eyes but finds that she is staring straight at him, through him, blankly; so he looks away. He moves again. Still no sensation. He closes his eyes and tries to recall to his mind the flying breasts and buttocks of his dream the night before: but they haze, cloud in his brain and he cannot hold them. At least he leans down and touches his lips to the soft material of the dress.

"No," she says, shifting away from him. "Don't."

He looks at her desperately. Realizes with a sudden flighty sensation that he is close to tears. He feels his granite-encased member beginning to decline. He moves again, harder this time. He can feel his face burning.

Then, slowly impinging upon his consciousness, he hears a sound.

A car.

"Oh God!" Marylou hisses suddenly. "Is that my mom? Stop. Stop for a minute." She puts both hands on his chest and cocks her head. Robin hears a car door shut. "Oh Holy Jesus!" she cries in a harsh whisper. "Robin, finish! Quick! It's my mom!"

"I..."

"Ro*bin!*"

"I...I *can't*..."

Her eyes are panic-stricken. She pushes at his chest. "Then get off! Robin, get off me!"

His vision blurring, he allows himself to be pushed aside as Marylou jumps up and arranges her dress before a mirror. "Put on your clothes!" she commands, not looking at him. She rushes to the window. "Oh, shit! There's no time!" Robin can hear the key turning in the lock of the front door. She looks back at him wildly. "Stay in here! Put your clothes on! Just…Robin, *put your clothes on!*"

She rushes from the room, slamming the door behind her.

Robin lies on the bed, the plastic prison attached to his body hanging uselessly. He cannot think. He sees his clothes lying on the floor. What is he supposed to do with them?

Hello, Mama, he hears in the hallway.

Hello, sweetheart.

You're home early.

*Well, do you know, I met our old pastor, that wonderful…*And the woman's fluttery voice recounts some story about someone or something. Robin cannot quite make it out. He hears the words: but cannot, somehow, make sense of them. He lies there, his nakedness strange to him. He knows Marylou will be appalled to find him still like this. And yet somehow it seems not to make the slightest difference. Let her find him this way. Who cares, really? The dialogue in the hall goes on. He wonders what would happen if he were to suddenly begin pounding his fist on the wall and yelling, *Hi, Mom, come look at what your daughter's brought home!* Then he could stand up as she came into the room and hurl the sensation-killing tube at her. That might be amusing. More amusing if he'd had an orgasm inside it, though. He giggles, twists on the bed. Yes, that's it! He could stretch the liquid-filled thing out like a slingshot and when the woman stepped in—

Dear, says the voice in the hall, *do you have a visitor?*

He hears Marylou's cutesy voice falter uncertainly. *I…Yes, Mama, he's come to help me…*

Their voices fade off as the two of them move toward the kitchen. Robin lies on the bed giggling crazily. Maybe instead of a slingshot he could make a catapult and...

A moment later Marylou bursts into the room. "Ro*bin!*" she says in a peculiarly shrieked whisper. She picks up his clothes and tosses them at him in a heap. "Go in the bathroom there and put your clothes on, for God's sake! What's wrong with you? Robin, *please!*"

He stares at her numbly. Wonders why she seems so frantic. For a moment he does not remember, exactly, where he is or why he is here. Or why he is stark naked on this girl's bed. He looks down at himself and pulls the slimy plastic away.

"We didn't need this, did we?"

"Ro*bin!*"

He stares at her dark pigtails, at her eyes filled with angry innocence, the small peach breasts forever locked away under the powder blue of the dress. Suddenly she grabs at his bare shoulders. "*In!*" she hisses. "*Get dressed!*"

Somehow it begins to come back to him, to focus like a film in a theater. He remembers. Feels a hot flush of shame or fear course through him suddenly. Finds himself standing. Feels her cold hands pushing him toward the bathroom. Realizes, as the door slaps shut behind him and he stands staring dully at the pink toilet, that he still has the plastic thing in his hand.

Meekly, he had met her mother; meekly, he and Marylou had gone to his car and he had given her the paper.

By then, she had made a complete return to her usual self.

"Oh, thank you, Robin," she had gushed. "I could never have gotten through Comparative Lit without you."

"I know," Robin said blankly, unable to look at her.

He had had fantasies—to force her into the bathroom with him, tear apart the powdery dress like so much tissue paper: but somehow he felt utterly drained, finished, as if some vampire had sucked his life's blood away and left him a sallow husk. He had lost even the slightest interest. There was nothing left. He felt only embarrassment, shame.

Marylou Kirk, however, seemed to harbor no such emotions. "Now isn't it wonderful," she said, her rows of pearl shining in the morning light, "when something like this works out so well? A perfect little arrangement!"

He started the engine and pulled away. His mind was free of all thoughts. He drove aimlessly for what seemed hours; finally, with the bright spring sun directly overhead, he had pulled off onto an old dirt road and turned off the engine and sat staring into a grove of trees. Formless desire began to grow in him after a long time and finally he found an old towel and used it mechanically. He kept his mind free of all images, sounds, odors. A frozen waste. A hyperborean snowscape.

7

The graduation ceremony arrives; Robin floats through it as through a dream. They sit in the big school auditorium, boys in black, girls in white (especially appropriate, he thinks sourly, for young virginal Marylou Kirk, who looks predictably adorable in her gown and pigtails; she has not spoken a word to him since that Sunday morning two weeks before). Michael Lyon is the class valedictorian and his likely wife-to-be Kathy Collins is salutatorian. Robin, seated near the back of the class due to the alphabetical arrangement, listens rather sleepily to Michael Lyon's vapidly inspiring words:

"...And so, honored guests, dear parents, classmates: let us always hold Hollowstone High close to our hearts, keep it vivid and alive in our memories and the memories of..."

His voice truly is golden, Robin thinks. A steady, pleasant tenor that inspires instant trust. He smiles wryly as he thinks of his own often reedy, thin voice; and he stares at the class valedictorian. He had talked with him last week in the locker room. Robin had just finished his usual quick, showerless change and was about to leave when Michael Lyon had arrived, fresh from tennis with Kathy Collins.

"Robin!" he'd said. "How are you? I haven't talked to you in weeks. How's the writing? Did the thing at the *Courier* die down finally? Have you thought about my advice?"

Questions, questions, pleasant inquiries rolled from his golden tongue. Robin had answered them absently; not because he was not interested, but because he found himself strangely distracted. As Michael Lyon spoke, the boy pulled open his gym locker, brought out his clothes, and began undressing. When he was completely nude he made the few steps to the open showers, turned on the spray for a moment, and rinsed himself. Then he came back, toweling himself off and reaching for his clothes. Michael Lyon's body was astonishing. The comparison to Greek sculpture was too easy, but nonetheless apt: the pectoral muscles glistened in the hard light of the locker room, the rippling stomach muscles gleamed. He was virtually perfect. The chest was hairless, and the legs were covered only with a light blonde patina. The behind was firm...and, Robin noticed with surprise, tanned.

"...So," he was saying, running the towel through his hair, over his smooth chest, onto his genitals and legs, "I've written something. Of course it's not as good as what somebody like you could have put together. In fact I thought of asking for your help, but then I said to myself, 'Lyon, you've got to do this one yourself.'"

Oh, perfect, Robin thought, gazing at the naked boy. Butter up the future constituent with a compliment aimed at his writing talents. Very nice. Robin knew that Michael Lyon had never considered for even an instant recruiting his help; but Michael Lyon was learning, yes, learning quickly, the politician's art.

"Well, it's a good little school," he said after Robin mentioned the campus in northern California. "It's got a good atmosphere." Robin knew that this was his polite way of saying he disapproved. "But I really think you should still consider my suggestion."

Robin smiled wryly, watching the boy dry his behind as the genitals dangled before him. He tried to imagine himself in an Army uniform with a big bull-faced idiot standing before him screaming and spitting into his face. No, it was not something he cherished. But Michael Lyon, he knew, would get better, as the years progressed, at suggesting directions for people's lives. He would become an expert.

But it was the body, not the conversation, that had held Robin enthralled. There was something tremendously exciting in Michael Lyon's nakedness. He found himself envisioning this body close to Kathy Collins, the two of them bare, glistening with sweat, pushing into each other. He heard their moans of pleasure. Saw Kathy Collins' breasts bouncing with each of the boy's thrusts. Realized, then, that he had not heard a word Michael Lyon had said for the past minute; and realized also that he had a warm erection inside his own pants. Robin the Rod, he thought, as Michael Lyon slipped into his clothes. Robin thought vaguely of passing a law that would prohibit the boy from covering such magnificent features. Really, it seemed to him, someone like this should be legally required to go about in the nude. Why not? At least on hot summer days.

Of course he did wonder, as he had wondered before, what such thoughts said about himself. Was he...? And yet it hardly seemed likely. When he fantasized it was inevitably about girls, breasts, vaginas: but when he stood before such a vision as Michael Lyon, it was hard to deny other, stranger feelings. Not that he ever saw himself actually touching the boy; but simply being able to gaze at him, that was, for Robin, enough....

The moment arrives when everyone stands and diplomas are handed out. Davy Carp receives only a few sporadic claps from the audience, while immediately after him Kathy Collins gets a big round of applause, as does Marylou Kirk; and of course there is a roar of approval when Michael Lyon's name is announced. Robin, near the end, receives virtually total silence. Then the school band starts up again, they march toward the exit, and it is over.

Outside the day is cool, clear: gowned students embrace laughing parents, the clicking of cameras fills the air, much handshaking and congratulating. Robin is greeted by a few neighbors. He searches for his father in the confusion.

"Hey, man." Davy, behind him.

"Hey."

"So now we're big-time operators, huh?" Davy grins vaguely and his face twitches.

"Yeah," Robin says. "Ready to step into the offices of any major corporation and be handed a vice-presidency."

He laughs. "Sure."

"So what are you going to *do*, Davy?"

The boy shrugs carelessly. "Maybe get a job around here. I dunno." He points. "There's your dad, man."

"I see him. Where's your mom?"

"Aw, she couldn't come. Had to work."

Robin glances at him. "So are any of your relatives here?"

"Nah."

Robin is suddenly filled with a deep sinking feeling. Strange to think: to be so totally abandoned that no one even comes to your graduation. He feels an odd guilt as his father arrives before them. The man says something, grinning, and shakes Robin's hand. Robin can tell immediately that the man has already begun his drinking for the day. He is not yet drunk; in fact no one else in the entire courtyard would have the slightest idea anything was amiss. But Robin knows. His mind is super-tuned to the subtle alterations his father's face and gait and manner go through: the dullness of the eyes, like old coins; the longer, more awkward stride; his too-boisterous voice and movements. They have probably three or four hours, Robin knows, until the danger arrives. And it will certainly come: once he has drunk enough to alter his eyes and voice (which is quite little, now, much less than before) there is no turning back.

"Well, what do you want to do?" his father asks. "Get some lunch? Some pizza maybe?"

"Sure, Dad. That'd be good."

They snap some photos; Robin tries to smile as his father shakes his hand. His mind is filled with how he will make his escape. He must be very careful, he knows. What will be essential in the next hour or two is to say nothing that might anger the man. That, of course, is difficult; but Robin has become an expert at it. If the man's mood were to change now, it would likely stay that way for the rest of the evening: but as the booze was consumed he would become ever more intense, argumentative, impossible, until either there was an explosion or the deadly silence descended, the obliterating, identity-erasing blank stare. Robin has analyzed all this with the cool detachment of a surgeon. All that is needed now is calm. That is the prescription.

As his father exchanges words with some neighbors Robin's gaze wanders to where Marylou Kirk is standing with her parents. They are positively beaming. Ten or twelve people, relatives probably, are bunched around her and she is laughing and displaying the rows of pearl as her pigtails bob up and down. He toys with the idea of saying hello. But what good would it do? She would simply be her usual Two Shoes (or Two-Face, he thinks grimly) self: *Oh Robin, how wonderful to see you! Mama, you've met Robin...* He had, of course, told no one of the escapade. It was much too shaming. Whenever he thinks of it his face begins to burn. He wishes he had had time, then, to ask her: *But how do I look? Am I ugly? Am I too skinny? Am I big enough? What do other guys look like?* It is quite a remarkable thought: to realize that of all the people here now, several hundred of them, Marylou Kirk is the only one to have seen him naked and ready for sex. The only one! But he cannot think of what happened between them as sex. He had wrapped himself into a slimy cement prison and poked himself into a department store mannequin for a moment. Technically, he supposes, he can say that he is no longer a virgin; but only technically, in the fine print. He feels no different than he had before, only more ashamed and embarrassed. He wonders what the girl's face would look like if he were to walk up to her just now and say: *Hi, Marylou! Gee, it sure was nice fucking you the other day!*

Michael Lyon's voice suddenly reaches him. "Robin!"

He turns. There, hand-in-hand and followed by beaming relatives, are the valedictorian and salutatorian coming toward him. Kathy Collins, it occurs to him, truly is a gorgeous girl. Smooth, liquid features; straw-blonde hair reaching to her shoulders; a body that is the subject, he is sure, of many a Hollowstone High boy's fantasies. But beyond that, she has a certain style, a grace, that gives the impression that she was born to be the hostess of rich and charming dinner parties, to be the loving and supportive and charismatic wife of, say, a young, charismatic politician on his way up.

"Robin, old man!" Michael Lyon says, shaking his hand. Kathy Collins also greets him pleasantly. "We have news for you—for everyone!" the boy says. "We just announced it to our parents..."

"What's that?" Robin asks.

"Kathy and I are getting married!"

Somehow it makes Robin want to burst out laughing. But he does not. Everyone congratulates them; and Kathy Collins holds out her hand to display the modest but exquisitely tasteful diamond ring Michael Lyon has apparently just given to her.

But as Robin looks at the glittering gem, an island suddenly emerges from his sea of consciousness. The light of the diamond flashes in his eyes and the smiling people, the laughter, the congratulations melt like sudden mist and he is sitting at the kitchen table in the house in the cul-de-sac. His father is across from him. The only light comes from the hanging lamp over their heads; the rest of the house is covered in oily darkness.

He is thirteen years old.

Between them is a small blue box which his father opens to reveal rings and necklaces: gold, silver, diamonds, big green emeralds, blue sapphires, milky pearls. They glitter strangely in the pool of light and attached to each of them, he notices, is a number. In front of his father is a handwritten list from a jeweler which catalogs each number and the appraisal value of the piece. Also before the man across from him is a big glass filled with the pungent amber liquid. The man frequently lifts this glass and drinks from it.

The box is pushed toward Robin.

"Go ahead," the man says.

Uncertainly, Robin touches the jewels; sifts tentatively through them. He is somehow afraid that to touch these things now, so soon, might make her cry out: as if she were being ripped apart, the way she was a few days before when the boxes of her had been carried from the house; the way she was only yesterday, when the bits of her were scattered into the depthless blue abyss. He touches the rings, waiting to hear her cry. He thinks of her coming into his room—when had it been?—and sitting next to him and telling him that she had come a long way and Robin looking down and noticing that her bare feet were dirty, mud-spattered. And then Robin descending into the fathomless blue of unconsciousness. He had been dreaming. Hadn't he? His mind wavers when he thinks of it, the images swim like a mirage, like something seen underwater. He wants to grasp it, hold the image firmly inside himself, but it slips around, eludes his pursuit.

"Go ahead," the man says again, raising the glass to his lips. "Choose."

Robin picks up a tiny gold band into which is set a bright, multi-prismed diamond. He holds it to the light, sees it glittering on her finger as she sits beside him on the bed, the reflections like a hall of silent black mirrors. He sees himself in the mirrors, naked, sees himself hacking away at his body and blood running over his skin. He thinks of the woman's humming, her cool palm stroking his forehead, the softness of her lap. Thinks of an earlier time, much earlier, water glistening like a melting curtain down her neck, her breasts, her stomach, and she holding him to her, warm wet softness and grace. Then he thinks of ovens; big, long Nazi ovens: the wetness heating and boiling on top of her and eating her body away like acid, great cavernous holes opening up in her face, her breasts, her stomach, smoking, blackening, burning, and the ring, the ring falling from her twitching black fingers, her mouth agape and her lips scorching and receding like an old skull's, her hair aflame: and soon nothing: black bits: only the ring sitting there undisturbed amongst the charred remains.

Of course it had not happened that way. Of course the white-shrouded automatons at the hospital had removed it, and everything else, long before she had been pushed into the terrible oven. He wonders who had stripped her clothes from her. Wonders who had pulled her panties down, seen her nakedness for the last time before all warmth left her forever, before she was a cold and rigid sack of bones and skin. Wonders if anyone washed the blood from her body, if they were gentle and careful around the big bruises that must have covered her.

He gazes at the ring in the light and at last sets it next to himself.

His father makes a check mark next to the item on his list and pulls the small blue box toward himself. He chooses quickly, immediately, and pushes the box back toward Robin.

They continue like this until the box is nearly empty. Robin picks up the rings and necklaces tenderly, chooses only after long deliberation; his father stares at him with his steel eyes and drinks from the glass of amber liquid. Then his father takes the box again and grabs something quickly, almost at random, and checks it off his list. When they are finished, the man takes his pencil and begins adding the totals.

"Dad," Robin starts to say, "I don't really..."

"Wait," his father cautions, glancing sharply at him. In a moment the tally is done: the values of their stacks are within one hundred dollars of each other.

"Okay," the man says, pushing the empty box toward Robin. "You keep those things in there. And take care of them. They belong to you now." He stands, drains the glass, and stuffs his own stack of jewelry into his pants pocket. He turns and walks out of the kitchen, into the silent darkness beyond. But then he turns, or nearly: Robin sees his profile, half-hidden in the blackness, one gnarled hand curled into a fist.

For a moment it is as if he wants to say something; his mouth opens; then closes again. He bumps against the door frame and then disappears.

A moment later Robin hears his footsteps thudding dully up the stairs.

Robin had gazed blankly at the jewels before him on the table for what had seemed hours. They were like pebbles, he thought, pebbles tossed up onto the beach at random, without any meaning whatever. He closed the man's voice off from his mind. He closed everything off, put it all away, as if into a secret chest only he had the key to. He only wished that he could lose the key, run out to the end of the pier in the darkness and hurl it away, far, far away, to sink into the deep and shadow-crossed sea.

And then, as instantly as it had appeared, the vision fragments and dissolves: the house in the cul-de-sac, the jewels, the darkness, they scatter like seagulls and he hears the laughing parents again, the click of the cameras, feels the bright spring sunlight pouring down on him again.

"It's a beautiful ring," he says, looking first at Kathy Collins, then at Michael Lyon. His vision blurs strangely. "A beautiful ring…It's beautiful. I don't think—I don't think I've ever seen such a beautiful ring!"

He had started a journal that year, and into it he had written these words:

Perpetual vertigo. That's what it seems like sometimes. A sudden falling sensation, like in a dream. It seems to me that other people don't live like I do, don't live this kind of vertiginous, terrified life (but then how am I to know?). As if the rug is constantly being pulled out from under me. Certainly it's that way with Dad. The not knowing when the outbursts will come, the inability to guess what's around the corner, never knowing when the sudden sinking fall might occur: perpetual vertigo.

Hours after the graduation ceremony, Robin remembers these words. They have long since finished the pizza; nothing remains of it but a few scraps of melted cheese. After that, his father had bought him a root-beer float from the ice cream bar and a big foamy mug of beer for himself at the beer-and-wine counter. Of course he had asked Robin, as he often does, if he had wanted a beer instead: his father often encourages him in such adult endeavors. But Robin had declined.

The place had begun to fill up as they drank; and soon his father met some people he knew, rough-and-ready types from the harbor. The harbor! A thousand centuries ago, that harbor, that boat, those early mornings in the cold spattering sea. The glistening, pop-eyed fish slapping in the garbage can, the smell of the salt cold. Shivering in his jacket and feeling nauseous as his father in his captain's cap steered the boat toward distant islands at top speed, the boat chopping rudely through the liquid glass of the sea....

His father's voice had begun to slur about an hour before, and it was then that Robin grew most careful. They had not said much, actually. They had talked a bit about the northern California college and the courses he would take there. But mostly it had been silence between them. Then his friends had arrived: and after a few minutes his father had said, grinning strangely, "Robin, I'll be right back," and had gone over to a table where four or five of them were sitting drinking beer and shouting crudities. They were all of a similar type: heavy fisherman's jackets, blue jeans glittering with dry fish scales and old blood, captain's hats or woven wool caps, unshaven. They were the ones who did it for a living, who went out each morning into the darkness with their big nets to catch the fish that were running that day, that season, and who sometimes did not come back for days and days, living on their boats, sleeping in the gentle sway of the sea. Robin can remember such nights. The soft rocking, it should have lulled him into sweet oblivion: but it did not: for he could not trust it, ever. As if some dark demon who could assume a pleasing and beautiful shape were trying to convince him that everything was all right, everything was fine, go to sleep. But he wouldn't. For he knew something was not right. After all, his mother never came along on such journeys: tried, in fact, to keep his father from taking him: he could hear, through the bathroom wall.

Leave him alone, she would say. *He doesn't like it. He's just not that kind of boy.*

Yes! he would want to shout. But his father would say: *Somebody has got to get him out of that bedroom of his. He never sees anybody. Doesn't have any friends. All he does is read his books and listen to his records.*

Yes, but—

I'm not saying there's anything wrong with that; it's just that he's going to have problems when he gets older if he doesn't learn how to live in the real world.

Robin sits in the restaurant watching his father. It is interesting to him what a chameleon the man can be. On the warm Sundays, when he is sober, they can have their pleasant games of tennis and their pleasant luncheon at the outdoor restaurant almost—almost!—as if they were friends of a sort. He could be pleasant, he could smile, he could ask Robin how he was doing in school, he could offer advice. How, he wonders, can he reconcile that man, the one of the sunny afternoons, with this one: the dangerous one: the one who, even now, is declining into a kind of nether world into which no one can follow? Who will erase Robin's identity by ignoring him—or who will shout at him in the darkness, look at him with wild, crazed eyes, accuse him of greed and thievery?

Robin remembers once stepping into the house, late, after he thought the man would have gone to bed. The man had almost run at him, stepped in front of him, too close, his boozy and musky odor filling Robin's head: *My money*, he said, his voice high and wild, his eyes fogged and hugely blue. *Have you been stealing it?*

What money, Dad? Of course not.

My money! my money!

Robin had tried to walk past him, tried to drown out the strange unreal voice. His father had kept pace with him, standing just inches away. The man was always careful not to touch him, instead looming over him like an enormous, malevolent shadow. *My money! Somebody's been taking my money!*

No one is taking your money. They stood at the foot of the stairs, his father on the first step looking down at Robin. *Why don't we talk about it in the morning?*

His father's eyes, huge and accusing, stared down at him with a mixture of revulsion and horror. *So it's you!* he shouted. *You're stealing my money!*

I'm not stealing your money, Robin said. *I don't know what you're talking about. Dad, it's late. I want to go to bed.*

His father stared down at him in the darkness and then suddenly moved out of Robin's way with elaborate, stumbling courtesy. *Of course, sir! You have the right of way! Thieves always have the right of way! Except sooner or later they'll find the joke's on them! Sooner or later when their father dies they'll find they're left with nothing! Nothing!*

And now he watches his father with the fishermen. He is too loud now, too drunk. He challenges them to arm-wrestle and one of the men, a short one with a squat face, sits across from him. Another man acts as referee. They begin: Robin sees the raised veins on his father's neck as he slowly pushes his opponent's arm to the table. A roar of approval goes up around him and his father calls and gestures for another challenger. Robin begins to wonder how he might escape. And yet there seems to be no way. They are too far from home, he cannot walk. But he wishes he could. Wishes he could just run into the night, into the cloaking darkness. Everything is too dangerous now...But, paradoxically, this may actually mean that the house will be safe when they get back: his father has peaked too early and may simply fade into nothingness by the time they arrive. But things are not safe now. Now they are very dangerous. The man's boozy boisterousness could easily make a sudden switch, blow up like a vessel of volatile chemicals into aggressiveness, paranoia, the bulging eyes and strained, unnaturally high voice. It happens even among his friends; although it is much more common with just Robin, in the house in the cul-de-sac. *I know what you're doing!* he hears the man shout, the voice following him up the stairs like a clinging ghost. *You think I don't but I do! I know exactly what you're doing!* And one night—when had it been?—when the man crashed into Robin's darkened bedroom, jolting Robin suddenly out of sleep, and tearing into his chest of drawers, digging through the clothes, tossing out socks, underwear: and then just as suddenly charging out again, slamming the door behind him.

It's amazing, he supposes, how little he actually thinks about these things. He is vaguely aware that this is not the way most people live. And yet he wonders. On TV, he sees what Hollywood producers depict as "normal" families: but he is not sure he has ever actually met one. Michael Lyon's, perhaps. But who could know what happened in the night, when the doors were closed and locked? For the Withers family had always appeared normal enough, even when his mother had been in her worst decline: for nothing ever happened while the sun was up, no, it was a specter of darkness, this malignancy, a thing of night...And so he wonders about this idea of "normality." Wonders if all families, every last one them, aren't hiding secret truths in the dark. Wonders if everyone's life is not, finally, secret.

He watches his father slam down another opponent's arm and the cheer goes up again. These are the kind of people his father had always wanted to live around, Robin guesses. Rough, rag-tag, seafaring types. He wonders what had ever made the man decide to strap himself down with a wife and child and all the attendant baggage. Certainly his father had loved the sea, once. He often used to talk about growing up poor in the Midwest and hitching out to the West Coast when he was a teenager—never going back. He had fallen in love with the ocean, he would say. What was there for him in the Midwest with its farms, dust, and endless dirt roads that led only to other farms, other roads? He had not looked back. Anyway, he had been an orphan: his own father had vanished when he was a baby and his mother had left him with relatives, saying she would be back for him: but never returning. He had not seen or heard from her since. He had bounced from job to job, worked on an aircraft carrier in the Korean War. Eventually, after his return, he had drifted into the insurance business and met Robin's mother. That was the story the man would tell: though Robin could never quite imagine it all, somehow. He tried to picture his father as a young man (wrinkles lifted away, skin tightened, hair full again) hitchhiking across America. He couldn't do it. Tried to picture him on an aircraft carrier, in a Navy uniform. Couldn't. There was something unreal about it, as if his father could not truly have existed before Robin's memories of him began. Old photographs, gray and crinkled, served only the heighten the sensation of unreality: they looked faked, posed. The man sometimes seemed aware of this and would try to impress upon Robin how real it all was. *Damn it*, he would say, *you don't know what it was like then.*

But that was years ago. Now his father said very little: except on those rare occasions when the drink put him into an expansive mood and he would tell Robin about the prostitutes he had known in Japan, the Philippines, Korea, the Midwest. Such stories embarrassed Robin, but they fascinated him too: to think of his father roaring through those distant, dark places…

"Robin! Hey! C'mere, kid!"

He is snapped away from his thoughts and looks over at his father. His heart sinks. Having beaten all comers, the man is now gesturing to him with a hearty, sloppy smile.

"C'mere, kid! Take on the old man!"

His friends are urging it on: "Come on, boy! Show this old fart what you're made of!" Robin flushes deeply and finds himself quivering. There is no way out. How he would love to run, just run screaming into the night: *no, no, no, no!* He feels twelve or thirteen again: hears the man's flat-footed footsteps on the stairs, their sound like the knocking on a door: feels his pulse race: and yet there is no escape. He tries to raise his hand in a polite declining gesture but they are all cheering him on. He knows he will have to stand. He stands. He walks toward the table, counting each step one two three four five because he feels that if he does not, he may collapse: may crash on his face into the restaurant's faded rug: the world is spinning, spinning: his father's arm is poised, ready, he is grinning, his eyes are two steel-blue searchlights boring into him; Robin's heart is hammering against his chest, threatening to burst out entirely.

And suddenly he is at the table, his father's poised arm before him like a scythe. He glances at the grinning face. Knows, vaguely, that an hour or so from now he will be driving the grinning face home, it will be mumbling in its stupor, and it may be that Robin will simply leave him in the car when they arrive, and the man will stumble up sometime later, when he is able, stagger upstairs and past Robin's room into the darkness beyond. Knows that it is all ending now. Knows that in a few weeks he will be in a dormitory in northern California, far, far away from the house in the cul-de-sac, far, far away from the thumping sounds in the dark; away from the fog-filled gray days and away from Marylou Kirk and everyone and everything, absolutely everything, far from it all, never to return, like his own father, this grinning apparition before him, never to return, but to go far away, ever farther, searching for the lovely ghosts and for his apple-half, his missing apple-half which is, he knows, there, in the distance, somewhere, waiting. He clasps the man's hand. Their eyes meet. The arms tense.

8

It is late summer when Robin arrives at the university. Located just off the coast, it is quite lovely, set as it is amongst seemingly endless mountains of redwood trees. A few minutes' walk from the campus, he discovers, he can find gorgeous, winding nature trails; if he turns in the opposite direction he will find himself in the town proper, a charming little affair with restaurants, book shops, and a town square. It is not, he supposes, bad at all. He is given a fourth-floor dormitory room which strikes some anxiety within him: it is but one small cubicle with two tiny beds and desks, which he is expected to share with another student. The bathroom, terribly public, is at the end of the hall.

These things are a concern: but, in the first few days, they fail to overwhelm him with worry. He has arrived at least a week earlier than necessary, and almost the entire floor is deserted; indeed, there is hardly anyone around the campus. It is very peaceful, and he finds that he is almost enjoying himself: there is something terribly unreal about being *at college,* but it is a pleasant sensation that fills him with a feeling of maturity. The house in the cul-de-sac, the footsteps in the night, the dark accusations, the whirlpool of memory: all of these are long, long past, in the hardly-recalled pages of yesterday. They no longer matter. He has torn himself free of them like a bird bursting from the bars of its cage. He is free! On his own!

In California!

In those first days he spends his time wandering the campus and the town. He finds the university library and puzzles out the complexities of finding titles in the "stacks": there had certainly been no such complications in Mrs. Klibo's library with its hissing radiator and the rain falling outside. He is initially daunted, but soon masters the system; and when he does, he is absolutely astonished at how many books there are, how many fantastic things to read, how heavy is the presence of the lovely ghosts. He obtains his student library card and immediately checks out a dozen titles, reading them one after another after nightfall in his room: Thomas Wolfe, Conrad, Dickens, thick anthologies of modern poetry. He does not understand everything he reads, but the sheer flow of words, their patterns and rhythms, fill him with an almost drunken sensation and he finds himself flowing into strange new places, leaving the school and the town far behind; they come back to him only slowly, hazily, when he has at last closed the books: then, like an animated sequence in a film, the walls of the room begin to compose themselves again, and the beds, the desks, the chairs, finally the sounds and textures and temperatures. Sometimes, in this deep and removed frame of mind when he is far from the school and the town, he does not even read a single title, but numerous ones concurrently—jumping from one to another, the dazzling ocean of words engulfing him like warm rain. It is the same in the day, when he goes downtown and visits the book shops. There are several fine ones, it being a "college town," and the prices are low. He loves most especially one shop tucked away on an out-of-the-way corner, called Sammy's Used Book Catastrophe. It is a remodeled old Victorian house with row upon row of dusty hardcovers and paperbacks in nearly no order whatever. The lighting is dim, the atmosphere mysterious, almost sepulchral. Sammy himself, Robin thinks, is half-mad. He skulks around the shop *sans* shirt or shoes and his wild shock of silver hair is inevitably a tangled mess. He owns a tiny brown Chihuahua that barks nastily whenever a customer enters and around whose neck is tied a red ribbon with a small placard attached: BEWARE OF ME. In addition, Sammy cannot add. He will take the books Robin has chosen, glance at the prices scribbled therein, and say: "Looks like about three bucks to me!" or whatever amount comes to mind. If he is reasonably close to correct, Robin pays; if the amount is too high, he politely corrects him. At which time Sammy will giggle: "Ha! Hey, *college* boy!" For all that, he is absolutely amazing in his knowledge of what is in his own shop. Robin has tested him on this. He can name any author, any subject; and if the answer is not "No, nothin'," then the man's pale gray eyes will suddenly begin quivering in their sockets, his brows will knit and unknit, and finally he will burst forth with the words: "*Yes!* It's *here!*" and bound up the stairs towards Robin's request.

In the first three days of his high, drunk-on-freedom orgy, Robin spends fifty-six dollars on books in Sammy's shop, thereby dissipating nearly all of the extra money his father had given him for "start-up expenses."

It is not really a problem, however, since he still has his first month's allowance in the bank as well as some leftover money from his birthday. A strange affair, that. With a gift of two hundred dollars from his father he had reached his majority: or, in California, quasi-majority, since he can still not legally drink until he is twenty-one. There had been a couple of cards from relatives, including one from the ancient, receded ghost Aunt Margaret, saying, "Happy Birthday and Graduation! We're All Very Proud of You!" On the bottom of this was added in a sloppy scrawl: "Me too! Cissy. PS Write me a letter sometime." Other than that, the momentous occasion had gone unrecorded by history. But it had gotten him thinking of that time again, years before. He had been rather surprised Priscilla even remembered him, for sometimes it seemed he could hardly recall her; but he did wonder what five years had wrought. Feeling strangely awkward, he had written a short, polite letter to her.

And so, walking the nearly deserted corridors of the dormitory in the evening, taking his showers alone in the cavernous bathroom, walking around the campus and the nature trails behind, walking the town, reading, going to films, Robin passes his first days: and, he thinks to himself, everything is just fine. He suffers no residual loneliness, no terrors, no night-dreams. He sleeps deeply and evenly with hardly even a thought of Wind Point or the house in the cul-de-sac.

A few days before the beginning of term, however, things take a drastic turn the worse.

In fact, many turns.

People begin arriving: first a handful, then a veritable flood. Soon the dormitory is packed with them. Soon there is nothing but the sound of shouting voices, laughter, boxes being pulled along the floor, doors opening and slamming shut. Soon the bathroom is exactly like the high school locker room he had so dreaded. Worse, an invader bursts into his room: his new roommate, a big gawky boy from Salinas who leaves his clothes everywhere and snores more loudly than Robin had ever imagined a human being could.

"Whatcha doin' with all them books?" the gawky boy asks him one day. "Readin'?"

Gawky Boy has arrived on an athletic scholarship.

And, just as suddenly, as rudely, his several days' pleasant routine of reading and book-shopping is utterly shattered by the beginning of classes. Life begins to whirl in an unpleasant cyclone. There is confusion about his schedule; three classes he registered for have no record of his registration; the school bookstore is sold out of two required texts; he gets continually lost on his way to classes. He knows no one. He cannot even begin to form an opinion of the classes or professors because everything simply blurs by in those first weeks: he can hardly tell one subject from another. Eventually things are straightened out with his schedule and he finds himself taking mostly general education courses in which he has not the slightest interest: Astronomy, Mathematics, Biology. It is exactly like high school, it seems to him. He had envisioned coming to college and studying nothing but literature, for months and years on end; but a careful perusal of the college catalog reveals that he is in for at least two years of primarily unrelated courses. The only subjects which interest him are Psychology and his only English course, an elective called "The Modern Short Story: Antithesis and Synthesis."

And when reality does begin to sort itself out—when he becomes able to distinguish this professor from that one, this room from the other, when he begins to recognize some of his fellow students by sight—he finds himself with the sinking feeling that he is in completely the wrong place. He has the unpleasant idea that everyone around him is somehow older, wiser, more mature: he sees groups of students arguing about intellectual things, making notes late into the night in the library: he feels that there is some mysterious river of academia that he has somehow failed to wade gracefully into. Quite beyond that, however, is that fact of...Well, just that day during lunch period he had seen a girl lying on the grass, her arms luxuriously stretched over her head, while a boy lying just to her side leaned over and french-kissed her. Worse, as he lay in bed at night he can hear, most distinctly, whispered female voices in the hall: *hush, hush,* giggle, *shh!* The dormitory is six stories high, and in theory, half those stories are reserved for boys, half for girls. In fact, although there are official rules and monitors, it appears to be quite easy to breach the void. Gawky Boy himself frequently disappears after dark: "Goin' huntin'," he says, a dull chuckle burbling from his lips. Not only is there an academic river Robin has failed to enter into, but a social and sexual one...It fills his mind at night with reluctantly-recalled visions of Marylou Kirk, and his face reddens with shame in the darkness.

The quiet little town he had initially greeted with such enthusiasm is utterly ruined by the presence of the thousands of students. The streets are crowded with cars, bicycles, pedestrians; the restaurants grow packed and loud; even Sammy's Used Book Catastrophe loses its sepulchral ambiance and becomes a stuffy, annoying marketplace. And all of these people, it seems to him, have *lives*; they seem so busy, so bright, so filled with things to do!

And what do *I* do? Robin will ask himself as he sits out on the lawn during lunch, staring vacantly at the academic groups and the couples strolling along in love. It shames him. Often he will lie back, stare at the bright cool blue of the sky (that is one thing, at least: the September afternoons here are glorious, cool and breezy and clear, with the sound of the ocean distant but audible) and go through his personal inventory. Number of dates in lifetime: zero. Number of girls kissed: zero. Number of girls seduced: zero. (He has decided finally that Marylou Kirk truly cannot count.) Friends: zero. What a checklist, he thinks, for an eighteen-year-old "young adult." What, he wonders, is adult about him? He has not changed a whit since he was twelve. All of the people around him, people his own age, do all these things—have all these things—but him? He has only his catalog of grimness.

Of course he has often considered dating. For years he has created fantasy dates within his own mind with this girl or that one; but when it comes to the actual preparation—the *asking*—he freezes as surely as a Cro-Magnon in an Alaskan iceberg. He cannot imagine how he would ask; let alone what he would do if the girl said no. Which she surely would. In high school, he had tried to use the telephone. He would work himself up for hours to the task, first writing down the girl's name, then looking it up in the phone book, copying down the number…and then sitting by the phone, staring at it. Sometimes he got up the courage to lift the cradle and begin dialing; but by the third or fourth digit he would slam it back down in breathless terror. Once, he had actually completed the dialing and heard the line ring. He had let it ring once and then banged the phone down again. He was absolutely positive that he would be rejected. After all, for each of the four years the school had sponsored a Sadie Hawkins dance, and not once had he been asked. It was proof positive. Adult! The world merely whizzes past him and he, he simply stands there stupidly like someone trying to leap onto a spinning carousel….

A month passes, then two; Robin has no idea whatever where the time has gone. When he thinks of it, the image that comes to his mind is that of water swirling down a drain. He seems to have no clear memory of anything, his mind is so filled with bustle and activity and homework. He studies his Astronomy and Mathematics and Biology and remembers the information long enough to be examined on it; then it, like time, swirls away forever. At night, blaring stereos keep him awake until late (along with the usual *hush, hush,* giggle, *shhh!*). His roommate develops a habit of stumbling in in the early hours of the morning, usually drunk. (How the students get past the guards and monitors is something utterly unknown to Robin, but it is obviously not difficult.) The food available in the dormitory cafeteria is atrociously bad: cold, green-tinged eggs, stale toast, watery soups: he comes to survive on the fresh sweet rolls delivered each morning from the bakery in town and the cold foamy milk that pours from the silver metal dispenser at the end of the counter. And, by the end of October, the clean blue skies which had greeted him each day have disappeared entirely. A constant low-lying fog sets in. Clouds. Rain.

The only class which interests him these days is Short Story. This is taught by a professor named Turnham, Leo Turnham, a well-preserved man in his late forties with a handsome stream of silver hair, a multi-toned mustache, and round wire-rimmed glasses which give his already-round face something of the appearance of an owl. To Robin's eye the man is as much a professor as any man can possibly be. Gray tweed jackets, baggy slacks, gray suede shoes; the appearance always amuses Robin. But Leo Turnham's academic accomplishments are impressive: a PhD from Berkley, published books of literary criticism. He is quite an affable sort, too, outside of class. Inside it, Robin thinks, he is pomposity personified.

He remembers the second day of the course, for which they had been assigned a story to read.

Turnham stepped into the room, and after a perfunctory good morning, he had taken his place behind the lectern and his eyes had assumed that glazed, visionary look one associates with religious zealots and bad Hamlets. Staring into some depth of infinity only he could see, he had announced the title of the story they were to discuss.

"'The Doctor,'" he intoned with grave seriousness, "'and the Doctor's Wife.'"

There was a long pause while students contemplated this revelation.

Then, just when Robin began to think that that might be the full extent of the lesson, Professor Leo Turnham's mouth had opened again. This time his eyes moved down to the rows of students and the eyes were filled with all the earnestness of spiritual devotion.

"'The *Doctor*,'" he proclaimed, and paused briefly. Then the words came: "...'and the Doctor's Wife.'"

Students stared at him in speechless awe.

The professor raised his left arm and gazed at his hand as if it contained Yorick's skull.

"'The Doctor,'" he said slowly, "'and the *Doctor's* Wife.'"

Each time he repeated the title his voice grew with emotion and a noticeable tremor had come into it.

Finally he walked to the window and stared out it for a long moment. Then, slowly, very quietly, he made a half-turn toward his audience and spoke:

"'The Doctor'..."

The class leaned forward as one.

"...'and'..."

The air was charged with suspense. Turnham's eyes, suffused now with the glow of madness or genius, swept slowly across the room until finally resting at that invisible point of eternity. Then, and only then, did he announce, suddenly:

"... 'the Doctor's *Wife*'!"

The catharsis in the room was tangible in the gasps, the sighs, and the girls fanning themselves with their textbooks.

For all that, Robin quite likes the man, and has taken to visiting his office in his free time. The office is exactly what he had expected: a huge bookshelf covering an entire wall, filled mostly with old and battered copies of critical works on the Elizabethans, the Romantics, the Surrealists, and nearly everyone else. His desk is a confusion of papers, books, pencils and pens, dirty coffee mugs. Robin likes it there. In the office is an old sofa which is more comfortable than any chair in the library, and it is amusing and a bit thrilling when someone else, another professor, comes into the office and the professor and Turnham engage in some high-level intellectual talk. Robin feels a bit out of his league, but somehow has the idea that it is a league he could one day enter into; quite different from the intellectual groups on campus and the social and sexual stream he has somehow been kept so apart from. This, he thinks, is attainable. Books. An office. Students. A bit dull, perhaps, but attainable. Unlike his other, grander dreams, the secret ones that contain glory and power and the marvels of the universe, this one seems obtainable...even easy. It would just be a matter of time. B.A., Master's, PhD: he could have it all, he knows, by the time he is thirty. And so he could have classes of his own, a cluttered office of his own, he could publish articles of his own—critical minutiae on this metaphor or that cluster of images. The way is clear to such a fate.

The question, of course, is whether he would *want* that life: and if not, if he is to choose that other, more marvelous path, the question is *how*. For there is no clear road map for such a destiny. No lamps to light the way. No compasses to give direction. He is alone, he knows, groping toward a strange door in the dark.

One misty afternoon Gawky Boy pushes into their room and says, "Hey, man, don't you ever check you mail? Here, they gave me these."

And to Robin's surprise, two envelopes sail across the room. One lands on his chest and the other dips suddenly and hits the floor. He picks it up and looks at both of them from his prone position on his bed. One is from Davy Carp. The other has no return address; its postmark is Santa Barbara.

He opens the one from Davy first.

Hey, dude, it begins. *Guess what!*

And as he reads, Robin begins to laugh. Davy is announcing to him that he has decided to take, "more or less," Michael Lyon's advice regarding Robin to himself: and he has joined the Navy! He has already signed the necessary papers and leaves for boot camp in San Diego next month...Robin shakes his head wonderingly. Little Davy Carp? Of the Withers/Carp cultural police and the *Personas Non Gratas?* In the *Navy?* It is more than a little difficult to imagine.

So you gotta write to me, dude, he closes. *I mean when I'm busy serving the Grand Old Flag (it's a high-flying flag). Carp.*

Robin muses on this letter for some minutes, staring at the gray drizzle outside. It fills him with an odd feeling that he cannot quite define. It is a bit like being abandoned, somehow. And yet he cannot puzzle it out. He thinks it a bad decision, certainly; he cannot imagine Davy Carp surviving some drooling moron spitting orders into his face. But then again, who could know? Davy was an oddly malleable type. Perhaps he would make it. The boy certainly suffered from a lack of direction (a common disease amongst Wind Point cultural policemen, Robin thinks wryly); at least this would give him something, a pre-set course.

He stares outside for some time, thinking about it, until suddenly he remembers the second letter. He slips it open neatly with his index finger and brings out a small sheet of paper with a red heart pre-printed on it. He glances at the flowery signature: it is from Priscilla Wilder.

Hi, Robin! it reads. *I hear you're in the wilds of the redwoods now. Guess what—I'm living in Santa Barbara. I'm on my own now (loving it!!!) Why don't you think about coming for a visit sometime, over a long wknd mebbe? Its really beautiful here—sun fun etc. Your Old Pal, Cissy.* An address is written on the bottom.

He stares at the writing on the paper for long moments. He finds her chummy tone odd: they haven't seen each other, after all, in years. Notices also the signature, *Cissy*: hears her voice from years ago in his mind: *I ain't no fluckin' sissy*. He wonders how she has changed over these years, what kind of a person she has become. He finds himself wishing she had enclosed a picture. It's very curious, this letter. He is rather surprised that she still remembers him. He has an odd sensation then, as he thinks of how Priscilla must have matured and grown: time, he thinks, truly exists outside him. People live outside him, outside his experience. This has never really occurred to him before. Somehow it had always seemed to him that, beyond of his own range of vision, people did not truly exist: did not truly live: that it was only in relation to himself that they had any life, any breath at all. But this, he realizes suddenly, isn't so. He thinks of Davy Carp en route to San Diego and the spitting moron in his face. Thinks of Priscilla, how she obviously must have changed. Thinks finally of his father, there in the house in the cul-de-sac. His life, his father's life, somehow continues: even though Robin is not there anymore. The man did not simply become vapor and vanish. *He lives.* The idea fills Robin with a heady, peculiar feeling, like the feeling he sometimes has when listening to Mahler: or rather, just after the final notes have died away and it is as if a fragile, untranslatable connection to something in infinity hovers there for a long moment before dissipating again into space. Like the feeling he has sometimes had of being so intensely *alive*: connected to the universe: that breathless sensation of being a part of a whole, a section of the universal. If these people truly have lives outside his, then they too are part of the connection, the universal everything of eternity: and it is a heady thought. That he is not the center, but merely a piece in a fantastically gigantic design: and that those others, all those others who have lives outside his, are part of the same design: disconnected from him in one sense but in another, one with him: the same breath, same bones, same blood. He is one with them, they are one with each other.

It reminds him of a story Turnham had had them read for Short Story class: "The Professor Remembers," by one Terrence Llewelyn. Robin had been moved by it in the same way Mahler moves him, that sensation of connectedness, that speechless bridge to infinity. Nothing much "happened" in the story, being simply an account—written in the gentlest, most lyrical prose—of the last few hours of an old professor's life, as the facts of his life blend together in his mind with mystical visions of God and the beyond. What was extraordinary was the vividness of the world Llewelyn had created: the smells in the professor's room, the light, the sounds of the children outside his window: it was all extraordinarily real, more vibrant, Robin thinks, than real life. It was a grim tale—the old professor was as confused at the end of his life as Robin is now—but at the conclusion, when the professor dies and the laughter of the children outside triggers a vision of himself as a boy rising before his own deathbed, it was exquisitely moving.

He stares out his dormitory window, thinking about it, watching the spattering rain come down. He wishes he had someone to talk to about all this. The ideas come into his head in a miasmic rush and he cannot sort them out. The concepts are too large, time, infinity, death. He wonders, like the professor in the story, about death. It has occurred to him that perhaps it is not the opposite of life at all. Such has he learned in his Biology class: that the essential aspects of the organism, its atoms and molecules, do not cease to exist at death: rather, they are simply redistributed to the soil, to future organisms, to space. There is something exhilarating in the thought. Thousands, millions of bits of Robin Withers finding their ways into the buds of lilies, the eyes of lions, the flames of the sun! And if we are made up of essentially nothing but these atoms and molecules, he wonders, then what is death? What is it *really?* A cessation of being; of consciousness; perhaps—but he wonders just what that means. What consciousness is, what he means when he says "I." He cannot make it out. Is it possible that he will someday look out from the eyes of a lily, a lion, the sun itself? That a million Robins will look out from a million places, see a million things with a million consciousness? Is life then just a temporary integration of these swarming, separate millions which will soon scatter themselves again through the corridors of the universe? He closes his eyes and thinks of it. Sees space, drifting, floating. Sees a glowing door in the distance. Swims toward it. Swims...

Sometimes, in a slight, superficial way, he discusses these things with Turnham. He is afraid of asking too deeply about them for fear of looking silly, ignorant, hopelessly undergraduate: for it seems to him that Turnham has probably long since figured everything out, and Robin feels like a clumsy and dim oaf trying to catch up. But they do discuss them, and what writers say about them. Turnham gives him William James and Nietzsche to read and helps him through it all. Robin finds Nietzsche fascinating, glorious: the epic, passionate quality of it, especially near the end (*For I love you, O Eternity!*)—those half-realized concepts from his high school days about man being his own

God are here fully, wonderfully articulated. It gives him the same feeling of connection of Mahler, of Llewelyn's professor.

Turnham seems greatly interested in Robin and in the discussions they have. He calls Robin "a fine English student, really fine, one the best we've had in years": and frequently praises Robin's critical mind. Such praise fills Robin with pride: but also with unease. He is proud of being so good in class, but class is not what interests him. The lovely ghosts, the connection-points of the giant design, these are what he wants! He burns in his desire to create. To make, produce! And yet he cannot seem to do it. In his second term at the college Robin enrolls in a Critical Writing course with Turnham: day in and day out they analyze poems by Blake, Donne, Shakespeare. Turnham praises his work, reads it aloud to the class while Robin preens; his ego in supremely gratified. And yet! And yet!

Sometimes, in the rainy misery of his dormitory room, he will bring out an old sheet of paper onto which he had once typed a few words:

when I come home from somewhere she is there waiting for me.

The words haunt him. It is the beginning, he thinks, of something. But he does not know what.

In desperation, finally, he sits down in the library one day and resolves not to stand again until he has created something.

For hours nothing comes.

Finally, despairingly, he begins writing words nearly at random; and in a few hours, much to his surprise, he finds he has something resembling a story. It excites him tremendously. He works on it over the next week, revises it ruthlessly: then one afternoon, presents it to Turnham. Robin is bursting with pride.

"My first short story," he tells him. "Be gentle with it, okay?"

But he says this with false modesty, for he knows fully well that the story is as good as any of his critical papers. Better. It is on the level of Mansfield, Melville, Llewelyn. It *flows*. He wonders if Turnham will recommend it to a good journal. He awaits the verdict with some trepidation; but mostly with supreme confidence.

Finally, a few days later, Turnham hands the story back to him during class along with a school paper. Ignoring the essay's usual top mark, he reads the note attached to the story:

Robin—

1) Slow-moving with too much extraneous detail.

2) Unconvincing dialogue, esp. love dialogue between James and Sarah.

3) James is totally unbelievable. (What do you know about Irish potato farmers circa 1800???)

Leo.

He nearly faints. He cannot believe it. His story! The one he sweated for, forced into being with hours of bloody labor in the library! To be dismissed so brutally! It's obvious to him that Turnham did not understand it, and he immediately resolves to explain it to him after class. But when he goes to Turnham's office, somehow he cannot speak of it clearly.

"Look, Leo," he says, "I think you missed the point. What I was trying to do was—you see, the whole Irish thing is a kind of—a kind of *metaphor* for—you see, it's not meant to be taken literally, it's—it's—"

Turnham looks up at him through his round owl-glasses. "Robin," he says, "calm yourself. Sit down."

Robin sits on the sofa, leaning forward tightly.

"You wanted my reaction, didn't you?" Turnham asks calmly.

"Yeah, but..." Robin stares down, ashamed of the papers in his hands. "But—but Leo, you're—" he grimaces—"so *brutal!*"

Turnham stares at him from his desk chair. Robin notices that he has quite attractively soft gray eyes. "Robin," he says again, taking off his glasses and wiping them with a tissue, "you yourself don't know what that story is about. You just proved it by trying to explain it to me and not being able to do it. And if *you* don't know what it means, how am *I* supposed to know?"

"I *know* what is means…"

The professor stares at him.

"At least…" Robin falls silent for a moment, uncertainly. Then: "At least—I *thought* I knew.…"

Turnham smiles beneficently.

Over the next months, Robin writes several more stories. He grows accustomed to Turnham's brutal responses, which slowly come to be less brutal: by the fourth story, Robin has even earned the comment: *You're improving.* Turnham actually seems to know quite a lot about the craft of writing, though not a writer of fiction himself. Robin is rather in awe of him. He wishes, too, that he knew more about the man: for although Robin has told Turnham a fair amount about himself, Turnham has been reticent. He knows that his professor has a daughter: her picture adorns his desk. He does not know about a wife, or anything else.

Near the end of second term, Turnham invites Robin to his home.

"Nothing much," the man tells him. "Just something to eat, some company. That's all. Would you like to?"

It is like a heavenly benediction, this invitation. A summons to dine with the great. Robin knows then that he is truly *in* with Turnham, despite the failure of his stories. The misery of the snore-filled torture chamber called his dormitory room seems to lift evanescently; he drifts through his other classes as through clouds. The brilliant Turnham has invited him to his home! Nothing else, for the time being, matters. Old realities fade away as he prepares to take his seat among the anointed, to ascend the summit. This is the beginning, he knows. A new life awaits him.

9

It is early evening when he pulls up before Turnham's house, prematurely dark: a heavy cover of mist and clouds has blotted out all but a feeble gray glow. It is uncommonly cold for early May and Robin has on his heavy jacket. All the way over the windshield had continually misted up and Robin had had to use an old towel to clean it off again.

He checks the address scrawled on a scrap of paper; looks toward the house across the street. Although smaller than the house in the cul-de-sac, it nonetheless reminds Robin of it: the same vintage, same basic layout. But Turnham's house seems in great disorder. His lawn is weed-infested and overgrown; stacks of wood and bricks lie scattered near the door; his garage, which is open, displays a monumental disarray into which the man's car hardly fits. Robin smiles slightly as he steps out of his own car. It is amusing... *human*, somehow, this mess of Turnham's. He had been vaguely afraid of entering some hushed mausoleum where everything had its certain place and nothing was to be touched without permission. He notices tiny droplets of rain pelting his hair and nose as he crosses the street and approaches the big door. He knocks; slips off his glasses, wipes them on his lavender shirt.

In a moment Turnham opens the door. He has a glass of wine in his hand and is wearing a gray cashmere sweater over typically baggy cotton slacks; his feet are in soft gray loafers. The professor at home, Robin thinks.

"Robin, hello! How are you?" The man extends his hand and they shake. Turnham tugs him into the house. "It's a terrible evening, isn't it?"

"I'm used to them," Robin says, his eyes taking in the house. The short hall leads straight into the main room, which, he can see, is decorated in soft earth tones.

"Maybe you are," Turnham says, smiling in his owlish way, "but I'm not, never will be. I'm from Iowa. No fog in Iowa. Come on into the main room...Let me take your coat." He disappears with the soggy jacket while Robin walks into the big, high-ceilinged room. It is quietly lovely. The fireplace has a small crackling fire sparking inside it; on the walls are reproductions of modern paintings (along with one or two originals that are quite attractive: swirling washes of color); one wall is covered with a glass-enclosed bookcase. The sofa and chairs look inviting. There is a television in one corner quietly playing a news program; a silent stereo is next to it. Robin walks over to the bookcase. The titles are predictably highbrow: but, he notices, under *T* (the books are carefully alphabetized, quite unlike the ones in Turnham's office), are three titles of particular interest: *Milton and the Pathetic Fallacy*; *Blake as Witness*; and *Christopher Marlowe, An Introduction*. All by Leonard Turnham, PhD.

"Ah!" Turnham says in a pleasant voice as he re-emerges. "You've discovered the library."

"Just noticing *your* books."

"Oh, yes. I have a few dry and boring—but I must say quite brilliant—titles by some old fart who goes by my name." He goes to the bookcase and slides the glass away. "But look at these. You're interested in contemporary writing, so these should be up your alley." Turnham brings out several titles—novels by Hemingway, Thomas Mann (in German), Andre Gide (in French). All are first editions and some are inscribed. Robin wants to ask how much they are worth but his instinct tells him the question would be gauche; instead he asks how long Turnham has been collecting.

"Oh, years and years," he says, crossing to the bar on the other side of the room. "Would you like something to drink, Robin? I'm having some wine from Monterey. Good cheap stuff. Want some?"

"I will, thanks." Actually, Robin virtually never drinks. He has never quite sworn himself to abstinence, and has occasionally sipped at beer or wine; but of course the odor always brings on memories of shoutings, dark rooms. Just now, though, he does not wish to appear a prude. He accepts the glass from Turnham while flipping carefully through the books. Turnham goes to the television, switches it off; puts a record on the turntable. A soft, bluesy ballad comes gently over the speakers: Billie Holiday.

After a few minutes, Robin looks up from the books he has been gazing at raptly. "Is your wife here?" he asks.

"No wife," Turnham says. He has seated himself in a fat chair on the other side of the room. "I'm divorced."

"Oh, I'm sorry."

"Don't be. Anyway, I'm all by myself here."

"And your daughter…?"

"Mauri? She lives with her mother."

Robin nods. At last he sets the books aside.

"Dinner will be along in a while," Turnham adds. "It's in the oven. A souffle. I hope that's all right."

"Anything," he grins, feeling the warmth of the fire soaking into him. "Remember, I live in the dorms. Cafeteria food."

"Bad?"

"Deadly."

Turnham smiles. "I lived in a dorm in Iowa when I was your age…which is to say about two hundred years ago. Sounds like dorm food hasn't changed."

"It's one of the eternals," Robin agrees. "God, Time, Dormitory Food. Leo—" Robin is always quietly pleased to use Turnham's first name—"listen, did you read the new story I left in your box? 'Laura's Dream'?"

The man nods.

Robin waits for a long moment. "Well?" he says finally.

Turnham shakes his head. "Warmed-over Chekhov. You've been reading him, haven't you?"

Robin falls back against the bricks beside the fireplace. "*Jesus, Leo!*"

Turnham laughs. "Don't be so offended. Listen, I'll tell you a secret: all good writers start out by imitating. It's inevitable; it's how you develop style. Your story is a Chekhov imitation—but it's a fairly good one. You're learning how to put a story together, the mechanics of getting your characters from A to B. You *are* improving."

"Yeah, but—" He sips at the wine. He wants to say: I don't want to be *improving*. I want to be there *now*. "But Leo, at this rate by the time I'm seventy-five I may have produced one halfway competent paragraph and that's about all."

Turnham grins. "What did you come here for, sympathy?"

Robin grins back, shakes his head. "Food."

"That's more like it!" He stands suddenly. "Let me check the progress of my culinary masterpiece...."

The evening begins like this, slowly, quietly. Robin moves to the big sofa and Turnham invites him to take off his shoes and stretch out: "Like Stanley Kowalski," he tells him, "my motto is: 'Be comfortable.'" And Robin is. They talk of literary things. Turnham amuses him with his wit, his outlandish opinions: "You realize, of course," he says at one point, "that these ambitions of yours are meaningless, because you are doomed to be no more than a footnote in literary history."

"Thanks!" Robin says, looking over at him, surprised.

Turnham holds up his hand. "Again I've offended you. And yet I don't mean to. You see, it happens to be a fact that, in our post-Christian, pre-apocalyptic culture, we are *all* footnotes to two works: the Bible; and the complete works of Shakespeare."

"And everything else is footnotes?"

"Everything."

"Milton, Blake, Spenser, Dostoyevsky, Flaubert, Rilke?"

"Footnotes."

"Stendhal? Kafka? Tolstoy? Proust?"

"Footnotes. Proust, maybe two footnotes."

Robin laughs. "So then how would you classify your own books about these footnotes?"

"I would paraphrase what Churchill said of Hitler. 'A footnote wrapped within a footnote.'"

"Anyway, how do you know I'm not destined to take my place next to those two non-footnotes?"

Turnham grins. "Maybe you are. How do I know? Then, if I live long enough, maybe I can write a footnote to a primary source—you. That would be a nice change of pace."

"You just wait. Give me a few years."

Turnham nods. "Granted."

"Bible, Shakespeare, Withers. The Big Three. I think that has a nice ring."

"You're right. It does." Turnham drains the wine glass and goes to the bar for another. "Stranger things have happened. Hitler was a house painter who became the greatest dictator the world has ever seen. Until recently a movie actor was governor of this state. More wine?"

"No, I'm okay."

"Choose some more music for us while I check the souffle again."

And later, during the dinner—which they eat in a tiny, simple dining room just off the kitchen, to the sound of Dexter Gordon on the stereo—Turnham amuses him with literary stories of a bizarre turn.

"Do you remember," he says, pushing his plate away and wiping his mouth with a napkin, "a few years ago, there was this writer named...what was his name? It's slipped my mind. Wrote little stories, very short ones, in a kind of 'See Dick Run' style. Very popular for a while. Reminded me of Vonnegut. Brannigan, that's it. I suppose he was a bit before your time. Anyway, this guy Brannigan—Robert Brannigan—committed suicide in San Francisco maybe four or five years ago. Terrible tragedy for his family, I suppose, although I must say that he did the cause of literature a considerable service by hastening his own demise. Shot himself in the head one fine morning—probably after re-reading his own books. I guess I shouldn't be so flip about it: but the point is that a couple of years ago I was in San Francisco looking for some things when this bookseller—he has a shop on Market Street, I've known him for years—called me aside and said, 'Leo, I have something *very* special that I'm showing only to my preferred customers.' He led me into this dusty back room. It was getting late, you know, dark—it was all very mysterious—and he flipped on the light, which was just one naked bulb overhead. At the end of the room was a safe. He glanced at me a minute and then flipped the dial and opened it. Inside was a cash box, some books too valuable to put on the shelves, and a big stack of papers. He brought out the papers and put them on this table under the light bulb.

"'Have a look,'" he told me.

"I leaned down to look at them: the first page was a typewritten sheet that read, *A Deliberate Heaven: A Novel by Robert Brannigan.* It was an original Brannigan manuscript.

"'Fred,' I said, 'why are you showing this to me? You know I don't collect this kind of stuff.'

"He gazed at me through these Coke-bottle glasses of his and said, 'Look through it. Just look. It was the book he was working on when he killed himself.'

"To be courteous, I flipped through the first few pages. It was typical Brannigan. 'The family lived in a house. It was a very big house. Uncle Harry was run over in front of the house one day and that was a very sad day for the family.' Et cetera. I could never puzzle out his appeal…Anyway, I glanced at a few more pages when I came upon something: a spot on the page. I didn't think anything of it, but when I turned to the next page, the last page of the manuscript, there was a huge brown splotch that covered the entire sheet and blotted out what was written there.

"'What is *this*?' I asked.

"Fred came over to me and lifted the sheet of paper up into the light. Gazing at me, he said—like a holy benediction, really—'Brannigan's brains.'"

Robin gasps, then laughs. "Leo, that's disgusting!"

Turnham laughs heartily. "True, though. I wonder who bought poor Brannigan's last, soiled manuscript."

Robin chuckles again, sips his wine. "You have an interesting notion of appropriate dinner conversation."

"Well, you'd finished your dinner. Anyway, you'll be blabbing that story all over campus on Monday."

"Nah."

"Why not? Not good enough?"

"Nobody to blab it to, really."

Turnham nods, understanding.

"I have dessert, too," the professor says after a moment. "First-class treatment here."

"Jeez. We're really going to town tonight. Hey, Leo, this was great, you know. Really."

"But not as great, I assure you, as Doctor Turnham's Chocolate Mousse." He grins and pushes back his chair to stand.

"Chocolate mousse? No kidding?"

"Made with mine own hands from an ancient French recipe known only to a few obscure American professors, and nearly every Frenchman who ever lived."

"Fantastic!"

They have more wine with dessert; Robin feels it beginning to go to his head slightly. He is not drunk—has never been drunk. But he is light-headed, and the sensation reminds him of many years before, in the field of long grass with Priscilla...He thinks briefly of the letter he has received from her. His curiosity is strong about her, about the changes the years have wrought. He thinks to ask for a picture the next time he writes. Then Davy Carp crosses his mind, and after him Michael Lyon, and Kathy Collins, his father....But he blots them all out suddenly. He does not want to be there, not now. He wants to be here.

Robin is a bit dizzy as they stand and walk back to the main room. Turnham has switched off most of the lights in the house, and only one lamp is on in the living room. Most of the light comes from the fire, to which Turnham adds some wood. It flares up prettily.

Robin takes a pillow from the sofa and lies on his stomach before the fire. He slips off his glasses and places them before him on the hearth. Turnham comes over and sits next to him and they both look into the fire.

"When I was a little kid," Robin says, staring into the flames, "my mom and I used to buy this...I don't know what you call it, this kind of dust you toss into the fire and for a couple of minutes it turns the flames green and blue and all these strange colors."

Turnham smiles at him.

"Except we hardly ever used the fireplace," he adds, scowling. "I don't know why. I can't even remember the last time we burned a fire there."

"Messy," Turnham offers. "Shoveling, afterwards."

"Maybe."

"Do you hear a lot from your parents?"

"Well—my mom's dead."

"Oh."

"Yeah. Since I was thirteen. My dad...I don't know."

"Distant?"

Robin nods. "Two islands. I'm not even sure we're in the same stream."

"What does he do for a living?"

"Sells insurance, if you can believe that. Runs his own office. The sign on the door says that he can 'Insure Your Future.'"

Turnham smiles. "Lofty claim."

"Mm-hm. But he couldn't insure his own family's."

Turnham is silent. Robin watches the fire crackle and sizzle. He doesn't think much about these things, not anymore...since coming to college he has thought of his father little, his mother hardly at all. But as he watches the fire the memory of her comes back with amazing vividness. He can see her on the pier, her white dress, her bare feet, the dark hair blown back by the wind: her face is indistinct, but he can hear her voice: she is talking about wrapping the sky-gems around themselves and floating to the moon. *Oh Robin*, she says, leaning down with her face close to his, her eyes and cheeks and lips inches from his own, *it's a real diamond day.*

Dimly he realizes that it has begun raining outside. He can hear the insistent pattering on Turnham's roof and the wind is blowing against the main room's sliding glass door, causing it to shudder slightly in the semi-darkness.

"Going to be a nasty night," Turnham says. The stereo has long since fallen silent and all that can be heard in the room is the fire, the rain, the wind.

"Yeah," Robin says. "Maybe I'd better get going."

Turnham sets his wine glass gently on the hearth. "Why don't you stay here?" he asks quietly.

Robin glances at him. "I couldn't impose like that, Leo."

There is a pause. The rain seems to lighten; the wind calms. It is a moment before Robin even realizes that Turnham has placed his hand, very softly, on Robin's shoulder.

"It wouldn't be an imposition," he murmurs.

Robin is suddenly aware of his heart inside his chest. The hand on his shoulder kneads his skin, softly.

"Leo…" he begins, then stops. For he does not know what it is he wants to say. For long moments he offers no reaction whatever. He stares into the fire exactly as before.

"Leo," he says again, suddenly resolved; and he turns onto his side to look at Turnham. But he does not pull away from the hand, which remains there. They look at each other. Finally Turnham's hand moves to Robin's face, touches it softly with the backs of his fingers. Robin closes his eyes a moment. Then he opens them again.

Turnham smiles slightly, almost wistfully. "Tell me when to stop," he says.

He remembers that a moment before he had had a resolve…but to do what? It has slipped his mind. He had made a decision, but he can no longer remember what it was. Perhaps, he thinks, the alcohol has dimmed his mind slightly. But he wonders if it would be any more definitive dead sober. Robin is intensely aware of the sound of the rain, the fire, the wind. Aware of the earth-colored carpet beneath them. Aware of Turnham's hand unbuttoning two buttons on Robin's lavender shirt and his hand slipping inside and touching his chest. The sensation makes him draw in his breath suddenly. Turnham's hand stops, hesitates, seems for an instant about to draw away; but Robin finds his own hand covering Turnham's, holding it there. He looks not at Turnham but at a space of darkness behind him. At nothing. He realizes abruptly that this is the first time any human being has touched him like this, for this reason…the first time another human being's flesh has willingly contacted with his own for this. The sensation makes him giddy. A shiver runs through him. The abruptness of it, the sudden tangible connection. He lets go of Turnham's hand and feels more of his shirt buttons coming undone. Tentatively he reaches toward the man's gray sweater. Lifts it slightly. Touches the silky shirt underneath, pulls it open gently and places his own hand over Turnham's heart. It is beating solidly, evenly. The chest is smooth, hairless, like

Robin's own. Exactly like his own, he thinks wonderingly. A living, breathing being. Like himself.

He is on his back, Turnham leaning over him, his lips on Robin's hair. He can feel the man's mustache, its oddly pleasing tickle causing his scalp to tingle. The lips course over Robin's face, his forehead, his cheeks. They are firmer than his mother's had been. He touches Turnham's cheek. It is firmer too; and yet soft to the touch, in a different way.

Turnham slips off his glasses, places them on the hearth next to Robin's. His eyes are like prisms, bright, deep-set prisms filled with glints of silver and gray and black. Robin smiles at him. It is the first time he has seen Turnham as a man, as a person, rather than as a professor: a living person, with flesh and breath…and a heartbeat. It is an amazing thing.

"You planned this?" Robin asks quietly.

Turnham shakes his head. "I swear to you. Of course…" He grins in a new way, indefinably new, a man's grin, not a professor's. "…Of course it may have crossed my *mind*."

Robin touches the sides of the man, the living, breathing man. Turnham leans close again and their lips touch gently.

"How long can I stay here?" Robin whispers.

"Forever."

"Until I have a PhD…and we're both brilliant professors?"

The lips touch again. "Don't be a professor," Turnham whispers. "Professors…they're children. Children with their faces pressed to the glass of the candy shop. Don't be a professor. Be a candy maker."

"I'll be a candy maker."

"Yes…"

"Stop talking now. Stop…stop talking. Stop talking," Robin gasps, feeling the man's heartbeat, and his own, the two heartbeats pumping in tandem, together, in the darkness.

10

That weekend Robin spends in something of a daze. Dozens of times he tries to forget what happened and concentrate on his homework; but he cannot. His mind floats back to the fire, the rain, the darkness. When he thinks of it his heart begins fluttering in his chest like a bird: and he feels a giddiness course through him. He takes long, misty walks around town, engages in conversations with students he meets, Sammy of the Used Book Catastrophe, customers in shops. He feels he has never done so much talking in his life, and so boldly, and about anything: for when he thinks of what happened between the two of them his mind begins to spin, to whirl. He wants to call Turnham, and several times steps into a phone booth to do so. But after depositing his coins he hangs up the receiver and listens to them tinkle down into the change slot again. He doesn't know if he should. Doesn't know quite what he would say...For they had said so much together, or rather Robin had, in their talk afterwards. He told Turnham of his virginity, or, as he phrased it, quasi-virginity. Of his painful shyness that had never allowed him to so much as pick up a phone to ask someone for a date. Of his childhood yearning to change his gender. His confusion, his fear, his terror.

By the time he'd finished, he is sure, he must have appeared a completely neurotic case.

And yet Turnham had listened sympathetically and not treated him as if he were a nut. He felt he belonged; that he could say these things that had been closed up within himself for countless years. Turnham listened, nodded, touched him affectionately. It was the touching, the reality of it, the heartbeat, that made Robin nearly rapturous: and, though he had been afraid he might end up crying after saying so many of the old, miserable things (although in fact crying is something he never does), Turnham had made him laugh instead.

A dozen times he thinks of calling Turnham, and four or five times steps into a booth; but each time he listens to the coins slip down into the change slot. He doesn't know the language to use, the tone. He imagines a hundred different conversations. None of them are quite right; or rather, he cannot be *sure* of any of them. He feels his nerves jumping inside his skin. He decides to wait for Turnham to call or to see him; then almost immediately reverses his decision and decides to drive over to the man's house. But he does not.

Class on Monday morning is a peculiar but quite pleasing experience. He sits back, watching Turnham do his usual pompous professor act, with a certain knowledge that, he realizes, no one else has. Odd: like seeing Marylou Kirk at graduation and thinking of what they had done together, or almost done. But here the feeling is far more intense. As if he is aware of the secrets of the universe. The others in the room, he knows, know Turnham—and Robin himself—only in this limited role, only in this public play-acting; but Robin has other, secret knowledge. It is a delightful, childlike sensation: *I know something you don't know,* he thinks, glancing around the room.

At the end of class Turnham is surrounded by students and so Robin decides to wait until later to see him. But as he is stepping from the room, a voice calls:

"Robin!"

He turns. Turnham, breaking away from his students and simultaneously apologizing to them, steps over to him. Their eyes meet momentarily and Turnham slips something into Robin's hand.

"Read this later," Turnham says.

Robin smiles. "Okay."

Turnham returns to his students, and Robin leaves the room. He feels the folded-up piece of paper in his hand, wonders about it as he would wonder about the contents of a surprise package.

Of course he realizes he must be careful about it; such a note is not for public consumption. He has a free hour, so instead of going to the library he hurries back to his dormitory room. Rain is splashing onto the pavement and into the grass but Robin hardly notices it as he rushes, nearly runs, to his room, holding the note carefully in his pocket and protecting it from the downpour.

He is out of breath by the time he bounces into the room; but he does not stop even to take off his wet jacket. He throws himself into the chair by the window, tosses his rain-streaked glasses onto the desk, and unfolds the note with shaking hands.

Robin:
I want you to know that what happened the other night was the result of too much alcohol on my part. While I cannot say that I didn't enjoy your company, I'm sure you understand that nothing of that nature must occur between us again. As I may have told you, I am currently trying to reconcile with my ex-wife.
I want to apologize if either that evening or this note have caused you any distress whatever.
I would appreciate it if we never mentioned the subject again.
Leo.
PS For obvious reasons I must ask you to destroy this.

Robin stares at the slip of paper thunderstruck. He feels as if the magic carpet he had been riding on has suddenly, for no reason whatever, been pulled from under his feet and he has tumbled headlong into an abyss. He gazes blankly at the words on the paper until they seem to break up and become random lines of blue ink. The tone of it, he thinks, is like one of those terrible rejection slips he has received on the odd occasion he has gathered courage enough to send something to a publisher: *Dear Contributor: We regret to inform you that* etc. Cold, unemotional…brutal. That's the word. Brutal. He cannot believe it. As if he were just anyone off the street! Some faceless moron he had never seen before and would never see again! He is suddenly enraged and he crumples the note, hurls it against the window, jumps up and paces the room. But a moment later he retrieves the paper from where it has rolled under his bed and shoves it into his pocket. Stalks to the other end of the room, his breath short. Pulls out the note again, uncrumples it, crumples it again. Throws himself onto his bed. He has a good mind to report the bastard for seducing him. That would fix him up good. He even has tangible evidence, the note, to back him up. It's a fine plan. Go first to the president of the school…or better yet, to the police! Circumvent the school entirely to be assured it wouldn't be covered up. That was it, the police…yes, I want to file formal charges…Oh, the shame, the embarrassment, the humiliation!

But after a few minutes of lying on the bed, staring at the ceiling and listening to the rain pelting the window, he begins to calm. His heart slows. Melancholy passes over him like a long shadow; his energy dissipates like the burnt-out fragments of a star. He lies there listlessly. What difference does it make, finally? What, really, had he expected from Turnham? He ponders this for some time. What could he have expected? What did he *want*?

He lies on the bed for a long time. He knows he is missing his Science class but he continues staring at the ceiling. Dozes, finally, for a few minutes, the note in his loose fist.

Finally, sometime later—he does not know how much time has passed—he goes to the window and opens it. It is still heavily raining and the cold blast of air hits his lungs suddenly. It is not an unpleasant sensation. He looks out at the drenched lawn beneath him and the buildings: other dormitories, classrooms farther in the distance; students moving about under umbrellas, some rushing with newspapers held over their heads. He can see the ocean from where he is sitting and he stares at it, at the gray sky that seems to melt into it. He cannot be sure where one leaves off and the other begins.

I must ask you to destroy this.

Carefully he unfolds it, smooths it on his knee; then, without re-reading it, he holds the paper out into the stream of falling rain. He watches as the drops pelt at the thing, like daws pecking at overripe fruit; and the letters begin to run down the sheet, bleeding into each other, dissolving into smeared veins of blue. When the note has become completely illegible he drops the soaked paper and watches it fall, not lightly or gracefully, but heavily, like a lead weight, toward the gutter below.

A kind of nervous excitement soon lights up the campus: the approach of Finals Week. Robin realizes with some astonishment that he has all but completed his first year in college.

In a series of *four...*

He sits in the crowded but quiet library one night, thinking about it. His Science textbook is open before him but he is not reading it: each time he tries, his eyes scan the lines in an apparent process of reading but by the time he has gone three or four pages he realizes that he has paid attention to nothing, learned nothing. And so he will turn the pages back, try again. But the same thing happens each time and so finally he sits at his table staring blankly at the text, no longer attempting to read it. The picture on the page shows a cell dividing, and lists the names of the various stages of the process. All of which Robin is supposed to know, none of which he knows. He could learn them if he could concentrate, but concentration is something in short supply now. He has not thought clearly since the episode with Turnham several weeks before. He has not spoken to the man since: says nothing in class: sits there, not meeting his eyes, feeling only humiliation and shame.

He thinks about categories: wonders if the incident, once and for all and forever, established him in the camp of the sexual minority. He supposes so, and yet he wonders. He has now had such intimacy with one man and one girl—sort of, anyway, in the latter case—and so it seems to him a rather open question. He knows many people would not think so, that on the basis of what happened with Turnham he would be *classified*. Grouped. Pigeonholed. But Robin does not feel ready to be so easily compartmentalized. He is not sure that he can see it as an either/or proposition, as most others do. Of course he has long felt this way about God, too. He could never stand the way one church invariably claimed to have the ultimate, absolute, final Truth, and that other churches...well, one had best stay away from *those* churches. And yet when one went to *those* churches, one found the same dogma, the same absolutism. What, he wonders, is the need for it? Either/Or. Black/White. This/That. What, he asks himself, if he feels both this *and* that? What if all the churches partake in a similar portion of Truth, but none have it all? Or, to look at it the other way, perhaps they are all equally deluded, equally wrong. And as to the other, closer question, the question of Turnham, he wonders if it is really necessary or logical to *classify* human beings. Robin feels utterly adrift on this issue, floating between islands of desire; and yet he knows that others would not have it that way. Others would tell him *You are this* or *You are that*. With pointed fingers.

   He sighs and stares at the picture of cell division again.

   A year of his life: and for what? What has he learned? He can think of little outside of his own reading. Already the details of his first-semester classes are fading in his mind; already he is sure that if he were handed an examination in one of those earlier subjects he would fail it miserably. A year in a tiny room with Gawky Boy. A year of hurried, embarrassed showers. A year of no friends. He sighs again; the list is remarkably depressing. He can hardly stand to eat the dormitory food. He belongs to no clubs, has attended no parties. At times the loneliness is like a physical ache, a deep awful emptiness somewhere in the pit of his stomach. Late at night, with Gawky Boy returned from his revels and snoring like a chain saw across the room, Robin will lie awake, sometimes actually grasping his stomach, pressing his arms to it, folding up his body fetally and holding himself tightly around his midsection. He does not like to think of it. It embarrasses him. Does not like to think of the humiliation he feels when, day after day, he receives not a single letter from anyone, not a line, not a scribble. Even his father rarely encloses anything with his monthly checks. Sometimes there is something like this:

Robin:

Hope you're doing all right. Everything is okay here. Keep studying hard.

Your Dad.

Interesting, he thinks, that he has not actually seen his father for nearly a year now. He had avoided returning home for Christmas by claiming he had too much schoolwork to do, which was a boldfaced lie; but somehow he could not face the hypocrisy of the season anymore, could have nothing to do with the tired decorations his father brought out every year and the tree and the perfunctory gifts they exchanged. It was horribly false and awkward. He hated it. It brought back memories he didn't like to have raised: visions of his father and mother shouting at each other next to the tree, once even knocking over a glass of their precious liquid, and Robin staring as the amber river splashed into the throw rug, filling the room with its pungent odor. 'Tis the season, he thinks, to be melancholy.

Slowly he becomes aware of the dull ticking of the clock on the wall opposite him. He thinks about Wind Point, about escape. He had thought, a year ago, that he would escape: that he would leave the house in the cul-de-sac far behind him: but he has not. He knows that now. He has not escaped. It is still with him, that house: those shadows: those thoughts, those nightmares. He hears the clock on the wall ticking. It seems to be growing louder and louder and there plays across his mind the image of the warehouse, the secret warehouse in which all his future seconds are stored, and how he would love to be able to pull the door of the warehouse open, pass through the door and see them there, all the seconds like sleeping birds awaiting his arrival...or would it be a pitifully low stack, just a few hurling themselves out second-by-second until there was nothing left at all but emptiness, disaster, blackout?

He stands finally, collects his books, and steps out of the library.

Outside it is growing dark. The rain cuts through the sky like splintered glass: the fog, thick and dark, weaves slowly around the tops of the buildings as if to choke them, drain their lives away. Robin stares at the top of the English building, shrouded in mist like a castle in an old horror film. He crosses the sidewalk and cuts across the parking lot toward the dormitory.

Suddenly there is the wet shriek of tires on pavement. Robin's head shoots up and he sees a pair if headlights skidding toward him. He half-turns, slips; there is a sudden dull pain in his hip and his books and glasses fly from him. Suddenly he is on his knees, soaked with water, dizzy.

"Oh my God!" He hears the voice, familiar, and the car door being pushed open. "Robin! Are you all right?"

For a moment he is not sure. He is unsure of anything: where he is, who he is. The rain pours down on him and on the dark figure standing over him. He looks up. It is Turnham.

"You stepped right in front of me!" the man says, his voice apprehensive. He leans down. "Robin, are you all right?"

"I...I'm fine," he hears himself saying. After a moment he stands, unsteadily. "I'm fine."

Turnham stands with him. "Are you sure? Let me take you to the hospital."

"No, I'm fine. I'm fine…Where are my glasses?"

"Here." Fussily, Turnham picks up the glasses and the books and hands them to Robin. "Are they scratched?"

"No…No, they're okay."

"Fine. Now get in the car. We'll go to the hospital."

"No, Leo, I'm…I'm all right. No broken bones."

"What about your hip?"

Robin touches it. It is slightly sore, but not seriously. "No, I'm okay." He slips on his glasses and they look at each other through rain-smeared lenses.

"You're absolutely positive?"

"Positive."

"Robin, I'm terribly sorry, *terribly* sorry."

He shakes his head. "It's nothing…nothing, Leo."

Turnham stares at him concernedly.

"You're sure?"

"I'm sure."

The man looks long and hard at Robin; then moves toward his car again.

"All right. If you're sure. If you have any problems…"

"I'm *fine*, Leo."

Turnham gives him a final stare, his face a confusion of anxiety and concern; then, finally, he nods, gets into the car again, and pulls away.

Shakily, Robin takes refuge in the nearest covered hall. He sits down against the wall of the building and slips off his glasses again. His knees are soaked. He is quivering.

"Excuse me," a voice says, "are you all right?"

He looks up, rubbing his glasses against a dry portion of his shirt. A dark figure, a young woman, is standing in the rain with an umbrella over her head. Without his glasses he cannot make out her face.

"Yes," he says. "Yes, thanks, I'm fine."

"I saw it happen," she says. "I was standing right over there. I thought for a minute you were done for!"

"Oh." He smiles weakly. Inside his mind he hears a clock ticking and sees the dark warehouse of time, the door open and all the mad birds screeching and fluttering from it. "No, I'm okay. It was no big deal."

"I'm glad."

"So am I, I guess."

The dark figure stands there a moment longer. Her silhouette is sliced through by the slivers of falling rain.

"Are you sure you're okay?" she says. "You look a little funny." She steps out of the downpour then and approaches him, leans down before him. She has dark hair which hangs down on either side of her face and big, round dark eyes.

"Look at me," she says. "How many fingers am I showing?"

"Two."

"And now?"

"One."

"Okay." She stands again. "You pass. That's the extent of my medical knowledge, anyway." She giggles.

"Well, thanks for the concern," Robin says, moving to slip on his glasses. "I appreciate it. By the way, what's your—"

But as he looks up, the world focused again, he sees her black-coated figure, umbrella over her head, disappearing into the mist and rain.

"—Your name?" he finishes weakly, to no one.

After a moment he stands, his mind empty. He brushes himself off and picks up his things; looks out at the parking lot and its slithering sea of moving lights. He pictures a foot stepping from a curb years ago. He stares into the gathering darkness and wonders vaguely when morning will come. He looks out toward the ocean then, an image crossing his mind of a faraway island, floating through a sunny sky toward a figure at its shore. But there is no sun here, he thinks, glancing again at the girl receding into the distance. No light at all. Only time, ticking with the precision of drums: drums for dark, unspeakable acts committed in an endless maze of shadows.

CHAPTER 3
ALL THE BEAUTIFUL DEMONS

And from then on, oh, we lived in a—world of light and shadow… But the shadow was almost as luminous as the light.

Tennessee Williams, *Suddenly Last Summer*

1

As he nears Greyfield the darkness becomes familiar. Sitting behind the steering wheel, the glow of the various gauges suffusing the interior of the car in a strange, unnatural green, he begins to recognize the lights and shadows and speechless forms outside: and knows that he is all but there. For the first time in a year, he is about to pass through Greyfield on his way to the turn-off that will lead him into the four-mile drive to Wind Point. It is nearly midnight. He had gotten a late start from the college, delayed by some unfinished paperwork; by the time he had finished loading the car the sun had begun to set. He felt an inexpressible melancholy as he pulled out of the parking lot. On balance, he could not say it had been a good year. At times it had been sheer agony. And yet, as the tall buildings of the school receded in his rear view mirror, he felt a sore lump form in the pit of his stomach: a lump which reminded him of curling up, fetal-style, on his dormitory bed in the darkness. Listening to the human buzz saw across the room. Thinking of Turnham. Terrible memories! But there was nonetheless a quality of nostalgia as the buildings disappeared into the distance behind him. Like someone who has gone through a war, he imagines. But of course someone who had gone through a war would know that he would never have to return to it; whereas Robin...

Lately he has thought a great deal of Priscilla Wilder. He has looked at her letter over and over again, studied the casual invitation which concludes it. It is tempting; tempting to take a week or two of this three-month break and drive down to Santa Barbara and visit her. Of course, he does not know how serious she had been in inviting him, but he certainly must do *something*. He hasn't a single plan for the long summer holiday. He and his father had discussed it over the phone a few days before: his father had told him it would be all right to stay there; but the prospect fills him with fear. The shadow-man! He pictures the bulging blue eyes, the hooked nose, the flabby skin on the neck, and feels his own heart pumping inside his chest. He pictures the house in the cul-de-sac: the glowing television, the glass tipped over onto the carpet, the staircase; the shouted voices, the footsteps. Of course, it is a year later now. Certainly everything will be different now.

But he does not really believe it. His father will be the same person he was. His voice will be the same. His clothes. His odor. Robin has tried to keep from thinking of this. Over the past few weeks, he has kept his mind filled with final exams, selling his textbooks, filling out forms, saying goodbye to teachers, helping Gawky Boy load his things when, one day, his parents (a man and woman who might have been siblings, so similar were their thick bodies, harshly angled shoulders, square heads) arrived for their son. It had been easy to keep his mind filled, to hold off the visions which now—as he sits in the car in the green glow, the radio softly playing pop music and the familiar shapes and shadows of Greyfield beginning to appear before him—rise like evil phoenixes from their well-deserved ashes.

He feels himself becoming afraid.

It's silly, he knows. Nothing in Wind Point is going to kill him. The mist will not reach out, encircle his neck and sap the life from him. The house in the cul-de-sac will not devour him. The sea, dashing itself against the rocks, will not call out in an alluring voice like a siren from an ancient Greek epic beckoning him to his death. He knows these things will not happen. But he also knows that there are whirlpools in Wind Point: swirling cyclones that threaten his sanity, his life: and it is only by keeping distance between himself and them that he can survive. It makes no difference that the whirlpools are entirely inside his brain, made up of ten million memories locking him in their deadly grip. They are there nonetheless. And as he pulls closer and closer, realizing that at any moment he will see the sign leading him away from the mainland and onto the old Scully Road, toward the house in the cul-de-sac and the shadow-man and terror and catastrophe, he slows the car. His hands quiver on the wheel. He applies the brake gently and pulls to the side of the road and the car sits there, idling motionlessly.

Suddenly he wants to scream. He shouldn't be like this! He's nearly nineteen years old! He shouldn't shake, quiver, become speechless at the idea of approaching his old home. He knows that he is sick; that he is mad; but he had thought that, with age, the memories would recede and he would be able to function without…without the terror. Without his heart slamming against his chest. His breath coming short. Fantasies of the giant glowering clock rising before him. He is suddenly disgusted with himself, revolted by his own self-pity.

He steps out of the car and into the cold night air and paces angrily, restlessly. Somehow he must stop all this. The cycle must end. He must pull himself up from the whirlpool. But how? When it has dominated him, controlled him for so long? His entire life!

And, if he were to do it, banish the swirling monsters, what then would be left for him?

He stops for a moment, thinking about this. What if he were to destroy the whirlpool...and find nothing beyond it? Just a blank screen, void, absence? How then could he live? What would there be for him?

He stares into the darkness. The oily ocean is before him. His father is out there, he knows, just a few miles along the Scully Road, waiting. Expecting him. Perhaps he would even have cooked a nice dinner, kept it warm for him. Perhaps there would be balloons and welcome-home presents. Perhaps...he looks at the ground, the damp soil underneath his feet. Of course his father would have done no such thing. It is midnight. His father is always asleep by midnight. When Robin pulls up to the house in the cul-de-sac, it will be dark. Dead. He will have to fish the old key from his pocket and fit it into the lock and open the door. He will have to switch on the light in the foyer and bring in his things. He will have to find his way up the staircase, alone, to his room. And then the lights will all be turned off again and everything will be exactly as before. Silent. Dark. Timeless. He does not know if he can do it. Does not know if he can lie there again, in that bed, that darkness, listening to the pepper tree rustling outside the window and thinking of Melissa Rosselli and Uncle Jasper and little Star-eyes and waiting uncertainly for the sound of unsteady footsteps in the night...He shakes his head suddenly.

He climbs into his car again, switches on the heater, and pulls away from the curb. But he does not drive toward the sign which he knows will soon appear: shaped like an arrow, it reads *Wind Point 4 mi.* He turns instead in the other direction. He has no specific, conscious destination in mind: merely turns onto streets slowly, at random, for several minutes. But after some time he finds himself pulling into a public parking lot and switching off the engine; and, although he is not sure where he is, the place is familiar. He sits staring straight forward at a line of night-darkened shops thinking vaguely that he has been here before, that he knows this place, but unable, for many minutes, to think of where he is. His mind is curiously frozen. Fragments slips across it: slivers of dreams, splinters of memory; isolated phrases, odd colors: but the pieces fail to coalesce into anything coherent. They remain fractured, meaningless, confused. He feels adrift; rather, he imagines, as an amnesiac must feel, with nothing but strange echoes to help him find his way in the dark. He stares into the night, trying to isolate within his mind some thread which he can wind out, building one image and sound upon another, to a sensible line of thought. But the thoughts will not arrange themselves so neatly. Turnham's voice and the touch of his hands tumble into his mother's *G'night, baby*, and her fumbling fingers at his pajama buttons; Star-eyes, squealing and clinging to him as they fly down a hill on his bicycle, becomes Gawky Boy stumbling into the dormitory room in the middle of the night; the hiss of the radiator in Mrs. Klibo's library melts into the sound of the river and he and Priscilla staring toward the doe across the field in the long grass. He shakes his head. Hears Davy Carp's voice. Sees the cherry blossom paperweight and hears his Uncle Jasper's raspy grumble, feels Sonya's knees touching his own under the table; hears Marylou Kirk's giddy voice and sees her vacuous eyes, the silly animal posters in her room, feels the crinkly material of her dress. Hears voices in his parents' bedroom. Sees his own image in the mirror, naked, hatred in his reflected face, the butcher knife raised in the air.

    He steps from the car. His inner confusion gives him a strange sensation of euphoria. Without knowing where he is going, he walks toward the line of shops. He has been here before, but his mind will not make the connection: refuses to acknowledge its own memory until he is standing directly before it, looking at it.

Mounted in one of the windows is a large, light-paled photograph of his father. A dim bulb illuminates it and the legend, written in bold, fearless black print underneath: *I Can Insure Your Future*. Beneath this is his father's name and the oddly threatening title: *Agent*. The photograph is not new; it is a studio portrait, rather stilted, from six or seven years before. He stares closely at it. The grin, intended to be warm and inviting, looks to Robin more like a grimace. The man's hair was fuller then, darker; the skin, tighter; the eyes more clear. The changes are obvious, and shocking. Had there ever been a time when his father had actually looked like this? When this had been the appearance Robin had been accustomed to? It seems impossible. Yet he knows it is true. Back when he was twelve or thirteen, this had been what his father had looked like. As Robin stares at the old photograph in the window he begins to feel frightened in a new way: for it is as if, comparing the two images of his father, some deadly demon had swooped down upon the man, drained the life from him, made his skin sag and his eyes blur, made his features grow disproportionate and hard, bled him until his skin became yellow and pallid. Like a scene in an old film after the vampire receives the stake through his heart and the body dusts away, first slowly, then faster and faster; and yet here, somehow, it is also reversed, his father is not only the vampire but also his victim, mute and helpless in the face of the terror. Of the two, Robin realizes, the latter is more true. His father is equally a victim of the ticking clock, the arms spiraling madly in their arcs. The thought has never really occurred to him before: his father, being a man like other men (though the idea is nearly inconceivable), is subject to the same laws of existence, rules of disaster. His father is growing older. His father, eventually, is going to die. The idea is unreal, and yet it fills him with a heady feeling. *I Can Insure Your Future*. And yet the man's own future, Robin thinks, is even now swirling darkly into eternity.

The Unspoken

He pictures himself at his father's funeral. The church, sepulchral, cavernous, hollow, rings with the sound of the minister's voice: the organ plays soft hymns which reverberate throughout the hall: the casket, polished oak with a silver satin lining, is before him. He is the only one in the church, and he hears the preacher's voice asking him to come forward for a final viewing. He walks toward the casket. As he walks, the distance between himself and the oak container seems only to grow, to become infinite; and soon he thinks he will never arrive there, that the minister and the organist will give up and go home, the lights will be switched off, the doors locked, and he will be left there, struggling to reach the box, walking as if on a treadmill toward unspeakable, unattainable things, alone in the empty darkness of the huge hall. But finally he is there. Finally he looks down at his father's body lying in the box. It is unnaturally colored: the cheeks rosy red, the forehead tanned and healthy. The man is dressed in an impeccable black suit, such as Robin has never seen him wear. His hands are folded across his chest; the veins, thick and ropy like worms, shine pallidly beneath the skin. The organ falls silent; the minister stops speaking. Robin can hear nothing but a slight dripping, somewhere far away, echoing and re-echoing throughout the church. He stares at his father, at the large forehead, closed eyes, drooping nose, the lips now permanently fixed in cold stillness. Then a voice, mysteriously distant and distorted as if it were being heard over a telephone, whispers: "Kiss him goodbye." Robin's eyes open wide. He wants to turn, but cannot; his eyes are fixed on the man's face. "Kiss him goodbye," the voice says again. He does not want to. Suddenly he is very young, very small, dressed in his neat blue suit with his mother behind him and there are people all over in the church, some of them weeping, some silently staring, all of them waiting for him to finish his turn in the line, and his mother is saying, "Kiss him goodbye, honey." He stares down at his father's still body in the oak box and, heart jumping inside his chest like a bird, leans toward it. They are nearly together. His lips are almost upon the man's skin. But then, just as they are about to touch the face, his father's eyes, blue and glowing, snap open. Robin tries to scream. Tears himself from the line. Stumbles blindly toward the exit. He hears a screaming, but it is not his own. It is his father's. His father is sitting up in the coffin screaming like a madman, wordlessly, hatefully, and the scream fills the echoing hall, mixes with the organ as Robin pulls and pulls at the locked church door—

I Can Insure Your Future.

Robin stares at the lit photograph in the darkness. The sky is quite clear, he sees, glancing up; the steel curtain has disappeared. Tomorrow's skies, he knows, will be brilliant. But not in Wind Point. It is still only early June, too soon for the curtain to have yet parted there. In Wind Point will still only be the gemless, colorless blanket. *We'll wrap them around ourselves,* she says; *and we'll float right up to the moon.* But it was a lie. They never floated anywhere. They only sat and mouldered right here on terra firma. He thinks of it as he looks at the photograph again. Lies. An infinity of lies. She had lied to him for years. They both had. They had lied to him every morning when he came downstairs and sat at the breakfast table and no one said a word about the night before—and there was always a night before: glasses spilling onto the floor, shouted accusations, fumbling with the door key at two in the morning, misaligned pajama buttons, slurred words, bumping into the wall of the hallway, slurping cold stew from a bowl, deadly snake-masks: there was always a night before, about which they would say nothing, which would disappear into the blackness of the past without so much as an acknowledgment of its ever happening, an admission that Robin had not gone mad, that he had seen these things, they had happened, they were as real as the three of them sitting at the breakfast table now in the apricot light. More real, in fact. Because it was true, the actual thing, not an unspoken mirage; not a silent dismissal, a mute denial. Not warm sweet buns and sugar flakes falling onto his plate and big cold glasses of milk. That was all lies. There was only one truth, but it lived in a different country, an unfamiliar landscape, which Robin could not locate. He had tried. He had thought, before, that it would be there at the college: when he had escaped, at last, the house in the cul-de-sac and all that was associated with it: but, finally, that was lies too. The empty promises of freedom, intellectual enlightenment, "personal growth"; the irrelevant, tedious classes; Turnham. All lies. There had been no freedom, no learning, no discovery of anything. Only boredom, busy work, the illusion of escape when in fact, every year, the school would close down again and he would find himself back here, contemplating the infinite four-mile drive back to Wind Point. He had thought he would somehow burst free, pass beyond the clouds to a smooth gem-clear blue, but here he was again, lost, left standing alone in the darkness.

He turns from the photograph.

His breath is shallow and uneven. He does not know if he can do it. He thinks about that house, four miles away. Pictures the driveway, the foyer, the rooms, feels the atmosphere there, breathes the odors, listens to the silence. It fills him with a kind of vertigo. He feels afraid; sees, within his mind, the whirlpool, vast, treacherous, growing like a malignant cell, reaching out to engulf him, drain away his life, leave him a sallow husk. He sits down on the curb and runs his hands through his hair. His nerves are jumping inside his skin. His palms are sticky and cold. Three months, he tries to tell himself. Only three months. He can stay in his room, he can go to movies, the library: three months won't kill him. No one will choke or stab him. He will survive. But will he? Or is this another lie? He cannot be sure of anything anymore; truth, lies, where he is, who he is. He feels dizzy. He senses his consciousness beginning to swirl. He puts his head in his hands and tries to breathe. It is difficult, nearly like drawing water into his nostrils. He knows he must do something; must break the descending spiral; but he does not know how to do it. How to free himself. He knows there must be a way but he is a blind man stumbling around in the dark; he has sat in the hallway too long staring at the sunrise and his mother has come up to him and seen his milky, vacant eyes, blinded forever, useless, like Oedipus. Or so he used to imagine. He did not realize, then, that it would not take any lengthy hallway vigils, no long stares into blazing sunlight, to cripple him. He is already blind and helpless, he knows, stumbling, always stumbling, toward an unknown door.

He looks toward his car in the parking lot. Inside it are boxes with books, cassette tapes, a portable radio, school papers, clothes. His empire, he thinks sourly. His estate. His entire world, really, packed into the microcosm of the brown car: letters, shoes, unfinished stories, finished stories, a camera, a small blue box containing his mother's old jewelry. He had drained his California bank account down to nearly nothing just before leaving, since there was no branch in Wind Point: he has about five hundred dollars on him, cold hard cash, crisp greenbacks. He has not decided what to do with all of it. It is more than he needs, certainly, for three months in Wind Point. For what is there to buy in Wind Point? A hamburger, an occasional milkshake? A ticket to a movie? He frowns.

Of course, a thought has long occurred to him, caressed his mind like balm. But he does not think he could really do it. And yet it continues to float to the surface of his consciousness. He has been thinking of it for months: he could, he knows, not return to Wind Point at all. He has a car, all his things, cash. He could go somewhere else. Anywhere else. Of course it might infuriate his father; but then his father would be far away. Perhaps he would never see his father again. Perhaps he would not even leave a forwarding address. Perhaps…the prospect fills him with fear. But, as he sits there at the curb, all the years of lies sweeping over him like wind, the glow of his father's photograph illuminating his own body and face, he suddenly realizes with perfect certainty that he cannot go back there. He has come within four miles of his destination but can go no farther. Nothing will kill him, his intellect tells him; but he cannot trust his intellect. Something may well kill him if he goes back to that place, that darkness. He already feels a force, malevolent, swirling, even here, even in Greyfield. What might it be like in Wind Point? Impossible to imagine. But he cannot, certainly, go back to it. He cannot return to that house and the flat footsteps in the dark. The staircase, the doors closing on empty rooms. The malignant cloud of silence that hovers within the rooms, roaming at will, smothering him. He cannot go back there. To go back there would be to die. He would die as surely as if he swallowed handfuls of pills and floated out of the world on a wave of oblivion. He cannot go back there.

He looks toward his car. He stands. He sees himself opening the door; closing it; turning the key in the ignition. He sees himself pulling out of the parking lot and the glowing photograph in the window receding into blackness. He drives all night.

2

Eighteen hours later it is dark again and he begins to see the lights of his destination rising before him: not the few straggling, lonely bulbs of Greyfield or Wind Point, but thousands of vivid electric stars, like a great sprawling Christmas tree laid before him on a bed of night. He has stopped only for a few hours during the entire journey, for hamburgers, coffee, gas; unable to keep his eyes open any longer, he had slept for two hours outside Salinas. Otherwise he has kept himself in continuous motion since pulling out of the parking lot in Greyfield. He had felt, somehow, that to stop for any length of time, to arrest his progress in mid-flight, might be to allow the past to swarm up behind him and envelop him and carry him back to that place, that darkness. Which he could not allow. So he had kept his hands wrapped tightly around the steering wheel as he neared the Oregon border, passed through darkened Crescent City, drove by—with barely a flicker of recognition—his university, and then entered the unfamiliar country: the hundred tiny villages between the redwoods and San Francisco. He passed by them with indifference, hardly seeing them. The sun had begun to rise, it was morning by the time he reached San Francisco; and, although he saw the city, drove across the Golden Gate Bridge, he did not stop or think anything of it. He kept on driving as the sun rose in the sky and the day grew warmer and sleepier and finally he had allowed himself two hours at the side of the road outside Salinas. Then he had continued, his eyes red now and puffy with fatigue, his muscles drenched with pain, his skin—as he saw it in a gas station bathroom—pale and drawn like a ghost's. He had kept on. Motion, that was the key. Not, he thinks, to be caught in stagnant stillness, but to keep on, ever-moving, ever-roaming, like a shark wandering endlessly through the murky dark.

But now, he sees, the end of the road is near; only minutes away. The freeway exit signs for Santa Barbara are coming toward him: LaCumbre, Mission, Carillo; he knows that he will have to make a decision, leave the now comfortable and familiar tunnel of darkness that is Highway 101 and find his way…to what? It is just past eight in the evening. The closer he gets, the more he realizes the silliness of his action—what if she is not home, what if she has no room, no desire to have him there? There are a thousand variables. Still, he has a contingency plan: if it becomes obvious that he is not welcome there, he will stay only overnight. Then he will move on to—what? That he does not know. Wherever a car and four hundred seventy-five dollars can take him.

He chooses a freeway exit at random and finds a gas station, pulls up to it and asks directions from the attendant there; he is given a complex maze of turns and counter-turns to follow. He writes it down carefully, noticing the clear, warm darkness of the town. He wishes it were daylight: the air is fresh, clean, and he wonders if the town is as well. He gets back into his car, rolls down the window, and drives off. He pulls back onto the glitteringly lit freeway again and sails along it for a few miles, then exits; and begins searching the streets for Priscilla Wilder's home.

He finds himself in a part of town that is very nearly a slum—decaying buildings, battered cars on blocks, ill-clad children running around the roads. Every half-block a different blasting stereo dominates the air. The streets are packed with people, blacks and Hispanics mostly, and as he drives along there are great pools of dark on the street caused by malfunctioning or shattered street lights. He finds it somewhat frightening, but keeps driving: until, at last, off Micheltorana Street, he finds what he is looking for.

It is a big three-story brick structure which looks like nothing so much as a penitentiary. There is only one entrance, at the front, and few windows. Robin might have taken it for a warehouse. But the street number is unarguable; and so he pulls his car up a block away, shuts off the engine, and climbs out of the vehicle. He locks it carefully and then looks toward the great brick building.

He realizes suddenly that the blaring rock music that he has been hearing for the past minute is coming from the building: and, at the same moment, he realizes that it is not a stereo. It is a live band, hard rock, with gnashing guitars and a singer bellowing:

> Give it to me *now*!
> Give it to me *now*!
> Baby, baby,
> Give it to me *now*!

Robin scowls and walks toward the place. A few of the passersby glance at him but he averts his eyes. He wonders if it is so obvious, as if a placard were strung around his neck reading: NAIVE SMALL TOWN TOURIST. He reaches the entrance of the building, which consists of several brick steps leading up to a dark foyer. A group of Hispanics block the entrance.

"Excuse me," Robin shouts over the music, heart jumping at his throat. "Does Priscilla Wilder live here?"

The mute doorstops glance at each other, then one of them—a powerfully-built teenager with a tight-fitting tank top shirt and jeans—nods lazily into the building. Robin swallows and steps past them. He wonders vaguely if he will ever step out again.

Inside in the dim light he sees that the entire downstairs consists of one giant room, occupied at this moment by a shouting and milling multitude numbering at least forty. The music, crushing in volume, comes from upstairs. The room is clouded with cigarette and marijuana smoke. Most of the men and long-haired and -bearded types in blue jeans, but there are many exceptions: older men with formless polyester suits; well-dressed, well-groomed executive types; the women are a potpourri of every style imaginable, from bangled and jewel-bedecked types to ones in mini-dresses and sheer black stockings like prostitutes. He wonders if they really are prostitutes. He wonders who all these people are. He feels painfully ignorant, a dirt farmer at his first city-slicker's dance. For a few minutes he stands in a corner, uncertain of how to proceed, overhearing snatches of conversation:

Tweed-jacked professor-type to black woman in business suit: "...And so Annemarie was going around telling people her wonderful new beau was an engineer. Turned out he was a diesel mechanic, but she went off to South Africa with him anyway."

Young tank-like Mexican with crew-cut to leather-vested man with sunglasses: "In Greece, I hear the old men sit at the table in the restaurants and play with themselves while they look at the little boys."

Long-haired man in denim, passing joint to another such (voice suffused with awe): "I know what Heaven is, man. It's a place where you just get fucked-up all the time...and Eric Clapton plays guitar twenty-four hours a day."

He wants to ask someone the whereabouts of Priscilla ("Cissy," he keeps silently correcting himself); but is so intimidated by the crowd that for a while he simply stands in the corner, staring and hoping he will see her. Of course, he realizes, he might not even be able to recognize her. He knows he will have to ask someone. He glances around for a likely candidate.

To one side of him there appears a tall man, or something resembling a man, dressed in denim rags, unshaven, with marijuana joints wrapped in his long hair like curlers.

"Hey, *dude!*" he say, his rheumy eyes glistening. He leans close to Robin. "Kansas City, last year, right? Grateful Dead? Jesus Christ, was Garcia *hot* or *what?*"

Robin looks at him, his brain beginning to feel strangely light. He shakes his head. "Sorry," he calls out over the music, "it wasn't me!"

The man looks at Robin again and grins. His teeth are black and rotted. He nods: "You're right, dude! Not Dead Kansas City. Stones New York! When Keith Richards was so fucked up he kept falling off the stage. Sounded like shit. But what can you expect from somebody who looks like Keith Richards?"

Robin shakes his head again.

The stranger scowls. "But I *know* I know you, man."

"I don't think so."

"Where you from?"

"Oregon."

"*Oregon? Shit!* No *wonder* I know you! *Incredible* grass in Oregon."

"We haven't met," Robin says. "I'm sure I'd remember."

"Well, consider yourself blessed, man, to be comin' from Oregon. That's God's Country up there. Grass with real *cojones*."

"Listen," Robin says, supposing this wastrel is as good as any, "do you know somebody here named Cissy? She's supposed to live here."

"Huh?"

"Cissy. Cissy Wilder. A girl. Does she live here?"

"Cissy?" He looks around. "Yeah, she's around, with Koofie somewhere. I dunno where." He begins to unwrap a joint from his hair. "See, man," he says, carefully lighting it, "I got all this weed arranged scientifically. Down back of my head is the Mexican stuff. Southern, you know. South of the border. So that's like the back of my head, like, you know, south." He inhales. "Then shit from Maui, that's west, see, so it's here on the left. Then Humboldt County and Oregon, that's north, so that's all right here, at the top." He points.

Robin smiles slightly. "But that would only work if you were always facing north."

"Huh?"

"If you're facing south, then north would be behind you."

Marijuana Man's eyes seem to glaze for a moment. Then he says: "Hey...hey, you're *right*. Holy shit. Now I gotta come up with a new system."

Robin chuckles. The blaring music is making his head ache.

"Here," the man says, offering the joint to Robin.

"No thanks."

"Hey, c'mon, man. Classic Maui Wowee. I ain't handing you shit. This is for real."

Robin's eyes move over the room and he wonders about the accuracy of the statement. The sweet smoke is starting to make him dizzy: but he is slowly relaxing, the tension easing out of him. The room is quite warm, nearly balmy: he has an image of himself as butter melting in a pan. He accepts the offering, inhales shallowly; remembers the first time, by the river, the glittering light of the water.

Marijuana Man is grinning and nodding. "Nice?"

Robin smiles, hands it back to him. "Yeah." And it is: he feels rather as if gravity were loosing its hold upon him. "Potent."

"Well," he says, inhaling again and passing the thing back to Robin, "all merchandise you see here on the trading floor—" he gestures to his head—"is available for purchase. Instant delivery."

Robin laughs. "I guess not. I really just need to find Cissy."

"Yeah—" he looks around the room—"maybe she's upstairs. Let's take a look."

Marijuana Man leads Robin through the crowded maze of people toward a dark staircase. The music, as they come near the stairs, is deafeningly loud—not even music now, but a sheer crush of distortion. The staircase is unlit and nearly as crowded as the main floor. A man in a shapeless brown suit is passed out on the lower stairs and they step around him.

"Nice company, huh?" the man shouts as they make their way up. "You ever been here before?"

"No. I just got in. From Oregon."

He nods. "I thought so."

Robin pictures the placard around his neck again, in more detail: NAIVE SMALL TOWN TOURIST. PRONE TO IDIOTIC BEHAVIOR. PLEASE DO NOT FEED.

When they reach the next flight Robin is shocked to discover that they have still not found the source of the music: there is still one more flight. Already the sound is so loud that it seems to bounce around inside his skull, threatening his equilibrium. This floor is not so crowded: but he can make out nothing beyond that fact, as it is almost completely dark.

"*Is Cissy here?*" Marijuana Man shouts over the din. But not far enough over: there is no response. At last he stops someone, a young man in blue jeans and no shirt, and says something to him Robin cannot hear. Then he turns to Robin and points upward. "One more flight, amigo!"

As they head toward the stairs again they are stopped by two youngish men, surfer types: clean-shaven, blonde, floral-printed shirts.

"*Carl!*" one of them shouts to Marijuana Man.

"Steve, my man!" They laugh and shake hands. "How was the waves?"

"Nothin'. Shit today."

"Where were you?"

"El Cap. We were gonna drive down to Malibu but we were too fuckin' lazy."

"*I* wanted to," the other surfer says, drinking from a flask of something.

"*You* wanted to!" the first surfer laughs. "All *you* wanted to do was go to Menotti's and get fucked up. Jesus Christ."

"Did you have a better idea?"

"Yeah. I said, 'Let's drive down to Malibu.' You said, 'Nah, I just wanna go to Menotti's and get fucked up.' "

They laugh. The second surfer looks at Robin: "Hi," he says. He offers Robin the flask. "Have some."

Robin's lightheadedness has engulfed his entire body. The sweet smoke of the room is swirling around him, soaking into him, making him feel as if he were a surfer too, but not on water: rather on pure, soft clouds. He also feels the fatigue settling into his bones and brain again. He is dreadfully tired, sleepy. He accepts the flask nearly without thinking—he is more or less beyond thinking at this point—and swallows.

It is as if he were a circus performer who swallows burning spears. The jolt nearly knocks him down and he coughs, trying not to. The surfers laugh. Marijuana Carl shakes his head.

"Shouldn't drink that rotgut shit, man!" he says, taking the flask and swallowing.

Eventually, after several more swallows, they take their leave of the surfers. Robin is no longer entirely clear as to where he is or why. The electric distortion bounces around inside his skull and in the dimness he sees figures flitting in and out of his vision. He stumbles as they mount the stairs. It occurs to him that in the fifteen or twenty minutes he has been in the building he has managed to get both drunk and high…Eighteen hours, he thinks, of driving and an empty stomach. They climb the stairs and the distorted music rings in his ears, vibrates them. His vision is growing blurry. And yet he feels quite good. In fact, all he really wants to do is smoke more and drink more. He remembers, dimly, sitting in front of his father's photograph in Greyfield, ten thousand years ago. He has entered a different world now, somehow. He is not even sure where he is, but he is somewhere that is not Wind Point: hence, he is somewhere good. But is that right?

They arrive at the top of the stairs and Robin sees before him, at last, the source of the monstrous din. A full band is on this big, open floor, amplifiers around them. There are five of them: a singer, guitar, bass, keyboards, drums. The noise is nothing short of breathtaking. Around the band are more people milling, laughing, drinking.

"She must be up here!" Carl shouts into his ear. "Let's look around!"

He follows his companion blindly through the semi-darkness. Carl meets more of his friends. Robin is offered something else to drink. He drinks. He notices that people, couples, are lounging around up here on big pillows. Suddenly he feels he would love to collapse into one of them and sleep forever. He feels he is not quite in the room, but floating somewhere above it, looking down on everything. His brain is swirling.

At last, for the first time since he arrived, the band blasts a final note and abruptly stops playing. There is applause. Robin stares blankly at the band while Carl converses with someone. He watches the guitar player, fiddling methodically with his amplifier; the guitar player, with dark hair and eyes the shape of teardrops, looks up at him suddenly, absently smiling; goes back to his amplifier.

"Man!" Carl cries out suddenly. "The quarry is within range!"

Robin looks to where Carl is pointing. Dimly, in the distance—or what seems the distance, in his current state—he sees what he makes out to be two women lying on some of the big pillows that are scattered around the room. He cannot see anything of them but their dark, hazy forms. He is overcome suddenly by vertigo: feels himself growing afraid. But he follows Carl through the maze of people until they are next to the women.

At first he cannot even tell which one might be his cousin. It does not help that his vision keeps blurring. But finally she comes into focus: a pretty, big-built girl in cute pink painter's overalls. Her eyes are round and dark; her hair is an attractive black bowl around her face. He looks at her, tries to smile as Carl says "Cissy! Someone here lookin' for you." Then he looks back at Robin: "I've delivered the goods, man."

"Thanks," Robin says. "Thanks a lot."

"Any time, dude. And any time you're in need..." He gestures to his head.

"Thanks."

Carl abruptly disappears.

Robin looks back toward Priscilla, who is looking at him strangely. Finally she stands.

"I know you, don't I?"

He grins stupidly. "Maybe you do."

Her voice is deep, husky, almost a man's voice. She is scowling in thought. "Are you who I think you are?"

"Depends on who you think I am."

"Robin?"

He grins, trying to remain upright. "At your service."

"Robin!" She suddenly throws her arms around him. "It's wonderful to see you! I recognized you right off! You haven't changed much—"

"Neither have you," he says, or tries to say, uncertain of whether the words are coming out or not. "You look…Uh, great…"

"Hey, everybody!" Priscilla shouts, taking advantage of the band's momentary silence. "Look who's here! This is my cousin Robin, from Oregon!"

A number of people in the room look toward him, seem to smile: but they all begin to blur suddenly, dangerously, and he feels his legs begin to fold up beneath him like twin accordions. He realizes that he is about to fall down in a stupor. The thought is quite amusing to him and he giggles as he feels, instant to instant, the strength of his legs fading, collapsing. He supposes he should say something to these people before he goes, however. Something to leave a good impression. After all, he wouldn't want everybody to think he is a mere falling-down drunk. Even if that is what he is. Must leave a good impression, he thinks, giggling inwardly, feeling the legs coming apart, crumbling like ancient Roman pillars. Very important. His daddy taught him that: *Leave a good impression.* And what Daddy says must be true. He tries, therefore, to find some words to say, but it is very difficult, because his legs are in the process of collapsing, and that seems to take all his concentration. Still. He will try: and he hears his voice, suffused with giggles, slur the words *God bless us, everyone!* before he tumbles into the pillows, and sleep.

3

"I must say, Robin, you have quite a knack for first impressions!"

Priscilla: she blurs into focus slowly as he opens his eyes. Light is streaming into the room too brightly and he closes his eyes again, rubs them; groans.

"What time is it?"

"Eight-ish."

He keeps his eyes closed for a long moment and feels himself uneasily drifting over a swirling sea. The previous night exists only in fragments: a door, a staircase. As he lies there, stilly, it begins to reassemble itself inside his mind, he begins to recall music, voices, conversations, until he almost thinks he remembers what happened. Not entirely, but almost.

He opens his eyes again, to slits, and tries to puzzle out where he is. Everything is still blurry. Priscilla, a vague, pink-clad form, is standing at the corner of the room leaning over something. Next to her is the bright window. Beneath it, a mattress lying on the floor covered with tangled sheets. A cheap plastic dresser hangs open, displaying clothes on hangers, shoes on its floor. Robin himself is lying on the floor, a blanket and some pillows under him, a sheet on top. He groans again and tries to sit up on his elbows; fails, collapses down again.

He hears a giggle from the corner and then the sound of footsteps coming near; suddenly his nostrils are filled with the odor of coffee.

"Have some java," she says, sitting next to him. "I put sugar in but we don't have any milk."

He opens his eyes again and looks at her. The focus is beginning to improve slightly.

"Where am I?" he asks weakly. Something thick and hard seems to block his throat.

"You're at our place. Second floor. Remember, you were here last night. You had to pass through here to get upstairs."

He scowls, shakes his head. It makes him dizzy, so he stops. Looks again at Priscilla.

"Here," she says. "Take your coffee."

He succeeds in sitting up this time and he takes the plastic mug from her hands. He says, "Thank you," and after a moment adds: "I'm not sure exactly what happened last night."

"Well," she says, grinning, "after you made your spectacular, shall I say, debut, I asked Carl...by the way, Carl is a real lowlife. You really don't want to be around him. He keeps getting arrested. Anyway, I asked him. He said some various, uh, illicit substances did you in. Almost instantly."

He nods.

"It was pretty funny," she adds.

Robin sips at the coffee, the pieces of memory assembling themselves around him.

"So why didn't you tell me you were coming, you bozo? You could have sent me a letter."

"I did," he lies.

"Oh. Well, I never got it. The mail service around here isn't all it's cracked up to be, and it's cracked up to be absolutely nothing."

He smiles, begins patting his body to find his glasses.

"Here they are," she says. She reaches to an upside-down milk crate just to the left of them. He slips the wire rims onto his face, squints for a moment, blinks, and looks at her. It is the first time he has seen her clearly, or almost clearly, since arriving. Five years have done amazing things to her appearance. Her face is still round, with the curious close-set eyes, but the face has softened, become feminine; not a beautiful face, certainly, but an attractive one, a bit heavy but with a fine grace. Her hair is no longer the unkempt, tomboyish mess it had been before, though she still wears it in bangs across her forehead. But now the bangs have been professionally cut, and her hair, bowl-like, seems sculpted around her head. Big gold hoops dangle from her ears. Her body is large, as big as Robin's, she is flat-chested; and yet the effect is one of a quite attractive young woman.

"It's great to see you," she says. "I was really hoping you'd come sometime."

"Well," he smiles groggily, "here I am, spectacular entrance and all." He sips at the coffee.

"How long you here for?"

"I don't really know. I don't have any specific plans...But if it's any problem, I don't have to stay here. I mean I know I've just *descended* on you. I can..."

"Oh jeez, it's no problem, at least if you don't mind sleeping on the floor. When does your school start up again?"

"August. End of August."

"Well, you're welcome to stay here as long as you want. You can see—" she glances around the room—"it's a bit Spartan, but it's a roof, anyway."

Robin looks around the big, empty room. "This isn't even an apartment, is it?"

"It's a warehouse."

"Why do you live here?"

"Are you kidding? Do you have any idea what rents go for in Santa Barbara?"

"Still—living in a warehouse..."

"It's not so bad," she smiles. She brushes through her black hair with her hand. "There's electricity, at least. And free concerts some nights...see, they use the third floor as a rehearsal space for bands. They rent it out. They guy who owns the place is this French guy who uses the main floor for his own storage. The second floor he rents to us and the third is for the bands. See, he owns a club in Isla Vista, the Burning Zombie, and the bands that play there practice here."

"Is it legal?" Robins asks. "Living here?"

"Oh, probably not. But it *is* cheap. Koofie and I—Koofie's my roommate, you met her last night—but you probably don't remember—can live on practically nothing."

He looks around again. "There isn't even a bathroom here."

"There's one downstairs. See, all the modern amenities."

They are silent for a moment. Robin drinks the coffee.

"So how's your dad?" Priscilla asks.

Robin shrugs. "All right, the last time I saw him. How about your parents?"

"They're fine. Same ol', same ol', you know. Not changes. My brothers are all in college now. The *same* college. Southern Methodist. In Texas."

They are silent again for a long moment.

"What do your parents think of you living here?" Robin asks.

"Well, they don't exactly *know*," she says. "See, we didn't part on the best of terms, you know?"

Just then he hears footsteps coming up the stairs. A dark, slender young woman enters the room.

"Hi!" Priscilla says.

"Hola," she answers. "You guys still lazing around here? Cissy, I thought you would've long since taken our guest for a tour." She goes to Priscilla and kisses her on the cheek. The woman's hair is blonde, remarkably so against her dark, rum-colored skin; her eyes are hidden behind octagonal sunglasses. She wears a tattered striped t-shirt, provocatively ripped up one side, with cut-off blue jeans and white sandals.

"Don't blame me," Priscilla says. "Blame the prostrate form lying there on the floor. He just woke up." They kiss again, and the slender girl looks at him, smiling. "Hi."

"Hi."

"My name's Koofie Mortenson. It was going to be 'Koffee,' like what you're drinking only spelled with a 'K,' except that on my birth certificate somebody made a mistake and nobody ever bothered to correct it." Her voice, Robin notes, is high and wispy; the exact opposite of Priscilla's.

Priscilla giggles. "Koofie doesn't wait for people to ask about her name—"

"—Because *everybody* does," she finishes.

"You can call her 'Louise,' though," Priscilla goes on. "That's her middle name."

"You may *not* call me Louise," the girl says, breaking away from Priscilla and moving over to the hot plate, pouring herself coffee. "That is, if you want to stay with us in this place."

"Well," Robin smiles, "maybe I should just be safe and not call you anything."

"Yes," Koofie agrees, "but that would be rude, and you wouldn't want to be rude like your cousin here."

"I'm not rude," Priscilla says. "Just obnoxious."

Robin grins, watching them.

"You're rude *and* obnoxious."

"Nuh-uh. Now you're telling lies." She grins at Robin. "She's telling you lies."

"Well, you guys," Koofie says, pouring sugar into the coffee, "I don't know why you're sitting around here doing nothing when you could be down at the beach or shopping or any number of things. It's a beautiful day."

"Talk to my cousin here," Priscilla says. "He's the one holding up the whole operation."

"Have a heart. After all, he *was* potted."

"I know!"

They look at him. His face flushes.

"Well, I'm not potted now," he proclaims,. Standing suddenly, boldly. A sensation of dizziness rushes into his head immediately but it passes. "No, I'm ready for whatever. Maybe if you could just point me to the bathroom…"

They borrow an extra bicycle from a neighbor down the street and the three of them ride through the downtown area toward the beach. The day is perfect: clear, crisp, the salt air fresh and invigorating. The town itself, Robin thinks, is lovely: the clean, Spanish-style buildings, the shops, the old houses, the views of the ocean and the mountains. The air clears his head quickly and he feels almost euphoric. They stay to the smaller streets as much as they can, so that they can all ride side-by-side, and Priscilla and Koofie point out things of interest: historic houses, well-known gardens. They stop at the county courthouse, a big, cavernous old building with polished wood floors, and wander in its cool silence, step up into the bell tower where they can see the entire vista of Santa Barbara laid out before them like jewels in a sea of blue. Robin's head is remarkably clear, free of the old thoughts, the old darknesses. It is as if, finally, he has shucked off like a useless husk the ancient, dry years, and found himself here, new, free. He wears a t-shirt, short pants, and thongs, and thinks to himself how far he has come, in distance, yes, but most of all in his own mindscape, from the land of the steel curtain and cold fog and footsteps in the dark. Those things are gone, utterly, completely. One simple act—getting into his car and going—has allowed him to shake it all off, Forever? He wonders. There is, of course, the problem of money. Also his school. And of course his father: interesting, he thinks—he has not so much as considered the idea of how he will tell the man where he is, what he is doing. He supposes his father must be concerned right now. Perhaps he has even called the school, only to learn: *He's left the dormitory.* And so visions would perhaps begin crossing the man's mind: his son, bloody and mangled, his car wrapped around a telephone pole. Eventually the police would be called. *Robin Withers, 18. Vanished somewhere on way north to Wind Point.* It gives him a peculiar feeling of power, a sensation, he realizes, he has never experienced with regard to his father. To be perfectly in control of a situation of which his father knows nothing. There is something heady in the thought. And yet, he also knows, he will have to contact the man. Somehow. Soon. But he doesn't want to think about it, not now: now all he wants to do is stand here, the cool breeze on his legs, looking down at the beachfront town and listening to the girls' descriptions.

"Look!" Priscilla points. "You can see our house!"

Robin's eye follows her finger until it locates a red-brown square somewhere in the distance. The excitement of the girls rubs off on him and he finds it thrilling too, spotting the big squat building. The entire view is gorgeous. He has never seen anything like it, certainly not in Wind Point or its environs. Not at college. Nowhere but here. And, abruptly, he senses a feeling of placidity pouring over him: calmness: everything seems so very right just now, the air, the breeze, the light, the company. He has never been so happy. He looks toward the girls as they lean over the wall of the tower, their bodies touching, and stare down at the ant-like people below. Robin moves and stands next to Koofie and looks down as well.

"Don't they look silly?" she says. "They all seem so *serious*."

"Like it's a matter of life and death," Priscilla adds, "to get where they're going."

"Maybe it is," Robin says. "For them."

"That's only what they think," Koofie says. "There's nothing that's really that important. I mean, think about it. If Martians came down and took a look at us from this angle, do you think they could figure out what everybody thought was such a big deal? We'd just look silly, like little bugs running around in mazes. I mean everything: even wars and stuff like that. The Martians wouldn't be able to figure out why any of it ever happened or what was going on on this weird planet Earth."

Priscilla giggles. "Louise is feeling philosophical today."

"I'll thank you not to call me Louise."

"Yes, Louise."

"Cissy, do you really want to die in an unfortunate accident off the top of this bell tower?"

Priscilla grins back at Robin. "She's beautiful when she's mad, isn't she?"

"No," Koofie says, "I'm beautiful all the time. Ask anybody. I happen to be a beautiful woman."

"Robin, is Koofie a beautiful woman?"

"Well," Robin hesitates, "almost as beautiful as me, I'd say."

The girls laugh; then they fall into each other's arms.

"Do we shock you?" Priscilla asks.

He looks at them. No, he wants to say, you delight me. But he says only, "No."

"Good. There's no room here for people who're easily shocked...like small-town boys from Wind Point Oregon."

He shakes his head, smiles. "It's all right, you guys. Really."

"See?" his cousin says, looking at Koofie. "I told you he was okay. I mean for somebody in *my* family."

They spend most of the day at the beach swimming, sunning themselves, wandering along the beachfront shops. They chatter incessantly, about everything: movies, restaurants, the best beaches, school, should we get ice cream or hot dogs, do you like sandals, I need a beach hat. They tell him his hairstyle is all wrong and troop him into a hairstyling salon: forty minutes later he comes out again wearing a short, sporty cut with a soft wave in it. ("Now you're a real California boy!" Priscilla grins.) The hot sun crosses the sky slowly, lazily, like the day itself, passing as in a soft and supple dream. Everything is far away now. Lying on the beach, watching the two girls frolic in the salty waves, he wonders who that stranger ever was, the lonely and confused neurotic who would wince when he heard the man's footsteps coming up the stairs or quiver on his dormitory bed, doubled over in inchoate pain. It all seems so distant now, unreal. He has made a bid to be accepted in a new kind of world, a carefree world, and that world has accepted him. He has never felt such peaceful, lazy happiness. He loves the young woman Priscilla has become; he loves her roommate Koofie. He feels welcome here. As if he belongs.

In the evening they sit in an outdoor cafe with white mesh tables and chairs (its name is "The Salty Peter"), drinking wine and watching the slow sun gently hemorrhaging into the sea. Priscilla's bright grin covers her face as Koofie, her face partially obscured by a huge, floppy beach hat, leans over and whispers something to her. Robin grins too, pouring wine from the carafe. Finally he giggles.

"What's so funny?" Koofie asks.

"I don't know," Robin says, truthfully. "Just this whole day, I guess. Everything."

"You're going to stay with us awhile, aren't you?"

He nods. "If it's okay."

"Of course it's okay, what do you think? Don't be stupid."

"Sorry. It's my nature."

Koofie laughs. "The only thing is, you'll have to cover your end of the food."

"Sure," he says, thinking vaguely, unhappily, of the four hundred-odd dollars he has to his name. "You wouldn't happen to know someplace I could pick up some money, do you? Mine will last awhile, but…"

The Unspoken

"We could get him a job at Touch 'n' Go," Priscilla says, and giggles.

"Touch 'n' Go International," Koofie interpolates with mock seriousness, "is our place of employment."

"Well, great. What kind of work is it?"

They both laugh. "It wouldn't be right for you," Koofie says.

"No, definitely," agrees Priscilla.

"Why?" He laughs with them, slightly. "What's wrong with it?"

"Nothing," Koofie says, pushing some of her blonde hair out of her eyes. "It's perfectly legal and everything."

"Well, what is it?"

Priscilla laughs again, a hoarse, throaty laugh that makes Robin's mind return for an instant to years before. "Robin," she says, "Touch 'n' Go International is a phone-sex service. You know. You dial up, give your credit card number and expiration date, and you get to listen to a girl talk dirty to you." She grins again. "It's all on the up-and-up."

"So to speak," Koofie says.

"You're kidding," Robin says. "You're putting me on."

"No joke," Priscilla says. "That's where we work. The pay's good and the work is easy."

"What..." He shakes his head, smiling. "What do you say to them?"

"The customers? Whatever they want. Rough, easy, tough, gentle, whatever. You know. Mostly you talk about how big their dicks are, *if* you'll pardon my French."

"And so," Robin says, after a pause, "the guys sit there in Keokuk or Peoria or wherever they are and play with themselves while you talk to them."

"Well, *we* don't know what they're doing while we talk to them. That's their business."

"How did you get involved in this, anyway?"

"We answered an ad," Koofie says, folding her arms behind her head, around the big hat. "We both did interviews, over the phone. See, it doesn't matter what you *look* like, only what you *sound* like. Some of the women who work there are fat and ugly…but when they're fat that sometimes gives them those kind of low, deep voices that guys like." She smiles. "Like Cissy here. Not that she's fat or ugly. But her voice: low, throaty. Husky. Whereas mine is more flighty. Marilyn Monroe-ish. There's a market for both types."

Robin chuckles and shakes his head, staring out at the satin-covered sea.

"Anyway, though," Koofie says, "we can look around for something for you. We know loads of people."

"Okay," he says. "Thanks."

They sip their wine—obtained without trouble from the waiter, since Robin looks older than his age—in the deepening darkness. After a while he asks, "Isn't your job a little…I don't know—sad?"

"Sure it is," Koofie says flatly.

"The funny thing," Priscilla adds, "is that some of them don't even call up to hear dirty talk. Some of them just want to *talk*. They pay a fortune just to have a female voice talk to them for a few minutes." She scoffs slightly. "Some of them seem like they might be nice guys, too. It's sort of weird, picturing these guys alone in their apartments calling up strangers on the phone. I always thought somebody could write a book about it."

"But it would be too sad," Koofie says. "You'd have to do it as a comedy."

"Yeah."

"Anyway," Koofie says, "Cissy and I aren't planning on doing it forever, are we?"

"Hm-mm. Know what we're going to do, Robin?"

"What?"

"*Travel.* Big-time. See, that's why we're living in such a dump. We're saving up. Luckily Koofie's family has money and she has a few stocks and bonds and stuff. We're going to take off together." She grins at her roommate, who grins back.

"To where?"

"Everywhere! Europe. Asia. Africa. Bumming around in sleeping bags."

"What do your parents think of the idea?"

"Well," Priscilla says, sipping the wine, "fact is, I don't have much contact with them right now. I mean they know where I am. But we're not really speaking."

"Oh."

"Mm-hm. See, I scrammed out of there almost as soon as I got my high school diploma. I bummed by way south until I got here."

"And met me," Koofie interjects.

"And met this…person." She laughs. "It's true, though. We met at the beach. One thing led to another, bim bam boom, and here we are."

"That's great," Robin grins. "It really is." He means it: looking at them together, the glances they give each other out the corners of their eyes, reminds him of nothing so much as Turnham: but he does not want to think of Turnham. Instead, he looks out at the darkening sea. He notices that it has grown quiet: the few customers who had been at the cafe when they arrived are gone, and stars like tiny electric eyes are appearing overhead. The air is growing cooler. If he looks behind himself, he can see the headlights of the cars on the street facing the cafe. Before him, nothing but a few empty tables; then the sand, and the sea. They are wonderful together, he thinks, Priscilla and Koofie. Sitting with them in the quiet darkness, the sound of the ocean near them and its dark glitter mesmerizing him, fills him with a quiet contentment. Everything is all right here, he knows: for the first time in his entire life he feels that everything is all right. He is welcome here. This world is right for him. Of course, vaguely flitting like wings across his mind are other thoughts: his father, school, Wind Point: but they are easy enough to deflect here, now. They continue talking, as they have all day. He learns more of Koofie: that she is originally from Minnesota, her father, long absent, was Mexican; she hitchhiked out to California two years ago; once she played a bit role in a porno film ("I didn't screw anybody, I just pranced around with my tits hanging out"), and decided after six months that she could never again live away from the sea. Fortunately her mother had been understanding and had not cut her off entirely; in fact, she receives healthy checks each year for her birthday. "She knows me," she says. "She knows everything about me. And she knows I'm not going to change. I mean about anything. California, my lifestyle—anything. So she helps me."

"More than *my* parents do," Priscilla says. "They couldn't care less."

"Now," Robin says, "that's not true."

"It *is*. They always told me I was abnormal. What kind of a thing is that to say to a kid, to call her abnormal?"

He smiles. "Maybe you were."

"May*be*. But they didn't have to *tell* me!" Laughter.

"So what are you going to do with yourself, Robin?" asks Koofie. "I mean, if you don't mind my asking. What do you want to do when you finish college?"

He glances away, involuntarily annoyed. "I don't know," he says. "I wish I did."

"What's your major?"

"English."

"Going to be a teacher?"

He shakes his head. "I don't know. I don't think so. I guess what I really want to be is a writer."

"Really? Writing what?"

He smiles again. "I guess I don't know yet."

"But that's exciting," Koofie says, looking closely at him. "I'll bet you can do it, if you try. I have a cousin who's a writer. Writes mystery stories for those, what do you call them, pulp magazines. *True Detective* and stuff. He doesn't make a living at it, but it helps him pay the rent. It can't hurt, if it helps pay the rent."

Robin wants to say: I don't care if it pays the rent. I want to do something, something that—what? What? But he cannot formulate the words, and knows that even if he could they would not come out right, they would sound stuffy, pretentious, thick hot air about Art and Artists and blah blah blah. The words can't communicate it. He thinks again of Mahler, of the final notes of the Ninth Symphony fading into eternity, and something, not music, not sound, but something, a mysterious connection to the infinite, hovering there like an elusive dragonfly: attractive, dancing, untranslatable. That is what he wants: to make something that can touch that dragonfly.

"Sure," he finally says. "But I don't know if I could really write that kind of stuff." He shrugs. "I don't know. Probably I'll never do anything. Probably I'll just talk about it."

"You never know," Priscilla says, looking toward Koofie. "Robin is one of these intellectual guys. He was the same way when we were kids." She grins back at him. "You haven't changed, you know. Even then you were real *serious* and *solemn* and always had your face buried in a book about a thousand miles thick."

Robin laughs. "I'm not that glum, am I?"

"You're pretty glum. Even now you are. Do you still bury yourself in those big books?"

"Sometimes. I can't *help* it, being an English major."

"Still. You *like* it. A professor, that's what you ought to be. Or a musty fusty old literary critic who farts dust."

He laughs again. "No, no, no! You're all wrong."

But he is not sure if she is or not. There is an appeal in the idea: an office, dusty Venetian blinds, a couple of thousand books lining the walls, all of them dog-eared and annotated and underlined. Coffee rings on his desk. Sloppy stacks of student essays. A bright wife and a couple of bright kids. Faculty parties. Maybe even a messy affair with one of his students sometime. A role he could step into, he knows, with ludicrous ease: it would only be a matter of time, of reading more books, writing more essays. And when he had read enough books and written enough essays they would hand him the pieces of paper that would give him official entrance into the world of people who spend their lives reading books and writing essays. Possible: attainable. And yet, when he thinks of it, it is as if there is something else there in the distance, something hovering in that instant of infinity between the final note and silence, the inexpressible beckoning to another world, one of marvels and dreams and wonders. But how to find his way there, how to discover the door that will lead him to that world, remains a mystery.

At last they notice the waiters taking in the tables and chairs for the night and, in pleasant silence, they begin riding back to the warehouse. It is silent and dark when they arrive: tonight, they tell him, is not a rehearsal night, and no parties are scheduled. The building seems lonely and abandoned in the quiet dark; and Robin lies on his makeshift bed for hours, staring into the night. Occasionally he hears the rustle of Priscilla or Koofie in the bed on the other side of the room. He finds himself wishing, more than anything in the world, that he could lie there with them, together.

4

After a week of lazy days spent wandering the book shops and the beach and sipping iced tea in outdoor cafes, they find him a job not far from the warehouse. He spends five hours a day, three days a week, unloading tires from big, soiled white trucks that arrive filled to the brim with them. He and four other young men—also college students on summer break—bring the tires from out of the trucks, load them onto the big dollies, and roll them into a big dank building which smells of dust and rubber. The easiest job is pushing the dolly, and he and his co-workers arrange that each of them will have that task for one-half day out of the week. Robin's turn at this comes on Wednesday afternoons. Otherwise, all the tasks are much the same, whether unloading from the truck or lifting the tires onto the high stacks in the storage buildings. It is incredibly tiring and Robin comes home constantly with sore muscles which Priscilla massages for him. And yet he does not find the job truly arduous. There is something pleasant about simple manual labor: and he realizes that he has never in his life done it before. When he had worked in the restaurant in high school he had merely delivered water and crackers to arriving diners and cleared their dishes away when they were finished. It had been wearying, and boring, but it had not given him the deep-down, sore-to-the-bone kind of ache that this work does. And there is something satisfying in it. Although he knows he has done no more than unload some hoops of rubber from trucks, he somehow has a feeling of accomplishment when he goes home in the warm, sloping afternoons. He somehow feels that this, after all, is the kind of work a budding writer *should* do.

That is, if he were budding. But he seems not to be. He spends a great deal of time thinking about writing. Often, on mornings that he does no work and Priscilla and Koofie go off the Touch 'n' Go International, he will sit on the floor with a pad of paper in his hand and a pencil and try to find what he is looking for. But somehow it does not come. A hundred images will play across his mind: voices, cries, echoes: but they fail to coalesce into anything he can write down. He supposes it's what people call Writer's Block. After all, in college he had been able to write; even if the writing hadn't been any good. But now nothing comes at all. The blank page remains blank. At times he brings out some lines he had once written: *when I come home from somewhere she is in the living room waiting for me.* He still thinks the clue may be there. But he cannot find it.

He is careful not to let on to his hostesses that he is accomplishing nothing, and they seem nearly awed by his apparent industriousness. "You really *are* a writer," Koofie said to him one morning as the two of them were going out. "What is it? A story?"

"Don't know yet," he smiled.

Koofie nodded knowingly to Priscilla. "A genius in our midsts."

"I know," Priscilla answered, brushing her hair in front of the mirror leaning in the window frame. "Did you see the book he's reading now? Another one of those million-pounders. By some Russian."

"Turgenev," Robin said. "But it's not that thick, is it?"

"It's pretty thick. And I bet it's old and boring. I hate old books." She began applying mascara to her eyes. "We always had to read them in high school. *Jude the Obscure.* Holy moley! Obscure is right. You know what I really hate about old books, though? The way people are always ejaculating on each other. You know? It says something like, '"No, I won't do it!" he ejaculated.' And then the other character will ejaculate right back at him. '"Yes," Count Whoozovich ejaculated in return, "you will, you will!"' I mean, didn't all those ejaculations get a little *messy?*"

They had all laughed. But it isn't funny, day in and day out, staring at his blank pages. It is depressing. But, depressing or not, it does keep his mind from dealing with other things that are potentially even worse:

Hello?

"Hello, Dad?"

Robin? Where are you? I expected you two days ago. I called the school....

"I know, Dad. I'm sorry. I...I ended up changing my plans. At the last minute."

A pause.

Where are you?

"I...I'm in Santa Barbara."

Santa...

"At Priscilla's. You remember her. Uncle Otto and Aunt Margaret's daughter? She...lives here now. She invited me and I—I decided to come."

Another pause.

Don't you think you could have called...

"I know. I should have. I'm sorry."

The conversation blurs at this point. He remembers apologizing over and over again, but the details are gone. What had they said to each other? Whatever it was, it was uncomfortable, and terrible. He had felt dirty, horribly dirty, when he hung up the phone, as if some unwashable grime were covering his skin. Not just this skin. His soul.

What he had done was unimaginable. And yet he had done it: refused. Forbidden the terrible darkness from swarming over him again. He realizes that this should be a victory, a personal triumph: years of dully accepting the unacceptable had been suddenly, brutally torn asunder: and yet he feels no sense of triumph, only embarrassment, shame.

That is, when he thinks of his father. But he does not, in truth, think of him very much. The man's milky, glowering eyes and sharply hooked nose seem distant now, lost in time, as does the house in the cul-de-sac and its rooms, the lurking silence and breathing dark. Another life: or perhaps not life at all, rather a long dream. And he has, he thinks, emerged from it. Unloading the big tires, laughing with Priscilla and Koofie, this is the new life he has sought: open, free: a place where he is accepted, where he belongs. Even the nightly band rehearsals are not so arduous. Often he will go out to movies, to plays, and it is only occasionally that such hard rock outfits play here as he had heard the first time. Many times the bands are soft jazz or blues players, and not a soul shows up to listen. Robin finds himself quite enjoying some of these groups, and gets to meet the musicians; this is thrilling, as they are, he thinks, genuine artists making money at their art. This he finds incredible. He has often thought of the day, somewhere in the far-flung future, that he himself might receive a check for something he has written; but it seems impossible. Still, to be around these singers and guitarists and saxophonists is a heady experience. How casually they talk of "contracts," "gigs," "deals"! To be able to swim through such a world as an equal—that would be everything.

One afternoon he sees a poster advertising a concert by the local symphony, and he immediately goes to the ticket office of the theater and buys a ticket. The program includes a Beethoven overture, a Richard Strauss suite, and Mahler's Fourth Symphony; and he awaits the precious day almost breathlessly. It is all he can think about. To hear Mahler played live, by a real orchestra! He imagines the musicians, their clothes and instruments and music stands, the rustling sheets of notes like cocoons about to burst to butterflies, and the conductor's dramatic entrance, clasping his hands before him and acknowledging the applause. Then the hush of silence that would fall as the conductor turned from them, looked down at his score (or perhaps, even more dramatically, there would be no score), and finally, lifting his head and surveying the orchestra like Eisenhower or MacArthur reviewing the troops, he would raise his magic wand, poise it in mid-air for just an instant, and then slice it down through the electric air, the horns majestically blasting the opening note of the *Egmont* overture.

But when the night arrives he is nearly crushed with disappointment. The theater is too hot; his seat is too close and too far to the side; the strings' entrances are sloppy; the conductor is a catatonic old man who hardly seems awake on the podium. Robin finds himself unable to concentrate on the music, instead

The Unspoken

hypersensitive to any of the audience's coughing, rustling, sighing; when he looks at one female cellist his mind floats clean away from the Strauss and instead wonders what she would look like with her black dress removed. He closes his eyes, trying to focus on the suite, but then worries that people might think him asleep; so he opens them again. Glances at the cellist, who his imagination again amends to a state of undress. He sighs. The situation is hopeless.

But it becomes absolute agony after the intermission. The delicate Fourth Symphony—which, with its sleigh bells and lilting melodies, always makes Robin think of fantasy Christmases and snowmen and hot rum before a crackling fire with a beautiful woman nestled against him—is utterly massacred by the corpse-conductor and his skeleton crew. Entrances are missed. Solo bits are muffed. Bum notes crash around the stage like half-deflated basketballs. It is tortuous. And yet, as Robin casts his eyes over the nearby audience members, he is shocked to find that they appear not to mind at all. Large women in tight dresses that make their bodies look like overstuffed sofas stare vacantly at the stage, frozen smiles on their faces. Their husbands, those whose heads are not nodding backward, look uncertainly at the conductor as if this were some new kind of endurance test, unlike the ones they used to run through in the Army; but they say nothing. And at the end, when the contorted performance at last grinds and scrapes to a halt, they all applaud. Robin sits scowling, wondering why these people, none of whom, it would appear, can tell good from bad, came at all. He takes one final, languid look at his cellist (*Farewell, my lovely*, he thinks), then turns and stalks up the aisle in disgust.

Of course, nagging at the back of his brain is the uncomfortable feeling that he is not, after all, much qualified to judge such things. Robin Withers, the great cultural arbiter of the Western World, who has never, before tonight, attended a concert; who has never been inside a first-rate art museum; who has never seen a ballet; who knows no foreign languages; who has never read Tolstoy, Milton, Dante…the list is endless. He winces inwardly as he remembers, just for an instant, Davy Carp and high school and the *Personas Non Gratas*.

But as he reaches the door of the theater and steps out into the bracing night air, his attention is diverted by something else. Standing under a street lamp, in a natty black sweater and dark slacks, is someone he recognizes: though he cannot, for some seconds, place who it is. Then, as the young man's eyes suddenly turn onto him, he does: it is one of the musicians, a guitarist, from the warehouse rehearsals. Robin had seen him on his first, drunken night, and has noticed him several times since.

"Hi," the guitarist says.

Robin smiles and approaches him. "Hi."

"Where's Cissy and Koofie? I saw you, thought I'd see them."

"Well," Robin says, "they don't go in much for this highfalutin' stuff."

The guitarist smiles. His face is dramatically angular, like a portrait by Kirchner or Heckel; his eyes slope downwards at their outer edges, rather like teardrops, and his sharp nose and thin mouth suggest the ascetic; but two or three days' growth of beard darkening his face make him appear more bohemian. His dark hair is chopped quite short on the sides and is long in back. Robin guesses him to be about twenty.

"Yeah," the guitarist says. "I've seen you around a lot with them."

"I'm living there, actually. Priscilla—Cissy—she's my cousin."

"Yeah, I remember, she said that. By the way, my name's Cape." He extends his hand, which Robin grasps. The hold is firm. "Cape Erikson Barnes. I know it's pompous to go by three names, but with a name like mine I can't help myself."

Robin introduces himself. "How did you like the music?" he asks, nodding back toward the theater.

"Oh, well. The local band, you know. They tried. But that—what's his name?—Mahler—puts me to sleep anyway. I had a nice snooze after the intermission."

Robin laughs. "I would've slept too, but I couldn't. It was too painful. But I *like* Mahler."

"Nobody likes Mahler." Cape's eyes flicker with amusement. "Unless they're *very* self-pitying."

"Maybe I am." Robin grins.

"So what's brought you to Cissy's place? I mean it's not everybody who could stand living like that."

"I'm just visiting. I'm from up north, actually. Oregon. We hadn't seen each other in a long time. I'll be leaving soon, I guess..." Robin glances around at the dark palm trees lining the streets in either direction. "But now I'm not so sure. Maybe I'll stay a while. I haven't decided."

"Where are you going now? Back there? To the warehouse?"

"Yeah, I think so."

"Need a ride? I have a van. Well, technically it's a van. Really it's a beast from Hell."

"Sure. Why not? If it's not out of your way."

"No, it's no problem." They begin walking up the dark street. Robin feels a kind of thrill coursing through him. After all, Cape Erikson Barnes—he runs the name through his mind several times, to remember it—is an excellent guitarist who plays with several of the bands that rehearse at the warehouse. Robin has seen him more than once, tuning up before a session, sitting on a stool and leaning methodically over his instrument, slowly turning the tuning pegs this way or that, instinctively leaning his ear close to the strings. His memory uncovers another fragment: Priscilla's voice, days or weeks ago, saying to Koofie: *Saw Cape in the supermarket, stealing things. He's broke as usual.* Robin glances over at him. Cape is tall, slender, walks with a confident—even brash—gait, exudes aggressiveness. He is not unattractive. They talk of Robin's college, life in dormitories ("I did a year in college back east," Cape says. "University of Maryland, College Park. The boredom nearly killed me, but the dorm food delivered the *coup de grace*"), Santa Barbara, movies, music. Cape, Robin quickly finds, is wonderful on the subject of music, tossing off casually knowing references to Django Reinhardt, John Lee Hooker, Erik Satie, Pink Floyd. Robin knows little or nothing about any of these people, but the sheer, excited flow of words, Cape's bright, living eyes and voice burbling with passion and laughter, beguile him.

"Well! Here is the sacred beast," Cape announces as they arrive at a bashed and battered metal box, powder-blue, which is his van. It is perhaps fifteen years old, with a cracked windshield, bald tires, and laces of rust running all over it like a macabre embroidery.

Robin scowls, then grins. "Is this thing safe?"

"Safe?" Cape laughs. "A more pertinent question would be whether it's even *legal*, and the answer is: certainly not. But don't worry, it won't kill you. Maybe just *maim* you a little. Here." He unlocks the side door and, with some difficulty, rolls it open. "Take a look at my castle."

Inside, Robin sees cheap wooden paneling coming unglued from the walls and ceiling; a mattress with dirty blankets on the floor; an acoustic guitar; a few books and rumpled paper bags.

"I live here, you know," Cape says, a curious pride finding its way into his voice. "At least, I do when I haven't made any other arrangements."

"Here?" Robin says. "In this van? But this is worse than the warehouse."

"But *immensely affordable*," Cape laughs, sitting at the edge of the van's floor. Robin remains standing in the street.

"But where do you put your guitars and amplifiers and things?"

"People's houses. The warehouse. Around. I don't have that much, really." He shrugs. "Say, if you don't mind, I'm going to step out of these fancy duds." He climbs into the van's interior. "They don't belong to me anyway, although I'll probably steal them." He strips off the sweater and slacks and slips into a baggy gray sweatshirt and worn blue jeans. "I don't mind dressing up like that, sometimes. Makes you feel kind of *classy*. But I'm basically a slob, as you can probably tell. I have no class. I come from pure peasant stock. Commoners, we is. How about you?"

Robin grins. "Slobs."

"Yeah, I thought so, I can always tell a fellow slob." He zips up the jeans and brushes his hair back with his hand. "I'm going for a drive down to the beach. Wanna come?"

Robin hesitates; Cape laughs again. "Aw, come on! What terribly important things await you at the warehouse? I know the band there tonight. Ziggy's Membrane, they're called. Awful. Not worth the powder it'd take to blow 'em up. So why don't you get in?"

A few minutes later Robin finds himself in the passenger seat of the dubious van, careening down the freeway at seventy-five miles an hour. A curious nervousness, a kind of thrill, charges through him as he thinks of this, his new life, and how far it is from his old, dead self, the self of frightened flinches in the darkness. He rolls down the window and feels the cold breeze on his face. Perhaps he has finally done it, he thinks—freed himself forever from the tyranny of the whirlpool of memory. He feels, just now, that he has, and it is a heady feeling, bright, wonderful.

"Cissy tells me you're a writer!" Cape calls out over the roar of the van's engine.

Robin shakes his head. "That's just an unfounded rumor."

"Well, she says you're working on something, a novel or something, every day!"

"Just trying. Not succeeding."

"Had anything published?"

He shakes his head.

"You'll have to show me something you've written!"

Robin nods, wishing they could change the subject. It is not a happy thought, writing. Literature. He sometimes thinks that it would be better to forget about it entirely—admit to himself that the vision of the cluttered desk and hundreds of dog-eared volumes in a crowded office darkened by dusty Venetian blinds is the direction he must inevitably take, that it is his destiny. Perhaps it is, after all. And what would be so bad about it? There would be money, comfort, even prestige. It wouldn't be such a bad life. He grins wryly. Wife, kids, car, three squares a day. Why not?

"Here we are," Cape says, down-shifting and pulling off the freeway. "I've got my own private entrance!"

Suddenly he jerks the wheel sharply to the right and crashes over bushes, nearly slamming into two trees, driving the vehicle over a steep dirt slope that, as they crest it, turns to beach sand.

"See?" Cape laughs. "And I'll have you know that I pay an arm and a leg for the privilege of that little private drive!"

"I'll bet you do—!"

"Damn right. I've paid more in traffic tickets than you could ever *dream* of...But this leads to one of the best beaches around here. It's a little cove. Not many people go there because it's too hard to get to. Except," he grins, "if you've got your own private entrance."

Cape motors the vehicle through more thick bush and Robin's head smacks against the van's ceiling. "Sometimes I sleep down here," Cape says, "when I'm feeling the need to get away from it all. But a lot of times I just come here to open up the back doors and play guitar." Finally the bush clears and Cape drives the van over a long, craggly series of rocks.

At last a steep, sudden decline leads them to a tiny, isolated cove surrounded on three sides by crumbling walls of shale. Cape turns the van around so that its back is facing the ocean and turns off the motor.

"Well! Hell of a ride, no?"

"No," Robin mutters, rubbing his head. "Hardly a *ride* at all."

Cape laughs and jumps out of the van, breathes in the ocean air and beats himself on his chest. "Ahhh!" he cries out joyously. "This is *it*, isn't it?"

Robin steps out and looks toward the ocean. It is undeniably lovely, lit this night by a low moon sending shimmering waves of silver over the water. The cove seems cut-off from everywhere else in the world. Its high walls make it nearly unimaginable that only a short distance away are the freeway, electric lights, civilization. He likes it here. What he thinks of his sudden companion, however, he is not so sure.

"It's a bit cool for a paddle, this time of night," Cape says, looking out at the waves. "Too bad. It's nice here when it's a little warmer." He pulls open the van's rear doors and Robin wanders toward the water's edge. He finds his heart beating rapidly.

He sits in the sand. After a moment Cape joins him, guitar in hand.

They sit in silence for some time, only the gentle strumming of the guitar adding anything to the ocean sound. Into Robin's mind float other shores: a woman in a willowy white dress, feet padding on wet wood, imagining gems wrapped around her. He shuts his eyes momentarily, tries to banish the visions. Thinks instead of the night's symphony. But, every moment, he is aware of his companion: and he steals glances at him, at his powerful profile, his large but graceful hands, his crossed legs.

"Anything you'd like to hear?" Cape asks. "I'm taking requests."

Robin grins, looking out at the water. "Play Mahler's Fourth."

His friend laughs. "Oh, that's good! But no, I think not. Maybe..." And he begins a soft, melancholy piece with a simple melody. Robin looks at Cape's face while he plays. It seems to change, chameleon-like, from the brashly confident mask of the crazy driver to something softer, more intense and sensitive. He plays the guitar extremely well. The notes, graceful as gulls lifting into a morning sky, seem to float effortlessly from his fingers.

"That's beautiful," Robin says after a few minutes, after the final notes have faded to silence. "What is it?"

"Just something I've been fooling around with. Variations on a theme, you know."

Silence again.

"Say, where did you study music, anyway?" Cape asks him.

"I never have."

His companion glances over at him. "Really?"

Robin shrugs. "I just like it, that's all. I don't really know anything about it. I couldn't tell you the difference between a bar and a measure."

"Hm." He strums the guitar. "That's rare. To like highbrow stuff like Mahler without a background in it."

Robin shrugs again, vaguely pleased with himself.

"Me, I used to take guitar lessons even when I was a little kid. My mama was convinced I was some sort of prodigy." He adjusts a tuning peg. "Wasn't, though. Thought I was, for a long time."

"But you play very well."

"Yeah, but millions of people play well. It doesn't matter. I remember what my last Music teacher in high school told me. 'You're *talented*, Barnes; but you're not *gifted*.' He was right."

Robin thinks of it for a moment; then says: "How can you be so sure?"

Cape shrugs. "After a while you figure it out, that's all. No, I'm quite good. I can make a living at it when I get off my ass and do it. But that's all...It's just as well my mama didn't live to see my conspicuous lack of success."

"She's dead?"

"Yeah. Since I was ten."

Robin looks at the dark sea. "Mine died when I was thirteen."

"Really." Cape resumes his quite strumming. "Charming coincidence."

They sit together for a long time. Robin sifts sand through his fingers, draws aimless patterns with his fingers.

"What did yours die of?" Robin asks.

"Cancer. Horrible, that slow wasting-away. I'll never forget it. The way she was in the hospital in those last few days, her skin all yellow, old, you know, like old paper...Anyway, it was a long time ago."

There is a pause. Then Robin says, "Mine died in an auto accident."

"Really."

"Mm-hm. One day she was there, the next—"

"Nothing."

"Nothing."

Silence.

"Where are you from, Cape? Originally."

"You mean back in the good ol' days? Kansas. Born 'n' bred, a real Kansas farm boy."

"No kidding?"

"Mm-hm."

"How did you come here? To Santa Barbara?"

"For school, at first. But then I dropped out." He brushes his hair back with his hand. "And I decided not to go back there. At least not for awhile. I don't know. My people are..." He shakes his head.

"Slobs?"

He grins. "Slobs. I mean, you know. The kind that throw their trash out the kitchen window. I decided a long time ago that I didn't want to be like that. I was different...I *knew* I was. Music, for one thing. And the fact that I'm gay. It was always obvious that..."

But Robin, inhaling sharply, does not hear the following words. His mind is frozen on just one. He doesn't think he has ever articulated it in his own mind, or used it to describe anything having to do with himself. *Gay*. There is something repellent about it, yet, at the same time, attractively mysterious. They talk for some time; but Robin's mind is preoccupied. He keeps thinking of the word, piercing him like an arrow through the heart. He cannot decide if he is excited or sickened by it. It seems unreal. And yet he remembers Turnham, the fire, the darkness: what had that been? But he had never thought of it that way. Had, in fact, hardly thought of it at all, since things had broken off. To be classified: to be *gay*. To call yourself by that word, to identify yourself in that way. It is an amazing, perhaps terrifying idea. But why? he wonders. He has been staying with Priscilla and Koofie for weeks. But they never used that one word; and anyway, he reasons, being women, perhaps their sex lives were too alien to him to be relevant, or understandable. After all—he realizes with an inward wince—however the technical definitions might have been altered by Marylou Kirk (a figure lost in the mists of forgotten time, and yet still with the ability to make his face burn, as now, with shame), the fact is that he is a virgin with women. Utterly inexperienced in the realm of breast, vagina, clitoris. And so, although he has heard them making sighing love-sounds in the darkness, it did not impact upon him the way that Cape's simple, open declaration has. Turnham, after all, would never have classified himself as *gay*. It has never occurred to Robin to use the word to apply to himself. He has never, in fact, met anyone who would have said such a thing. And yet here he is, in this sea-filled dark, sitting with someone who can casually mention: *I'm gay*.

"Yeah: I thought so," he hears Cape saying beside him. Robin looks over at him suddenly.

"What?"

"I said, I thought so." Cape looks at him. "I mean, why do you think I invited you out here?"

They sit in silence again. Robin finds himself quivering slightly.

"You look nervous," Cape says.

"Maybe I am."

Cape chuckles. "It's the thought of this wonder next to you."

Robin grins, giddily. "Maybe."

Cape strums the guitar, meditatively smiling.

"Tell me about your mother," Robin says, after a long time.

"Not much to tell. She was sick ever since I can remember. Got worse and worse. Finally died."

"You don't want to talk about it."

He shrugs. "It's done, really. Finished. I try to move forward, not back."

Robin stares out at the ocean for several minutes.

"I'm sorry," Cape says at last. "You want to talk about something, don't you?"

"No, I guess not."

"You do."

Robin shrugs.

"It *is* a bond, I guess, a kind of a bond." Cape silences the guitar for a moment. "Having your mom die when you're young. People that's happened to, they understand each other."

"Do you think so?"

"Sure. At least that's been my experience. It's just one of those things. I'm not real big on psychology myself, but it's not hard to figure it out. The feelings of…I don't know. Betrayal. Abandonment, guilt. Guilt that you couldn't save her. All that kind of boloney."

"Yes," Robin says. "Yes, that's it."

"I don't like to talk about it because I've tried to flush that whole life down the toilet. All of it. My dad is this hypocritical religious bastard. Exactly the kind of guy you'd expect to find on a farm in Kansas. If you put him in a book nobody'd believe it because he'd be too much of a cliche. But there *are* people who are walking cliches. My daddy used to read to us out of the Bible every night. TV wasn't allowed. Only religious music could be played on the stereo, and maybe, once in a while, as a treat, Mozart's *Requiem*."

"So how did you get involved in music?"

Cape smiles. "Pure contraband stuff. Bought me a little radio from a guy at school, with one of those little white plastic earphones you stick in your ear. I used to listen to everything, late at night. He never knew. He was too stupid to know."

"And at school…?"

"He didn't mind my taking Music at school. Somehow thought it would be good for my character or something. He never came around to listen, so it didn't matter that he thought we sat around playing hymns when really I was in Jazz Band."

"Do you still stay in touch with him?"

"Nah. I've got some sisters, I send one of them a card now and then to let them know I'm alive. Otherwise, I've chopped that umbilical cord. With a vengeance."

"So have I," Robin says, after a moment.

"Nah, you haven't. Who's paying for your college?"

Robin looks away. "He is. My dad."

"See? You're still securely tied. Don't feel bad, though. Daddies can come in handy sometimes. Like when you're hard up for dough." Cape smiles.

"Maybe," Robin says. "I don't know. I *feel* independent of him, though. Like I'm my own person." Even as he says it, he knows it is not true: but he nonetheless feels he must say it, as if to convince himself.

"Well, maybe you are. I don't know. I don't know what Oregon boys are like. Although," he grins, "I hope to find out very soon."

Robin grins widely; his heart jumps. Cape strums the guitar, humming along with the melody softly, evanescently, the notes blending with the sound of the sea like gentle whispers in a falling rain.

After, the blankets wrapped tightly around them, the rising wind pushing at the sides of the vehicle like soft hands, Robin grips him tightly and presses his face into his companion's chest hard, as hard as he can, and he intertwines their legs, and dimly, only half-consciously, he becomes aware that he is emitting tiny whimpering sounds, hardly more than squeaks, like a small bird in pain: Cape's soft voice comes to him as through a thick haze, vague, distant, disembodied: for some time he does not make out the words, only the sounds of them, gentle, comforting; but finally they materialize, become not sounds but words, phrases, understood language.

"Robin? Hey. What's going on? Are you crying? What's wrong?"

After a long moment he moves his head away from Cape's body slightly. "No, I'm not crying."

"What is it? Did I do something wrong?"

"You were perfect."

"Then what...?"

"It's nothing." He shakes his head, puts his lips to Cape's chest. "Nothing."

"I have the feeling we're avoiding something here."

"Cape, no."

"Was that your first time?"

He shakes his head. "Second. Did it show?"

"Only because you didn't act like most guys. Stick it, squirt it, stuff it back in the jockey shorts. That's more par for the course."

Robin smiles slightly. "I didn't even stick it."

"I know. Do you have something against my ass? I mean, a political thing or something?"

He giggles. "I have nothing against your ass. I love your ass. I don't particularly want to shove parts of my body up it, though."

"But Robin, *give* and thou shalt *receive*..."

He laughs. "I know...Maybe that's what I was afraid of."

"You haven't done it?"

"No."

"It's not bad," Cape says, "really. It won't kill you. Maybe just maim..."

"Maim me a little, yeah, I know. But I take my philosophy from Ginsberg. In one of his poems he says: 'Who wants to be fucked in the ass, really?'"

"What a spoil sport."

There is a short silence.

"Did I disappoint you, Cape? Seriously."

"Seriously: no." He kisses Robin's forehead. "You were great. Seriously."

"Seriously?"

"Seriously."

Robin touches his companion's back softly, breathing the musky man-smell of semen and sweat that emanates from his body. "Thank you," he says. "I'm not very confident in matters of the bedroom...or the backs of vans..."

"Hey, what was all that noise about a minute ago? You seemed..."

"Cape, it was nothing. Please. Forget it."

"I think you want to talk about something."

Yes, he thinks; but it's not one thing, it's ten, a thousand, all mixed together in a hot, confused jumble; and he doesn't know how he could express it all in words; for it is complicated, and mixed-up, and he is afraid that if he opens his mouth it will all come out nonsensically.

"I don't know," he finally whispers.

Cape runs his fingers through Robin's hair. "Give it a try," he mutters quietly.

"I don't know what I want to say."

Cape is silent for a moment. They are close together.

"Okay," he whispers.

They lay in silence for a time. Robin can feel Cape's heart, firm, even, pulsing near his ear. He intertwines their fingers and becomes super-aware, again, of the sensation of touch: of the living warmth underneath the skin of Cape's fingers, and his own; and as he touches the fingers, as their fingertips meet and he gently glides his own down through Cape's, resting them finally in the space between Cape's fingers, and as they squeeze each other's hands and he feels the strength, the softness of the flesh and the hardness of the bone underneath, he feels an old sensation coming upon him, swarming over him like sudden clouds. Life! he thinks. He is alive! He hears the ocean rolling outside and the whistling wind and, through the window of the van, he sees the stars: the connection-points of the vast design, the huge oneness of the universe; and he thinks of lilies, of lions, of the sun and light and distant galaxies traveling through dimensions of time and remembers that this, too, is part of him: every swirling nebula, every spinning sphere, the vast cold emptiness of space, they are part of him: he is part and parcel of the endless chain, of that which *is*.

"Do you believe in God?" he asks Cape.

"Me? No."

Silence.

"Do you?"

"I don't know," Robin whispers, the strange, delicious life-feeling coursing through him, making it difficult to speak. "I'm not sure. Sometimes I do. Sometimes God is the only thing I believe in, in the whole world."

"And tonight?" Cape whispers.

"What?"

"What do you think about God tonight?"

Robin closes his eyes and buries his face in Cape again, breathing in the heady sex-odor and feeling the powerful heart pump in the smooth chest and picturing galaxies, impossibly distant, weaving majestically through their tapestries of night, stitching their connections to him throughout unspoken immensities, wrapping him with them in their cloaks of infinity.

"Tonight I believe in God," he whispers.

5

Priscilla turns over onto her stomach, simultaneously adjusting the sunglasses on her face. Robin watches her struggle to reach the clasp of her bikini top for a moment, then says: "Here, let me."

"You're a dear."

He reaches over and unclasps the top. Priscilla lies flat on the big towel, the summer sun making her body glisten with sweat; Robin, on his back, stares up through his sunglasses at the lazy blue sky and listens to the waves ceaselessly hammering the shore. It is a perfect summer day and the Tuesday morning beach is nearly deserted. Only a few mothers with small children pass occasionally; otherwise they are by themselves.

"So are you really in love with him?" she asks.

Robin grins, sleepily. "I think I am."

"He seems like a good guy."

"He is."

"Still, be a little careful. He's got kind of a reputation. And you've only been together a week."

"I know."

One week: and yet it seems they have been together always. It seems, really, as if he had never truly been alive before: or as if what had gone before was an old, cracked black-and-white film, whereas everything now has suddenly burst into glorious Technicolor. He has a hard time picturing life before Cape. He feels utterly new. They have spent every night together, and every night, as they become more familiar with each other—with each other's bodies, their patterns and responses—has been better than the last. Even in the cramped space of the old van, he had never felt uncomfortable or cheap or anything but warm, satisfied; loved. That was it. He felt loved, every night. And will feel so again, he knows, tonight. Loved.

"But I've never known anyone like him," Robin says, absently.

Priscilla nods, smiling.

He wants to say more, but somehow cannot express himself. The feeling of Cape's arms around his body when they wake in the morning: the smooth hair on his legs: the morning stubble on his chin: it all fills him with a warm, wonderful light. And to know that it is his, that it belongs to him and to nobody else, is exhilarating. A day or two before he had watched Cape playing his guitar with a blues band at the warehouse: Cape had been dressed in artful sloppiness, a big gray T-shirt and patched blue jeans and a white hat with a big brim: and, as Robin watched him play the instrument, sometimes breaking off and shouting "Whoa! Whoa! Dudes, that's *all* wrong!" he had beamed with pride. Every move Cape made, he felt super-conscious of it: every fold in the clothes as they hung on his skin, every movement of arm, hand, finger, every darting of his eyes, every flash of a grin, and, most of all, every time their eyes met: it was like a gloriously warm chill running through him. To sit there, watching him play a slow blues, improvising a one-string solo, and to picture him in other landscapes: to watch the strong hands moving up and down the frets and strings, to watch the powerful ropy veins rise on the backs of his hands, to see the faint patina of sweat starting to cover them, he would see his body in the van at night: the strong, thin build, the incisive teardrop eyes close to his, the hands touching his own, the lips brushing his face. He would feel Cape's long hair in his hands, sifting through his fingers. Feel the gentle curvature of his back underneath his fingers. He would hear the music they played on Cape's little tape player: blues, mostly, some jazz, some rock ("But *none* of your buddy Gus Mahler!" Cape would proclaim). A few times they had played light classics—a Tchaikovsky suite, a Mozart concerto. Often Cape would play slide guitar inside the van, gentle, sad blues songs, and would talk about the blues: about Robert Johnson and Blind Lemon Jefferson, Howlin' Wolf and Willie Dixon, Lightnin' Hopkins and John Lee Hooker.

"It's my first love, blues," he would say. "On my little radio at night I could pick up some stations in the south, black stations that still played the originals, the real stuff, not soul and disco and Motown crap but the real stuff by the real people. It was fantastic. Technically, you know, most of them were terrible by today's standards. But that sound! That's what all the whitey bands are trying to copy, the Stones and all of them. But they're *nothing* like these guys." And Cape would play him tapes. At first Robin heard nothing in the primitively-recorded, primitively-played recordings, but after he had been listening a while he began to hear a purity, a simplicity, an honesty in them which was compelling. And so they would listen, late at night, under their blankets, to the sound of old black men, most long dead, singing of their loss, their joy, their pain. They would snuggle together and listen to the music coming quietly over the little speaker and Robin would picture cotton fields, juke joints, smoke-filled rooms filled with blacks.

"Listen," Cape would whisper, "can't you just *hear* it?"

And Robin could. He could hear it. And he knew that what he was hearing was a thousand light years from anything his other, former self had ever experienced in those distant, nearly-forgotten days. That boy has dead now. Now he had become someone, something else.

"What time is it?" Priscilla asks.

"Almost ten."

"Mm." She sighs. "I'm due at Touch 'n' Go at noon."

"You've got time yet."

"Sure." She grins. "But I don't want to leave here. I'm a real beach bunny, lemme tell you. 'Course I guess you've figured that out by now. My only ambition in life is to find the ultimate beach and sleep on it forever." She giggles, then yawns.

"It shows," Robin says, smiling down at her. "You're nearly as dark as Koofie now."

"I know! I'm practically a mulatto! Well, it'll come in handy when we go off on our world jaunt."

"You aren't really going to do that, are you?"

Priscilla pushes her sunglasses down and looks at Robin for a moment, then slips them up again. "Of course we are. That's our plan. What, you don't believe us?"

"I don't know. It seems..." He searches for a word. "It seems *impossible*, I guess. And so expensive."

"It won't cost that much. We've saved more than enough for the plane tickets already and Koofie has been looking into how to cash-in some of her bonds and stuff. We want to leave next month."

"Next *month?*"

She glances over at him. "Sure, why not?"

"I don't know, I..." But he stops talking then, looks out at the morning sea. He realizes abruptly that somehow he had hoped to keep the current arrangement forever. He cannot remember a time that he has been as happy as he is now, with Cape, Priscilla, Koofie, the warehouse, unloading the heavy tires, movies and afternoon tea at warm outdoor cafes....

She grins. "Will you miss me?"

"Of course I will."

She puts her chin in her hands. "Well, I'll miss you too, you know. Even if the past weeks *have* been the first time I've seen you in five years. Does it seem like that long to you?"

"I don't know." He thinks about it. "Sometimes, I guess. Other times not. Time does funny things to me. Like now, thinking about all that—when I was at your house, and my mom died, and all that—it seems very recent. Like a few months ago or something. But then again, thinking of Cape just now, and thinking that we've only been together a week, it seems incredible. It seems like I've been with Cape forever."

She nods. "I know what you mean. I think that happens to everybody."

"And looking at you…" He hesitates. "I don't know. You've changed a *lot*."

"Well, Robin, I *was* only twelve years old the last time you saw me."

"I know. It's not that. You just seem so…so *sure* of yourself now. So…'together,' I guess that's the word."

She smiles. "I guess I am. I just made up my mind in high school to be who I was, and that's that."

"You make it sound easy."

"Oh, I don't know if it was or not. I just always knew I would have to get away from that place, and I wouldn't do it in any 'normal' way."

"Right. You were abnormal."

She laughs. "Maybe I was, at that. I mean, look at me now. A big, deep-voiced lesbian."

"Do your parents know?"

"I'm not sure," she says thoughtfully. "I've never *told* them. They know I live with a girl here. Probably my mom suspects. But it's not real to them. I mean, *I* was never real to them, so why should *that* be? I think that deep-down they just suppose I need a good man with a big cock."

Robin giggles. "Ever had one?"

"Cock, yes. Big, yes. Good, no." She grins. "And that's how I got to be where I am today—wherever that is." She looks towards

The Unspoken

him, through the dark glasses. "What about you, Robin? Did you have girlfriends?"

"No."

"So you always knew. About yourself, I mean."

He shakes his head. "I didn't *know*. I guess I still don't. It's all kind of confusing to me. I guess I just take it as it comes."

"So to speak."

He smiles. "So to speak."

"Well," she says, "you haven't changed so much. I mean, it's easy to picture you now when you were thirteen. Still serious and studious—"

"I hope you're not going to say *glum*."

She laughs.

"That goes back to time, though," he says. "The way things always seem to change, but somehow stay the same too. Like with my mom. I remember when I was a senior in high school, I used to calculate to myself how long she'd been gone. Four years and however-many months, whatever it was. But when I'd lay in bed at night, even though years had gone by, I'd think to myself that, you know, it wouldn't really surprise me if she walked into the room right now. And it wouldn't have. Because it all seemed so recent. If she'd walked into my room and sat down on my bed and said, 'Well, honey, it was just a misunderstanding, really I just took a long vacation,' I would have believed her and accepted it. It would only have been later that I would have thought to myself that it was impossible."

Priscilla nods. "She was cremated, right?"

He nods. "Mm-hm. But there's no memorial. Maybe that's another thing. Maybe it's never been really *real* to me. Maybe it isn't even now. Because it was—I don't know, absurd. In a way. One day she was there, the next day she was gone forever. But there was no tombstone or marker or even a container of ashes or anything."

He thinks for a moment, looking out at the water and noticing a vessel on it, somewhere in the indistinct distance. "I always wondered why my dad did it that way."

"Ever ask him?"

Robin smirks. "We don't discuss those things. We've *never* discussed them. After the funeral, and after all her things were sold or whatever, we never discussed her again."

"C'mon. Never?"

"Never. I swear to you. Not once."

There is a silence between them. Robin watches the distant ship on the horizon.

"I've been thinking about her a lot lately," he says, absently. "I don't know why."

Priscilla looks at him through her sunglasses.

"See, I've never thought about her much," he says. "I mean, not really. All through high school, I can't remember thinking much about her. Mostly I would have dreams. I would always have these dreams that she was alive again and I'd see her in the living room or something and say, 'But Mom, I thought you were dead.' And she'd say, 'Oh yes, I was, but it doesn't make any difference.' Or something like that. And we'd sit together and watch TV or listen to music or eat ice cream and even though I knew she was dead, it didn't matter." He shakes his head suddenly. "Crazy."

"Oh Robin," Priscilla says chidingly, "you're not going to get all serious on me now, are you?"

Robin laughs. "No. I don't want to be accused of being glum. I guess I'm talking too much."

"Look." She points. "That concession stand is open. Why don't you get us some Eskimo Pies or something?"

"I'm not sure I should. Maybe I need to keep an eye on my girlish figure."

Priscilla laughs, a low, throaty laugh that reminds Robin of years before. "Go, go, go," she says. "I don't want to see you sitting around here getting mopey."

"Yes, Mother."

He grins and stands up, slips on a pair of sandals and walks toward the wooden booth. What brought all that on? he wonders as he walks across the hot sand. All that talk about his mother? He never discusses her with anyone; never thinks about her anymore, really. It's gone, smoke in the wind, lost in time. He thinks of the first night with Cape, and feeling an urge then also to talk about it. He has wanted to talk to Cape about his mother. He has wanted Cape to talk about his own. But the subject has not reappeared since the first night. What is the point, really, of talking? What will it change? Nothing. But still he feels the compulsion. He shakes his head. Silly, he supposes; think about something else, about Cape. He smiles then.

So this is love? he had written in his diary that morning. *It feels like it. I can't think of anything but him. I don't want to think of anything but him. When I'm not with him, all I want is to be with him. Which, I suppose, is what people talk about when they use that L-word. Love? Love!*

He buys two ice cream bars from the vendor and returns to Priscilla.

"Here," he says. "Do you want the Eskimo Pie or the Fudgesicle?"

"Gimme the Fudgicle."

She sits up, having reclasped her bikini top, and Robin sits next to her. They unwrap the papers from their ice creams.

"So are you really going to miss me?" Priscilla says.

"Sure I will," Robin says.

"I'll send you postcards."

"Sure."

She nibbles at the ice cream. "'Cause you're kind of important to me in a way, you know?"

Robin nods.

"I mean, after all," she grins, "you *are* the first man I ever tried to jack off."

There is a brief silence; then, suddenly, they both burst out in laughter.

"Before you changed course!" Robin laughs.

Priscilla giggles, throatily. "Before I change course, right!"

One thing Robin finds endlessly fascinating about Cape is his ability to compartmentalize his life in such a way that he has entire groups of friends who are utterly unknown to other groups of his friends. "It's my way of leading different lives, I guess," Cape tells him. And that is exactly what he does: in the evenings, for instance, they spend time with his musician pals. "But none of them know I'm gay," he says proudly. "See, that's not real *big* on the music scene. So I keep my mouth shut about it." But on some evenings he takes Robin to gatherings of his homosexual friends. There, Cape is transformed from a musician to a fairly militant gay: Robin is amazed at the change, how on one evening Cape is a laid-back blues player, on another an articulate, passionate defender of gay rights.

The first such meeting Robin attends is a peculiar experience. Try as he might, he cannot grow accustomed, even with Cape, to the sight of men arm-in-arm with each other; it makes him feel vaguely dirty, somehow. The room where they meet is upstairs in someone's old house, a room decorated with *Gay Power* posters. There is much discourse among the twenty or so men there about gay legislation and gay tactics and *gayness*. There is something about the word Robin finds repulsive. The people at the meeting, most of them, seem obsessed with that single subject: their own sex lives. Robin stays conspicuously silent that evening, speaking only when he is riding in the van later, with Cape.

"You were pretty quiet tonight," Cape says.

Robin shrugs. "I didn't have much to say to those people."

Cape scowls. "But you should, you know. I mean, they're fighting your fight."

"I never thought of it as my fight."

"But it is," Cape says, down-shifting and exiting from the freeway. "Yours and mine—right? Laws. Prejudice. Hate crimes. This weird gay disease that's killing people and the government says doesn't exist."

Robin stares out the window at the lights of the city. Cape, he wants to say, I'm not really very interested in that stuff. I'm interested in you, not in *gayness*, whatever that is. But, he wonders, *should* he be interested in such things? Shouldn't he be involved with what one of them tonight kept calling "our struggle"? Why, then, does the subject fill him only with boredom and a vague embarrassment?

"Cape," he says, "let's not talk about it. Please? Haven't we had enough gayness for one evening?"

"What's the matter?"

"Nothing. But can't we talk about something else now?"

"Like what?"

Robin laughs. He much prefers, he suddenly realizes, other incarnations of Cape: the blues player, the sensitive lover in the back of the van.

"I don't know," Robin says. Then he grins. "Tell me how much you love me."

Cape laughs.

Robin leans his head against Cape's shoulder for a moment. The warmth, the firmness of that shoulder fills him with a warmth of his own. He takes a tape cassette and slips it into the player: Etta James.

"Oh, good choice," Cape says approvingly. "That woman can sing like nothing human."

He leans his head down and puts it in Cape's lap while Cape drives. The warmth begins to fill inside him wonderfully. And yet he is disturbed, somehow: uneasy: he does not know why.

"Cape?" he says, looking up at him when the van stops at a red light.

"Mm-hm."

"Do you really love me?"

Cape glances down at him. "Robin, what's wrong?"

"Nothing," Robin says, burying his face in Cape's blue jeans. "Nothing's wrong. Nothing's wrong."

6

Sometimes, when he lays for a long time in a dozing, semi-conscious state, he can wind out like a thread a long series of interrelated memories, in a sort of imagistic free association. Lately he has been doing this more and more often with his mother. He sees her as she was, years ago, in the house in the cul-de-sac, sees her face and hears her voice and watches her body moving within a willowy white gown or a low-cut black dress with lilies on it. He can conjure up, like a stage magician, a nearly endless thread of pictures and voices and sounds. He thinks mostly of the early days. He thinks of her as she was then, very long ago, before some stranger (dimly remembered now, hardly thought of) invaded the house and captured her and hid her somewhere in a dark dungeon. He can picture her teaching him to write, to form a and b and c. How old would he have been? Three, four? And he can hear her voice as she reads to him from Mother Goose and Hans Christian Andersen and Dr. Suess. He can feel her arms around him and the big book open before both of them with its wonderful color pictures and he can hear her talking in the voice of a witch or a wolf, turning low and gravelly and funny-scary; then she is a little girl, light, lisping; then a father or uncle, rounded and low like a big bass drum; and he sees it all rise before him, all the stories, all the characters and scenes lifting from the pages of the book, suddenly animate, suddenly three-dimensional and alive. And it was wonderful, that sudden life, that abrupt creation of something real where nothing had been before but pictures and print and pages and his mother's voice. Later, when he was a few years older, she would read poems to him, long heroic poems by Keats and Shelley and Lord Byron and Tennyson and Wordsworth and Coleridge. Later still, they would read together silently on lazy summer days, he with his head in her lap and a science fiction novel before him or a mystery or an adventure story, she with a thick romance or thriller. He sees the fruit of summer, the soft fuzzy apricots and smooth black plums and hard fat cherries in the wooden bowl that was always on the kitchen counter. He sees her canning them and making pies and jellies and jams and he smells the sweet steam filling the kitchen. He can see the clean blue skies of summer over them, can feel the shirt-sleeve-and-shorts warmth soaking into his body. He sees her in the bathtub, steam rising before her body; and her voice: *Honey, did you have a nightmare?* Then he hears her voice through the wall, the quiet sighs, feels his body tingling with shame, and feels his arms around her, tightly, holding her tightly, feeling her dissolve to ashes in his arms, melting to nothingness, and hearing his own voice crying to her, Don't go, come with me, Mom, look at me, I'm here, Mom, look at me.

When his eyes open he is looking at the stars through the window of the van.

Cape rustles next to him.

"Robin?" he says groggily. "Why are you tossing around? Do you have to go to the john?"

Robin sits up in the darkness. The night is warm and he pushes the blanket off his shoulders. "No, I'm all right. I'm sorry. Go to sleep."

"What is it?"

"Nothing."

Cape rubs his eyes. After a long pause he says, "Mmm...You're not real big on telling the truth, are you?"

Robin glances at him. "What do you mean?"

Cape yawns and stretches, then says: "I thought we had something nice going...."

"We do."

"But now all you do is clam up and tell me nothing's wrong when it's obvious something's eating at you."

He looks away. "I don't know...Maybe I'm thinking about Priscilla—Cissy—going away. And Koofie."

Cape grins sleepily. "Yeah, that's wild, isn't it? Looks like they're really going to do it."

"I know. Maybe I'm thinking about that. And maybe I'm thinking about college and my dad and what's going to happen to us."

"Ah-hah," Cape says. "I think we just hit the jackpot."

Robin smiles slightly. "Well?"

"Well, nothing. I don't know."

"Haven't you thought about it?"

"Sure I have. That doesn't mean I have any answers." Cape sits up and reaches toward a brown paper bag near him on the floor. He brings a donut out of a plastic package.

"Midnight snack?" he says, offering them to him.

"No, thanks. It's past midnight anyway."

"What time is it?"

"I don't know. But we didn't go to bed until past eleven."

"Mm." Cape chews on the donut, puffs of white powder falling from it and onto his chest. "Must be three or four."

"I don't know what to do," Robin says.

Cape watches him, chewing.

"I've only been here...what? Five weeks? Six? But it seems like I've known you all my life. And Santa Barbara." He shrugs. "Everything. I don't want to go back there now. I'm like...I'm a prisoner. You know? Like I've been in solitary confinement all my life and suddenly somebody granted me the right to live in the free world for a few weeks. Or maybe I should say for one week," he says, looking at Cape. "Now I'm a genie out of the bottle."

Cape smiles. "A very sexy genie."

Robin flushes and looks out the window at the stars. He sees a white gown, feet bare on wet wood, pictures a glittering shroud of stars around her and her body rising, levitating, floating toward the distant moon.

"It's weird," Robin says in a small voice. "I'm so...I don't know, *distracted* these days. My mind just darts all over the place. It can never settle on anything. I think about you and school and my cousin and...I don't know. Old things."

"Like what?" Cape touches his arm.

"My parents. My mom especially."

There is a short pause.

"What about her?"

"I...Just—her. The way she was. I keep remembering all these things like pictures, recordings. Does that ever happen to you?"

"Sure, sometimes."

"What kinds of things do you remember?"

Cape sighs, staring at the ceiling of the van.

Robin mutters, "You don't want to talk about it. Sorry."

"No, no," he says quickly, "it's okay. 'Cause I *do* think about it. Sometimes it's hard to—to articulate. I don't know. Mostly I think about the months before she died."

"Yes..."

"And that's bad, you know, because you want to remember people as they were when they were alive, not when they were in the process of dying."

"Mm-hm. I know. That's right."

"Still. When I think about her I mostly think about the hospital, at the end. The last two months. Her body was all bloated, her stomach I mean, from this huge tumor. Like she was pregnant, practically. It screwed her up so bad her liver stopped working so her whole body got…puffy. Jaundiced. That's what she really died of, when her liver quit. She drowned in her own—fluids."

"Yes."

"Sickening. Terrible. I remember the sound of the oxygen, the day she died. The way it hissed…"

"Yes."

A long silence. The wind rocks the van softly. After a time, Robin realizes Cape will say nothing more.

"I just don't want to go back there," Robin says finally, to break the silence.

After a pause, Cape says: "So, don't."

"And do what? Load tires all my life?"

"Be a writer. I thought that's what you wanted."

"It's not that easy. You have to pay the bills too."

"Why? When you can skip out on them?"

Robin chuckles. "Facile! Very facile."

"But not flaccid."

He grins. "Never flaccid."

"Anyway," Cape says, "I don't see what the big deal is. If you don't want to go back, don't go back. Stay here. Stay in Santa Barbara."

"I can't live in a van all my life. Or in a warehouse either. I'm used to showers. Clean clothes. Three squares a day."

"And Daddy?"

Robin frowns. "Cape, come on. He's paid my way through one year. Don't you think I at least owe it to him that I finish—"

"You don't owe him anything. Not from the stories I've heard. Hell with him."

Robin sighs. He remembers thinking exactly the same thing, a few weeks before—it seems like years, now—when he approached the dark turn-off to Wind Point and suddenly knew that he could no longer be there, could no longer return to that darkness, that night. When he knew suddenly that the time had come to change forever, to fly like a bird away from the lurking demons in that darkness. But now, he thinks, he is being drawn back into it again. The whirlpool is swarming over him again, returning him to the darkness and terror and sentient silence of the rooms. The house in the cul-de-sac had merely loosened its hold briefly, allowed him a momentary glimpse. But he knows he must return. Knows he must go back there, that he is being sucked toward it, hurled inevitably into it again. Perhaps he can last a few more weeks, no longer. He is running low on money. The tire-loading job will soon end. Priscilla and Koofie will be disappearing, flying on wings of money he does not possess. There is no hope. He will have to return there, to face the glowering silence in the boozy dark, the footsteps, the breathing. The nights spent doubled up in his dormitory room, the endless timbercut of words in the stupid textbooks, Turnham's lying beneficent smile in the hallways. All of it. The whirlpool is drawing him inexorably in. Time is ebbing away, the vacation is nearing its end, and he has no way of not returning. It is impossible. Even if he were to get another job, what would it pay? He could not afford a place to live. And certainly he cannot continue in Cape's van. Even now he itches from dirtiness. Icy salt-showers in the waves of the cove are not enough, he knows. Eating from paper bags is not enough. He sees the white-shrouded figure ascending toward the moon, floating through airless darkness.

"Maybe...you could come to Oregon?" Robin asks in a weak voice.

Cape does not say anything for a moment. Then, quietly: "I'd die in a place like that."

Robin smirks. "Join the club."

Cape brushes the donut powder from his body and touches Robin's waist. "We'll work it out," he says. "Let's talk about it in the morning. Talk in the dark is always lousy and everything always looks different when the sun's up. You know? Not so many problems and junk and...*mothers.*" He smiles.

Robin nods, returning the smile weakly, and they lie down again. Cape turns away and Robin puts his arm over Cape's body and in a few minutes he hears Cape's breathing become soft, deep, even. Robin puts his nose in Cape's hair and breathes in the salt-sweaty odor of it and closes his eyes. He can feel that sleep is still far away. He tries to relax his mind, tries to settle the images and sounds into a smooth nothingness; but the effort is too great. Within moments of his mind growing silent, something rises in it again. A picture. A voice. His mother's body settling itself next to him on the bed. Asking him if he is asleep. The sound of a window being shut. He shakes his head suddenly: pointless, he thinks, to allow these things to play in his head over and over. He settles in again next to Cape. He switches the images to more recent, more pleasant ones: Priscilla and Koofie in the bell tower on a warm, windy morning; the three of them giggling breathlessly as they tromp into one shop and out another along the beachfront; eating hot dogs from a vendor, mustard spurting out of Priscilla's and her voice laughing, *Oh no! Not another ejaculation!*

Then he pictures someone, himself perhaps, alone in an apartment calling the anonymous number and hearing a woman's voice saying obscene things to him. Pictures the man playing with himself in the darkness, listening to the breathy voice moaning and sighing over the telephone. Pictures the window of the apartment and the man looking out it and the sound of city traffic below. Hears the horns honking and sees, suddenly, a foot stepping from a curb and dim headlights rushing forward and the sudden flat *thump* of impact—

His eyes snap open.

He lies there, stroking Cape's forearm absently.

Awake, he thinks about the image of the man in the apartment with the telephone in his hand. Naked. Naked in a desolate, empty apartment. Listening to the faceless voice on the telephone, the fantasy voice, disembodied, breathing its rented passion out over the distant lines. The room dark. The man's voice cracked with emotion: *Talk to me. Will you talk to me?* Yes, he thinks. Yes. This is it. The story, poem, novel, whatever it is to be. It is within these images, these sounds. He sits up in the bed. He sees the faceless man before him with extraordinary vividness, sees the glistening sweat on his naked body, sees the phone quivering in his hand. One call? Or a series, night after night, to the same hired woman? Or even different women? No. The same woman. The same woman, night after night, running up hundreds of dollars in interstate phone bills. The man living for the calls every night. Talking to her longer and longer each time. Falling in love with the faceless voice. Growing obsessed with it. Yes. Yes.

Quietly he reaches into his bag for a notebook and pencil he keeps there. Cape stirs momentarily, then settles again. The moon is bright and allows in enough light so that Robin can just see the marks his pencil makes as it scratches across the small pages.

<hr>

The next few days pass in a curious blur. There is no shortage of activity. One morning he helps Cape haul his various guitars and amplifiers from an assortment of houses in Santa Barbara and they take the lot to the Burning Zombie, the club in Isla

Vista owned by the owner of the warehouse. That night Robin, Priscilla, and Koofie sit at a small round table in a dim, cramped room, cheering Cape on with fifty or sixty other patrons: he has several very fine solos with the blues band and sometimes shares vocals with the lead singer. After, they all sit at a crowded table drinking until the club closes. Priscilla and Koofie begin packing: "We've got the tickets!" Priscilla announces one day. "Hawaii, Australia, Europe, India, Africa, the Orient! Robin, we're going *everywhere!*" When he thinks of it, it saddens him; and in a strange, unknowable way, frustrates him as well. But the fact is that he thinks of nothing very much—not Cape, not Priscilla or Koofie—besides his story. It lives in his mind with the vividness of a fever dream—the man in the dark room, the telephone, the cracked voice. They continue to spend their nights together in the van, but during the day Cape is taken up with band rehearsals at the Burning Zombie and Robin visits the beach: each morning he finds a comfortable place, sets out a towel and a beach umbrella borrowed from Priscilla, brings out his notebook, and proceeds to work. He finds that he does not necessarily *write* much in any one day. More often he sits, staring at the ocean through his sunglasses, letting images and sounds play across his mind. He continues to hear his mother's voice and soon he has begun to puzzle out how to put her, or someone like her, into the story. Why would the man be so desperate as to make calls like these? Who is he? What is his background? He builds lives for the man in the story, many lives, tearing them apart again with the casualness of a small boy knocking down houses of wooden blocks. Certain details he keeps. His mother. He thinks of her. Thinks of the long dark curls rolling on her shoulders and her Siamese-shaped, sky-colored eyes, her moon-round face, and her body in the black lily-sprayed dress. He wonders why he is so haunted by her now. Haunts. Ghosts. Monsters: demons. Both of them. For he thinks now also of his father, the footsteps in the night, the shouted accusations, the milky eyes grown hazy with alcohol. The huge photograph in the window glowering at him and proclaiming: *I Can Insure Your Future.* But too there are the warm mornings, too often unthought of, when they play tennis in the rising light and eat lunch in a nice cafe on the mainland. It is a jumble of image, sound. He thinks of demons, ghastly black figures in the night. Thinks of his mother, sees her eyes glistening in the darkness. Demons. Beautiful demons.

Often he will walk out onto a nearby pier in the early evening, after having spent the entire day writing and thinking of writing. The sunsets are clear and gorgeous in the southern California summer and he will stare out at them for long minutes, thinking vaguely of the blinded Oedipus and the warm yellow box of light in the hallway in the house in the cul-de-sac. He will listen to the sound of the ocean. He will think of her, the thousand blackened bits of her sinking and dissolving into deep blue eternity. He begins to picture in his mind his character, his faceless man, standing at the shore. Standing there, transfixed by the vision of the sunset and the clouds, pink and orange in the vivid light. Pictures the man walking slowly into the water. Why? he wonders. Although he has written many pages of manuscript, the images have not yet coalesced into anything resembling a coherent narrative. He sees the figure on the beach. Thinks of the darkness, the telephone. Thinks of the beautiful demons.

7

And when it ended, Robin thought later, it ended with the swiftness of a scythe slicing through flesh.

"Robin, what am I supposed to do?" Cape asked him. "New York! It's a real opportunity."

Robin looked at the teardrop eyes, the dark hair through which his fingers had run, the strong hands.

"I don't know."

"Then why are you looking like that?"

"Can you blame me?"

"I guess not. But goddamn it, Robin! I can't turn down an invitation like this!"

"No."

"And anyway, we'll write, right? And next time you get a long holiday you can come out and see me. Or next time I'm in California..."

"I love you, Cape." The words were strange in his mouth.

"Robin..."

"But I don't even know you. You're just a blur. And now you're going away and leaving me here."

"Don't."

"You jump into my life and then jump back out like a...a..."

"That's not fair. Did I know this was going to happen?"

"Still..."

"Still what? What?"

Robin shook his head.

"When are you leaving?" he asked.

"Soon. As soon as I can get packed and set. Tomorrow."

Robin nodded.

Cape looked closely at him, his voice growing softer.

"Do you want to stay together tonight?"

Robin looked away. For a moment he could not speak. Then, with effort, he forced a croak from his throat.

"No," he said.

And still later, when he thought of it again, he would visualize a cell dividing: but not in the slow graceful way he vaguely remembers from long-ago films in Biology class, but with a sudden awful ripping, an amputation, which left him raw and open and bleeding and only half-conscious, half-alive. One day Cape was there and the next day he was not. He wanted to talk of it to Priscilla or Koofie, but they were busy in their own preparations for flight and anyway, it was obvious they could never understand: for he and Cape had been together, he realized with a hazy shock, exactly twelve days. He would sit out on the grass in the park on Anacapa Street watching the cars and pedestrians and think of the faraway dormitory, curling up in the darkness and holding his midsection close, trying to hold back an enormous darkness he could feel growing inside him, a sickness, a madness, that he could, at times like this, feel growing within him like a cancer, a deadly black cell reproducing itself wildly, in a frenzied orgasm of its own re-creation, and the darkness spreading—like the silence of the house in the cul-de-sac—malevolently, and seeping into every crevice, every corner of his body, into his brain and heart and lungs and liver and spleen, and he could not control it, the darkness, he could only hold himself tightly, try to keep it from overwhelming him, from devouring him from within. It was at these times that he was terribly reminded of his madness. His sickness. His depravity. It was not a thing traceable to any single, observable trait or quality: rather, it was an all-encompassing, ubiquitous truth of himself. He was alive, yes, but what was his life, what sins had he committed, and how had he destroyed his life? How had he become what he was? That he was a monster was obvious. That he was diseased was evident. But was there a way to change? He could not find one. Even in the dormitory, he had sometimes found himself running the word through his mind: *God. God. God.* But it left him cold, barren. He could sense no shaft of light leading him to the stars. Only solitude, fright, the darkness within. He would feel, at times like this, that he knew the darkness intimately: that he understood it: that, just perhaps, it was not something alien, an intruder—like the woman in the snake-mask—but rather an integral, essential aspect of himself, unable to be severed or altered. Perhaps he could no more alter the darkness, the sickness, than he could alter his bones or his blood. But what was the darkness? he would wonder. This thing that he knew and yet could not describe or comprehend? Of what did it consist? It was alive, surely; but what was its life? How did it live? Was it too connected to the enormous oneness, the connection-points that, once or twice in a dozen years, he had glimpsed as one glimpses a ship as it approaches through a dank, low-lying fog, appearing and disappearing? He would sit in the cool shaded grass, thoughts and images playing across his mind-stage. He saw himself ripped apart, stumped limbs spurting blood on some indistinct battlefield. He saw the boxes that had been his mother being carted out the front door into a waiting van that took it all away, like garbage, to unknown destinations. Saw bits of bodies flying apart, hers, his own, and great blooms of night blossoming from their exploded chests, their burst lungs, huge animate forms like crazed mutant orchids devouring the dismembered limbs, swarming hungrily over the air itself, wrapping everything in their cloaks of living silence. Heard her voice, bobbing up like an island in the sea: *We'll float right up to the moon.* Saw the moon floating in the sky, and the sea, heard the profound thunder of the tides, and the moon and the sea were inextricably linked across the vast galactic gulf of darkness, reaching to each other, and the sea reflecting the moon back upon itself in a thousand fragmentary glimpses. Reflections of each other. Inexorable connections across the dark void. And he saw her floating there, a ring of glittering gems around her pale neck, suspended like a ghost under the moonlight, over the sea...Then the glitters coalesced, melted together into two lights, two malevolent orbs in a foggy dusk, rushing, rushing toward the foot stepping from the curb. Stepping. Without seeing? Drunkenly? Accidentally? Had it been an accident? Had she stepped out deliberately? Had she killed herself? Had she sliced their hearts apart on purpose? What had happened? What had happened? And then the two globes come at him and he feels a dull pain in his hip and Turnham's voice reaches him filled with rain: *Are you all right?* His vision blurred and a shadowy woman in the halls—*Look at me. How many fingers am I showing?*—a figure of darkness with an umbrella, disappearing into the mist. Are you all right? Look at me.

He would try to control the thoughts and the visions by thinking of his story. Picturing instead the man in the dark room, the telephone, the rented voice tinnily in his ear. But every time he thought of the man in the dark room he was led back again to the sea, to the man standing watching the tides and the skies before him. And as he thought of the sea he would be led back to the blackened bits floating through their dark eternity and the thread of his story would dissolve, leave him with only disconnected images, sounds, cries, and the sense of the great darkness. *when I come home from somewhere she is there waiting for me.* A melody sung by a siren. For, although it came to him again and again, it would speak no more: it would not yield up its secrets. And so things merely whirled by in his mind senselessly. He would think of Cape again, or try to think of him. But at times he would find that he could not summon up the image in his mind. Could not find the voice, the touch, the odor. Yet it had been but a day, two days, three: how could Cape have vanished inside him so completely, so utterly? When the figure floating to the moon was so vivid, nearly tangible? So nearly alive? As if time itself had somehow stretched and distorted, sand in a melting hourglass weaving madly to and fro, and bits of memory, shards of time weaving in and out of him like disjointed chunks of film. Old slivers suddenly new and bright and clearly visible. And recent pieces missing; suddenly, mysteriously gone. And yet, even without his image, even with only a shadowed recollection, constantly fragmented, of his face or body or voice, he would find himself missing Cape: with a terrible, aching longing nestled securely within the darkness inside him. Gone. Smoke in wind. Off to an unimaginable life in an unimaginable city, just gone, severed from him utterly. For twelve days it was as if a magic door had been opened and an electric, supernal light had shone upon him: then, as suddenly as it had opened, the door had slammed shut again, leaving him in the darkness.

    He would wander in the dusty-dark book shops, seeking solace in thumbing through tattered copies of Sara Teasdale and Edna St. Vincent Millay, trying to find the charm he had once seen in their fragile, melancholy lyrics; but where before he had seen delicacy, now he saw only brittleness. He would bring Nietzsche down from a forgotten shelf and search out the wonderful incantations of eternity; but they seemed overblown now, hysterical. One day he found a hardcover copy of a Terrence Llewelyn book, *The Professor Remembers and Other Stories*—a first edition some thirty years old—and purchased it, studying for hours the photo on the dust jacket: Llewelyn's jet-black hair dramatically slicked-back, his long, aristocratic face, the dark, almond-shaped eyes that seemed to glow with intensity. A cashmere sweater was tossed casually over his shoulders. Behind him were books: and Robin studied the titles closely, what he could see of them, wondering if reading every one of them (Virgina Woolf, Kafka, Mansfield, Trollope, in no apparent order) would make him into someone who could write a story like Llewelyn's. Who could find that exquisite, profound connection, who could create a scene as timelessly perfect as Llewelyn's professor on his death bed and the children's voices outside causing a vision of himself as a child to rise before him at the moment of his death. But, although he considered trying, he knew it would be futile. And as he looked across the rows and rows of "contemporary fiction," he knew only despair. All of these were living writers, his reason told him. Alive. Breathing. They ate and drank and talked and had sex and went to the toilet—or so his reason said. Instinctively, he knew it was false. Instinctively he knew that those names, Llewelyn and dozens of others, did nothing of the sort, that they were not flesh-and-blood beings like himself, but rather heavenly glowing angels of light who floated somewhere in the silver stratosphere and held communion with the gods, with Dickens, with Shakespeare, with Flaubert and Marlowe and Keats. And that was why, he knew, he was destined to fail. For he was mere skin, mere marrow and bone and blood. He was one with the universe, perhaps, but those names on the shelves were not of his universe; they existed somewhere else, on some plane of super-reality he could never hope to touch.

But now, thumbing through titles aimlessly, at random, he found he could concentrate on none of it, think of none of it. It all seemed to him false, unreal. He would shove a book back onto the shelf and yank another down, glance through it, and shove it back again. He did this over and over in the book shops, in the library. He could read the books for a minute or two but then the words would begin to break up, to become only random black branches in a sea of white: meaningless. He would wander then to the music shops, where thumping rock or sensual jazz or noble classical musics were pouring from loudspeakers: and he found himself rather enjoying the primitive raucousness of the rock 'n' roll shops, where groups with names like Black Sabbath and Aerosmith would scream out of the speakers and inside the darkened, dope-smelling shops he could see under dirty glass cases things like roach clips, rolling papers, many a mysterious item of drug paraphernalia. The blasting music did not clear his fragmented mind, but it covered it, made it imperceptible. He rather like the sensation. To have the darkness *screamed* out of him!

But finally he knew that it was over, that his burst into the sunlight, his re-creation of himself, was in the end an illusion. He would have to go back to school. Cape was gone and Priscilla and Koofie were leaving and, as impossible as it seemed inside his mind, the whole marvelous dream—for that was what it was, or what it seemed—was dissolving like mist in morning, or like a stage set being carted away by hired hands, broken up and sent in a dozen different directions. The play was over, the revels ended, and he was left alone, he thought to himself, in his darkness. He would have to pack his meager belongings and make the long drive back to Wind Point. It was over. Cape was in New York and Priscilla and Koofie were beginning a trip that would take them around the world and Robin Withers was going back to the damp dormitory room in foggy northern California, to listen to more jabbering in desultory classrooms while the rain pelted the window panes and he stared out at the fog-heavy mountains of redwoods and wondered when, when he would ever really break free, become an angel of light, if he would ever free himself of his darkness and float with the celestial ones. For a few weeks it had seemed possible: now, he saw nothing before him but the cluttered desk with sloppy stacks of student essays on top. His destiny, he would think. His absolutely inevitable fate. A vision beckoning to him: but was the vision a siren too? Would it lead him to the life that must be his, or was it only a devious illusion? A helping hand toward the final darkness, a surrender to the dreamless void?

8

A few days after Cape's departure Robin drives his car up into the Santa Barbara foothills, warm and gorgeous this time of year: filled with winding nature trails, thousands of green trees. He drives the narrow roads interminably, for hours, echoes and dim shadows playing across his mind: formless, voiceless, in a hazy jumble. He feels confused. While the pain of Cape's departure is still with him, he finds himself thinking less and less of it: more and more, instead, of the story he is trying to write. The man in the dark room, the telephone. Only days before he had been bursting with excitement about it; now he feels used-up, useless, a dry husk where once had been a mighty green stalk. Somehow the piece had gotten derailed. One morning he took up his pad and paper at the beach and found that there was nothing there anymore. The story simply stopped, in the middle of a paragraph. And it refused to move a word further. After the ease with which the first pages had been written, it was shocking: what was happening? Where did it go? The room, the man, the sounds, the atmosphere? Lost. He had wandered the beach aimlessly, trying to recapture it. The woman's voice. The man's, pleading, naked in the room. The traffic going by outside. But it was no good. It was gone.

    Robin stops the car at a small clearing where there is a tiny trickle of river, no wider than a rope or a ribbon. He gets out of the car and goes to the ribbon and puts his hand in it and splashes some of it on his face. It is cold and fresh. He stands up and looks around at the infinity of green foliage around him and at the sun above him, the rays fractured by the endless limbs and branches, pouring brokenly down through the trees and landing in jagged pieces on the floor of the forest. He hears blackbirds and blue jays in the trees and the wind passes through the high branches like distant echoes. As he stares up into the trees the wind begins to rise and the echoes grow louder, more insistent. He feels the wind at his back, blowing his hair and ruffling his shirt. The light breaks up as it shines through the waving trees and the bits of light on the ground shift, change their shapes, blink brightly on and off, here and there. The wind grows, whips the branches, and a torrent of leaves whisk past him and tumble along in the bushes and over the earth. He stares up at the mad trees and the line comes to him again: *when I come home from somewhere she is waiting for me.* He thinks of a letter, a note really, received yesterday: *I'm very disappointed that you've decided to waste your summer this way. I trust you're coming home soon. Home is where you belong.* The wind whips the trees savagely and suddenly he is in his room again and the window is ajar and she is sitting next to him on the bed, and he hears her voice and the wind outside intermingling, becoming one. He sees her hair blown back in the wind on a summer afternoon. Words suddenly begin to tumble forth in his brain as he stands there. The line, the brief, siren-like line, *when I come home from somewhere*, which he had written so many eternities ago, suddenly and magically begins to run on, like tickertape, the entire piece suddenly filling his mind and soul, arriving to him nearly entire, and he is only vaguely aware of having brought out his notebook in the torrential wind and the leaves blowing across the pages: he is elsewhere now, in the room with her, with her there, she is waiting for him, and she has a drink in her hand, and her breath smells of it and her voice is slurred mysteriously, dangerously, and he feels sudden fright, no, not fright, terror, sheer unspoken terror of the woman in the chair, sitting there, waiting for him. His pencil flies across the page but he is hardly aware of the process. Then something else begins to happen. He sees his father. He sees his father and himself and suddenly there is an enormous rush of memory pouring over him, far vaster than the vision of his mother in the chair, and suddenly, without pausing even for an instant, he finishes with the woman in the chair and begins on something else, he sees a dark room and a telephone but the man is not calling some anonymous voice, no, he is calling someone else, someone important, and they are talking, saying things to each other, but there is a hollowness, a meaninglessness to the conversation, he hears them speaking love-words to each other, *I love you, I love you*, but the words have no meaning because the man in the darkness feels the darkness within him, and Robin sees the man on the phone and then on the beach staring at the light in the sky and the clouds and suddenly the man has a face, and the woman on the phone, and the rooms, the atmospheres, they are suddenly real, he sees them all rise before him, he hears their voices and sees them moving in the rooms and suddenly, somewhere within himself, he realizes that this is it, what he has been waiting for, the pencil is flying across the page as if he were in a trance, the faces and voices and rooms come alive at last, alive, and he sees the faces and hears the voices and walks among the people in their rooms and the pencil flies across the page faster, ever faster, the pencil flies, it flies.

9
DROWNING
by Robin Withers
Chapter One

As they pull up in the driveway it all seems the same to him; only a new rear porch overlooking the ocean indicates that there has been any passage of time whatever. The illusion holds as long as he doesn't look at his dad in the driver's seat. Then, of course, it rushes back to him, like fire through a tunnel, how long it's been since he was here: nearly unbelievable, he thinks, how five years have changed his dad's face, made it gray, sallow, made the skin sag around his mouth and jaw. He has seen his dad now and then over these years; but only just now, studying his profile as they pull up in the driveway in the late-afternoon sun, has he really noticed the changes. He wonders if his own face has changed so much.

His dad brings the car to a stop and shuts off the motor. They stare at the closed garage door for a moment and then his dad says, "Well, how's it all look?"

"Good," he answers. "Fine."

His dad nods and grins too heartily and they step out of the car. It's warm and windy, good late-spring Santa Barbara weather, and only a few distant, wispy clouds are dabbed upon the otherwise unbroken blue sky above them. The sun is sinking slowly into the horizon and it makes the sea so bright he can hardly look at it—a dazzling thing, a brilliant green plain with hundreds of flashing silver coins tossed onto it. It's beautiful, he supposes.

"Tell you what, Seeg," his dad says, opening the car's trunk, "we'll get your stuff inside and you can unpack and then I've got a real dinner for us. Got filet mignon."

He nods. "Sounds great."

"We'll barbeque out here on the porch—my *new* porch," he says, grinning and winking. It's a habit of his, whenever he's showing something off, to grin and wink. He's done it ever since Siegel can remember.

"I'm kind of tired, though, Dad—maybe I could lay down for a while beforehand?"

"Oh, sure, sure, sure," his dad agrees quickly, hoisting the bag onto his shoulder and closing the trunk again. "It'll take some time for the coals to burn down anyway." His dad looks at him briefly. "Yeah, you look tired, kiddo."

He shrugs.

"Well, come on," his dad says, "you know where the room is."

Inside, it is as if he is looking at his own life through a pane of strangely flawed glass: the polished wood floors are the same, the Indian throw rugs, the off-white walls, even some of the furniture. But the old TV has been replaced by a shiny new home entertainment system, complete with VCR and fancy turntable (my dad? music? he thinks); the old hackneyed ocean scenes on the wall have disappeared and been replaced by several art nouveau prints in elaborate metal frames; the too-low coffee table which sat in front of the sofa is now a bright glass-and-gold affair, and the sofa itself is new. He has a curious sensation of being *here* and *not-here* simultaneously. He feels a touch of dizziness but it passes.

"What do you think?" his dad says. "I'm fixing it all up."

"I can see," he says. "It's nice. A lot different."

His dad stands there, turned half toward Siegel and half toward the room, hands on his hips and a look of satisfaction on his face. His dad: a big man, well over six feet, an impression of solidness: he stands there with his legs wide apart, the stance of a man comfortable with his own body, its weight, its balance. He is older, no question about that—the past five years have added ten to his appearance—but his figure is still formidable. His face helps this impression. Wide and sharply angled as if cut from wood, a big face, with a long mouth and thick white mustache and pale, intelligent eyes; the creases in his skin are deep, like dark canyons, and his hair is a thick, loosely curled mass of pure white.

"Let me show you this baby," he says, going to the stereo. "You've got to listen to this for a minute."

He puts on an LP of some country music and Siegel stands next to him listening to a woman moan in a Nashville twang about her heart being an empty bottle tossed into the sea. It's a lousy song, Siegel thinks, and the stereo isn't much better, but it's all right because at least the music relieves him for a moment of the problem of talking—an activity he has terrible trouble with around the man next to him. Always has. In the institution, during the many long stretches of having nothing whatever to do, he would imagine long conversations with his dad: shining, brilliant dialogues in which they said witty and meaningful things to each other. Sometimes he would actually say his part aloud, pretend his dad was in the chair across from him. It was something he'd always done, make up imaginary dialogues with people, things he would never say to them in real life. (*Real life*, he thinks, a sticky concept.) He suspected everyone did it, now and then. But it had become a regular pastime with him. Usually they were with his dad, but sometimes with old friends, or others in the house (house? institution?); once in a long while with his mom. But those not often.

His dad shuts off the LP abruptly. "Not bad, huh?" he grins.

Siegel smiles. "Pretty snazzy."

He nods, apparently satisfied with Siegel's response. "Let me show you some of my other new toys," he says. He shows off the new sofa, the TV and VCR, the paintings; they move into the kitchen, where all is new tile, new appliances, a microwave, shiny new surfaces. He tells Siegel about the virtues of a microwave: "I'll tell you, you pop a potato in there, zap! Six minutes and you got a baked potato. Hot soup? A minute or two. It's amazing!"

"It sure is," Siegel agrees. God, can't they think of anything better to say than this? Isn't there something more to talk about than baked potatoes and hot soup? After all this? Why has it always been this way? They'll go to their graves, he thinks, talking about potatoes and soup. He remembers that his mom had never allowed a microwave in the house, said it wasn't real cooking.

"And look here!" he continues, opening the door to the new refrigerator. Although it is nearly empty otherwise, there are two big steaks under some plastic wrap. "Pretty good, huh?" he says, lifting the plate out and winking. "Choice stuff. Figured we deserved it."

Siegel smiles. They are nice steaks, though food is the furthest thing from his mind; still, the idea of steak does sound good, if only because his dad is almost childishly excited about it. He has always had this quality, his dad, this ability to become so wound up in a thing that his excitement rubs off on Siegel. Siegel wonders sometimes if he himself has any capacity left for getting very excited about anything.

He stops thinking about it as his dad replaces the steaks in the refrigerator. "Well," he says, "I'm going to bring out that barbeque and get the coals going. You heading upstairs?"

"Yeah, I think so. For a while."

"Okay, kiddo. Take your time. I'll come get you if you don't come down."

"Okay. Great." He is about to step out of the kitchen when instead he turns and, vaguely embarrassed, says: "Thanks, Dad."

He turns quickly and leaves the kitchen. It occurs to him that he might have stayed; maybe his dad would even have asked him what he meant, and perhaps that could have led into a real conversation. The kind he used to fantasize about during those long stretches of tedium. But, even though he wants such a conversation, or thinks he does, the idea is nonetheless quite terrifying—just like walking the plank, he thinks, blindfolded and with a sword at your back, until *sploosh!* you hit those shark-infested waters.

But is his dad the shark? Or the one holding the sword?

He smiles to himself as he picks up his bag and heads upstairs. Dream interpretation, another common pastime. Searching for hidden meanings in everything—and not only in dreams. He could do it right now. Why, for instance, did he sling his bag over his left shoulder and not his right? Why did he hook his right thumb in the pocket of his jeans? Why is he even thinking about it at this specific moment? He chuckles quietly. In the institution, though, his self-analysis had been dead serious. He had scrutinized everything he did. Everything he thought. Tried to leave nothing unanalyzed. He gave himself a much more thorough going-over than any of the people there ever had....

And to what end? Did any of it—his own earnest self-evaluations, the long sessions in Hewitt's office—did any of it ultimately mean anything? Or do any good? He doubted it. He was the same person now that he had been. All his life, it seems to him, he has been trying to reach some new level, some other self—as far back as the very first day of kindergarten, he has been waiting. Kindergarten, he thought, would make him different: he would be in school, which meant maturity, grown-upness. But it turned out that it hadn't really made him feel any different at all. The next step was grade school. No difference there, either. Junior high.

High school. Virginity-loss. Emotional...what to call it? Collapse? Breakdown? Anyway, here he was now, at the other end of it, and he could swear that he still doesn't feel any different at all. Was it possible that the sum total of his knowledge, everything he'd learned in twenty-two years of life, amounted to zero? And if that were so, well, did anybody anywhere ever really learn anything? *We work in the dark. We do what we can.* Henry James. Remembered from an aborted attempt at college a few years before. The dark is right, he muses. An image flashes across his mind of a bunch of blindfolded people stumbling about in a dim room.

He smiles as he reaches the top of the stairs and opens the door to his bedroom. Here things are not so eerie, somehow—the same bed, rug, mirror, but everything else has been removed, repainted, changed, so that it hardly seems like his old room at all; more like a pleasant hotel. He slips the bag off his shoulder onto the foot of the bed and then goes to the window and opens the curtain a crack. That, at least, hasn't changed: a perfect, unobstructed view of the Pacific sunset, all splashed just now with bright pink and gold. And yet it has, he realizes abruptly as his eyes fall on the new rear patio and his dad wheeling the barbeque out onto it. Nothing is quite the same here anymore. He watches his dad for a few moments, then turns away from the window.

What now? He could unpack his meager belongings, but that can wait. He could lie down. He could shower. *Decisions*. He stands motionlessly and lets the word flutter around in his brain. He remembers the problem with decisions too well.

There in bed (this was years ago, in his apartment), he would wake suddenly in the morning and be faced with an infinity of choice. A shower or a bath? Glasses or contacts? What shirt? Pants? Shoes? What for breakfast? And all of it seemed so terribly irrelevant as he lay there, his eyes closed against the bright morning light. What difference did it make, finally? What possible difference to anyone? Why, then, decide at all? If it made no difference what he decided, he could simply avoid any decision whatever. That in itself would be a decision, of course, but a much easier one: a decision *not to act.* To stay where he was. Not move. And often he didn't move, not for hours. Until late afternoon, sometimes. Instead he would lay there and drift. That was the best way. Neither here nor there. The terror was being *somewhere,* pinned down to a particular point in time and space, subject to the laws of existence and choice. As long as he could maintain his place in nowhere, in nothing, it was all right: and so he would lie there, drifting.

It's a mark of maturity, he supposes, that he now finds being nowhere the source of unease; whereas somewhere—a particular, firm point—is now comforting rather than terrifying. Gives him a feeling of certainty. So much so that he can no longer sleep at all: he is afraid of that nether world of drift. And he is terribly conscious of himself, the fact that he is trying to sleep. He is always self-conscious now. Super-aware of himself. But no one back there, at the institution, would listen: he remembers pleading with Hewitt to give him something, anything, so he could sleep: but Hewitt was not generous with prescriptions: though Siegel did manage, finally, to locate some Valiums, through a fellow lodger...lodger! He grins. Guest? Inmate? The semantics were such a problem.

He considers lying down, but his thinking about it has made him wary. Instead he steps to the bathroom and prepares for a shower. Even the bathroom is changed: a tub has been installed where there had only been a shower before. He sets his glasses on a shelf and strips off his T-shirt and then sits on the lid of the toilet to pull of his shoes. He still has a pretty good form, it seems to him; pale, yes, but the muscles are fairly solid, the overall shape is okay. He stands and strips off his pants. He can see the shadow of his ribs under his skin; his nearly hairless legs have become rather thin too, but it's hardly noticeable. He wonders what he'll look like at his father's age.

As he turns on the water and feels it pour down his body he can hardly keep from thinking about Rachel. She has hardly crossed his mind in months, but suddenly, in this place, this house, she is unavoidable. When he shuts his eyes he sees her with dazzling clarity, just as if she were standing before him, showering with him, as she used to do when his dad and mom went out for the evening. They took crazy chances, losing all track of time up there in his room. But they were never caught; he doesn't suppose anything too bad would have happened even if they had been, but at that time, when they were both sixteen, it was more the excitement of trying to hide, the assumed danger. In retrospect, he realizes, neither of his parents could possibly have been fooled. Certainly his dad knew from the very beginning. His mom must have, too. But oh, those evenings: he would call her the second they left, she would be there in a few minutes, and as soon as they met at the door they were practically at each other's clothes—it was an effort to get all the way up the stairs. God, he wonders, were they ever that young? And he remembers what had occurred to him a few minutes ago, about feeling just the same as he always has, eternally unchanged. He realizes that it's not quite true. He feels *older*. Tired a lot of the time. He never remembered being tired with Rachel, not, at least, until the very end of a long evening of acrobatics. Today he could never go that long, that many times, not with the Lithium and Valium and dizzy spells and shortness of breath.

He wonders what's become of Rachel. She sent him a couple of letters at the beginning of his…what? Semantics again. *Internship*, he thinks, smiling. A couple of cheery, false letters that prattled on about people they knew in high school and things like that. Very unlike Rachel; it was obvious how uncomfortable the whole thing made her. And, as he never answered the letters, they stopped coming very quickly. It especially disappointed him that she never visited. He couldn't really have expected her to;

after all, she became engaged, engaged to that...what was his name? Anyway, it had been broken off a few months ago. She could have visited then, but she hadn't. And now he had actually lost track of her. Was she still in college? Or would she have graduated? An odd sensation, not knowing: for nearly five years they had been so wrapped up in each other's lives, maybe too wrapped up, knowing every detail of the other. Now, at this very moment, she might be in her parents' house only a few miles away; or she could be anywhere on the globe. He really has no idea. He doesn't want to think about it anyway. He prefers the past. Memories are usually a trap for him, he thinks, but not with Rachel. He enjoys thinking of those times. It occurs to him how much she would have loved this new bath. But then the shower had been plenty of fun too....

He suddenly realizes he has an erection. It's been a long time since he's seen one; what with the drug treatments and everything else, sex has been the furthest thing from his mind for... how long? Nearly a year. He looks at it with a detached sense of amusement. He has always thought there was something intrinsically absurd about the erect penis. Rachel had told him he was crazy, that it was beautiful, that he shouldn't be ashamed of his own body. But he had never been ashamed, really. Amused was the word for it. A woman's body, now, there was softness there, tenderness, inner space, a capacity to *bring in*. But with a man it was all external, a big stick, a meat-club. There was something funny about it.

When he was a teenager, before he'd met Rachel, he'd often wondered if he should have been born a woman. He remembers studying his face in the mirror for long minutes, visualizing what it would be like with long lashes, lipstick, hair flowing to his shoulders...Not that he'd ever truly wanted a sex-change or something like that. No, it was more a feeling that he was in some unknowable, unsayable way, simply more woman than man. The feeling had faded as he grew older, but still, now and then, he would suddenly hear its echo, in strange and unexpected places.

But there remains the problem of the erection. He has, it seems to him, three options. Deal with it in the shower; get out of the shower and deal with it in the bedroom; or don't deal with it at all. He tends toward the last. He is tired; there will be plenty of time, he thinks, to worry about that kind of thing. Now that he's here...But it does seem a pity to waste a perfectly good hard-on. He touches it briefly, feels the sudden tingling sensation course through him. It is tempting. But so is the thought of slipping between the cool sheets in his room and blotting out everything, falling into an endless dark—if he can, that is, if he can let go. He closes his eyes and forces his body to relax.

Finally he shuts off the water and steps out of the shower. He towels himself off and then goes to his bag on the bed and fishes out a fresh pair of shorts. He puts them on and slips into the bed.

He remains there for a long time, his eyes closed in the semi-darkness of the room. He can hear his dad on the patio below, removing the barbeque grill and pouring the charcoal briquets. Tearing paper for kindling. Then there is silence. It is some time before he realizes that his fists are balled tightly at his sides. He relaxes them. He tries to think of nothing, to make his mind a smooth blank. But Rachel's image keeps coming back to him. Then his dad, the dad he grew up with, younger and healthier. He wonders when was the last time they touched each other. He can't remember.

He turns over in the bed. He suddenly realizes that his hands are balled into fists again. He relaxes them. Then he tries to relax his shoulders and neck. His body is a wire of tension. He thinks about Rachel. He sees her shoulder-length dark hair, her small, pretty face and deep blue eyes: never a showstopper, Rachel, but pretty. Perhaps a bit too *together* for him sometimes: she never seemed mystified by anything or confused, or frightened, at least not until near the very end. Very logical, Rachel. Not that she wasn't passionate, she was, but there was something about her, a deep calm or certainty, that he had always found a little disconcerting. It was at such odds to his own nature. It became a problem for them at the end: she became exasperated with him, asking him over and over, What is *wrong* with you? What do you *want?*

But it was something words couldn't explain.

How could he describe the feeling that something, a totally undefinable, unknowable thing, was waiting for him somewhere just beyond the edge of his consciousness? Some dark, awful thing, like a cold black ocean? How could he explain that feeling? When he didn't even know what it was? Madness? Death? How could he ever explain it to her, this thing, this presence, that frightened him...not even frightened, exactly. Frightened wasn't the word. There were no words. That was the problem. There were no words, and words were all he had.

He shifts in the bed again. They had all looked for the absurdly simple answers. He could have told them even then that what they were looking for couldn't be found in convenient psychological pockets. It was something within him, something everyone knew, everyone carried, but could not speak of. He remembers the long sessions with the first psychiatrist—what was her name? Liona. Long wet winter afternoons sitting in her office telling about his mom while outside the light failed and it grew dark and the rain cut through the night like slivers of glass. They had attributed it to grief, but it wasn't grief. Not the heart of it. The heart of it was that dark something waiting just beyond the edge of consciousness. Something no one could utter. And so instead they talked about trivial things, stupid things: how do you *feel?* she would ask him, as if it made a difference. And he would play along, he would give her long irrelevant monologues about his parents and his feelings toward them. Sometimes he would just make things up. She never knew. Or if she did, she didn't let on—maybe she thought she was learning more from his lies than she would have from the truth. He didn't know; he didn't care, because it was all silly, a game they played, he and the psychiatrist and Rachel and his dad. It didn't make any difference. So he would just say anything that came into his head.

He remembers talking one afternoon about nuclear war: about growing up with the number *twenty* burned into his mind, that being the number of minutes, he had been told once, it would take the missiles to reach them. If some shadowy underground people somewhere decided to launch the missiles. Twenty, twenty minutes. The psychiatrist liked to hear things like that. It gave her pleasure. She could pigeonhole him then: *Depression about mother's death. Anxiety about world situation. Some paranoid tendencies.* He had hoped, had a vague, nearly empty hope, that she would be different, that she, the psychiatrist, would not pretend that the problem could be found in textbook definitions. That she would tell him she understood. But she never did. Nor did Rachel, or his dad. There was only one person who had, and who had admitted it, had told him. Who had cried with him about it at night in a dark room. Who had drunk with him about it. Who had understood, had known. Her image suddenly floats into his mind. He hears her voice. His eyes snap open.

At first Siegel isn't hungry for the steak, toasted bread, salad—the idea of eating is somehow repulsive. But after he has taken a few bites he finds his appetite coming back to him, realizes he hasn't eaten all day, and midway through the meal he is ravenous. He finishes the steak and has a second helping of salad. His dad looks on with apparent satisfaction, not eating much of his own food. They sit out on the rear patio, the smell of barbequed meat thick around them, the sunset slowly growing to a deep red stain across the sky.

"It's great to see you eating like this," his dad says, smiling. "Good sign."

"Well," Siegel says, sopping up the last of the beef juice with a piece of bread, "it's just that you're such an expert with the fire." He smiles at his dad, feeling quite good at the moment. He finishes his wine and pours another glass.

His dad leans back in his chair and looks out at the sunset. He glances at Siegel. "Didn't they feed you...?"

"Sure they did," he answers, knowing his dad can't bring himself to say *in there*. Semantics again. But more than that: an inability to really say anything directly about it at all. "Sure, they fed me," Siegel reassures him, smiling, "but not like this." In truth, the food he'd gotten back there had been uninspiring to say the least—lumpy potatoes, limp gray vegetables. But all that seems very far away as he looks out at the sea, at the sky, as he feels the cool early-evening breeze touch his face. The conversation has lagged throughout the meal, but the silence has not been uncomfortable; he is content. There is nothing troubling in his range of vision. No reminders. It's almost as if there is an unspoken understanding between them; but this is probably wishful thinking, for his dad seems uneasy—controlled, trying to be casual, but working too hard at it.

"So," his dad says, after a few moments' silence between them, "how's that book coming?"

And suddenly, instantly, Siegel's body tenses again. He doesn't want to think about the book. He has tried to forget about the whole thing. But now it rushes back to him, and with it all sorts of other things, associations, quicksand memories. He downs his glass of wine quickly.

"Great," he answers finally.

"Been doing much on it lately?"

"Sure," he says. "Yeah, it's almost done."

"That's great. Heard from that publisher?"

"No, not for a while. They won't have much to say to me until it's finished."

"No, I guess not. When I get to read it?"

He shrugs nonchalantly and tries to smile. "When it's finished."

His dad returns the smile, a bit stiffly, and stands. As he collects the plates from the table he says, "Oh, I forgot. Your friend Dusty called."

Siegel looks up. "He did? When?"

"Yesterday. Wanted to know when you were coming home."

"Hm." Dusty Moran. Now there is someone he hadn't thought of in a while. He had, in fact, nearly forgotten about him entirely. "Okay," he says, "I'll give him a call."

He follows his dad into the house and dials the number on the downstairs phone. Odd, he still has it memorized. It occurs to him suddenly that Dusty might not still live there. But before he can hang up the line rings and it's picked up almost instantly.

"Hello?"

"Hi, Dusty?"

"*Siegel?*"

"Boy, you must have been sitting on top of that phone."

"Nah, I was just watching TV. How *are* you, man?"

"Well, you know. Terminal but not serious."

Dusty laughs. "Same old Seeg. God, we've got to get together. How long are you going to be at your dad's house?"

"I'm not sure. A while. I don't really know what I'm doing right now."

"Yeah, I guess not. How long have you been back?"

"Couple hours. I just got here."

"That's great."

There is a silent pause.

"How you feeling, man?" Dusty says.

"Oh, pretty good. Fine."

"That's great, man. God, we've got to get together...Hey, you know what? You'll never believe what I heard the other day. Do you remember Sarah Diamond?" At this point Dusty launches into a long story about some girl they knew vaguely in high school. Instead of listening, Siegel thinks about Dusty, big bruiser Dusty, the guy the football coach tried for four straight years to get to try out but never succeeded. Dusty was too gentle, too harmless for football. Dusty Moran, often called "Dustbin Moron" in grade school...known affectionately to Siegel and Rachel as Dusty. Siegel likes him but he has never been sure quite why. They have little in common. But he and Rachel and Dusty had been a sort of threesome: Dusty as their eternal mascot, always seeming to be ready to go wherever they wanted, to do whatever they said. For some reason Dusty has always had a dog-like devotion to Siegel. It doesn't surprise Siegel that he called the house, that Dusty had kept tabs on him: he would have been surprised, he realizes, if he hadn't. And yet there is always something sort of pathetic about Dusty, too. He never seemed to have any sort of life of his own. Siegel remembers how sometimes he would duck telephone calls from him, tell his dad to say he wasn't home, just because the guy called so much. But he always liked him nevertheless. He's the only person Siegel knows, he supposes, who would make him feel completely at ease about the whole thing, his recent history. Oh, it was okay with Dusty. Everything was always okay with Dusty.

This story, this story Dusty is telling about this girl Sarah, is typical of him too. Dusty never had anything at all to say about himself—instead he filled in by talking about everyone else under the sun, no matter how (as in the case of Sarah Diamond) irrelevant. At last he comes to the end, an abortion or something.

"Wow," Siegel says, knowing it to be a satisfactory response to any of Dusty's stories. "No kidding. Listen, how are you doing, Dusty?"

"Me? I dunno. You know."

"Still living with your mom?"

"Me? Yeah. I mean you know. So how about we get together, man?"

"Sure. Okay. When?"

"How about tonight?"

Siegel sighs, quietly. He doesn't think he's really up to seeing anyone now, especially not a ghost like Dusty. But he finds himself agreeing.

"Great," Dusty says. "Hey, this is great. How about I come over?"

"No," Siegel says, too quickly, "no, I'll come over there."

"Aw, you don't want to come over here." That's another thing about Dusty—Siegel has rarely been to his house. The guy is ashamed of it, always has been; perhaps because his mom is not in the same league financially with Siegel's dad, or come to think of it, with Rachel's parents. Dusty has tried to steer Siegel away from his house. "Why don't we meet somewhere?" he suggests. "Like the Wharf?"

"The restaurant?"

"Yeah. In the bar there."

"Okay, if you want."

"I'll see you there in a little while, okay?"

"Okay."

"Seeg?"

"Hm?"

There is a brief pause. "You'll be there, right?"

He laughs. "Of course I'll be there. 'Bye, Dusty."

"See you, man."

Siegel hangs up.

The Unspoken

In the kitchen his dad is doing the dishes. They have a dishwasher, but his dad has never liked using it: doesn't get them clean enough, he says. Siegel takes a dish rag and begins drying the dishes that his dad has stacked on the counter. They don't say anything for a time. The sound of the running water and the clattering of the dishes seems to lift the need for talk. He finds himself enjoying the work. He has not been allowed to work, to do much of anything, for a long time: *rest* and *relaxation* are words he has grown to hate. Rest until you pass out, he thinks. Relax until you die. And so it gives him pleasure, this simple action, drying dishes: he turns each one over carefully in his hands and wipes it until it's as dry as he can make it. Then, as his dad rinses out the sink, he stacks them carefully in the cupboards.

At last they are finished and they look at each other. A moment seems to dangle between them: an instant when they might say something, make an overture, an offering.

It passes quickly. "Great dinner," Siegel says instead.

His dad smiles and nods. "Getting together with your friend?"

"Yeah. If I can have the car."

"Sure you can."

"I don't want to leave you here, though. You know, 'all alone by the telephone.'"

"Don't worry about me," his dad says as they walk into the living room. "I've got more than enough to do around here. You go have fun, kiddo."

"Well, okay. If you're sure."

"Sure I'm sure. You go ahead. I've got plenty of work to do."

Siegel nods and heads upstairs. When he gets to his room he looks at the bag sitting on the bed and realizes that he hasn't yet unpacked. Now is as good a time as any; and so he unzips it and brings out some clothes, miscellaneous toilet things, a couple of paperbacks; then, at the bottom, he finds what he has been trying not to think of, what he has tried to forget. On the top is the letter from the editor of the big New York publishing house. He has read it a hundred times, has it memorized: the editor has read Siegel's little book of poems and vignettes, *Unspeakable Acts*, published by a tiny press in West Virginia, and she is very impressed with it; she wants to know if Siegel has an idea for a novel. Oh, the arrival of this letter—out of the clear blue sky, nearly two years ago: a glorious confirmation of everything he had been trying to do since he was fifteen—an honest-to-God New York editor, with a major house, had somehow got hold of his little book—hardly more than a pamphlet—and been so impressed that she wanted to read a novel! And then under this letter, several more: Siegel had replied immediately, for he did have an idea for a novel, one he'd been thinking of for years. He'd hastily written a first chapter—a prototype for one, anyway—and sent the whole package off. The editor responded with enthusiasm. Here's the letter, right in front of him—the woman calls it the best writing of his she's seen, the whole idea is a winner, keep at it, and meanwhile on the strength of this chapter and outline let's sign a contract, shall we? O heavenly day! He'd signed the contract, was sent a five hundred dollar advance for a novel-length manuscript to be called *Drowning*. If acceptable, it would be published in the house's "Young Americans" series of "Distinguished First Novels," an auspicious place to debut by any standard. He flips to the next letter, dated a little over a year ago. The editor is asking where the manuscript is, why she hasn't heard from him. Then, under that, there is a shorter, much curter note dated several months later saying that his contract is about to expire and he had better serve up a novel or else return the advance. That is the last letter he has from her.

    He digs still deeper into the stack of old papers and comes to a tattered copy of his little book-pamphlet of poems and stories. He flips it open at random and looks at what is on the page:

ALCOHOL

when I come home from somewhere I
do not recall she is
in the living room waiting
for me hands clutching
the glass like claws eyes
cloudy yellow but with sharpness
somewhere inside that sees
knows

where have you been she says I
have been away but I do not
remember where and now all that is
and was is the woman in the big
chair ice cubes rattling in the
glass the glass with beads of
sweat running down in
rivulets I come closer to
her but the expanse is
forever and I walk walk then
run and suddenly I am
there Mother
I say

I take the glass throw
it away and she opens her
arms and I place my head against
her breast warm
and soft and
soap and
perfume and

she strokes my head and I
begin to fall asleep

then in my back a
ripping a
burning and trying
to turn and something
twisting I
back away she raises
the knife slashes
my stomach tears it like
a dress red
soaks my fingers and
falling back and
looking up she is
laughing or is it
crying claws
clutching the glass and
beads of sweat running
down it and onto
my face

    my face

He smiles slightly. Not bad, he thinks, not bad. But it's the work of a stranger, the poem of someone whose psychic landscape is very different from his own. He can hardly even remember writing that poem, now. Over four years ago. He tosses the book aside and finally comes to what, for some reason, he has been looking for: his novel, such as it is. He finds his copy of that first chapter, the prototype he'd sent the editor two years ago; beneath that is a second chapter, very rough, and a piece of a third. That's all there is. Forty pages or so, all totaled. That's all he has ever been able to write on it. All, in fact, he has been able to write at all. In the past year he's written nothing. Zero.

He flips through the pages, wondering whatever happened to the whole thing. But then, of course, realizing. Somewhere between the thing with his mom and his...incarceration, he had lost control of the book. It had fluttered away.

He stands there, looking down at the pieces of manuscript. Then he turns suddenly and tosses the whole thing into the wastebasket, manuscript, letters, his book, everything. He grabs a note pad out of the bag, finds a pencil, and sits down on the bed and begins writing a letter to the New York editor:

Dear Bitch, he writes,

I suppose you're wondering whatever happened to my manuscript "Drowning." Well, I'll tell you, you cunt. I never wrote the fucker. Or I should say that I did write it but that is was so breathtakingly brilliant that I couldn't allow this fallen world to see it. So one night I went out and threw the whole thing into the ocean, page by page. It belongs to the fish now, to God, if you like—who is a hell of a lot better publisher than your cruddy little house. I want a $100,000 advance on my next novel. Send it immediately. But harbor no illusions. You won't see this one either.

Love and Bullets,

A Distinguished Young American Writer.

He looks at what he has written and chuckles slightly. Nicely paranoid, this. Hewitt would love it. Maybe he should mail it to Hewitt...But no; he knows he wants nothing to do with any of that scene. He has to move beyond it forever, for good and all, no looking back.

But he isn't sure that he can. When he starts feeling like this, like he's feeling now, angry, afraid, he begins to wonder if he's not sliding down the slippery slopes again, wonders if he can keep himself together, at least well enough so that no one will notice how crazy he is. And he *is* crazy. He knows it even if nobody else does. Has always known it. When he was very young he used to think he was the strangest person who ever lived—and wondered if everybody else didn't know it. In other words, what if he were somehow totally different from everyone else—super-intelligent, say—and everybody else in the whole world was simply humoring him, or trying to keep from upsetting him? That could be it. Perhaps he had secret powers they'd made him forget about and they all lived in abject terror that he should ever discover them again. Sometimes he would sit in class trying to make them work. All right, he would think, I want this whole classroom to burst into flames, now! But it never worked. Never, that is, but once, a little bit: he had closed his eyes and wished that the whole world be flooded, that everyone be swept away in cool cleansing waters. And as he wished, rain had started hitting the roof of the building. It was the beginning of the biggest storm of the season.

Still, there was no flood, no one was carried away. But it gave him hope, encouraged him that his theory was correct: that he was different, had powers—and everyone knew it. Everyone. Not a person in the world didn't know it, not a person in the world didn't live in awe and terror of *him*. It was comforting to realize this. Comforting to know that he was, in fact, the center of the universe.

The funny thing, he supposes, is that he still hasn't entirely ridded himself of these thoughts. Even now, he occasionally finds himself wondering if everybody isn't just humoring him. But not, now, because he has super-powers; rather because he is so woefully inadequate. They all feel sorry for him. They all need to make him feel real, feel human, though he isn't really, he is really totally inadequate, everyone knows it, but they try to make his life easier by making him feel like the rest of them. But the illusion is always breaking down because, after all, he *knows*, in a very deep, instinctive way, his inadequacy. He knows.

It's sometimes like that, even today.

He looks at his letter to the New York editor for a moment, then tears it off the sheet and stands and tosses it into the wastebasket. After a moment he bends down and picks out his manuscript and the letters and the rest of it. He replaces them in the bottom of his bag and puts the bag away in a drawer. He closes the drawer softly, as if there were a sleeping child inside it.

10

And these goodbyes, too, are swift and final.

"Robin, I'm going to miss you something awful!" Priscilla says as he stands outside his car, the door open in the bright sunshiny morning. She puts her arms around him. "It's seems like you just got here—"

"I know." He had finished at the tire-loading job two days before—loaded his last tire, pushed his last dolly—and packed his things yesterday. He has been in Santa Barbara for two months. "So you're going when?"

"End of the month." Priscilla grins and looks at Koofie, who is standing just behind her. "First we hit Hawaii, just for a couple of days. Then Australia and New Zealand."

"It sounds great," Robin says, smiling wanly. "Really. Really... great. I wish I was coming with you." The fine art of understatement, he thinks to himself.

"Aw," Koofie says, taking his hand, "you finish with your college and you'll be able to do anything you want. With a degree you'll be able to go anywhere, do anything."

"Maybe."

"So you'll be going back to your dad's?" Priscilla asks.

"I guess so," he says, swallowing. "The semester starts in three weeks."

"Well, that's not so bad."

Robin shrugs.

"But I wonder," Koofie interjects, "how we're ever going to get to see this great novel of yours."

"I'll send you a copy," he says. "When it's finished. And published. And I'm a big multi-millionaire."

"Don't be so sure you won't be," Koofie laughs. "I've got a feeling about you."

"Well—that's nice to hear. I think."

They laugh in the bright blue morning and the obligatory inanities come from their lips. *It was great seeing you. Let's keep in touch. We'll send you a postcard from Down Under.* Robin, his mind a dull blanket of gloom, gets into the car and starts the motor. He pulls out of the parking lot as Priscilla and Koofie, the two soon-to-be world travelers, wave after him. It is over.

He stops a little over a half an hour later at a grubby little hamlet called Buellton and telephones his father from a gas station. His voice seems disconnected from his body as he hears himself saying, *I'm on my way. No, I'll do it in two days. I'll spend the night at a hotel somewhere.* And his father's voice, perfectly sober, Robin knows, sitting there in his office in Greyfield, saying *All right, Robin, see you then.* The voice bloodless, noncommittal. Like a recording. Robin hangs up quickly.

The road then, for hours on end: on his left the glittering ocean, on the right mountains, towns, other roads, trees, cafes. After many hours, vineyards: endless green shrubbery in the sharp afternoon light. He finds himself thinking of nothing in particular. He plays music on the radio, but does not hear it. His mind tries to re-enter the rooms of Siegel and his father, but right now, he knows, it cannot. The road precludes the possibility. Still, he feels a warm satisfaction when he thinks of those pages, flying along so effortlessly in a matter of days. If he can continue at this rate, he knows, it will be only a couple of months and he will have a finished novel. For that is what it is. A novel. The idea fills him with a tingling thrill. He will have written a *novel*, he, Robin Withers, and the effort will have been nearly nothing. For every time he sits down and thinks of Siegel and Siegel's father and Dusty and Rachel, the pencil begins scratching across the page with virtually no conscious effort. The problem, he realizes, with the idea of the man calling up the anonymous sex service, and falling in love with the girl, was not that it wasn't a good idea: he is sure someone could make something out of it: but it was too far outside himself. He could not enter the thoughts of that man, could not find his inner music. But Siegel, now: Siegel he knows as he knows himself. Siegel is *not* himself: but the creative leap, to get inside Siegel's mind, is not great, for Siegel has the same sickness, the same darkness inside him. He knows Siegel's melodies. He knows his face and voice and how he thinks. It is enormously easy. Long before the end of the semester, he thinks, he will be a *novelist*. The idea fills him with pride; and also with arrogance. Let the rest of the undergraduate mob muddle around in their short stories and poems and deep-think freshman essays. He will leave them all behind, and with all the effort of a dragonfly humming into the darkness. And, to cement his satisfaction, he will not show a word of it to Turnham. Screw Turnham. He will show it to some other teacher who will be overawed by its brilliance and who will tell Turnham all about it. Then Turnham will have to come to *him* and say, "Robin, I've been told about this extraordinary manuscript of yours…"

But he begins to scowl when he thinks of Turnham coming to him and saying this. He does not like to picture Turnham in his mind. The figure seems lost in distant time: he had thought he might never see the man again. And yet here he is, heading back again to all of it, the college, the classrooms, and the turn-off which says *Wind Point 4 mi.* and the drive out onto the point in the darkness and then the old salt-stripped sign reading: *Wind Point—Where the Shore Meets the Sea.* A thick melancholy settles into his brain, his bones, his being. The darkness again. The silence. The fear. He finds some hard rock music on the radio and turns it up loud, trying to drown out the thoughts, the awful images. Wind Point. The footsteps. The lying darkness. The dorm room. Everything. He must keep his mind a smooth blank, he knows, or else something terrible will happen. He will become like Siegel, raving away somewhere, totally disintegrated. Shh, he thinks to himself, the music blaring within the car. Shh...

He stares up at the ceiling of the damp hotel room and listens to the sounds of the city outside. Cars, buses; a voice shouting, "Hey! *Hey!* Son of a bitch!" He had checked in just before dark: Highway 101 had brought him abruptly into downtown San Francisco with its mad sloping hills, and he had decided to stop for the night. Somehow the hotel near the bus station had not seemed so bad earlier, when some sunlight still remained in the sky; but when the darkness came, the streets quickly filled with blacks in big overcoats and women in hot-pants and muscular Chicanos shouting to each other in Spanish. Robin had been eating in a fast-food place down the street when this unruly menagerie had begun to appear, and had hurried back to his hotel room and locked the door. He had hoped, earlier, that he might take in the sights of the city, late into the night: wander the darkened streets, perhaps find a recital or a play somewhere; but the streets were too filled, too brimming with frightening specters, for him to venture out. He grins wryly, lying on the bed. So much for the grand Frisco adventure. Well, his money was low anyway, less than two hundred dollars; though only two days before the tire-storage manager had paid him his final wages, his expenses in Santa Barbara had been enormous: all of the eating in restaurants, all of the books he had purchased and tickets for movies and plays and the one lamentable symphony. Still. He glances around the dim room, where there is not so much as a television. He needs to do *something*. His car is only at the back of the building; if he could gather the courage to go to it, he could at least take a drive. Of course very likely he would get lost, as his sense of direction is practically nonexistent; but he could always ask the way. Surely he could do that much, go to his car. Surely he need not stay here like a restless log. He deserved something, didn't he? After all, it…

It's my birthday, he thinks. He sits up abruptly in bed. August the seventh. Yes. He is nineteen years old today; the thought hadn't so much as shadowed his mind until this moment. Nineteen, he thinks: halfway to thirty-eight, an unimaginably distant age; yet he has attained fifty percent of it already. It is an amazing idea. He and his mother going to the bakery in the wee hours of the morning, to get the fresh hot bear claws and twisters, seems only a few months ago. His mother reading to him from Tennyson and Poe, or "The Rime of the Ancient Mariner," seems last week. But it has been years. The idea is faintly frightening. Anyone in the world would think of him as a young man, he knows; as a mere boy. But he feels terribly old at the moment. He has a sudden, sharp image of himself as he might be at thirty-eight: skinny, stopped-over, his hair an unpleasantly dull gray….

And still a virgin. *A virgin.* He contemplates the word. How could he be a virgin, after Cape? And yet he realizes that he still thinks of himself as one, for the mysteries of vagina and clitoris are still impenetrably closed to him. But Cape—even Turnham— what had all that been? Surely it wasn't innocent. No. It was real. But Cape had been wrong, or at least only half-right. For Robin still feels no identification with *gayness*. He remembers the meeting they attended, where the men had been holding hands: one of them, an otherwise pleasant sort named Jeffrey, had patiently explained to Robin that *gayness* (a word that makes him grit his teeth) had to do not so much with the fact that one went to bed with other men, but with a way of looking at the world, a style, an attitude. But it is an attitude Robin cannot connect with, any more than he could connect with the man in the dark room calling the anonymous sex service and falling in love with the invisible voice. Cape had told him he was repressed. But is he? He wonders. Is anyone? Or is the whole issue nothing but a delusion on the parts of a few people so unhappy with themselves that they must pretend to be perfectly secure, hysterically happy? He can hear Cape's voice and how it would argue with him about this. But he shuts the voice off abruptly. He does not want to think about Cape.

But there is nothing else to do in this damp, dim room. He stands and looks out the window. He is on the third story and he can see clearly the cars and buses and moving masses. It is crowded and loud. Santa Barbara had not been like this, not even when the warehouse became packed and manic. There was none of the dirt that is here, none of the grime and shouting of dangerous voices. He doesn't like it. But it is his birthday; and he should, he thinks, do *something*.

Finally he slips on his jacket and, without any particular plan in mind, steps out of the room and down the dingy hall to the stairs. He walks down them and through the yellow-grimed lobby, quiet and still with only a single clerk dozing behind the desk. He stands at the glass door looking out at the crowded city street and finally, checking to see that his money is firmly ensconced in his breast pocket (with a few emergency dollars hidden in his left shoe), he steps out into the vivid herd.

The instant he steps onto the sidewalk, a huge Chicano comes running toward him, screaming: "Hey! Hey, *muthafuckah!* You! I'm talkin' to *you!*"

Robin's heart freezes and he gasps as the mad Chicano comes rushing up to him, still shouting, "*You!* Son of a bitch! *You!*"; and then passes by, without slowing.

He resumes his breathing. It is a colorful crowd, no question of that; but he feels a trembling terror coursing through him. There is too much noise here, too many people, too many cars rushing crazily past and people walking out before them and horns blasting into the night air. He resolves to get to his car. He turns then, for he must reach the end of the block where he can go left to the parking lot. He has just begun walking, hands deep in his pockets and his head hunched low, when a young black in an overcoat comes up to him.

"Man," the man says, "you want some Thai stick?"

"No," Robin says, hardly slowing, "no, thanks."

"Uppers? Downers?"

"No...No, thanks, no."

He keeps moving. The scene takes on an unreal quality. He imagines that every pair of eyes meeting his own are somehow after him, chasing him, something out of a Kafka nightmare. Joseph K., he thinks, in a vast courtroom.

He reaches the end of the street and turns. The street is forbiddingly dim but he keeps walking. He sees his car in the lot, its comfortable brown familiarity curiously soothing; but then he sees something else. A group, or gang, of ten or eleven black youths are in the parking lot, gathered around a big fiery-colored hot rod. They are only twenty or twenty-five yards from his own car; and while they are not looking at it, are paying no attention whatever to it, he is suddenly filled with fright. He can picture himself trying to go surreptitiously to the car and one of them shouting, "Hey! Hey, look at that white boy!" And then all of them suddenly descending on him, pummeling him, robbing him, leaving him broken and bloody on the sidewalk. He giggles nervously. No. No, he will not go to his car just now. He stops in the middle of the street and looks around; two bars side-by-side, a pool hall. He turns back in the direction he came from, resolving to find a way into the safety again of light, of numbers. He arrives at the corner and then, from behind him, a voice reaches his ears.

"Lookin' for a date?"

He half-turns. From a narrow crevice between two closed shops, a figure emerges: a hooker, dressed in a flashy purple top and pink mini-skirt and high spiked heels. Her unnaturally blonde hair is wildly frizzed, pouring onto her shoulders in crazy waves. Her face is small, rather pinched, not especially attractive; but the purple top emphasizes almost obscenely her large, pendulous breasts. Her skin is pallid all the way down to her legs, but the legs themselves are muscular, and the little dress, absurdly small and tight, displays what appear to be curvaceous, full hips. She holds a cigarette between her fingers.

"I said, you lookin' for a date?"

For a moment Robin is struck speechless. He gazes at her stupidly, in a breathless combination of excitement and horror. He can hardly believe it. An honest-to-God prostitute. Thoughts run crazily through his frozen brain: *So they really do dress like that, they really do hide in shadows, they really do come up and offer themselves.* But for a long moment he cannot bring forth any words from his lips. The image of Joseph K. vanishes from his mind and is replaced for an instant by Woody Allen.

She smiles slightly, impatiently. "Well? C'mon, baby. You lookin'?"

"I—Well, I..." Easy now, he thinks. Act as if you know the score, even if you don't. Even if you don't know the score or the game or even what league you're playing in. He tries to look relaxed. He straightens up and smiles and pushes his hands into his pockets deeply, casually. He leans back on his heels, his head smacking against a light pole behind him with an audible *clang*. His head is suddenly filled with a sharp searing pain, but he refuses to raise his hand to it.

"I..."

"C'mon," she says. "You're lonesome, aren't you?"

"I...Well, maybe. A little. Yeah." His head aches dully.

"So?"

Well? he thinks to himself. The dark iron cell of his virginity, he knows, can now, tonight, be marvelously torn open, flooded with delicious light. True, it might not be in quite the fashion he would have preferred, but after all, he is nineteen today—nineteen!—and, he thinks, what prisoner cares about who helps him escape? As long as the escape is made. He looks at her, at her sharply angled face and voluptuous bosom. It is difficult to tell her age; twenty-four, twenty-five? He tries to say something, but the words get strangled in his throat. Instead he nods and tries to smile.

"Okay," the woman says. "Great. You stayin' around here?"

He swallows hard, manages to point and say: "There."

"Oh, yeah. Good. They don't give us problems there. C'mon then, let's go." She grinds the cigarette into the street.

And to his complete, open-mouthed stupefaction, he finds himself walking back to the hotel with an honest-to-God woman he is about to go to bed with. They say nothing and she does not walk close to him. He does not look at her. He is sure when they reach the door of the hotel that she will just keep on walking, but no: he opens the door, she mumbles, "Thanks," and walks in ahead of him.

He is shivering now. He feels as if he is at the brink of some enormous cliff, about to drop into untamed regions of the unknown. He is utterly terrified. Does he have enough money? he wonders. He has no idea what it costs. Ten dollars? Twenty? A hundred? How much can he afford? He makes a quick mental calculation. Not more than a hundred, certainly. But how much is in his shoe? He can't remember. And then another thought assails him. What if she tries to rob him? What if a small pistol is hidden in that little black bag of hers and as soon as they get into the room she pulls it on him and demands all his cash? What could he do? How could he get home? How could he call his father and say, *Sorry, Dad, but could you wire me fifty bucks so I can get home? I was robbed by a whore.*

They mount the stairs, still silent. Of course, he thinks, that scenario is unlikely. But it is very possible, if he lets her see where he keeps his money, that she might try to take advantage of a moment's inattention on his part to clean him out. Therefore, he reasons, he must be very careful. But he looks behind himself suddenly. Good God, he thinks, what if a cop had seen them? What if an undercover policeman watched the whole thing and is even now following them up these stairs? He stops for a moment, listens. Nothing. But maybe the cop is waiting. Hiding. Maybe... *Sorry, Dad, could you wire me fifty bucks so I can get home? I'm in jail for hiring a whore.*

He comes up to the door of the hotel room, not looking at her, and reaches with trembling fingers into his pockets for the key. For a moment he cannot find it. Oh Jesus, he thinks. I've locked it in the goddamn room. Great. Nothing like looking stupid in front of a woman you're about to go to bed with. But then he finds it, hidden in his jacket pocket; brings it out, drops it on the floor; picks it up, drops it again; as he rises the second time he bangs his head against the doorknob, striking the exact spot he had earlier with the light post, and a dizzying sting spreads across his scalp. This time he rubs it, muttering, "Goddamn it," as he inserts the key into the lock and they enter the room. He is shaking uncontrollably. He closes the door and locks it while the woman steps over to the window. Then another panic hits him. What if, instead of a policeman following them, *she works for the police?* Maybe as soon as they agree to something the handcuffs will come out and the door will be broken down from outside and—

But as he looks at her standing there in the city-lit dimness, he knows it is not true. She had approached him; that would be entrapment. No, she is a prostitute, the genuine article. It is unreal, her standing here in this room. He is not sure he believes it is really happening. But then he knows it is when she looks toward him with a steady stare and says, "Well? What do you want?"

"I...um..." Words have a hard time escaping his mouth again. Eventually he manages: "Well, how much do you, you know, charge?"

"Depends," she says. She stands there at the window with one hand on her bag and one hand on the window sill, her hip jutting out to the side. "Hand job's twenty. Blow job's thirty-five. Costs fifty to fuck me. You can fuck me in the ass if you want."

"Uh..." The ache rings in his head like a bell, and, absurdly, he notices a piece from Poe's "The Bells" running through his mind: How they tinkle, tinkle, tinkle in the icy air of night...

"Uh..." he says again. "How much—time?"

She shrugs. "Fifteen, twenty minutes. Unless you want to pay for more."

"No, I...That's all right. I...I guess I'd like—" He swallows and thinks: It's like ordering a hamburger and large fries. "I guess I'd like...to have sex. I mean intercourse. If that's all right."

She laughs harshly and takes the bag from her shoulder. "Okay," she says. "Show me the money."

He fishes fifty dollars from his pocket.

"Okay. I'll be back in a second," she says. "Go ahead and get yourself ready." She enters the bathroom and shuts the door.

Deja-vu all over again, he thinks, standing uneasily in the middle of the room and Marylou Kirk fluttering across his mind like a malevolent moth. He sits on the bed and slips off his shoes and socks. Then he strips off his jacket and waits. After a moment he hears the toilet flush and she comes out of the bathroom again.

She glances at him as she places her bag on the night stand. "Well, come on," she says. She sits on the bed, shakes her wild blonde hair back out of her eyes, and pulls off her high-heeled shoes. Robin watches her, fiddling nervously with his shirt buttons, trying to keep his fingers from shaking. Then the woman stands again and quickly pulls the purple top over her head to reveal two soft pink-nippled globes nearly blue in the dimness. He is astonished at how they bounce as she moves to a chair to place the top on it. Then, glancing at him again, she reaches to her short skirt and in one smooth, quick motion, strips it off herself and places it on the chair. She is naked now and Robin stares at the hair between her legs, the color, he thinks, of wheat, as she walks to him and puts her hands against his cheeks. Her stomach, inches from his face, is pale and flat.

"Come on," she says. "You shy?"

She pulls his face into the cool skin of her stomach and strokes his hair. He feels a tumescence rising in him slowly, hesitatingly. He kisses the skin of her stomach and tentatively reaches his arms around her and touches her smooth back.

"Come on," she says. "Take off your clothes."

He stands. She is several inches shorter and she lifts her head and french-kisses him suddenly, deeply, for a long moment. Then she moves to the bed and pulls back the coverlet. He pulls off his shirt and then his pants. He looks toward her, her naked body sitting now on the bed, cross-legged, and he can see the slit between her legs. He strips off his shorts and sits next to her on the bed. He is suddenly cold and goose-bumps rise on his skin. She reaches over to him, placing one hand on his shoulder and the other between his legs. She pushes him back on the bed and begins french-kissing him again, hard, aggressively, and pumps her hand methodically between his legs. But his body seems strangely absent now of sensation. He reaches around her body and strokes her back and then, hesitantly, reaches to the two ample buttocks and touches them. She sticks her tongue into his mouth rhythmically. He watches the two soft globes bounce lightly with her movement. He should be wild by now, he knows, insatiable. But something is wrong. He has a warm female body next to him but nothing is happening. Her face, he looks at her face, the eyes closed and the brows wrinkled into a scowl, the too-sharp nose, the unnaturally pale cheeks. She presses her breasts against his chest and he watches how their shapes flatten against him. He touches her hair. She does not smell as he thought she would. He had imagined a vulgar, perfume-and-cigarette odor; but she seems to have no odor at all. She kisses him over and over. The tongue is like a slab of meat in his mouth. Finally, still pumping him heroically, she takes one of his hands and places it between her legs. He strokes her there. But nothing is happening. He tries to concentrate on the kissing, the pumping, the warmth between her legs. He reaches a finger tentatively up into the warm, slippery canal and realizes that this is it, the Holy Grail, the initiation into the mysteries. But one thing is needed to finalize it once and for all, this initiation, and it seems not to be available. He is nothing but a shrunken, shriveled worm. He wonders how much time has passed. He still feels cold but he notices sweat trickling down his brow.

"What's wrong?" she says.

"Nothing. I—nothing." But suddenly he feels like sinking into the bed, through it, into the earth, into a place of darkness. Nothing is going to happen, he realizes suddenly. Even when she moves from his mouth and applies herself between his legs, nothing happens. He watches the curve of her back and the swaying of her breasts. Nothing happens.

"Look," she says finally, after a few minutes, "is it go or no go? I don't have all night."

He feels his face burning and the sweat runs into his eyes. His head throbs. He cannot speak.

Finally she sighs and moves away from him.

"I'm still gonna charge you, you know."

"I know."

"'Cause it's not *my* fault."

"No, I..." He shuts his eyes briefly, wipes his brow. He covers the place between his legs with a sheet. "I didn't say it was. It's okay."

She sighs again, stands. She looks at herself in the room's mirror, brings a lipstick out of her bag.

"What's...What's your name?" he asks her, his voice a thin whisper.

"Lolita," she says, applying the lipstick. "Yours?"

Robin smiles grimly. Now why did he suddenly want to know her name? he wonders. Why does he, now, suddenly want to reach out to her, cry to her, say: I'll save you! I'll take you to Wind Point! We'll get married! We...

There is something thick in his throat as he says, hollowly: "Humbert...My name is Humbert."

"Humbert? Funny name."

Silence descends in the room again. He watches as she wriggles into her tight little dress. Finally he stands and slips on his own pants, his body feeling like an awkward, out-of-whack machine, unbalanced. When he looks back at her again, she has put on the purple top and is slipping into her spike heels.

"The fifty?" she says.

He nods, reaches for his shirt. He counts fifty dollars out and puts it on the bed. He looks at the rest of the money in his hand: an orderly stack of tens and twenties.

"Jesus," she says, consulting a watch inside her bag, "it's been a whole half hour."

He looks at her. "I'm sorry. Should I pay you more?"

She nods, looking at him flatly.

"I..."

The Unspoken

I'll save you, he wants to say. Tell me your name. Tell me where you're from. I'll save you. Come with me.

He is trembling again as he strips a twenty from the stack of bills and adds it to the fifty on the bed.

She goes to the money and picks it up, puts it into her purse without speaking or looking at him. Instead she goes to the mirror again, checks herself a final time.

"Okay," she says finally. "See you around."

"Wait," he suddenly blurts, standing by the window. He cannot seem to think. His thoughts keep breaking off, uncertain, confused. He is not sure what has even happened here.

She looks at him, a trace of annoyance in her face. "What?"

"Wait, I..." His breath begins to come to him in short, uneven gasps, and he is suddenly afraid he will fall down. He feels dizzy. But he does not move from his position at the window. "I... It wasn't your fault."

"It's okay. No problem." She turns, about to step out of the room.

"Wait!" Robin shouts.

She looks back at him, sharply. "For *what*, man?"

"Don't..." He stands by the window with his arms outstretched. Don't go, he wants to say. Not so fast. I'm not just another customer. Come with me. Look at me. "I..." He searches desperately for something to say, anything to say that will keep her there, that will keep her with him always. He sees two orbs glowing in a rain-flooded dark: blurred fingers before his eyes: *Look at me. How many fingers am I showing?* Mist, shadows.

"I...I'm writing a novel," he says weakly, utterly disoriented now.

She scowls. "I gotta go, man." She moves toward the door.

At that moment, Robin feels something snap strangely inside him. He is trembling uncontrollably and his vision is blurred and he feels something break off, like a branch broken by wind. He is hardly aware of what he is saying. "I'll pay you!" he suddenly shouts. He grabs the stack of bills and starts flinging them, one by one, onto the floor. "I'll pay you! *I'll pay you!*" The bills fly from his fingers, fuzzy green leaves before his blurred eyes. "Isn't that what you want? Look! I have money! Take it! Take it! *Take it, goddamn it! Take all of it! Take it all! I've got money! Lots of money! Take it! Take the damn money!*" He stumbles then, falls onto the bed, his breath shallow and erratic, his eyes blinking rapidly. I'm here, he wants to say. Look at me. His head, bathed now with cold sweat, aches dully. His fingers are numbed with cold. After a long moment he looks up. Through the wavy air he can see, dimly, green bills like patches of grass on the floor. The door is hanging open like a stupefied sentinel. The room is empty.

CHAPTER 4
THE SONG OF THE EARTH

...what did become
   Of my heart, when first I saw thee?
   I brought a heart into the room,
   But from the room carried none with me.

John Donne: "The Broken Heart"

Oh, Mac, dear, love me, love me *big!*

Frank Norris: *McTeague*

1

Robin watches her from the stairs as she moves, a small stack of books in her hands, toward the checkout counter. Behind him he can hear the hushed whispering of students gathered around conference tables; the soft, ghostly clacking of a woman's high heels on the floor above; the hum of the air conditioner, a gentle, throbbing rumble. She is dressed in a black pin-striped pants suit which hangs somewhat baggily on her thin frame; a beret with a red feather rests on her head. He watches the feather bob with her movements as she places the books on the counter, searches her pockets for her student card, chats with the librarian; her hair—dark, straight, rather mousy—sways across her neck as she shakes her head in answer to a question. She does not know that he is watching her. He feels his heart beating as he considers the idea of descending the stairs and following her out. But he wonders if she even recalls him.

He watches as she turns from the checkout counter, her eyes aimlessly wandering over the paintings on the walls as she waits for the librarian to finish his work. She is small: short, skinny, with a tiny, pinched face and big dark eyes. Her nose is small and sharp and her mouth slightly pursed. The beret, Robin thinks, gives a somewhat forced effect: too self-consciously an "artistic type." And yet it fits her well. He watches as she stands with her hands together, the fingers picking at one another thoughtlessly. She is not, he supposes, particularly pretty. He watches as she balances on one foot, using the other to scratch her ankle. He is not even sure that he likes her much. But as she turns again to the counter and picks up her books, nodding and saying a few words to the librarian, and as she moves toward the electronic theft-detection panels at the exit door, he finds himself descending the stairs.

They had met two weeks before, although Robin had seen her many times over the semester in the hallways of the English building. The semester was passing in a gray, emotionless haze: Turnham had gone on a sabbatical to Turkey; Gawky Boy had been replaced by a cow-eyed young freshman with a tendency to leave his mouth hanging open, whom Robin had privately dubbed "Zero"; and time, unmarked by event or change, ticked on in its endless arcs. Robin was living a life, he thought, as close to unconscious as one possibly could. It was easier that way. It was, in fact, a good strategy for survival. He did not dwell in personal darknesses now; did not curl up in his dormitory bed at night clutching at his stomach; when he slept it was deep and black and dreamless. He was not, it was true, doing any writing, but in this numb, careless state it didn't seem to matter much. Occasionally he would bring out the first chapter of *Drowning* and stare at it; and would feel, perhaps, a vague longing, as for someone he had loved once long ago; but it was easy enough to file those feelings away in a deep and inaccessible place. He did the same thing when he thought of Cape, or Priscilla. The longing—and in their cases the pictures, the voices, the remembered touches—he folded up and put on the secret shelf, allowing himself only the numbness, the lack of feeling, the blissful absence of sensation. He did well on exams. He pleased his teachers. The fact that he was not really there, that he was a somnambulist, made no difference. He was accomplishing what made his teachers happy, what made his father happy, and therefore what should make him happy. He was tired of being the boy he had been for so long: tired of jumping away from shadows, of sentient dark masses swarming around him, of terror and shame. Life, he had discovered, was much easier this new way. He had, for the first time, no problems at all. For the first time he had succeeded in placing aside the lovely ghosts, the faraway dreams and wild ambitions, and instead simply existed, rather like one of the amoebas from his last year's Biology textbook. But unlike the amoeba, he would not split. He would not be torn asunder. He was whole, entire, for all time.

Occasionally something would happen that would stab into his slate-like haze. A letter from his father, for instance: *I'm glad to see you've come to your senses after that wasteful summer.* Involuntarily then, the pictures and echoes from the house in the cul-de-sac would flash before him: his father, the night Robin returned, a glass of whiskey in his hand: sitting in his chair in front of the television, the rest of the house dark and silent, the glow of the television screen like an electronic oasis in the sea of blackness; and the man saying nothing, only looking up vaguely with his eyes rheumy and unfocused, unfeeling, his silence a kind of suffocation, like being buried alive, a sort of death. Or a picture postcard from Davy Carp, stationed now in the Philippines: *Hey man, It's sweaty as shit here but the prostitutes are practically free, not that I'd know ho ho ho.* Or cards from Priscilla, every few weeks: Australia, New Zealand, Thailand, Nepal, with cute hearts drawn in red and sometimes a scribbled postscript from Koofie. Or a news clipping about Michael Lyon, off at Harvard or Yale or wherever it was, setting academic and athletic records and leading his team to the national debating championship.

Or when he thumbed through his record collection, pausing briefly at Beethoven, at Bruckner, flipping through finally to Mahler and needing only to see the words *Symphony No. 9* to remember, like a far-off echo in an empty canyon, those strings of depthless sorrow fading into infinity, the threadlike connection to forever hovering inside his mind, hesitating, not wanting to let go. But he never listened to such things anymore. They were part of his past, of another Robin, not the pragmatist he had transmogrified himself into. Echoes of distant lands and timeless dreams he had submerged under his islands of consciousness, and was determined to hold them there until they drowned.

He had met her two weeks before in the courtyard of the English building. It was a cold, overcast afternoon—the sheet of gray iron had long descended onto the season's skies—and Robin's mind was preoccupied with a Mathematics assignment he found completely incomprehensible. He noticed her sitting on a stone bench in the grass, gazing pensively at a book in her lap. She was dressed even then in black, with a black overcoat; the beret sat atop her head at a jaunty angle. Without particularly thinking of it, he sat down on the other end of the bench.

"Hi," he said, glancing at her momentarily while bringing out his Mathematics book.

She glanced up at him. "So?"

He looked at her, puzzled. Her eyes were large for her tiny face and they were nearly black; her lashes were long. Her hair hung down either side of her face, not quite touching her shoulders. Finally he smiled slightly. "So, nothing. Just hi."

She looked at him a moment longer, then her head turned back to her book. They were silent for a time, then she said: "Hi."

Robin looked at her, amused. He couldn't decide if she was serious or kidding. He said, "I think I've heard that somewhere before."

"I was quoting you."

"I didn't think it was a particularly quotable line."

"Is it supposed to be a conversation starter?"

"Yeah, if you like. Fact is, I've been working on it all semester and I've just been waiting for the perfect opportunity to try it out."

"I like it."

"Good. That's a load off my mind."

She grinned suddenly. Her teeth were rather crooked in her mouth and they made for an odd, lopsided effect. "Is your name Robin? Withers?"

"That's right."

She nodded. "I've heard of you."

He chuckled. "What does that mean? And in what dens of iniquity have you 'heard' of me?"

She shrugged. "I've just heard of you, that's all. You're this school's reigning genius in English."

"According to whom?" he laughed.

"Everybody. I always hear about this arrogant jerk with glasses who goes around the English building looking down his nose at all the peons."

His smile faded a bit. "That's not exactly fair."

"Well, it's what I've heard."

"Are you an English major?"

"I'm undeclared."

"What's your name?"

"Heather. Seabright."

"Pretty name."

"I didn't choose it myself."

"That doesn't mean it's not a pretty name."

She smiled again and looked away toward the gray sky. "So are you really all that arrogant?"

"I'm not arrogant."

"What are you?"

"Shy."

"Mm." She nodded. "That's a good answer."

He looked down at her open book, turning his head to try to see the words on the page. "What're you reading?"

"This?" Keeping a finger in place, she closed the book so that he could see the cover: *Paradise Lost*.

"Pretty highfalutin' stuff," Robin said.

"Don't I know it. And the teacher is a total dork. Ives. You know him? He spends most of his time talking about fishing at Shasta Lake."

"I've heard of him," Robin smiled.

"He wasn't even supposed to be the teacher anyway. It was supposed to be...what was his name? He went on sabbatical."

"Turnham?"

"Yeah. Is he good?"

Robin thought for a moment before answering. "Yeah; I guess so."

"Well, anyway, I'll never know. I'm stuck with the village fisherman."

"Poor you," he chuckled. He looked at her again and found himself enjoying the conversation; he felt relaxed, at ease; as befitted, he thought wryly, a somnambulist.

"What other classes are you taking?"

She shook her head, her dark hair swinging lightly. "Nothing. Just this one. I just thought I'd take it so I could learn something."

"You're not after a degree?"

"Not really. I just wanted to learn about Milton. Now every time I think of *Paradise Lost* I'll see glistening trout in Shasta Lake."

They were silent for a moment. Robin tried to think of something further to say. Finally the girl put down her book and began rummaging in her black bag.

"What have I got to eat in this thing?...I'm starving. But then I'm *always* hungry."

"You don't look it," Robin said. "I mean, like you eat much. You're pretty thin."

"Mm. Sometimes I'm a little bulimic, actually. Swallow it down and barf it back up. Kind of a sick habit, I guess. Ah!" she exclaimed, bringing out a hard green apple. "Here. This will help." She brought out a knife. "Want some?"

He shrugged. "Sure." He took a sliver she carved from the fruit and put it in his mouth. It was sour. As they ate the apple the gray sheet of sky began to grow slowly darker, as if some enormous mouth were sucking the light from it.

"Getting too dark to read," she said finally, finishing off the apple. "Too cold, too. I better go home." She organized her things and stood. "Bye-bye."

That was all there had been to it. No earth-shaking revelations or dazzling wit; nothing memorable in any way. And yet he had thought of it constantly. He could not, after a day or two, quite recall her face: but he could see vividly certain features of it, the crooked grin, the big eyes, the swaying hair. He found himself hoping to find her in the hallways or in the library. He could see her in the trademark black, her self-consciously arty getups, could see her thin body, the slight shoulders, the narrow hips. He resolved to ask her for a date the next time he saw her; although he was well aware that most of his resolutions of that nature collapsed into tongue-tied fits. It was an abominable situation. He had still, after all this time, never really gone out on a "date": this in the face of two sexual partners and an actual "relationship" with one of them over the summer. Still he had never asked a girl to go to a movie with him, picked her up at her house, taken her to dinner. Never! And still he remained, at least in the realm of breasts and vagina, a virgin; a stuttering, stumbling idiot. It was possible that he was not meant for such conquests, that Cape had been right all along; that he was denying the truth, even to himself...And yet he could not quite believe it. The night-dreams of soft female voices, of sweet breasts and nipples and smooth hairless stomachs, were too maddeningly persistent.

Trailing some distance behind her, Robin walks across the library's lobby and out the door. She is walking away down a path that leads through a small grove of trees and finally toward the town itself. He does not approach her. He wants to but cannot. Instead he simply continues behind her, watching the dark hair sway as she moves quickly along the path. They head into the trees, which are damp in the afternoon mist. His heart races. He can hear her footsteps on the path before him; he wonders if she can hear his.

At last she comes to a wooden bridge which overhangs a small gully and stops, leaning against the wooden rail.

"Aren't you even going to say hi?" she asks, looking back at him for the first time and smiling slightly, bemusedly.

He comes up to her, heart pounding now, with the vague idea of giving the impression that he had been trying to catch up with her. "I wanted to," he says breathlessly, "but you were walking so fast that...Anyway, hello."

"'Hi.' That's the proper greeting. Remember?"

He smiles. "You're right. Hi."

"Hi."

"How are you?"

"Fine."

Robin tries to catch his breath. She stands on the bridge, her arms folded over the rail.

"*Will you go to a movie with me?*" He blurts it out loudly, stupidly, breathlessly.

She grins, looking at him. He has made a fool of himself, he knows. As usual. A nice smooth build-up all right. Jesus.

"Yes," she says, her dark eyes meeting his own. "Yes, I will go to a movie with you. What took you so long to ask?"

The night is frosty. Inside the theater they buy popcorn, jelly candies, chocolate of all kinds: "But I'm going to make you eat most of it," she says, taking some of the popcorn out of the bucket he holds in his hands and putting it into her mouth. "Otherwise by tomorrow I'll be a zeppelin."

"You won't be a zeppelin," he says, grinning. "You're a million miles from being a zeppelin."

"A million miles maybe, but not so many pounds. Do you want to sit upstairs?"

They sit in the balcony, in the back row, watching a double-feature of lurid horror films (she had suggested them: "Milton has fried my brain. I need something light, like some nice butchered bodies"). Robin sits in the old lumpy chair only vaguely aware of the happenings on screen; instead noticing only the girl next to him, mere inches away. She fills him with a giddy, euphoric feeling; to think that she is here, with him: only him! He glances at her face as she watches the movies: he would like to gaze at it, he thinks, forever. But he tries to keep from being obvious about it. Her nose is small, her lips thin; he had seen earlier that she wore no makeup. He likes it that way. He feels a small thrill when she reaches her hand toward his legs, between which is the popcorn bucket. He deliberately reaches for popcorn at the same time so that their hands can brush together. He wishes his own weren't so clammy. He wonders about her: where she is from, why she is in college, her past, her future. He wishes he could ask; wishes he could lean

The Unspoken

over and whisper into her ear. He considers bending toward her and saying something, if only to have an excuse for putting his own face so close to hers. He has not detected any perfume on her, but he has not been very close. He wonders. Inhales; registers only the musty smell of the theater balcony. He sighs, tries to watch the movie. Considers reaching for her hand, which is resting on the arm of the chair next to him. But dares not. What if she drew it away? Would it not wreck the whole evening? Better, then, not to take the chance. Instead he sits motionless, tense.

"Wasn't it *great?*" she says a few hours later as they exit the theater. "That was just what I needed. Some good gratuitous violence!"

He smiles. "You're a morbid one, aren't you?"

She looks up at him. "Didn't you like it?" They reach the exit and walk out into a cold blast of night air. "Shit!" she cries, suddenly wrapping her arm around Robin's own. "I *hate* the cold! C'mon, let's get to the car, quick!"

They run up the street together, the icy air filling Robin with wild energy. The warmth of her arm on his own is electrifying. When they reach Robin's Brown Bomber he hurriedly unlocks the passenger door and she jumps in.

"Jesus!" she says breathlessly as Robin gets in and slams shut his own door. "When does *summer* come around here?"

"Not for about another nine months," Robin says, switching on the heater.

"Oh, God. I'll be dead for sure by then." She rubs her hands together. "When is this thing going to heat up?"

"Give it a break," he says, grinning at her. "It's fifteen years old."

And suddenly, with a perfectly natural, effortless motion, he finds himself dropping his arm smoothly around her. She leans closely into him.

"Ohhh..." she sighs, pressing her face to his chest. "You're warm."

"Am I? Then why am I shivering?"

"You're warmer than the *car*. Mmm." She closes her eyes and they sit there for a long moment without speaking. Slowly Robin reaches his hand toward her and touches her hair lightly. She nestles against him. He looks down at her, at the long lashes covering the closed lids, at her slightly parted lips. He lifts the beret from her head gently and drops it in his lap, runs his fingers through her hair. It is intoxicating. He can smell her now, unperfumed, only the natural odors of her hair and skin. He could breathe this, he thinks, for the rest of his life. He touches her cold cheek softly and her arm reaches around his ribs.

After a time, when the vehicle is fully heated, he says quietly: "Maybe we'd better go."

"Mmm..." She nestles against him again.

He giggles slightly, euphorically. "The..." Something thick and wonderful seems to block his throat. "Heather, the...the problem is that my...battery is on its last legs, and if we sit here much longer—well, they might have to dig us out of a glacier ten thousand years from now."

She giggles sleepily. "Okay," she mumbles. But she does not move away. Robin leans over with his left hand and switches on the motor; stretches to put the gearshift into drive.

"Need me to move?" she mumbles.

"Nope. Just stay where you are."

They sit together in warm silence as Robin drives back to her apartment. She has a studio of her own, a small room built as an add-on to a residential house. He has no trouble finding it again in the darkness.

When they pull up to the house Robin switches off the engine and says, "Hey, sleepyhead."

"Mm." She moves away from him at last and rubs her eyes. "I'm awake."

"I should be insulted," he says. "You find me so dull that you just sleep in my presence."

"I find you so *warm* I just sleep in your presence." She smiles groggily. "Want to come in?"

He feels his heart beating. It is past one in the morning.

"Sure," he says. "But I think maybe you're too tired."

"Huh-uh. I'll perk up just as soon as I hit that night air again. Just you watch—" She opens the door suddenly, gasps and cries, *"Jesus Christ!* C'mon!"

She runs around the house to her own entrance at the back. Robin follows briskly. She fumbles with the key for a moment, then quickly pushes the door open. "Come in and shut the door behind you! Quick, quick, quick!"

He does; and stands in the darkness while she tosses her beret on the bed and finds the light, a small table lamp on a desk in the corner. The room remains pleasantly dim. She leans over then, toward the floor, and switches on a space heater which glows orange in the room.

"At least it's not *too* bad in here," she says, rubbing her hands. "Anyway, here we are."

He nods, smiling. He had not seen the room earlier. It is extremely small, with space only for a bed in one corner and a long counter which she has divided up: one section is her desk, on which the lamp sits with numerous school books; a double hot plate rests in the middle; and past that the counter is covered with a checkered tablecloth. Underneath the counter is a small refrigerator and some storage drawers. The image of Cape and his van crosses his mind for an instant.

"Here, I'll burn some water," she says. She reaches under the counter for a pan and then goes to a window and opens it. She reaches over and Robin hears the sound of water running.

"Ingenious, huh?" she says, bringing the pan back in. "Outdoor plumbing."

"Ingenious," he agrees.

"Sit yourself down," she says. "As you can see, there's only one chair. So you shouldn't be overwhelmed by your options."

He grins and sits. She crouches by the space heater for a long moment, rubbing herself. "Did you want coffee or tea?" she asks, her back to him.

"Either."

"Don't say that. You must prefer one or the other."

"Tea."

"Tea." She stands again and begins bringing out cups, spoons, tea bags, sugar. The water on the hot plate begins to help warm the room. Finally it boils and she pours water into the cups. She glances at him and smiles as she mixes her tea; then she moves to the bed and sits on it, her legs crossed.

They nothing for a long time. Once their eyes meet and they both chuckle quietly. At last, after minutes have passed, Heather's voice breaks the silence.

"Tea okay?"

"Mm-hm. Fine."

There is silence again.

After a time Robin mutters, "We seem to have run out of things to talk about."

She looks at him. "Does it bother you? I was kind of enjoying it."

He looks at her in the lamplit darkness. "Actually, I was too. I was afraid you weren't."

"I was." She sips the tea. "People don't have to talk all the time."

"No. I guess not."

She grins, displaying her uneven teeth. But it is a charming grin, Robin thinks; nearly goofy.

"You're funny," she says.

"Why?"

"I don't know. You just are." She looks at him. "We've met before, you know. I've kept waiting to see if you'd remember."

"When? In another life, you mean?"

She laughs. "No. But maybe that too. I mean we've *met*. We really have. But you've forgotten."

"What do you mean?"

"Don't you remember? At the end of last year? It was raining?"

For a moment his mind is blank. Then, suddenly, the memory strikes him: the accident, Turnham's car, being knocked to the wet pavement, and then the dark figure: *Look at me. How many fingers am I showing?*

"That was you?" he grins. "After I was hit by the car?"

She nods. "Mm-hm."

"So we've known each other for ages."

"Maybe it was *destiny*," she says. "Have you ever had any problems? I mean, after the accident?"

"Oh, no." He shakes his head. "It was nothing. But it *was* a little strange. You see, my mom was hit by a car. That's how she died."

"Oh." She looks at him seriously. "I'm sorry."

He shrugs. "It was just strange, that's all. I wasn't hurt. But it did bring back…you know, memories."

"I suppose it would."

"Mm." He looks at the floor. "Anyway."

"Anyway." She smiles. She swallows the last of her tea and stands, places the cup on the checkered tablecloth; moves close to Robin.

"Finished?" she asks.

Robin swallows, his heart pumping inside his chest. Her stomach, covered by a black blouse and jacket, is inches from his face.

"Uh-huh," he manages to mutter.

She takes the cup from him and places it on the counter. Then she turns to him again and reaches her hands out to touch his hair.

"Hi," she whispers.

He giggles nervously. "Hi."

"C'mere." She pulls him up and over to the bed, then pushes him gently down. She reclines next to him, her face inches from his. He stares at her and finds himself trembling. She reaches toward his face and takes off his glasses and puts them on the night stand next to the bed.

"Maybe you'll like me better if you can't see me so well," she whispers.

He swallows, feels the tremors growing worse. "Heather, I...I do like you...You're beautiful."

She smiles. "Liar." She leans her face close to his and their lips touch softly. Her hand rests on his shoulder; after a moment she pulls back.

"Robin, what's wrong? You're shaking."

Goddamn it, he thinks. Not again. Not this time. *Stop.*

"...I'm okay," he says.

"Are you cold? It's not very cold, is it?"

"I'm—I'm okay." But the tremors are uncontrollable.

"You're not. Something's the matter. Is it me?"

"No...No, I swear to God. I..." He feels his eyes welling. "This..." He is short of breath but determined to speak this time. No more secrets. No more disasters. "This always—always happens...I don't know why." He shuts his eyes, ashamed to look at her.

There is silence between them for a moment. He moves to stand up and go when her hand reaches to his shoulder again and holds him back.

"Robin, don't leave."

He looks at her again. Her eyes are wide and deep and gazing straight at him.

"Don't go," she says.

She touches his hair, gently pulls his face to hers. She wraps her arms around him tightly. "It's all right, baby," she whispers, her lips near his ear. "Everything's all right. You don't have to go anyplace. I'm here. I'm here."

2

It is only the next morning that the suddenness of it hits him. He finds himself under a blanket, still fully clothed even to his jacket; looking around himself he recognizes the room from the night before, bright now with morning light shining yellowly through the thin curtains. The room is filled with windows: three along the counter, one to the side of the bed and one over it. It all seems cheery enough—a pleasant clutter of books, cassettes, plants, and scattered clothes. It takes him a moment, in his grogginess, to realize that she is not in the room.

He sits up, fumbles for his glasses. "Heather?"

After a moment the window over the bed snaps open and he starts, his eyes darting upward. Heather's face appears in the frame, pushing aside the curtain and looking down at him. "Hi!" she says brightly.

"Hi—" He twists on the bed so that he can see her without craning his neck. "What—uh, what's up?"

"Nothin' much. Are you a vegetarian?"

"No."

"You will be. I'm digging up breakfast."

He yawns, covering his mouth. "Actually, a bowl of corn flakes—"

"Ouch! *Corn flakes*. I can see you need somebody to teach you how to eat. The bathroom is that door on the right just as you go out, if you want to clean up. I'll be with you in five minutes." Her head disappears from the window and the curtain shifts back into place.

He looks around himself again and stretches his muscles. He stands, noting vaguely the black beret lying tumbled on the floor, and steps out the main door into the bathroom.

It is a simple affair with largely portable plastic fixtures. She has left a clean towel over the edge of the sink which he picks up; under it is a new, still-in-its-box toothbrush, a disposable razor still in its plastic wrap, and a half-squeezed tube of toothpaste.

"Are you going to take a shower?" she calls to him.

He glances at himself in the mirror: mottled hair, bleary eyes, stubbled face. Terrifying.

"Maybe I'd better!" he calls back to her. "If you don't mind!"

"Just a second!"

There is a pause; he hears her footsteps. He slips off his glasses and splashes water onto his face, rubs his eyes; relieves himself, flushes; and is just thinking of stripping down when there is a quick knock on the door and she pokes her arm in, holding a bathrobe.

"Use this!" she says from behind the door.

He takes it from her hand. "It's all right, I'll just put on these clothes again and go—"

"No, no, no. Just dump them outside the door and I'll throw them in the landlord's washer. It'll only take a half-hour and then you'll be clean and ready to face the world again." She closes the door. "Okay?"

"Heather, you really don't need to go to so much bother. I mean, I really appreciate it. But..."

"Oh, for corn's sake, it's no bother. The Seabright Hotel treats its guests well, that's all. Just clean up and then we'll have breakfast, okay? Did you find the toothbrush and razor?"

"Uh-huh. For me?"

"Uh-huh!"

"But I don't want to waste a perfectly good toothbrush—"

"Oh, don't be silly. You can take it with you. Unless you want to use *mine*, which might be a little gross."

"Well—"

"Leave the clothes outside the door, okay?"

He stares at the door. "Okay." Then, after a moment: "Heather, thanks. Really."

"No prob!" He hears her footsteps moving away.

The shower is deliciously, steamingly hot and Robin stands under it motionlessly for many minutes. The water beats against his closed eyelids and pours down his face and body in hot streams. He feels as if he will soon melt away, all tension and anxiety and tiredness seeping out of him, through his pores, into the open sky. He feels wonderful. Heather Seabright, he thinks. He runs the name through his mind a dozen times, thinking of the sound of each letter, each syllable. Heather. Seabright. He has just spent the night with Heather Seabright. Nothing happened; but she didn't criticize him, or tell him to get out, or laugh, or anything. She simply stayed with him. As the water rolls down his skin, images play in his mind: in the darkness, last night, half-waking to find her nestled against him, the both of them under the blankets, she in the bathrobe that even now awaits him when he steps from the shower, and gently, gently her palm touching his face, moving across his cheek and chin and lips, and snuggling her soft little body against his, one of her legs warmly over his own, her breasts against him gently, and the warmth of her, the softness of the bathrobe under his hands, her black hair tickling his nose, her quiet breathing: all to himself, every bit of her to himself, the two of them alone there together. He rubs his hands over his slippery body. A simple, delightful progression…But still he had been unable to function. Why? Could Cape have been right all along? He thinks of Cape, the sea, the van. It seems a thousand centuries ago: past tense: but this is the vivid, living present. He hears her humming in her room, and the sound of a knife on a cutting board.

Who is she? he wonders. And how could she have offered him this—everything!—so freely, so effortlessly, and how could it all seem so perfectly natural and inevitable that he would be here? Not surprising in the least—not even after the years of Marylou Kirks and prostitutes and shameful acts done in the darkness with nothing but evanescent nude fantasies for company? All of that, every bit of it, is suddenly, miraculously gone, and there is nothing surprising about it, it all makes absolutely perfect sense; as if his mindscape, cluttered for so long with misshapen, horrible figures, were suddenly wiped clean and smooth again, made innocent again and pure, everything made new, and only one figure was left there: Heather Seabright. It's all so simple. He sees her dark, blurred form before him: *How many fingers am I showing?* If he were a bit more of a mystic, he thinks, he might believe there was something preordained about it: inevitable: for it does feel that way, even now, even at this moment. Heather, he thinks. Heather Seabright.

He shuts off the water and glances down at himself, at the erection he abruptly realizes has planted itself there. *Where were you last night?* he wants to ask; but somehow, here, with Heather humming and chopping in the room, it seems not to matter much. There will be time, he thinks. For everything. Now, for the first time, there will be time.

He dries himself and, after he has given his body a moment to calm itself, he slips into the bathrobe. He realizes with a delighted sense of recognition that it smells like her. He ties it and steps out, breathes for a moment the cool sunshiny morning, then knocks and steps into her room again. It has grown steamy with her cooking. For once, she is not wearing black: instead, a gray sweater and sweat pants with dirty tennis shoes. Her hair is tied back with a red ribbon. The effect, Robin thinks, is amazing: the sarcastic little artsy girl at school has utterly vanished and been replaced by an image of healthy outdoorsiness, openness.

"You're getting the absolute *last* of the season," she says, glancing up at him and smiling before going back to her chopping. "You'd better appreciate it."

"I do," he says, grinning at her. "Last of what?"

"The carrots. Actually I'm amazed they're not all *kaput* by this time, especially after a night like last night. But I found a few. So I'm steaming together some mixed-up vegetables and I'll make us some eggs and that's going to be breakfast and you'd better not complain."

He grins again. He cannot stop grinning. "Who's complaining?" he asks. "It's fantastic."

She glances at him again, smiling crookedly.

He stands against the door, watching her.

"There's some water for tea there," she says, motioning toward a Thermos on the counter. "You can see I've got kind of limited cooking facilities."

"No prob." He pours some of the hot water into a cup. "For you?"

"Sure. Thanks."

He prepares two cups of tea. Standing close to her at the counter, watching her toss the last of the vegetables into the steamer, he is overcome with a desire to put his arms around her. He reaches out gingerly and touches her shoulder. She turns to him instantly and wraps her arms around him, buries her face in his chest. She is a full head shorter than Robin. He caresses her shoulders and back and they press against each other for a long moment.

Finally she pulls away from him slightly and smiles, moves forward again and kisses him lightly on his chest.

"You look good in my bathrobe," she whispers.

"So do you. I saw you last night."

She pulls away from him again, gently.

"Let me check the vegetables," she says.

While she lifts the lid from the steamer and prods the colorful mixture with a fork, he touches her shoulder again. "Heather," he says, "about—about last night..."

She shakes her head; for a moment he is not sure if she is thinking of him or the vegetables. "It happens to every man, Robin. You were nervous." She smiles and spears a piece of broccoli on the fork, moves it toward his mouth. He bites down as she says, "Don't worry about it, okay?"

"Still," he says, swallowing. "I—I'm sorry I...disappointed you."

"I wasn't disappointed. How's the broccoli?"

"I'm not an expert. But I'd give it another couple of minutes."

She nods, replaces the lid of the steamer. "Can I just ask one question?"

"Mm-hm."

She stares at the hot plate. "Is there anything...you know—physically? Wrong?"

"No. There isn't."

She grins again, picking up the two teacups and handing one to him. "Then stop worrying," she says, "and drink your tea."

There is a wire table and a set of chairs in her landlord's big grassy backyard. They take their breakfasts outside and sit under a sprawling tree whose leaves cast shadows of broken light onto Heather's face as they talk and eat.

"As a matter of fact," Heather says, "the landlord's out of town. I think he runs a spy ring or something. He's very mysterious. But anyway, we've got this whole landscape to ourselves."

The morning is unexpectedly warm after the previous night's cold, and unseasonably clear; Robin is comfortable in the bathrobe and slippers she has provided. They sit close together, her knee touching his own, and he is acutely aware of his nakedness under the bathrobe. An image flits over his mind like a bird's wing: years before, when he was unfathomably young, and a little blonde girlfriend—Sonya, that was it—playing checkers with him at a little table, she across from him, their knees touching under the table; and later, her damp palm in his as he was driven home by her parents. He had not thought of it in ages. And yet this scene now, he thinks, is nearly the same: like a recapturing of an earlier moment, a happier one, one when there was still innocence and excitement and the possibilities of the future. He thinks of the walking zombie he has been recently. He had not been living. He had not been conscious. Now for the first time in months he feels alive again: breathing, seeing, sensing, knowing: connected. And as with Cape, he is vividly aware of the living being next to him: every motion, each breath; and she fills him with a giddiness, a heady euphoria. She is so very *alive*, next to him.

They talk, at first quietly and hesitantly, then in a joyous rush, about everything: school, teachers, northern California, writing.

"I told you," Heather says, "I've heard all about you. You're a budding author."

"Maybe *budding* isn't the word," he says, chuckling slightly. "Maybe the proper term is *dying on the vine*."

"No, you're not. Have you had anything published?"

"No. My biggest claim to fame was a play I wrote that was produced in high school."

"Well, that's something."

"It was a disaster," he says, wincing at the long-buried memory. "A catastrophe. The author should have been taken out behind the barn and *terminated*."

She laughs. "What are you writing now? I mean, right now? You must have some project in the works."

"A novel," he says with a trace of pride; although he is all too aware that months have gone by since he has written a word on it, or anything.

"What's it called?"

"Drowning."

"Cheery title. What's it about?"

"Some guy."

"C'mon."

He grins, immensely pleased with the direction the conversation has taken. There is nothing he enjoys more than discussing his own writing; the joy is tripled by the fact that she is the one who has brought up the subject. "Maybe I'm not quite sure yet," he says, willfully mysterious. "That's why I'm writing it. To find out."

"Clever. But you're not being honest."

"How do you know?"

She finishes her tea in a final swallow. "I happen to be very bright."

"Had me fooled."

She looks at him sourly. "Are we going to start up the sarcasm?"

"Sorry. I was just trying to be honest."

"Stop it."

He smiles. "Sorry. You know I don't mean it."

"So don't say it. At least not right now." She leans her head onto his shoulder and touches the arm of the bathrobe. His skin seems to tingle and he is aware again of his nakedness under the robe. "Finished with breakfast?" she asks.

"Mm-hm."

"Good. Because I don't have any more food."

They giggle. Robin looks out at the big lawn, gently sloping and immaculately trimmed, a cobblestone pathway leading to the house. It is an idyllic vista.

"Will you show me some of your stuff?" she asks.

"Such as...?"

"The stuff you've *written.*" She slaps him playfully on the cheek.

"Oh. I thought maybe..."

"Well, I figured I didn't have to *ask* to look at *that.*"

They laugh again. Robin strokes her arm, covered by the gray sweatshirt, as she reaches between the folds of the robe and touches his chest.

"What day is it?" she asks.

"Sunday."

"What shall we do today?"

"I—I don't know." He smiles giddily at her as the scent of her hair wafts into him. "I didn't make any plans. I mean...I didn't think I'd be here. Now."

She runs her hand along his chest, strokes his nipple with a finger. "Don't you want to be? You can go if you want. I just thought..."

He looks at her. "Heather, no. That's not what I meant. I *want* to be here. More than anything. I..."

He leans forward and kisses her. Suddenly their tongues are intertwined and Robin's hand is on her neck and she is stroking his ribs under the robe. His entire body tingles wildly and on some level of consciousness he is aware that the robe will not be adequate camouflage; but he keeps on kissing her, his tongue running deeper and deeper across the ribbed roof of her mouth, and he hears himself moaning softly, whimpering with joy. He feels her hand moving across his stomach. He kisses her eyes and hair and cheeks wildly, drunk with the sensation, and briefly he opens his eyes to see the limb-fractured light pouring down through the tree onto them, the shifting shapes and shadows playing across her hair. Her hand moves still lower and suddenly, flickering like the light through the tree, he sees himself again at the river with Priscilla, her boyish body glistening in the summer noon, her hair dripping with river water, the sky dissolving in soft prisms of blue, and vaguely he sees the robe, fallen open now, and Heather's small hand there, and feels her tongue on his neck and running down his chest and stomach and light breaking through the trees, yellow beams splashing across the grass, the blue sky behind them swaying and shimmering like seawater, and then all sight dims and grows black as he feels his body arching, convulsing, hears wind seething through his teeth and feels her hair tangled in his hands.

"Well," she says later, "you were right about there not being any physical problem. I'm lucky to have escaped with my teeth!"

He laughs and pulls her on top of him. It is hours later; they lay warmly together under the blankets of her bed. When they had come back into the room they had locked the door and she had pulled the robe completely away from his body and he had gently lifted off her sweatshirt to expose her small, dark-nippled breasts; she had kicked away her tennis shoes as he undid the red ribbon and watched her hair fall to the sides of her face and then knelt before her to pull down the sweat pants, to breathe in the briny odor of her, to bury himself in it as she fell back onto the bed gasping and arching her body before him. Afterwards they slept for a time. He would wake now and then, feel her warm skin pressing against his own, and draw her nearer. What did he need with writing? he thought to himself. Or school? Or anything? This was all there was. All that mattered. All he needed.

Finally they woke, looked at each other; and all Robin wanted to do was hold her tighter, tighter, until he was drained of strength, until he blacked out forever.

"Your teeth?" he giggles, looking up at her and running his hands over the small of her back, watching her breasts bounce lightly with her movements. "What about my tongue? Do you know how much work it is to do that to a woman?"

"Aw, c'mon," she grins, "it's easier than sucking cock."

"Ho, ho. At least a cock is right there and all you have to do is act like it's an Eskimo Pie. With a woman it's all hidden away in there so deep you think your tongue is going to fall off."

"At least a woman tastes better than a man, though."

"Maybe. If you like fish."

"I like fish better than I like raw egg whites."

"It doesn't taste like raw egg whites."

"The texture, I mean." She puckers her lips in distaste. "Yucky."

"Anyway, how do you know it's not as good as fish? Have you tasted fish?"

She looks away, says nothing for a moment. Robin runs his hands along her waist. "I guess I should be honest with you," she says. "I mean, since it seems like something is kind of starting up here. Fact is, I *have* slept with girls before. A long time ago. I'm not a lesbian—at least I don't think I am. But sometimes I've gotten…lonely." She looks at him, her eyes questioning. "Is that okay?"

He looks at her, at her small naked body on top of him: the flat stomach and dark pubic hair pressed onto his own. He considers for a moment, then says: "Well, I guess it had better be. Considering that I've gone to bed with men."

She cocks her head, grins. "Really?"

"Mm-hm."

"So we're both experts on fish *and* egg whites."

Robin giggles, feeling his face growing hot, and looks away.

"Robin? You're blushing. What is it?"

"I don't know," he laughs. "Just…talking. Like this."

"What do you mean?"

"Well—" he looks up at her—"in my house those things weren't discussed. At all. I never even heard about the birds and bees. As far as the official party line in my house went, I was delivered by a stork."

"What about with your...boyfriends?"

He shakes his head. "We never really talked about it. I *couldn't*, I guess. That's what makes all this so strange to me. How I can make jokes like this so easily with you."

"You couldn't with girls either?"

He falls silent, staring at her navel pensively.

"Hm," she says, after a long moment. She sits up, straddling him, and cups his face in her hands. "I think maybe I just figured something out."

He nods, not looking at her.

"Well—" She moves her hands to her genitals, pulls them up so that Robin can see them more clearly. "What do you think of the brave new world?"

He giggles again, touches her legs. "I've seen worse."

She laughs and tumbles down beside him again. They snuggle together for a time.

"Heather?" he say finally.

"Mm."

"I'm not sure if I should ask you this..."

After a short pause she says: "The answer is yes."

A silence falls between them.

"I'm sorry," she adds, finally.

"Nothing to be sorry about."

"Well, anyway—I'm afraid I won't be wearing white on my wedding day."

He grins. "What do you have to worry about? At least you don't have to wear *black*, like us guys."

She giggles and her tongue finds its way to his earlobe.

"Heather?"

"Mm."

He stares at the ceiling as the afternoon shadows lengthen across the room. "Is something happening here?"

Her hand runs through his hair and she presses her body against his. "Something very special is happening here," she whispers. After a moment she adds: "Darling."

3

Nothing ever existed before now, he writes. *It's strange for me to think back to the things I wrote about Cape because it all seems unimportant now—just vague gray memories compared to the vividly-painted present. Or a brief flash compared to—what? Because even now, I've known her only a few days. But something tells me that this is not heading for another quick flame-out. Heather is not one to bounce into a life and bounce right out again when another offer comes up. She calls me every day—if I don't call her first; we spend all our off-hours together, reading or going to movies or just lolling around in her room for hours. I hardly spend any time in the dorm anymore. My roommate Zero wants to know what's going on but I won't tell him. I'm not telling anybody. I'm too afraid that if I open my mouth it will dissolve away.*

He considers the page he has just written; glances up at the school library all around him. Amazing, the hours he has spent in this library: mostly melancholy hours, studying amoebas ripping themselves in two and wondering how he could escape it all. And yet good hours too, especially those spent alone with no assignment due, roaming the stacks and bringing down half a dozen books of poems and stories and biography, losing himself in the world of print the way he had years before when his kindergarten teacher Mrs. Balfour-Ritchie read tales from the Bible to them—Samson and his hair, evil Cain and hapless Abel, nutty long-suffering Job. Or, a bit later, his mother and the big heroic poems by Lord Byron and Coleridge (her favorite: he can see the albatross in the sky to this day): her voice different for each character, alternately sweet and seductive or manly and authoritative or sinister and cruel. It has been, he knows, much the same here, sitting cross-legged on the floor amongst the stacks with a heap of books around him, perusing, tasting, sampling, the scenes and characters and language coming alive to him just as they used to years before. And it is, perhaps, the reason he finds his classes, even his English classes, so dull and depressing: such magic is not there, not within stuffy lectures and minute studies of image-clusters and patterns and deconstructionist theories. Try as he might, he has never been able to discover what relevance those things have compared to the simple exquisite pleasure of opening a book and having it come alive before his eyes, to hear the voices and see the scenes and dwell inside the minds of the characters. Turnham himself had called professors kids with their faces pressed against the window of the candy store; and told Robin to be a candymaker.

He shakes his head, closes his diary. He doesn't want to think about that time or any previous time at all. And yet, since Heather, he has found his mind stepping back increasingly often to Cape, to Turnham, to his father and mother and the house in the cul-de-sac.

"I thought memory lane was a road only old people went down," he had told Heather yesterday.

"Who says you're not old?" she had replied, smiling at him. "Maybe you're old before your time. People with backgrounds like yours usually are."

Of course some of it had been triggered by Heather's questions. He had told her everything: she knew about his mother, his father, writing, loneliness, Cape. (He had eliminated only Turnham, changing him into an unnamed high school teacher.) She listened. She asked the right questions. She was better, he imagined, than a fleet of psychiatrists: she did everything they could do and looked pretty with her clothes off too.

The Unspoken

And she *did* look pretty: gorgeous, in fact: her tiny little body was intoxicating to him. Her feminine odor, quite different from a man's, filled him with wild desire. When they were together in the little room he could hardly keep his hands from roaming over her for hours, feeling her softness and smoothness.

Yet his problem remained. Everything else, anything else, they could do with ease; but the other remained impossible. But even then—even then!—she would not complain. "Look, darling," she said, "after a lifetime of *your* mother, not to mention people like— what was her name? Marylou?—and then that teacher of yours, and your father, and *everything*, it's a wonder you're not permanently *derailed*. It's just a matter of time," she giggled, "until your little friend learns to trust mine."

And he has discovered that, incredibly, she shares his tastes in nearly everything. Her bookshelves are crowded with paperbacks of Dickens, Flaubert, Dickinson and Whitman and Baudelaire; as well as Christopher Isherwood, Graham Greene, Tennessee Williams. "But I like dead writers better," she has told him. "I don't know why. I guess I just like them because they can't screw up. You know? You don't read a great book and then open up the paper the next day and find out the author has stabbed his wife or had to be carted off the stage at some university because he was so potted he couldn't stand up. They don't *disappoint*, dead people. They're just there. Forever."

They like the same movies; like Robin, Heather can equally well squeal with glee over an after-midnight TV presentation of *Invasion of the Saucer Men* or be struck mute by the flowing nostalgic elegance of *Jules and Jim*. And music: just yesterday he had been nearly toppled with astonishment when he opened her tape cassette case and found, dotted among the Wings and Fleetwood Mac, symphonies by Sibelius, Beethoven, Copland—and Mahler.

"What's this?" he asked, his voice high-pitched with surprise as he held up a cassette of the *Resurrection* symphony.

"Oh—just some classical stuff. You probably wouldn't like it. I have strange tastes—"

"I *love* classical music," he said, gazing at her delightedly.

"You do? Really?"

"Mahler's my favorite composer in the world. I've never met anybody else who cared anything about him."

"I love Mahler too," she said, propping herself up on her elbows on the bed. "But I can't listen to him very much. He's so intense—"

"He tears you apart. I know."

"*Das Lied von der Erde* I love, though. I can listen to it—just barely! So unhappy, so…sad. Such an awareness of death…"

"I know!" Robin cried, enormously excited. "I know! 'Everywhere, forever, horizons are blue and bright…forever…forever…'"

"'*Ewig…ewig…*'" Heather echoed.

"You speak German?" he asked.

She shrugged, smiling. "A little. I can stumble through."

"Maybe that's why I like his orchestral stuff better…It's frustrating, not knowing the language. The voice becomes just another instrument."

"Some classical pieces are nice that way, though. A lot of times the lyrics are kind of stupid."

He laughed. "I guess so. But still. If I had to throw away every other piece of music in the world and keep only one, it would be the Ninth Symphony. No words. He didn't need any."

"I never listen to the Ninth. I can't take it. I'm reduced to a blubbering mess, way before the end. Can't talk for days!"

"Yes," he said, gazing at her. "Yes. Yes."

"I like Tchaikovsky more," she said, brightening. "I mean for everyday listening."

"Now there I can't agree with you," he said, shutting the case again and sitting next to her on the bed. "Slick, tuneful, and totally superficial."

"Do you know the *Pathetique?*"

"Sure. But how can you like Mahler and then also say you like that little Tinkertoy version of the same material?"

"It's not Tinkertoy," Heather smiled, wrapping herself around his waist, "and I have the distinct feeling that I'm hearing a little bit of your famed *arrogance*."

He ran his fingers into her hair. "It's a legitimate aesthetic judgment."

"Legitimate maybe, but wrong. Tchaikovsky has gotten a bum rap for years from stuffy people like you—"

"—I am *not* stuffy—"

"—Who think that it's a crime to write melodies a person can actually hum. He was a great composer. I played his Violin Concerto once, in a competition."

"I didn't know you played the violin."

"Used to. Haven't touched it in years. But I got second place. It was a statewide thing."

"Congratulations. Why didn't you keep it up?"

She shrugged. "Other pressing concerns in life, I guess. Besides, I wasn't really very good."

"I want to hear you play sometime."

"Sure thingie. But my main goal is to prove to you that Tchaikovsky isn't what you think he is. Jesus, he was even a faggot, you know. So you should like him for that."

She giggled wildly as Robin tickled her across her waist.

So easy, he thinks, gathering his books from the table. It is all so easy with her. Everything is open, possible, free. That is the way she is.

"I don't want any secrets," she told him. "I want to know everything about you."

"What about *you?*" he said.

She smiled. "Oh, you'll hear about *me*, all right. I never stop talking about my family. My daddy is wonderful. He's an under-under Secretary of Commerce in Washington. And Mama—she makes the best fruit pastries in the world, I swear to *God*. And my three brothers. Oh, you'll hear everything! And I really *need* to tell you about us, because we're a *happy* family and you need to know what that's like. So don't worry, you'll hear *all* about us!"

"Will I meet them sometime?"

"Sure you will. But they're way back east, you know. I think I should meet your pappy first."

"I'm not sure that's the best of all possible ideas."

"Yes, it *is*, because I'm going to prove to you that your daddy isn't the rotter you make him out to be. I'll use my feminine wiles to charm him something silly and we'll all have a great time."

He pictures her face as he drives along the glistening twilit street. The longer he spends with her the more vividly and accurately he can bring her into his mind. He can see her now, a little dark-haired girl with pale skin and big black pool-like eyes; her crooked teeth ("the result of a hack dentist, I'm afraid"), her black outfits ("gimme a break—I'm trying to look artsy, like all the leftover hippies around here"), her tiny hands and feet. He finds himself grinning stupidly whenever he thinks of her. She already has their first vacation planned: over an upcoming long weekend they are to go to San Francisco for two days of museums and symphonies. What a difference, he thinks, from his first time in that city!

And, against all his own predictions, he is writing again: or at least approaching it. *Drowning* has begun to live again in his mind: the characters, the sounds and shadows and rooms: he can see Siegel again, hear his voice, be with him inside his mind. Heather's enthusiasm was the trick. She had read the opening chapter and liked it, encouraging him to keep on with it: "Don't let it just sit there," she said, "go with it!" He has not yet dared to insert a sheet of paper into his typewriter but the images are there again, surfacing inside his mind like unexpected islands. He knows he must do it soon, that the pictures and sounds will not wait. They are alive again within him. And if they are alive, he knows, then *he* must also be alive, in ways he thought had deserted him forever. Or which, perhaps, he himself had deserted—for the sake of survival. But now he is back, he thinks wryly. Better than ever. *Robin Withers Part 2: The Legend Continues.*

A few minutes later they are together in her room, lying on the floor near the glowing space heater and listening to the rain softly spattering on the roof. Heather's breath smells like chocolate.

"What have you been eating?" he asks, kissing her.

"Almond Joys."

"I thought you were afraid of getting fat."

"I am. That's why I barfed them back up."

"You didn't barf them back up. Your breath would smell like barf."

She giggles. "You're right, I didn't. But I thought about it. Isn't that a funny word, 'barf'?"

He looks at her. "Do you really do that?"

"I have before," she says. "I only told you because I want to be honest about everything."

"Sure. You should be. I appreciate it."

"Mm-hm. Anyway, I don't do it anymore. I saw a counselor last year for a while and got over it."

"A psychiatrist?"

"Psychologist."

"What's the difference?"

"Hundred bucks an hour."

Robin smiles, begins unbuttoning her dark blouse. It is amazing, he thinks, that he needn't even ask permission to do this. It comes so naturally between them that the conversation is not even interrupted.

"I've thought about seeing somebody," Robin says. "Somebody at school, maybe."

She nods, stroking his hand. "You never know," she says. "Sometimes they're helpful. I've seen enough of them myself."

He looks at her. "You? I thought you were just as slap-happy as can be."

"Well, I am...But my parents are just that way. It's because they're so concerned. Every time little Heather had a problem, off to the shrink she went."

Robin considers this as he pulls the blouse open gently and kisses the pale skin between her breasts. "Why did you come to California, anyway?" he asks. "I've never been clear on that."

"Change of scene," she shrugs, touching his hair. "After nineteen years of loving family care I thought it was time for little Heather to enter the big bad world."

"And look what you found," he grins. "Big Bad Robin Withers."

She laughs, touching between his legs. *"Bad* is right," she says. "Say, I've got an idea."

"Does it have anything to do with my penis?"

"It might."

"I'm listening."

"Stop. Here's the idea—why don't we take off a couple of days from school and start our long weekend early? We can take four or five days in San Fran instead of two."

He considers as he kisses her nipples. "I don't know...I'm falling pretty far behind, school-wise, ever since *you* entered the picture. I just don't care about it anymore. If I ever did."

"So? Then we'll go ahead and leave early, right?"

"Heather, I'd love to, but maybe it's not a good idea for me to start cutting classes. There's going to be a test in Math just before the weekend anyway—he probably scheduled it that way on purpose, to catch us potential miscreants."

"Come on," she says, running her fingers around his ears. "Don't be a goody-goody. Live a little."

"I am living," he says. "I got a check from my dad the other day, I'm writing again, and I've got your left tit in my mouth. What more could a man ask for?"

"Robin, really. I want to go early."

"Heather, give me a break. You've got one class. I've got a full load."

They fall silent for a long moment. Robin pulls away and looks at her.

"What's wrong?"

"Nothing."

"Come on."

"Nothing's wrong."

He sighs. Then he smiles. "You look nice with your shirt open like that," he says.

"Thank you."

They are silent again.

"Heather, come on."

"Come on what?" She does not look at him.

"Don't be mad."

"I'm not mad."

"You act like you are."

She sighs. "I just want to be with you more," she says. "I thought this would be a good opportunity. I thought it would be great."

"It would be. It *will* be."

"Then why don't we go two days early?"

"Because of my *test*," he says, a trace of irritation finding its way into his voice. "Come on. You understand that."

She gives him a sour look. "You could do it as a make-up, I'm sure," she says. "Or take it early."

He frowns and props himself up on an elbow. "Yeah, I could. But it wouldn't be very convenient and—"

"Don't you want me to suck on your prick for hours in an expensive hotel overlooking the San Francisco nightlights?"

He chuckles. "Of course," he says. "It's just that the timing is bad. Let's just wait and go on Friday, like we agreed—okay?"

After a moment she sits up and crosses her legs.

"I want to be with you," she says. "I just want to be with you."

He scowls. "Heather, come on."

She looks at him, her eyes large. "Are you angry with me?"

"No."

"You are."

He shuts his eyes for a moment, then opens them again. "You know what?"

She looks at him sulkily. "What?"

"I think we're having an argument."

They look at each other in the rainy twilight. The space heater hums gently.

"No," Heather says, shaking her head. "Let's not do that. Please. I never want to fight."

He shifts so that he can place her head in his lap. After a minute of silence he chuckles.

"What?" Heather says, smiling tenuously.

"Nothing," he says. "Just a minor milestone. Our first spat."

She runs her hands over his chest softly. "And our last."

"And our last."

4
DROWNING
Chapter Two

He spots Dusty at a table near the corner. Even in the dim light, he knows him instantly: the same huge, soft build, thin blonde hair, blockish face. He seems to have changed hardly at all. Their eyes meet and a big grin spreads over Dusty's face.

"Seeg!" he calls. "C'mon over, c'mon over!"

They shake hands and Dusty embraces him quickly. "God, how *are* you, man?" he says, taking Siegel by the shoulders and looking at him. "Hey, you don't look half bad, you know?"

"Well, you look as bad as usual," Siegel says, and they both laugh. They sit at the table.

"What are you drinking, Seeg? What can I get you, man?"

He shrugs. "Wine, I guess. White wine."

Dusty beckons the bar maid and makes the order. "This one's on me," he says. "On me, man. God, it's great to see you."

"Well, it's good to see you, Dusty. Long time."

"Don't I know it. You got your nerve, leaving me all alone in this town. Going off and becoming a famous writer."

"I'm not famous quite yet."

"Yeah, but you will be."

"So tell me what you're doing, Dusty. What are you up to?"

"Me? I dunno. You know, same ol', same ol'. Still at the theater." Dusty has worked at the local movie theater since high school. "Assistant manager now."

"Really. That's good." It's unbelievable, he thinks. Siegel has always found it fascinating to look into his own past and compare it with what others were doing at the same time. The night his mom died, Dusty was working at the theater. The day he got the letter from the New York editor, Dusty was working at the theater. The day he went off to la-la land, Dusty was working at the theater. A veritable rock is Dusty. No matter where he goes or how badly he screws up, Dusty will be there when he gets back, a loyal puppy. It annoys him somehow. And yet he knows he's not being reasonable. *Treasure your friends,* he thinks. Something his mom would tell him. And he does, he does treasure Dusty in a way; but at the same time he despises him for his loyalty, his unquestioning acceptance of everything Siegel does. But, he supposes—thinking of Rachel—he would probably despise him even more if Dusty ever questioned him, challenged him.

The wine arrives and Siegel drinks it slowly, or tries to. He is just beginning to feel the effect of the wine at dinner—a pleasant mellowness, a warm expansive feeling inside. He would like to chug the wine in front of him down, swallow it in a few seconds flat, to increase the feeling, relax him even further. But he can't, not with Dusty right in front of him slowly sipping his soda pop.

He swallows half the glass and then puts it down and tries not to think about it.

"So how are you, man?" Dusty says. "I mean really."

"Really? I'm fine, Dusty. I really am."

"We just haven't talked in so long. You know? I mean I sort of thought you didn't want to talk to me anymore."

"No, no, nothing like that," he says, shifting in the chair. "It's just that I was kind of busy, you know? Being crazy took up pretty much all of my time."

Dusty laughs, a good, real laugh. Typical of him. Anyone else would have given him a nervous glance, but Dusty just accepts a thing on its own terms. "You crack me up," he says finally.

"Well, I'm pretty cracked myself."

He laughs again. "Same old Seeg."

"Same ol', same ol'."

"That's it." Dusty wraps his big hands around his glass. His face turns serious and they don't say anything for a moment. Siegel glances around the nearly-empty bar and it occurs to him that he shouldn't have come here at all.

Finally Dusty breaks the silence.

"What *was* it, man?" he says. "I mean...What happened?"

Siegel glances at him. For an instant he thinks he is back in high school again, they are sitting in the cafeteria, he and Dusty and Rachel...But that passes and he is left with the question lying there like a heavy weight between them. Again, that was Dusty. No self-consciousness, squeamishness, tact, whatever you wanted to call it. He just asked you, straight out. And how to answer? What is there to say? What words can he use? How can he talk about what it is to wake up in the morning with nothing but a palpable dread, the feeling of a dark awful *something* hovering near you, just out of reach? And you don't know where it's come from? Or what it is? Words can't communicate it. It's beyond words, or rather, it precedes them. As he sits there he suddenly grows very afraid. It's like this sometimes—he thinks about those days too much, they become too vivid, and suddenly it's as if he's there again, sinking into those sensations, feeling the encroaching darkness swarm over him. Just how had it happened? He was fine—he thought he was fine—in the months after her dying, the months after he took the apartment up north and got the night job at the motel and wrote mornings and slept afternoons. He remembers feeling good then, sometimes. On cold crisp winter days, walking to the library. Visiting old sloppy, sexy Valerie across the street for drinking and cards and laughs. Seeing Rachel every few weeks when she drove up from Santa Barbara, going to the fair, night carousels, making love afterward. How had it happened? How had it crept up on him? When he stopped showing up to work, when he was due on his shift and the phone would ring and ring and he would just listen, how had that happened? When he started telling Rachel not to come up anymore. When he stopped getting out of bed entirely. When he just wanted to drift in that half-world, lose himself in silence that was not silence, darkness that wasn't darkness. When his neighbor Valerie finally looked in through a crack in the curtain, when she saw him collapsed there, head hanging over the side of the bed—he remembers it this way— hallucinating his child super-powers bringing on the torrential floods, the end of the world, the final collapse of the universe, nuclear missiles exploding into the endless sea, explosions you could ride on, all the way to the stars, past them, for all the stars were falling too in blinding white jets of light, splashing into the sea, and later, people in the room, doctors, ambulances, have you taken any pills, son? any drugs? How could they have known that he didn't need drugs for it, all he needed was a little wine, a little wine and the darkness that approached him always, the vast, unknowable darkness, that was all.

How had it happened? When he got the phone call from his dad telling him to come to the hospital. And getting there, seeing him through the glass door as he walked up, knowing everything immediately from his face, and slowing suddenly, there being no more reason to hurry. The funeral director there only an hour or so later, already taking his notes, making his arrangements, a stooped-over man who spoke apologetically and constantly cleared his throat. He remembers feeling totally calm, logical, as if this were all just a small ripple in the smooth lake of existence. Wondering why his dad was sitting in the corner with his hand over his face. Someone behind Siegel asking about a final view, did he want a final view? And turning and looking at her, an ax-faced nurse looming over him darkly, what was he supposed to say? What in the world kind of a question was it?

Dusty's voice suddenly pitches him forward again to the bar, the present.

"Jesus. You want another drink, man?"

Siegel looks at him. He realizes abruptly that he has been talking through all this. He notices his glass is empty.

"Another," he says, and coughs. "Yeah, that sounds good. Yeah."

Dusty, rather grim-faced, makes the order.

There is an odd silence between them for a moment. It occurs to Siegel that he has finally succeeded in making happy-go-lucky Dusty ill-at-ease. He wishes he knew what he'd just said to him.

Dusty looks at him. "How are you feeling now, Seeg? I mean really. I mean *really* really."

He laughs. "I think we've already covered this territory."

"Yeah, but...I dunno. I mean, are you really okay now?"

"Sure I am. They wouldn't have let me out otherwise."

"Well, but you could leave whenever you wanted, couldn't you?"

Siegel looks at the table. "Yeah, I guess. I wasn't really *committed*. But still, they said I could leave. I didn't just walk out."

Dusty nods. "That's good."

He smiles. "Mm-hm. Well, you know me. Can't keep a good loon down."

"I know, man. I know."

They are silent for a moment. The wine comes and Siegel resolves to only sip at it. He feels a little high. And a little bored. He could talk to Dusty all night, tell him the most intimate details about everything, and it wouldn't make any difference. Just like talking to that first psychiatrist, Liona. Like talking to a recording. *Yes. Mm-hm. I understand. I know what you mean.* No connection. No...exchange. Just a rambling monologue. And anyway, he knows that Dusty doesn't understand, though he wants to. God, how he wants to. He has always wanted to understand everything about him. Siegel remembers Dusty smoking pot when they were sixteen, mellow, conservative Dusty actually smoking pot with him and Rachel, just because he didn't want to be left behind. That's exactly what he'd said. *I don't want to be left behind.* But it was futile, of course, Dusty would never understand the tiniest thing about him. Or he about Dusty. How could somebody live like that, the way Dusty lives, the routine, the monotony? He can't help but think that Dusty's inner life must be dead, dead as an old mother.

He grins wryly.

At the same time, it makes him wonder about his dad. If he can talk like this to Dusty, so intimately, and yet feel nothing but boredom, would a real dialogue with his dad be any different? It could be just the same sort of thing. And yet something tells him it wouldn't be. Why this would be, he can't say; perhaps their shared experience…and yet he and Dusty shared experiences, and even when they talk about those, Siegel only feels bored and removed.

"Have you heard from Rachel, Seeg?"

He looks up. "Hm? No. No, I haven't heard from her in six months. Have you?"

Dusty nods, looks at his glass. "I see her around now and then."

"Is she out of college?"

"Will be. End of the year."

"Mm. So she's still in town."

"Oh, yeah. Yeah, you should call her."

He smiles vaguely. "I don't know about that."

"You should. She talks about you."

He sips his wine, trying to keep from chugging it. "Oh? What does she say?"

"I dunno," Dusty says, sounding defensive. "I mean, I don't remember exactly. But she talks about you."

"She should talk about that…what was his name?"

"Her fiance?"

"Yeah."

"Saul. Biberman."

"Saul Biberman, that's it. She should talk about him."

Dusty sighs. "That's all over, man," he says. "You know that."

"She hasn't told me."

"Your dad must've told you."

He nods. "But she didn't. She hasn't said a word to me." At this moment he feels very angry toward Rachel, something he hasn't felt before. Before he just felt sadness, a sense of loss. Anger is new. Where did she get off, anyway? Abandoning him when he goes to the bin and then turning around and getting engaged to some other clod. And now he finds out she *talks* about him. Well, what does that mean? He certainly doesn't talk about her.

"You know, man," Dusty says, clearing his throat, "I mean, maybe it's none of my business or anything, but I think you shouldn't worry much about that Saul guy. He was nothin'."

"She was going to marry him."

"Well..." Dusty's eyes look a little uncertain, a little melancholy. "Just between you and me, man, I pretty well figured that whole deal would never come off. I mean, she got involved with him right after you went away, and she...well, you just don't know. I mean you really don't. I mean how broken-up she was. She was just in terrible shape. She used to call me in the middle of the night and ask me to come over. She used to call when I was at work."

Siegel is listening.

"What did she say?" he asks.

"Oh, you know. The kind of stuff you'd expect. How much she missed you and how bad she felt about the whole thing and how she felt guilty that she didn't do enough."

"She shouldn't have felt guilty. I was the one who cut it off."

"I know, but you know Rachel. She cares about you, man."

"Then why'd she plan on getting married to that other guy?"

"She was on the rebound." Siegel winces a bit, inwardly, at the cliché. He has a vague image of a basketball court with Rachel bouncing off a backboard and he and this faceless other man scrambling for possession. "She just needed somebody. Saul was the guy that came along."

Siegel grins sourly. "She should've used you. You were right there."

Dusty looks miffed. "Hey, that's not my style, man. You know that. I mean, it crossed my mind, sure. But no way."

"Well, thanks for that, anyway."

"Why don't you call her, man?"

He glances away, out the window at the darkness and the black ocean sparkling in it. "I don't think so."

"C'mon." Dusty smiles a bit, cajoling him. "You know you want to. It'll be just like it used to be. I mean the way it was back in high school. And a little ways after that, too."

Dusty, he wants to say, it won't be the *same*. How could it possibly be the same? Four years later? With all that's happened? But, he realizes, for Dusty it *would* be the same: that, perhaps, is the pathetic part of it: for Dusty hasn't changed at all, he *is* the same. Dusty is a time machine. Looking at his big blonde bulk, Siegel can feel the years slipping off himself, or seeming to. Just as he'd felt a few minutes before. But he knows it's a lie, time has passed, things have changed, the person he was back then is now a long-dead stranger. But then something else occurs to him. How he has so often felt as if he's never changed at all, has never developed in the slightest, is the same person he was when he was five years old. And yet, at the same time, there is this, this feeling of his high school incarnation being a stranger, an odd figure lost in mist. He feels both of these sensations simultaneously and yet there doesn't seem to be a paradox, except when he tries to work it out logically. Logic has always been a trap for him. But that, logic, is what he'd tried to base his life on all the time in the institution: if he could only achieve perfect reason, perfect logic in everything he did, all confusion would vanish. Because there would be no place for confusion or problems in a logical existence, one based on pure mathematical principles. But it hadn't worked very well. Other things, non-logical things, emotional things kept blocking the way, confounding him—until logic itself began to confound him, to seem illogical. Until he had no idea what logic meant anymore; the way any word, if repeated often enough, seems to break up and become meaningless. He'd given up on a logical existence.

He says none of this, however. All he says is, "No, I guess not." Then, as an afterthought: "You call her if you want."

Dusty looks at him. "You want me to?"

Yes, he thinks.

"No," he says.

"Why not? I will. C'mon, let's get her over here."

"Dusty, really. It's not a good idea." Besides, he thinks, what a silly way to reunite, with their puppy Dusty hanging on. He will have to call her, he knows. But this isn't the right place or time.

The puppy sighs. "Whatever you say, man."

"I'm just not up to it," he says, swallowing wine.

"Okay."

"Another night."

"Whatever, man."

They sit in silence for a long moment.

"Besides," he says, taking off his glasses and brushing a speck from them, "I think I'm starting to get a little drunk."

Dusty smiles. "You were a teetotaler once, Seeg."

"I know. But all I drink is white wine. You're not going to catch me heading down my mama's road." As he says this a memory flashes into his head: taking her big bottle of Calvert's whiskey, pouring half of it into the sink. Not all of it, he couldn't just throw it away—he was only fifteen, God only knew what the repercussions would be—so instead he would just pour out part of it, now and then, thinking that maybe, somehow, if she had a little less available, maybe...But of course that half-empty bottle would be replaced the very next day by a shining new full one, an endless succession of them, all filled with that same pungent but strangely beautiful amber liquid. He had learned to hate alcohol. Whiskey, anyway. And anything connected with it. Liquor stores. Bars. And yet here he sits, he thinks, getting slowly drunk on white wine, thinking about his mother and alcohol and the great darkness at the edge of his consciousness. Suddenly the fear comes back to him. Suddenly he is very afraid.

"Dusty?" he says hoarsely.

"Yeah, man."

He looks up, half-panicked. "Call Rachel," he says.

5

"Why not?" she asks insistently, her lips moving to cover Robin's. The smell of the street is a heady melange of fried food and cut flowers; when he pulls away from her slightly and glances upward he can see the swirling rain clouds that have gathered overhead but do not cover the setting sun on the horizon: as they stand on the San Francisco street corner, bristling with winter cold in the sunlight, rain begins to patter down on them: fat intermittent drops splashing into his hair and over her eyes, sweetly icy drizzlings on her tongue as it meets his in the vibrant air: and their black-gloved hands around each other, a shopping bag draped over Robin's forearm, Heather's small purse over her shoulder. It is their fourth, and last, day in San Francisco. Robin wishes only that it could go on forever: every day has been filled with museums and galleries, book shops, restaurants; every evening with plays and recitals and symphonies. He cannot believe how happy he is here. How he looks forward with exquisite anticipation to each new event, every new moment, and how full he feels, how satisfied, how whole and complete. And how much, as he wraps her tightly in his arms, she has begun to feel not like a separate being but an extension of himself: an inseparable, irreplaceable element of his own being, in a way he had felt before with the entire universe in those occasional moments when something, a thought of freedom or a touch of Cape's hand, had triggered his sudden re-awareness of the vast everything, the infinite oneness in which he lived. With Heather comes that same sensation, that stunning lift of consciousness into some other plane of being, yet modified now: now that oneness is no longer a faceless expanse but a warm vision of Heather: the abstract has become concrete, personified. For by being connected to Heather, he thinks, he becomes connected to everything else. By being one with each other they are one with the universe. By holding her here on this simple street corner he feels part and parcel of everything, the odor of the flowers, the sounds of the autos, the voices and giggles of children as they pass: and he thinks of lilies, of lions, of the rays of the sun shining through millions of miles of airless space, and they are all of those things together, the two of them, the tiny seeds and the vast intergalactic gulfs, perfectly melded into a single contiguous whole.

"Why not?" she says again: whispers.

"What?"

"What I suggested..."

The sweet smell of the flowers is overwhelming. The drops of rain fall onto them like buds, suddenly bursting into transparent petals.

"Do we have to talk now?" he whispers.

She giggles breathlessly. "No," she says, "I just thought..." And then their mouths are pressed together again, the cold air thick with lilies and roses and orchids as the buds drop from the sky and explode over them and soak into their hair and their skin and their eyes.

"Seriously," she says, grinning. She splashes the hot bath water at him as they sit facing each other in the big hotel tub. It is past midnight.

"Seriously what?" He runs his hands along her slick hot legs. "By the way, how often do you shave these tree trunks?"

She laughs. "They're *nice* legs, and you know it. I don't know. Once a week or so. But that's not what I'm asking."

"What are you asking?" he says, taking each of her legs and drooping them over his shoulders.

"About my idea. About the end of the semester."

"Aren't we going to have a little money problem?"

She sighs and rolls her eyes. "I *told* you, baby, that I've got the money to cover most of it. You supply the car and whatever you can extort from Daddy. I've got enough money to last us at least a few months."

"And then...?"

"And then we come back here."

Robin frowns. "And what do I tell my dad about spring semester?"

She glances away toward the ceiling, thinking. "Tell him...tell him you're going on an *educational tour*. Which is what it is, after all. From one coast to the other and back again. That's bound to be pretty educational."

"He's already mad at me for running off over the summer. He thought I should have enrolled in summer school. Instead I went to Santa Barbara and spent money."

"Well, you also *worked*, you told me, so he can't say that you weren't *doing* anything. Anyway, who are you living for, anyway? You or your father?"

"I've been asked that before."

"Oh? And what was your answer?"

He smiles. "I don't think I had one. But the fact is, he's paying for my—"

"'Paying for my education,' blah blah, I know, you've told me. So you take a lousy semester's break. So what? What can he do?"

Robin says nothing, stroking her feet absently.

"Hm?" She leans forward slightly. "I think that's a very good question for you to answer. What can he do?"

He shrugs.

"What did he do when you took off last summer? What was the punishment?"

He looks away. "There wasn't any. He didn't punish me."

"So...?"

He shakes his head. "That's not the way it works between him and me. He never *punished* me. Not even when I was a kid. He never hit me or grounded me or anything like that."

She looks at him. "Then I don't understand the problem."

"It's hard to explain," he sighs. But he wonders if it can be explained at all, if the English language is a medium that can communicate what he means to say. He has noticed this before: the gap between the reality and the language used to express it, the gulf between the thing and its symbol. Quite a thought, he imagines, for someone who fancies himself a writer: that language itself is a falsifier, a deceiver. But how can he say it? How can he bridge the gap and give voice to what he means? "It's..." He hesitates, falls silent, tries to start again. "Heather, it's never been 'punishment,' in that sense. It's more like an *assumption*. An assumption that I won't go too far...too far out of line, too far afield. Like it would never even enter the realm of possibility that I could do certain things. I don't have to ask or get permission or rebel against him or anything. Just..." He falters again. "Just... well, certain things are impossible, that's all. They're not done. Not talked about, either. Like, when I was a kid, I never dared ask anything about sex or girls or anything like that. I *couldn't* have. That wasn't the kind of thing I could ask him, and he didn't need to *tell* me that...It was like an unspoken understanding between us that he was there for certain things and that the others just didn't exist." He thinks for a moment. "I guess that's why I never went through any great soul-searching or guilt when I... started up, with men. I mean, those kinds of feelings never even occurred to me. Because *all* that kind of thing was so inconceivable. We never got to the *point* where something like that would be...shameful—I mean any *more* shameful than anything else. It was *all* shameful. I think to build that kind of special, particular guilt in somebody you have to talk about it, on *some* level, even if it's just...I don't know. Hysteria." He frowns. "But sex didn't exist in our house. And questions weren't allowed."

"What if you'd asked him?" she says.

He shakes his head. "I couldn't have. I *never* could have. Like with my mom—I told you all about that. We've never discussed it. To this day I don't know exactly what happened the night of the accident. I mean, what *really* happened. Where he was standing and what they were talking about and what she did and...what happened. Everything. That subject is closed." He takes her feet from his shoulders.

"Robin," she says, looking intently at him, "what would happen if you opened it again? I mean, if you just sat down with him and said, 'Dad, I want to talk about some things,' and then just launched in? What would happen?"

He stares at her navel in the water. "I can't imagine ever doing that," he says.

"But what if you did?"

"If I did, I suppose my dad would get upset and change the subject. But it doesn't matter, because it'd never get to the point that I actually asked him something. Those things aren't discussed between us—no, it's more like they don't *exist* between us. So he doesn't have to punish me or anything. The issues never come up. And if I do...do something wrong, like that trip this summer, then he just ignores it and it's understood that I won't pull anything like that again. Don't ask me how it happens, but that's what happens. He gets drunk and looks at me with these sort of rheumy eyes, unfocused—and it's like..." He scowls, searching. "It's like every terrible thing in the world is inside him and the threat is always there that they might all come out suddenly at me and..." He stands abruptly, reaching for a towel. "I don't know. I'm babbling."

"No you're not," she says. "Keep talking."

"I've talked enough for one night. C'mon, let's go watch some TV in the boudoir."

"Robin…"

"Robin nothing. I don't want to talk about this anymore."

"Well, *I* want to talk about it." She pulls the tub's plug, then stands and takes part of his towel for herself. "And I think you need to."

"There's nothing to say, really."

"There is too."

"Look," he says, helping her to dry herself, "I know that it's not logical. I know everything you're going to tell me, and you're right. But it doesn't change a lifetime's worth of lessons. All the logic in the world goes right out the window when I'm in that house in Wind Point with him. Then it's like I'm thirteen again, listening to his footsteps coming up the stairs and feeling my heart pound."

He steps out of the bathroom into the dark bedroom, moving to the curtain and opening it slightly. The streets glisten with still reflecting pools.

After a moment Heather comes up behind him and touches his hips. "Okay," she says. "Maybe we should drop the subject. I'm sorry."

He reaches behind himself, touching her. "Nothing to be sorry for," he says. "It's just that you guys from great big hysterically happy families don't know what these things are like. I mean, dead mothers, alcoholism, all that. And both my parents were alcoholics, you know. It's not just my dad. In fact my dad wasn't that bad until after she died—that was when the roof caved in…But anyway, it was my mom too. I don't think about it much anymore, but it's true. I used to think of myself as having two mothers—the one that smelled like booze, the one that scared me; and my real mother, who was hidden away in a dungeon somewhere by the bad one. I used to have fantasies about saving her—I would be on this great big glowing white horse." He chuckles.

"How does your dad keep his job, Robin? I mean if he drinks as much as you say?"

"Well, Mom and Dad were—are—whatever—two different kinds of alcoholics. By the end, my mom was starting to tie it on first thing in the morning, sometimes. But my dad *never* drinks until after the office closes. He's never missed a day of work, as far as I know. He's a disciplined drunk."

Heather's cheek rests against his back. Her hands roam between his legs.

"And that's another problem," he says, watching her hands.

"Don't worry about him," she says. "He's my project. I've got to get your mama and your papa and all the evil hobgoblins out of his little brain."

"Does he have a brain?"

"He has a head, he must have a brain."

"Would you like to take a closer look and find out?"

A chuckle fills her breath. "He has a ready-made hole I can explore. I'll send my tongue up it as a probe. A sensory probe."

"In the name of science."

"Mm-hm."

"You have a dirty mind."

"You have a dirty body," she says, her hands moving. "You're a dirty boy. You're a regular monster."

"And you're a disgrace to feminine propriety."

"And you love it that way."

He grins and turns to her. "You've got that right."

"See? So I'm good for something." She pokes her finger playfully into his navel. "What are *you* good for, I wonder?"

"Me? I'm keeping you healthy with all that good sticky egg white flowing into your tummy."

"You'll turn me into a zeppelin."

He laughs. "Not true. Fifteen calories a go, I read somewhere. Of course you can probably double or triple that for me."

"At least. When you gag me to death, you get to explain to the cops how I died."

"They'd be so impressed they'd let me go."

She smiles. "If they were male cops."

He pushes her gently on her chest. "Lay down on the bed, you fishmonger."

Later, their bodies damp and their arms and legs lazily intertwined, Robin thinks again of the lilies and the lions: and how easy it is here, how perfect, how absolutely right. He would never have believed, only a month before, that he could ever be like this with anyone: open, free: without embarrassment, without guilt. That was it: guiltless. He cannot remember ever feeling guiltless in his life.

He makes a small involuntary noise in his throat and Heather stirs. "What's that, baby?" she says.

"Nothing…"

"I thought you said something."

"Not really. Only…"

"What?"

"Only that I love you."

The words sound peculiar as they escape his lips. He remembers saying them to Cape and having the same sensation: an odd, indefinable feeling of unnaturalness, as if he were speaking a foreign language. The words seem not to fit quite perfectly in his mouth. It is an awesome thing, he knows, a huge unimaginable concept that those three words symbolize; and perhaps that is the problem: how can he convey what he means, the depth and the complexity and the profundity of it, in a three-word set phrase? Impossible; and yet he knows of no other way to do it. The limitations, he realizes again, of language: the vast unbridgeable gulfs.

"Oh, Robin," she says breathlessly, looking at him, "oh, God, I love you too." She clings to him tightly in the dark room, her arms wrapped around him and her legs intertwined with his.

He chuckles slightly, giddily. "Do you mean it?"

"Yes."

He holds her closely. His mind is whirling, flying about somewhere in interstellar space, lost in a dizzy void.

After a long moment they relax again and Heather nestles her head under Robin's chin.

"I just wish…" she begins; then trails off.

"What?"

"That we could go away together," she says, kissing the hollow of his neck.

"Heather…"

"I know, I know. Daddy."

"I'm sorry. If we could just wait until summer…"

"I don't want to wait."

He smiles. "You're a very impatient girl."

"I'm used to getting what I want. I'm spoiled."

"Comes from being in a happy family."

"Mm-hm."

"But it's not very practical for me. Right now."

"I know. I understand. But we'll at least go to Wind Point at Christmas, right?"

He sighs. "I don't think that's a very good idea."

"Yes, it is. I want to meet Daddy."

"You think you do. Later you might not be so sure."

"Come on. It'll be great."

"Yeah, unless he starts drinking and shouting at me that I'm stealing his money."

"Does he do that?"

"When he drinks."

"How is he when he doesn't drink?"

Robin considers. "Distant."

"So we'll keep him from drinking."

He chuckles. "What are you going to do? Hog-tie him?"

"I'll use my feminine wiles."

"No siree. Your wiles are reserved for me."

She giggles. "Not *those* wiles. Anyway, I want you to promise we'll go to Wind Point."

"Heather..."

"Come on. Don't be a poop. I want to sleep in your old bedroom and do the kinds of dirty things there you used to only dream of."

He laughs again. "I didn't even dream of them, much. I didn't know enough about them."

"So, promise."

He stares at the ceiling in the darkness. For a moment he thinks he can hear footsteps, a television, a thick-set body settling into a leather chair.

"Okay," he sighs. "We'll go to Wind Point."

6

The remaining weeks of the semester pass in a happy haze. Assignments flutter past; exams come and go; but Robin is not too much aware of them. He spends virtually all his time at Heather's.

The December rain turns icily cold as they prepare to drive to Wind Point. He is surprised, really, that he does not feel more trepidation about this proposed journey than he does: he remembers just scant months before being so terrified of the idea that he had been literally incapable of it—turning, he recalls, before even reaching the old Scully Road, never getting past the faded photograph in the office window at Greyfield: *I Can Insure Your Future.* Now it is a worry; but not an unconquerable terror. After all, he knows, he can always turn and leave with Heather. He needs to take nothing he doesn't want to take, accept nothing he doesn't wish to accept. He is in control now, he thinks. The tables have been turned at last.

He smiles to himself in his dormitory room as he packs his suitcase. O courageous and all-powerful man! he thinks. A mere handful of moon-turnings before he was no more than a quivering bowl of gelatin; now he is an all-conquering warrior!

He does wonder, though—as he drives through the gray and misty afternoon toward her house—about Heather. Sometimes he has the odd feeling that her core, her center, is something he has not reached. And yet he does not know how that could be. She is open with him about everything: "No secrets," she will say. Perhaps, he thinks, it is merely the way of women, with which he is still unfamiliar: but more than once he has found her in strange moods, crabby and snappish or peculiarly distant. They do not last long, these moods, but they appear suddenly like clouds on a clear horizon; and Robin is unable to puzzle out their source. At first he had suspected her menstruation. But the moods came more frequently than that, and not on any schedule he could determine. In the morning she could be fine, ready for fun; but in the afternoon she might fade somewhat, wilt, and retreat into silence. When he asked her what was wrong she would smile and say, "Just homesick, I guess"; which was a reasonable answer; but it did not account for her moments of sudden churlishness, as when they might be deciding which movie to go see and she would throw up her hands abruptly, saying: *"You* decide, then. I'm just a stupid girl who doesn't understand these things." Then, just a moment later, the clouds would disperse and she would look at him with regretful eyes, saying, "Oh boy, I just made a boo-boo. Robin, darling, come here, I'm sorry, baby."

Most of it, he imagines, can be chalked up to new-relationship tensions. It is not as if he himself has always been perfectly behaved, especially when they experimented with each other sexually. Then his frustration could come out suddenly. Still, that was an observable, diagnosable problem: a cause. With Heather there sometimes would appear to be no cause at all. She could become suddenly obstinate, and over the least important things; which would lead them into, if not arguments, at least disagreements. He remembers the first of them, insignificant in itself, when they had gone in circles about how many days they would spend in San Francisco. Unimportant; but it seemed in retrospect to be the keynote for many discussions which followed. It frustrates him. But then again, realistically, it doesn't matter much. They are so close now, so intensely together so constantly, that things like this, he supposes, are bound to come up. And what difference does it make? He loves her company, loves having her arms around him and listening to her small soft voice whispering to him. When he is with her it is as if the rest of the world fades into a thin vapor. He has everything he needs with Heather. Nothing else matters.

She is waiting for him on her landlord's front porch as he pulls up in the driveway. She waves her black beret, grinning, and picks up her bag, scurrying out into the drizzling mist toward the car. "Hi!" she says brightly, tossing the bag into the back seat. "I hope you have the heater on in this beast!" She drops herself into the seat beside him and slams the door shut, rubbing her hands together. "Oh yes, you *do*, you warm little rascal…" She leans over and kisses him. "All set?"

"Guess so," he smiles.

"You be cool. Everything's going to be just jim dandy."

Robin backs out of the driveway and heads out of town as Heather asks, "Does your daddy know when we're coming?"

"Uh—" he hesitates—"Well, sort of."

"What do you mean, sort of? Did you call him?"

"No."

"Why not, baby?"

He shrugs. "He knows when the semester ends. He'll be expecting me. I told him a while ago that I'd come back for Christmas this year."

"Still…did you tell him I'd be coming?"

He grins and chuckles. "No."

"You naughty boy. You should have."

"Sorry. I didn't want to talk to him on the phone."

"Now how do I know if I'm welcome?"

"It's my house too," Robin says, glancing at her. "Anyway, don't worry about it. You'll be as welcome or unwelcome as me."

She leans her head against his arm. "You'll be welcome. He's your daddy. He loves you."

"Mm. Where'd you read that Commie propaganda?"

"Stop," she says, punching him lightly. "Be a good boy. We're going to have a wonderful time."

It is nearly midnight when they reach Wind Point; the house in the cul-de-sac is enveloped in darkness. Robin feels his heart beating as he crosses the familiar walkway, ascends the remembered stairs. Heather stands behind him as he glances back and says, "Well, here we go. Merry Christmas."

Heather nods. "Knock."

He knocks.

They wait a long moment. He knocks again.

Finally he fishes into his pocket for his key and opens the door, stepping into the dark foyer.

"Dad?" he calls, flipping on the light.

Heather steps in behind him. "Nobody home?"

"I guess not. I wonder where he is," he says, suspecting that he knows the answer. "Oh well. Shall I show you the place?"

"You bet. Where's your room?"

"Up here." They move up the stairs in the shadows of the foyer light. When they reach the upstairs hall Robin turns on another light and gestures. "Spare bedroom at the end there.

Then my daddy's room. That's a bathroom there. And here," he says, opening the door, "is the late empire of one Robin Withers, Esquire."

He switches on a lamp and looks. It has not changed. The dark throw-rug; the lavender bedspread; the curtains over the window; the desk, the dresser, all are the same. He moves to the closet and opens it.

"Here's my youth," he says, looking at the array of books, magazines, old record albums, board games, his high school graduation gown on a hanger.

Heather looks. "Any old love letters in there?"

"Ho, ho! Don't I wish."

She holds onto his arm. "I'll write you some."

"Not necessary," he says, glancing over at the curtained window, the image crossing his mind for an instant of the woman standing there in the darkness staring out into the leaves of the pepper tree and the night beyond. He sees her black dress, the white flowers sprayed on it, the pearls around her neck; hears her softly slurred voice. *You asleep, baby?*

"Well," Heather says, crossing to the window and looking out, "when do you think Daddy will return?"

"I don't know," Robin says, sitting on the bed. "He must be at one of the bars. Sometimes he gets back pretty late."

She looks at him. "Maybe he's not at a bar."

He shrugs.

"It's Christmas time," Heather says. "Maybe he's visiting friends."

"He doesn't have any." Robin leans back on his elbows. "Anyway, we're here."

She grins and jumps onto the bed beside him, the bedsprings squeaking. "And we'll be just like Siegel and Rachel in this room. I'm going to do all those nasty things to you I promised."

"Like what?"

She rolls onto her back and writhes mischievously. "Tell me what that little boy who used to live here dreamed about," she says. "I'll do it."

Robin chuckles, touching her stomach. What *had* that little boy dreamed about? he wonders. He is not sure he can remember. Most of that time is lost. Irretrievable. "I'll think about it," he says. "Say, have you called your family?"

"Mm-hm. Yesterday."

"Oh. I thought you were going to call them from here."

"I decided to do it on my landlord's phone. They were disappointed, of course. But they were really happy to hear about you. They want to meet you."

"Oh, is that right? I wonder what you said about me."

"Well, I said that I've got this big beautiful boyfriend with big blue eyes who's a brilliant writer and he's got a big dick and this time it's the real thing."

Robin grins. "Brilliant writer, huh?"

"Robin," she laughs, "you were supposed to pick up on the 'real thing' part!"

"Big dick, huh?"

"Stop. Now what do you think about that I just said?"

"Well, I can't deny it. I *am* a brilliant writer and I *do* have a big dick."

"Not that part! I'm asking you a serious question."

"Then why are you giggling?"

"Because you're *tickling* me…"

"I'm massaging you."

"That is *not* a massage…Robin, cut it out. Now I'm serious."

"Okay," he says, moving away from her slightly. "What was the question?"

"Wait." She jumps up suddenly, switches off the lamp. "There. That's better."

Robin stares at the pepper tree's limbs silhouetted against the window; hears their soft sighing as they brush against the glass. The foghorn sounds in the distance.

"Will you open the window a little?" he says. "It's stuffy in here, isn't it?"

"Sure." She moves to the window, stands near it for a moment in her dark coat as she finds the latch. She opens the window a crack. "Okay?"

Robin nods and Heather returns to the bed.

"Now, as I was saying..." she begins.

But his attention is distracted from her words as he hears again the wind brushing through the pepper tree and feels the cool air touching his face. For a moment he thinks he can feel a familiar weight next to him on the bed but then he realizes it is Heather. He is sure he can smell whiskey in the air, sure that someone must have been here just moments before he came into the room. At any moment he expects to hear footsteps, soft bare feet on the wood floor padding back to the bedroom where the shadow-dark Other waits...Where they made mysterious sounds in the darkness as he leaned his ear against the bathroom wall and listened. He can see himself crouching at the wall and the bathtub next to him, can see himself coming into the bathroom and the hot steam making her curls droop across her chest and shoulders as she says, *What is it, honey? Did you have a nightmare?*

"...Robin?"

"Huh?"

"Have you heard anything I've said?"

Before he can answer he hears the door downstairs being opened and muffled voices in the foyer.

"Is that...?" Heather begins.

"It's my parents—my dad," Robin says, sitting up.

"He's talking to somebody."

"Yeah." He stands. "Well, we'd better make our presence known, I guess."

A low thudding sound which Robin cannot identify comes from downstairs. He goes to his bedroom door and looks down the hall, his heart jumping in his chest.

"C'mon," Heather says brightly, taking his arm, "let's go meet Daddy."

"Heather..."

"Come *on*."

They move toward the stairs and when they arrive there Robin looks down and can see into the lighted foyer. His father, laughing raucously and stumbling, is attempting to pull a huge Christmas tree through the door while a woman Robin does not know makes a clumsy, giggling attempt to help. Time seems to suspend itself as Robin stands staring at the scene: he feels as if he had never left this place, never gone off to college or Santa Barbara or anywhere, and soon, he knows, soon the woman with the moon-round face hidden behind the snake-mask will appear and there will be shoutings and accusations and amber-colored liquid spilled into the rug. He sees her years ago—or was it last night?—lying here, exactly here, having managed to ascend the stairs and then collapse, and he sees himself with a wet washcloth moving toward her and wiping away the fluid running from her mouth and saying Mom, it's okay, Mom, it's okay. He feels suddenly as if the huge black jaws of the past are rising before him, empty and awful like a black hole in space, about to overcome him, envelop him forever.

"*Robin!*" His father's voice suddenly pierces through the haze. "Hey Susie, look who's here, it's my boy Robin!"

The woman looks up toward him as his father's face fills with a sloppy grin. Heather propels him forward as they move down the stairs.

"Hi, Dad." They shake hands. "This is my friend Heather."

"Well, that's nice," the man grins. "This is *my* friend Susie." He chuckles; the smell of alcohol on him is overwhelming. "So this Christmas everybody's got a friend. What a Christmas it's going to be. Robin, help me with this goddamn thing, will you?" He begins pulling at the tree again, stripping some of the branches as he tries to force it to come through the door.

"Let me help!" Heather says cheerily, and somehow the four of them manage to pull the green behemoth through. His father has not shaved for days; Robin finds himself tense each time the man's unfocused eyes, like foggy blue searchlights, fall on him. Within a few minutes they have the tree standing in the living room, where it takes up nearly half the floor space and pushes against the ceiling.

"Beautiful, isn't it?" his father says proudly, clapping Robin across the shoulders. "I told Susie here that this year I wanted a *real* tree, because my son Robin was coming home for Christmas and I didn't want any *dink* tree, I wanted a *real* tree, *big* tree." He laughs. "And I got one, by God."

"I tried to talk him into a smaller one," the woman called Susie says. She is short and hard-looking and when she speaks it seems to Robin her voice is hard too. "But he wouldn't go for it. He just kept saying, 'Big! Big! Real tree! Real tree!' Of course," she giggles, pressing against his father's arm, "he said it a little more often after we'd been to a couple of bars."

His father grins and looks at him. The rheumy eyes, the hawk nose, the shining forehead: he has not changed a bit, Robin thinks. *I Can Insure Your Future.* "Don't say that around my boy, honey," his father says. "Robin doesn't go in for that kind of low-class stuff us *drunks* like to do." He breaks away from the woman and heads into the kitchen, opens the refrigerator. "But *I* do! Do you want something, uh...Heather? Is that it? You want something to drink?"

"No thank you, Mr. Withers." She squeezes Robin's hand, not looking at him.

"Two teetotalers, good God," his father mumbles as he brings into the room a bottle of red wine and two glasses. "Guess it's just you and me, honey."

"Pour away!"

"How's life at that school of yours, Robin?" he asks, pouring the wine and handing a glass to the woman.

"It's okay."

"Still knocking 'em dead?"

He smiles weakly. "Trying."

"Well, that's great. Around here, me and Susie have been spending a lot of time together, especially since I closed the office for Christmas. God, it feels good to be away from there." Robin's attention escapes the scene as his father asks Heather a few questions about herself, his voice slurred and too loud, his big bulk dropping into the leather chair. He knew it would be like this, of course. It is not as if he hadn't warned Heather that it was not a good idea, coming here. He closes his eyes briefly, feeling the past drawing close like a black shroud. Nothing has changed, he thinks. Except himself. There once was a time when he would not only have not objected to this, but would hardly even have been consciously aware of it. Now he is super-aware. And soon, he suspects, his father will mount the stairs with this woman and go with her into the bedroom. The thought of it makes his heart race. He feels dirty. The idea is appalling. He pictures himself sitting at the upstairs hall window, yellow light pouring in and rendering his eyes pale and useless, and the hushed thumping sound of his mother's bare feet coming toward him. To be blinded, he thinks. To have it all burned away, made clean again. Filth. Disgust. Waste.

"Hey, we should take some pictures!" the woman called Susie exclaims.

"Great idea!" his father agrees boisterously. "Robin, get the camera, will you? It's on the mantle over there."

Robin takes the camera and holds it carefully, trying not to quiver. He snaps a flash-photo of his father and the woman.

"Now you two!" the woman says, taking the camera from him. "Stand in front of the tree there! Oh, this is so Christmasy!"

Heather squeezes his arm, snuggling against him and grinning as they stand before the tree.

"Smile!" The woman commands.

The flash pops: Robin sees a pair of useless blind eyes suspended in the air.

"Is it still raining?" Robin asks after a moment.

The woman seats herself beside his father on the arm of the chair. She says, "Huh-uh. Stopped a while ago."

"Let's take a walk," he says to Heather. He tries to smile toward the two figures in the leather chair. "I want to show Heather a little of the old hometown."

"At this time of night?" the woman says.

Robin shrugs. "The streets are safe here." For an instant he sees headlights in a starless dusk. "C'mon, Heather, let's go, huh?"

They rush in silence through the residential area, past the shops and businesses. The night is bracingly cold and they stay separate, not touching, not looking at each other. Robin moves faster and faster. At last, without slowing, he points toward a darkened building.

"That was their favorite bar," he says.

They walk some distance further.

"That's where she used to buy booze," he says, pointing at a stationery store. "It wasn't a stationery store then."

They walk in silence again, rapidly.

"See that building down the road?" he says. "The big white one? That's the hospital. That's where they took her at first."

They keep moving, arriving finally at an intersection.

"This is where she got it," he says. "She was standing somewhere around here. It's hard to tell because the roads have been redone since then. I don't know what direction she was standing in or what direction the car came from. It was sunset and they were drunk. They must have been. Nobody told me that, but it's obvious. They were probably fighting about something. She stepped off the curb. I don't know who was driving the car. That's another thing nobody ever told me. I might've met him sometime. The headlights were turned on. I remember hearing that, once. That's why the driver got off. It wasn't his fault. He was inside the speed limit and his headlights were on and she just—she walked right in front of the car. Smacko, just like that. Killed instantly. At least that's what I've always been told. I've wondered sometimes. Maybe they just said that to spare my feelings. It's possible she lingered awhile. Stands to reason, because they took her to the Wind Point Hospital...I think if she'd really been dead they would've taken her straight to Greyfield, to the big hospital there, for the...the preparations. You know. But they didn't. I could be wrong, but—"

"Robin, baby, baby," Heather says, taking his hands firmly, "stop. Stop it. Come on. It's past two in the morning. Let's go home. We'll get some sleep and then we can leave tomorrow if you want."

"I want to show you something." He pulls her through the icy omnipresent darkness, their breaths puffing fast and hard into the night. Within a few minutes they come to the pier and he can hear the sound of the water splashing against the wood and the hulls of the boats in the harbor.

"Did you see the sign coming into town?" he says, pulling her by the hand along the damp pier. "Did you? It says, 'Wind Point—Where the Shore Meets the Sea.' I don't know what madman came up with that, because it's a lie. There's no shore here.

Nothing but rocks. Hazardous as hell. Boats crack up a lot. My dad used to have a boat. He used to make me go fishing with him on the weekends. I hated it. I was afraid. I didn't like the cold. But he told my mom she was turning me into a sissy." They rush toward the end of the pier, their footsteps sloshy against the wet wood. "So every weekend he dragged me here, to the harbor at four in the morning where he kept his boat. And out we went. I never caught a fish, after the first one. I caught one and it scared me so much I threw it back when he wasn't looking. After that I put the hook in the water without any bait on it." They reach the wood rails at the end of the pier and stop. "But my mom brought me here too," he says, the words rushing out unstoppably. "She would bring me here when I was a little kid, we'd walk here and then she'd take off her shoes and walk along the pier barefoot. She'd wear a white dress. She used to tell me that if you looked at the fog close enough you'd see that it was really a million little sparkles all suspended together in the sky, like diamonds. 'Robin, it's a real diamond day,' she'd say, and..." Something seems to overwhelm him suddenly. "...And then later it all stopped because of her drinking and then..." He forces the words from his throat. "...And I've never even known whether it was an accident or if she did it deliberately, if..." He whirls away and stares into the darkness, into the black waters. "Oh, fuck her!" he cries. "Fuck them! *Fuck both of them! Fuck them! Fuck! Fuck—!*"

"Robin, darling," Heather whispers, her hand on his arm, "let's go home. Come on. Time to go home now. Time to go home."

7

"This was a truly fine idea," Robin says, later, in the darkness.

Heather says nothing.

"I told you I didn't want to do this," he continues, staring at the ceiling. "I told you it wasn't a good idea. Did you listen? No. You just railroaded me into this wonderful family reunion, the way you've been railroading me into everything else. I say I want to do *this*, we end up doing *that*."

"Robin, please," Heather says.

"If you'd listened to me, we'd be at school right now, in your room, having a great time. But no. You had to get this great idea into your head."

"Robin," she says, turning to him in the bed, "what do you want me to do? I've already apologized. What am I supposed to do now?"

Robin sighs, his eyes moving over the familiar dark. The curtain sways in the breeze of the window and the limbs of the pepper tree brush against the glass. Nothing here has changed: the room is the same, and the bed, the walk to the bathroom, the footsteps on the stairs: nothing has changed but himself. He thinks of the boy waiting for his mother to enter the room and open the window and sit next to him on the bed. That boy is a separate entity, lost in the vortex of time. He can feel the same sensations here, in this room, this bed; but in a deeper untranslatable way, he knows, he is no longer that boy; memories cannot make him so. That incarnation of himself has vanished forever. Lost. And that perhaps is what makes him feel so much fear, so much imbalance and vertigo and tension. There is nothing left to that boy but a few dots of memory, and to be able to see that, to be able to look back at an earlier version of himself and realize how finished and dead it is, is itself a kind of death: a reminder, he thinks, of how, as time in its whirling arcs continues unceasingly to rush past, there will be still more incarnations that will sink away into the darkness: he himself, as he is now, at this moment, will one day be as dead as the twelve-year-old; until the moment arrives that all the Robins, all incarnations of the past, and all memory of them, are digested by time in a final definitive instant of oblivion. He wonders when he is going to die. And wonders if, after all, there is any continuation of any kind, if his million atoms and molecules will ever look out from the buds of lilies or the eyes of lions or the rays of the sun. Perhaps it is nothing but darkness, or non-darkness, unending, unbeginning nothingness. But how then to explain the connectedness, the sudden wild sensations of being part of the vast design, a tiny but inextricably connected bit of space fluff which is a piece of the earth, the sky, the stars? But then, if he is connected to everything in the universe, how can it be that he cannot connect with his own earlier self, cannot see that boy except as a dark receding figure in a whirling cyclone of devouring time? Time, he thinks, is the destroyer. He is reminded of a line of Faulkner's he once read: the theme of the artist must be "the human heart in conflict with itself." But that is not it at all, Robin realizes suddenly. The final, overarching theme of everything is not the heart in conflict with itself but in conflict with time.

"I felt so confident, coming here," Robin hears himself saying. "Now I just feel…"

Heather touches him. "Let's not fight, okay? I told you I never want to fight."

"I don't want to fight either."

"But we seem to do it, sometimes."

"I know. But later on I can't figure out what we were fighting about."

"So we have to stop it."

"I'm sorry."

"So am I. For bringing you here. I shouldn't have pushed you like that. I thought it would be okay."

"All I want is to get out of here," he says, not looking at her. "There's nothing for me here. This place is just a graveyard to me."

"I know. I know *now*."

"And I'm not dead yet—am I?"

She chuckles. "Not yet."

"I hate this place," Robin says. "I hate what it does to me. I hate what it turns me into."

"I know."

"I want to leave."

"We'll leave."

"Now."

"Not now. Now you sleep. And we'll stay a day or two for appearance's sake."

"Christ."

"After that, we'll never come back."

He looks at her in the darkness.

"Never?"

"Robin, we'll never set foot in this town again. Ever."

The branches of the pepper tree brush against the window in the darkness.

<hr />

After that it is a foregone conclusion. They say nothing to his father; Heather does not call her family. They say nothing to anyone upon returning, three days later, to the university. They say little, in fact, even to each other. They discuss not *whether* they will do it but *how;* and within a few days they have packed the car, stored their belongings, and closed out their bank accounts. Robin finds himself completely calm about all of it, perfectly placid, like a still and motionless lake. For this, he knows, once and for all and forever, is finally it: the real journey, the true bursting onto another level, the new plane, the fresh life. All the others—the trip to Runningwater when he was a child, the beginning of college, the escape to Santa Barbara—they were all but dry runs to this: not even dry runs, perhaps, but illusions: each time it had proven to be a lie. This time it is no lie. He knows it because he is already in the process of self-renewal; it is already happening:

he is becoming something other than what he was, someone new and fresh and vivid, it is no mere promise now but solid reality. And it is Heather who has made him so, he knows. Heather who has filled him with the confidence first to return to Wind Point at all, and not be reduced to a quivering mass of quicksand; the courage, at last, to say *no* (if not directly, then at least through his actions) to the shadow-man. To leave: to ask no permission, to not concern himself with the foggy glares or the accusing eyes in the glowing dark: to say *no*. Yes, he had been knocked off-balance at Wind Point. Yes, he had lost himself for a while that first evening. But he had survived it. No demons had gripped him in the shadows. No ghosts had stolen the breath from his body. And to know that at last, to face it and see it with dazzling clarity, to understand it in his deepest being, in his brain and in the marrow of his bones, is exhilarating. He had been free all along, he thinks. The freedom had been sitting there on a silver platter simply waiting for him to come by and pick it up.

And it is Heather who has made him take it into his hands. Straddled in her only chair, he watches her now as she goes about the room picking up her last things and putting them either in a box for storage or a bag for the garbage. Late December: she is wearing a dark pullover sweatshirt and gray sweatpants, her feet covered with thick fuzzy socks striped like two barber's poles.

He smiles, studying the curvature of her buttocks as she bends over for something on the floor. He would not have thought it possible, mere months before, that he could be like this with anyone. Together—inextricably bound into the weave of each other's lives. It had been conceivable once, with Cape. Perhaps he had been in love with Cape. He had thought he was. He can see Cape now in his mind, the properties of his face and body assembling themselves like an animated film, can smell the semen and the sweat emanating from his body like an earthy perfume. Had he been in love with Cape? He thinks of the word *love.* He had told Cape that he loved him; he had spoken the same words to Heather. What was their truth? What, in fact, was their meaning? He has not been able to puzzle this out in spite of all his efforts. It seems a central issue, an absolutely indispensable point to be decided between two human beings: do you love me? And yet the word somehow eludes him, escapes his grasp like smoke in wind. *Love.* He had said it to Heather because he knew it would please her; and because, whatever his feeling for her actually was, he knew that it was strong enough and intense enough and so all-encompassing that he could use the simple shorthand, the easy generalization, and that she would understand, at least vaguely, approximately, what he was trying to tell her; but the specifics of it, the true core of the matter, seemed to totally elude such facile definitions. What he felt for her was indefinable; language could not encompass it. It had been the same, in a different way perhaps, with Cape. The words, though easy and pleasing, had nothing to do with what he was trying to express; they were mere symbol when what he needed was the solid reality.

"Hey," Heather says, bringing something out of a drawer. "Look at what I found."

It is a Halloween mask, an evil green face which she places over her own, growling and then giggling. "What do you think?" she says.

"It becomes you," Robin smiles.

"Or do *I* become *it?*" she asks, laughing and tossing the mask into his lap. "It's left over from some Halloween party somewhere."

"Are you about finished?" he says, turning the mask over in his hands. "I thought we were going to get moving soon."

"Yes, yes, yes. Possess your soul in patience."

"You're late, as usual."

She smiles. "Whoever said a woman had to be on time?"

"Whoever said you were a woman?"

She gives him a sour look. "You think you're so smart," she says. "Are you really ready?"

"Really ready."

"Everything packed? Car checked? Gas?"

"Ready for take-off, commander."

"Then I guess I *am* late. But I'm nearly done."

Nearly done: and then, he knows, they will be gone. They will travel across the country with money enough for months, they will head across the warm southern states toward Florida and then up to New York. Along the way they will work, if necessary, and eventually they will meet Heather's family in New Hampshire. Maybe they will return and maybe they won't. But if they do, he thinks, it will be as different people: glowing giants, unstoppable, in total control. And that is the central issue, Robin knows: control. Sanity and balance and control.

A few minutes later she says, "Well! Wise guy, I think I'm finally finished. Everything's put away, I'm dressed—I guess I'm ready!"

"Great," Robin says, standing and moving to her. He places the goblin mask on top of her head like a hat. "Shall we do this deed, then?"

"Why are you putting this thing on my head?" she says, taking it off. "Are you trying to tell me something?"

"Like what?"

"Like I'm a *hobgoblin*." She bugs out her eyes as she says the word.

"No. But you *are* something unworldly." He kisses her.

"Oh? What am I?"

"I don't know yet." He runs his face through her hair slowly.

"What do you mean, you don't know?" She puts her arms around him and works her hands into the back of his pants. "I think you know me pretty well. Inside and out."

"Do I?"

"Don't you?"

They nuzzle each other for a long moment, then slip out into the December drizzle toward the car.

8

"I don't know about you," she says, "but I'd like to die in a place like this. Isn't it *beautiful?*"

They are somewhere in the Mojave desert, drinking raspberry sodas as they stand beside the car and look out into the endless desert horizon, brilliantly sharp and clear in the cool morning light. The quiet is enormous. There is nothing near them but the empty road. A few birds glide past. Heather looks around herself, grinning.

"Isn't it?" she says.

And, he realizes, it is. He remembers last summer, standing in the bell tower with Priscilla and Koofie and looking out across the entire vista of Santa Barbara and growing excited by it all on the strength of their own excitement: their own enthusiasm making it more than it would have been otherwise. It is the same here. He had thought it a pleasant-enough scene: but Heather's thrill makes it thrilling to him as well. She is right about the beauty of it, the huge peacefulness and serene majestic quality of it all. The feeling of eternity: the unobscured sun lifting inexorably into the sky, as it has done for millions of years and will do for millions more. Is he part of it all? he wonders. Sometimes he feels that he is only connected, truly connected, to Heather: that the rest of the universe does not even really exist. It is all so complicated, so impenetrable.

"It's beautiful," he says, "but not as beautiful as you."

She grins. "Liar."

Connection, separation: interweaving, isolation: which is it? Which, ultimately, is the true state of things, the final, absolute truth? It seems essential that he find out; for how can he claim to be a writer if he has no answer to give, nothing to say but only to ask, no light of understanding but only fumblings in the darkness? He must *know*.

"Hey, baby," she says, coming up to him, "what are you thinking about? You're a million miles away."

"No I'm not. I'm right here. Right here."

<hr />

Later, Robin would trace the trouble back to Las Vegas—or at least the trouble's beginning. For it was there that a tension began to grow between them. It was not an obvious thing; and the incidents in which it was at first manifested were so minor in themselves, so insignificant, that it was a stretch for his imagination to conceive that they were any more than tiny ripples on their smooth lake. On the first night in Las Vegas, for instance, there was a fight about which hotel to stay in. It began as their earlier disagreements had begun, with a gentle verbal jousting, an entreating tone in Heather's voice, a defensive one in his own: "C'mon, Robin," she said, "don't be a poop. Let's live a little. So what if it costs more?" And his answer: "Heather, if we start that we'll be through our money in a month. Let's go to a cheap, decent place." The issue bounced back and forth between them as they sat in a fast-food restaurant over milkshakes. They talked about it, it seemed to Robin, for far too long; eventually he grew irritable and agreed to the expensive hotel. This, he thought, would smooth out things. But somehow it failed to.

In the car, heading toward the hotel:

"Now you're mad at me."

"Heather, I'm not mad at you. Stop telling me what I am. I agreed to the hotel. It's fine. Now why don't we just drop the subject?"

"I don't want to drop it if it's unresolved. Then it will just fester."

"Nothing is unresolved. We resolved the issue. I don't even know what you're talking about."

On and on, that first night in Las Vegas: around and around. Even after they had checked in and put their things in the room it had not quite ended.

"I just want us to be totally honest with each other," she said. "Otherwise…"

"Shh," he said, covering her lips with his own. "Stop talking."

And finally it was all right, hours after it had begun. But something happened between them as a result of it which lingered. It was nothing immediately definable; they saw the sights together in Las Vegas, wandered the smoky casinos, laughed and saw movies; at night they slept wrapped tightly around each other; still, it seemed to Robin, there was a slight alteration between them, a kind of imbalance, which persisted for days. Heather was also aware of it, for finally, on the morning they were to leave, she leapt onto him as he sat on the bed, pushing him backward and straddling him, tousling his hair and saying, "Robin! Listen! Where are we?"

"Las Vegas."

"Not where. *Where*. There's been something wrong between us for days."

"Has there?"

"Haven't you noticed?"

"I guess I have."

"What is it? What's wrong with us?"

"I don't know."

"Are you still mad at me?"

"I was never mad at you, Heather."

"Then what is it?"

He touched the dark material of her pants. "I don't know. Why don't we try to put it behind us?"

"I think we should talk about it."

"I think talking is what caused it in the first place."

She looked down at him thoughtfully. "Maybe you're right. But I'm sorry, baby. For whatever happened. Really."

"So am I."

She grins brightly. "So we forget it, right?"

"Right!"

"Pals again?"

"Pals, you cocksucker."

"I didn't suck your cock *last* night."

"I know. And he's feeling the strain today, let me tell you."

"Is he?"

"Take his pulse and find out."

"Oh…Oh, you're *right*. I guess Doctor Seabright had better perform some oral surgery, huh?"

"Whatever you think is best, Doctor."

"Don't worry about a thing. When I get finished you'll be good as new."

We're on our way to New Orleans, he writes in his diary. *We've been gone nearly a month; never have I spent so much uninterrupted time with another human being. It has changed, I think, our relationship in certain ways. Maybe this is what marriage is like? But not necessarily, perhaps. We seem to be getting into an odd cycle of silly arguments over insignificant things—arguments neither of us want and both try to avoid, but which surface anyway. What I wonder is whether our arguments are really about what they appear to be about.*

Clever boy, he thinks to himself.

And yet there must surely be some truth to it, too, the idea that perhaps they are really fighting about other, less apparent things. Why else, he wonders, would they get themselves into these circular situations? Why would they allow them to come between the thing that is pure and fine that they have together?

As they head east the climate grows warmer; they find snow in Arizona, icy rain in Albuquerque, no more than cold winds in Texas—they had realized they would have to stay to the south if there was to be any hope of avoiding snowstorms and blizzards. They had molded a huge snowman outside the hotel in Flagstaff in the middle of the night, giggling exhilaratedly; Heather had attached a big snow-penis to it, a sight which made Robin burst into hysterical laughter. She looked like a little girl, he had thought to himself, watching her in her mittens and boots and wool cap scampering around in the slush. They had a snowball fight; Heather, being more accustomed to snow, was easily victorious, pummeling and peppering him with dozens of the crumbly cold balls while Robin struggled to form the strange spheres within his clumsy gloves. In the morning they had borrowed sleds from the hotel manager and raced each other down a nearby hill, the freezing wind vibrant in Robin's face, her laughter and the swooshing sound of the sleds imprinting on his mind a sense of innocence, of freedom, of pure breathless joy. As they careened down a particularly steep slope they had accidentally bumped their sleds together; they both lost control, tumbling hilariously into the snow and rolling down it madly, ending together in an intertwined tangle of limbs and kissing each other's frozen faces. This, he thought to himself, was how they should be, the two of them. As they entered New Mexico the snow turned to rain: and this put them in a quieter, mellower mood, less wild but no less exhilarating, as they stayed in empty restaurants for hours drinking hot spiced tea, talking, holding hands, and watching the gentle rain fall. And this was how they should be, he thought to himself, the two of them. On the road, heading from town to town, sight to sight, they alternated behind the driver's wheel. The played music on the tape player, loud beat music, as the constant hum of the car was hardly amenable to Bach or Beethoven. He would read to her aloud, fun stories, car stories, Saroyan and Thurber and Mark Twain. They sang. They talked. And mile after mile was chewed up by the car and left behind them, more and more distance was pushed between them and all the swirling cyclones of lost time; more and more distance from the other Robins, the earlier incarnations which like parasites would try, back there, to latch onto him, suck the life from him and leave him a pale and empty husk. More and more distance. Albuquerque and Portalis and Lubbock and Fort Worth and Alexandria, town after town, distance upon distance, leaving them all behind, all the Robins, and the man in the house in the cul-de-sac, and the barefoot ghost who dwelled there, everyone, everything. Lost in sheer distance, in vacant sky-filled space. And only the two of them entering, minute after minute, a newer intensity.

But in New Orleans the trouble had struck again, more viciously. Robin had been delighted with New Orleans, especially the French Quarter: the live music coming from every bar and hotel and strip joint, the dancing, the spicy Creole cuisine, the sidewalk artists, the packed autoless streets and the architecture and the overstuffed old book shops: it was exciting, thrilling, alive. They took a room in a nearby hotel ("Rent by the Week or the Month"), complete with a small dirty kitchenette, and resolved to stay there at least a few weeks. At first it was excellent. In the early morning, just as a crisp dawn was beginning to pour over the city, Robin would write in longhand for an hour or two while Heather slept; then when they were both up and ready they toured the city—one day the French Quarter, one day the downtown, one day the Garden District, on and on. They saw plays and Dixieland concerts, historic sites, went to peep show palaces, studied the famous gardens of flowers and bougainvillea. It was, if anything, even more of a highlight than the snow of Flagstaff or the rain of Albuquerque: the winds, fierce, icily brisk, were invigorating, enlivening, the occasional rains sharp and stinging, and huddling close together as they walked or ran was fun, crazily sensual.

"*Ohhh,*" Heather would cry, banging her mittens together, "Robin, it's like our first date all over again!"

And never had she looked so beautiful, he thought, as one evening near darkness when he had stood outside the door of their room and watched her returning from a walk, head hunkered low against the cold, wool cap over her ears, mittened hands stuffed deep into her pockets, and, seeing him watching her from across the open patch of frost-filled grass, she had suddenly broken into a run toward him, calling in a delighted voice, "*Look at me!*" as, halfway across the grass, she went into a perfectly balanced slide on her shoes straight toward him, her eyes open and vivid with life, her arms wide, happily shrieking as she skidded into his embrace.

It was at the zoo that the trouble had struck again. They had gone on an afternoon which rumbled with coming rain, the sky rolling and swirling. Heather had not much wanted to come ("I'm not sure that I like zoos"), but there had been nothing else to do that day, and Robin wanted to: as amazing as it seemed, he had never been to a zoo in his life. They paid their admission and bought a container of popcorn, making their way around the cages: gorillas, monkeys, chimpanzees, leopards, tigers, crocodiles, elephants, a hundred kinds of birds; as an afternoon's amusement Robin found it adequate. But Heather had grown quieter and quieter as they made their way around the cages. Her face was pensive.

"What's wrong?" Robin asked her.

"Nothing," she said, her eyes not meeting his, her voice small.

"Does this place upset you?"

"No..." She looked over toward the tigers' cage. "I mean, it's educational and everything. It's fine."

"Why don't we leave?"

"It's okay."

Robin weighed the matter in his mind, decided that pushing her to leave might cause more friction than simply continuing, so they visited more cages. Heather said nothing.

"Hey," Robin said finally, taking her by the shoulders and smiling, "that's enough wildlife for one day. Let's go take in a movie or something."

"But we haven't even seen half the zoo."

"We'll see it some other time."

She shook her head. "Your mommy and daddy never even took you to a zoo. You should see this one."

"Heather, you're not having a good time."

"Yes, I am."

He sighed. They sat on a wooden bench near a cage of screaming red birds.

"Tell me what's the matter," he said.

She stared straight before her. "Nothing's the matter. I don't know why you keep saying there is."

"Because I want you to stop worrying so much about whether or not I want to see this whole place. I want you to tell me you don't like looking at all these animals caged up and you want to leave."

"I don't."

"Heather, come *on*."

She scowled. "Why don't you just go on? I'll wait here."

"Why don't we leave?"

"I want you to finish seeing the zoo."

"I don't *want* to finish seeing the zoo."

"Now you're mad at me."

Robin sat back suddenly, exhaling.

"I am not mad at you."

"Yes, you are. I can hear it in your voice."

"Heather, stop it. We're just going to end up fighting again."

"We're not fighting."

"Look," he said, breathing slowly, "I think we should leave here. I think we should go get something to eat and then maybe catch a movie. How's that sound?"

"What about the zoo?"

"I don't care about the zoo."

It was a moment before she spoke. "You're just saying that to placate me. I'm disappointing you."

"You are not." He stood. "C'mon. This isn't a good place. Looks like it's going to rain anyway."

In the car later, as rain splattered across the windshield, she spoke again.

"I'm sorry about the zoo."

"Forget the zoo. It's not important."

"I just couldn't stand seeing all those beautiful animals in those...those cages."

Robin sighed, watching the blurred headlights in the other lane.

"I knew that was it," he said. "Why didn't you tell me?"

"I didn't want to disappoint you."

"Heather, you wouldn't have disappointed me. If you'd just told me in the first place then we wouldn't have had to go through that whole rigmarole."

"I'm sorry. Don't be mad at me."

"I'm not mad at you."

"Yes, you are."

"*Damn* it, Heather!" he said sharply. Then he quieted. "I'm sorry. I didn't mean to raise my voice. But this gets so frustrating, us ending up in these circular...*things* all the time. This is just like Las Vegas. If you would just tell me what you *wanted* at any given moment..."

"I'm not a dictator, Robin. I don't want to be telling you what to do all the time."

"It's not dictating. It's being clear. If *you're* clear and *I'm* clear then we can make a decision together."

"But I didn't mind the zoo that much. I really didn't."

"You hated the zoo."

"Robin, I did not hate it. It made me a little sad. But I was willing to stay there—"

"You see?" he said, glancing at her. "You see what's happening right now? I make a statement, an obviously true statement, and you hedge and contradict me. Then we end up going in circles."

She looked at him sharply. "I wonder what makes you so sure that *you* know better than *me* what *I* think. How do *you* know I hated it?"

"I could see it in your face."

"Hm." For a moment she says nothing. Then: "You can *see* me fine, but you don't seem to be able to *hear* very well."

He glances at her. "Meaning what?"

"Meaning you never *listen* to me."

He felt the blood in his checks. "I *listened* to you, darling. I listened to you hem and haw there in the zoo, refusing to tell me what you wanted to do."

"Don't call me 'darling' in that tone."

"Heather…"

"You think you're so smart, like you've got the answer for everything."

"I do not—"

"I guess it's not worth bothering to listen to me, I'm just a stupid girl who doesn't know what she wants."

"I never said that!"

"You did," she said, glaring at him. "That's *exactly* what you just said!"

"I said you weren't being clear. I did not call you stupid."

"You might just as well have. It's what you think, anyway."

"Now, goddamn it, that's not fair."

He had hoped the argument would subside when they arrived back at the hotel, but within a minute of walking in the door it started up again.

"I just don't see," she said, tossing her coat on the table, "why you couldn't be just a little more understanding about some things."

"Like what? When am I not understanding?"

"Like today! Like when I was upset at the zoo and all you could think of to do was start picking on me!"

"I did not pick on you. I simply tried to get a straight answer—"

"There you go again. That superior tone."

"*Stop* it, Heather!"

"Now you're giving orders."

He stared at her, then turned away. He tossed his glasses onto a counter and rubbed his eyes. "This is making me tired," he said. "I don't want to talk about this anymore."

"It needs to be talked about, Robin." She dropped herself into a chair at the other side of the room.

"I don't even know what we're talking *about.*"

There was a long silence. At last Robin went to the TV and switched it on, hoping that the sound and light would distract them from further talk. But he found himself speaking again.

"I notice," he said, "that you got a little quiet when I asked you what we were arguing about."

She looked at him, frowning.

"Know what that shows?" he said. "That we're not arguing about anything at all. Maybe we're just spending too much time together, that's all. Maybe we need a break from each other."

"What are you suggesting?"

"I don't know." He stared at the television: an old black-and-white movie, *The Snake Pit.* "Maybe just some time apart, that's all."

"I don't think that will solve anything."

"I don't think there's anything to 'solve,'" he said. "I think this whole thing is just a product of too much time together."

"You see?" she said. "So nothing I said is important at all. It's all just because we're 'spending too much time together.'"

"Well, maybe we *are*."

"And maybe you just need to listen a little bit more."

"Oh, goddamn it," he said, turning from the television, "I've *been* listening to you for *hours* now."

"Then why haven't you heard a word I've *said?*"

"Maybe because you haven't *said any*thing!"

She looked at him fiercely. "I have been trying to explain myself for this long and you have the nerve to say that—"

"Heather—"

"No!" she shouted, standing. "You stop cutting me off and telling me what to do and say and everything else! I'm sick of it! Every time we have a little disagreement it gets blown way out of proportion because you won't *listen*—"

"I'm listening! I hear you loud and clear!"

"All I'm asking for is a little sensitivity sometimes and instead I get Mr. Big Brain telling me all the answers like I'm some retarded five-year-old!"

He realized suddenly that he was still wearing his coat. "Heather, maybe I'll just go out for awhile."

"To where? And leave me stranded here?"

"I'm not stranding you anywhere. I'll just go out for a couple of hours and—"

"And leave me here! No!"

"Heather, goddamn it—"

"Don't give me any 'Heather, goddamn it'! I'm not going to have us start running away from each other every time there's a problem, especially when you've got the car and I've got nothing. I—"

"Then *you* take the car," he said, throwing the keys on the table between them.

"I don't *want* the car!"

He looked at her sharply. "Then what *do* want?"

"I want you to be a little bit sensitive and caring and to listen to me—"

"I have *been* sensitive," he said, hitting his fist on the table, "I have *been* caring, and I listen to you *all* the damn time!"

"If you're so sensitive, why did you pick on me in the zoo? If you're so caring, why do we always get in these fights? Will you explain that to me, Mr. Big Brain?"

"*I'm* not causing the fights!"

"Oh, fine! It's all my fault! We're back to the retarded five-year-old routine!"

"You're twisting my words. You're changing *everything* I say into something else. I believe that I've been sensitive *and* caring—"

"Well, if you're so *caring*," she spat, glaring at him with her hands on her hips, "then why can't you *fuck* me, that's what *I'd* like to know!"

The room crashed into silence.

He stared at her unbelievingly for a long moment, his entire body quivering wildly; then he grabbed his keys from the table again and stormed out into the rain, slamming the door behind him.

His mind is frozen, thoughtless, as he sits through a long double feature of foreign films at a downtown theater. He sees the moving images on the screen, follows vaguely the plots, but he finds the images and the stories fracturing inside his mind, breaking apart, becoming jumbled and confused. A grinning girl becomes Heather; a woman's shouted voice becomes Heather's voice. She overlays the pictures and the sounds no matter how much he tries to say focused on the films themselves. At last he stops trying, lets the fragments tumble across his mind however they wish; it is too tiring to stop them. But he can think of nothing, no questions, no answers; his mind is like the movie screen before him, blank, featureless, a passive receptor of pictures and color and voices. It is easier that way. For if he were to let the thoughts slide into his mind, allow himself to ask the questions and run over the scenes again and again, he would grow upset, terribly upset, and so he does not: he remains frozen. Hours pass. He is not entirely sure what he is watching; the pictures run on into confusion. A love story, perhaps. A man and a woman. Grand sweeping passions, swelling music, torrid French pouring from their lips. A war. Separation. He is wounded. She is seduced by another man. The soldier returns from the war with a limp, then their bodies together, their clothes thrown carelessly on the floor, wild desperate embraces, hot tears, and the woman's body becomes Heather's, the face dissolves away and becomes dark and small with a crooked smile and big dark eyes, he sees her in the room in northern California that first morning, she pulling away his robe and he pulling off her sweater and pants, pushing her back gently onto the bed, her legs opening to him and burying his face in the intoxicating aroma; hearing her gasping cries, feeling his hands grow damp as sweat pours from her legs onto him. The pictures on the screen become her face and arms and stomach and legs, the fingers her fingers, the breasts her breasts, and he can feel her hands around his head, her skin next to his, he can hear her voice suffused with softness whispering into his ear.

He stands finally, makes his way out of the theater and toward his car. It is freezing cold and raining heavily. He turns on the heater but the drive back to the hotel is not a long one; the vehicle is still cold a few minutes later when he pulls into the parking lot. The rain is sharp and stinging as he steps from the vehicle. He is soaked by the time he gets back to the room.

He can feel his heart beating as he opens the door slowly.

The room is dark. He can see, dimly, her shape in the bed: turned on her side, her shoulders and arms bare. He says nothing as he closes the door behind him. The figure in the bed does not stir.

He slips off his shoes, then makes his way around to his side of the bed in the darkness. He looks down at her. She is turned away from him. He feels a peculiar vertigo attacking him from within, as if he might shortly fall down. He strips off his shirt and pants and stands by the bed naked for a long moment before he gently pulls back the blankets and slips into the bed.

He does not move for minutes; hardly breathes. Her body is less than two feet from his but it feels like an interplanetary gulf, a cold vacuum of space. He finds himself shivering.

At last, hesitantly, he turns partially toward her and reaches his hand out to her bare shoulder.

The instant he touches it she turns over to him and in one smooth, instantaneous motion, wraps her body tightly around him and begins to weep.

9
DROWNING
Chapter Three

The reunion is hearty, happy, false. Rachel, looking very sophisticated in a black pin-striped pants suit—and yet cute too, in a hat with a dark band and a bright feather in its brim—greets him too warmly, too cheerfully: "Siegel!" she says animatedly, putting her arms around him and kissing his cheek, "How *are* you?"

He mumbles something in reply and retreats back to the table quickly. Rachel and Dusty follow and as the two of them sit she says, "I heard you were back but I wasn't sure. Just like you, not to call me!"

"I would've called," he says, looking at his wine nervously.

"Oh, sure," she continues with false cheeriness, "*you* would've called. When hell froze over."

He smiles weakly, tries to play along. "I was going to call you tonight."

"Well, then," she says, leaning her head forward and supporting it with her palm, "why didn't you? Why did you leave it up to your cohort here?"

Dusty interrupts. "Hey, this is great," he says. "See, man, I told you, just like old times! We need some more drinks. What are you having, Rachel?"

"Just 7-Up, I guess."

"7-Up it is. Where's that waitress? Never mind, I'll go get 'em." He is positively beaming. "I guess I should let you two get reacquainted for a minute, huh?" He winks and walks toward the bar.

They sit with a heavy silence between them for a long moment. She looks good, no question about that. Her hair is shorter than he remembers it: two dark raven's wings peeping out from under the hat. She looks at him with her big blue eyes—pale eyes, almost clear—and he looks down at the table.

"What'd he say to you?" he asks. "To get you over here so quick?"

She smiles slightly. "Just said you were here, that's all."

"I was going to call you."

"Were you?"

"Mm-hm."

"Well, it doesn't matter. Here I am."

"I know. It's great to see you."

"It's great to see you, Siegel. It really is. How long are you here for? What are your plans?"

"I don't know. I guess I don't have any, really. Not yet."

"Staying at your dad's?"

"Uh-huh."

There is a brief silence.

"How's your book coming?" she says.

"Great. It's almost finished."

Rachel glances down at her hands, at the painted nails. Then she looks at him again. "Do I look okay?"

"That's a funny question."

"Well, I just...I don't know. I wasn't sure if I should dress up or what."

"You look great." And she does. He can't help but think of those long evenings upstairs, the long showers together. He feels a mild swelling between his legs. *Down, boy*. That would be just great: five minutes after he meets her again for the first time in nearly a year he'll ask her to have sex with him. That would go over just dandy. And yet the desire is undeniable. He could walk into the back room right now and be ready to go. He feels slightly ashamed of himself for this. He likes Rachel, he really does, he wants to talk to her for a long time, wants to see how she is...and yet, he thinks, if there were only some way to have sex *now* and talk *later*, instead of the other way around. As it is he'll just have to suffer and try to forget about it.

There, too, that childhood notion comes back to him of somehow being the wrong sex, of having been born with the wrong instruments. It always seems to be this way—he sees a pretty woman, begins to talk to her, and the first thing he is thinking of is how to get her into bed. There is something very base about the male, it seems to him. He likes to consider himself a sensitive person, an artist even, and yet he can't seem to escape his own biology, its reflexes. He wonders why he didn't jack off in the shower earlier. It would have made life much easier right now.

"It really is great to see you again," she says.

"You too, Rachel."

Silence between them. Siegel begins to wish Dusty would come back.

"How are you doing in school?" he asks.

"Great. I graduate at the end of the semester."

"Good."

"Are you going to come and watch the ceremony? I'm Phi Kappa Phi and everything."

He smiles slightly and shrugs. "Sure, I'll come. If I'm invited."

"Of course you're invited."

"Then I'll come."

Dusty comes back with two glasses of 7-Up in his hands. "I was going to get you something, man," he says, "but it looks like you're still working on that. Besides…"

"Yeah, I know. That's fine."

As Dusty sits down Rachel says, "What is that, anyway? Wine?"

"Mm-hm," Siegel says.

"I've never known you to drink."

He shrugs and swallows the wine casually. "Just white wine, that's all."

Dusty says loudly, "So what do you guys want to do, huh?"

"I don't know," Siegel says. "Any ideas?"

Rachel suggests a movie. "What's playing at that theater of yours, Dusty?"

"Hey, great idea! There's a horror double feature."

"Ick," Rachel says. "I can't deal with horror movies. All that splatter and splat."

"What do you mean?" Siegel says. "You and me used to watch horror movies all the time."

"Yeah, but that was at your *house*. And it was just old ones anyway. Like *The Wolf Man*."

"Aw, come on, you guys, it'll be great!" Dusty says. "I can get you in for free now that I'm assistant manager. I'm not supposed to, really, but nobody'll know."

"C'mon, Rachel," Siegel says, enamored suddenly of the idea, "why not? Let's go see some good red gore."

"I don't like those movies," she says, sipping her 7-Up through a thin red straw. "Isn't there anything good playing?"

"Not for free," Siegel says. "See, I knew we had this guy around for a reason."

"The money doesn't matter."

"C'mon."

"Yeah," Dusty says. "C'mon, it'll be great! I haven't even seen these two yet. They just started yesterday."

"C'mon Rachel." He looks at her. She is quite pretty in the dim light of the bar. The fiance, or ex-fiance, crosses his mind suddenly and he feels a pang of jealousy.

Of course if you don't want to go to the movies, he thinks, we could always have a wedding. I'll be the fucking best man. Though if I'm the best man I don't guess I'll get to do much fucking. Unless old Saul baby is as good-hearted about sharing his woman as it looks like I am. He wonders how Saul was to her in bed. Probably better, he supposes; probably gave her screaming orgasm after screaming orgasm, which he'd never been able to do. Orgasms, yes, but wild ones, one after another, never. Rachel said that she just didn't have them that way. But he always wondered if she didn't just need a real man, a real lover.

The swelling in his pants has become even worse. He swallows the last of the wine and watches the world grow momentarily blurry around the edges. Stupid of him, he knows. Ridiculous. As if he owns her, as if she should have remained faithful to him until the day she died—as if he'd given her any reason to, in those last months...as if he himself had been faithful. He and his neighbor up north, Valerie, had flopped around a few times; but he somehow couldn't view that as the same. It wasn't serious. Not like Rachel and her goddamn fiance. But he can't help it—he feels like a kid, wondering what they did in bed, if Rachel sucked him, if she rode him, if she got on her hands and knees, if...

He shakes his head suddenly.

"Siegel," she says, "you okay?"

"Hm? Oh, yeah. Just a funny feeling in my head."

"Nothing serious?"

"Nah."

"Well, all right, you guys," Rachel says resignedly, "I guess you talked me into it. Let's go to the horror show."

※

He stares at the images on the screen, absorbed in them, a nuclear holocaust: blinding white flashes, cities disappearing: he can't take his eyes away, he is fascinated. The number *twenty* crosses his mind, that magical, awful twenty, twenty minutes. He gawks at the pictures, emptily mesmerized by them, until finally there is a fade to black and the main part of the story begins, something about a group of survivors coming up against a bunch of mutant horrors. It's very stupid and much more dull than he'd thought it would be; he hasn't seen a movie in months, he'd supposed the novelty of it would keep him entertained; but he is bored. Nor can he keep his mind on what's happening on screen. Instead it drifts to his dad, wondering what he is doing, to the institution and Hewitt, and finally to Rachel. He looks at her. The light of the screen flickers strangely on her face as she watches the movie and munches on popcorn. After a moment she notices him.

"What is it, Siegel?" she whispers, half looking at him, half at the screen.

"Nothing," he whispers back.

"Don't you like the movie?"

"It's all right."

He glances around in the darkness. The theater is mostly empty. Finally he looks to his other side at Dusty. Dusty's eyes are big and wide and childlike, staring at the screen.

"Rachel?" he whispers.

"What?"

"I don't like the movie."

She smiles. "Neither do I. I thought you did."

"I don't."

At that moment Dusty leans over to them. "Hey, isn't this a great movie, guys? I told you!"

Siegel and Rachel look at each other as Dusty goes back to the movie. Then they giggle and whisper softly into each other's ear.

"Well," he says, "I knew we were here for some reason."

"You were the one who wanted to see a horror movie."

"I made a mistake. Everybody's entitled to one in their life."

"Ho, ho. Do you want to leave?"

"Yeah, but we shouldn't just leave Dusty here."

He thinks about the trip over. Rachel had driven him, while Dusty had come in his own car. Alone in the familiar BMW, the radio playing softly, he'd been content; they had spoken little, but it wasn't an awkward silence—not a lack of words, but a lack of their necessity. Finally, as they neared the theater, he put his head on her shoulder. She had smiled and touched his hair.

"There must be some graceful way out of here," he whispers.

"Any ideas?"

"You could go to the bathroom. Then a minute later I'd go. We just won't come back."

"Oh, that's graceful, all right."

"He'll think one of the mutant monsters got us."

"I know. This *movie*. Is there anything he doesn't like?"

"No, Dusty loves everything. He's a good puppy."

They giggle again. Siegel feels slightly dirty, laughing about Dusty when he's only two feet away, but he keeps laughing anyway. He doesn't suppose they've said anything that's really very funny, but here, in the darkness, the furtive whispers, it is: there is something of a forbidden quality about it that reminds him of the long evenings upstairs with her when his parents were away. It creates a secret electricity between them. The wine helps it, too, floating pleasantly on its waves. And in the past few minutes his shortness of breath has come back, making him light-headed—he can't quite inhale fully; he is not left gasping, in fact no one notices at all, but at the same time he feels a giddy sinking sensation, feels his pulse accelerating. Taken together, the darkness, whispers, wine, the breathing, they are something like a euphoria.

"Let's get married," he whispers to her.

"What?"

"I said, let's get married."

She smiles at him quizzically. "What brought this on?"

"I don't know. Let's just do it." At this moment it seems like a wonderful idea. Marriage. A couple of kids. House in the suburbs. Station wagon with wood paneling on the side. PTA meetings. Suddenly he wants it, wants it badly. Crazy, he knows, but he is suddenly in love with the idea. "C'mon, really. Let's get married."

"I think we've got a lot to talk about first, sweet."

"What's to talk about?" He nuzzles his face into her neck and she giggles.

"What's gotten into you?" she says.

"I dunno. *Love*, I guess."

He kisses her neck and her chin and she puts her arms around him. He wants to stand up and shout, laugh, call out to the whole world…what? He doesn't even know. All he knows is that he's suddenly euphoric, really cloud nine, uncontrollably so.

"We've got to get out of here," he whispers.

"I know. Maybe at the end of the movie."

There is a noise on Siegel's other side and he looks over to find Dusty conversing with a teenage girl from the snack counter. After a moment Dusty looks over at them and sighs. "There's a problem with one of the cash registers," he says. "I gotta go straighten it out. No rest for the weary, right? Or whatever it is."

"Oh, okay," Siegel says.

"So you'll tell me what I missed, right? When I get back?"

"Sure."

Dusty nods and follows the girl up the aisle and past the rear exit.

Siegel looks at Rachel. "There'll never be a better opportunity," he says quietly.

Rachel giggles. "It's so *rude.*"

"But at least we won't have to look him in the face and tell him we're going off somewhere by ourselves."

"So instead we just duck out like criminals?"

He grins. "Why not?"

"Well, okay. Let's do it."

Giggling furtively, they get up and make their way down the aisle to the front exit. They pass through a heavy curtain and past the redly glowing *Exit* sign into a tiny room leading to the door. Suddenly Siegel turns around and wraps her in his arms and kisses her deeply. She makes a small sound of resistance but then puts her arms around him and returns the kiss. He is incredibly horny. He moves his hand to her bottom and she does not resist. He presses his pelvis against her.

"Well," she whispers, "somebody's missed me."

"I'm sorry," he says. "I can't help it."

"Don't be sorry. I've missed you too."

He wants it so badly that crazy fantasies pop into his mind. But he has to wait. He knows he has to wait. Even this, here, now, is dangerous, Rachel might misread it, tell him that all he wants is sex and leave him cold. But sex isn't all he wants. God, how could he ever explain? Sex, yes, but that's only the first part of it, the crazy part, the part that won't wait. He wants everything else too. The touching and the talk and the intimacy and the laughs. But he needs the sex now, needs it badly. He kisses her again, their tongues intertwining, and the need is like a series of hot, dark waves crashing inexorably into him. He needs *her,* he realizes. Not just a female body. No one else would do. He needs her.

There is no choice but to take the crazy chance. He whispers raggedly, "Rachel...can we go someplace—?"

She smiles beautifully at him and cups his face in her hands. "Of course we can."

He feels tears welling in his eyes. "You won't—I mean, you won't think that I'm just after sex or something? I just…" The euphoria and the need are hopelessly mixed together, what he feels is indefinable, an incredible high. "I just…I just really need you right now. Do you know what I mean? I…"

"Don't be silly," she says. "I understand. I do."

"You always have. I've never known why. I've always treated you like—"

"No, you haven't…"

"I have."

"You shut up. How about my folks' house?"

"Are they home?"

"Nope. Out of town."

He looks at her, his vision blurred, and smiles and nods. "That'd be great. Really. Just—great."

"Come on."

They hurry into the parking lot, giggling breathlessly. Like little kids, Siegel thinks—little kids with a secret. He nuzzles her again and she playfully reaches over and squeezes his groin.

"Jesus," he laughs shakily, "don't do that. I'll lose the whole store."

"You *have* missed me, haven't you?"

He looks at her. He wants to give a serious answer but he can't keep from laughing. They both laugh in the black, star-filled night. Then, when they are almost to the car, a voice calls from behind them:

"Hey, you guys!"

"Oh, shit," they whisper in unison. They look at each other and giggle again.

Dusty is standing at the theatre entrance, a long, unwound roll of cash register tape in his hands. He looks incredibly helpless. "Hey you guys, where you going?"

They start to get in the car. "We've gotta go, Dusty!" he calls back. "We'll see you later!"

"Yeah, but—hey—"

They slam the car doors shut and Rachel starts the motor. They both begin to laugh hysterically as she zooms out of the parking lot, Dusty's voice fading rapidly behind them: "Hey, you guys! Don't you want to see the rest of the movie? It'll be great—!"

10

Florida they find glorious. The skies are clear, the temperatures summer-warm; their boots and snow-jackets are consigned to the trunk as they bring out sandals, shorts, T-shirts, swimsuits. They spend warm childlike days at theme parks with a hundred ways of playing with water: rides, slides, tunnels, pools: in the evenings they soak in the hotel's sauna until a pleasant sleepiness overcomes them, and they doze long hours in their room together, lazily bathing and calling room service. Robin tries to keep writing each morning, but the days are long and slow, and a perfect peace settles over him, a serene lethargy; the days pass, slip away as gently and quietly as smoke through his fingers. They find an out-of-the-way cafe with outdoor tables and they sit there for long hours drinking wine (purchased courtesy a marvelously realistic fake I.D. of Heather's) as the light dims in the slow afternoons. They both grow relaxed and expansive with the wine and Robin enjoys her more and more this way: it is so easy, he thinks, to avoid any troubles at all—warmth, sun, a bit of wine as lubricant, and then everything is as easy and wonderful as it could possibly be. It reminds him of the lazy happiness he had felt in Santa Barbara with Priscilla and Koofie: but this happiness is a far greater, far deeper one. He loves to watch her when she is looking elsewhere, loves the subtle changes in her expression when she sees something which interests or amuses her, loves the sweat glistening on her chest above the halter top, loves the supple movements within her throat when she swallows wine from a sweating glass. They talk for long hours, but later it is difficult for him to recall what they talk about. They eat, but he forgets what. And in the hotel room he pulls her halter top gently away and buries his face in her breasts, her stomach, touches and kisses her, but later he cannot remember one time from another; they all melt together in a smooth seamless haze. Sometimes he tries to read but he cannot concentrate on anything for long. Nor can he listen to anything but the simplest rock music. Mahler's symphonies, Terrence Llewelyn's stories, his own novel: they all recede before him into a careless, sunny horizon. None of them matter here in this dazing and gemlike light. He drifts from day to day, happily.

But finally, reluctantly, they decide to move on. They drive through the Florida Keys, all the way to Key West: there they take a tour of Hemingway's old house and drive past Tennessee Williams'. The Hemingway does not particularly interest Robin except in a remote way, for it seems dusty and dead; but Williams' house, hidden behind dense shrubbery, is a source of enormous excitement to him. They go past it again and again, Robin hoping—though not admitting it to Heather—to see the man himself, to see him moving and breathing and speaking. A part of him says that this of course is impossible: that while this may be known as the man's house, he does not actually live here, cannot live in a structure made of wood and plaster and paint that is simply a house like other houses: no, he must reside elsewhere, in the silver heavens about the clouds, talking with the ghosts of Chekhov and Lawrence and Hart Crane.

But the mere sight of the house pulls him out of the lethargy he has lately fallen into. He resolves to begin working again, every day, and hard: he tells Heather she may have to go to see some things on her own and leave him in the hotel so that he can work, that he has wasted too much time, that if he waits any longer the whole book may slip away from him.

"I love you when you're impassioned," Heather grins.

And he does more. He must, he knows, begin to step into the world of literature: that it is not enough to simply doodle away privately, showing nothing to anyone. He must submit—must publish—or else he is not really a writer at all. The few tries he made at this in college had resulted in such gruesome rebuff ("Dear Contributor: While your work does not suit our present needs, we wish you the best of luck elsewhere...") that he had been too frightened to continue. But he must, he knows: it is the only way. And so, one evening while Heather watches a movie on television, he sifts through all his manuscripts, searching for material suitable for mailing to an editor. It is a depressing experience. Looking over his college stories, it is very clear why they were never printed: and clear that Turnham was horribly correct: derivative, immature, half-baked kid's stuff. There is a certain undeveloped talent behind them, true, an ability to turn a phrase or write a pretty paragraph, but there is no vision, nothing that is his own: it is all borrowed, and obviously, from others—a bit of Chekhov there; some Dostoevsky there; a cake of Hemingway's with icing by Steinbeck. He reads through story after story with increasing dissatisfaction and alarm. No, none of them will do. They are all apprentice work, unpublishable.

He stares out the hotel window, despair spreading over him. Perhaps he is not a writer, after all. Perhaps it is to be the cluttered desk, the packed and dusty bookshelves, the student essays and coffee rings on old papers. Perhaps he has been living in illusions. For among the hundreds of pages and dozens of stories, he can find nothing that works, nothing sustained, nothing but a few well-wrought sentences and clever metaphors.

He sits there for a long time, unmoving.

"Baby?"

He starts, looks up at her. "Hi."

"Hi. What's up?" She touches his hair.

"Nothing. How's the movie?"

"It's over. Kirk Douglas won."

"Congratulate him for me, next time you see him."

She grins. "What's wrong? You look unhappy."

"No."

"Liar."

"Really."

She drops herself into the chair on the other side of the table, looks at him.

"It's just these," he says finally, pushing away some of the manuscripts.

"What about them?"

"Nothing. That's the problem. They're terrible."

She scowls. "No, they're not."

"They are. Just college junk anybody could have written." He stares quizzically at the papers before him. "The funny thing is, I used to think they were so good."

"Robin, stop it. You're talented. You are."

"So's everybody," he says, looking out the window again. "The question is what you *do* with it, and I haven't done anything. Not a thing. Maybe I'll just give it up. Pack it in. I haven't written anything in weeks anyway. I think I've just been fooling myself for a long time."

"Don't be silly. You're not going to throw it all away now."

"I might as well, Heather," he sighs. "This stuff is just a bunch of crap."

"What about the novel?"

He stares into the darkness. "I don't know."

"Have you been re-reading it, too?"

"No. Just these stories. I was looking for something to submit to an editor. I can't go on like this, working in a vacuum."

"Well, you dope," she says suddenly, standing, "where's the manuscript? I've got an idea, if that's what you want to do."

"It's over there," he points. "By the bed."

"Oh, yeah." She moves to pick it up. "Your problem, baby, is that you're not *assertive*. Lookie here—where is it?" She moves again to Robin, stands near him as she flips through the pages of *Drowning*. "Here." She is pointing at the poem, "Alcohol," in the first chapter, ostensibly written by Siegel.

"What about it?"

"Publish it! Send it out to somebody."

"It's supposed to be part of the book, though."

She rolls her eyes, knocking him on his head with the papers. "Robin, you are so *dull!* The hell with the book—I mean, for the moment. Get a piece of paper, type the poem onto it, and send it to a journal. They'll publish it. *Somebody* will. Guaranteed."

He stares at the poem on the page. "You think so?"

"I know so. So cut your sad clown routine."

He smiles. The poem does seem to work, at that. He recalls sitting in the Santa Barbara foothills by the river and the wind rising and the line, the poem's first line, which had been with him for—how long? years?—suddenly running on and on, a vivid fever dream. But it had not stopped there. It had grown, suddenly including the boy in the house and his father and the light and the sounds in the rooms; and, almost without thought, his pencil had moved and moved across the windblown pages. But Heather is right, he realizes. The thing does stand by itself. It does work.

"Maybe I'll try it," he says to her, smiling uncertainly.

Later he would wonder if those happy productive weeks in Florida had only been a mirage.

Later, when he came to consider the texture of his life with Heather, its rhythms and patterns, he would find that he could discover no answers, only more questions. When he would wonder later how it had happened, how their lives together became a series of shattering windows endlessly replicating themselves in a tunnel of darkness, he would find himself unable to find answers or even theories for answers. Arguments, disagreements, misunderstandings, all of these were comprehensible; what he could not grasp was the sudden viciousness of which they were capable. And not only Heather. When provoked, he discovered, he could reply in kind; and even when he could see the fight going nowhere, and when he knew what it would take to solve the problem (a kiss, a caress, a long walk together), oftentimes he did not do it, stood his ground instead, became intransigent and dug-in like an infantryman under fire, and so the trouble would grow, fester, become malignant, overwhelm them until they were screaming at each other. And about what? he would wonder later. Each fight followed a pattern: a minor disagreement, attempted deferment to the other party, refusals of the deferment, a temporary switching of positions, sensitivities growing frayed, impatience, frustration, a blundering onto tangential subjects, an attempt to return to the issue, brief success followed by a resurrection of the tangential business, and finally hopeless distortions and confusions ending in shouting bouts. It could be mapped, he thought, charted as one would chart a fever. They resumed even before they left Florida. An argument over which road to take one afternoon escalated into a fight about who controlled rights to such choices. A disagreement over whether or not they should have the car looked at by a mechanic became an argument over their sex life. The transmutations were endless, as were the shouting matches.

Somewhere in Georgia he began to think that they should bring the trip to an end.

Don't ask me how it's happened, he wrote in his diary. *I do not know. There is something dark and terrible developing between us which appears at periodic intervals and is leading us I-don't-know-where.*

In Atlanta, coming back from a walk, he discovered her throwing up in the bathroom. She claimed she was ill; but two days later, in Savannah, he found her doing it again. A discussion of this led into an argument about personal rights, truth, lies, trust, control. Robin's mind began to whirl. He had stopped writing altogether. Silence descended between them on the long trips from one place to another. They would lie in bed for hours without touching each other, and if one of them would ask, "Why are you so far over there?" the other would respond, "I'm not. I'm just comfortable here, that's all," and it was accepted silently.

Why is this happening? he wrote in his diary.

And yet they were capable of sudden bouncings-back: an especially good museum, a breathtaking view, a funny encounter could lift them suddenly, toss them back to an earlier time before such things had taken place, and they would cuddle together and apologize for all their wrongs and kiss sweetly and Heather would say, "Robin, we'll never fight again, never ever," and Robin would say, "Never ever," and he would become lost in her aroma, her warm skin, her deep eyes, the sensation of her arms around his naked body, her breath, her lips and hair, lost, floating as if to a place with no gravity, no up or down, perfect free-floating timelessness, far from ticking clocks and endless arcs, a place of serenity, peace. Days could pass in this way, together and unaware of anyone else in the world, only the face of the room-service clerk at the door or the actors on a TV show; lost, vanishing into one another, dissolving together, becoming extensions of each other, inextricably connected to the other's hands and arms and voice and mind. "Who are you?" one of them would ask, and the other would answer, "I'm you," and it was true; but the moment would end and it always came to Robin like the amoebas ripping apart in his imagination, rudely, gracelessly, a bloody and violent separating and retreat back into solitariness and silence and darkness. Each time it happened it shocked him, drove him into sadness and depression and confusion. A room-service bill, a wrong number on the telephone, anything could ignite them like an unstable acid and suddenly their extensions, like roots from the earth, were retracted from each other or burned away, huge trees aflame, noise and terror. He would wake abruptly with Heather shaking him, saying, "Baby, baby, it's just a bad dream, it's just a bad dream," and he would lay there breathing quickly and sweating. "What were you dreaming?" she would ask, and he would reply, "Things dying."

As they passed through South and North Carolina—by now it was nearly March—he found himself thinking more and more of Wind Point, of the house in the cul-de-sac, of college. He had done no more than send his father a few postcards, leaving no forwarding address; he had communicated with no one else. He wondered what his father thought about it, what he told that girlfriend of his; if, in fact, he thought of it at all, or cared. Of course it was impossible to return now, even were they to end the trip. His father had made his choice, it seemed to Robin; his father had issued his statement. It was over. And so all he could really do was keep moving, searching for light, sun, new intensities. Strange thought, to realize that he would never again see the house in the cul-de-sac, never walk up those steps or open that door or ascend the stairs into the upper darknesses, never lie listening in the night for sounds from downstairs, never feel his heart smashing against his chest as the clumping footsteps neared him in the hall. Never again. He had at last severed the umbilical cord, for all time.

But for what? he would wonder, lying in the darkness with Heather's body far away across the gulf of cold sheets and blankets. A girl who, even now, he failed to understand: who was not, in a way, even real to him, whose focus in his mind would blur and change, whose core remained untouchable. He would tell her he loved her; but the words were nonsensical; they refused to fit in his mouth. *I love you,* he would say. But it was a triple confusion. Who, he would wonder, is "I"? How could he use the word when there were in fact many Robins, Robins from whom he felt increasingly estranged, dark distant reflections of selves he no longer knew? "Love"? He could not define the word; suspected no one could: four letters alternately miraculous and dangerous and inexplicable. And "you"? Who *was* she? And if there were many Robins, would there not also be many Heathers? It was meaningless. Human connection itself was not possible, he began to think, because we have no single self, only a potpourri of selves existing over time. If there were a way, he thought, to integrate those many selves, unify them into a real organic whole, then it could be possible. But there was not. Unity was only a necessary illusion.

A deep melancholy began to come over him. He saw little of the budding eastern spring as they drove through it, the leaves and blossoms and endless swaying fields of grass; he felt only hopelessness. Everything was coming to an end. His writing was gone; he and Heather hardly spoke to each other now—they were not fighting exactly, not usually, but rather had arrived at a point of deep, unspoken mental separation. They could still enjoy each other's company. They could still laugh at a funny movie or make sexy jokes with each other. It was nothing obvious, nothing definable. But they were, Robin knew, apart. They had tried to talk about it, but had gotten nowhere. There was nothing to say.

"What's happened to us?" Heather would ask.

Robin would shake his head.

They made efforts. They experimented with spending days apart. They tried to collaborate on a short story. They talked. They did not talk. And yet the disillusion continued, grew, blossomed like an awful flower between them. At night Robin would dream of a dark house engulfed in flames, and running, running through the house, Heather crying to him from somewhere, but unable to find her, unable to find his blazing white sun-horse on which he could carry her away. Something had happened between them that neither could define and yet was ripping them in two. Robin's depression grew dull and thick.

"Heather?" he says.

"Hm?" Her voice comes through the closed bathroom door.

"Can I come in?"

A short pause. "Since when do you have to ask?"

He opens the door. She is sitting on the toilet.

"I don't know," he says, looking toward the bathtub where water is running steamily.

"Anyway, what's up?" She wipes herself with toilet paper, stands and flushes. "Want to take a bath?"

"Not right now."

She steps gingerly into the tub. "Ouch! Hot! Just the way I like it." She settles herself into the tub and turns off the water. "Kill the light, will you? I want to relax."

Robin shuts off the light and the bathroom is in darkness.

"Heather," he says, standing in the doorway, "maybe it's time to end this."

"What?"

"This. The trip. Everything."

She does not answer. Slowly his eyes adjust to the dark and he can see her sitting in the tub, her eyes glistening and her breasts slick with water.

"Why?" she says finally.

"You know why. We don't have to talk about it."

Another silence.

"Is it the sex thing, Robin? Because if it is…"

"It's not the sex thing. Or maybe that's just a symptom."

He hears the water splash gently.

She says, "We can't end it like this."

"I think we may have to."

"I don't understand what's wrong. I know there's something wrong between us but I don't know what it is."

Silence.

"Do you love me, Robin?"

"Heather, stop it."

"Do you?"

"It's a stupid question."

"Why?"

"Because it is. It doesn't mean anything."

"It means something to me."

"It doesn't mean anything to you. It doesn't mean anything to anybody. It's just something people say to keep from…from saying anything."

"Maybe you're too intellectual for me. Maybe I'm just too stupid to understand."

"Heather, don't start. Please."

He hears her sigh. After a moment passes he moves toward her and sits on the edge of the tub, touching her wet shoulder softly.

"We can't end it like this," she says again.

He touches her cheek with the back of his hand, strokes it softly. "We're killing each other," he says. "I've never been so depressed in my life. I can't write. Can't eat. Can't *think*. And you're the same way. Throwing up your food…"

"I haven't—"

"You did when I went out for the paper today," he says quietly. "Clean the bowl better next time."

"Oh, God…"

"So maybe it's time to call it a day."

"Why is this happening?" she asks quietly. "Why?"

"I don't know. But we can't seem to solve it. Maybe if we separate for awhile."

"How long?"

"I don't know. A few months, maybe. You go to your folks in New Hampshire. I'll go somewhere else. After a while we'll see."

"You're all I have," she says in a small voice.

"You have your family."

"Them! A lot of brothers and sisters! They're not you."

Robin stares at the dark wall for a long moment. Then, glancing at her, he says: "Sisters? I didn't know you had sisters. I thought you only had brothers."

"I've got two sisters."

"Hm." He thinks for a moment. "That's funny. I could have sworn you said you only had brothers."

"Two sisters. I'm the oldest."

He looks at her. "And how many brothers?"

"Three."

He smiles slightly. "Tough, keeping this kangaroo court straight in my mind."

She smiles in return, places her wet hand in his.

"I don't want us to separate," she says.

"Neither do I. But what else can we do?"

"Stay together. Keep trying."

"For how long?"

"As long as it takes. Robin, I love you. No matter what you say about it, I do." She squeezes his hand. He suddenly realizes that tears are flowing down her face. "And I'm sorry, baby, I'm so goddamn sorry for everything that happens between us…"

"Heather, stop."

She sniffs. "Nothing like this has ever happened to me before," she says shakily. "Never. I've never felt this way about anyone.

You're all I think about. You're all I care about. All I want to do is make us happy together and all that ever happens is..."

"Heather..."

"All that ever happens is this *shit* which is all my fault..."

"Heather, honey, stop, no it isn't."

She presses her face against his arm. "Oh my God," she says. "Oh my God, Robin, don't leave. Don't leave me. Please."

"Heather, stop crying. Come on. We can't talk about this if you cry."

"I can't *help* it..."

He tussles her hair softly. His vision has grown foggy and there is something hot and tight in his throat. "Calm down, Heather," he says. "Come on, sweetheart. Calm down."

"Just don't leave me. Promise you won't leave me."

"Shhh. Quiet down. Here, wipe your eyes a little."

She splashes the water slightly. "Maybe...maybe if we just agree never to fight, never to fight about anything in the world..."

"We haven't been fighting, lately," he says. "That was before."

"Or we agree to talk whenever there's a problem..."

"We talk all the time. All we do is talk."

They are silent for a long time. Heather stirs the water listlessly with her hand.

"Maybe I'll go into the other room," he says finally, standing. "I'll let you finish your bath."

A few minutes later he is on the bed watching TV when she comes in, drying herself with a towel.

"So what do you want to do?" she says.

"I made a suggestion," he says. "I can't think of any other answer."

She walks to the curtain, holding the towel in front of her, and looks out. "You want to leave me," she says.

There is a change in her tone of voice that puts Robin immediately on his guard.

"Unless you have a better idea, honey," he says. "What do you think?"

"It's fine," she says, looking back at him. "Go ahead and leave."

"Heather, don't be like that. Please."

"No, I mean it. It's fine. Let's split up the money. I'll go visit my parents and you go back to California or whatever you want to do. You call me when you decide you're ready to see me again."

"It's not just when *I'm* ready," he says, sitting up.

"You're the one who wants to leave."

"Heather, I don't want to fight."

"I'm not fighting."

"You've got a tone in your voice I don't like."

"Sorry. I didn't realize that you don't like my voice either."

Robin sighs, looks away. He decides against speaking.

"So," she says, "go ahead and leave. Pack your things. Go."

"Heather…"

"Go. I'm not stopping you."

"Darling…"

"Leave. Tonight."

He stands and walks to her. She holds the towel in front of her body. The look in her eyes is cold and impenetrable. "Heather," he says, reaching to her, "come on…"

"No," she says, brushing his hand away and moving from him. "If that's what you want to do, then do it. Go! But don't stay around here. I don't want you here if you don't want to be here."

"Heather…"

"Go! You always say we get in arguments because we're too sensitive around each other and won't take positions. Well, here's a position! Go! Get out of here!"

He feels suddenly deflated, defeated. "Heather, listen for a…"

"There's nothing to listen to." She tosses the towel on the bed and grabs her robe from the closet, pulls it on. "Come on. Let's divvy up everything right now." She pulls open a suitcase. "I'll throw your stuff to the left and my stuff to the right. Here's my clothes." She tosses a heap to one side. "But this is your shirt." She throws it to the other side. "Here's your sandals—these are my panties. This is…"

He moves to her quickly, takes her by the shoulders. "Heather—"

"*Stop it! Stop touching me! You said what you wanted, now we're doing what you wanted! Leave me alone!*"

He watches as she hurls things this way and that. He feels abruptly as if he were twelve years old again, watching his mother at the bedroom window.

"Yours!—Yours!—Mine!—Yours!—"

"Heather…"

"*Shut up!* Help me with this! The more help you give the faster we'll get it done and the faster you can be out of here!"

He sits on the bed, trembling. She rips through the bags and suitcases with furious intensity. Clothes fly. Papers. Books. Tubes of toothpaste. His diary, which falls open. He picks it up.

"Go ahead," she says, tossing cassette tapes to either side, "go ahead and write something else nasty about me in that little book of yours! Go ahead and write about your 'inability to communicate' with me!" She does a whining imitation of his voice. "Say a little more about 'the vast gulf between us' and all your other lousy intellectual shit!"

He stands suddenly, aghast. "You've been reading my *diary?*"

"No shit, Sherlock! Of course I've been reading it!"

He cannot speak. He stares at her, his eyes wide.

She laughs derisively. "Big shock, huh? Well, what did you *think* I was going to do? I wanted to help you! I wanted to see if I could find out why your fucking *prick* doesn't work!"

He is shaking violently. His breathing is erratic. He looks around the room wildly, feeling suddenly trapped, claustrophobic. "You…" he starts to say, his voice strangled. "You…!"

"*What? What?* Say it!"

"*You...!*" He hurls the diary against the wall.

"Oh, great!" she shouts. "Beautiful! Destroy the hotel, why don't you! Then we'll have to pay for it!"

He grabs his hair, pulls at it in rage. His face is burning. He glares at her.

"There!" she says, tossing the last suitcase on the floor. "Now collect your shit and get lost! But we're divvying up the money so that I have enough to get home. You're not getting out of here with everything!"

"I—I don't care *what* you get—!"

"I know!" Her eyes blaze darkly. "I know you don't care! That's been the whole problem from the beginning! For God's sake, you just *told* me you don't love me! You don't care! I know you don't! As usual, Mr. Big Brain, you've hit it right on the nose!"

"You...Heather, you have *no right*—"

"Stop it! I don't want to hear anything you have to say! You told me you want to leave, so leave!" She takes the money from her purse, hurls it on the bed, begins to divide it by leaving half on the bed and throwing half on the floor. "Get your wallet out!"

His hands tremble as he reaches to it; he drops it as he brings it out. He picks it up, looks inside, fumblingly brings out about half of the total amount and tosses it toward her. She crams the bills into her purse.

"Pick it up!" she says, pointing at the floor. "Pick up all this shit and get out of here!"

He takes his suitcase and throws his things into it while Heather stalks into the bathroom and slams the door shut. He hears the lock snap closed. He tries to keep his mind free of thoughts, free of the rage he feels boiling inside him. Just do it, he thinks. You wanted out and now you're out. Just do it and go.

He pockets the green bills on the floor and takes the suitcase to the car. There he finds a few items belonging to Heather and he tosses them into a paper bag and brings them back into the room.

The room is silent, like a village after a black storm.

"I've brought your things from the car," he says to the bathroom door. "I'm leaving them here on the bed."

He waits. Silence.

"Heather, we'll talk about this tomorrow," he says. "I'll call you tomorrow."

No response. The rage within him dissipates, vanishes, leaving him dull and blank: he feels suddenly deflated again, an empty husk without thought or life.

"I'll call you tomorrow, Heather," he repeats, and stumbles out of the room.

In the car he sits staring into the darkness for long minutes. If he is connected to anything, he thinks, or ever was, that connection is gone now. He feels burned-out, blackened and aimlessly floating like a dwarf star. Alone. Dead. His heart beats rapidly and yet he is utterly exhausted. He wants no more than sleep, long deep deathlike sleep, nothing else: escape, oblivion, peace. He understands nothing, he realizes; and so how could he ever claim to be a writer, or even an intelligent human being? He grasps nothing, has no answers, knows only darkness and confusion.

From where the car is parked he can see the door to their room. At first he does not register the sight of the small figure in the terrycloth robe who opens the door and stands silhouetted there, her arms folded under her breasts. She does not move for minutes. He stares back at her blankly, thinking distantly that if he ever knew her, anything about her, he does not now; she is a stranger, lost to time, nothing but a collection of disparate fragments, just as he is, broken bits of glass pressed crazily together in an uneasy frame. Unconnected, unintegrated, shards sailing around blindly in the dark: spears of glass hurling through black space.

Finally she moves away from the doorway and out into the parking lot. Her steps are quick. In a moment she is standing next to the car door, looking down at him. She has been crying: her eyes are swollen and deep black rings have appeared under them. Her eyes and her cheeks glisten with tears and her entire frame is shivering.

"Baby?" she says, her voice tiny and shaking.

He looks away from her.

She taps on the glass.

"Baby?"

He begins to quiver. He watches his hands in his lap, vibrating as if a motor were running them. His breath is quick and short.

"Robin?" She taps again.

He stares at the steering wheel, unable to respond.

"Robin, come back inside," she says, her voice unsteady. "Please?"

Neither of them move for long minutes. Finally she taps on the glass again.

"Baby, please come back inside."

He glances up at her. She is hugging her body closely as tears flow down her face. Her lips quiver and her hair falls in a tangle over her cheeks. As he looks at her, as their eyes meet, he suddenly feels deeply afraid, as if somewhere in her eyes were all the unleashed darknesses of the world.

"Please, baby. Please...At least open the window a little. Please..."

He reaches toward the window handle and cranks it once. The window opens a crack. Heather reaches the fingers of one hand into the crack but it is not wide enough for her hand to come through. Her fingers remain in the crack, dangling.

"Baby, please open the window..." Her voice is engulfed in tears. "Please open the window, Robin...I'm sorry...Oh my God, Robin, I'm *sorry*..."

His breath is rushing through him in gasps. He watches her fingers writhe in the crack of the window like snakes. He is terrified.

He reaches forward suddenly and turns the key. The engine fires into life.

"*No...!*" Heather cries. "Robin, please, *please* don't leave...I'm *sorry*, baby...Come inside, please just come inside and we'll... we'll..."

He places his hand on the gearshift and pulls it into drive.

"*Robin...!*"

Staring straight forward, he presses lightly on the gas. Her fingers pull against the glass.

"Robin, open the window...please open the window...Robin..."

The car begins to move. The fingers disappear from the window and he hears her behind him weeping wildly, hysterically. He is shaking so that he can hardly hold onto the steering wheel. He feels as if an explosive has gone off in his chest and left his heart a shattered, blown-apart mass of blood and sorrow. He could stop, he knows. He could put his foot on the brake pedal. He is probably wrong about it all. He is probably a cold-hearted bastard, an uncaring monster. But then he has always known that. He has always understood from his earliest childhood that he is sick and depraved, evil and monstrous. He has known it since he listened trembling at the bathroom wall, since he had fantasies of hurling Melissa Rosselli into a dungeon and raping her, since he had imagined having two separate mothers and killing one of them, murdering her ruthlessly with his flashing sword, he has known it since she had faded into the dark haze and it was his fault that he had not saved her, his fault that she had wanted to do it in the first place, it was his own flaws, his own monstrousness that made her do it, and he has known this all along, that if he had been better it would not have happened, nothing would ever have happened, and now here it is again, his sickness, his monstrousness, he can hear the voice wailing in the darkness behind him as he presses down on the gas pedal, and he will go to Hell for this, he knows, he will surely go to Hell if there is a Hell and if there is any judge to decide, he will go to Hell for this, but he presses down on the gas pedal anyway, keeps pressing down on it, he presses down on the gas pedal and does not let up.

11
DROWNING
Chapter Four

Rachel's house is in the foothills, a big five-bedroom affair isolated by trees and thick shrubbery all around. Siegel stands on the rear patio, which faces a sharply descending slope and affords a lovely view of the Santa Barbara lights. Crickets chirp in the darkness. For Siegel, it is the time machine effect again—over two years since he's been here, he realizes, yet it hasn't changed at all. It is amazing to him, how little anything around him has changed in this incredible period. The inside of his own house, yes, that is different; his dad is older; Rachel's hair is shorter, her voice slightly deeper than he remembers. And yet that seems to very little considering how much he himself has changed, how far behind he has left that boy of years ago. But has he? he wonders. Has he really? Or is he really just the same person he was that first day of kindergarten, always waiting for some breakthrough, some new, different level of existence, and never attaining it? Strange, this paradox, this feeling of both being true….

The euphoria, such as it was, has worn off for the most part: he stands on the patio in the warm night waiting for Rachel to return, and happily so, cheerfully anticipating; but the overwhelming need seems to have gone for the moment, that enormously intense desire that made him have wild fantasies in the theater. Just as well, he figures. Much more of that and he would have burst right out of his jeans. But his want is still there. He wonders if this isn't a pattern with him, this mad, hot desire for something he may not be able to get, and then, once it becomes apparent that he will get it, a cooling. His novel crosses his mind, unpleasantly. He has a scene in mind that he supposes he really should write; but he certainly isn't going to do it just now, waiting for Rachel. He feels his groin swelling pleasantly.

"Hi, sweet," she says, behind him.

He turns to her. She has removed the hat and shoes and the vest of her pants-suit and, in the dim light, she seems almost ethereal. He smiles as she comes into his arms.

"You're something," he says.

"Shall we go in?"

"Mm-hm."

They step inside and Rachel pushes him gently onto the sofa. Then she crosses to the stereo, puts on a record of soft piano music, and comes back, sits next to him.

"Pretty, huh?" she says. "Do you like Windham Hill?"

"Never really listened to it."

"We went to a concert," she says. "That's where I heard it."

Something happens to Siegel abruptly. The vision of the faceless man, the fiance, Rachel's fiance, suddenly flashes into his mind. He doesn't have to ask who the *we* is that she is referring to. And then suddenly he finds himself wondering again what they did, if they did it in this house, on this sofa.

"I want you to talk to me first," Rachel says, her face close to his.

"What about?"

She smiles. "What do you mean, what about? I think we've got a lot to catch up on, don't we?"

"I don't know. I guess."

She looks at him closely. "Are you all right now, Siegel?"

"Me? Sure I am."

"I mean, do you feel good? Or do you feel…" She leaves the sentence unfinished.

"I feel fine."

She looks down at his hands.

"What was it like in there?"

He looks at them as well. He clears his throat. "I—I don't know. It was all right. It was just a lot of psychiatric sessions and drugs and things. No straitjackets, nothing like that. It wasn't so bad. Really. You should've visited." He says the last sentence without thinking; immediately wants it back.

"I wanted to visit," she says. "But I just…I don't know. I thought it might do more harm than good. And then there was…" Again she trails off.

And then there was Biberman, he thinks.

"Things were just strange then," she finishes weakly.

"I know. I was the strangest of all."

She smiles slightly. "I let you down, didn't I."

"What do you mean?"

She sighs. "Those dopey letters I wrote. And then not writing at all. And not visiting. And…well, you know. My…plans."

He shrugs, shakes his head.

"Siegel, I want to explain about all that. About Saul."

"You don't have to say anything. He's gone, right? So he doesn't matter." O generous man! he thinks. Gone, yes, hence forgotten, right? But Siegel can't forget him, especially not when he keeps getting tossed in his face. His groin tingles. He really wishes they could get down to business; plenty of time, he thinks, to talk about all this nonsense. First things first…But of course he can't say such a thing to her. He crosses his legs.

Rachel begins to talk. Siegel tries to listen, but the attempt is unsuccessful. He hears isolated snatches: *if you knew how I felt then…he was just a nice guy and I was…it was crazy, a crazy time…*But he can't concentrate on the words, they don't have any meaning.

His mind drifts to her breasts. He tries to concentrate on her words. Drifts to her breasts again. Abhors himself for it. Here is his old girlfriend, perhaps still his girlfriend (this, apparently, has yet to be decided), pouring out her heart to him, and all he can think of is—Ridiculous. *Males,* he thinks. No matter how much they try to fight the stereotypes, their biology always trips them up.

He remembers his guilt when he and Rachel first started having sex: the feeling that he was violating something, damaging it, something pure and clean. Bruising it with his trogloditian meat-club. And earlier, an earlier memory, a distant mind-picture, of himself and his mom when he was very young: the room dark, curtains drawn, a hazy yellow half-light filtering through: Mom alone in the room in her chair with the TV and the pungent amber liquid. *Mom,* he'd said, *I don't want to be a boy. I want to be a girl.* Her dulled eyes staring at him: no answer, as if he hadn't spoken at all, the river of amber pouring into the glass, the sound of it, the lifeless doll eyes wandering back to the TV screen.

Not that it had ever been a serious thing, this desire to switch sexes. No, it was more just a basic shame. In the institution he had analyzed it no end. He and Hewitt had talked about it; but the conclusions they came to were too obvious, too pat: father not around much as a child, lack of male role models, domineering mother…But didn't all that come together a bit too easily? he would wonder after the sessions. Isn't there something more to human psychology than cubbyholes, textbook definitions? Lying there, staring up at the white ceiling in the darkness, he would know it was true: for then he would feel the other darkness, the huge one, the awful one, drawing near, and know that that darkness couldn't be explained away, pushed aside. It was a connection to something beyond words, something eternal. Something terrible and forever.

The Unspoken

The name *Saul* invades his consciousness again and he is whipped back to the present, the room, Rachel's voice.

"It's all right, Rachel," he says, suddenly realizing she is crying.

"It isn't," she is saying. "I—I just couldn't face it anymore, Siegel. I couldn't face what you'd become. I just didn't have the... courage, I guess. I didn't—"

"Don't be silly," he says, holding her. He keeps his legs crossed so she can't bump against his hard-on. "You were in there for a long time. A *long* time. You put up with so much." Which is true. She had. Frequent bouts of irrationality and paranoia. Depression. He even hit her a couple of times, in his foggier states.

"And so Saul was just...a way out. You know? That's all he was."

"I understand." He wishes that name wouldn't stab at him so much. He feels vaguely violent toward the whole thing. As if he would like to punish her. But it passes.

Still, he is beginning to feel irritable. He's really heard enough of old Saul baby and Rachel's problems and all that stuff. He has enough problems, he thinks, he doesn't need to sit around talking about them. Not when he could be having sex. Or, failing that, drinking. Rachel Clayton, he thinks. Rachel Biberman. Rachel Clayton-Biberman.

Tonight's Self-Pity Rating, ladies and gentlemen, is a record 9 1/2 on a 10 scale! He smiles to himself wryly. He'd invented the Self-Pity Index in the institution. Hewitt had loved it, asked him every day what the rating was. He had never broken 9, although he usually felt worse then than he does now. The depression, after all, was real. The self-pity is so much garbage...He realizes this intellectually, but there doesn't seem to be much he can do about it. It's like a flood when it comes, uncontrollable, overwhelming.

"I don't even know why you kept coming up, those last few months," he says, trying to comfort her. "Things were so bad. You should've hated me."

"I didn't hate you. I hated your—your sickness. Your problems. I loved you. I—I still do. That's why I'm getting all sloppy now. Because I don't know what you think of me anymore and I don't know where we're going or what's happening."

His groin swells again. He is listening, it's nice to hear this, but at the same time he can't help but think of her breasts. He kisses her softly. Then more passionately. She yields to him easily. He touches one of her breasts. He presses her back onto the sofa. He is sure, finally, that this is it. Then, suddenly, she makes a moan of protest.

"Siegel," she says, "not right now. Not yet. Please?"

"Come on," he says, unthinkingly.

"No, not right now. I'm not in the mood."

"Rachel…"

"Please, Siegel?"

He sighs and sits up quickly. It comes out of his mouth before any thought even comes near it: "I'll bet you never turned your friend Saul down."

She sit up. "What?"

"Nothing."

"What did you say?"

"I didn't say anything."

"Siegel, I haven't seen Saul in…"

"I know, I know."

"Then why did you—"

"*You're* the one who keeps talking about him."

"Well, I'm just trying to explain that—"

"I don't need any more explanations. I'll just bet you never turned him down, that's all."

It is a moment before she replies. "Siegel, I'm sorry, but it's really none of your business *what* Saul and I did."

"I didn't say it was."

"You inferred it."

"I don't give a shit, really."

"You're jealous."

He glances at her, his face hot. "Just interested, that's all," he says. "Just interested in who you were balling while I was going nuts."

"You bastard."

The words keep coming, even as he knows that every one of them makes the sex sail further and further away, makes it more and more hopeless, and the anger rises in him, the desire to hurt her, to smash her lying face in, but he controls it, filters it through words: "I'm a bastard, huh? What about you? You and your little friend Saul? How do you think it felt, every day, in those goddamn psychiatrist's sessions, talking about Mom and Dad when all I could think about was you fucking your new boyfriend?" It's more than that, he knows, he's making it stupid, superficial: it's not the fucking, it's the closeness, the sharing, the looks they must have given each other, it's all that together; but none of that comes out, he can't form the words, and so more of the stupid things come out, the oversimplifications, the nonsense: "What do you think it was like thinking about some guy porking you while I was in the looney bin? Huh? Couldn't you have waited? Couldn't you at least have done that much, you, you—?"

He suddenly realizes he is standing over her, his face burning, his fists balled tight. She looks up at him fiercely.

"You're an ungrateful shit," she says. "All you've ever done all your life is feel sorry for yourself and try to make everybody around you feel sorry for you too. Well, I don't! So you have problems. So your mother died. I tried to help you through it. But you know what I think? I don't think you *want* to come through it. You *like* it! You *love* feeling sorry for yourself!" Siegel turns away and looks out the sliding door at the Santa Barbara lights. "You'll never do anything, Siegel, the way you are! When are you going to stop it? Like that book of yours. When are you finally going to finish it? Are you even *writing* it?"

He whirls around. "I'm writing it."

"Prove it. Show me some of it."

He looks at her sourly. "Well, I don't have it *with* me."

She stands. "Then let's go to your house. Show it to me there. I dare you."

"Fuck you. Nobody gets to look at it until it's done."

"Oh, sure. When will that be? Before or after the Second Coming?"

"What business is it of yours?"

"What *business*?" she shrieks. "It's five years of business of mine! I stuck by you. I *helped* you. When your parents thought you were crazy!"

"Well," he says, going to the door, "turns out they were right, huh?"

"Where are you going?"

"Out."

"I *drove* you here."

"It's only a mile back to the bar. I'll make it."

"Don't be stupid. I'll drive you."

He glances at her as he reaches the door and is seized with an overwhelming desire to hit her, fuck her, make her pay. For something. He doesn't know what. All he knows is that his sex drive has somehow turned violent tonight, as it used to sometimes before the institution, when she would come up from Santa Barbara for the weekend and he would wind up hitting her, never badly, but hitting her, and liking it.

"Stay out of my life," he says, and storms out.

12

It is past seven in the morning by the time the fat summer sun begins to amble over the blue mountains to the east, sending streaks of corn-colored light across the rustling long grass and still, sleeping houses dotting the landscape like hard-edged cocoons. The world wakes slowly here. For a long time there is no sound whatever but the wind picking up gently with the coming of light and running through the grass with a sound like rushing water. Presently sparrows and bluejays begin to fuss about their nests in the trees, calling and twittering and fluttering from limb to limb. A door opens; a dog barks and charges into the morning, disappearing into the acres of wild and uncut grass which rises waist-high in the valley behind the house. And then rustlings in the house itself: pans rattling; voices, adults and children, indistinctly audible. Finally there is the slap of a screen door and a boy and a girl run onto the lawn in front of the house, happily shouting.

Robin loves to watch this gradual process of awakening. An hour before sunrise his radio switches itself on, pulling him gently from sleep with the graceful strains of Faure or Borodin or Debussy from a classical station in Baltimore; he will rustle, twist about, and after a few minutes manage to sit up and rub his eyes. Then he will walk the length of the trailer to the tiny bathroom, turn on the shower to allow time for the hot water to arrive, relieve himself and shave and brush his teeth in the light of the dim globe overhead. By then the water is steaming and he will luxuriate in the stall for many minutes, feeling the soap pour down his skin and the shampoo run from his hair, until finally he turns off the water and dries and dresses. Then he will make tea and sit at his small table drinking it in the darkness, waiting for the sun to appear over the eastern ridge and the sound of stirring life to reach him. He will open a window to feel the cool breeze slowly fill itself with morning warmth. And after a while, after he has watched the beams of light appear over the grass and heard the dog bark into the valley and the children bound into the front yard to begin their play, the trailer will be filled with yellow light; and Robin will pull his typewriter toward him on the table and glance over the previous day's work before winding a fresh sheet into the machine to begin. By eight-thirty or nine o'clock Mrs. Pierce, a comfortably-built woman in her forties with hair streaked red and silver and a propensity for wearing her husband's baggy overalls, will be digging in the garden behind the house. Mr. Pierce will back his pickup truck out of the driveway and pull away, heading toward what they call "The Factory," which is in fact the headquarters of their produce-shipping business. Soon the boy and the girl will pester their mother for permission to ride their bicycles to a friend's house or into town, and they will disappear down the long road. After that it is quiet again, very nearly as quiet as the moments before dawn; only an occasional car passing by the road or Smithy, their golden retriever, barking in pursuit of a rabbit or cat.

That he is here at all, he realizes, is a miracle of random chance.

He had had absolutely no destination or even direction in mind that night three months before when he had fled the motel parking lot and the weeping voice behind him. All he had known was that he had to get out. Everything had become impossible. He spent two days—or was it three?—on the road in a foggy state, unaware of where he was going or why. He remembers calling her from a gas station phone booth but receiving no answer, only the information from an anonymous desk clerk that Miss Seabright had checked out early this morning, sir. She haunted his dreams for weeks afterward: tears running from her dark eyes as if the eyes themselves were melting away: he was afraid in the first few days that she was following him. But he had not seen her again.

A hard loneliness had swept over him darkly then, especially at night when he involuntarily reached for her familiar form and found next to him only cold sheets: something he occasionally does even now. But now he does not find himself thinking of her much, or when he does, it is in the abstract: only a name, an uncertainly-remembered face and voice hurled into the dark pit of the unreachable past. Lost. Which is, he imagines, a good thing, for when something does trigger his memories of her they fill him with melancholy and old anger. It is not that he hates her; he simply cannot reconstruct in his mind an image of her, a persona, that holds. He remembers aspects only; fragments, glints; like glimpsing someone through a patchy fog, now there, now gone. He had made an effort to contact her a few weeks later, calling Information in New Hampshire and trying to obtain a telephone number. But there were no Seabrights listed in any county he tried. At last he had given up.

He was, he realized at the time, in danger of plunging into a black despair. But one evening he had pulled into this anonymous northern Virginia town—*Ashersburg*, the sign said—and been charmed by its cobblestone sidewalks and wide streets, its old white Colonial houses, its endless miles of grass and hills all around in every direction. He stayed at a bed-and-breakfast inn—there were no standard hotels—and walked the streets the next day, pleased by the quiet and tranquility, the clean wind blowing through the blossoming spring trees, the local accent which was not precisely Southern, but something indefinably different, more flat and nasal in tone. He visited an historic cemetery and felt a sense of awe at the sight of the graves of Confederate soldiers: so many Lees and Hagars and Barristers killed within a year or two of each other, and all for a cause doomed to be dropped into the greasy ashcan of history. He was delighted with the local library, a spacious old two-story house with a bright wiry lady behind the desk, a library which reminded him of years before, of the hissing radiator and Mrs. Klibo.

It was on the second night, talking with Mr. Terg, the owner of the bed-and-breakfast, that he had learned of a job available in town.

"Can you pack fruit into boxes?" Mr. Terg asked.

"Well," Robin answered, "I can load tires into warehouses."

Mr. Terg called his friend Mr. Pierce; told him that he had a guest, a young man from out west (Robin smiled) who might be wanting some temporary work; Mr. Pierce told Mr. Terg to send Mr. Withers to him directly; and within an hour Mr. Withers was hired. Pierce himself was a gruff barrel of a man with crewcut gray hair and skin grainy as wood who smoked a pipe incessantly. But he liked Robin, called him "Rob"—just as everyone else in town soon did; and despite the fact that he had never been called "Rob" in his life, Robin rather enjoyed it. The name was well-suited, he thought, to this strange land of Hanks and Stans and Bills. Upon learning that he had no place to live, Pierce offered the trailer he had, he said, "just sittin' in the yard," and within two days of his arrival Robin found himself with accommodation and employment. The fact surprises him even now. And it had worked out marvelously well: Pierce allowed him to work basically any hours he liked, so Robin would generally go in for a half-day four or five times a week; it was more than enough to pay the minimal rent on the trailer, and he has hardly any other expenses. Mrs. Pierce frequently defrays his food bill by leaving things on his doorstep, and once or twice a week, usually on Sunday, they have him "to table" in their home. It is, he thinks, a perfect arrangement.

And he is quite happy, in a calm and mellow way he has experienced only very rarely in the past. He gets a great deal of work done in the mornings; and he takes a peculiar pleasure in his menial work at the fruit factory, hefting the hard red apples in his hands and deciding into which box, which fate, they will be sent. He only wishes that he could, once and for all and forever, escape the shadows that dart like birds' wings over his consciousness: sudden visions of Heather in her black beret, head tossed back in wild laughter, or her dark eyes close to his own, or the feel of her skin next to his, sudden snatches of her voice striking him at unexpected moments. Troubled dreams. And when he thinks of her too much, a pain in his gut that sends uneasy tremors throughout his whole body: the amoebas again, he thinks, ripping themselves apart, just as with Cape. But the sensation is different too. With Cape it had been a sudden intense longing that burned out quickly like a match. His memories of Heather are more like a flashlight beaming through fog, occasionally bright and blinding, mostly dim and indistinct, but never entirely absent: he does not *think* about her much, not really, but she seems always to be there, hovering, pricking his consciousness unexpectedly. Clearly it had had to end; his mind is settled on that point; there was something about the combination of the two of them that sent an indefinable feeling of doom through him. But then, he realizes, he did not know Heather, not in any real way: she remains like a mirage to him, uncertain, unfocused. He does not know where she is from, knows nothing of the source of her emotional problems, her hysteria and distress and bulimia and sudden paranoias. He knows nothing of her, he thinks, absolutely nothing, and yet he spent more time with her, more intimately, than any other person in his life. How then could she remain a mystery? How could she still be an incomprehensible melange of contradictions and confusions? Why doesn't he grasp anything? Why does every step he takes toward understanding lead only to greater darkness?

 Nor is Heather the only source of anxiety. He looks to the side of his work table, where an unfolded sheet of paper whose contents he has memorized sits. *Robin*, it says, *I will never understand why you do not discuss these things with me. It was with great surprise I learned you were not enrolled in school this semester.* He pictures his father in a pool of light at the kitchen table, achingly scribbling these words in his stilted, clumsy style. *If you were not satisfied with the university you should have come and talked to me about it*. The letter, like all his father's letters, has a limping, unnatural feel to it: of course, he realizes, his father writes them when he is sober, and Robin is not accustomed to listening to the man in that state. The man staggering in with the ridiculous Christmas tree is what he is used to, what he understands; what he knows how to deal with. This man in the letters is a stranger. He flushes with embarrassment every time he looks at the final words, *Love, Your Father.*

Enclosed with the letter, which had arrived a week before, came a postcard from Priscilla, this time from Morocco: Robin had had to look at a map to learn where the place was. *Took a fantastic cruise on the Mediterranean*, she writes, *in a yacht owned by a rich English faggot who took pity on a couple of poor scruffy American gals. We're heading south now. Be a good boy. Kisses from C&K*. Also a letter, long delayed (sent first to his college, then to his father, who had had to hold it until he received Robin's address), from a literary magazine in New York: for a long time he had not been able to understand its contents.

Dear Mr. Withers:

"Alcohol" is excellent. It will be appearing in our Autumn number, coming in August. You'll be sent 2 copies gratis. Enclosed find a check for our standard rate, $25. Many thanks and best of luck.

And indeed, there was a $25 check in the envelope. But for days it had not made any sense to him. It appeared that they had accepted the poem for publication; but could he be sure? He re-read the letter dozens of times, studied the check closely. He felt sure that there was some trick, some subtle catch. And yet he could find none. He took the check to the bank and they cashed it without asking him a thing, handed him two ten-dollar bills and one five and said thank you. But it was somehow not as he thought it would be. He did not know what he had expected. Expressions of ecstasy from the editor? News headlines? Celestial choirs? It seemed rather mundane, really. A simple business letter and small check. Mundane, and less than real. For he continued to live in the little trailer, continued to pack the apples into boxes; nothing changed. Nothing had been printed, he had nothing but this strange, impersonal, dry letter.

He said nothing about it to anyone. He would wait and see.

At times he felt a small thrill course through him, when he pictured the magazine and its serious, stolid print, and thought of his own poem appearing in it as if by magic on one of its pages. But he did not really believe that it would happen. There was the letter sitting on his table, true, but this somehow seemed entirely unconnected to how the stories and the poems actually appeared in the magazine. He felt sure there was something more to it, something no one had told him. It was inconceivable that they could print his poem in this way. And so he waited. Something would happen, he knew, something would ultimately be explained to him, something that had been forgotten would be remembered.

And that, perhaps, is the real answer to all the mysteries—to Heather, his father, writing, everything: that things are forgotten, that they drop into the deep well of the past, into the unyielding darkness, and cannot be returned. And the more things are lost, the more confusion comes to reign; the more the dark well fills, the less substance the present has. He pictures the arms turning in their arcs, swirling like a spinning vortex into which everything drops and falls, all the bits and pieces of shattered glass disappearing into the cavernous jaws of time. If there was a way, he thinks, to halt the arcs in their motion, to close the gaping and voracious mouth, a way to bring the contents of the dark pool to light again, then perhaps he could understand something, see connections and patterns where all now seems random and chaotic. But there is no way. And so the best he can do, he supposes, is drift on in his lazy, thoughtless happiness; to forget about meanings and bridges, to live only in the eternal *now*, breathing and writing and packing apples. Perhaps this is what he must come to accept, he thinks: that there are no answers, no ways out of the darkness.

※

Finally, a few weeks after receiving the mysterious letter and check, a manila envelope arrives: in it are two copies of the journal and a slip offering a discount subscription. Nothing else. As he opens the envelope and examines the journals he thinks that this must be some kind of promotional pitch and doubts that it has any connection to the letter and check. The cover is light tan, and lists the contents of the issue: a glance down the list does not reveal his name, and so the nervous tension drains out of him. Indeed, it is a promotion. He flips through the pages carelessly and for a moment it does not register in his mind that on page seventeen appears a poem called "Alcohol." He reads two other poems first; then, his memory curiously piqued, turns back to the earlier page. Indeed, the bold black print reads "Alcohol," and the lighter, smaller print below the title reads "Robin Withers." And the poem beneath appears to be his poem. How odd, he thinks. He looks back at the cover again. Still he does not see his name. Turns back to page seventeen: "when I come home from somewhere..." Yes, it is his poem, all right. He reads through it once, his heart beating skittishly. Then he reads it again. It is his poem, typeset in the magazine with his name on it. How interesting. It gives him the peculiar, unreal feeling that he had not really written the poem at all, that he has merely read it before somewhere; it is familiar, yes, but certainly not his. How could it be? On the facing page is a poem by a writer whose name he recognizes, who has appeared in other journals. A glance through the journal reveals several known names, and two quite famous ones. Thus it is not possible that it is his poem, and he turns back and reads it again, trying to understand. For all the world it appears to be his; but he knows this is impossible.

Finally he turns back to the cover and stares at it, scanning the list of contents once more. No, his name is not there. But wait: centered at the very bottom are words he had not noticed before: "*And Poetry by Chaney, Dale, Messinger, and Withers.*"

He gasps. It is his name; he flips to the poem; yes, it is his name again. It is his poem! It has been published! His heart thunders in his chest as he sweeps the other copy up from the table, turning to page seventeen quickly to make sure there is no mistake. Yes, it is in this copy also. He cannot believe it. It has been published! He stands, paces the trailer rapidly for minutes, then hurls himself into the chair again and re-reads the page, gazes at his surname on the cover. His name, his title, his poem, all are there in the journal. Suddenly terrified, he searches for any typographical mistakes; sighs with relief when he finds none. It is exactly as he wrote it. And it is *there*, published, permanently printed and bound and finding its way into mailboxes and university libraries all over the country, perhaps the world. One hundred years from now, he thinks, a student will be able to refer to the old indexes and find his name and the title and the issue number and page, and he will be able to go to the Periodicals section and ask for the journal and it will be given to him. Because it is *there*. He must order more copies. He must order five copies, ten, a dozen, and ship them to Priscilla and Koofie and Davy Carp and Gawky Boy and Zero and…Turnham. Yes, and Turnham. And his father. Cape. Mrs. Klibo! They must all read his triumphant arrival on the literary scene, they must all be humbled and awed by his accomplishment. *Print.* He must send copies to his old teachers, Mrs. Balfour-Ritchie and Mrs. Peterson, yes, and to Sammy of Sammy's Used Book Catastrophe, yes, to the whole world, to everyone he has ever known! And to Heather—

He calms at last, the name filtering across his consciousness. Odd, he thinks. In a way it is really Heather's publication. It would never have occurred to him to send out the poem—that had been her idea. He finds himself abruptly wishing she were here, to watch her laugh with delight as she sees the familiar name on the cover and on the page, as she looks up at him with deep pool-like eyes and says, Robin, I'm so proud of you! He wishes she were here. Wishes he could put his arms around her now, bury his face in her, feel her hands roaming over his body...He shakes his head. Ridiculous, of course. It had had to end, of that there could be no doubt. It was over. Still, he wishes he had her address; he would mail her this second copy. He wishes he could speak to her on the phone and tell her the news. But it is impossible; and just as well, he supposes. It is finished forever, the amoebas have been torn asunder and there is no hope of ever bringing them together again.

He sits back in the chair, grinning and staring dazedly at the journal's cover in his hand, flipping over and over again to page seventeen to be sure that the words have not disappeared. But they do not disappear. They are there, he knows. They are there.

13

As the months roll past in a lazy haze the echoes from his old, lost life become increasingly dim and distant. He spends many of his evenings with a local girl, April Ashers, who works with him at the fruit factory. She is seventeen, just out of high school, with long blonde hair burnished with red and a plain, somewhat pretty face with cheeks covered by pink freckles. They had often chatted during break-times in the big drafty warehouse. She is a bright girl and pleasant-enough company. Several nights a week they have dinner at one of the town's few restaurants or go to a movie at the sole cinema; he supposes it could be said that they are dating, though Robin does not think about it much. She is someone to pass time with. He enjoys listening to her Virginia twang and her talk about local people, local events and scandals: her entire frame of reference, he realizes, is local: she has traveled slightly in the nearby states, but has never really been far from home. She is, he supposes, as he was. But she is sweet, finds Robin somewhat exotic for being from the wilds of the west, and they enjoy each other, though it never even occurs to Robin, when he is with her, to kiss her or hold her hand or, in fact, anything. He sometimes wonders about this. Could Heather have derailed him permanently? he asks himself. His sexual desire seems to be zero.

But then, perhaps he has merely gotten smart. His life is peaceful now, pleasant, actually enjoyable: it is the intense emotions, he realizes, the boiling inchoate stews of love and confusion that have been causing him his misery. A quiet life of work, he thinks, and reading, and listening to his little radio; dinners with the Pierces or a movie with April; this is what life should be. No echoes, no dark vortexes. A Tolstoyan simplicity. And he has a right to it, after all. Two decades of fear and darkness and perplexity have earned him the right to a little quiet happiness, it seems to him, far from the nightmare bangings on the wall and cries in the night which are all he has known. He is so very *tired* of being afraid, of jumping away from shadows. Here there are no shadows. Here there is only warm sunlight.

And with April such things are easy. In April, he thinks, there are no darknesses at all. An inveterate baseball fan, she will meet him in town with her Baltimore Orioles cap on her head, her grin shining in the sun, and say in her twanged voice: "Well, Rob, what's the deal?" Often they bicycle around the Virginia countryside, April happily blowing pink gum-bubbles and chatting about this and that. She is a child, of course—Robin is entirely aware of that—but her company is so cheerful, so altogether *pleasant*, that it invariably lifts his spirits. And he must admit that his ego is gratified when she comments on what an adventuresome traveler he is or how she has "never met a real writer before."

Ah, he thinks, if she only knew...But she does not, and will not, for he has no intention of trying to tell her anything of the darkness. She would not understand. And he does not want to wreck their happy friendship: their bicycling, their long walks, eating at local hash-houses together, going to movies. It is all so easy and carefree, very different from his earlier life with the girl with dark pool-like eyes. But he does not like to think about that; prefers it to vanish like everything else into the black jaws of time. He will, he supposes, never understand what happened between them. And perhaps it would pay not to inquire too deeply. Things are so much simpler now; the way he has always hoped they could be. Easy, sunlit, free.

One day, after re-reading some of Terrence Llewelyn's stories once again, he impulsively slips a sheet of paper into his typewriter and taps out a short letter. *Dear Mr. Llewelyn,* he writes, *Please forgive the presumption of a youngster like me writing to you; but I wanted to send you the enclosed, as a token of appreciation for your work and what it has meant to me, most especially your story "The Professor Remembers," which I think is one of the finest examples of the short story to be found anywhere. The enclosed journal represents my first published effort, and I hope it gives you some small fraction of the pleasure your work has given me.* After a few minutes' hesitation he puts the letter and journal into a big envelope, addresses it care of Llewelyn's publisher, and sends it off. He does not suppose he will ever receive an answer, and indeed, weeks pass and nothing arrives. He has nearly forgotten about the letter entirely when, to his amazement, one day he goes to the post office and is handed an envelope whose return address label reads "Terrence Llewelyn" and a street number and a town in Connecticut. His heart races as he gazes at the envelope. In a way it is more thrilling than seeing his first work in print: something in this envelope has been written by the author of "The Professor Remembers" directly to him: to Robin Withers! Personally! He cannot believe it is true; and as he stands outside the post office in the warm August air he hesitates before opening the envelope. It is possible that it is merely a form letter of some sort. Swallowing, he slips the envelope into his shirt pocket and gets into his car. He will not be humiliated in public, if that is what it is. He will go to the trailer and open it there.

Ten minutes later he is in his trailer and his hands tremble as he carefully slips his fingers under the flap of the envelope and pulls it open. Inside it is a single sheet of paper, typewritten on one side.

Dear Mr. Withers,

Sorry it's taken me so long to answer your letter—it followed me to the West Indies and then back again. Anyway, thanks for the kind words—which are most gratifying in these dark days when damn near everything of mine is out of print—and the journal. No doubt about it, "Alcohol" is fine work. I'd be curious to see more of your stuff. Be that as it may, all best wishes to you.

Terry Llewelyn.

The paper shakes in Robin's hand. The sloppy typing, the signature in blue ink: all produced, he realizes, by the man who wrote "The Professor Remembers," that story so perfect in tone, so beautifully wrought, that it had brought tears to Robin's eyes the first time he read it: as it still does. He studies the typeface—a manual typewriter, an old one—and the signature, a nearly-illegible scrawl in blue. Then he searches the words more carefully. "Out of print"? Terrence Llewelyn? It seems unimaginable. And then the words "fine work." Fine! To think that Terrence Llewelyn has read something written by Robin Withers and found it "fine"! And the kicker: "I'd be curious to see more of your stuff." An open invitation, he thinks, to continue—to write more! To write again to Terrence Llewelyn, *the* Terrence Llewelyn! He pictures the man in his mind, the photo from the dust jacket: the incisive eyes, the sharp aristocratic nose; the dramatically wind-swept hair, the sweater casually tossed over his powerful shoulders. He studies the return address, a perfectly normal-sounding street and town in Connecticut; but like Tennessee Williams' house in Key West, he imagines, not really inhabited by him. And yet here it is: a perfectly ordinary piece of paper with typing on it, a totally unexceptional-looking signature in standard blue ink that does not dance or float evanescently from the page.

An hour later, having re-read the letter so many times that he has it memorized, another thought occurs to him. He goes to the refrigerator and opens a soft drink while he thinks about it. This letter, he realizes, is really the result of Heather. If it had not been for Heather goading him into sending out "Alcohol," it would never have been published; without that publication in hand he would never have dared to write to Terrence Llewelyn. The idea fills him with a vague fear: so many roads, he thinks, lead back to Heather: Heather who is no more than a dark ghost to him now. He knows he is being silly; that it is inevitable that the past would affect the present; but he is still uncomfortable with the thought. He would rather, he knows, have attained all this entirely on his own, not in collaboration with someone else; and surely not with Heather. To this day he cannot think of her without growing melancholy or angry. Although she is lost to him, swallowed up by the black jaws of time, her echoes nonetheless return unpleasantly to him even now. He does not want to think about her. He wants to think about his writing and Llewelyn and the Pierces and his friend April and the quiet sweet life he leads here, free from darknesses and catastrophe. But Heather's memory continues to reach out its dark tendrils to him. He had thought he had found the answer with her; the missing piece, the other apple-half of his soul; but he had been wrong. Terribly wrong. He had found nothing with her but more darkness, more confusion.

And he has turned away from the darkness now, he knows. Now he will live in the light.

A knock at his door pulls him from his thoughts.

"Rob?"

He grins and opens the door, looks down at his friend standing there in the sunlight looking up at him. She has on a blue blouse and cut-off jeans and her hair is pulled back in a pony tail. Her head it covered with her baseball cap. She looks, he thinks to himself, so young; so much younger then he himself looks. When he looks in the mirror he sees a man who could easily be nearing thirty. April could be fifteen.

"I thought I told you not to call me that," he says, smiling.

She grins, cocks her head to one side. "Sorry. I forgot. So what's the deal?"

"What's behind your back?"

"Surprise." With her accent it comes out as *suprahz*.

"What?"

"Come out 'n' see."

He grins and steps out into the long grass surrounding the trailer. He notices her ten-speed bicycle leaning against the wall of the house.

"Which hand?" she says.

He points.

She laughs. "Wrong! Choose again."

He points to the other hand.

"Wrong again!"

He laughs. "Now, April..."

"Ha! I don't have anything in my hands." She holds them out, palms open. "See? But I wasn't lying. I *do* have a surprise."

"Which is what?"

"Which is I'm not working today, so we can spend the day together."

"Sounds great to me."

"Unless you're writin' stuff."

"No," he says, thinking of Llewelyn's letter, "I've done all I'm going to do."

"Why don't we have a picnic? You can borrow a bike from the Pierces."

This is what he likes about April, he realizes: her happy impulsiveness. When he makes a decision it is always with suffering and confusion and second thoughts; April just does things. He wonders if it is because she is so young…Then he catches himself, remembering that after all, he is only three years older than she is. And yet, in some way, she is much younger than that. Or, more likely, he is much older. At any rate, there is a difference between them that way, one that he enjoys immensely.

Of course, he remembers, things had been like this with Heather too—in the beginning. But had they? he wonders. Had they really? Or had he, from the very start, sensed a mystery with her, felt a preoccupation and compulsion, known fear?

"Okay, you lousy Baltimore Oriole," he grins, flipping up the bill of her cap, "you've got a deal. Let me put on some short pants."

They sit together in a field of long grass staring up at the cloudless blue sky above them, chatting about this and that, light things, sunshine things. The green hills seem to stretch forever in every direction, and the hush of the wind stretches too, never-endingly, across the hills and fields. As she talks about going to college, her mom and dad, things she wants, he half-listens: his mind drifts across years and miles, pictures slowly and vividly materializing of other fields, other skies, Priscilla standing above him, and the sound of the wind in the grass like a sea; his body next to Cape's in the old van, the wind pushing at it from outside as if to enter but the two of them there together, warm and still; and then April's voice reaches him again, and the past and the present roll peculiarly and pleasantly together, focus and refocus themselves, waft gently through him like the wind in the grass, and he feels alive, vividly alive, not in the strange mystical way he had sometimes felt before but in a quiet way, a subtle and easy way. He looks at April, at her pale eyes sparkling in the sunlight and her plain-pretty face and her freckled cheeks tanned by the summer and her straight shining hair falling over her shoulders. He takes her hand, the fat summer sun rolling slowly across the sky.

14
DROWNING
Chapter Five

A dramatic exit. He'd rather enjoyed it. Still, as he hurries down the street, fists at his sides, he wishes he could have controlled himself; not screwed it all up; Rachel deserved better, she always had, he had no right to say any of the things he'd said, he should have just shut up and taken it and maybe right now she'd be whispering to him in the darkness...He tries to keep the image from materializing in his mind.

The night is warm and clear and the wind has died down. It isn't a bad night for walking at all and soon enough he finds himself back at his car, his dad's car. He stands outside and inhales the clean night air, tries to catch his breath from the long walk, feels his body relax, his fists uncurl. He wonders what he should do. The bar is inviting; he could step in again and chug some more wine. He seems to be coming off his high and he doesn't want that to happen, not yet. He has been having too much fun floating along on the waves. Even this thing with Rachel hadn't seemed too bad, because he had the waves. Now they were calming, settling. But the bar is more crowded now than it was when they left. He could just give it up, he supposes. Go home. But nothing waits for him there but his dad and those awkward, circular conversations and he doesn't think he can face that just now. He could go back to the movie theater and see Dusty; but his mind quickly disposes of that possibility. He could drive back to Rachel's...

He steps into the bar again.

The place is about half-full, noisier than before but not bad. He makes the order at the bar and while he is waiting for the wine he looks around. Men with women. Men in groups. Women in groups. Everyone seems connected with someone else. He sighs. He wouldn't mind a decent conversation just now, like the conversations he used to have with Hewitt on the days he was feeling good and didn't have any terrible agonies to impart. Hewitt was very well-read in literature and philosophy and, much as he hated Hewitt a lot of the time, he'd enjoyed those conversations. But no one here looks ready to have a discussion about Locke or Descartes or existentialism or much of anything else. Just as well, it was mostly crap anyway. Fun to talk about, but crap. He takes the wine and sits on a stool next to the wall.

After a while he notices a big blonde girl get up from her table at the other side of the room where she is sitting with her friends. She heads right for him, smiling; but just before she reaches him she turns to the bartender and orders a drink. He studies her profile in the bar's dim light. Beautiful, no question about that—long lashes, full red lips, honey-blonde hair reaching to the middle of her back; big breasts, big hips. A sort of *sprawling* girl, he thinks. Rachel's smallness, her dark features cross his mind. He swallows more wine.

The girl glances at him and smiles. "Hi."

He opens his mouth to say something in return, but no sound comes out. He covers it by nodding.

She looks back toward the bartender but keeps talking. "I haven't seen you around, have I?"

He suddenly realizes that this girl is going to try to pick him up. There is no doubt about it at all—he doesn't even know how he knows. He has *never* been picked up in a bar before. But he is absolutely certain.

"I haven't been around," he says, a sudden thrill of anticipation running through him—even though, truth to tell, this girl isn't really his type...lovely, yes, but too big, too buxom, too much makeup. Still...

She gets her drink—something colorful and frothy—and looks at him again, smiling. "Anybody sitting here?"

He shakes his head and she sits. She is dressed in a tight cashmere sweater and blue jeans and looks maybe twenty-five. There is a brief silence.

"What's your name?" she asks. "Mine's Clarissa."

"Siegel," he says, trying to smile. "Hi there."

"Hi."

Silence again. The bar seems to be growing louder.

"Where you from?" she asks.

"Here. Santa Barbara. But I've been away for a while."

"Oh." She nods as if he has really told her something.

It goes on like that. Stupid talk. He lies, tells her he's been at college back east. Some description of his dad's house. The discovery they went to the same high school, she two years ahead of him. She tells him where she works, some secretarial thing somewhere. He doesn't really listen. They drift onto movies, always reliable, it seems to him, for stupid talk. She mostly sees comedies and horror films. She asks him if he has seen that new double feature over at the what's-its-name theater. She's talking about the film he and Rachel ran out on. She tells him how great it is.

Siegel pays little attention to the whole conversation, though he knows he appears to. His mind is taken up with wondering what she looks like without the sweater and jeans. But somehow he can't get especially excited about the prospect. They have another drink and he gets nicely back on top of the wave, finds himself smiling and laughing though nothing she says is particularly funny or even intelligent. He supposes this kind of conversation should be tense with ambivalence, unfulfilled sexual energy, but he is perfectly relaxed. Because he really doesn't care. She could walk away right now and he wouldn't be disappointed. Or she could ask him back to her apartment. Either way. Who cares? Riding the wave is what matters.

After a time her outline begins to blur slightly and he eases up. He has to stay on the wave, not tumble into it.

"...So I just told him," she is saying. "I just said, like, *look*, if you keep changing what you want from me, how am I supposed to know what to do, you know? I mean when he tells me to type this letter and then five seconds later he says type these forms and then I'm supposed to do this other thing, I'm like, come on! But he's all, 'Well, you should be able to get it all done.' But I mean..."

She goes on like that, prettily perturbed. He doesn't need to listen to the words, he just keeps himself vaguely aware of the tones, the pauses, so he knows where to insert a "Yeah" or "Uh-huh." God, she loves to talk, no doubt about that. He is tempted to order more wine but he's still a little too high. Has to wait. A few minutes and he'll be in good shape. Meanwhile he wonders what Rachel is doing. He hopes she's crying her heart out, all broken up. Because *he* sure isn't. He's just sitting here with this chick who most guys would think is much better-looking than Rachel and he's talking to her and maybe he'll get to ball her pretty soon. Everything's hunky-dory, by God, couldn't be better.

But he can't keep it up, not even in his own mind. He wishes he could rewind time, reverse it, go back to him and Dusty and Rachel at the theater. Or even earlier, in the bar. A little less wine. A little less shitheadedness on his part. He could have been wrapped around her in her big bed right now, falling asleep in her arms, if he hadn't screwed it all up. He thinks of calling her: he could talk, ask her to forgive him, maybe he could drive out there again. Shit, she was only a mile away. One lousy mile. Why did he even give a damn about that Saul, anyway? She'd chucked him. Why should he care if the guy's dick poked around in Rachel's territory a few times? What difference did it make, really? Why should he *care?* But he does. He can't help it. It drives him crazy—O happy word choice! He smiles grimly to himself. His intellect tells him that he doesn't own her, she's not his property, since when did he care about all this hypocritical middle-class morality, anyway? Yet the whole thing fills him with illogical, inchoate rage.

He suddenly notices the blonde bimbo beside him laughing, apparently at something he said. He wonders what it might have been. Then he notices that she is closer to him now, leaning toward him, her face only a couple of feet from his own. Her breath is boozy and he can smell a strong perfume on her. The combination is not, surprisingly, entirely unpleasant. Happy, drunk, big-boobed women, he thinks. God love 'em.

"Did you hear me?" she says quietly, huskily.

"Hm?"

"I said, do you want to talk more at my place? My apartment?"

Well, this is it, he realizes. He's being propositioned. He had hoped the moment would be more thrilling than it is. But he does feel the tingling in his groin again, a mild flush running through his body. Incredibly, a woman is tossing herself at him—on his first night back yet. He looks at the stranger next to him, wonders what peculiar diseases might be hidden within that hot figure. Doesn't matter. If it's okay with her, it's okay with him; he doesn't care, it's irrelevant, all he wants is her body, relaxation, relief, he doesn't care about anything else. And Rachel: let her go to Hell. He'd be damned if he was going to sit around frustrated when this big blonde was ready, willing, and able.

He smiles at the bimbo and finishes his wine. "Sounds good to me," he says, grins. They leave the bar together.

Her friends drove her to the bar, she tells him, so they take his car back to her apartment. It's down in a shoddy neighborhood near the freeway: faded buildings, cracked streets, cars on blocks. As they pull up he can hear a lot of noise, stereos and loud talk, coming from the apartments.

"Don't they ever go to bed?" she says. "My neighbors, I mean. Sorry. The place is kind of loud."

He shrugs. "Doesn't matter."

These, actually, are very nearly the first words they've spoken since getting in his car. He wonders if all pickups are like this—cheery, false conversations in public and awkward, embarrassed silence in private. They get out of the car and Siegel breathes the night air which is growing slowly cooler. He can draw breath easily just now. She leads him past a long line of apartments until finally they ascend some stairs and she brings out a key.

"This is it," she says, opening the door. "Looks like my roommate's here."

The inside of the apartment isn't bad; a lot of hanging plants liven it up. It's quite warm and there is the smell of baking.

"Louie?" Clarissa says.

Suddenly a short girl with glasses pops her head out from the kitchen. She is perhaps nineteen. "Hi there! Makin' cookies."

"Why?" she asks.

"I don't know!" She ducks back into the kitchen again while Clarissa and Siegel stand in the living room where the little TV is running an old horror film he recognizes, *Night of the Living Dead*. "It was just like, why not? I was watchin' this weird old movie on

TV and I just had a cookie attack. It was terrible. I couldn't control myself!"

Siegel smiles. He likes this Louie already. But then Clarissa turns to him—she is his height, even a shade taller—and smiles and says, "Well, do you want a drink? Or do you…" She leaves it unfinished.

"You gotta try some!" Louie says, coming into the room with a plate of cookies. She has on a big apron that is covered with flour and raw dough. There is even flour on her glasses. She pushes the glasses up on her face and peers at him. "Oh, hi," she says, smiling. "Sorry, I didn't see you there. You have a cookie too."

He does. Clarissa makes the introductions and they stand around looking at each other for a minute.

"Did you want that drink?" Clarissa asks him.

"I don't know. Sure." He is somewhat embarrassed to be discussing this right in front of her roommate, but he supposes there isn't much to do but trudge onward. "Why don't we drink them in the…you know—?"

"Okay," she says casually, and goes into the kitchen while Louie sets herself in front of the TV again.

"Have you ever seen this movie?" Louie asks him, eyes glued to the screen

"Uh-huh."

"Is it weird or what? Except the zombies aren't weird enough. I mean, some of the people I know are pretty much like these guys." She laughs at her own joke and hears Clarissa laugh in the kitchen. He smiles. He finds himself almost wanting to watch the movie with this funny little girl rather than disappear into the bedroom with Blondie. But just then she comes back with two glasses of wine, hands one to him, and says: "We're going to bed now, Louie. Keep it down, okay?"

"Huh?" She barely glances away from the screen. "Oh, okay. Have fun."

Clarissa tousles the girl's hair affectionately and then says to Siegel, "C'mon."

She leads him down the hall. They pass one closed door and then she opens the door at the end. There is light in the room from the outside lamp. He sees more plants, some rock 'n' roll posters, an odd-sized bed somewhere between a single and a double.

"Well, this is it," she says quietly, closing the door behind them, They look at each other briefly in the darkness and then she leans forward and kisses him. He feels his groin swell with anticipation. He can hear the movie out in the front room and Louie rustling in the kitchen. He realizes vaguely that the outside lamp is faulty, buzzing and flickering irregularly. They move to the bed and lie down, putting their drinks on the night stand and touching each other softly. Her long hair spills onto him and he touches it; thinks fleetingly of Rachel and her dark wings. He has trouble concentrating on the girl beside him. How darkly ironic, he thinks. In the institution he would have killed for a woman like this. Now that he has her, he doesn't care much one way or the other.

After a time she gets on top of him, her legs inside his, and presses her pelvis between his legs rhythmically.

"Good?" she whispers.

"Mm-hm."

She begins taking off her clothes, slowly and sensuously. She pulls off the sweater and shakes her hair free and then smiles and unbuttons her blouse. She strips it off and then unclasps the bra. He watches as her big breasts spill out and she leans forward for him to kiss and caress them. Finally she stands and pulls off her pants, quite gracefully—that particular action had been a running joke with him and Rachel, always

The Unspoken

an awkward, off-balance thing—and then her panties. She lies down next to him.

"Now you," she says.

He starts with his shirt. She watches him, looking interested and perhaps a bit amused. As he begins removing his pants she kisses him, wetly and deeply, and he feels her hand moving down to him as the pants and shorts come off simultaneously. She stops kissing him long enough to look and says, "You're nice."

He smiles. "I bet you say that to all the guys."

"Uh-uh," she says, missing the joke. "You really are nice."

She is an expert, no question about that. And utterly unashamed. With Rachel, now, sex had been a dark thing, done under the covers; they had a lot of fun, but on both their parts there had been a feeling of...what? Shame? Rachel would touch him, even take him in her mouth, but immediately after finishing she would move away and there would be no more talk about it. Same with him going down on her. It was fun with a touch of danger, a tingle of the forbidden about it. Here there is no such feeling. All seems easy, free: she leans down and kisses him casually, plays with him. He is floating just right on the waves and is totally relaxed and quite enjoying himself. She sucks on him expertly until he is nearly ready to explode and then stops suddenly.

"Not yet," she smiles coyly. "Me first."

He grins. "You're the boss."

He goes down on her, not unhappily. She is utterly without reserve, sighing, moaning, her pelvis undulating. He begins to worry that her roommate will overhear. Then it occurs to him that it's obviously no secret what's going on anyway; he wonders how two of them can be so open with each other, so honest. In his house sex had been something you didn't talk about whatsoever. Totally off-limits. He had never even gotten a birds-and-bees lecture—he'd had to pick up information, such as it was, from briefly confiscated copies of *Playboy* he found in his dad's bureau drawer. When he was fifteen he'd felt he must have been the most ignorant horny young man ever to walk the earth. He remembers that as the time he began having the fantasy dialogues with his dad. A habit he has kept up ever since. In his fantasy dialogues he would tell his dad everything, all that he was feeling, all that scared him, his worries about being a boy, his fear of girls' strange bodies, his worry about his mom, her sickness, and his simultaneous terror and euphoria at the darkness, the vast, cold darkness that even then he felt coming toward him, rushing at him.

But of course none of this was ever actually spoken. He remembers the silence between him and his dad as being like that of the tomb. Icy. Dead. But it was never really dead, he realizes now; no, it was always charged with life, with tension, and still is. But silence is still silence, he supposes. Alive or dead. What difference did it make? He begins to feel depressed somehow…As his mind shifts back to the present he smiles wryly to himself. Here he has a beautiful blonde's crotch in his face and he's depressed.

Just what do you *want?* he hears Rachel asking, some forgotten time ago.

But these thoughts are drowned out as Clarissa begins to come. She is positively volcanic about it, her pelvis bouncing, moans that are nearly screams, pulling at his hair. He is not sure if it delights or annoys him. At any rate, it is over soon enough, and she lies there panting, sweat glistening on her bare body, and Siegel strokes her legs absently, kisses them.

"That was nice," she says finally, catching her breath. "Thank you."

He crawls up next to her and he can smell the light odor of sweat under her arms. He finds himself liking her more than he had before. She doesn't seem quite so empty-headed, lying there next to him. He sips his wine and then holds the glass to her lips.

"Hope I didn't wear you out," she says.

He shakes his head. "I'm still ready." And he is, he realizes, glancing down at himself.

Just then there is a knock at the door.

"What?" Clarissa says.

"Sorry, Clare," Louie says, "I left my Algebra book in there. Can I get it?"

She pulls a sheet over them casually. "Sure, c'mon in."

The girl in the flour-covered apron scurries in and goes to the desk, glancing at them casually. "I didn't mean to interrupt anything. But you guys were quiet."

"No problem," Clarissa says. "We were taking a break."

"I'll be out of your face in two seconds," she says, digging through a pile of papers.

"What happened to your horror movie?" Siegel asks, trying to sound casual.

"It ended. Freaky movie. There's another one on now but I've got to get my Algebra done."

"You go to the university?" he asks.

"Oh, here it is," she says. Then she looks back at him. "Yeah. Geology major."

"Siegel's just back from college," Clarissa offers. "Where did you say you went?"

"University of Maryland."

"Really?" Louie asks. "What major?"

"English."

She sighs. "My *worst* subject." Then she goes to the door. "Well, carry on, you guys." She shuts it behind her.

They lie next to each other for a time without speaking. Finally, wordlessly, Clarissa reaches down to him and he feels his body surge, flow. She pulls on him gently, draws him inside her. She spreads her legs wide and bends her knees and holds onto his bottom as he thrusts himself inside her. At first he feels that he will explode almost instantly; but then he levels off.

"Make sure to pull out, okay?" she whispers. "I don't have any protection."

He nods. But he can't concentrate. He doesn't like being this close to her face, she is too real to him, he likes her too much. He likes the whole house, likes her roommate. He suddenly realizes that somehow it was his contempt for her that had turned him on. The feeling of just using someone, no hassles, no Rachelian dramas, just pure *use* of a dumb bimbo, like using a toilet. But now he likes her and it makes him feel dirty, wanting to use her. It's no good. He leans close and kisses her deeply, shuts his eyes. Fantasizes about Rachel. But that's no good either: this girl doesn't feel right, doesn't smell right or hold him right, and anyway, when he tries to visualize Rachel under him it only lasts a moment and then turns into her shouting at him. He switches the fantasy to an old standby, a sequence in a favorite porno film. Listens to the moans and the sighs on the soundtrack, watches the guy thrusting himself into her. But tonight it doesn't work. It isn't getting him anywhere. Clarissa is real, too real, he can't escape her.

"What's wrong?" she asks.

He shakes his head, embarrassed. He rolls onto his side.

"Am I doing something wrong?" She touches his nipple.

"No...no, you're fine. You're great. I'm sorry. Maybe I drank too much."

"Do you want to just lay here and talk? Try again later?"

He nods. "Yeah. That's a good idea." He sighs. Very sensitive, considerate, helpful. Exactly what he doesn't need in order to feel contempt for her. They lie in silence for a time. She seems not impatient or unhappy; she strokes him softly, his chest and shoulders, kisses him gently. His mind wanders: he thinks of his dad, Dusty. His mom flits across his mind and is gone again.

"You and your roommate," he says quietly, only half-listening to himself, "sure have an open relationship."

She smiles. "I hope you didn't mind. I didn't even really think."

The Unspoken

"I didn't mind." He didn't; in fact, it was rather sexy. But his mind moves to Rachel again. He thinks about how badly he'd wanted to hurt her, before. He'd controlled himself, thank God. But oh, he'd wanted to hurt her. Physically. Not just mentally, that was too easy. His mind was too quick for her and he could always come up with the worst sorts of things to say to her. No. Physically he'd wanted to hurt her. For betraying him, running out. For goddamn Saul. One part of him—a deep, secret vein of himself—told him that she'd failed the test, it didn't matter how long she'd hung in, how much she'd endured, she hadn't lasted long enough, she'd failed him. Everybody had always failed him. And he felt the rage rising in him again, rage against them, all of them, rage against himself for his deplorable self-pity, for even having such thoughts. But he couldn't help it, they surfaced like corpses in an ocean. And that's what they were, after all. He understood that. Corpses. Dead weight. Useless baggage. But they surfaced anyway, uncontrollable as the zombies in Louie's movie.

"...Louie and me are real, like, close," Clarissa is saying to him. "We've known each other for a long time. I really love her, I mean as a friend. She's helped me through a lot. I had a sort of... breakdown, I guess you'd call it. A while ago. She really helped me."

He looks at her. "You did? A breakdown?"

"Well, sort of," she says, her head on his chest. "It was like, you know, I just couldn't face things anymore. I was scared all the time. Do you know what I mean? I was just so scared that I couldn't...function, I don't know, do anything. I know it must sound weird to you."

"No, no it doesn't."

She keeps talking. Much of it is familiar; much of it he remembers himself, the same sensations, similar feelings. And he thinks *no, no, no,* for every second he is liking her more, forgiving her silly teenage dialect and brainless chatter, finding she isn't a stupid bimbo at all, really; and he can feel no contempt for her at all, only empathy, sympathy, and he feels the sex rushing away from him, the impossibility of it. He thinks of Rachel again. Only when he thinks of Rachel do the contempt and hatred rise in him. He knows it's irrational. But there it is: her image, the desire to smash the image, hurt it, mangle it.

"We sleep together sometimes," she is saying. "Louie and me. We're not, like, lesbians or anything. I mean we've played around with it. But neither of us are really into it. We just sleep together. Hold each other. We trust each other." She pauses. "It's funny, I've never told anybody that. Nobody else knows about it."

"I can keep a secret," he says.

"I know you can. Maybe that's why I'm telling you. It's funny. I really love her...You know? Except it isn't a sex thing. I love her every way except that way, I love her as much as I've ever loved any of my boyfriends. In a way it's better because there's no sex thing. That just screws everything up. You know?"

"I know."

"Sometimes I think we've worked out the perfect deal. Louie and me. We're like soul mates. When either of us gets horny we call somebody. We've both got, like, casual boyfriends. They don't really know what's going on. And then sometimes I just go out and pick somebody up...like I did you." She smiles and kisses his chest. "Just for sex. And because there's no sex thing between Louie and me there's no jealous stuff. We never have to be jealous. Jealousy is what ruins everything. Without a sex thing it just isn't there."

"Sounds good," he says lamely. Actually it sounds better than that. But utterly unworkable, for him. For him and Rachel. He feels his body tense as he thinks about her again. Rachel. The rage, the anger, the desire to hurt. They fall silent and his mind races around: images of Rachel and that faceless Other, may he

The Unspoken

fry forever in the Stygian darkness…Her smart-ass know-it-all face when she asked him if he really was writing, when she challenged him about it. God damn her. Then he realizes that he is stiff again, Clarissa is stroking him.

"Want to try again?" she whispers.

But he knows what will happen. Why bother?

"Want to try a different position?" she offers. "Maybe…?" She flips her hand over gracefully.

He feels his face flush. He nods.

She gets on her hands and knees and spreads her legs and he puts himself into her. At last: he knows it as soon as he goes in. He feels himself swelling and growing harder. She is disembodied now, an ass sticking up in the air, a face hidden, just a female body for him to use, to do with whatever he likes, and Rachel's image floats into his mind again as he begins to slam it into her, hard, feels his pelvis slap against her bottom. He shoves it in as deep as he can get it. Faster, deeper. He is making her pay now. He will hurt her. He will make her scream in pain. And he is loving it, hurting Rachel. It feels wonderful, to slam it inside her, to violate her precious body, to just bang away with no thought to her or anything. To just screw the living daylights out of her. The fantasy quavers; he hears Clarissa's voice saying, "Ease up a little, honey, okay?" But it becomes Rachel's voice; and he'll be damned if he'll ease up for *her*, she'll take it and like it the way she took it from Saul baby. At last he feels the spasm beginning to hit him and in some distant part of himself he remembers, and as the wave slams into him he pulls out and squirts the stuff onto her, loving it, shooting it onto her ass, her back, it's glorious, like pissing on her, at last she's getting what she deserves, at last!

Then the wave subsides.

He looks at Clarissa and suddenly wants to cry shamefully. He does not meet her eyes as she looks back at him and smiles.

"Jeez, you really *go*, don't you?"

"I'm sorry," he mutters. "Did I hurt you? I'm sorry."

"You didn't hurt me. Don't worry about it." She reaches for some tissues from the night stand and hands them to him. "Now clean me off so I can roll over, okay?"

He feels the shame and embarrassment rise in him again as he runs the tissue over her wet skin. The grossness of the male. But worse than that, what he'd done to her: how he'd treated her: of course she didn't know, couldn't know, that he hadn't been thinking of her at all, but Rachel, and that he'd been hurting her inside his mind; nonetheless, he is ashamed of himself for it, for using her that way. Even if she doesn't know.

They lie beside each other in the dim room and Siegel watches the flickering light on the ceiling. It's all tied together, he supposes. Sex as pleasure, sex as pain: for anyone from a childhood like his, where things weren't talked about, nothing ever surfaced, wasn't it always destined to be a hopeless muddle? He remembers the one time he saw his mom naked, when he happened to come into the bathroom once when he was young, seven or eight. She was in the bathtub and he remembers uttering a shocked gasp and covering his eyes.

It's all right, she said. C'mere.

He had slowly uncovered his eyes and gone to her. The bathroom smelled like steam and the amber liquid in the glass at the side of the tub. Her hair was coming down in moist dark curls and he remembers being astonished at her breasts, at the size of the nipples, but more than that, at the plain fact that she was *different* from him. He remembers staring at that place between her legs, unable to take his eyes away, the hot bathroom steam rising between them. Whatever had happened after that, he cannot recall. All he remembers is the shock of her body, that and the embarrassment, later, at the fact that he was not like her. The feeling he had failed her.

"Siegel?" she whispers to him. Then he realizes the voice is Clarissa's.

"Hm."

"Were you asleep?"

"Just dozing."

She touches his cheek. "It's been nice," she says. "It really has."

"Well...maybe we can do it again." The idea is a good one, it seems to him. He likes this apartment. He likes Louie. Clarissa is smashing in bed, no question. He would like to come back here. Come back and smell cookies baking and watch old movies on TV and help Louie with her Algebra and English and stroke Clarissa's gorgeous body and maybe Louie's too her in the flickering darkness. He would like to stay here. To never leave.

She looks down. "I don't know...I don't like to lead guys on, you know? I like to tell the truth."

"What do you mean?"

"Well...I like you a lot, Siegel. That's the problem. I like you too much."

"Hm?"

"Don't you see?" she says, looking at him, her face close to his. "Me and Louie. It would ruin everything if I got involved with somebody I really like."

He smiles humorlessly. "You don't want me to come back because you like me?"

She grins sadly, shrugs, her bare shoulders moon-pale in the dimness. "Something like that, I guess."

He sighs. "Do you want me to go?"

"Well, you don't have to go right now. Do you want some more?" She touches him.

"No. No, I guess not."

"You're welcome to take a shower." She runs her fingers through his hair. "I'm going to go check on Louie, okay?"

He nods. She pecks him on the cheek and gets up, stretches, and goes out of the room, not bothering to close the door.

He lies there for a time, not thinking about anything. Then he gets up and scoops up his clothes and finds his way to the bathroom. He considers a shower but then decides to forget it, simply splashing cold water on his face instead. He puts on his clothes. Then he sits on the edge of the bathtub and puts his head between his legs. He listens to them laughing and talking in the front room. He feels a thick sourness clogging his throat. His body quivers. He clenches his eyes shut and tries not to move.

15

April sits across from him in the hot cafe, perspiration glistening on her skin. She grins at him under the bill of her baseball cap as she adjusts a strap on her tank top. An overhead fan lazily moves the air about.

"You look sleepy," he says.

"Mm, I am. It's the heat."

"But you should be used to it, shouldn't you?"

"This year's worse," she says. "Here it is the beginning of September and it's still baking."

"Ah, well. You're an Ashers. The place is named after you. You'll tough it out."

"We could go to my house. Nice and air-conditioned."

He sips at his cola. "I don't know," he says. "I always feel like your parents are interviewing me."

She smiles. "They are. I mean, they do that with every guy I bring home."

He looks at her and narrows his eyes in mock-seriousness. "Oh? Have there been that many?"

She flicks her fingers at him. "You know what I mean. "Nothin' *serious*. High school boys." Robin listens to her accent: *high* comes out as *hah*; *boys* as *boahs*.

He nods, smiling. He does enjoy her company, no doubt about that; but he is increasingly aware, every time he sees her bright eyes and pink-speckled cheeks, of her youth—her emotional youth—and of the vast gulf of experience that exists between them. It is a curious phenomenon. In Wind Point, and later at college, he had always felt himself hopelessly naive about everything; here it is different. And not just with April. The people of the town treat him as an exotic figure from "out west," a young man who in Mr. Pierce's words "knows words we never heard of here," and, strangest and most exhilarating of all, "a writer." It is a source of continual astonishment to him when he is introduced to someone and that word is used to describe him. A *writer*. Not a fruit packer, not a college boy, not Mr. Withers's son, but a *writer*. He supposes he is one, in truth: he has the poem in the journal to prove it, the novel-in-progress: and yet something about it makes him feel like a charlatan. He is not a *real* writer. He does not float in the celestial clouds conversing with the ghosts of Dickens and Flaubert. Nothing, in fact, has changed at all in the time since the poem appeared and he made the jump, at least technically, from "unreal" to "real." He has experienced no tremendous and sudden understandings of the universe; still feels overburdened with questions, roaming in darkness when he should, being "real," be in bright sunlight. It is rather like the sensation he had had after being in Marylou Kirk's bedroom in high school. Technically, yes, the definition had now changed. But in reality it hadn't. He still feels like an ignorant oaf in regards to most everything.

But when he is with April, this sweet little girl from a small town who has seen and experienced nearly nothing, and when he talks to the people of the town who treat him as someone different, alien and special and interesting, he wonders just what he means when he thinks of "experience." *They* seem to think he is experienced. Why, then, does he still feel like an awkward idiot?

"Anyway," Robin says, "let's not go to your house. We can go to the trailer. It's not air-conditioned but at least it's in the shade." He smiles. "I think we could survive the afternoon."

"Whatever," she says, brushing her hair back from her shoulder. "You can read me more of your story."

"I keep telling you, you're not going to like this story. Especially the part I just finished."

"Why?" It comes out as *wah*.

"Well, it's kind of sexy, for one thing."

She laughs. "You think I don't like sex?"

"I don't know. I've never tried to have sex with you."

She laughs again. "Rob—Ro*bin*—I may be from a small little town, but they teach us about the birds and the bees here too. I'm not that stupid."

"I didn't say you were stupid, April."

"I'm kidding. It's just that you big-time world travelers sometimes get a little…I dunno. *Protective*, I guess that's the word."

"I don't mean to be," he says.

"I didn't say I minded. It's just the way it is."

"Well," he says, "are you finished? This place is too sweaty for me."

They spend the hot afternoon out in the grass, under the shade of the big tree in the front yard, playing with the two Pierce children and talking. They play touch football, squirt the boy and the girl with the water hose, play keep away with April's cap; later they sit under the tree while Robin answers the burning questions of the two children about what California is like. Innocence and experience, he thinks: and which is which?

"God, this is lazy living," he says to April after the children have gone. He stares up at the sky with his hands behind his head.

The Unspoken

"I'm sure my daddy can find you some work around the house, if you want to work all that bad."

He laughs. "I'm too frail and weak for these macho guys around here. I couldn't keep up."

A wisp of hair falls across her eyes. "You're not supposed to, anyway. You're an outsider. You've probably noticed, this is a pretty closed-up little place."

He nods. "How long has your family lived here?"

"Since the seventeen-hundreds."

"Jesus. And they've always been here?"

"There's always been Ashers here, yeah. Some of them move away. But it's a big family."

"Yeah. Still, that must be nice in a way. Big family, always somebody to talk to. Always someplace to *go.*"

She smiles down at him. "It's a little boring sometimes. Everybody always knows everything you do."

"Well, at least somebody *cares* about what you do."

She shrugs, picks cloverleaf from the grass and deposits it on his chest. "I'd like to do what you did," she says. "Just pack and go, sometime. See some things. I'd go with somebody, though, not alone like you did."

"Mm." He has never spoken of Heather to her; or to anyone else, for that matter. He prefers to leave the subject in darkness.

He thinks of the Ashers family, motionless since the seventeen-hundreds. The children grew up, became men and women, had children of their own, grew old, died, and their remains are all to be found in the same cemetery, line upon line of them, Josephs and Elizabeths and Marys and Fredericks stretching across the smooth grass. It is an amazing thought, that kind of perpetual existence. He thinks of his father as a young man, the stories he had told Robin: the orphaned wanderings, the hitchhiking and cat houses, poverty, Korea, aimlessness, anonymousness. For that is what it must have been. To have not known one's father, to have been abandoned by one's mother, left to grow up among people one did not know in a place one had never seen and could never belong to: perhaps it was no wonder things had happened as they did. How could a person even hope to have a stable family, a sense of direction, calm and peace, when his own life was no more than roaming, searching for those same things? Wandering blindly in the darkness? Odd, he thinks. He has never thought of it quite this way; that he and his father, in their vastly different fashions, have faced, perhaps, much the same dilemmas. And so perhaps were destined to be what they were. Perhaps it took the long line of family graves, the sense of solidity and permanence and perpetual renewal that they gave, to bring any kind of sanity to one's life: the sense of being anything but a randomly floating bit of space-dust in the void.

As the sun tumbles low in the sky they sit at the little table in Robin's trailer and Robin reads her a short section from *Drowning*. He doesn't enjoy doing this, but April claims to be interested; the problem is the darkness of the manuscript, the unrelenting bleakness of the story. He is sometimes surprised at directions it has taken, directions which seem only to drive it into further darknesses. At times Siegel and Rachel and Dusty seem to have lives of their own, refusing to obey his commands; sometimes he wonders if they won't suddenly appear in the room with him. The thing is so close to him, so inextricably bound to him, that he feels uncomfortable reading any of it to anybody else. Rather as if someone were to rip open his soul and set it on a display stand for public view. But he reads, and they talk lightly about it. The shadows stretch outside and the light within the trailer grows to a deep warm fruity color.

Finally April stands. "I guess I better go. Drive me?"

Robin looks at her. "Don't go yet."

"It's gonna get dark in a little while." *While* becomes *wahl*.

"Stay here, why don't you?"

The Unspoken

"And do what?"

He grins, feeling suddenly light and giddy. His heart is skipping quickly. He moves between April and the door, puts his hands on her waist, and leans forward to kiss her. She emits a small sound of surprise; then her hands touch his arms softly.

They look at each other in the deep light.

"That was nice," April says quietly.

"Why don't you stay here for a while?" he whispers, his face close to hers.

"Robin..."

He kisses her again. Somewhere across the dark gulfs of his mind he wonders where all this has suddenly come from. He does not think he had been considering it, even moments before. He, Robin Withers, is attempting a seduction! Even as he kisses her he cannot believe it. He is excited, but feels no fear; she is a sweet girl, pretty, he likes her bubble-gum breath and her soft voice, he likes everything about her.

"Robin, I better not."

"Why?"

"I just better not..."

He kisses her again. Her arms move around his waist. He presses her against the door of the bathroom as her arms move up along his back and he breathes in her odor of grass and earth, outdoor things, sunshine things.

"Robin, I better not..."

Their breaths come fast together and he reaches under her tank top and strokes her skin. She makes another small sound and begins to pull away, but he holds her fast and kisses her. Soon her hands are moving in his hair. As he kisses her he pulls her toward the bed at the other end of the trailer. They sit on it together, kissing deeply, and Robin pushes her gently down into the sheets. Her baseball cap tumbles to the floor. His body is rushing, pounding. Dimly he remembers his problem; realizes suddenly that there will be no problem here. He can feel it as surely as his heartbeat.

"Robin, I..."

"Shh."

He pulls at her tank top, at her bra, kisses her big pink-nippled breasts, buries himself in her as she pulls away his shirt and runs her fingers across his back. He can taste the dried salt on her skin as it melts onto his tongue. He feels her lips on his neck, his shoulders. He reaches toward her cut-off jeans and unbuttons them, pulls the zipper, tugs them down, is shocked and amazed by her long and wild pubic hair the color of burnished copper. Her hand roams between his legs. She unbuttons his pants and reaches her hand inside. His pulse is pounding wildly. Then they are naked together and pushing against each other, Robin's hands running over her hot skin, April's breath quick and shuddering, and he sees her legs open for him and he rolls on top of her, kissing her over and over, realizing suddenly that he is inside her, feeling the warm slippery tunnel seeming to engulf his entire being, wrap around him tightly and totally, hearing their bodies slap together, breathing in her sweet quick breath and gazing into her open eyes as her mouth opens and emits a twisted, impassioned sound and her hands press against his buttocks, pulling him in again and again, faster and faster, plunging him deeper and deeper into her slick secret passage, feeling his entire body melting into it, rhythmically dissolving, feeling her legs wrap around him and watching her breasts bounce with his thrusts and the sweat running under her arms, and the sights and sounds and sensations begin to blur, to swirl as he feels himself arching and convulsing and suddenly releasing, bursting and gushing and streaming into her, exploding deep up inside her body, at last, he thinks, at last, and he feels everything flowing from him, out of him, endlessly....

A minute later their breaths still come quickly and Robin can feel the sweat on her skin.

"I've never done that before," she says.

He glances at her. "You're not a virgin…?"

She smiles. "Come together, I mean. At the same time."

"Did we?"

She laughs, still out of breath. *"I did."*

"Did you?"

"Yeah. And I *know* you did."

"Jesus," he says, his body shaking slightly. "I've never…never *done* it like that before." He knows what he is thinking of: the incredible all-around feel of it, the melting together, the complete bonding. He says: "I mean, usually there's a little foreplay or something…"

April laughs. "I liked it."

"Except…"

"What?"

"I hope you're going to tell me you use some kind of birth control."

"I take the pill," she says, her breath beginning to slow. "You don't think I'm *that* stupid, do you?"

"I'm sorry for not asking," he says. "That was terrible of me. I just sort of lost—"

She laughs again.

"—Lost control. Oh my God, that felt good."

They remain together, tangled in the white sheets, as the light in the trailer dims.

"I better go soon," April says. "My parents'll be wondering what happened to me."

"Mm." He pushes his body next to hers, pulls her to him. "Just stay here," he mutters. He does not want her ever to leave; they will just lie there, he thinks, forever. "Here," he says, reaching to the floor for her cap. He slips it over her head. "Put this on.

There. That's exactly the way I want you to dress from now on. Just a baseball cap and nothing else."

She giggles. After a moment she says, "Robin?"

"Mmmm…"

"You don't think—" she hesitates—"I mean, you don't think I'm bad, do you?"

He glances up at her hazily. "What?"

"I mean, for…this. Doing this."

He laughs. "Why would I think that?"

"I dunno. Some guys would."

"What do you mean? Afraid you'll get a 'reputation'?"

"Don't laugh. It can happen in a little town like this."

"Mm." Across his mind flutters a girl he knew in grade school, Lisa Robinson, a little girl with carrot-colored hair who had disappeared from classes abruptly and was never seen again. Thirteen, she had been.

"Yeah, I suppose it can," he says.

"I've only been with one guy before."

"You don't have to tell me that, April. It doesn't matter."

"It's true. Just a high school boy I used to go out with. That's when I started taking birth control. There hasn't been anybody since."

"Okay."

"I just wanted you to know. So that you don't think I'm…"

"April, stop worrying." He kisses her. "I think you're perfect. Just the way you are."

His mind flits over other, earlier scenes like this: Cape: Heather: the quiet pillow talk afterwards: he wonders what she would think if she knew that what had just happened was a historic, first-ever-in-the-history-of-the-world event. But he cannot tell her; she would never believe him, anyway. It would cast a shadow of doubt between them that does not exist now. There are many things he cannot tell her. Certainly Cape must remain in darkness. Even Heather, were he to say anything, he could discuss only in severely edited form; April is too young, these things would hurt her, and the gulf between reality and expression is there always, perpetually limiting his ability to say anything of what he means to say. And so he remains silent.

And here, in this warm and fading light of late afternoon, it does not make much difference. He pulls her close to him again and breathes the grassy air coming in through the open window. He thinks of his novel, the poem in the journal, his newest letter to Llewelyn. But mostly he thinks of the warm breathing softness beside him, and the ease with which she has solved everything for him, all the problems, all the darknesses. It is all so simple here. What had once seemed eternally impossible all just falls smoothly into place now like well-oiled gears in perfect synchronization. As night seeps slowly into the trailer he smiles, knowing that the other, more sinister darknesses are all far away, lost in his new, bright sunlights.

16

As summer gradually gives way to autumn, as the dogwood trees flush red and begin their silent seasonal rain onto the lawns and streets and autos, Robin exchanges letters with Terrence Llewelyn. Each envelope he receives with the familiar address label and postmark causes a thrill of anticipation to course through him and he will rip it open eagerly. Llewelyn is alternately encouraging to Robin and despairing of himself. For every *You have a real talent, keep it up*, there is a *This whole game of being an artiste is really only for the desperate or stupid. I should never have taken it up*. The letters are filled with advice: *You should probably go back to college—at least it will give you a captive audience, and some teachers to work with*. Or: *Forget all the faddish crapola, whether it's minimalism or whatever's current at the moment. Do your own thing. "To thine own self be true"—Polonius. Of course he was an idiot, and Hamlet did him in good. But he had a point*. The tone of the letters surprises and delights him: to think that the author of the elegant, elegiac short stories uses words like "crapola" is wonderful. He can hardly believe that Llewelyn would bother with a nobody like Robin Withers; but the fact that he does fills Robin with enormous, boundless confidence that spills over beyond his writing to affect everything else.

Still, he finds his emotions becoming oddly mixed about his life. Pleasure and happiness he has, in abundance: April comes by nearly every day, and they merrily exhaust each other. Frequently they go for bicycle rides through the paths in the hills, have picnics. But they do not really talk about much, he has noticed. They actually do not have anything in common. She speaks of local people, local things, talks vaguely of "going off to school"; Robin thinks only of the lovely ghosts, of his novel, of Llewelyn and the life that seems to beckon to him. When he thinks of April, what he thinks of is her naked body tangled in his bed sheets, her smell, the heat inside her thighs. He does not like this fact, and realizes that it was not always this way. Before they had brought sex into it, it seems to him, he had spent time with her because he genuinely liked her, was interested in how her mind worked, her limited frames of reference; he felt energized around her bouncy youth. But something had changed after going to bed with her. She became vastly more important to him, yes, but for a far more limited reason. She became body parts, parts for which he felt an insatiable hunger: breasts, vagina, a mouth.

He is becoming, it occurs to him, like Siegel.

He does not want it to be like this, and he makes efforts to become interested in what she says, to the point of even taking her to a baseball game all the way in Baltimore; but when he is with her, unless they are in bed together, his mind wanders. He can hardly believe this to be true, but it is. He can hardly believe that, having a happy, healthy girl of his very own for the first time in his life, he does not dote on her, cherish her, seek to spend every minute with her; and when he thinks of this he compares his actions toward April with his behavior around Heather. They are two totally different worlds. April is a sweet child; Heather was something else, something indefinable and strange, a person who seemed to be an extension of himself in some way, an aspect of him, a reflection. It had been a dark feeling when he was with Heather, whirling into something unknown, something new, a melding-together unlike the simple bonding he and April share in bed: something infinite, unending. It had frightened him, that limitlessness. He had pulled back from it. And yet surely, he thinks, there must be more to experience than this trailer and packing fruit and April Ashers. He enjoys all of it: but Ashersburg is not where the lovely ghosts reside. He realizes this all too well, and grimly. There is a stultifying quality here, a mundaneness, that is inescapable: perhaps April is right after all, wanting to escape the destiny of the hundred graves lined up in symmetrical rows across the green grass, stretching on and on, all the same, every Ashers landing in the same final destination forever and ever. And it is an illusion, after all, this kind of grave-filled permanence; it is not permanence at all, merely its appearance. Did it matter if graves with one's surname were to be found in a grassy valley somewhere? Did it make a difference? If Robin stumbled one day upon a valley filled with granite-carved stones reading *Withers*, would it answer any of the questions, light any of the darknesses, help him toward the lovely ghosts? No. It would solve nothing. The individual still had to find his own way, discover his own path, uncover his own meanings. Grass-covered graves could not help.

He begins to feel strangely as if he is merely treading water here, floating in a kind of stasis. He does not want to feel this way: he has, he supposes, most everything he has been trying to attain: the shadows have given way to bright sunlight: and yet as the weeks wear on his dissatisfaction continues to grow and multiply. He begins to produce less and less each day on his novel; more and more time he wastes in sleeping, daydreaming, wondering about the source of his unhappiness. The simple pleasure of manual labor at the fruit factory gives way to a desultory numbness. The people of the town, whom he had once found so invigoratingly different and charming, begin to appear small-minded and predictable. Even April begins to wear on him. He grows tired of talking about her little concerns, her little worries, when all he can really think of is those things he cannot express, the mute connection to the lovely ghosts, the new lives and intensities and meanings. And yet he feels guilty too. Surely he cannot become a Siegel, cannot be interested in April only as Siegel is interested in Clarissa. No. But there is that element: and he knows it is wrong of him, that she is a nice girl and a vulnerable one, that he must remain concerned with her as something besides a bed-partner; but it is difficult. The things April talks about are not really very interesting. Her parents, her friends, horses and dogs, baseball, when she will have enough money to buy a car: kid's things, he thinks, and that is why, although the difference in their ages is slight, he thinks of her as a child. Her concerns are childish. How could he ever express anything of the lovely ghosts to her, Mahler's silken thread to infinity, Llewelyn's resonant, rapturous echoes? He had given her "The Professor Remembers" to read once. Her reaction: "It's okay, I guess. Kinda boring. I don't really like, you know, *stories.*"

No, he realizes, the two of them do not really inhabit the same universe. But is that true? Why then can they share each other so wonderfully well in bed? Why can he release himself with her in a way he had never been able to accomplish before? Is it possible that the mind and the body are entirely separate, then? No connection? That the mental planes he wants to find he must discover entirely alone, unaided, and that sex is only an instantaneous flash of the purely physical? It cannot be. The mental life, he thinks, cannot be all there is of life. The physical must somehow have its place; and the spiritual also. But he cannot balance them; they never come together into anything coherent, anything unified and comprehensible; they remain disjointed, disconnected. One distracts from another, throwing off the balance. It is maddening. With Heather, his mental life had been amply filled: she had liked the same things, lived in the same passions, understood the same realities. But physically that final opening, giving, merging had been impossible. With April it is the reverse. And God? he wonders. Only a sporadic, unpredictable presence, now here, now gone, eternally indefinable and void. None of the theories explained it; not the messages he had heard years before in the churches, not Nietzsche; they had, perhaps, glints of it, tiny chutes of the rainbow light flashing off the spinning gem, but the reality of it remained hidden and uncatchable. And perhaps it will always be that way, he thinks. Perhaps, like Siegel, he will simply continue wandering in the darkness, no connections, no answers, only endless confusion.

But there must be something else! he thinks. Another solution, a different way! The way of Mahler, of Dostoevsky, of Shakespeare! They had found the way, he thinks, but had left only the dazzling fruits of their revelation; no road map, no indication of how they got there. And without that he is lost. He cannot find it himself. He has not the strength, the drive, the genius. He is only a pitiful pygmy to them, a shrunken shadow to their enormous spirits traversing the earth and sky like giants. He can see them, hear them. He can see the bursts of diamond-light in the sky and hear the song of the earth as they stride across it. But that is all. He cannot reach them.

"Rob?"

"Hm." He opens his eyes to look at her. The light pours through the trees brokenly, illuminating her face in bits and pieces. She is a beautiful child, he thinks. Not in a way which announces itself, but there nonetheless: the simple smoothness of her skin, the clearness of her eyes, her clean glowing hair: she seems so fresh, so untouched. She smells of grass and soil. When she speaks, her voice seems never to have known terror or shame.

"Can I ask you a question?"

He touches her arm and the soft blue cotton of her blouse. "Go ahead."

She looks at him and the light catches her eyes, makes them glisten brightly. She smiles.

"Do you love me?"

He stares at her sunlit arm, at the light blonde hair covering it in a glowing sheen. He knows what she wants him to say. But he also knows how meaningless it would be, how pointless, to say one word; how mean and hurtful it would be to say another. In truth, he does not know what he feels; he is an ever-shifting quicksand of emotion and memory and feeling, and how can it ever be reduced to such an absurdity, a handful of words?

"Why are you asking me that, sweetheart?"

She looks down and the glistening eyes vanish under softly-lashed eyelids.

"Because I think I'm in love with you," she says.

"Me?" he says, trying to make light. "Why would you be in love with an old scumbum like me?"

She smiles. "I dunno."

"We don't even have anything in common."

"I think we do."

"We don't know each other."

"You know me. I'm trying to know you. I know you well enough to know that you're not like anybody around here. You're not like anybody I've ever met."

"Oh, we pretentious would-be artists are a dime a dozen."

She glances at him, then away again; something in her expression is sad. "Please don't make jokes, Robin," she says.

The Unspoken

After a moment he says, "Sorry."

He looks at her. Her expression is far away, her crystal eyes in some other place. And here again, he thinks, is that mysterious phrase, those unfathomable three words attempting to bridge the endless gulfs. He feels suddenly guilty. For what has April been to him? A pleasant shadow; unreal, unconsidered in any serious way. A little girl in a little town. Suddenly he despises himself, looking at her distant eyes: feels shame. He had thought he was being impulsive when he had started up sexually with her. Now he knows he was being callous, selfish; interested in her only—yes, this is it—because she was not threatening, not his equal. The psychology of it comes at him in a rush: no wonder he could not function with Heather, or with a prostitute, or even with the ancient ghost Marylou Kirk. He was afraid of them. With April he felt no fear; could easily direct and dominate any conversation, any activity; but he had not bothered to consider her feelings for even an instant. And so their bonding, their closeness that he felt when they were in bed together, was entirely an illusion. She was not real to him; he did not really care about her; there was no melding, no real enveloping of each other besides the momentary burst and release. All else was false. The breaking-through to the new level, the greater intensity, was impossible.

April looks away, down the deep valley spotted with wildflowers.

"You don't," she says, "do you?"

"What?"

"Love me."

He cannot answer. He sits unmoving in the grass.

After a moment she says quietly, "I guess you think that I just do...*that* for everybody."

"April, no."

She looks at him sharply. "Don't you?"

"I..."

"I don't think it matters to you," she says. "The feelings, I mean. I guess you think you can just jump on top of a girl and..."

"April, no, I swear to God, if you knew what—"

"...And just go bam-bam-bam and walk away."

"Have I walked away? I'm right here."

"You're not here. You're with your books and your writing and whatever. You're never with me." She looks at him, her eyes brightly shining in the light. "I want us to be together."

"I don't understand what you mean."

She takes his hand and studies his palm. "I want you to love me," she says. "And you don't. I know you don't."

"April, stop it."

"You don't understand. A girl can't just do it over and over with a guy and not have feelings about it. About *him*."

"April, I *do* have feelings about it. *And* about you."

She drops his hand into the grass.

"You have pretend feelings," she says.

He cannot speak: feels suddenly as if someone had ripped out his heart, studied it with searing accuracy, found it wanting and thrown it in the trash. He suddenly wants to apologize to her, to everyone, to every person who has ever lived for everything that has ever happened in the world.

But he cannot speak. He feels only mute grief. After a while April stands and brushes the grass off her jeans and walks to the edge of the valley and looks down it and does not move for a long time, except to stroke her hips slowly with her open palms.

17

The letter could not quite be construed as an invitation, but it was certainly a second cousin to one. *Since you say you'll be traveling,* Llewelyn had written, *look me up if you find yourself in my little corner of Paradise.* Robin's pulse had raced as he read the lines and re-read them. He pictured the Llewelyn photograph on the back of *The Professor Remembers and Other Stories,* the black hair slicked-back, the sharp, vivid features that observed and understood everything; the big cashmere sweater over his shoulders, the books lined up behind him in unalphabetical splendor—Trollope leaning against Katherine Mansfield, Virginia Woolf rubbing shoulders with Kafka and Fitzgerald. He had wanted to respond immediately, the instant he received the letter; but he forced himself to wait. Over-eagerness, he thought, was the mark of the gawking amateur. He had had to tear up five different responses to the letter, none of which caught the exact tone he sought: cool appreciation combined with a sensitive—but not pandering—deference. At last he had finished a response that pleased him; he left it sitting on a shelf for two weeks to let it mellow, then did a final revision and sent it off. He told Llewelyn that as a matter of fact he had been hoping to make the trip to the university there to look into their English program (which was a bald-faced lie), as it would be easy to get there from Ashersburg on the train. Was the train near Mr. Llewelyn's home? (He knew it was; he had studied a map and train schedule at the local library.) And could Mr. Llewelyn, if he was sure it wasn't too much bother, suggest a day and time? They had confirmed the arrangement in subsequent notes to each other.

And that is how, on this cool, airy morning with gray clouds ringing the horizon, Robin finds himself nervously clutching a shoulder bag borrowed from April which contains some money and his copy of *The Professor Remembers.* He cannot believe that this is about to happen; it is unimaginable. Llewelyn is one of the gods, one of the giants majestically striding the earth, taller than the tallest redwood, vibrant and supernal: it is impossible that he could actually *meet* him. And yet he has the letters, the amazingly ordinary pieces of paper with typing on them that Llewelyn has sent; the perfectly unexceptional signatures and address labels. Robin can feel his pulse pounding inside his head as the train slowly begins to squeal to a stop, as he realizes that what he is seeing outside is the Connecticut town named on the address labels, and that Llewelyn lives here in this town, he *lives* here and buys his groceries here and goes to the post office here and has his car serviced here. Or so it would seem....

But as he disembarks, stumbling off the steps in the press of the morning crowd, he knows it is not true. He had been searching the faces outside as the train pulled up; but there had been no Llewelyn, no princely-looking man with dramatically swept-back hair and a luxurious cashmere sweater tossed casually over his shoulders. And as he moves his eyes over the many bodies rushing this way and that across the platform, shouting at each other over the whistling and hissing of the train, he feels despair combine with a curious relief. It is just as well, he knows; he would only have made a fool of himself in the company of such a man; would only have been a clumsy gnome trailing in the wake of his supple golden light. He looks around the crowd dully for several minutes, thinking that it is possible Llewelyn is late, or is having trouble finding him, but the chances of such things are remote. Llewelyn is not here. Llewelyn never had any intention of being here. It had probably not even been Llewelyn who had written those letters, but some under-under secretary. Llewelyn has never heard of him. Llewelyn is preoccupied in the heavens, somewhere above the clouds conversing with the ghosts of Joyce and Shakespeare. Llewelyn cannot lower himself to such dull oafs as Robin Withers.

"Robin Withers?"

He turns at the sound of the voice: loud but raspy, emphysemic, full of harsh air. A short pudgy man with a cigar in his mouth is standing before him. He has on a baggy, ill-fitting sweatshirt and his hair is pale and colorless, hanging in loose strands over his ears and eyes. His skin is mottled and yellow like old paper.

"Yes?"

The man grins through the cigar and extends his large, meaty hand, shouting over the din: "I think you're looking for me!"

"Oh." Robin shakes the hand. "Terrence Llewelyn sent you?"

"I'm Terry Llewelyn!"

Robin's hand freezes for an instant as he stares at the stooped, diminutive figure before him. Someone is playing a joke. This is not the man of the dark ocean-wave of hair, the beautifully casual sweater over the shoulders. Of course, Robin realizes, that photo was taken some time ago; but he had assumed that the only difference might be a few strands of silver weaving gracefully through the majestic black. This vision before him is something completely different. Unlike the old photograph, sharp, crystalline, the small man standing before him seems soft and unfocused, his outline ragged, his eyes blurred; and yet, in the instant he stares bewildered at this little man who calls himself Llewelyn, he begins to see how it could be. If time had swooped down like a vampire on him, sucked away the color and life, if gravity had pulled ever more insistently at his features, drawing them down toward the earth and death, if his body, in fighting the process, had been diverted from keeping his frame slender and elegant and allowed it to soften and expand, to grow and molder like a compost pile, if all these things had happened, then this could be Terrence Llewelyn.

"Well, it's great to see you!" Robin says heartily and too loudly even for the noisy platform. "I hope it wasn't too much bother for you to get here!"

"Can't hear a word you're saying!" Llewelyn shouts back at him. "Let's get out of this place!"

Robin nods vigorously and follows Llewelyn's rather bearish figure as it pushes through the crowd. In a few minutes they are inside Llewelyn's car, an old battered Volkswagon beetle which emits belches of blue smoke each time it starts to move.

"Glad you could make it here," Llewelyn says. He leans forward in his seat, peering through the windshield. His face is pensive and annoyed as his eyes dart around the road. "I don't get many visitors, out here."

"I would think you'd have lots," Robin says, uneasy with the aged specter beside him.

"Nah, that was all back in the old days. Nobody knows who I am now."

"Well," Robin says, trying to calm himself and sound easy and natural, "'The Professor Remembers' is still a required text in a lot of English classes. That's where I first read your work."

"That's too bad," the man says, his eyes moving suspiciously. "Being a required text is a lot of crapola. It's like being stuffed and put in a museum. 'And here is *Great Art,*'" he says in a voice like a museum guide's. "'Do not touch. Do not think. *Admire.*'"

"Well, it keeps your work being read—"

"By who, though? A lot of know-nothing college kids."

Robin smiles, glancing at him. "Like me?"

"Well you seem a little livelier than most of them." He grins through his cigar.

"I thought you said in one of your letters that it was a good idea to go back to college, though."

Llewelyn frowns. "Did I say that? Well, maybe. I guess it's good from a writer's point of view. Gives you an audience, and somebody to evaluate your stuff who, I suppose, knows their ass from a hole in the ground." He pauses, moving the cigar in his mouth. "But for Christ's sake don't go to college to *learn* anything. Just use it for what you can get out of it and then get out."

Eventually they arrive at a rather run-down little white clapboard house at the end of a street filled with such houses. The grass in front is overgrown and weed-infested and there are big splotches of grease in the driveway.

"This used to be a nice neighborhood," Llewelyn says as he pulls the vehicle into the driveway. "Then something happened. I don't know what it was. Maybe the fact that *I* moved in!" He laughs suddenly, a throaty, hoarse laugh emanating from somewhere deep down in his lungs. "Careful of the dog turds," he says, stepping out.

Inside the house is a dark shambles. Dirty, heavy curtains keep all but the dimmest light from entering the sepulchral main room, which is furnished with tattered chairs and a lumpy-looking sofa. Books lay in great collapsing stacks all over the tables, the chairs, the shelves, the floor; one coffee table, he notices, has no legs at all, but rather is supported by four stacks of hardcovers. Bric-a-brac of every description is everywhere. Record albums. Dirty ashtrays. Bits of clothing. A vacuum cleaner sprawled in a corner. Soiled blankets in heaps on the floor.

"Sit down!" Llewelyn commands, pulling one of the curtains open slightly and displaying a backyard which is similarly abandoned-looking: patchy brown grass, weeds, large spots of clumpy earth and piles of wood. He opens the sliding glass door and a huge black dog suddenly bounds inside, barking.

"Hey! Cut it out!" The dog leaps delightedly at Llewelyn, whose cigar tumbles from his mouth onto the floor. The dog immediately takes it up, shakes it violently as if it were a fresh kill, and shreds it all over the carpet.

Llewelyn glances at Robin. "Domestic bliss," he says.

Robin smiles uncomfortably.

His host drops himself into the easy chair at the other side of the room and rummages around on the table nearby. Finally he produces a fresh cigar and shoves it into his mouth, not lighting it. "That goddamn dog is always eating them," he says. "Damndest thing I've ever seen. Jumps up onto me and pulls them right out of my mouth sometimes. I can't control it. Even Sher can't."

"Sher?" Robin asks.

"Sherrie," he says. "She lives here with me. Hey, Sher!" he shouts raspily. After a moment an indistinct voice comes to them from another part of the house. "Come out here, why don't you! We've got company!" Llewelyn stares woefully at the dog eating the cigar, shaking his head. "Sher is my assistant," he says. "Every aging idiot needs one. Something to drink?"

"A Coke would be fine. Whatever you have."

"Sher, bring some Coke in here when you come!"

Robin hears the voice, which seems to have drawn nearer: "Okee-doke..."

"This house," Llewelyn mutters, glancing around himself. "This is all Sherrie's fault, you know, not mine. I wouldn't have a dog like this. Something smaller for me, something proud, like a bull terrier. A clean little critter that doesn't leave turds in the yard so big you've got to bring a dump truck in to clean them out." He shakes his head again, looking vaguely at the opposite wall. "I hope you don't think you're going to find any peace when you reach your old age. That's what kids always think, but it's a bunch of crapola. You don't find any wisdom, either. Eliot knew that. It's in 'Four Quartets.' I knew Eliot, a little. Polite guy. Had a sense of humor. Couldn't stand anybody thinking of him as a barbaric American, though."

Robin's attention is suddenly super-wired; he breathes in every word Llewelyn says. This, he thinks, is what he has come for; but as soon as the subject appears it vanishes again.

"The problem with old men," Llewelyn says off-handedly, as if merely thinking to himself, "and I'm not *that* old, I'm only sixty-three, but I'm old enough to know, is that they become like kids again around women. That's why you always see these things in the newspapers about old men humiliating themselves around girls. They lose their minds, can't think straight. And that's like being a kid, like being in your twenties again. Somehow when you hit middle age all that calms down a little. Not totally, but a little. But when you're very young, and then again when you're old, it's all you can think about. I guess it's because those are the two times in a man's life when he really has to prove something. To himself. When he's young he has to prove that he has it. When he's old he has to prove he hasn't lost it." He laughs suddenly. "And both times he's wrong. A young man has it but doesn't know how to use it. An old man knows how to use it but he's lost it."

Robin smiles. "That reminds me a little of something in that story of yours, 'A Daily Dilemma,' when you have Archibald—"

"*Ahhh*, my little princess!" Llewelyn breaks in suddenly, looking toward the doorway. Robin turns slightly. A woman is standing there with two bottles of Coke in her hands. She is tall, with a full, rather sprawling figure and a frizzy shock of red hair which looks slept upon. She is wearing a sheer nightdress through which Robin can see the dark shapes of her nipples. Her feet are bare. She cannot be more than twenty years old.

"Hiya," she says sleepily, glancing at both of them and stepping over to Robin to hand him a bottle.

"Robin, this is the love of my long life, Sherrie. Sherrie, this is Robin Withers. He and I have been pen-pals of late."

"Mm. That's nice." The girl smiles at Robin through half-closed eyes. She turns to Llewelyn and holds out the second bottle. "Did you want this?"

"Maybe you'd better spike it a little for me, baby."

"Mm-kay." She moves blowsily to a dark corner of the room where, Robin notices for the first time, there is a small, high counter with bottles of liquor lined up on it. "Cut it out, Pee-Pee," she says to the dog as it tries to push its nose between her legs.

"Pee-Pee." Llewelyn looks at Robin dryly. "Is that any name for a massive beast like that? I ask you."

"I don't know," Robin says, swallowing Coke and feeling his heart beat. "I'm not an expert on dog names."

"I am. We had tons of them, growing up. Alexanders and Samuels and Johnsons and Maxwells. All very aristocratic-sounding. *Pee-Pee* is a poodle's name."

"It's a good name," Sherrie mumbles, pouring the Coke into a glass and picking up one of the bottles. "It's Vietnamese...or something."

"Of course, dearest," Llewelyn says, winking toward Robin. "Its name is purest music, wondrous to the ear."

The girl swallows some of the mixture she has prepared, then replenishes the glass and turns to hand it to Llewelyn. "It's too early in the day to be poetic, Lew."

"I have to be, precious," Llewelyn grins, taking the glass. "My young disciple here expects it."

She sits on the arm of the chair and drops her arm over Llewelyn's shoulders. "What's a disciple?"

"An understudy, baby. A student."

"Oh." She smiles hazily toward Robin. "Like me."

"That's right, little one." He pats her hand, then swallows some of the Coke mixture and puts the cigar in his mouth again. "I'm teaching Sherrie here all about life. Literature. Music. Love. The whole nine yards. She's my little Frankenstein monster."

"Lew taught me everything I know," she says.

Robin looks at the two of them in the sagging easy chair.

"And what do you know?" he asks her, a thin smile on his lips.

Her eyes roll around the room and she pushes some of the matted red hair out of her face.

"I don't know," she says.

"You should know that I'm sick, Robin," Llewelyn says as he sits down on top of his desk in the study. "Deadly sick. Arthritis. Cirrhosis. Cancer of the lung, pancreas, gonads, asshole, anywhere you can think of."

Robin studies him through the slatted light beaming in through the half-closed Venetian blinds. Images pop into his mind of years ago, when he was very young, sitting in a rather similar room with his Uncle Jasper: the room cluttered, stacks of things falling over onto each other, and dim light casting shadows like bars across the walls.

"I'm—I'm sorry to hear that, Mr. Llewelyn," Robin says lamely, unable to think of anything else.

"Please. 'Lew' is fine. Anyway, here it is." He opens his arms in a gesture of grand display. "Asylum Heights, I call this room. Want to know why?"

Robin nods and Llewelyn gestures for him to follow him to the window. When they are standing there together, Llewelyn pries open a slit between the blinds. Robin looks through: past the low fence there is nothing but open field until, perhaps half a mile in the distance, he can see a large white rectangular building surrounded by trees and fences.

"That's the local madhouse," Llewelyn chuckles.

"You're kidding."

"Scout's honor. I didn't know that when I bought this house, but it was a comforting fact to learn. So I call this place Asylum Heights now. Where all lost souls find themselves, sooner or later. So anyway, when I finally snap, they won't have to carry me far."

Robin stares at the bone-colored building, tiny in the distance. He thinks he can see figures moving about on the lawn, but he cannot be sure.

"Anyway." Llewelyn turns from the window and Robin can hear his breathing, wheezy and whistly. "Other than that, this is a pretty standard workroom, I'd say. Not that I do much work." He moves back to the desk and sits on it; Robin sits in a hard-backed chair in the middle of the room.

"Are you working on something now?" Robin asks.

"Always," Llewelyn says. "But it's crap. All my work is crap now. That's the same thing I told you before. I know how to use it, but I've lost it."

"Come on," Robin says. "You've written some of the best—really the *best*—stories I've ever read, so many of them…"

"All years ago, though. All that's gone now." He shrugs. "I hit early and faded fast. A few of the first stories are still around, but they're going too. 'The Professor Remembers' is about the only one that still gets read these days. And I wrote that when I was twenty-five."

"It's a beautiful story, though," Robin says seriously. "Really beautiful. It's one of my all-time favorites."

"Well, thanks. That's nice to hear." He swallows more of his drink. "Every now and then I still get letters about that story. Always from young people like you. I think I know why it is, too. It's because it's a young person's view of what it's like to be old, and to young people it sounds right. It's not, though. That story is fucked-up."

Robin sits forward. "Mr. Llewelyn—Lew—you're being too hard on that story. Really. I can't—I can't even *tell* you what it's meant to me."

Llewelyn shrugs. "Well, maybe. Who knows? My judgment is all shot to hell. I can't think straight anymore."

Robin glances around the room. A huge Rothko print covers one wall: two rectangular pulses of red floating in a sea of darkness. His eyes move to the desk again, where a small glass paperweight rests on a stack of papers: and he remembers, like a vivid film suddenly projected onto the screen of his mind, Uncle Jasper giving him the cherry blossom paperweight, tossing it casually into his small hands and telling him to give it to his first mad, all-encompassing love, Sonya, who later had him to her house where they played checkers together in her bedroom, their knees touching under the table while Robin's heart smashed against his chest so hard he thought it might burst out entirely, flutter away like a lark, and later still, the two of them in the back of her parents' dark car, not looking at each other but their hands coming together, and the wetness in her palm, the soft warmth of it: it was all he wanted in the world, he thought then, to hold that damp little palm forever, back in a time before there were things like pain and terror and shame…He tries to fight a heavy melancholy he feels coming over him.

"I'll tell you something else," Llewelyn says, pushing up the sleeves of his dirty sweatshirt to expose hairy gray arms. His eyes, dull and colorless, seem to sag down his face like a bloodhound's. "You know as much now as you're ever going to know."

Robin shakes his head. "That's a depressing thought."

"It always is, to young people. They always seem to think they're going to *learn* things as they grow old." He chuckles and drinks from his glass. "Oh, you can read. Travel. Meditate. Think. But none of that really *teaches* you anything…Agh!" he cries suddenly, glaring at the glass in his hand. "This is all I need, to be drinking on top of my ulcers. I quit drinking for a while but then I went back to it. Anyway, if you want to know my opinion, it's this: after we leave puberty we never learn a single goddamn thing. We already know everything there is to know. All there is after that is trying to find a pattern, a plan, a scheme for dealing with what we know—" he searches for a phrase—"and for accepting what we'll never know. That's it. End of worldly wisdom."

Robin smiles, looks down at the floor. "But artists create their best works when they're older—"

"Do they?" Llewelyn says. "Tell it to Keats. Shelley. Mozart. Chris Marlowe. Older people have just had more time to reflect, that's all. More time to think. So they can come up with more novel approaches to the problem. But they don't *know* anything, they've just had a longer time to think about what they *don't* know."

"That's a kind of wisdom, though, isn't it?"

"Maybe. It could also be a crock of crapola." The telephone, hidden somewhere among the stacks of papers and books, jangles suddenly. "Pardon me, Robin," Llewelyn says, reaching behind himself and picking up the receiver.

Robin looks away and listens to the conversation. Llewelyn is talking to an editor, or an agent. He is complaining about "the lousy goddamn percentage," the "puny advance." Such talk makes Robin uncomfortable, though he knows that this is it: the real world of books: aggressive telephone conversations, negotiations, deals. He finds the idea frightening. Llewelyn talks for quite some time on the phone, but the only subject seems to be money; never do any of the familiar words come up which Robin knows, not "truth" or "art" or "perception" or "feeling." He feels depression coming over him in thick clouds. This is not the world he had sought—a gruff, opinionated old man spouting homilies, his red-haired bimbo-companion; a world of sourness, darkness, complaints about money and dogs. He had thought he would find something else here, a new level, a shining and vibrant place: but what he sees is exactly like any other house, any other people, any other life. There is no difference. The man on the book jacket, he thinks, does not exist anymore—if he ever had. Llewelyn is a man like other men.

He checks his watch: he has been here nearly two hours. It feels like two days. He shifts in his seat uneasily. Finally the red-haired woman walks past and stops in the doorway.

"Sometimes he's on the phone for a long time," she says to him in a hushed tone.

"Maybe I should go?"

"No, Lew wouldn't like that. Come into the kitchen."

He follows the negligee-clad figure through the dark hall and into a kitchen strewn with dirty plates, pans, pots, bread crumbs, hard dog food spilled across the counter. Robin sits on a stool at the kitchen counter.

"Something to drink?" she asks.

"No. No, thanks."

"Mm. Well, I'll have something." She rinses a glass at the sink and then takes a bottle from the cabinet and pours. Robin finds himself wondering if this woman ever gets dressed; it is nearly noon.

"It's nice that you've come to visit Lew," she says, her voice slurred and her eyes looking toward him but focusing somewhere else. "He's real lonesome. I do what I can but he's still lonesome. He doesn't have many friends."

"I would think he'd have lots of friends," Robin says tightly. "He's a great writer."

"That's what people say," she sighs, gesturing vaguely with the glass toward a stack of books on the table. "I've read a couple of them. They're...I don't know. Descriptions of what trees look like and stuff. Nothing *happens*."

He looks at the floor. "Some people think that's what makes him so great. His stories, I mean. At least some of them."

"Maybe. I don't know. I guess I don't get it."

He looks at her. The sun comes in through the kitchen curtain dully, shining on her like unpolished brass. Her skin is pale and her negligee rumpled.

"Can I ask you a question?" Robin says.

"Sure."

"How old are you?"

She smiles indistinctly. "Nineteen."

"You're younger than I am."

She shrugs, looking off into space. "Lew and I take care of each other," she says. "Our age doesn't matter."

Robin glances away. "I didn't say it should."

"Mm. He *is* an old man, though...Sometimes that makes it hard..."

"How long have you known him?"

"A year, maybe. I'm not sure."

"Does he have any family?"

She giggles sleepily. "Besides me? Not that I know of."

Robin frowns and stares at the floor.

"Where are my partners in crime?" Llewelyn suddenly bellows from his study. Robin and the red-haired girl glance at each other. Llewelyn comes out then, stumbling over a shirt in the hallway. "Goddamn this place...shit all over the floor...Ah, there you are!" He grins as he comes up to them and takes the drink from the girl's hand. "Robin," he says, swallowing, "I'm afraid I'm going to have to cut our interview a little short. I've got to make some phone calls to these liars and shysters who call themselves my publishers. They're like children, you know. They try to steal whatever they can from you and you have to slap them back, tell them to stop it. Then they'll behave, for a while." He laughs hoarsely, looking at Robin's face. "You'd better get used to it, kiddo," he says. "You'll be dealing with them soon enough. Honey," he says, looking toward the girl, "put some clothes on, why don't you, so you can drive Robin here to the station." He looks at Robin again. "You have to get to the university anyway, right?"

"Oh. Yes, right," Robin says, looking away as the girl saunters into one of the back rooms.

"It's easy to get there from here. Only a half an hour on the train. You might meet a teacher there name Radley. Derrick Radley. I know him well."

"Friend of yours?"

"I hate his guts. If you see him, shit on him." Llewelyn bursts into hoarse laughter again.

Robin smiles. "Well, if I do, I'll make sure to tell him it's a gift from you."

"Oh, sure. I'll take full credit. That son of a bitch wrote an article about me in this little review they have at the college there. It was *not entirely positive,*" he spits in a sarcastic tone. "Smart-ass jerk. I'll never understand people like that." He swallows again.

"I mean, he could have gone after somebody important. But instead he takes a sitting duck like me. Most of my books aren't even in *print* now. But I guess there's enough left over of my so-called 'early reputation' that there's still a few people out there who want to skewer me. It'll happen to you too, you know. Especially if you make it too early, like I did. They hate you then. They never forgive you for it. So when you get older and fade, when you're lying there in your grave but still conscious, they stand over you and laugh and kick dirt in your face. And there's nothing you can do about it because, like I told you earlier—you just don't have it anymore."

Robin looks at Llewelyn's face, profiled in the brass light. He can hear sprinkles of rain popping on the roof. "Lew," he says, "look, I don't know about any of that, but I can tell you that you've been extremely kind and helpful to me. I can hardly tell you what it's meant to me."

"Ah, well. That's one thing I can do, anyway."

"Lew, look—" He pulls his shoulder bag close to him and brings out his copy of *The Professor Remembers and Other Stories*. "Would you mind scribbling in this?"

"Huh." Llewelyn takes the book in his hand, turns it over and looks at the photo on the rear panel. He scoffs. "I haven't seen this in a long time. My first one, you know. Look at that prissy bastard on the back." He takes a pen from the counter and opens the book to the flyleaf.

For Robin, he writes. *Who'll make it. from Lew*. He hands the book back to Robin. "There you go," he says. "Best I can do, under the circumstances."

Robin smiles at the small man. "Thanks, Lew. But I'm not convinced that I'll 'make' much of anything."

Llewelyn shrugs and pushes a cigar into his mouth. "That's because you're trying too hard. Relax. You're just a kid. Don't try for it all at once."

"I don't feel like a kid."

Llewelyn grins. "Wait'll you get to be my age. Then see what you think of that statement."

"But I thought," Robin says, looking at the floor, "that when I got to be your age I'd *know* something. That I'd have arrived somewhere."

The man shakes his head. "Nobody ever arrives anywhere," he says. "They just keep moving. Like sharks in the water. And that's a bit of worldly wisdom you can take to the bank."

The girl comes into the kitchen again, having slipped a pink dress over herself. "Okay," she says, "I guess I'm ready, if you wanna go." She pushes her feet into a pair of sandals sitting on the floor. The weird combination of the pink material and her red hair make her look, Robin thinks, like some kind of frothy cocktail.

"Okay, Robin," Llewelyn says, taking his hand. "Nice to have met you. Keep in touch. Let me know how that novel of yours is coming."

Robin smiles wanly. "I sure will, Lew."

Llewelyn nods and disappears back into the hallway, slams the study door shut. Within moments he is shouting into the phone again.

"C'mon, Pee-Pee!" the girl calls, and immediately the big black dog leaps into the room and bounces its body against the door—barking, Robin thinks with wry grimness, for its freedom. He thinks of the photo of Llewelyn on the back of the book and glances at the red-haired girl. Then he pictures the rectangular building down the hill, hidden behind shrubs and fences. Asylum Heights, he thinks. Where all lost souls find themselves, sooner or later.

The girl takes him to the station in an old green convertible. Though the skies have grown thick with clouds she leaves the top down, and the dog sits between them panting its jowly breath into Robin's face. As they rush through the downtown streets, pictures flutter across his mind of Uncle Jasper, an ancient figure he had not thought of in ages, and he thinks of Sonya and the cherry blossom and a time when the world was simple and everything lay before him like a glittering bed of pearls. And what, he wonders, does he have before him now?

They do not speak until she pulls into the parking lot and stops the car.

"Hey," she says, her eyes hidden behind rectangular sunglasses, "do you know anything about cancer?"

"Not much," Robin says. "Why?"

"I have a question. Only I'm too afraid of Lew's creepy doctor to ask it."

"What is it?"

"Well…" She frowns and runs her hands along the steering wheel. "Is it, I mean—cancer—you know—is it contagious?"

Robin scoffs. "I don't think so."

"Really?"

"I'm pretty sure."

"Gosh…I don't know." She looks forward. "When Lew and me make love I always wonder if he's going to—you know—leave it inside of me."

He shuts his eyes briefly, opens them again. "Don't worry about a thing," he says. "It's not contagious."

"Oh." She smiles brightly and looks at him. "Good. That makes me feel real good."

He nods. "Goodbye, Sherrie. Thanks for the ride."

"Okee-doke."

"Take care of him."

She nods vaguely and Robin steps out of the car.

"Oh," she says, "Wait. Do you have a cigarette?"

"No."

"Tough luck. I wanted to give it to Pee-Pee."

"Sorry."

"Oh, well. I'll buy some on the way home." She starts the engine. "Bye-bye!"

The little green car whizzes away.

Robin watches it go, then looks up at the fat gray clouds overhead. He finds his way to the Ashersburg-bound train and sits down in his compartment.

Just then the sky bursts, like a handful of silver blossoms pouring their soft exploding petals into the open and receiving earth: trying, he imagines, to wash away all terrors and confusions, all shames and disappointments, trying with its gentle, sweet flood to soften and dissolve all the cancers of the world.

18

Depression, he writes. *Triggered by T.L. turning out to be a boozy, self-pitying bumbler no better than anyone else and less interesting than most; but really involving everything, the terrible ennui and directionlessness I feel now. I'm very tired. Not sleeping well. I feel like all my gods are being washed out to sea.*

<hr />

"I talked to your father this morning," April says.

Robin turns and looks at her suddenly in the warm light of the trailer. "You did?"

"Mm-hm."

"How?"

"He called the Pierces. You must have told him you were living with them. I was there with Mrs. Pierce."

He scowls. "And?"

She looks up at him, her eyes sharp. "And nothing. We had a very nice talk."

"About what?"

"You. What did you think?"

"What did he say about me?"

"He said he missed you."

"Ho, ho. I'll bet."

"Really."

"He must have been drunk."

"He didn't sound like it. He wanted to talk to you. He wants you to go back there and finish school. He sounded like a nice man. Did you know that he used to live around here? Back when he was a teenager, he said, he lived in Lawtonburg. That's only a hundred miles from here."

"Well, isn't that charming."

"So will you call him?"

"No."

"Why not?"

He shakes his head, sits down on the bed.

"He's just about all you have, Robin," she says, looking at the floor. "Besides me, I mean. You shouldn't throw away your daddy like that."

"He threw me away a long time ago," Robin says. "He had a choice between booze or me. He made his choice."

"People make mistakes."

He frowns and glares at her. "What do you know about it, anyway? And who assigned you to be my conscience?"

Her voice is smaller as she says, "I didn't mean it like that, Robin."

"You have no idea what you're talking about," he says crossly. "You don't know what's happened between us or the kinds of things that have gone on. When he drinks he's off his rocker. And he *always* drinks. My mother *died* because of him."

She looks at him. "That's not true. Not from what you told me. It was an accident."

"It's pretty damn near true. If he had stood up to her instead of—" He breaks off suddenly. "Never mind. This is none of your business."

"I thought your business *was* my business."

He shakes his head. "You were wrong."

They say nothing for a long moment.

Finally April speaks. "I feel like I just got a door slammed in my face."

"Sorry."

After a minute has passed April stands. "I'm going to go, Robin."

He looks at her. "When are you coming back?"

"I don't know."

⚔

Darkness: drifting. Unmoored islands tumbling into a savage stream. Distant forgotten voices crying over canyons. Giants as tall as redwoods stumbling and crashing down into the undergrowth. Faces floating out of an oily sea of black. An island far away in the sunlit waters, swimming closer and closer through the sky toward it, and a figure, microscopically small in the bright distance, standing at the shore looking out into the endless sea.

⚔

Hi, Sweetheart (Koofie says Hi too), You'll never guess where we are now. In the middle of the Kalahari Desert! Sand dunes, camels, and everything! We were invited here by this Peace Corps guy we met in the capital. He's lived here for 3 years and it shows—sits on his porch and throws pebbles at his chickens for hours! There's also a British " fellow," pip-pip, who seems to do nothing but kick soccer balls against his fence all day long and talk about the English countryside. Last but not least there is a long-haired guy with the longest beard I've ever seen who claims he is writing the Great American Novel. Sound like you have competition, you better watch out!!! But that's it for the white folk. The Africans are nice, though. They speak English here! Anyway, we're scramming tomorrow for South Africa, then flying to India. Lots of love. Cissy.

---

1 October
Dear Dad,
I would appreciate it if in the future you refrained from

---

1 October
Dear Dad,
I understand that you called here recently and talked to my friend April. I think that

---

2 October
Dad,
I am leaving here soon. I may end up back in California but I can't be sure what

---

4 October
Dear Davy,
Thanks for the most recent postcard. Sorry I haven't communicated in so long. As you can see, I'm far from "home"—took a cross-country trip with

a girl I've since split from. I seem to be in the process of becoming a genuine "drifter." In fact, I'm planning on drifting from this little place sometime soon—to what destination I don't know. I feel like hell these days. Writing a novel, I guess, but it's not going well. I told you before about the poem I had published—but I've had absolutely no success since. Everything comes back with rejection slips just like before. I somehow thought that things would change once I got one in print. SIGH. I met the "great writer" Terrence Llewelyn a couple of weeks back—turned out to be a big-mouth jerk with a teenage bimbo hanging on him. Another illusion shattered! In a long line of same. At least you're getting some sex there—important for every young man's development. Builds strong bodies twelve ways. Tell me more about the Philippines. It seems as if everybody I know is somewhere far away, doing something INTERESTING, quite unlike Yours Truly who just continues to plod away in the darkness. I try, but nothing ever happens. Maybe I should get smart and follow Michael Lyon's advice of way back when, just like you. There are worse fates, I guess.
Robin.

Disconnection: faces fragmented, flying apart like spears of glass and sinking into darkness.

And perhaps it is all illusion, after all. Perhaps there are no new levels, no bright intensities, no connection-points to the vast design. Perhaps it is all mad dream. Things fall apart and fly directionless in a murky dark without reason or logic, bound in their madness to the endless arcs circling wildly, unstoppably, rendering everything pitifully wasted and pointless.

He tries to write more about Siegel but it does not come. Or rather, it does; but somehow he is reluctant to put it on paper. The material makes him uneasy. There is something frightening about Siegel. And yet he keeps returning to the manuscript, adding a word or two, a sentence, a paragraph. No more. He thinks of abandoning it; but each time he files it away in a drawer, he brings it out again within a day or two. The pages seem startlingly white, naked.

And then will his morning arrive? When will the darkness at last dissipate, break apart and dissolve and leave him in bright sunlight? When will the demons, beautiful and unbeautiful, at last melt away, sizzle to nothingness? When will the mirrored reflections in the endless hall coalesce and solidify and become one? When will meaning and understanding come?
Splintering. Breaking-up. Loss.

"I don't understand what's come over you," she says. "We used to have so much fun. Now you never smile, never tell a joke, never laugh. And you won't tell me what's wrong."
"Nothing's wrong," he mutters.

Melding, integration, escape, glorious new intensities: illusions like glass shattering. Rain spitting down like splintering mirrors. The sky the color of lead, clouds a blanket of fists. Arms swirling, swirling.

"What's wrong?"
"Nothing's wrong…"

African sunsets. Indian street-scenes. New York nightclubs. Filipino cat houses. Unfamiliar scents and lives and rooms. Reaching toward them like holding smoke. Darkness.

And how could I ever tell you, sweet little April with your baseball cap and strawberry hair and bubble gum, how could I ever tell you of the great darkness waiting to swoop over us like a thick black cloak? Of the silence that is malevolent and listening? What words could I use for you? What would make you understand? The gulf of intergalactic space is vast and impenetrable and airless. Words will not float. They break apart and sink into the darkness like ashes, dissolve into eternity. And we remain motionless, waiting in mute terror for the moment we are to follow them. There are no escapes, no new intensities, nothing but a few instants of hazy broken light like a candle in fog until the night crashes down again forever.

"Your dad called again."
"I don't want to hear about it.…"

His hands on her body, rain streaming down outside: his cheeks on her stomach, his face pressed into her breasts, their tongues winding together, tears running from her eyes.

What's wrong?
I'm sorry.
I'm sorry, I'm sorry.

An island in the sunlit distance, the sea shimmering vividly around it, and floating through the warm sky, slowly descending toward the figure on the shore who stands there unmoving, staring out into the endless waters.

19

The bar is dark and warm: warmer, at least, than the hotel at which he is staying, where the heaters do not function and the windows are cracked and split. He spends as little time as possible there. And there are, after all, many things to do in San Francisco. Some of them are even free, which is important now, down as he is to his last few hundred dollars. He swallows the wine before him. Interesting thought, the future. He is all but penniless with no immediate prospect of being anything else. He supposes this should worry him; but somehow it fails to. It does not, after all, make any real difference. He has no options anyway. He had abandoned life in the little Virginia town months before; going back to Wind Point is out the question; and what else is there to do, really? His life is no more than some old clothes in his car, his typewriter, and some pages of an unfinished, perhaps never to be finished, novel. Nothing else.

He stares straight forward, feeling the wine enfold him in a pleasant mellowness. Over the past few weeks he has been enjoying the sensation more and more, the warm kick of the wine in the back of his throat, the gentle expansive feeling that flows over him: problems seem to dissolve before him like clouds dispersed by soft light. White wine, he thinks, Siegel's preferred beverage;

but unlike Siegel, he has no interest in picking up bimbos in bars or taking anybody home to screw, no interest in old friends or lovers, no interest in the past at all. It is all over and done, vanished, smoke in wind, all of it unlighted and irretrievable and lost. There is nothing but the ever-shifting moment, the instant of existence like a clock's perpetual ticking, moment upon moment, instant driving into instant, nothing but the eternal *now*. All the rest is meaningless.

He has found himself, these past several weeks, remarkably unencumbered with the past: shadow-men on the stairs, ghosts wrapped in pearls, voices and cries: it has all disappeared, delightfully, and he has found himself thinking of nothing, really nothing, sensation following sensation without old memories weighing him down. It is wonderful. It is also, of course, somewhat abetted by the wine he swallows each evening. But what of that? Perhaps, he thinks, that is what he has needed all along: to loosen up a bit, take it easy, go with the flow, mellow out. He has taken himself awfully seriously, he knows, for a very long time. Perhaps it is time now to stop, to live as other people live, no worries, no cries in the darkness, no trembling terrors: just good pleasant life: and why not? He is intelligent; not too bad-looking; in decent physical shape; surely those blessings are enough for anyone. For all of his tortured shyness, he thinks, he has had no shortage of lovers since leaving high school. In fact he has acquitted himself rather well on that point; he has done a good job of masking his inherent sickness, driving it so far down that it is invisible to all but himself. Some even seem to find him attractive, desirable. It is an amazing thought, and often he wonders if they are not really just playing, just pretending in order to salve his feelings. He can look around this very bar, see men much less good-looking, less intelligent, picking up women and taking them away. It is possible that they have some strange subterranean quality, a style or charisma, which Robin cannot see: but it does not seem likely. Women even come to his table sometimes, talk with him; he imagines that the only reason he has been unsuccessful is that he has not tried. He is not really interested, anymore. All that is illusion, he knows; there is no melding, no coming-together in any but a fleeting, physical sense: no miraculous bonding, new intensity: nothing.

He stands, his legs slightly unsteady, and pulls on his jacket. Perhaps that is the answer to everything in the world: that there is nothing: nothing, that is, except darkness, silence, isolation: and the only answer is to curb the sounds and pictures, all the whirlpool of clutching time, to escape it, break free and live only in the infinite instant, the perpetual tick of time: for only by escaping the whirlpool can he be truly free.

And there is no reason he cannot do it, he realizes as he makes his way out of the warm room into the cold darkness of the December night. He can drown himself in today, lose himself in it, and by so doing loosen the clutch of the whirlpool until finally it falls away, once and for all and forever, like a cancer dissolved and defeated. Because after all, those old voices and whispers and cries were not his anyway, but rather some earlier incarnations of him, one of the many images in the mirrored hall, the jumble of Robins which have existed one after another over the course of his life. There is no connection to be found anywhere, he knows, because they are not essentially connected. The consistency granted by the single name *Robin* is entirely an illusion, for the selves continue to fall away into the darkness, into the black jaws of time, unstoppably, never to return. How could there be any connection between the self that he is now and the boy who sat across from the little blonde girl Sonya at the tiny checker table, their knees electrically touching, and later, her damp palm in his in a world that knew no night, only bright morning? There could be none. That boy has been dead for years, he thinks, and many others too, similar in some ways but vastly different, all of them dead and burned and their ashes hurled on the vast speechless sea. And so the only way to deal with it is the perpetual instant, the ever-living present. It is the only thing that can be trusted; that does not betray. Only the past betrays.

He walks down the dark street which glistens after a cold December rain. A year and a half since he was first here, he realizes, in the hotel room with the girl with frizzed blonde hair. He finds himself trying to recall her face, trying to reassemble the qualities from the chambers of his mind. But he stops himself. No, he thinks, that is the trap rising before him again, the great gaping mouth of memory, and therein all danger and deceit lie waiting. He continues walking, slipping once, regaining his footing. He will live, he thinks, without memory, without old agony, without feeling. It is the only way. The only solution. His foot slips again but he keeps moving. Nothing matters but to keep everything that has ever happened far, far away, washed away like dirty water swirling down a drain. He will make it all vanish into darkness and he will live in pure, soft sunlight, as he did once, as an earlier Robin did years ago before there was terror, betrayal, pain. He will recapture his Nietschzian Superman, he thinks, who existed once, long ago in another life when the little girl held the cherry blossom paperweight in her hand and her lavender eyes looked into his and her tiny fingers moved the checker pieces across the board and her warm palm rested softly in his in the dark car, in a time before memory, before whirlpools and loss. He will find the timeless moment again. He must. And to do it he will reject the whirlpools, the jaws, the breathless vortexes. None of them will exist now, for him. He will be as he once was: innocent, clean, sun-warmed, young.

He slips again and bumps against the wall of a shop next to him. He is drunk, he supposes; a rather disgusting conclusion to have to come to, but there it is. The world seethes uncertainly before him. He is dizzy. Finally he makes his way into the hotel and through the dark lobby. He stumbles up the stairs, slipping on one and banging his knee against it hard. He winces. But he will make the ascent, he thinks, he will not collapse like a stumbling drunk on the stairs. He holds the rail tightly as he moves up. Finally he is there; for a moment he cannot remember which direction his room is in. He thinks about it for a moment. He turns left finally and brushes against the wall as he searches for the number. There it is. He stands staring at the door, searching his pocket for the key. For a long time he cannot find it. Then he does. The door blurs before him as he tries to put the key into the lock. He pushes against the metal once, twice, three times, not quite able to find the slot. It seems terribly sad, this state of affairs. He pushes and pushes but the key does not fit into the slot. He giggles vaguely, looking up and down the unfocused hall for anyone coming by. Perhaps his father, he thinks, that would be good, or even the ghost of his mother. He had met the ghost of his mother once, years before, when he was another Robin, he had seen her come into the room and sit down on the bed and say, "I've come a long way, honey," and "I'll come back someday." But perhaps it had only been a dream, after all. He knew it had not been but that was what he had decided to think anyway. So, if she were to come along any time now, a drunken ghost, that would be just jim dandy.

He slides down the door and sits with his back against it, trying to focus his eyes on the opposite wall. He feels sleep coming over him suddenly, swooping down on him like dark wings. His eyes begin to close. But as they close the door to his room opens slowly, from the inside. Now this is very curious, because there can be no one in the room. But the door opens and he feels himself fall back, giggling gently, onto the carpet. He is staring up at the ceiling of his room now; it is fuzzy and strangely doubled. He giggles again. Then a figure comes into view, blurred, indistinct. "Look at me," its voice says. He tries to look but his eyes will not focus. He sees the figure's hands reach toward his face and pinch his cheeks. He shakes his head slightly, groggily. The sight before him begins to come into a shimmering clarity, as if he were underwater. Someone is leaning over him and touching his face. For a long moment he cannot make out who it is. Then finally he blinks, and he can see the figure, if only for a moment, in perfect focus: the face, the hair, the dark eyes.

"Hi, baby," Heather says, smiling.

CHAPTER 5
A DARK AND VICIOUS PLACE

The dark and vicious place where thee he got
    Cost him his eyes.

    Shakespeare: *King Lear*

1

In the dim, uncertain light, through the haze of sweet smoke lying thickly in the air, his eyes follow the sound of her tinkling laugh. For a long moment he fails to see her; and finds himself wondering vaguely just who all these people are. Friends of hers? Several he has never seen before: one, a pale youth with wispy white hair, pounds discordantly at the piano while another, with long black hair and a distinctly Satanic mustache and goatee, hangs over him giggling. The room is packed with people, with noise. He smiles without knowing quite why as he steps down from the kitchen and moves through the mass of bodies. A woman with the straps of her dress falling down dances liquidly to the piano, staring at the floor; she reaches to him, wrapping her arms around his neck and grinning.

"Dance wid me," she slurs.

He escapes her sloppy grip and moves further. He makes his way past a motley-looking group passing a joint amongst themselves and at last glimpses her, her tiny frame obscured by bodies. He hears her laugh again. Struggling through the crowded room, sweating, he makes his way to her. She grins when she looks up and notices him, slipping her arm around his waist.

"Hi, baby!" she says.

"Hi," he says. "Listen, who—"

"I want you to meet Lotar," she says, gesturing with the glass in her hand at a big stupid-looking bear of a man with bangles on his wrists and a shirt open to the waist which displays a hair-tangled chest. "Lotar works for the Big Blue Savages," she says.

"The who?" Robin says, frowning, shaking the man's beefy hand.

"The Big Blue Savages! The band. You've heard of them. They're really hot in California right now."

"Oh. Oh, right," he says, having no idea what she is talking about.

"Lotar sets up their drums."

"Oh. Well, congratulations, Lotar. Heather," he says, turning to her, "can I speak to you for a second?"

"Sure thingie." She glances at Lotar and grins. "Back in a sec."

"*Lotar,*" Robin says as he pulls her toward the bedroom which, he remembers with satisfaction, he had had the foresight to lock hours before. "Do you suppose that's the name his mother gave him, *Lotar?*"

She giggles. "That's nothing. Did you see the black guy in the hall? He used to be called Lennie Adams. Now he's *Akinwumi Sofala.* He says it's Nigerian."

"Mm. I wonder what he knows about Nigeria."

"He's never been to Africa. It's a Black Pride thing."

"Didn't that go out of style a while back?"

"Not for Akinwumi!"

He unlocks the bedroom door and they step into the dark room. He looks at her: her hair, longer now than it used to be, lighter in color, is fixed in a soft wave and brushed back off her forehead; her skin, almost ghostly pale, seems to glow in the dimness. She wears a bright, baggy outfit in a patchwork of colors with several necklaces and bracelets draped over herself. She is almost unrecognizable, he thinks, from the mousy little girl he had met back then—when had it been? But then, she has always had this ever-changeable, chameleon-like quality: one moment one person, the next someone else.

"Heather," he says, running his finger over her hair, around her ear, "I thought you said we were going to have a *few* people over tonight."

She grins lopsidedly. She is a bit drunk, a bit high. "I know, baby," she says. "I swear, I only invited a couple of people. But people told people. Word gets around."

He frowns. "I think we must have every lowlife in San Francisco out there."

"Baby..." She pouts prettily.

"Come on, Heather. Let's try to bring these festivities to a close pretty soon, okay?"

"Aren't you having fun?"

"Sort of. But come on, it's past midnight."

She smiles and leans her head against his chest. "You said I could have this party, baby," she mumbles.

"I know. You can. I'm not mad. I just think there's too many people, that's all."

"Live a little." She giggles.

"I'm alive."

"Here. Drinkie." She holds the glass to his lips and he swallows. Something slips evasively down his throat, like mercury, then hits his stomach and lights it on fire.

"Potent," he says.

"Relaxing."

"Anyway, Heather, can we please put a lid on this sometime soon?"

"Okay, okay. In a little while." She looks up at him impishly, her eyes big and dark. "You never know what I might do to you after the party."

He kisses her forehead. "We've stopped that. Remember?"

"*You* stopped it."

He swallows from her glass again. "Go back to your party, little soldier."

She moves back into the main room again, where the white-haired young man has been replaced at the piano by his Satanic friend. Robin follows her, the sweet marijuana odor easing his tension. He is not angry with her, but he grows tired of these parties—nearly every week now, and always with too many people he has never seen before. Not that they own anything that might be fodder for a thief: there is nothing in the main room but a few bits of thrift-shop furniture, a small black-and-white television, an ancient bookcase, and the old tuneless piano which the landlord forced upon them because he had no other place to store it. And in fact, some of the people who show up are quite interesting: San Francisco artists, designers, would-be actors; hangers-on, perhaps, but amusing enough for an evening. But not constant evenings, week after week.

An intense-looking dark man, very short and nattily dressed, comes up to Robin. "I am leaving now," he says.

"Oh. Okay," Robin says.

"I have only one testicle."

Robin looks at him. "Is that right?"

"The other was removed by surgery."

"I'm sorry to hear that."

"I am still fully functional in all respects."

The man turns then and weaves out of the house.

There was once a time, Robin muses, when such encounters would have shocked him. Now it all seems par for the course. Once he would have been acutely uncomfortable at such a gathering: nervous, ignorant: now he is, if not exactly one of them, at least familiar with their types. It is amusing for him to consider that he is, after all, the host of these parties: that, although most of them come out of acquaintance with Heather, whom they meet through her job at the boutique, when they arrive they meet him: and like him, apparently, for they come back again and again. Painters. Graphic designers. Actors. Amateur writers who print little typewritten magazines. He has quite good conversations with some of them, sometimes. It is good for him to know these people, he supposes; left to his own devices he would know no one. And the constant presence of people does serve to relieve the tension that sometimes—often—builds up between the two of them. It is not a tension like the screaming fits they had gotten into before, in that other world, ages ago. It is something more subtle, indefinable: a kind of competition: and yet what they could be competing for he cannot imagine.

He watches her as she resumes her animated conversation with the wastrel called Lotar. After a moment he turns away, walks back toward the kitchen; but her voice seems to follow him, weaving between the dozens of people in the main room. All the other voices fade into an indefinite hum while hers stabs at him: the flighty giggles, the tinkling laugh; he wonders if the others in the room can hear her so clearly. But he knows they cannot. It is as if he is a receiver tuned only to her wavelength, and all others are no more than faint whispers and static. He goes to the refrigerator and pours some wine into a cup. Soon he finds himself involved in a conversation with two young writers he knows from the cafes and coffeehouses that he and Heather occasionally visit. He goes not like the work of either of them, but finds their grand pronouncements about art and literature and life amusing enough:

they seem so young, he thinks; and so much like he himself used to be, back in the far-lost past. They still see things in clear, black-and-white terms; have not yet learned that everything is in some way muddy, nebulous. And yet as he listens to them, offering an occasional comment, he remains super-aware of Heather's voice. He cannot even see her now, through the crowd of bodies. But he can hear her distinctly. He feels as if he could find her even in total darkness, even if he were blind. Her voice is such a clear signal, like a tin-can-and-string telephone stretched between them. He wonders if she is as aware of him. He does not think so. And yet it could be: often at gatherings like this one he sees her studying him, her eyes darting from the person she is talking to to his face, back and forth. He wonders if she is aware of him right now; or if his existence has blinked into nothingness for her, only to be revived again upon hearing his voice or seeing him coming toward her. He does not like to think of being dropped into a void of nonexistence; it makes him want to go to her again, look her in the eyes, touch her arm, say, I'm here. Look at me. But he knows that would be foolish. He sips at the wine, listening vaguely to the coffeehouse poets before him. They are attacking different well-known writers for being "facile," "cheap," "sentimental."

"Cheap?" Robin says suddenly, looking at them and grinning. "Sentimental? Let me tell you about cheap and sentimental. Let me show you something." He goes into the main room, to the bookshelf, and brings down *The Professor Remembers and Other Stories*. He brings it back into the kitchen. "If you want to hear some cheap and sentimental writing," he announces, loudly enough that several people turn to look, "you should try *this* guy! Let me find a good passage…" He flips through, knowing what he is looking for: finds it and, giggling, begins to read. It is the death scene from "The Professor Remembers": the slow, aching fade-out into eternity; the vision of the professor as a child rising before his dying body, the sound of children's laughter outside. Robin reads it in an overblown, declamatory voice thick with derision. All the people in the kitchen start to laugh, and Robin laughs with them, wondering how he could ever have believed this nonsense was any good at all. What once seemed gentle and evocative and haunting is now sticky and bitter like saccharin. He thinks of clumsy Llewelyn and his nineteen-year-old paramour; thinks of the house filled with garbage and booze. Llewelyn! He should have realized long before that there was a perfectly good reason for Llewelyn's books to have fallen out of print. They were bad books, pure and simple. Yet it had taken him years to realize it. Everything he reads now, every word of it, is wrong: corny, overwrought, second-hand emotion. He is glad that he is sophisticated enough to see it now; but cannot understand how he could ever have been so ignorant.

He finishes the final long, winding sentence to a chorus of giggles and guffaws and then says, "And *that*, ladies and gentlemen, is truly bad writing!" He grins and closes the book as the listeners laugh and applaud.

Even before he places the book down on the counter his attention is focused again on Heather. He hears her voice as clearly as if she were standing next to him; and yet he cannot quite distinguish the individual words. They do not seem to matter: it is the voice itself: the rising sounds and the falling ones, the undulations, their peculiar music. Sometimes he tries to fight this awareness, tries to think: Stop. But he cannot stop, especially when other people are around. He moves a few steps so that he can see her, at least in glimpses, through the many bodies. He studies her face, the movement of her lips and throat, watches her head tilt back in laughter. He can do this even while carrying on a conversation with the two amateur writers: his glance moves to them, then off again, apparently into vague space but in fact directly toward Heather. It bothers him that she refuses to look his way. They have played this game innumerable times: she must know that he is looking: and he wonders what it means, if it means anything, that she will not return his look, seems unaware of his eyes or even his existence. Has he blinked out for her, then? Has he been tossed into the grave of non-being, only to be revived and resuscitated when he imposes on her by force, as he had a few minutes before, moving to her and taking her by the arm as if to say: Look at me? He does not like the feeling. And yet he can think of no reasonable excuse to go to her again. His glance moves with annoyance to the simian Lotar. He does not like the look in Lotar's eyes, the way he stares at her so absolutely unblinkingly, as if he were the Creature from the Black Lagoon. It seems to Robin very nearly indecent; and yet Heather takes no notice, continues chattering merrily and laughing. Robin wishes she would look toward him. It is like being buried alive, this nonexistence. Like being a mirage.

At last he sees that people are beginning to move toward the door. The amateur writers take their leave. The white-haired boy and Satan allow the piano to fall to silence and prepare to go. Akinwumi Sofala is nowhere to be seen. The drunken dancing woman is escorted out by two men. Robin smiles and grins at all these people as they find their ways out into the misty dark, saying goodbye to them, wishing them well. He is, he imagines, a fairly charming host. Certainly none who were listening will quickly forget the hilarity of his Llewelyn reading. But he feels an immense relief at their going, as if a tremendous weight has been lifted from his chest. At last Lotar, too, makes his way into the night, the laughs and goodbyes fade, and he and Heather are alone in the house.

"Tell me about Lotar," he says, later.

She stands before the dresser mirror, unbuttoning her shirt and placing it over a chair. She glances back at him lying on the bed. "Lotar?" she says. "I don't know. I'd never met him before."

"Oh. I thought you had."

"No." She unclasps her bra and Robin watches the small familiar breasts appear in the dim light. "Why?"

"No reason." Robin turns onto his side. "You just seemed to be paying him an awful lot of attention."

She smiles slightly. "Jealous?"

"Should I be?"

"Don't answer a question with a question. It's bad form."

"A little. Should I be?"

"Why should you? I told you, I'd never seen him before." She slips out of her pants and stands naked before the mirror. Looking into it, she says, "Besides, I thought we had that whole issue behind us. I thought we had an agreement."

"We do." He stares at her. "I'm not arguing."

"And it was your idea anyway, you know. The agreement."

"I know it was."

She turns to look at him; then walks toward the low bed and sits down beside him. She touches his hair softly. "But we can change it, you know. If you decide you want to."

"Let's not get into that again."

She sighs.

"Haven't we been getting along better?" he asks. "I mean, since the agreement?"

"I guess we have."

"What do you mean? No fights, no arguments, no problems. Pure paradise."

She smiles wanly. "Robin, I…"

"Don't start. Please."

"I wasn't starting anything."

"You want to run over old territory."

"No. I just…"

"Heather—"

"Okay, okay." She sighs again and slips under the covers. Robin reaches to the light and shuts it off and they lie there for a long time in the darkness. Although she is turned away from him he knows she is not asleep. He can tell from her breathing, from the small movements she makes. He wraps his body around hers and feels her move into the pocket his body creates.

After a long time with her warm skin pressed against him he feels his body beginning to respond. He moves uncomfortably against her. Minutes pass; finally Heather's hand reaches around and touches him.

"Don't," Robin says.

"Robin..."

"We have an agreement," he says. "I'll go into the other room if it's a problem."

"It's not me. I'm thinking of you—"

"Forget it," he says.

Finally she moves her hand away again. The room quiet and still except for the sound of the foghorn, somewhere in the far distance, lowing its warnings into the gray and icy San Francisco bay.

2

Something had changed between them. Their personal equation had changed. The two of them together no longer equaled what they once had: instead of screaming fits, there was elaborate politeness; in place of the loss of himself to her there was a curious, unspoken distance. He could not be sure whether this politeness, this distance, was real or feigned, whether it would continue or dissipate suddenly at some unexpected moment; but something had changed.

She spends her days at the boutique while he tries to work on *Drowning*. In the evenings, three times a week, he drives to the nearby liquor store where he loads crates until midnight. It is an arrangement such that they actually do not spend much time together, often communicating through notes left on the kitchen counter. It is better this way, he thinks. The problem before had been that they spent every waking moment with each other, coming too close, growing too intensely one with each other: it had seemed good then, but it had not been. It had been a mistake. We work in the dark, he thinks, alone: anything else is illusion.

But is that true? Had it been an illusion, what they had had together before? Had there never been any melding, any newer intensity, had they both been merely deluding themselves? He wonders. Illusion or no, however, it is quite gone now; the selves that had created the events of before have fallen away like old husks and new selves, physically identical but psychically altered, have taken their places. They are two new people in a new relationship with utterly new dynamics between them. And he had not anticipated that at the beginning: at first he had been overwhelmed with fear, thinking of the old world, considering what they had done to each other and assuming it would still be the same now: but of course it was not: nothing, he realizes, is ever the same, not after it has passed through the relentless refracting prism of time.

Not that, at the beginning, they had not tried. Or, rather, assumed: for the first few days it had seemed as if no time had passed at all, as if everything was exactly the same as it had been. Melding: asking, Who are you? and answering, I'm you. The other patterns had reappeared too, the sudden terrible tensions, the voices rising. But soon they had passed through them. He does not know if they will come back; but for now, with their agreement, it is under control. And how tired he is, after all, of endings: April, Cape; his father; on and on, further and further back in time, ending after ending, all of them draining and exhausting. But they all had had to end, of course, because he is not the same person that he was, he ended and began constantly, shed his old lives like snakeskins left behind in the swirling dust. And so his old relationships had to end as well.

It is impossible to imagine, he sometimes muses, how people can stay together for thirty or forty or fifty years. How do they do it? How can their identities continue to grow and change in the same ways? They cannot. And so what is it that keeps such couples together? It seems an absurd idea on the face of it; and yet there is an appeal to it: he quite likes the idea, waking up fifty years from today and finding the same familiar face next to his own. Heather's face? He is not sure. He tries to imagine what Heather will look like when she is old: tries to superimpose in his imagination wrinkles and hardened skin and gray-streaked hair: but he cannot hold the image in his mind. But himself, now: adding silver hair and eyes sunk back into his face and a small paunch to his stomach: he can imagine that perfectly. But as he thinks of the image, he realizes suddenly that who he is really picturing is Llewelyn: Llewelyn, with his features distorted into his own. He shakes the image away. He does not like to think about Llewelyn. A man in his sixties in a dirty little common house, a teenage bimbo for company, his career in tatters, his health fading: what a fate! Will it be his own? he wonders. Will he end up in the same way? Will his career establish itself, then decay and crumble and leave him with nothing?

He sighs. For that to happen, he thinks, he must have a career first.

But that does not seem to be happening. He still has the journal, the one journal that published the one poem: but now, instead of being a source of pride, it is more like a mockery. He can look at his name printed there, and the words that he had written, or somebody with his name had written, ages ago in the Santa Barbara hills; but instead of being first in a long series of such publications, it remains all by itself, alone. Nearly a year has gone by since it appeared, and yet there is not even the slightest hint of anything else that might appear anywhere. It is an embarrassment to him, now; and try as he might, he cannot seem to change the situation. He writes little these days. Oh, he pretends to be working on *Drowning:* but in fact he manages little on it. He does not like thinking about *Drowning*, the characters, the sounds, the rooms: its echoes are too insistent. He has become afraid of it, or afraid of finishing it, or something. He does not know what it is. But something keeps him from doing more than doodling on the project, making minor changes on earlier chapters, fixing a line here or there. But something has occurred to him about this. He has realized just recently, and literally for the first time ever, that he has no idea how *Drowning* will end. It is an extraordinary thought in itself, but all the more so to realize that it had never even occurred to him before. Everything in *Drowning* is real to him: Siegel, the father, Rachel, the bar, the houses, all of it: so real that he had never even wondered just where the entire manuscript was going to ultimately take him. The ending would somehow take care of itself. But now as he is approaching it he is not so sure. What should happen? What *could* happen? There seem a thousand possible ways to take it, but which one is the right one? And how could he know? How could he be certain?

There is no way to be certain of anything, he knows. He thinks of the postcard he had received the week before: *Hey, Amigo! I got yr. address when I passed thru yr. old college town. So you've dropped out? Become an eternal rebel like yours truly? Cut the old umbilical cord? I'm back in SB-land for a while—gimme a call or something sometime. Miss you. Cape.*

And what, he wonders, is he to make of this? He would like to see Cape again, but Cape is only a ghost now, a faded specter. He thinks of the van and the ocean, Bessie Smith coming over the tinny speaker. The guitar and the spicy man-smell. *Miss you.* Lost.

He rolls onto his back on the bed, staring at the ceiling. He is so very tired of confusions and questions! He is tired of remembering what Llewelyn had told him, that he already knew everything he was ever going to know. That could not be correct, certainly, for he knows absolutely nothing. And yet there is a kind of sense to it: what else, really, is there to *learn?* He sighs. The bed creaks. At least he knows, now, that the cluttered desk and the stacks of student essays and the dirty coffee cups will not be his destiny. That old life has truly vanished, completely, utterly: Cape might drive through and obtain his address but Cape would not find him there, working his way toward such a fate. Never. No more desultory classrooms and sleepy students, no more knocking on that strange door to an unwanted future. He had gotten rid of that.

He wonders what his father would say about it. He has not even seen his father in nearly a year; has not spoken to him. A few postcards have been the extent of their communication. He tries to picture the man's face in his mind, finds it soft and wavering, unclear. He listens for the man's voice: hears it, somewhere within his mind: *He asleep?* It is always like this—the more recent memories are faded and impossible to bring forth; but the older ones, from years before, ages ago before the disaster, are perfectly clear. But none of it makes any difference, he supposes, in the long run. All of it is gone now, never to return, and he will never be in that house again, never hear those footsteps on the stairs in the dark. If it all remains in inchoate confusion, then so be it. He is tired of being wrapped in warped confusion, stumbling in the darkness. The instant of existence, he thinks: that is the key. Instant to instant, one flashing into the next; otherwise the jaws of time open and he is drowned, lost.

He listens.

In the bathroom, behind the closed door, he can hear the sound of Heather weeping softly.

"Do you love me?"

"I thought we weren't going to talk about this kind of stuff."

"I think we need to."

"Heather…"

"What?"

"Don't start."

"I'm not starting anything. I just want to *talk*."

"Isn't talking what gets us into trouble?"

"Used to. Not anymore. When was the last time we had a fight?"

"I don't remember…"

"We *never* do. We never fight anymore. All that's gone. All I want to do is talk."

"About what?"

"About the question I asked you."

"We've talked about this a million times."

"I've talked. You've copped out."

"I have not copped out."

"You have."

"Please leave me alone."

"No."

"You're going to start a fight, aren't you."

"No."

"You are. I know you."

"Do you?"

"Mm-hm."

"I don't think you know anybody. You're a million miles away."

"No, I'm not."

"You are."

"Well, maybe that's what we needed all along. A little distance. Maybe that was the whole problem in the first place."

"I don't like distance."

"Without distance, you and I would be killing each other again. You know that."

"There must be some other way. Robin, I'm so lonely. You're not even here with me anymore."

"I am."

"You're not. And I don't like it. I don't like the way we are together anymore."

"You miss the screaming matches? Are those what you want?"

"I want *you*."

"I'm right here."

"You're copping out again."

"You keep saying that."

"It's true."

"You don't even know what you're talking about."

"Stop it. Please. You don't understand how I feel. Sometimes I think you hate me."

"Don't be silly."

"You act like you do. You won't even let me touch you."

"You touch me all the time."

"I mean *touch* you."

"Look, Heather, if that isn't going to work, then it isn't going to work. What's the sense of torturing ourselves about it?"

"It can work. You told me it worked with that girl in Virginia."

"That was different."

"How?"

"I don't know. Different. Different time, different place, different person."

"So I'm not good enough."

"Heather, that's not what I said."

"Then what *is* it?"

"If I knew *that*..."

"You loved her, didn't you?"

"Who?"

"That girl in Virginia. You were in love with her."

"Don't be silly."

"You were. That's why you could do it with her but not with me."

"That has nothing to do with it. I wasn't in love with her. I'm *here*, aren't I? I'm not there."

"Please, Robin, let's try again."

"Leave me alone."

"Robin…"

"Heather, we had an agreement. We've been getting along fine lately…"

"I don't *want* to just 'get along'…"

"Then what *do* you want?"

"I want *you*…"

"I'm right here."

"Stop it. You know what I mean."

"No, I don't. Neither do you."

"You're not giving me anything. You think we can just live together like this—"

"What am I supposed to be giving you?"

"*You.*"

"We've *tried.*"

"Robin, I don't mean the sex thing…I mean…goddamn it…"

"Heather, stop crying. You're just trying to manipulate the situation."

"I can't *help* it…"

"Maybe I should just go out for a while."

"No. That's your solution to everything."

"Do you have a better one?"

"Stay here with me…"

"Heather, stop crying."

The Unspoken

―――

Party after party in the little house near the bay. The fog overhanging each morning, the color of stone.

―――

"Maybe we should give it up. Split."
"Robin, no. We *can't*."
"You're not happy."
"Are you?"
"I'm all right."
"That doesn't answer my question."
"How's your cold?"
"Better. The doctor gave me these capsules. See? Green and yellow. Lemon-lime. Aren't they pretty?"
"I don't think we're very good for each other, Heather."
"Maybe we're not. But we could be."
"Stop. Take your pills."
"I'm taking them."
"Have you been throwing up in the bathroom lately?"
"No. What makes you think so?"
"I just wondered."
"No."
"I like your hair like that."
"You're trying to change the subject."
"Maybe. But I do like your hair like that."
"Thank you."
"It makes you look older. You look a lot different than when I first met you."
"When was that?"
"Oh, a million years ago."

Mist across the grass. The steps outside beaded and cold. The walkway glistening in the gathering darkness.

3

"Here," Robin says one windy Saturday when they are together in the house. "I've got something for you."

She is lying on her back on the couch reading a Dostoevsky novel. She has on a red jumpsuit and her feet are bare. "What's that, baby?" she mumbles, not looking up from the book.

He walks over to her. "Here."

She looks up, her eyes round and dark. He holds out a small blue box to her.

"A present?" she says, suddenly grinning.

"Mm-hm."

She sits up quickly, her face child-bright. "You got me a prezzie? Why? What is it?"

"Well, you'll have to open it and find out."

"*Thank* you!" She grins widely as she takes the small box from his hands. "But it's not my birthday."

"I know." He sits beside her on the couch. "Do I always have to wait until your birthday to give you a present?"

"Uh-uh. You can give me a prezzie anytime."

He smiles. Things have been better between them lately, he thinks. Both of them have been in decent frames of mind and the circular discussions which are not, anymore, quite arguments, have mostly ceased. They live together, like other people.

He watches as she opens the box, finds the tiny object wrapped in blue paper. She starts to undo the paper, finally discovering the gold ring with the tiny diamond. She inhales and her mouth opens slightly. She looks at him.

"Robin, it's beautiful!"

He nods. "It was my mom's."

She looks at him a moment longer, then back at the ring. "Are you sure?" she asks, gazing closely at the small gem. "I mean...are you sure you want me to have it?"

"Mm-hm. I mean, it's not an engagement ring or anything. It's just a ring."

She nods, slips it onto her finger, grins. "It fits."

"I had it altered. My mom's hand was bigger than yours."

"It's beautiful."

"Let me see." He takes her small hand and looks at the ring. He hears the pepper tree rustling against his bedroom window, feels the familiar weight pressing down on the bed beside him. "It becomes you," he says.

Heather grins lopsidedly, gazing at him. Her eyes are vivid with life. "Robin—thank you. Thank you for this. I'm so touched..."

"Well, I've had these rings and necklaces and stuff for years. Ever since she died." He can see a younger Robin sitting across the kitchen table from his father, the single overhead light like a pool of gold in a sea of blackness, and the box moving between them, each of them choosing, taking out, separating, and his father carefully annotating each choice on a piece of paper. "I just thought it would be nice to...do something with one of them."

"Thank you. I love you, baby."

He smiles and squeezes her hand. "Like it?"

"I love it. I'll keep it forever."

He looks at the gold band, the little diamond, the golden leaf cluster surrounding it.

"Did she wear it a lot?" Heather asks.

"All the time. It was her favorite."

"Thank you. I don't even know what to say."

He leans forward, tousles her hair. "You deserve it," he says.

"Do I?"

"Sure you do."

"Sometimes I'm not so sure."

"Forget the past. Never mind. It's all gone now."

"I guess. Want some wine?"

"It's a little early in the day, isn't it?"

"So what? We're celebrating."

"I guess we are."

She smiles and touches his cheek briefly, then stands and walks into the kitchen.

"Robin?" she calls.

"Yo."

There is a brief pause. Then: "Have you ever given a ring like this to anybody else?"

He scowls. "No."

There is a long silence. Finally Heather appears again with two glasses of red wine in her hands. As she gives one to Robin she says, "Not even that girl in Virginia?"

"What a lousy thing to say." He puts the wine on the table next to the couch.

She sits and looks at him. "I didn't mean to make you mad."

"I'm not mad."

Her eyes grow wide as she looks at him. "Robin, I'm sorry. Please. It was a dumb question. I'm sorry I asked it."

He stares at his hands in his lap, fidgeting. "You shouldn't be so suspicious."

"Baby—" She places her wine on the table and folds herself into his arms. "I'm sorry. Forget it. I'm sorry. Dumb question. Please." She kisses his neck softly. They sit in silence for a long moment.

"By the way," Robin says quietly, "the answer is no. I didn't give any ring to the girl in Virginia."

"Robin, never mind." She nuzzles against his neck. "I'm sorry."

"What about you?" he asks. "You weren't a virgin the whole time—"

"Robin, let's not get into that."

"Well—"

"It was a terrible time. I made mistakes. You made mistakes. But we're together now. We're okay."

She changes the subject then, makes a remark about Dostoevsky. They talk about Dostoevsky for several minutes while they sip their wine. Robin stares at the ring on her finger, watches how it catches the light and tosses it in different directions. It is pleasant between them, just now.

Finally a silence falls between them. He breathes the odor of her hair and her hand touches his chest softly.

"What was her name?" Heather asks quietly.

"We seem to be back on a subject we were trying to avoid."

"I'm just curious."

"Her name was April."

"That's a nice name."

"She was a nice girl."

"Was she?"

"Mm-hm."

There is another pause.

"What was her last name?"

"Ashers."

"Ashers. April Ashers. Too many A's."

Silence again.

"Did you like her?" she asks finally.

"Heather, stop it. That's enough."

"I'm sorry, I'm sorry." She presses her face against his neck. "I'm just jealous."

"I know you are."

"I won't ask you any more."

"Good."

"I don't want to start fighties."

Robin chuckles. "No fighties," he agrees.

"Thank you for the ring, Robin. It's beautiful."

"No prob."

She giggles and nestles against him. She sighs happily. "This is how it was when we were first together. Remember?"

"I remember."

"We would just lay together for hours, talking…making out…" She giggles again.

He kisses her forehead. "I know."

"Then something changed and everything got…"

"I know…"

"But it's never going to be like that again. I won't let it."

"It wasn't all your fault."

"Most of it was."

"No, it was mine too. I would let things happen when I should have stopped them."

She smiles. "Ancient history," she says.

"Ancient history."

"Never again."

"Never again."

He remembers the little room she had had near the university and the little space heater and her perpetually black clothing. He remembers how quickly it had all come together, how quickly and how easily, there in the little room: her touches and caresses, her body arched back on the bed. Another vanished place, he thinks, another lost time.

The gray light outside begins to dim as they lie there together on the couch, silently. There are so many, he thinks: so many vanished places and times: so much light hurled into darkness. He stares at the blackening sky, musing. What if tonight were the last night of the world? he wonders. What if the pallid light draining slowly away were going forever, to leave them in cold darkness, empty void?

"What are you thinking about?" she asks in the dimming room.

"Nothing."

"Liar."

He glances down at her. "Well, what were you thinking about, then?"

"I was thinking about how I wish we could be like this forever."

"Everywhere," Robin quotes, "forever, horizons are blue and bright...forever..."

"Ewig...ewig..." Heather grins. "You know, we haven't listened to any Mahler in a long, long time."

"I know. I guess I don't have the patience for him anymore."

"You love Mahler."

"Yeah, but I don't particularly want to listen to him these days."

She nestles against him. "We never listen to much of anything. When was the last time we went to the symphony?"

"I'm not sure. Five, six months ago, I guess."

"We should do things like that more. Together, I mean."

He smiles slightly. "Why bother? When we can just be together like this?"

She looks at him, her eyes bright. "You're right. Here." She takes the glasses from his face and places them on the table. Then she kisses him gently. Robin feels soft electricity pulse through his body.

"What are we going to do?" Robin whispers.

"About what?"

"You. Me. Everything."

"We'll stay like this forever." Her eyes glitter in the gathering dark. *"Ewig."*

"No, we won't. Sooner or later we'll be hardly talking to each other again and you'll be off crying in the bathroom."

"Robin, please," she whimpers, pressing her face to his chest. "Don't talk about things like that."

"Why not? It's what happens between us."

"I know. But things'll be different now. Look." She holds up her hand, displaying the multi-prismed diamond on her finger. "It'll bring us luck."

"Forever?"

"Forever."

"Must be a pretty lucky ring."

"I'll make it lucky. I'll use my feminine wiles." She drapes her leg over him.

The visions continue playing in his mind: the end of the world, coming not with bombs and shrieks but quietly, smoothly, like this, the slow end of light, pulses fading to faint erratic taps like drops of rain spattering a window, silence descending. There is nothing terrifying in it. It is all calm and gentle, drifting out into the seas of eternity. *Ewig...*

"Heather, don't," he whispers. The room is dark now.

"Shhh..."

"We have an agreement."

She presses her finger to his lips softly.

"Heather..."

"Shush, baby. Shush."

"I don't think I'll be able to—"

"We won't try that," she whispers. "Shhh."

He watches her as she moves. She smiles at him.

"If you unzip me," she whispers, "I can be out of this thing in two seconds. One-pieces are nice that way..."

He reaches to her, visions of the final darkness still fluttering in his mind like blackbirds loosed from the warehouse of time. He tugs at the zipper. It gives easily. Soon she is completely nude and the jumpsuit is in a collapsed pile on the floor.

"Heather…"

"Shhh." She guides his hand between her legs. She kisses him deeply, her tongue warmly tickling the roof of his mouth. She strokes him for long minutes and then touches the hand that is between her legs. She whispers, "You haven't kissed me there in a long time."

"I know."

"Do you want to?"

Seas of darkness.

"Yes…"

She smiles again, kisses him on the face, then down the neck, unbuttoning his shirt and kissing him down his chest. She moves her legs over him and puts him in her mouth. It is as if he is floating on the eternal sea even now, he thinks: flowing, flowing, forever. After a time the flow grows quicker and he imagines nothing but the perfect eternal dark of the end of the world, forever, forever. Who are you? he hears a voice ask from a distant place, and his own voice answers, I'm you, and then the dark sea gushes, it gushes.

4

Drifting within each other, time wafting gently as on a placid sea. Voices intermingled: soft sighs and whispers. Eyes, darkness.

Who are you?

I'm you.

New intensities. Living night filled with breath. Hands together, stomachs pressed flat to one another, feet curled into feet. Grasping, pulling. Closer. Never again, never again. Weightlessness, dissolving together, vanishing. Closer. Wordlessness, melding. Communion, binding like roots, limitlessness. Closer.

I have been drawn into her again, he writes.

―※―

"I've missed you so much, baby..."

"Shhh."

"Why?"

"We don't need to talk about anything. Let's just be quiet."

"But I *have* missed you. Even when we were here, together, living together, you were so far away..."

"Heather..."

"What? What's wrong?"

"Let's not talk. Please."

"Why not?"

"I'm afraid of talking. It always takes us someplace we don't want to go."

"Not anymore, baby. Look—the ring you gave me. See? It's our good-luck charm."

"Still..."

"Still what? We don't have any more problems, baby. That's all in the past. We're two new people now."

"Same old problem, though."

"Don't worry about it. We'll get it. You got it with...what was her name?"

"You remember her name."

"I don't."

"You never forget anything. You can't fool me."

"Robin, I don't remember her name."

"Her name was April."

"Oh, yes. I remember now. April Ashley."

"Ashers."

"Ashers, sorry. How did you like it with her?"

"Stop. Please."

"I'm not starting anything."

"There's no point in talking about her."

"There is. Maybe if we can get to the bottom of your feelings about her we can figure out why it doesn't work with me...."

"You're just jealous and you want to talk about things that make you jealous. Let's talk about *your* boyfriends."

"I'm not the one with the problem."

"Oh..."

"I'm sorry. I'm sorry, baby. I didn't mean it like that."

Eyes dark and depthless. Tangled sheets, hair. Lips together in darkness. Sweet breath. Skin smooth, warm. Closer.

"Was she pretty?"

"Yes."

"What did it feel like when you were inside her?"

"I don't know what it felt like. I don't want to talk about this."

With April it was the closeness of one human being to another. Heather and I are two aspects of the same person.

"You're throwing up in the bathroom again."

"I was sick."

"You weren't sick."
"Okay. I'm getting fat."
"Heather, you have to stop it. Right now."
"I'm sorry, baby. It's just…"
"Just what?"
"She was skinny, wasn't she?"
"Oh my God, not again."
"She was, wasn't she?"
"It's none of your business."
"Oh, no. *No.*"
"I'm sorry…Look, honey. I'm here. I'm not there. I'll never go back there. Now stop worrying about it. You're already plenty skinny as it is. You're just the way I like you."
"Do you love me, Robin?"
"Stop it."
"Do you?"
"The fact that you even ask the question means you'll never be satisfied with the answer."
"Do you or don't you?"
"Why do you want to fight so much? Can I ask you that?"
"Who's fighting?"

Tears hot and bitter on the tongue. Odor of sweat. Feel of bones under skin. Closer.

I am afraid of what we become when we are together and whole.

"No. No. No. No. No." She holds her head in her hands, hiding her face. The sky outside is filled with mist nearly white in the bright afternoon: a blanket, he thinks, of bone.

"I'm only looking for a few *answers*, Heather," he says.

"You don't trust me."

"I don't *understand* you. Now look. I've got some questions, that's all. And I think we need to get them straight or else we're just going to be confused all the time."

"I'm not on trial."

"I didn't say you were." He sits next to her. "Now, I've noticed some things—"

"Robin, stop talking. Please stop talking."

"—And I'd like you to clarify them. Now, first of all…"

"Robin—"

"Heather, be quiet." He looks at her, sitting beside him on the sofa. She is wearing blue jeans and a bra without a shirt. She picks up a brush and runs it through her hair briskly.

"I'm not going to answer to an inquisition."

"Stop it. Now let me tell you some of the things I've noticed. First: I want to know once and for all—"

"Robin—"

"—How many members there are in your family."

"I've *told* you."

"No. You've lied to me."

She looks at him with an expression of horror on her face. "What?" she gasps.

"You've been lying to me from the beginning."

She clenches the brush in her hand. "How dare you—!"

"I want to show you something." He stands, feeling his heart beat, and walks to the bookcase. He brings down a black book; opens it to a marked page and starts to read. "'She told me she has three brothers and her parents, all in New Hampshire.'" He looks over at her. "That was a week or two after we met. Six months later—" He flips through book.

"Stop it!" She stands and faces him, her eyes furious. "I'm not going to stand for this!"

"Six months later: 'Odd thing: just before we had our big blow-out fight she told me she has two sisters. I've never heard of them before. Strange, considering how 'close' she says her family is.'"

"Robin—"

He looks at her flatly. "And then the other night," he says, "when we had those people over, you were back to the three brothers routine."

She glares at him a long moment; then the anger drains from her eyes and she smiles. She tosses the brush casually on the sofa. "Baby," she says, coming toward him, "I can't believe we're even arguing about this. I've never kept any secrets from you. I *do* have three brothers and I *do* have two sisters. I'm just not close to my sisters, that's all. I don't like to talk about them much."

"I thought you were all hysterically happy."

"Okay," she sighs, "maybe I wasn't totally honest there. Maybe we're not as close as I led you to think. We *are* close, though."

"What are the sisters' names?"

She looks puzzled. "Robin, why are you doing this?"

"Because there's too many questions," he says, sitting on the bar stool beside her. "Too many mysteries."

"What mysteries?"

"You once told me you played Tchaikovsky in a competition."

"Oh, that was just a joke."

He scowls. "No, it wasn't. You told me that seriously. And yet whenever anybody brings music for that broken-down piano there you say you can't read music."

She stares at the wall. "Baby, I was just trying to impress you. I told you that stuff about Tchaikovsky when we first met. I wanted you to like me."

"Why couldn't I find any Seabrights listed in any county in New Hampshire?"

"We're unlisted, that's all."

"That great big family, and not one person lists his name in the phone book?"

"I guess not. Robin, you always say that we get into trouble by talking. Maybe we should stop."

"Why?"

"Because I don't like believing that you think I'm a liar. I thought we trusted each other. I trust *you*. I love you—"

"Let's not get into the love routine again."

She picks at her fingernails, frowning.

"Heather, why is it that we've lived here over half a year and I've never once heard you talking to your family on the phone?"

"*Stop* it, Robin!" He watches as she stalks into the bedroom and brings from the closet the vacuum cleaner. She pulls at the cord and plugs it in, not looking at him.

"Heather," he says, "don't do that right now."

She switches the machine on and the air is filled with its mechanical whine. Robin watches her push the thing back and forth across the rug. She does not look at him; her face is tight. Within a few minutes she is finished and switches the machine off again.

"There," she says tightly, under her breath, as she wraps the cord around the handle. "Finished. Since no one *else* does it, *I* have to do it. Even though one person here works *full*-time and the other only works *part*-time."

"Heather, come over here. Sit down. Please?"

She does not look at him. She takes the machine back into the bedroom and Robin hears the closet door slam shut. Then silence.

Finally, after minutes have passed, Robin walks into the dim bedroom. She is lying on the bed, turned on her side away from him.

He sits next to her on the bed. "Sweetheart?"

She does not respond.

He reaches his hand to her shoulder. She draws away.

"Heather, don't be like that. Please." He moves closer to her and touches her hair. She does not move. He leans toward her then and kisses the back of her head.

"C'mon, Heather," he says quietly.

Her voice is tight as she says, "You think I'm a liar."

"No, no I don't."

"You do. You just said it in there. You said I've been lying to you from the beginning. That's what you *said.*"

"I know. I'm sorry. I was angry at how you were reacting. I didn't mean it—"

"You *did*—"

"Sweetheart, all I needed was some answers to some things. That's all. Is that so much to ask?"

"I've answered everything. All your interrogation."

He sighs. "I didn't mean it like that. I'm sorry I took that tone with you. I really am. It's just that..." He reaches for the words.

"Just that what?"

He strokes her shoulder gently for a long moment. "Heather," he says finally, "I don't think I know who you are."

She looks back at him. Her emotion is unreadable.

"What do you mean?" she asks.

"Just what I said."

"Robin, we've been together for—"

"I know how long we've been together. And I don't think I know who you are."

"I'm you," she says in a small voice. "We're the same."

"I mean—" he hesitates—"I mean, on a more practical level."

"Are you going to start interrogating me again?"

"Stop it. Don't be like that."

"Are you?"

"I'm not interrogating you. Please."

"Why don't you get a bright light to shine in my face? That's the way they do it in the movies."

He scowls. "Look," he says, irritated, "if you want to talk about interrogations, how about the fact that I've never once asked you to talk about the boyfriends you had when we were separated and yet all you ever think about is the girl I was with?"

"We're back to *her*," Heather spits, sitting up. "You just can't seem to get your mind off *her*."

"Stop it."

"Why should I? You live with me, you let me go out and work eight hours a day at the boutique to pay for your writing, and all day long you sit in this house and dream about *her*."

"*You're* the one who brings her up all the time!"

She jumps up and moves quickly into the main room, her bare feet making a hard thumping sound on the carpet. "That makes a lot of sense!" she calls back to him. "Your old girlfriends, that's just what I would want to talk about, twenty-four hours a day! Good thinking, Mr. Big Brain! That's all I want to hear!" He can hear her pulling open the refrigerator door and then slamming it shut again. "All Heather Seabright wants to hear in the whole wide world is about how you loved screwing a teenage—"

"*Stop* it!" He follows her into the kitchen, his pulse suddenly pounding in his head. "Heather, I am *tired* of these games of yours. I don't want to play them *any more*."

"Games?" She has taken a bottle of red wine in her hand and is pouring some into a glass. She slams the bottle down on the counter and swallows the wine in the glass. *"Games?"* That's all my feelings are to you, is *games?*"

"That is *not* what I said. You deliberately misconstrue everything—"

"You just *said* I was playing games! And what I'm doing is expressing my feelings! So my feelings are just games to you!"

He grabs the wine bottle, pours some in a glass, and swallows it quickly. He notices the diamond on her finger sparkling in the light. "I did not say your feelings were games," he says intensely. "I said you were *playing games with me.* There is a *difference.*"

"Big difference," she says, glaring at him and swallowing from her glass again. "One of those big intellectual things I just can't *understand,* I guess. I guess I'm just too *stupid.* Maybe you should go back to that little cunt of yours in Virginia—"

"Leave her out of it—"

"—And *screw* her a few more times, and explain it to *her.*"

"Shut up."

Her eyes are wide, furious. "Don't talk to me like that. Don't you *dare* talk to me like that."

"I told you to shut up." He finishes the wine in his glass and reaches for the bottle again.

She nods. "Mr. Big Brain's giving the orders now, huh? Mr. Freeloader is going to decide how things are going to be, huh? Who's *paying* for this house you live in, I wonder?"

"You are—"

"That's right! Mr. Big Brain is right again!"

"—Under an agreement that we came to *before* we started living together again. I'm living up to my part of the agreement."

"Oh, you are, huh? What about the other part of that little agreement of ours? That I wasn't going to have to play Mommy to poor little Robin because he can't *fuck* me? You were finally going to leave me *alone.* What happened to *that?*"

"*You* started that again."

"Oh, great!" She swallows again. "Poor little Robin can't take any responsibility for his own life now! Now everything that happens is the Dragon Lady's fault!"

His pulse is thundering in his ears and the wine is rushing to his head in black waves. "Knock it off," he says, his teeth clenched together. "Knock it the hell off. Shut up."

The Unspoken

"Don't tell me what to do!" she screams, slamming the bottle on the counter.

"*Shut your fucking mouth!*"

"*Goddamn you! I wish I'd never met you! I wish you were dead!*"

Her hand lashes out suddenly, striking him hard across the face. In the instant before it connects he sees her face, contorted and ugly and unrecognizable: then he sees nothing: as the palm strikes his skin something bursts inside him and it is as if he is suddenly within a dream, a participant but also an observer, inside himself yet also close behind. He sees his hands reaching toward her, knocking one of the wine glasses across the counter. It flies off the end and the wine splatters across the refrigerator and the glass bounces off a cabinet door and careens to the floor, bursting like a translucent blossom. He hurls her against the refrigerator. She slaps back at him. He hears her voice only distantly, as from a faraway place, and he cannot distinguish the words. He grabs at her hair and her face twists in pain. Glancing down he sees that she has stepped on a shard of the blossom glass and blood runs from her heel into the floor. He shoves her rudely over the kitchen steps, she stumbles and falls onto the carpet. Then he is on top of her but also behind himself, watching, and he sees shades of red spinning around him madly like a carousel of blood, and there is darkness too, darkness whirling, endless swirling streaks of black, he slaps at her and wrenches the bra from her chest and pushes his hand into her pants, between her legs, and the rage is uncontrollable now, he cannot stop it, but he also watches, watches over his own shoulder, pulling and tearing at the pants, slapping at her face, prying open her legs, then holding her by the neck as she slaps and slaps at him but she is a mere insect now as he holds her and tugs at his own pants and pulls himself out and drives himself into her. He hears her cry out. He hears her from the distant place crying to him Robin stop it hurts Robin it hurts. But he drives himself into her and he has never felt so powerful, so completely in control, as if the entire universe were flowing into him and through him, and he watches himself, watches the lilies and the lions and the galaxies and all things and all time rushing into him in the single endless moment of perfect ecstasy, hears her crying, sees her eyes filled with terror and awe, and then the moment releases, bursts like an ecstatic blossom, opens, unleashes, and he is free, completely free, a spirit floating in the sky, over oceans and islands and through space and into the moon and the stars....

He stops moving.

The red light and the streaks of darkness recede slowly; and he finds himself fading into the room again, dizzily, nauseously.

Oily sweat covers his body. He is panting heavily. Heather's eyes are closed tightly and she is weeping in short, erratic gasps of shallow breath.

He rolls away from her.

For minutes the floor seems to sway and buck. Once he tries to stand but he hardly makes it to his knees before the carpet rushes toward him again. He lies there then, eyes open and staring at the ceiling, breathing hungrily through his gaping mouth.

Finally he turns his head and looks toward her. Her arm covers her eyes and her mouth is disfigured as she cries, her body bouncing with her convulsions. But she is nearly silent. Robin listens. The sound is eerie, ominous. His eyes move down her body. There are red marks on her side where the bra was ripped away. There are speckles of blood around her vagina. There is blood on both her feet from the broken glass and the blood has run up her ankles; trickles reach as far as her calves.

He closes his eyes for a long moment and then opens them again. His vision is blurry as if strange webs were draped before his eyes. He manages to get to his knees and he glances out the window at the dimming light and the fog which covers everything in a glistening mist. He stands. The floor continues to sway but by holding to the wall he is able to make his way into the bathroom. He falls onto his knees then, in front of the toilet, and vomits into it. It is as if his entire body wants to pour out of itself and be flushed away into an eternal darkness. He convulses three times, four. Finally it is done and he reaches to the handle and flushes the mess away. He staggers to the sink then, coughing, and rinses his mouth.

At last, shakily, he moves to the bathroom cabinet and opens it and brings out bandages and gauze and iodine and a towel and a washcloth which he wets with hot water. He takes these items into the main room where Heather is lying, curled-up fetally now and weeping, her face hidden in her hands. He places them next to her feet. Then he goes to the kitchen, stepping carefully around the glass, and finds a silver metal bowl which he fills with hot water. Another, smaller bowl he leaves empty. He searches for a drinking glass, cannot find one; settles for a coffee cup; he fills this with cold water and takes the bowls and cup to her. Finally he moves to the bedroom, his vision still grayly fogged, and strips a blanket from the bed. He brings it into the main room and sets it next to her and he kneels down near her feet.

He reaches toward her and touches the bleeding foot gently. She inhales sharply and pulls the foot away. She is quivering.

"Heather," Robin says quietly, "you're bleeding. Let me have your foot."

He reaches to it again. When he touches it she pulls it away a second time. Her breath is erratic and she makes a small whimpering sound.

"Heather," he says gently, "come on. Let me fix it."

She looks at him through her fingers, her eyes wet and frightened. "No," she says in a strangled voice.

He looks back at her, trying to stay calm and emotionless, trying to keep the bile from rising in his throat again. He looks down at her foot again and reaches toward it. She tries to draw it away but he grasps it firmly this time and brings it near him. He holds her by her ankle and tries not to hear the uneven whimpers coming from her as he looks at the red-smeared thing and sees that a large chunk of glass has lodged into her heel.

"Hold still," he says, his voice barely a whisper.

In a smooth motion he pulls the glass shard from her heel. She gasps once. He drops the glass into the empty bowl, then takes the washcloth and begins wiping away the blood. There is a tremendous lot of it. He discovers several more bits of glass in her foot and he pulls them away and drops them into the empty bowl. At last when he has her foot reasonably clean and has wiped the stains from her ankle and calf he takes up the iodine.

"This may sting a little."

He paints some of it into the bottom of her foot. She does not resist. Finally he affixes a large bandage over her heel and two smaller ones elsewhere. Then he takes her other foot in his hands and discovers only one minor cut there. He cleans it and affixes a small bandage.

He looks at her. She is staring at nothingness now, her hands before her in a vaguely prayerful manner. Her face is soaked with tears and her eyes are dark-ringed and puffy.

Her pants are bunched down around her thighs. He reaches to them, touches her softly.

"Let's get these off you," he says, his voice hollow in his ears. "I brought you a blanket."

"No," she says, trembling. But she does not move to resist.

He pulls the sweatpants from her legs as gently as he can and she lies there naked, curled up like a seashell. He places the blanket over her shoulders and around her legs. He moves to where he had seen the speckles of blood and, after rinsing out the washcloth in the bowl of water, touches her there. Her legs clench together.

"Heather," he whispers, "it's all right. Let me get you cleaned up." He touches her again. After a long moment her legs relax slightly and he wipes her gently with the washcloth. Then he covers her with the blanket.

"Let me see up here," he says, and lifts the blanket away to see her breasts. He studies the red streak on her skin, touches it softly.

"It's not bleeding," he whispers. "It's just a…an abrasion. I think we'll leave it alone."

Finally he looks at her face. Her eyes are like broken prisms. He rinses the cloth again, thoroughly, and cradles her head in his arm. He uses the washcloth to wipe away the glistening wet on her face and the mucous under her nose. Then he takes the cup of water and holds it to her lips. She swallows once, coughs. Her breathing has slowed.

After she has finished drinking they do not move for a long time.

"Do you want me to call the hospital?" he asks at last.

"No."

There is silence between them for several minutes.

"Do you want me to call the police?"

"No."

They sit together and the darkness in the room grows. At last it is nearly night and Robin says, "Let me put these things away, Heather." He stands and picks up the bowls and cup and other things and puts them in the kitchen. He sweeps the kitchen floor and wipes off the door of the refrigerator.

When he turns back to look at her again she has dragged herself up to the window and is staring out at the darkening gloom, holding the blanket tightly around herself. Robin's legs seem ready to give out under him so he moves close to her and sits down. He does not touch her. He tries to keep his mind perfectly blank.

After a long time, after it is completely dark in the room and Heather appears no more to him than a blanketed white ghost, her voice, far away, small, old, reaches him. She asks him a question to which he can think of no reply. In a whisper she asks, "Robin, what's going to happen to us?"

5
DROWNING
Chapter Six

He feels the wave beginning to decline so he stops at a liquor store and buys a bottle, gulping a good half of it down thirstily as he drives. He should be happy, he realizes, all things considered. He's free. Half-drunk. Just been laid. It's a beautiful night, the stars like lighted crystals above him. A night good enough to write a poem about. If he still wrote poems. If he still wrote anything. He drives slowly, with no particular destination in mind. He thinks about Rachel and tries not to think about her. Screw her; who needed the crap? He just got a first-class lay from a beautiful blonde, and really, there wasn't much that Rachel could give him that the blonde hadn't. A truckload of horseshit, maybe.

Eventually he finds himself in front of Dusty's movie theater again. The sign is still bright but the place looks deserted.

He sighs. He wouldn't have minded sinking into one of those cushiony chairs and pleasantly dozing to the sound of mutant monsters from outer space terrorizing virginal white girls. Ah, well. He parks the car around back and decides to get out anyway. Just then Dusty comes out the rear door.

"Seeg!" he says.

"Hi, Dusty. You still here?"

"Aw, we've been training this new guy. My assistant. But he got everything screwed up tonight…turns out they'd been calling me ever since I left for the bar. So I been busy straightening out the mess."

"That's too bad."

Dusty glances back at Siegel's car. "Where's Rachel?"

"Home…she went home."

Dusty glances back at him. "Oh," he says, simply. "You guys should have stuck around. The second movie was a lot better."

"Well…" Siegel rubs his cheek. "Sorry about that."

Dusty leans up against the theater wall. "Hey, I know how it goes," he says.

"Don't you ever turn off your sign?" Siegel asks. Around the corner of the building he can see the neon shining in the window of the store across the street.

"Nah, we leave it on so people can see what's playing. If they want to come tomorrow or something, I mean. You okay, Seeg?"

"Hm? I'm fine."

"You look kind of funny. I dunno."

He shakes his head. "I'm fine."

"Where's Rachel?"

"I told you. She went home."

"I wouldn't've thought I'd see you again tonight. With Rachel's parents out of town and all."

He shrugs. "She was tired."

"Oh." He nods. "Boy, she didn't look it. She looked like a million bucks, didn't she?"

"Yeah, I guess."

They stand there in the cool night.

"Late," Dusty says finally. "Guess I better get home, man."

"Yeah…okay."

"You call me tomorrow?"

"Sure. Sure I will."

Dusty smiles. "Nah, you won't. But I'll call you. Okay? Maybe we can get together again. You and me and Rachel. Or just…or just you and me, man. If that's better."

"What do you mean?"

There is a brief pause. Then Dusty shrugs.

"I dunno."

"We'll get together," Siegel says. "The three of us. We'll go someplace. Sailing, maybe. Rachel can get her dad's boat."

Dusty smiles. "Sure, man. That'd be great."

"I'll call you. I will. Tomorrow."

"Sure, man. Great."

"I guess we'd better get some sleep."

"Yeah. Late."

"I'll see you, Dusty."

"'Night, man."

They look at each other a moment longer. Then Siegel turns and gets into his car and pulls away. He picks up his bottle again and drinks. He looks in the rear view mirror at the theater but Dusty is already gone.

At the old high school he wanders down a long, dark row of colorless lockers until he comes to his own. That is, the one he had back then, ten thousand years ago. It looks much the same, a little more dented maybe, but it hasn't been repainted; an unfamiliar *Pink Floyd* sticker is affixed to the lower left corner. Then he glances at the locker next to it, Rachel's locker. It is the same too. He sits down with his back to the lockers and stares up at the ceiling of the long hall. It is very quiet. When he'd approached the lockers he could hear his footsteps echoing up and down the hall but now all is silent. They met at these lockers, he and Rachel, when they were sophomores and Rachel still wore those shiny silver railroad tracks on her teeth. God, she looked younger then, he realizes. He wonders if he has changed that much. Down the hall he can see the door to Mrs. Rocca's room, or the room that was hers back then at any rate, where he and Dusty had English together. High up on the walls are photos of each graduating class, each student with his own picture. After a time he stands and wanders to his own class. The faces are familiar but seem to belong to people he knew hundreds of years ago. Even Rachel's picture is like that. He remembers the wallet-sized print she gave him of that shot, with her looking so fresh and young and happy-go-lucky: *Dear Siegel, she'd written in loopy, microscopic print, What is there to say that you can say on the back of a dumb little picture? I love you. I really do! You're all that matters to me in the whole world. Keep your head above water and be good. Write me every week from that college of yours, Sweet. See ya at Christmas. Love, Rachel XXXXX.*

College! He can hardly recall that brief debacle back east. He can vaguely summon up misty visions of a cramped dorm room, idiot roommate, green-tinged cafeteria eggs; but it had lasted only a few weeks: then he received the call from his dad, the distant voice quavering, saying that Mom was in the hospital. He remembers the plane going back and Rachel picking him up at the airport. Getting to the hospital and seeing his mom there surrounded by all those sterile white death things, needles and tubes and plastic pieces in her nose, the slow, evil hissing of the oxygen. Her eyes dull, unfocused.

Hello, Siegel, she said. Vaguely he heard Rachel and his dad closing the door, leaving him alone with her.

Hi, Mom. When you getting out of here?

Soon…I'm getting out soon.

How had it happened? He had been gone only a month and yet she looked a decade older. It was incredible. Her hair was white, her face sickly yellow and puffed out, her hands fat and soft. How in the world had it occurred?

That's good, he said. Can't have you in here being sick.

She closed her foggy eyes and smiled slightly.

But it was all over, he knew. She was gone, lost. He stared at the woman in the white bed and tried to connect her somehow with the person he remembered, the woman in the bathtub when he was young. The woman alive with mystery and love, even if it was tempered many times by the amber liquid he detested, even if it was often fractured, distorted. She no longer existed, that woman. In her place was this charlatan, this impostor. He felt like lifting her and yelling in her face: *What have you done with my mother?*

Instead he stood over her silently and listened to her ragged breathing and the hissing of the oxygen. Soon he realized she'd fallen asleep. All he wanted to do was get out of there; run; hide; but he stood unmoving. He thought that somebody should stay. He stood there for a long time. Finally his dad came back in and touched his shoulder.

C'mon, Siegel, he said. There's no more we can do now.

He remembered his breath coming fast and shallow, not unlike the woman's there in the bed. Something came over him suddenly and he turned from his dad and ran out of the room and up the hall and found Rachel in the waiting room.

Come on, he said, strangled. We've got to...I...

What? she said. What?

But he couldn't form the words. He had an incredible, overwhelming urge to push the nightmare away, put it as far from him as possible, wipe the death away like he would some kind of grime on his skin, wipe it away with life and being and forgetting. Rachel had understood. He hadn't had to tell her. She took him for a long, silent drive into the foothills, darkness falling around them. They didn't speak a word for hours. They made slow, gentle love.

She had understood.

How? How could she have understood him then?

And what had happened later? When she had stopped understanding?

Who had he become in those following months? Years?

He thinks about the times later, in the apartment up north, when his vision would blur and he would forget where he was, overcome with visions of floods and falling stars and bombs: sometimes it would happen as he was walking down the street, or in a restaurant; he would try to cover it, say to himself, *This isn't real, doesn't matter how real it looks, remember you're in a restaurant, don't freak out, keep it together, don't go under.* And the weekends together, trying to explain it all to Rachel, trying to describe it in words; an impossibility; for what he could describe were only the images, the fantasies, the superficial things of it, not where it came from or what it meant. The failure of words. He thinks back to earlier this night, trying to tell Rachel why friend Saul pained him so, but talking about the sex alone, though sex was only part of it, not even the most important part, but he hadn't been able to find words to describe the rest of it; and so it was lost. And so nothing they said to each other meant anything. He remembers other pointless conversations: the first psychiatrist, Liona; Dusty; Hewitt. So much empty verbiage, meaningless sounds—none of it mattered: it was a waste, so much so that he'd finally started lying to Hewitt, telling him what he wanted to hear, for the textbook definitions were so easy to follow; and sure enough, a few weeks later he was pronounced fit and ready for the world again. But he was, of course, unchanged from before. *You're only cheating yourself,* he hears some high school teacher telling one of his classes. But that was where they were wrong: for they assumed that the answer could be found in words, in talking, arguing, forgiving. But none of that mattered. Bombs were still bombs and death still death and we were all still sentenced to life imprisonment inside our own skulls. There wasn't a chance of ever making anything but the most superficial, illusory contact with anyone else. And so he had decided his world, of the floods and falling stars and bombs, was as good as anybody else's. What did it matter? Until all he could hear was the end of the world, everything else was far back, like a telephone voice hidden under static.

Until they took him away from his apartment, injected things into him, made the universe's collapse fade to a distant hum, a faraway cry; until it disappeared almost completely.

He lies down in the hall and shuts his eyes. Perhaps he can sleep now, he thinks, with all the alcohol in him, all the tiredness. He doesn't feel especially anxious as he usually does when he tries to sleep. He can sense the hall slipping away from him, rushing back down a long corridor, and a new world coming up to greet him. Darkness and silence. Sleep, he realizes. He's going to go to sleep. He feels a tingle of satisfaction run through his body. Sleep. He feels his body settle in, relax, his eyes calm and untwitching. Peace…Quiet…He thinks of nothing as he drops into a black void.

But then suddenly the bloated white dead form in the bed rises before him and he gasps and shakes his head violently and he is awake again in the long school hallway. Awake. Breathing. Alive.

He can see her bedroom window from where his car is parked. Her light is on; he watches for any sign of movement in the room. He had planned to knock on her door, to just get out of the car and walk up and knock. But it hadn't worked out that way: when he actually arrived, looked at the house, he hadn't been able to go through with it. So instead he sits and looks at the yellow-curtained light in the window, thinking about getting out of the car. But knowing he won't do it.

Hi, sweet. He hears her voice in his mind.

He wants to go to the door, but what could he say? There was never any explaining it. He would just end up saying something else, something different from what he meant. And that would just make things worse. He wishes there were some other form of language, something besides words which only made everything cheap and shallow and ridiculous.

His mind flutters across the novel again, the great unfinished novel. He has never thought of it quite this way before: but that, really, is the reason he'd never finished it. Words. After his mom's death, after realizing that there was no hope of bridging the gulf between him and his dad, it had all begun to seem silly. The novel. Writing. Literature. He'd looked over everything he'd written since high school and it all seemed ludicrous, a joke. He read others' books. None of them were any better, none of them could overcome the medium, none of them communicated anything. They were all just silly contraptions that purported to have Great Meaning but really were just stupid little stories made up by people who'd failed to bridge the chasm, the enormous space between idea and expression: and he'd looked at more art, at paintings, at films, and found the same thing, that none of it communicated what it wanted to, what it *meant* to, it could grasp only an infinitesimal fragment of the idea, the vision. A microscopically small portion of the great darkness.

He'd given up.

He thinks of the manuscript there in the bureau drawer back home, and wistfully the fantasy of having it published, his name in print on a book by the big New York publisher, crosses his mind. He supposes he could still do it if he wanted. But when he'd realized the failure of words, of art, it had become pointless. What was the use of another stupid little story that said nothing? That cheated, that simplified, that suggested some pattern of existence when all was really random chaos? Not a bit of it could ever be understood by anyone. We work in the dark. We do what we can.

He sighs and drinks from the bottle and looks at Rachel's bedroom window. He takes off his glasses and wipes them. That was when the split had come, when he'd decided that all was uncertainty and confusion and there was no hope of ever communicating anything to anyone. That was when Rachel seemed to fade into the horizon to him, vanish into the sun, become unreal; when everything became unreal. When the bombs and falling stars were as real as the floor under him. When the strands of what he'd thought of as "reality" pulled apart. When he'd hit her in a desperate attempt—yes, this was it!—to be *with* her, together, in the same world. But it hadn't happened. At the end of it she was as unreal as she'd been before. And so he stopped calling her. Stopped writing. Stopped going out, except to the corner grocery for wine now and then. Mostly he just sat in his room marveling at the stars and bombs and great explosions and how they would disappear sometimes and be replaced by the game show on the TV or the sound of cars going by outside. But that world was no more real to him than the other. They were the same. He lived in one as much as the other.

Finally he notices some movement in the bedroom. He watches as Rachel, a dark shadow behind the curtain, moves about in the room. She is taking off her clothes. He imagines her naked body pulling back the bedcovers and slipping in between the cool, fresh sheets. The outline of her body under the covers. The look of her dark hair on the pillow. Her arms opening to him. He wants to run to her. She turns out the light. He starts the car.

The ocean is dark and quiet as he gets out of the car and breathes the night air. He stands in the driveway of his dad's house—he can't think of it as his own anymore, or as the "family's"—and is vaguely surprised to notice that the lights are still on. His dad is not a night person, never has been: "Night's for sleeping," he'd say. "Give me a bright morning with a little breeze and the sun coming up over the mountains any day." Very unlike his mom. His mom thrived at night, laughed and drank at night, stayed out at the bars at night. And she had died, he realizes, at night.

He remembers the autopsy, or its results anyway, being told that cirrhosis had made her liver stop functioning and the fluid therefore had begun to back up in her body, which explained her

The Unspoken

grotesque fatness and softness and shortness of breath; until the liquid had backed into her lungs and she'd no longer been able to breathe. He'd asked the doctor how it could have happened so suddenly, in just a few weeks. He'd said that these things sometimes happened this way (he was an old man and a compassionate one, but a tired one, one who had seen this many times), that a person could by sheer power of will keep her body together, functioning, as long as she had some reason for it, some purpose. Had anything bad happened to her lately? Anything that might make her lose that will?

And he realized suddenly that her abrupt decline coincided exactly with his departure for college.

Why didn't you *do* anything? he wanted to scream at his dad.

But how could anyone have known? How could Siegel have known that it was him, his mere presence, that held her together, that in losing her son to a college back east she was losing the final thread that connected her to this world? That she was that sick? Why didn't she tell him? Why didn't she...

Words, he thinks. She could only have used words, and those would have communicated nothing, meant nothing. She had understood that. And so she'd said nothing, hoped that somehow he would understand; but he was too young, too immature, he didn't have any idea. Not like he does now. Standing there leaning against the back of the car and looking out at the dark ocean he feels he understands her perfectly.

He remembers her sitting cross-legged on his bed in her flimsy white nightgown with a cup of coffee in her hands that smelled like the amber liquid and looking at him, asking him about his writing, his stories, having him read them to her. She would touch her dark curls and twist them as he read. She would smile sometimes, at odd moments, and look up at him from the bed with love in her eyes. Pride.

You're going to be a famous writer someday.

He would grin nervously, bashfully, he would shrug.

He was fifteen. He was sixteen. The amber liquid flowed in rivers. His dad was a vague sometime presence, often gone at work, on long trips to distant cities; he was no more than a silhouette, really, a dark shadow-man. Staying away. Doing nothing. Nobody doing anything. The rivers flowing. She no longer going to the bars, staying in her room, her eyes dull, lifeless. Darkness falling in the room, yellow-tinged half-light. The TV in the room droning mindlessly. Refusals. Recriminations. Partial recoveries. Bumping against the wall as she walked. Bowls slipping through her fingers. Her voice quavering and harsh. Partial recoveries. Almost total recoveries. Walking along the beach together, Dad in one of his faraway cities, talking about the future one early evening. She only slightly drunk, barefoot in her long flowing white nightgown. He remembers thinking about the past, thinking how it was like a road that got longer and longer every day, and yet the longer it got, the more he wanted to travel it. Wanted to return to the softly smiling woman who sat cross-legged on his bed listening to his stories and telling him he would be a famous writer someday. Sometimes when he was young they would splash about in the ocean together under the bright moon, laughing and giggling and then charging back to the house, their bodies glistening with crystals of sea-water, where she would run a warm towel over his body, they would shake water onto each other breathlessly. Later they would listen to music on the stereo, or watch old movies on TV, his head in her lap, her cool fingers running through his hair. But then later, in her own room, the amber liquid, the doll eyes...

Suddenly the front door opens and he hears his dad's voice: "Siegel?"

He clears his throat. "Yeah?"

He sees his dad leaning out the front door, holding the screen in one hand. "Coming in?"

"Yeah. Just getting a little fresh air."

He walks toward his dad and the light in the house. "Not like you to be up this late, Dad," he says.

His dad smiles and shrugs as they go inside. "Thought I'd wait up for you."

"You didn't have to do that."

His dad shrugs. "Well, your first day and all, I ought to make sure you make it back in one piece, shouldn't I?"

Siegel grins. Has it really only been one day? Hell, less than that. A few hours, really. His dad goes back to his chair in the living room. On the TV is an old western with Gary Cooper.

"Sit down," his dad says. "Made some popcorn. Have some."

Siegel sits on the sofa and stares at the movie for a few minutes.

"Have a good time?" his dad asks finally, during the commercial.

"Hm? Oh, yeah. Great."

"So how's your friend Dusty?"

"He's great. Same ol', same ol', you know. He never changes."

"He's a good kid, that Dusty."

He doesn't answer. The movie runs for a few more minutes and then another commercial comes on.

"So," his dad says, "you guys do anything special?"

He shrugs. "Went to a movie, that's all."

"What movie'd you see?"

Siegel names it. It seems to him that his dad is asking an awful lot of questions. But instinctively he realizes what is happening, and is even touched by it: his dad is trying to have a conversation with him. But it isn't working. All they can talk about are the dumb things, the meaningless things, the stupid talk. They can't even make an attempt to say anything more to each other, even if it were possible. Which of course it isn't.

"Have a little to drink while you were out?" his dad asks.

Siegel smiles. "A little. Does it show?"

His dad returns the smile. "A little." There is a pause, then he gestures at the TV. "You like Gary Cooper?"

Dad, let's have a real talk. About Mom. And you and me. Let's talk about everything. So what if it won't make any difference in the long run. So what if words don't mean anything and everything is made cheap and simple by them. Let's try anyway.

"I don't know...I don't remember much that he did. *Meet John Doe*, I remember that. And *High Noon*."

The thing is, we've never talked about this kind of stuff at all, Dad, it's like Mom never existed, like nothing ever happened. Well, it all happened. She happened. And we need to talk about how it happened and why and what it means and what we're going to do with the rest of our lives.

"Have you ever seen *Sergeant York?*"

I want you to tell me why you were never there. Why you let everything happen the way it did. Why you were so damn weak about it.

"No, I never did. I saw *Farewell to Arms*."

You're so manly and all that shit. Why didn't you do something?

"I remember that one. Helen Hayes was in it."

Why didn't we talk about it? Why didn't you just admit it, tell me that you were too weak to deal with it? Instead of pretending it wasn't happening?

"Was it Helen Hayes? Really? The nurse?"

Because if you'd said that, you bastard, maybe I would have understood and not hated you so much.

"Yeah. I'm pretty sure it was."

Look, you shit, I was in the same boat. Why didn't we do anything? You're my damned father. I was sixteen. You should have led the way.

"How about that. Hard to believe. So young then."

Instead of running off all the time. You should have been here. She needed you. I needed you.

"I know. She's so old now. That's the way life goes, I guess."

I still do, goddamn it.

"Well, Dad, I guess I'm going to hit the hay."

I love you, damn it. Whether I like it or not. Even though I hate you, I love you.

"Okay, kiddo. Get some sleep."

I love you, Dad.

"Okay. 'Night."

Dad...

"'Night, Seeg."

6

"Welcome to Skid Row!" Cape Erikson Barnes says, grinning. "Robin, it's *great* to see you!"

They embrace briefly. "How are you, Cape?"

"Snafu. I don't want to talk about it. C'mon in!"

Robin steps into the apartment, dim and dingy in the late afternoon light. It is all one room: a rumpled bed in the corner; a tiny kitchenette across from it, the sink piled with dirty dishes; a bathroom next to it, the door hanging open, the sound of water dripping into a tub. Crates and cardboard boxes cover the floor, giving the dark room a feeling of temporary occupancy, through traffic. Guitars are propped up against the walls.

"Pull up a crate!" Cape says, laughingly inverting one of the wooden crates and making a show of dusting it off with his hand. "First-class accomo's here, let me tell you."

"But it's a room," Robin says, his eyes moving over the stained, bare walls. "That's more than you had before."

"Well, I still spend a lot a time in the sacred beast," Cape says. "Truth is, I'm borrowing this place from a guy who's out of town for a while. In jail, actually."

Robin looks at him. The most immediately noticeable change in Cape is a light, tidy beard covering his cheeks and chin, and for some minutes this is all the change that Robin notices. It is attractive and Robin finds himself trying to visualize exactly what Cape had looked like before, nearly two years ago. He has no photographs. He had remembered Cape as being rather taller than he really is; the face somehow differently proportioned. It is a strange sensation: Cape is simultaneously familiar and unfamiliar. His hair is somewhat longer than Robin remembers it, spilling now in graceful waves over his collar; is he perhaps a bit heavier? He wears faded blue jeans and a close-fitting black T-shirt which Robin almost thinks he recognizes. The eyes, like descending teardrops, are the same. The quick grin is the same.

"I can actually offer you some refreshment," Cape says. "Yesterday, after you called, I went out and got some junk. I figured it wouldn't be all that swift to agree to host a foreign student like you and then dehydrate him to death. Want something?"

Robin shrugs, smiling. "A Coke, maybe."

"Coming up. Pronto." Cape goes to the tiny refrigerator under the sink, brings out two cans of Coke and tosses one to Robin. "So what do you think of my new empire?" he asks.

"Rustic," Robin says, popping open the can.

Cape chuckles. "I haven't been here long. And I don't really spend much time here. It's kind of nice, you know, having four walls to call your own." He opens the can and takes a long swallow. "I mean, for a change of *pace*."

"What happened to New York?"

"Well," Cape says, finding a crate to invert, "I played that gig, sure enough. Six months' worth. Made some money, even. But it was a dead-end thing. It never went anywhere. So after the gig I hung around New York, got a few jobs, you know, here and there. Didn't light any rivers on fire. Finally I decided I liked the West Coast better and wandered back here."

"Sorry it didn't work out."

"Yeah, well, that's the breaks, you know. Hey, how's Cissy? I haven't heard from her forever."

"Well, you know they went on their world trip." Robin lists the places from which he has received postcards, the most recent being Japan. "I think they'll be coming back in not too long. Priscilla mentioned that their money was starting to run a little low."

Cape nods. "I always liked those two. I really did. Two peas in a pod."

Robin smiles. "I know."

"And they're still together."

"Mm-hm."

Cape shakes his head. "It's hard," he says. "Hard, for two girls. Harder for guys, though, I think."

"Well," Robin says, "history has never cared much about lesbians. It's usually homosexual men who get shot."

"Don't I know it! And now there's this AIDS thing. Creepy crap. But what brings you here, pardner? I mean, it's great to see you, but I'm a little surprised."

"I just wanted to come to Santa Barbara again," he says. "And I needed a place to sleep, that's all." He smiles. "Don't read into it more than what's really there."

Cape grins. "You're not in school, right?"

"No, I dropped out. I'm living with someone there in San Francisco. Or…I was. I'm not sure now if I am or not."

"Mm." He nods and touches his beard. "I get the picture. Family crisis time?"

Robin chuckles. "Something like that."

"Well, you've come to the right place." Cape stands and moves to a small tape player. "We'll take care of you here. It's a home away from home."

The music comes on: slow blues. It takes him a moment to recognize the voice. Bessie Smith—he has not heard her in ages; the voice pitches him back abruptly to the van, the sea, the darkness.

He had made the decision to come here with almost savage suddenness. He knew that he had to escape. He knew that, whatever happened, he and Heather could not stay together; at least not for the time being. Every time he looked at her he felt a thick, dark cloak of guilt pass over him. For he *was* guilty, after all; at last, he had found something of which he was incontestably guilty. There was a certain sardonic satisfaction in it. He had felt guilty his whole life anyway; now, at last, his guilt had been confirmed. This was despite the fact that in the days following the incident, Heather had said nothing about it; had not shied away from him or accused him silently with her eyes; they continued together as before. Oddly, she seemed less affected by it than he was. It replayed itself in his mind over and over again; and he could hardly believe that it had been him, that he had done such a thing. He was guilty. It was as if something had broken inside him once and for all; as if darknesses he had kept at bay all these years had suddenly ripped themselves free of their bonds and were now on a mad, destructive spree. And yet there was nothing different about him externally. Heather did not seem to think anything was amiss. Cape does not, now. But within himself, he knows that something has changed.

And you dropped, lost, when something broke / And let you from a Dream.

Emily Dickinson: he had been considering it as an epigraph for *Drowning*. But now it seems just as appropriate to himself. He had felt afterward as if he were literally descending, dropping wildly into a place of darkness, tumbling downward like Orpheus into the underworld. He had to escape. What was coming was black and frightening. He did not need Heather to be his Eurydice. He did not want to drop into this darkness, this unspoken nothingness.

And so he had gone. He had said to Heather simply: I have to go. She asked, Will you be back? And he said, I don't know. This time she did not argue the fact; no screaming scenes or fits of weeping; she had merely nodded, said, I love you, and he had left. Cape had seemed happy to hear from him on the telephone; and Santa Barbara seemed somehow to beckon to him. He had known, after all, happiness here. At least he thought he had; his memory could, he knew, have played tricks on him. He had been a different person then, another Robin; and so who could tell if there would be anything in the city for him now? Possibly, very possibly, there would be nothing. But he had to leave. Run, flee.

"How long will I have the sunshine of your smile?" Cape asks, grinning at him from the tape player.

Robin glances up at him. "I'm not sure," he says. "A few days, maybe a few weeks. But if it's any problem…"

"Shit, it's no problem. It's great to see you again. You look good. A little pale, maybe, but good."

No one can see it, he thinks. No one knows of the unleashed, speechless dark.

"So do you," he smiles. "The beard is a nice touch."

"How's the writing?"

"I had a poem published a while back."

"Oh, yeah. You told me that. So you're moving up in the world, huh?"

Orpheus, dropping. Lost.

"Sure," he says. "Little by little. How about you? Are you with a band now?"

"Yeah, I've got a steady thing at Pat O'Bannon's down on lower State. Three nights a week." He shrugs. "At least I don't have to work now. At a job, I mean. I don't even shoplift much these days."

"That's bad," Robin smiles. "You'll lose your edge."

Cape laughs. "Don't I know it. But what the hell!"

That night he sleeps demurely on the floor and the next day, after Cape leaves for rehearsals, Robin takes his car and drives to the old familiar places. He looks in at the tire warehouse but sees no one he recognizes. Then he goes past Priscilla and Koofie's place, the old, squat brick building: but boards have been hammered over the windows now and it appears to have been abandoned. He is filled with melancholy, sitting in the car staring at the decaying brick structure. How vividly he recalls his first appearance here! And being accepted by them, totally accepted, sleeping near them in the second floor room, going to the beach with them, receiving back rubs from Priscilla. Open, free.

He steps out of the car and tries to enter the building; but the door is locked tight. He peers through a crack in the boards over one window and sees that the ground floor is covered with boards and sawdust and empty crates. He sighs and turns away.

At the old courthouse he takes the elevator up to the observation tower and stands there, leaning against the railing, just as the three of them had on the day after he had arrived. But now fog and intermittent clouds spot the vista and the view is limited. He remembers the simple happiness he had felt here then; the childlike sensation of delight at having actually done it, come here, and having been accepted so totally. He wishes the two of them were here now. But even if they were, he knows, it would not be the same: nothing, he realizes, is ever recapturable: nothing tossed into the swirling vortex of time ever returns.

He feels suddenly lonely.

Then Cape had come into it; and for a few days it had seemed that he had everything he could ever have possibly wanted. But it had not lasted. Soon the amoebas were ripping themselves in two and it was over, all of it, finished. He had been forced to return to Wind Point in defeat.

He stares out at the Santa Barbara vista. Somehow it is less interesting than he had thought it would be; he has, he thinks to himself, seen it all before. But then the first time he had seen it, it had not been the vista itself that was important; it was a mood, a tone, that no longer exists. The possibility of freedom was so alive in him then: and that was what had charged the moment, filled it with magic. Now, he knows, he is broken; and the darknesses have begun to take over. There is no magic left. There had never been much, not since the woman in the lily-sprayed dress had pressed her weight down on the side of his bed and looked at him with her hazy eyes, talking of diamonds suspended in the sky and floating trips to the moon; now whatever had been left has been snuffed-out. Crushed.

7

"I haven't been here forever," Cape says, stepping out of the van. "Hasn't changed much, huh?"

Robin steps from the van into the darkness. He follows Cape to the ocean's edge. And it does seem, for a moment, the same: quiet, isolated, like a single little honeycomb hidden in the wilderness. He stares at the moon over the waters, picturing vaguely a woman in a white gown with gems sparkling on her neck and fingers floating, slowly floating, up through the black sky.

"It's pretty much the same," Robin agrees.

But it is not. Or rather he is not: and so it is all different.

"I'm glad we came out here," Cape says, looking at the ocean, nodding to himself. "It's a nice place."

"Mm-hm."

They look at each other awkwardly. Robin chuckles. After a moment Cape turns and moves back toward the van. He opens the rear doors and sits, his legs dangling down. "You know," Cape says, "you've been here for days and yet you haven't once made a comment about the sacred beast."

"What is there to say about it?" Robin asks, smiling back at him.

"Well, I don't know. You could kneel down and say some hosannas or something. When we first met you were a bit *dubious* about this fine machine. And yet here it is, still smokin'." He laughs.

"I stand corrected," Robin admits, walking up the sand toward Cape. "It's a hell of a machine."

"Damn right. I think it's immortal. I never do *any* work on it. Sometimes a tire blows out. That's it. Never any engine trouble at all. Which is good. I'm not real big into engines."

Robin smiles and sits down next to Cape. "Do you ever hear from your family?"

Cape frowns, touches his beard. "I stopped by for a few minutes on my way back from New York. I didn't stay long."

"Still no-go with your father, huh?"

"'Fraid so. How 'bout yours?"

"I haven't talked to my father in a year."

Cape nods. "You needed to get rid of that umbilical cord. It was strangling you."

Robin shrugs. They fall silent again. Robin listens to the waves.

"So what are you doing to do?" Cape asks quietly. "About your crisis thing, I mean."

"I don't know."

"Well, you can stay here as long as you want. I mean with me. It's no problem."

"Thanks, Cape."

They fall silent again. The night is warm and still.

Suddenly, and without thinking about it at all, Robin leans over and kisses him.

"You're taking the lead?" Cape asks quietly, their faces close together. "That's a switch."

"I'm not as innocent as I used to be," Robin smiles. "Anyway, it's pretty much inevitable, isn't it?"

"What?"

"You. Me. Ocean. Night. Van."

Cape chuckles. "Yeah, I guess it is."

⇌

Later it is pitch-dark and slow, soft blues songs play quietly over the speakers and they are wrapped in each other and the warm blankets but it is not the same.

"What's wrong?" Cape asks him, his eyes glittering.

"Nothing."

"You never finished."

"I finished *you*."

He laughs. "You know what I mean."

"I'm all right. I'm tired." He looks at the van's ceiling, different emotions coursing through him.

"You seem a little…"

"What?"

"I don't know," Cape says. "Distant?"

They are silent for a time, hardly touching.

"I don't know," Robin says finally. "Maybe this isn't quite what I thought it would be."

"Meaning?"

"Meaning nothing. That's all."

There is a short pause.

"Well," Cape says, "I'm sorry."

"Don't be. I was being unrealistic."

"What did you expect?"

Robin smiles at him. "It used to be me asking all the questions."

"Look, Robin," Cape says, propping himself up on an elbow and looking at him, "I told you that you can stay here as long as you want. Under whatever circumstances you like."

He touches Cape's chest softly. "I can't do that."

"What?"

"Get involved with you again."

"Why?"

Robin sighs. "Because of what happened last time."

Cape looks away. "Robin, what choice did I have?"

"I didn't say I blamed you. But I have to look out for myself. Being involved with Cape Barnes means being involved when *he* wants to be involved. Disappearing when he wants you to disappear."

Cape scowls, not looking at him.

"Anyway," Robin says, "I *am* living with someone at the moment. Maybe I still am."

Cape nods. "A *woman*, no less."

"No less." He smiles.

"You have a picture of her?"

"Mm-hm. Want to see?"

Cape nods. "I'm curious."

Robin digs in the pile of abandoned clothes for his pants; finds them, pulls out his wallet. The photo he carries was taken in Florida, at an outdoor cafe; the camera has caught her looking up toward the sunlit sky, her head tossed back in laughter, a dark hat with a bright feather in it at a jaunty angle.

Cape switches on a flashlight and aims it at the photo. "Mm," he says. "Cute. What's her name?"

"Heather. Seabright."

"Pretty name." He switches the flashlight off again. "So what *are* you these days, Robin?"

Robin puts away the photo and the wallet. "What do you mean, what am I?"

"Are you gay? Straight? What?"

Robin sits up in the bed. "I don't think of myself like that, Cape."

"Everybody else will."

"I don't think anybody else particularly cares."

The Unspoken

"You'd be surprised. Are you bisexual, then?"

"Cape," Robin says, frowning, "I just don't *classify* myself like that. I don't think in those terms. That's pigeonholing people. And you've always got to cut off people's arms or legs or something to fit them into the pigeonhole."

"That might be true," Cape says, "in an ideal world. But we live in the real world. You want to know what I think?"

"What do you think?"

He touches Robin's stomach gently. "I think you're gay and you can't stand it."

"Cape..."

"You told me you have sexual problems with this girl. Doesn't that tell you something?"

"It tells me I have sexual problems with that girl. There was another one I didn't have any problems with at all."

"Still. Maybe you're trying to be something you're not. Bisexuality is a cop-out."

"Being dishonest with yourself is a cop-out too."

"Exactly. I agree with you." He smiles. "And at this particular moment you're going to have a hard time convincing me you're straight."

"I didn't say I was straight, Cape. I also didn't say I was crooked. Those are your words."

"Not mine," he says. "The world's. The U.S. of A's."

"Mm." He thinks about it for a long moment. "And you 'gay' people have fallen right into their trap," he says. "They told you that who you like to go to bed with is the deciding factor in who you are as a person—and you agreed with them. You even say nowadays that there's something called a 'gay sensibility' that makes you different from everybody else in the world."

"There is."

"Crap. People are people."

"People change, though, when they're hated just because of who they sleep with."

"Maybe. But don't you see, Cape? By accepting the world's idea that you're somehow 'different' just because of that, you've already lost the war. It's already over, because you're fighting it on the enemy's terms."

Cape looks at him dryly. "Would you like to tell me what choice gay people ever had? What else could they have done?"

Robin shrugs; strokes Cape's hips. "I don't know. But becoming obsessed with your own sex life isn't the answer. Neither is deciding that people have to make some kind of either-or choice." He kisses him. "Natural inclinations aren't something you can make 'commitments' to. It's not like voting for a candidate or something." Briefly, absurdly, the vision of his old high school acquaintance Michael Lyon flits across his mind.

"If everybody thought like you do," Cape says, running his fingers through Robin's hair, "we'd still be burning homosexuals at the stake."

"Let's not talk about this anymore, Cape. You and I will never agree on this. Why are we talking politics now, anyway? Let's forget it." He studies Cape's hand, the soft flesh wrapped over hard bone, the craggy raised veins. "Let's just enjoy each other...okay?"

They move into each other again, wrapping limbs around limbs. He tries to lose himself in Cape's heady man-smell, his broad naked shoulders and hard legs, but cannot quite do it. Their discussion comes back to him, and how meaningless such talk is, how little any of it matters. It is nothing next to his darkness, he knows. His darkness is everything now...He drifts, thinking of the sorrowful and joyous music coming over the speakers, thinking of time and distance. He thinks of Cape's voice, years ago, talking about the mother in the hospital and the evil hissing of the oxygen, the religious farmer-father, and a young, unimaginable Cape playing his little radio in his bedroom in the darkness.

All gone now, he knows, never to return, smoke in wind. Lost. He thinks about the last night of the world and the slow gentle end of everything. Softly now. Softly fading.

He is, after all, guilty. He knows that now. All his explanations and justifications have failed to disguise the fact that he is guilty, has always been guilty. He is to blame: and so it is no wonder that this life has been as confused and frightened and unhappy as it has been. He is guilty. It is a guilt which no one in the world had recognized until now, until Heather.

But is that true? Perhaps his father had known all along. Perhaps that is the reason for the years of eyes boring into him like searchlights, coldly accusing. And his mother? That is why she left him….

"Goodbye, Cape."

Cape smiles sadly. "You're sure I can't get you to stay?"

"Hm-mm."

"Where are you going?"

"Back, I guess. To San Francisco."

He chuckles. "To your *woman*."

"Something like that."

"Well…You're welcome to stay here, you know. You really are. Maybe we could make a go of it."

"No," Robin says, looking at the floor. "We can't."

Cape touches Robin's cheek. "You're a fence-sitter," he says gently.

Robin takes his hand in his own. "That has nothing to do with it. You think it does, but it doesn't. Cape, I just wanted a place to stay. And…to see you again, I guess, that too. But you can't ask me to get involved with you again after what happened." He looks at him. "I loved you."

Robin is not entirely sure what he means by this; the words, as always, sound strange and foreign in his mouth: but he needs the simple phrase, the easy approximation.

Cape nods. "I'm sorry about that, Robin. For what it's worth. I did throw you away." He nods. "Guilty as charged."

Robin's voice is tight. "It's not a question of guilt."

Cape shrugs. "I was a couple of years younger then. Maybe I'm looking for something different now. I don't know…this gay disease thing is scaring the shit out of me. I'll be honest with you. It really is. I think—I think a lot of things are going to change. Soon. For a lot of people. And so I want something…something that'll last. Something permanent."

"I can't be it, Cape."

Sighing, Cape says, "Okay"; and embraces Robin. "Have a safe trip."

"Thanks."

"Send me a postcard now and then."

"Sure." He smiles weakly.

Cape frowns. "You okay, Robin? You look pale."

Robin nods. "I'm fine. Goodbye, Cape."

Bits of the past like leaves swirling. He had lied; he was not going back to San Francisco, not yet; but he had to get away from Cape Barnes. Being with him was too depressing and hopeless; too many scraps of lost time fluttered around him, time that could never be grasped in their hands and made whole and pure again. Everything had changed and time had never stopped trundling past. It was hopeless. He does not even know, now, quite why he came here: hope? curiosity? spite? But it does not matter very much now. His guilt is total, his darkness complete.

And they are, he realizes now, the same thing.

⇌

"Hello?"

"Hello, April?"

"Who's this?"

"It's…April, it's Robin."

"Robin?"

"Yeah. You remember. Robin Withers."

"Yeah, I remember."

"How're you doing?"

"I'm fine. Why are you calling?"

"I…April, I…I thought I might be coming out that way sometime soon."

"Yeah?"

"And maybe we could…could see each other."

A long pause. The telephone line hisses.

"April?"

"Yeah?"

"What…what do you think? If I come out, can I see you?"

"Jesus Christ!" she cries suddenly. "Robin, of *course* not!"

"I…"

"You really have the nerve to call me now? After you up and disappeared?"

"April, I…"

"One day you're here, the next day presto! Like magic! And now you call me and want to see me *again?* After what you did to me?"

"I…"

"Did you ever stop to think for one second how I would feel? Did you ever care? Did you ever even *notice?*"

"I…" His breath comes fast and hard. Strange spots appear before his eyes and his head throbs suddenly. "I'm—sorry…"

"You're *sorry?*" she shrieks. "You came here and got me into bed and made me fall in love with you and then you disappeared without one word of warning and now all you have to say is you're *sorry?*"

"April…listen…"

"Have you ever stopped to think about anybody's else's feelings in your whole *life?*" she cries. "Do you have any idea how humiliated I was? Did it ever cross your mind to wonder what the people in this *town* would think? Did you even stop to think about how I feel about this call right *now? Did* you?" Her twangy accent becomes thicker as she grows increasingly upset. She is weeping.

"I…I thought maybe…"

"One postcard! That's what I got from you after you left! One postcard!"

"April…"

"Go to hell, Robin! Just go to *hell!* Don't ever call here again!"

"April…wait…"

There is a click. Then a dead buzz.

⇌

They stand in a line facing him and pointing their fingers and he is guilty. Heather is there and his mother and his father and April and Cape and Priscilla and Turnham and the prostitute in the hotel room and Davy Carp and Marylou Kirk and Michael Lyon and Terrence Llewelyn and Uncle Jasper and Aunt Margaret and Sonya Skyler and he is guilty. He understands it at last. His guilt is total. His darkness is complete.

⇌

The Unspoken

Demons clutch at him in the dark. The sun has been drowned in the sea.

And there is no redemption. Words are useless. Apologies are meaningless. The past is absolute, unsalvageable, a terrible clanking weight that can never be escaped or understood. It is simply there, always, impenetrable, a massive stone sphinx that will never yield up its secrets. He sees arms swirling in the night. Blackbirds soaring into the black sky, shadow upon shadow blotting out the stars.

Later there is light again. Strange, unreal. He is floating in a crystalline blue sky, high above the sea. Below him, far below, is an island: and he drifts down toward it, slowly, wafted gently on the warm sea-winds. There is a figure on the island looking out into the waters. He floats closer and closer. He cannot quite make out who it is. The scene is old and familiar to him, an ancient, often-repeated dreamscape. The sea sparkles like an ocean of diamonds. He can hear the cries of seagulls. He floats down toward the figure, closer and closer now, closer than he has ever come; and he sees that it is a woman. She is standing there, nude, with her arms at her sides, looking out at the diamond sea. She is turned away from him. He floats closer: can make out the smooth sculpted shoulders, the dark hair, the small curved buttocks, the slender legs: he floats closer: her body is convulsing, he sees, as if she is crying: closer: emotion overwhelms him: he loves her: he must be with her forever: closer: she cries: closer: at last he is but a few feet from the figure on the island and she begins to turn toward him, her back twists gently, her shoulders circle around: he feels wind brushing his face: she turns: his breath is fast and hard:

he loves her: she turns: and finally her face looks toward his and the dark hair blows back away from her cheeks and he sees the tears running down and the trembling lips: and he floats there, speechless above the diamond sea and the pebbled shore, gazing into Heather Seabright's face.

8

"Look," Heather says. "Aren't they pretty?"

She sifts the multicolored capsules through her fingers and as they tumble over each other onto the bed they make a sound like hard winter leaves rolling in a street. She sits there, cross-legged and nude, a strangely faraway smile on her lips. Her hair hangs greasily around her face. There are black, baggy rings under her eyes. The room is dim and still.

"Aren't they?" she says again.

He studies her in the dimness, watches as she raises the wine glass to her lips and drinks. Reflexively he takes his own glass and drinks as well. They look at each other across the bed. He says nothing. All around him, on the bed, scattered across the floor, are the disordered pages of *Drowning:* pen in hand, yellow legal pad before him on the bed, he scribbles slowly, not sure anymore of what he is writing, the process of writing itself nearly unconscious, not a matter of making decisions but of simply letting the pen scratch across the yellow lined paper as it wishes. He has lost track of how long they have been in this room, this darkness.

Finally Heather moves on her hands and knees toward him. She grins lopsidedly, kisses his stomach. Then she reaches into his shorts.

"Why are you hiding away your stuff?" she asks.

"I'm not."

She pulls the shorts away and fondles him, grinning. "I want you to fuck me," she says.

"I just fucked you a couple of hours ago. And a couple of hours before that."

"I want you to fuck me again."

He moves the pen away from the legal pad, twirls it aimlessly in his fingers. "Doesn't that little tunnel of yours get tired?"

"Nope." She kisses him. "You give it a shot of vitamins every time."

"You have a dirty mind."

She giggles. "C'mere. I want to feel you on top of me."

"Don't you want me to finish this?"

She pulls him to her. He drops the pen on the bed and the yellow pad falls to the floor. They are wrapped around each other now. He looks into her bloodshot eyes. They are limitless.

"Isn't that better?" she whispers.

"I like your hair like that," he says.

"Like what? I haven't washed it in weeks."

"That's what I mean. Rumpled. It's sexy, a naked woman on a bed with rumpled hair."

"So, since I'm so sexy, you'll want to fuck me."

"Well…"

"He's just about ready. I can feel him."

"Well, he's always ready. But he's tired."

She grins. They kiss deeply.

"Maybe you want to put him someplace else," she says. "Do you want me to roll over?"

"Is it okay?"

"You've done it before."

"It doesn't cause you any pain?"

"Sure it does," she says, moving. "I want you to do it to me."

"Why?"

"I just want it, that's all. Don't ask questions."

"Like this?"

"Mm. But you're bigger than that. Put it in there. *Really* put it in. Hard." She gasps and cries out. "*Oh!* That's it," she says, her voice strangled. "Do it. There you go. Hurt me. C'mon, hurt me. Hurt me. Really hurt me."

Closer: time dissolving. The darkness growing and growing in the room. Closer. All barriers broken. Perfect timeless melding. No words, no apologies, no pasts. Living within each other, the same cells, same breath. Who are you I'm you. I don't want to leave here, never ever. We're the same. The same, baby. Closer. The same hands, same skin. Closer.

And there is no other possibility. He knows that now. Knows, from his dream of the island and the diamond sea, that he has arrived at his final destination once and for all and forever. All escape routes are closed. All passageways blocked. The thing will play itself out until the end. The darkness unleashed inside him melds together with her and they become something else, some new kind of Nietzchean Superman, a giant taller than any redwood traversing the sky and taking cups of stars in its enormous hands. The old world flat and dull and gray; the new world with as many colors as the capsules running through her fingers and across the bed and tumbling into the floor, bright like the sparks from a fireplace. And old selves falling away, lost, dry useless skins dropping into darkness forever. Only the present moment now, microsecond to microsecond, the perpetual instant. All else gone in the swirling vortex, chopped to pieces by the circling arms like scythes.

The Unspoken

And no words now. Words lost in the dark sparkling seas, drowned. Laotzu: *Nothing that can be said in words is worth saying.* And at last he understands it, that it is the speechless things, the unspoken ones, that bring whatever meaning there will be: that What do you want and Let's talk and I love you are all stupefying inanities. They have nothing to do with it, with the unbound darkness inside him. Or with them together, becoming one.

Look at me. How many fingers am I showing?
   Two.
   And now?
   One.
   Look at me.

And God, and the universe, and the lilies and the lions and the rays of the sun and the feeling of flowing oneness coursing through him? Lost. The product of other Robins, other times, other vanished selves. Only the two of them now, becoming one. Closer.

Inside. Inside. Inside. Limitless. Closer.

Like Siegel, time unwinding; like a watch-spring stretching out to infinity. Day and night and day but always darkness growing, blooming and blossoming and flowering darkness. Darkness budding everywhere, orchids bursting in the air over them.

And perhaps there has never been any choice, after all. Perhaps when the first neutron interacted with the first proton, when the first atom multiplied into the first molecule, when the first cell was formed and divided into a second cell, it has all been inevitable. Perhaps everything now is inevitable until the end of eternity. Each new cell division, each atom and molecule bouncing around the galaxies, every one on a single predetermined course, completely unalterable. Perhaps everything has been preordained from the beginning: from the moment his father's sperm sought out his mother's egg and they dissolved together and hooked onto the wall of her womb like a butterfly fluttering onto a summer blossom and something like consciousness began to grow. Something that would ultimately think and talk and call itself *I*: perhaps there has never been any choice at all. There is an open door out of which blackbirds fly. There are arms in the sky circling madly, madly.

Yes. Yes. Yes. Yes. Closer...

"Aren't they pretty?" she says, the red and green and yellow and sky-blue capsules tumbling through her fingers. "Aren't they, Robin? Aren't they pretty?"

9
DROWNING
Chapter Seven

In the bed, in the darkness, he listens as downstairs his dad turns off the Gary Cooper movie and locks the doors and comes upstairs. He remembers when his mom and dad would come upstairs together, rarely speaking, his mom stopping outside Siegel's door and sometimes opening it a crack so that a thin ray of light peered in. He would pretend to be asleep as she whispered Goodnight, honey, and shut the door again. Then he would hear them in the bathroom down the hall. His own bathroom stood between his bedroom and theirs but nonetheless he sometimes heard sounds from that bedroom, voices, bed creakings. He remembers wondering what went on in that bedroom, behind that door. What did they talk about, lying there together? And what did they...But that was impossible to think about. Later his mom took to sleeping in the spare bedroom down the hall. And he wondered about that too.

He remembers other listenings.

He remembers listening for Rachel's car on the weekend evenings. Listening to it pull up on the street outside and feeling the swelling between his legs and the rush and tingle at the ends of his fingers and on his scalp. He remembers listening to her footsteps coming up the walk.

And he remembers the bombs. The bombs that exploded during the torrential floods that submerged the earth. And the stars exploding into the sea in giant sizzling crackles. The sound of Armageddon, he supposed, listening to the winds howling and buildings being smashed by the force of the endless seas. Loud. Violent. But maybe that was the way it had to be, he reasoned, the end had to come in a tremendous crash, a monumental noise. And it *was* the end....

But it wasn't, not after they took him to the institution and shot him full of things and Hewitt undertook to "spif him up"—that was his term, a rare attempt at Hewitt humor. Then he realized that nothing had ended. Yet. Of course, as he told Hewitt, it could all end still. In twenty minutes. If they set off the missiles that he'd been living with for these past months. It could still end.

He turns in the bed. The wave is quieter now, mellow, but he is still riding it, and while he's on the wave he can't slip off into sleep. He opens his eyes in the darkness. Thinks about Rachel lying there in the bed, about how he could have been with her at this very moment, in her arms. He could have called his dad, he would have understood, and told him where he was and been with her even now. If he hadn't screwed everything up. It's the story of his life, screwing up. He thinks of the doll eyes and the TV and the fat shapeless thing in the sterile white bed. Unnecessary. Stupid. And what of the man watching the Gary Cooper movie? Waste. Waste. Idiot fantasy dialogues. A galactic gulf between them never to be breached. Waste. All waste. Stupid screw-ups.

He sits up in the bed. He can hear the surf crashing smoothly against the shore.

Oh, for a world like that girl's, the one he laid tonight, Clarissa. Free of jealousy. Open, true: communication beyond words: how did they mange it, he wonders, that perfect sort of relationship, jealousy-free? *We trust each other,* she'd said. That was why he'd wanted to stay, he realizes; to find out about their world, how it was that they could live in such total harmony with one another, so peacefully. It didn't seem possible, and yet it was. She had told him the truth. But how? In *this* world?

He suddenly begins to miss Rachel so much that it is a physical thing, an empty, sick feeling in his stomach. He presses his arms against his belly and closes his eyes again. Screw-ups. Even the whole Hewitt thing, the institution, was a screw-up. A joke. He'd simply caught on to what they wanted him to say and a few weeks later he was free. Easy. And a waste.

He listens in the bed for several minutes, until he knows his dad is in bed and probably asleep. The house is silent. Finally he gets up and opens his door softly and pads downstairs. He sits in his dad's chair and dials the number in the darkness.

"Hello?" Her voice is sleepy.

"Rachel?"

"Siegel?" She makes an indistinct sleep-sound. "What are you doing calling so late?"

"I…needed to talk to you."

"What about?"

"This evening…tonight. You know." There is a brief pause. "I fucked up. I'm sorry. I totally fucked up."

"It's all right, sweet," she says. "So did I. I shouldn't have pushed you like that. I should've…"

"No, it wasn't you," he says, his throat thick with something. "It was me. You were perfect. You always are."

"Oh, Siegel. Are you drunk? You sound drunk."

"Only a little."

"Will I see you tomorrow?"

"Try and stop me. I mean if you want to. See me, I mean."

"Of course I do."

"I'm sorry, Rachel."

"Don't be sorry."

"I hurt you tonight."

"You didn't hurt me. I understand."

He thinks of Clarissa, thinks of slamming it into her, trying to make it hurt. "I did hurt you," he says. "I really did. You don't even know. But I did. I fucked up. I've always fucked everything up. But not anymore. I'm not ever going to fuck anything up again."

She laughs slightly. "Don't be silly," she says. "Of course you will. Everybody does. You think you're the only one?"

"I'm going to treat you right," he says. "I'm going to stop being a fuck-up. We'll see each other every night. I'll be a model of good behavior. And I'm going to finish my damned novel. Once and for all."

"Good," she says. "That's good."

He inhales deeply, his breath strong. He feels strong now. Feels good. "I really mean it," he says.

"I know. I know you do."

He laughs. "How do you know? I'm a notorious liar."

"Are you lying now?"

"No. But how do you know?"

"I trust you, that's how."

He laughs again, feeling the euphoria return a bit. "Everybody lies," he says. "But it doesn't matter, because nobody listens."

"Ha, ha. You sound like your old cynical self again."

"No," he tells her, seriously, "not him. I'll never be my old self again."

There is a brief pause.

"Good," she says finally.

"I love you, Rachel."

"Well, I love you too."

And for a moment, a brief, wild moment, it is almost as if the words do mean something, as if they are truly communicating, bridging the gulf, and the illusion is exhilarating, breathless.

"I do love you," he says. "I swear to God, I do."

"Oh, Siegel," she says, "I love you. I mean it."

"I do too. I mean it too."

They go on like that, convincing each other of it, assuring each other that they do mean something, the words, the phrases, the sounds, all of it; that there is something there, a connection, a bridge.

"So?" she says. "Do you really want to get married?"

He grins. "We'll be a modern family. Two-career couple. And a boy and a girl. Daycare. Station wagon. All that."

"Sounds pretty good, sweet. After I graduate?"

"After you graduate. I'll have the book done by then."

"Can we really make it work?"

"Sure we can."

"We have a lot to talk about, though. Seriously."

"I know. We'll talk."

"I love you, Siegel."

"I love you…"

And, for a moment, he almost believes it's true.

10

"Finish it. You have to finish it."

"Finished…it's—it's finished."

"It's not finished." Her eyes glitter in the darkness. Her voice is a whisper.

"It is."

"There's still a little more to go."

"No…"

"You have to end it."

"I—I don't know…how it ends…"

She gazes at him. In her eyes is every darkness in the universe. "You know how it ends," she whispers.

11

DROWNING

Chapter Eight

In the bed again, much later, he listens to the swoosh of the surf outside. He does not close his eyes. He feels the darkness close to him and he lies in the bed staring at the familiar ceiling and breathing shallowly.

He wonders about the conversation with Rachel. Just more words spewing out of both of them, grandly unmeaningful, stupendously wasted. Did they know each other any more, any better, now that they had talked? Had they breached the gulf?

Of course not.

But it had felt good then. As they were talking. It had *felt* as if they were making a connection. And that, he supposes, is enough—that illusion, that feeling of connection, that sensation. Enough because it has to be enough. It's all anybody can do. A life sentence inside our skulls. We work in the dark.

He feels the shortness of breath come back to him with a vengeance. He gasps as he sits up in the bed and bends over so that his head is touching his knees. That eases it. No doctor had ever diagnosed his breathing problem. Bacteria? A blood clot in his lungs? As far as anyone knew there was no reason for it.

He leans back again, his head against the wall. The problem has calmed, for the moment. He can see out his window the dark driveway and, beyond it, the sparkling black ocean. He remembers falling asleep to the sound of the ocean when he was young. The gentle rumble as the waves crested, like distant thunder. Sometimes the furnace would start up, a low, cozy hum, and the two sounds would mingle in his mind, come together, and the combination always sent him off to dreamland.

Not anymore, though. Now he listens to the ocean with sleep the furthest thing from him. Even the furnace wouldn't help, he knows. No sleepy-bye tonight, he realizes grimly. Hopeless.

And all the alcohol isn't doing any good. If anything, it has wired him. He would like to come down but he can feel that it won't happen for a while. He'll have to ride this one for a time longer. Jesus, what had happened tonight, anyway? It seemed like a month had gone by since his dad had pulled up with him into the driveway and helped him with his bag and showed off his new stereo. Had it really only been that evening?

He sighs. He thinks about Rachel and Dusty and the possibility of going sailing or something. It seems very distant, part of another life: he remembers that they used to sail in high school, the three of them. They had had a lot of fun. But was that even him, back then? Or an impostor? Somebody who dressed and talked and looked like him, but really had no connection to him at all, a faraway stranger? He doesn't know. Perhaps he will never know. Whether he is the same person he has always been or if he had truly changed, shed his old identity the way a snake sheds its skin. Who could know for sure? Very likely both are true, paradoxically. He has no problem with paradox anymore; feels, in fact, that it may be the key to everything. Perhaps, he thinks, the fallacy of the human heart is in the idea that a paradox cannot be true, that by its very definition it is impossible. Maybe that's the secret. Because it occurs to him that the world only begins to make any kind of sense at all when he accepts that two contradictory things might be true at the same time: he is the same and he is different, he loves Rachel and cannot love anyone. It begins to make a kind of sense beyond logic, beyond thought. He stares at the ceiling and tries to puzzle it out. But it would seem to require a new sort of thinking, one not based on language. Language is the trap.

But he can't think without it and therefore can't quite discover what he's looking for. He listens to the surf. Thinks about the events of the evening. It is very quiet.

Finally he gets out of the bed and goes to his bureau drawer. He pulls it open softly and brings out the pages of manuscript, feels their weight in his hands. He stands close to the window and can just make out the words on the pages. They are good, it seems to him. But they are words. And so it is an artificial thing, this novel—this fragment—a creation, a falsity. Existence is not as he has portrayed it here; and it never would be, he realizes, because there is no way to communicate the essence, that hidden something, that darkness. He will never finish the novel, he knows. He will never write another word on it again.

He sets the pages on the bed and slips into his pants. Then he stands for a long moment looking at the room, still and silent in the night. He never lived here. The stranger did. The one he once knew but with whom he has now lost all contact. It *was* him. It was him at one time. But now? Just a stranger, a face he could pass by on the street. Lost.

He picks up the manuscript and goes out into the hall and down the stairs. All this, too, unfamiliar and strange. Not a part of him, not who he is now. Even the man whose low wheeze he can hear from upstairs. There is no longer a connection, if there ever was. They do not know each other.

Has he moved beyond all this? he wonders as he moves toward the front door. Maybe. But where, then, can he go? If he is no longer in the same world with Dad and Rachel and Dusty and the rest? It is an impossible thing. But now, as he crosses the driveway and opens the car door and brings out his bottle, still a third full, he fully realizes what he has known instinctively all along: that he has never found the world where he belongs, that he is a stranger everywhere, a face pressed against the glass. All the problems are a smokescreen. The feeling of being the wrong sex, of not knowing whether he is still the same person he was, the failure of words: all are just symptoms of the bigger problem. And he doesn't know what there is to do about it. He drinks from the warm bottle of wine and walks down the sandy hill to the beach. The surf seems very loud tonight and the moon is bright and full, its white rays shining on the ocean and making it glisten.

No one had ever known him. He has never known anyone.

A memory floats into his mind. Not long before he left for college, before he departed for what he thought would be a new world, one without the rivers of amber or night screams, different, fresh, alive, his mom sat on his bed the way she had when they were younger and asked him to read a story. A drink was in her hand. But he had nothing to read. I don't have anything, he'd said. Something's happening to me. I don't know if I can write anymore. And he sat beside her on the bed and noticed how much older she looked now, not old, but not new and vibrant the way she had once looked. Her hands were heavily veined now and her hair was tinged with gray and she had put on weight. What's wrong? she'd asked. Why can't you write? The room was dim, the curtains drawn against the late-afternoon light. I don't know, he'd said. I don't know. It's like there's some giant terrible dark something near me.

She'd poured more of the amber river into the glass. They'd sat there on the bed, drinking from it together.

I know what you're talking about, she said.

You do?

She nodded, looking into the glass.

You feel it too? he asked.

She nodded.

There was a long pause.

What is it? he whispered.

She shook her head.

They sat there a long time.

Is it a bad thing or a good thing? he asked.

She didn't answer.

I'm afraid, he said.

She looked at him and smiled slightly, touching his hair. The air smelled of age and amber.

I'm afraid, he said again.

She pressed his face to her breasts.

Mom, I'm afraid, he said.

He cried softly into her breasts. He thought there was a question he wanted to ask her, but he couldn't find the words. They looked at each other in the near-darkness. The room was silent. Her eyes were wet. In the dimness she almost appeared as she had years before, the damp curls, the steam. They looked at each other. They were close together.

He sits at the water's edge, just beyond the damp sand. He props the bottle up in the sand and sets the manuscript pages beside him. He stares out at the ocean. Occasionally he drinks from the bottle. He tries to keep his mind as blank as possible. He'd had a lot of practice at this in the institution. Keeping his mind a clean slate. No thoughts, no words. Words creep in sometimes but he quickly banishes them.

I love you, Siegel. Rachel's voice. Gone.

There's no sex thing. We trust each other. Clarissa. Banished.

Have a good time? Dad. History.

Eventually they are all gone. All of them. He concentrates on the ocean and keeps his mind blank. Sometimes an image crosses it but that's all right, as long as there are no words. Just blissful silence. Peace. The sound of the ocean, like the sound of forever.

Eventually he notices light starting to appear in the sky. It begins as a dull red, barely discernible, and after a time grows to a soft pink. He notices the stars beginning to disappear. The light seems to absorb them like a living thing. He watches this dispassionately.

Finally there is enough pink light in the sky that he can make out a cloud at the edge of the horizon. It is thin, light, like a wisp of steam, and he can tell that it is moving, swimming slowly across the sky. He stares at it for a long time.

Then he hears a sound. At first he can't make out what it is, and he listens closely. It is familiar, yet somehow different. He listens as he stares at the cloud moving in the sky.

It is a long time before he identifies the sound. When he does, it is not a scary thing, not a worry, but rather comforting, familiar, peaceful.

Bombs.

But not the bombs he is used to. The bombs he hears do not crash and blast and tear things apart: rather they are like the ocean waves, a quiet whoosh of arrival, a smooth cresting, like distant thunder. Not violent...Smooth, easy, like the light in the sky swallows the stars, naturally. He watches the bombs landing in the ocean. They are quiet. They do their work peacefully. And then there are other landings and he realizes it is the stars: they are falling from the sky like white rain, thousands of them. But they too are quiet, peaceful, they sizzle comfortingly when they splash into the water. It is like riding waves of peace, these bombs, these stars, waves of pleasant sound and vibration. No noise. No bursting or screaming. Just waves, pulses, like music. He sits on the beach and watches the world end. The final collapse of the universe.

And he watches the cloud. It comes toward him, swirling, assuming a shape. It dances before him sensually. It is beautiful to watch: the streams of white seem to recreate themselves, to twist luxuriously, to play to him. It is only a few yards from him now, suspended just above the water. The bombs and stars land behind it, and their music fits the dance of the cloud perfectly, they are made for each other, they are one. And finally he begins to recognize the cloud in the sky. The face, the open arms, the flowing white wisps of gown: and he stands, knowing that at last he has found it, the world where he belongs. It is all so wonderfully familiar. He knows this world. Trusts it. He has been lost from it for a long time but now he has found it again. And he realizes that it, too, has been trying to find him, sending hints to him. He hadn't understood. But now it is clear.

As he steps toward the water he notices only dimly that the bits of manuscript, the pages, have been caught by a breeze and are whipping off the stack one by one and sailing into the ocean. He drops the bottle in the sand. He feels the other world receding into the sunrise behind him. The water swirls about his feet, his legs. It is warm. Like bath water. And at last he feels it coming over him, the great darkness, he is one with it, and he realizes that it is not terrible or awful or cold or horrifying. It is warm. The cloud-woman's arms reach to him. He hears her gentle laugh. He feels an indescribable joy.

THE END

12

In the slow, multicolored dawn, the road is like a strip of night stretching into eternity. Sitting in the passenger seat, fading gradually into consciousness, he gazes at the silent vista: nothing stirs but the shadows, moving slowly across the sands. There is not even a hint of breeze: only stillness.

Heather's head lolls back in the driver's seat, her eyes closed in sleep. It takes Robin a moment to remember: his car, the sands, the road: when he does, he feels a tension tighten within him like a slowly-stretched wire. He closes his eyes again and tries to calm his breathing.

After a time Heather begins to stir. Although his eyes are closed he is super-aware of her every movement. She sighs; then she stretches. He feels as if she is doing these things inside his own head.

Finally she opens the car door and he is forced to open his eyes.

She steps away and he glances back at her as she kneels down behind the car. After a long moment he opens the passenger door and walks back to her.

"Bushwhacking," she says, standing and buttoning her pants.

He smiles slightly and uses a nearby bush for the same purpose. Then they move back to the car again and sit there, leaving the doors open.

He is amazed at how clear and empty his mind is now. No thoughts, no shadows, no echoes. Nothing but a smooth sea of nothingness. As if he has become a spirit, floating somewhere above the clouds...He stares at the full moon still hanging in the morning sky.

"Here," Heather says, handing him a piece of white bread.

"Should we be eating?" he asks.

"I told you before," she says, chewing and not looking at him, "it works better with something in your stomach. Otherwise you might barf."

Robin chews. The bread feels strange in his mouth: the texture is like nothing he has ever felt before. The formless tension begins to grow in him again; he concentrates on the clarity and emptiness of his mind. They eat the bread and then split a banana between them and drink from a flask of water. Finally they step from the car again and stretch their muscles.

"You want to drive?" Heather says.

He shrugs. "Okay."

He moves around to the driver's side of the car and starts the engine. After Heather settles herself in the passenger seat he starts the car moving across the loose soil and sand of the Mojave, away from the black road behind them. The path is rough and bumpy but they will be driving, he knows, for only a little while. They pass cactus and scrub brush and behind them the sphere of the sun grows to a full circle on the horizon, splashed all around with red and pink and yellow. It is still very cool. The car's progress is slow across the sand and once they nearly become stuck.

"No," Heather says, scowling. "We're not far enough yet."

He keeps the vehicle moving and after some time they are out of view of the road and all around them is nothing but sand and bush and stone. They drive a while longer and the sand grows deeper. The morning grows hot with astonishing quickness; soon Robin is sweating. He thinks little of anything as he maneuvers the car along in the sand: feels no tension inside him. It is a drive like other drives, no different. The sand grows deeper. Soon he is having difficulty keeping the car moving.

Finally he feels it sink into the sea-like sand and the tires spin uselessly.

He reaches forward and shuts off the engine.

"End of the line," he says.

Heather nods, her expression intense. She steps out of the car. All around them is desert: in every direction, as far as Robin can see.

As he steps out of the car he looks at her and she nods, her eyes strange. He glances at the enormously blue sky above them as he takes a bag of tools from the back seat and moves to the front of the car. She watches him as he digs a small bed for himself under the front of the car and then crawls into it on his back.

Once he is there he locates the screws which hold the oil and radiator fluid. Carefully moving himself so as not to get drenched with the black muck, Robin carefully undoes the first screw. Black oil comes burbling out into the sand.

Then he moves forward slightly, to the radiator, and opens it as well. A greenish-brown liquid splashes out.

He crawls out from under the car again and crouches down, watching the two liquids flow away into the sand. After several minutes neither of them are more than a trickle.

He stands again, wipes his hands, and looks toward Heather. She is sitting on a large, smooth stone, her arms folded before her.

"Finished?" she asks.

"Finished."

They stay where they are, in an unmoving tableau, for a long moment.

"Okay," Heather says finally; and moves toward the car. The morning sun glares down on them now.

And this is all there is to it, Robin finds himself thinking with wonder. This is actually all there is to it. It is an activity, an action, like others. It seems as if there should be more to it, more ceremony, or that there should be some final marvelous statement of profundity to make; but there is none. Llewelyn had told him never to expect any; no arrivals, only journeys; and perhaps Llewelyn had not been such a fool after all. Except, he thinks, that this *is* an arrival. A destination. The only destination, it seems to him, there can ever be.

And perhaps there had been other arrivals, at that. Heather herself had represented an arrival: a new kind of being. Together they became one person, a person who was neither him nor her but rather a third body, independent of the two of them, an altogether new person, and when they breathed together they created this new person with their breath. The creation of the third person was an arrival too.

They sit together in the car, leaving the doors open. There should be something else to say, he thinks. There should be words spoken; but there is nothing. This makes perfect sense, he knows, for after all, Siegel knew all about words: he was under no illusions, the way Robin himself had been: but none of it makes any difference now.

They had left the house in San Francisco quite clean and neat. Whenever anyone got around to looking in, they would find an orderly array of crates and boxes, all their plates and books and cassettes nicely put away. It had seemed the best thing to do. They had destroyed all the personal things: letters, photographs: he does not know if they found everything, but they had gotten most of it. They had crumpled it all up and burned it in the fireplace because it seemed indecent, like grave-robbing, to have others come along later and paw through their pictures and their words and their lives, others who would never have any understanding of who they had been together. And so they had gotten rid of all they could find. When they vanished, they would vanish completely; nothing but a few dishes and bed sheets and books. Lost.

Heather rustles in some paper bags and brings out several small prescription bottles.

"Where's the water?" she asks.

Robin brings it out from behind the seat, a big plastic canteen.

She nods. Then she opens the first bottle.

"We should take these at about one-minute intervals," she says, pouring some of the sea-blue capsules into her palm. "If you take them too fast you might throw them up."

He looks at her. She is beautiful, it seems to him, sitting there in the morning light: beautiful as a ghost is beautiful: her face, moon-pale now, her eyes darkly ringed, has the shattered look of the survivor of a wild storm; her hair, tossed back away from her forehead, is tangled and wind-blown. She wears a simple blouse and an old pair of blue jeans and tattered sandals.

He feels the both of them becoming as evanescent and blank as a pair of ancient spirits.

As she pours some of the capsules into his hands he glances at himself in the rear-view mirror. His eyes, behind the wire glasses, are hollow. Old.

He stares at the capsules. And now he will know, he thinks, of the lilies and the lions and the rays of the sun, the million molecules splintering from himself and floating and ascending into other lives, other matter, Robin Withers becoming one with the universe, a part of forever, wafting across infinity in millions of different consciousnesses. This is the sensation of life, he knows, that he had felt before, at odd times: it is coming into him again: that speechless sensation of limitlessness, endlessness, eternal expansion into everything. It floats into him now, at this moment, and as he looks across toward Heather it is almost as if the thing is already done, he is already drifting into other dimensions and realities....

But it is not quite done, not yet, and he looks at her sitting there in the morning light, the open canteen in her hand. He notices the diamond on her finger, glinting. It is odd, but they do not speak. They do not even say goodbye. They look at each other for a long moment in the orange light of the dawn and then Heather puts a capsule into her mouth and swallows from the canteen.

She hands the canteen to Robin. He can feel his heart beating as he places a capsule on his tongue and then raises the canteen to his lips. He swallows. The capsule plunges smoothly down his throat.

He hands the canteen back to her.

They go on like this for many minutes. He knows that they will not feel the effects yet: but soon a wonderful flowing sleepiness will overcome them and they will begin to lift into infinity, like the closing notes of a Mahler symphony, *ewig*, the final graceful sigh into a peaceful forever. It will all go away now, he knows. All of it. There is nothing more to fear. He rests his head back on the seat as he takes his turn swallowing the capsules. There is no terror now, no sorrow, no regret. There is nothing at all. And finally, very slowly in the arid desert morning, he feels his darkness start to turn to golden light. He feels terror turn to wonder. He sees Siegel standing at the ocean shore, the water splashing around his ankles. He sees the moon high in the morning sky.

It begins as a blue speck floating toward him through a sea of black. At first it moves slowly, then picks up speed, coming at him faster and faster until his entire range of vision is filled with the vibrant blue, supernal, all-encompassing. He hears a sharp buzzing in his ears. He can feel, distantly, the car seat under him and the heat of the sun on his face: but he holds his eyes closed and these things seem far away, unknowable. The blue light begins to pulse inside his head and the buzzing is very loud. Not so fast, he thinks. Not so fast. His heart seems to be beating within his skull, pounding as if to burst his head from the inside. He feels his head being stretched, warped into unrecognizability, and for a moment he has the image of a newborn baby's head being pulled and scraped and dented under some mad doctor's forceps. Then comes another sound, pouring in behind the buzzing: it is like rain, hard rain on metal: but as he listens he realizes it is more like a piece of meat sizzling in a hot pan. The two sounds blend and mix as the blue light pulses with his heartbeat. His heart has begun to beat very fast now; or at least that is how is seems; perhaps it is actually slowing and only the strange stretching sensation makes him think otherwise. He does not know. The blue light grows very bright, nearly blinding. He wishes he could look away. The buzzing and sizzling are painful in his ears but he cannot plug them. He is breathing heavily, he thinks; or seems to be; it seems to him that he is nearly gasping.

Now he seems to lose his balance. It is strange. He is not moving, knows instinctively that he is still sitting in the car, but suddenly there is no top or bottom to the blue light pumping inside his skull and he feels abruptly cut adrift, falling through vacant space. The sensation frightens him. He tries to reach forward to grab onto the steering wheel but he cannot open his eyes and he does not know whether he is holding the steering wheel or not. He does not know where his hands are at all. He cannot feel them. Nor his legs. He can feel nothing but his heartbeat, and that is inside his head, not his chest. He no longer has a chest. He no longer has anything but the blue light and the thumping and the buzzing and sizzling.

He is afraid now. This is not how he thought it would be. Where are the peaceful waves wafting him into eternity? Where is the final gentle sigh of the orchestra coming to rest? He tries

The Unspoken

to move his hands but he cannot feel them. Now, gradually, another sound enters his head: his own breathing. It is an enormous sound. Each inhale, each exhale is like a hurricane within himself: he pictures trees soaring through the air, shacks knocked to splinters in a frenzied wind. He can hardly believe that there could be such a sound in the world.

He resolves to open his eyes. He is afraid of the blue light and the buzzing and the hurricane winds and so he will open his eyes. He will open his eyes. He tries to open his eyes. His eyelids weigh tons. He cannot move them. His heart slams inside his head. He must open his eyes.

Finally they are open or he thinks they are. Everything is bathed in a bright wash of blue: his hands, the steering wheel, the dashboard, the sands outside. They are blue and the blue pulsates and with each pulse the distance between himself and what he is seeing seems to change. He begins to feel a thickness inside his head, a muddiness. It is becoming difficult to connect one thought to the next. Difficult to

Don't worry about a thing, honey

He tries to keep his eyes open. There is a thick, awful clanging inside his skull and he thinks of Quasimodo with the huge bell, ringing it over and over. It is like that now. He wants to hold his head in his hands but he cannot raise his hands. He can see them, just, through the blue veils: they are gripping the steering wheel tightly and ropy blue veins are standing up on them and it seems to him that the veins are pulsing. But he cannot raise them. He tries to. He thinks: I will raise my hands to my head now. But they do not move. The thoughts themselves are nearly buried under the cacophony inside his skull. His eyes begin to close but he forces them to stay open. He tries to think. His pulse is like a horse kicking him in the head over and over. He is frightened. He is terrified. The terror: he thinks of the terror: when he was a child, over and over, sudden attacks of unreasoning blind panic:

they have come again: he is *crash! crash!* honey something terrible has happened something terrible has He tries to shake his head clear. He cannot shake his head. The blue waves grow thicker.

Then he hears another sound. For a moment he thinks it is inside his head but then he realizes it is coming from somewhere else. He tries to focus his mind on the sound, hold it there. Whimpering. Soft high sounds of pain. Where are they coming from? He tries to move his eyes away from the veins on his hands but they do not seem to want to move. He hears the sound again. Like an animal, a small animal in pain. He tries to move his eyes. The sound again. His eyes seem stuck inside their sockets as in concrete. The sound, the sound! A moan now. He decides to turn his head. He decides to turn his head. His head begins to turn.

Hang on, Star-eyes!

He sees her on the island once more, standing there naked and weeping, the island of his dream, her eyes darkly shadowed, broken and hopeless, and here now is that same face: her eyes are closed, clenched shut, her head is lolling from side to side in the ocean of blue, and sparkles appear before his eyes as he looks at her: her hands bounce up and down in her lap senselessly: he wants to say stop, stop that, but the power of speech is hidden somewhere far away, behind the pulsing and clanging, her legs move in and out uselessly, and she makes the small sounds over and over. Open your eyes, he wants to say. He tries to move his mouth but cannot. Open your eyes. Open your

He falls against the car door suddenly. It is as if the world has suddenly tipped on its side. For a long moment he cannot seem to sit up straight again. It is almost funny. Except that it is not. Crunched against the side of the car he feels he is drowning, that the blue waves are flooding over him inescapably. He thinks of Siegel standing in the dawn and the warm water around his ankles. Lies. All lies. It is not warm. It is cold and thundering and hard. He tries to pull himself from the side of the car door. He tries. He cannot move. The world is blue. He must move. He knows now that he must move. His eyes want to close again. His eyes want the mad cacophony to take over forever. But he is afraid of it. He tries to shake the windstorm in his mind away. He cannot. He start the car / but it won't move we planned it that way didn't we?

out of the car get out of walk

His hand begins to move. His hand begins to move. His hand moves. It weighs tons, unimaginable tons. It falls as it moves to the door latch. He raises it again. It seems to take years. Then he pulls. The door opens and he tumbles into the blue sand.

walk / stand and walk.

There are two of them now, and he stands there dispassionately observing himself stumble away from the car. He is standing now. Moving. He can hardly breathe. The world pulses savagely. He looks at the girl in the passenger seat lolling her head this way and that. He must get to her. He watches himself move around the side of the car. He falls. Stands again. Falls. He lifts his fingers to his mouth and pushes them down his throat. He feels a convulsion but nothing rises. He tries again. He gasps and when he coughs it is as if someone is firing a shotgun into his brain. Nothing rises. But he stands. He makes his way to the passenger door. He opens it. She does not seem to be aware of his presence. Her head lolls and lolls methodically. She does not open her eyes.

Heather / Heather. *Heather*

He does not know if the sound is coming out of his mouth or not. He tries to say her name, over and over. He hears it inside his mind but does not know if he is actually saying anything. Finally he watches as he reaches his ropy hand to her and pulls. She falls out of the car, slamming her head hard against the door frame. Her legs are in the car and her arms and chest in the sand. Her eyes are open now and huge and blank and staring. Spittle trickles from her mouth across her cheek. He kneels down to her. Heather, he tries to say. He reaches his blue fingers to her mouth and tries to put them in but her teeth are clenched shut. Heather. Heather, can you hear me. Heather. Her hair is spilled into the sand like a wine stain. Her eyes stare at him, but seem to see nothing. Her breath comes in erratic chatters.

Heather / *Heather* stand up. stand up / here I'll lift you.

He loses his balance again and falls to his side. The world has tilted again and he cannot seem to stand. He sees the sun, a huge blue ball glaring down at them.

He watches himself as he finally stands and pulls her to her feet. She is heavy and lumpy. He has carried her before but it was nothing like this: this is dead weight. Heather wake up / wake up

we have to walk sweetheart / walk / *walk*

He drags her along, holding her under her arms. Her head lolls. Her eyes roll in their sockets. Her teeth shine bluely in the blue desert air, her lips drawn back tightly. She falls into the sand. He kneels over her.

look at me / *look at me.* Heather look at me

Her eyes are as empty as marbles. Breath hisses through her teeth.

come with me Heather.

He lifts her again.

come with me. *come with me.* we'll walk to the road we'll

In the pulsing blue before him there is a graveyard. A huge, limitless graveyard, row upon row of identical stone markers, the remains of generations of families in the freshly-mown grass.

Heather *Heather* talk to me say something

He lifts his feet through the loose sand. He weighs hundreds of tons now. His brain is pressing against his skull and he knows that at any moment it will burst through, explode into infinity.

They will get to the road. He will take them to the road. He can do it. He can take them to the road. He watches himself walk now. He must merely continue to walk. He must walk. The ocean is blue and thick and completely enveloping them but he will walk.

She makes a sudden sound and her body jerks out of his hands. Prone, in the sand, she twitches.

Heather / *Heather* stand up stand up

There is an enormous whooshing in his ears and he feels wind slapping at his face. The grass-lined graves hover before him. He can hear a clock ticking somewhere. There is a dim light glowing in her eyes and he slaps at her face. Heather. Heather. Wake up. Wake up. Wake up

Their eyes connect. He sees life in her eyes. She is looking at him.

Heather Heather

Her mouth moves. —Robin.

Yes. Yes. Yes. Yes.

—Robin I

Stay awake. Stay awake sweetheart. Stay

—Robin I / I / I'm not going to / to be able to / to make it

The eyes turn to glass again and the breath grows faint.

Heather. / *Heather*

He stands suddenly, trying to shout. He tries to shout. He does not know if any sound comes out. His head is crashing and clanging. The ticking is like needles jabbing into his brain. The malevolent eye of the sun glares down. He tries to shout into the desert morning. He tries to shout. He tries to

He watches himself fall; and knows suddenly that he will not stand again. He trembles and twitches. He can see her from where he has fallen. She is on her back in the sand, her breasts hardly rising or falling now.

lilies / lilies lions / lies lies lies

He can see the diamond on her finger shining blue light into the blue morning and everything is blue covered with blue.

lies. / oh deep dark helpless

Overhead there are blackbirds streaming into the sky, shadow upon shadow against the blue, thousands of them, the sky packed with them. And there, just there among the graves, is a young doe, its eyes perfectly innocent and blank, staring toward him in the dewy grass. He gasps and feels something burst inside his brain, opening incredibly like a strange door flying wide into a vast emptiness. His vision flashes white and blind, his eyes pouring from their sockets like Oedipus.

lies birds sky light. / live love oh love

I I I I

CHAPTER 6
WHERE THE SHORE MEETS THE SEA

From deepest dream I have awakened.

Nietzsche: *Thus Spake Zarathustra*

1

As I draw near the close of these pages, some six months after beginning them, I find that in the time since I have returned to this house my attitudes toward it have undergone a great change. Why this should be, I am not sure; but I can look back to the early pages of this manuscript and sense the fear and trepidation that was coursing through me at the idea of being here again after so many years. I think that childhood houses and rooms, even entire towns, take on rather mythical dimensions after one leaves them: there is no doubt, at any rate, that the reason I had for so long failed to come to any decision about the house is that I was, on some level, afraid of it. When I first walked through the front door and stepped into the dark foyer, when I made my way up the lightless stairs and into my old room, I somehow expected something to happen. What, I do not know. It seemed impossible that the house could be, after all, no more than a collection of wood and plaster and paint: and yet that is what it is. And as the months have passed here, as I have worked on these pages and eaten my meals and talked on the telephone, I have become increasingly aware of it. Indeed, when I pull my car up in the front drive now after a visit to the bank or the post office, I feel nothing at all. Sometimes, of course, something touches me: if I look into an unopened drawer and find something unseen for years, one of my mother's knitted pot holders, for example, or a bowl or a book; but there is no longer anything threatening in this.

And so I have decided to sell the house. There is no reason for me to own it anymore, and the money I will make from the sale will keep me quite tidily for two or three years; I have, therefore, been boxing things up in my spare time. The accumulation is nothing short of astonishing. I suppose I shall have to have a sale of some kind. Of course it is a peculiar sensation, going through all the old things, especially those belonging to my parents; but I have found virtually nothing of a personal nature left over from either of them. In a way I am sorry for this. It might have been revealing, somehow, to have come across a few old letters they had written to each other or diaries or something of that sort. But there is nothing. It is a collection mostly of junk.

That last sentence may seem harsh. And yet it is the truth. For the meaning of things, whether it is a pot or a plate or a book or a ring, is not in the object itself but in its associations: the pot or the plate is merely a stimulus for memory. Still, I confess an odd feeling within myself when I sort through things, placing them in boxes marked "KEEP," "SELL," or "THROW AWAY." And an even odder one when I take the accumulated contents of "THROW AWAY" to the curb, walking past the realtor's sign which now impales the front lawn.

As I write this it is night; the house is soundless save for my tapping at these keys. When I stop for a moment and look up from the paper, the silence swoops down: and I will admit to a melancholy as I look across the floor at the many boxes sprawled over it. But it is a temporary feeling, for I think too of New York and my life there and my agent, the dilapidated but effective Simon Stillman; and my new-found, or rather soon-to-be-found, financial independence. A great many things await me there.

I stand for a moment, glance out the window through which my mother stared so many times; and see only darkness. But beyond the darkness, I know, there is light. There is light.

Awakening begins with the word *I*. Submerged, distant, it floats there like a perpetual faraway echo. It is not as if his mind has suddenly conjured up the word from nothingness, created it in a definite gesture of imagination. Rather it is as if a nameless something, not quite conscious, had been searching through his subterranean depths, not quite reaching it, watching it slip away like hazy light in a dark fog. *I*.

For a long time that is all there is, that single word floating inside him. There is an enormous darkness enveloping him: and he hears nothing, sees nothing, thinks of nothing but the single faraway word, *I*, hovering there. The sound of the word stretches and bends, fades in and out, bounces gently inside his skull. It echoes and reverberates. *I. I.*

Then he begins to disintegrate again, and *I* starts to fade, lost in the endless depths, and the nameless something swirls slowly and sinks, and there is nothing again.

Some time later it resurfaces; and *I* wafts gently around inside his mind, not harshly or insistently but like a soft hum: a whispered mantra, soothing, hypnotic. Soon it begins to have a kind of pattern, a slow, pulsing rhythm, regular and steady. After a while he realizes that what he is hearing is his own breathing, and wrapped inside each inhalation and exhalation is *I*, filled with breath, with air, each drawn slowly in and out. *I...I...*

The Unspoken

He becomes aware, dimly, of time passing. It is not something that worries him. He feels no anxiety about it at all. But he grows slowly aware of the phenomenon, that between one listening to the breathed *I* and another there is unaccounted time: that he is still rising and sinking in his own consciousness, awareness giving way to blankness and back again. But as the unknown time passes he begins to believe that the periods of blankness are shorter than they once were. More regularly now, with fewer empty gaps, *I* floats inside him, connected inextricably to each time he breathes. *I...*

It is a long time before he grows aware of another rhythm within himself. The realization comes when he notices a soft thumping within his head and understands that he is hearing, or rather sensing, his own heartbeat. He listens to the way in which the breathing *I* and the heartbeat blend together, each rhythm connected to the other; and he finds after a time that he can even control them if he wishes, can speed up his breathing slightly or slow it down and the heart will stay perfectly in tandem. This fact fills him with a sense of warmth and well-being. They are so perfectly balanced, these two. He experiments with controlling them between long periods, or what he dimly perceives as long periods, of blankness.

Finally there comes a time when it seems to him that he hears voices. At first he cannot be sure, and they sound very distant, as if spoken across some great canyon. He cannot make out the words at all. But they are, something tells him, voices. *I...*he thinks. *I...I am.*

There follows another period of blank nothingness.

Much later, *I* surfaces again. He hears his breathing and the heartbeat and it does not seem to take long for him to connect again the two concepts: *I...I am.* He is. He knows nothing else in the world but he knows that. He is. He exists. He is something that is not nothing. A fixed point. *I am.*

Voices impinge on his consciousness again: distant vague murmurings: he tries to listen but finds them fading in and out of him like faraway stations on a radio. He cannot be sure whether he is hearing them or not; can be sure of nothing other than the fact that he *is*. He listens to his breathing, feels the heartbeat inside his skull. He is. A positive in a sea of neutrals. Is. Am. *Being*.

Other sounds now: a door closing: hollow clicking footsteps: an indistinct swish. He breathes and as he breathes some invisible sensors within himself send small tingles out to the ends of his fingers. He had been unaware that he had fingers; that he had anything at all besides the omniscient darkness. He knows that he exists; that he *is;* but fingers! That is a new concept. Fingers. Hands. *Body*.

I am, he thinks; and then he remembers his name, each sound of it arriving achingly slowly as if from a far-lost place: first comes the sound *rah*, distant, whispered; then, some time later, the brief, cut-off *b;* and finally the long soothing *ihnnn*…The sounds come together at last, reconstruct themselves inside his mind, fuse, and he finds the name "Robin." He lets it play there, listening to each special sound (imagined now, inside his mind), each component of breath it takes to create the unique and peculiar fusion of consonants and vowels needed to form "Robin." And later still he knits together other sounds into another tapestry and finds "Withers."

I, he thinks again; and there is such a thing as *I,* and since there is, he realizes, then *I am;* and he has, he thinks, a form, for everything that exists has a form because everything that exists is made up of atoms and molecules. The form may be vast and unknown like the universe or infinitesimally tiny like an amoeba but they exist and so they have form. And he has form. He has a body. The body has even been given a name, a label: Robin Withers. And he exists, he knows. He is here now, in this particular instant of space and time. *I am.*

The Unspoken

It occurs to him sometime later to wonder just *where* he is. He has become aware that, since he exists, other things must as well: surely he cannot be the only *I,* the space occupied by his body cannot be the only space. No: there are other persons, other spaces. He has heard voices, after all, voices that he does not think emanate from some vein of his mind but rather are there, real, outside himself. And he has heard doors, and footsteps receding into distant places. But for a long time, sinking in and out of himself, he cannot imagine how he might reach toward these outer spaces. His darkness seems endless, inviolable: so he remains there, motionless, breathing.

After a time he notices tiny bits of sound reaching him from somewhere within himself. He is sure they are not coming from outside. He hears rhythms, modulations, tones of voices: he remembers them. He cannot quite make out the words but he recognizes, dimly, the sounds. He has heard them before. Where, when? In another world, sometime long ago; an ancient, dead world, long-lost. It is as if the voices reach him through the thicknesses of walls or closed doors: they are muffled, indistinct: he cannot make them out. But finally the abstract tones begin to coalesce and focus. Soon he can determine emotions: a sorrowful resignation, or a gruff dismissiveness; and then the words themselves come together, surface, tumble over each other:

Everything's going to be fine, baby.
He asleep?
We'll wrap them around ourselves and float up to the moon.
He asleep?
Right up to the moon.

He remembers then. His mother, his father: pictures now, synchronous with the voices, piercing the darkness. Her face, the dark curls on her shoulders, the blue Siamese-shaped eyes, the weight of her sitting next to him, the smell of her skin, the touch of her lips lightly on his own. His father's shadow in the doorway blending into the hallway's darkness; only his gnarled hand exposed to the light. And then other pictures, passing as in slow pantomime. He begins to remember names and faces. He sees himself, or younger versions of himself, in different rooms, lights, atmospheres: lying before a glowing television on his stomach; biting into a dark plum; reading a paperback book. The heft of a baseball in his hands. A warm bag of baked things against his stomach. Knees touching knees under a tiny table with a checkerboard on it. He thinks again: *I am.*

Time passes. He feels tremors around his eyes and realizes, dimly, that they are beginning to open. He has made no conscious effort to do this: has not decided *I will open my eyes;* rather, it seems simply to be happening outside his own will. It is like waking from the deepest of sleeps, an involuntary response. He does nothing to stop or encourage it; leaves his eyelids to tremble as they choose.

Light begins to glow inside his eyes and he realizes that they are opening. It is a very slow process and a great deal of time goes by: light glows, then vanishes; blinks on and off; and he becomes aware of the sounds outside himself again. They are not many. Once he hears a door and carpeted footsteps and feels, or thinks he feels, a cool palm on his forehead. He cannot be sure. The light glows and fades, then glows again. Silence surrounds him.

He opens his eyes.

He is looking at a ceiling. For a long time his eyes do not move from it; he listens, but hears nothing. He breathes. The ceiling is a plain stark white. As he looks at it he remembers the rooms of his life: they come back to him in quick succession: a house in San Francisco, near the bay; a trailer in Virginia; a dingy dormitory; the ceiling of a van, wood paneling coming unglued: many ceilings, he thinks, many rooms, many atmospheres, and time, time present in all of them always like a silent and secret fifth columnist.

It is not until his eyes drop to the chest of drawers across from him, and then to the window and the pepper tree branches brushing against it, that the realization blossoms within him as to just where he is. He feels no emotion as it enters his mind. He feels nothing at all. His eyes move from the window to the familiar throw-rug on the floor, across the bed and toward the door leading to the bathroom. He listens. He can hear wind pushing against the house; and as his eyes move to the window again he hears the tiny scratching sound of the branches against the windowpane. Beyond the crisscrossed patterns of the branches he can see, in small patches, pieces of a gray sky. It looks to him like a morning sky.

He looks toward the door. It is closed; but he has the feeling that someone has been here quite recently. His eyes move over to the shapes of his own legs, covered with blankets, to his own stomach and chest. He is wearing a flannel shirt he is not sure he recognizes. He studies his hands on top of the blankets: raises one to his eyes and stares at the pronounced veins. They look to him something like branches.

After a time he feels the need to visit the bathroom so he pushes back the blankets and slowly lifts his legs over the side of the bed to the floor. They seem heavy, clumsy: and as he sits up he is not entirely sure they will support his weight. He presses his feet to the floor, feeling the muscles in his legs tense strangely, uncomfortably. Keeping one hand firmly on a bedpost, he lifts himself up. It is all right: his legs are strong enough: but his sense of balance is confused. The floor seems to sway and he holds tightly to the support of the bed for a long moment. Finally he lets go.

He nearly falls; but manages to keep himself upright. He makes his way across the cool throw-rug to the bathroom door and opens it. Hardly registering the bathroom itself, he moves to the toilet and uses it, hearing dimly in his mind his father's voice: *Don't pull your pants down like that. Kids will laugh at you.*

He flushes and goes to the sink, splashes water on his face; looks into the mirror before him.

He hardly recognizes the image staring back at him. His skin is a pale, sickly-gray color. His hair has been cropped very short, hardly more than a butch; there is beard stubble covering his jaw line. But it is his eyes he sees most vividly: red-rimmed, pale, they seem to have sunk into his face, receded, and the heavy black rings and lines under them appear to have taken over. He is looking into a face, it seems to him, much older than his own: the face of a middle-aged man, bleary and wasted.

As he looks away from the image he catches a glimpse of something. He looks into the mirror again. He can see the reflected image of the bathtub behind him: and as he looks at it, for just a fleeting moment he thinks he sees a woman there—in steaming water—her skin slick and glistening, her hair falling to her shoulders.

Baby, did you have a nightmare? she asks.

Inhaling quickly, he turns and looks at the bathtub. It is empty.

He moves unsteadily back to the bed then, falls into it exhaustedly. The walk to and from the bathroom seems to have taken all his strength and, shivering, he pulls the blankets up to his neck. He has never felt so tired. He is utterly drained of everything: strength, thought, emotion. He feels sleep swooping down.

Later—hours, perhaps days—his eyes open again at the sound of a door handle being turned. He shifts in the bed and looks blankly toward the door. The room is half-lit.

The door opens and a woman backs into the room carrying a tray. He watches the form moving and wonders vaguely where his glasses are; he cannot make out who is there. The form turns toward him in the half-light, moving to him with the tray.

"Oh," she says. "You're awake."

He recognizes the voice: it reaches to him as across canyons. For a long moment, however, he cannot place it.

"I brought your breakfast," she says.

In dull, automatic response, he sits up sorely; and as the woman leans toward him with the tray he recognizes her.

"Hello, Priscilla," he says. His voice is cracked and hollow; hardly more than a whisper.

She sits next to him on the bed. "Hi."

He wishes he could see her more clearly, but the light is dim and she is unfocused. He can make out her dark, short hair, her big arms; nothing else.

"Where—" Something catches in his throat and he tries to clear it. "Where—where are my glasses?"

"Here." Her voice is low-pitched. She reaches to the small table beside the bed.

Fumblingly, he places the glasses on his face. Priscilla is sitting there in a pink blouse and black denim jeans, looking at him with her close-set eyes. It seems to him that she has gained weight, but he does not really know. He cannot picture her as she once looked, cannot think of her clearly: as if cobwebs were wrapped stickily around his mind.

"Orange juice," she says, gesturing toward the tray. "Scrambled eggs. Toast." She smiles slightly. "It's the best I can do. I'm not that much of a cook."

He stares at the tray dully.

"Go ahead, eat," she says gently. "Give it a try."

He looks at her, then at the tray again. It seems to him that he should say something, or ask something, or…but his mind is fogged.

"My mom would have brought it," Priscilla offers, "but she had to go to the mainland today. I'm the deputy nurse." She smiles.

"Your mom?" he says in his hollow voice. He has difficulty forming the words and they sound strange when they come from his mouth. "Aunt Margaret?"

"Mm-hm."

He studies the orange liquid in the glass. The glass itself is familiar: he pictures drinking milk from just such a glass between mouthfuls of hot bear claws and twisters fresh from the bakery.

"I..." he begins to say; but the words do not come.

"Shush," Priscilla says. "Eat your breakfast." She reaches toward him and places her palm across his forehead. "I think your fever's gone," she says.

He reaches for the fork on the tray. His fingers seem to have glue in the joints and he feels clumsy, awkward. The fork trembles, suspended in the air; then clatters down onto the plate.

"It's okay," she says, leaning toward him and picking up the fork. Her face is close to his and there is an odor of lemon. Her hair is cropped short on the sides and hangs nearly to her shoulders in back: a picture materializes of an earlier Priscilla, a black bowl surrounding her head. "Here," she says. She takes his hand and places it around the fork. "Try again."

He stares at the fork in his hand, moves it slowly to the spongy heap of egg on the plate. He manages to scoop a bit onto the fork and lift it to his mouth.

"Good," Priscilla says. She smiles. "Good."

He chews the soft, strangely-textured food for a long moment, then feels it slide lumpily down his throat. It makes him cough once.

"Drink your juice," Priscilla says, lifting the glass.

He places the fork on the plate, takes the glass and touches it to his lips. A cold, acidic liquid tingles his tongue.

They continue like that for several minutes. He drops the fork again but picks it up by himself; some of the juice dribbles down his chin. Priscilla takes a paper napkin and wipes him. After a while he has finished the egg and juice and has taken a few nibbles from the toast.

"Finished…" he says with difficulty. "I'm finished."

"Don't you want your toast?"

He stares at her, manages to shake his head.

"Well, you did pretty good." She stands and takes the tray, begins moving toward the door.

"Priscilla?"

She stops and looks back at him. "What?"

He stares at her. "I…" But he cannot finish and so merely sits there, his mouth open.

Priscilla places the tray on the chest of drawers and comes back to the bed. "Here, Robin," she says, lifting the glasses from his face, "lay down again."

"I…" He tries to stand suddenly, not knowing why. Priscilla's hands push him gently back against the pillows.

"Lay down, Robin," she says.

He relaxes his body again and Priscilla adjusts the bed sheets.

"Priscilla…"

"What?"

He touches her hand and she sits next to him again. "Priscilla, how…" His voice is weak and harsh in his throat. "How did you… you get here?"

Priscilla sighs, smiling slightly. "Robin, you ask the same questions over and over."

"I don't remember…"

She looks at their hands, together. "Your dad called my mom just before you came here. For some…help. He needed help to take care of you. My mom said she'd come. I was there, so I came too."

"How long have you been here?"

"Couple weeks."

"How long..." It is difficult to finish the sentence. He swallows. "...How long have I been here?"

"Couple weeks," she says. "Since you got out."

"Out...?"

"Out of the hospital."

"Hospital...?"

"Rest home," she says. "Whatever. The hospital, that's what your dad calls it."

"Where is my dad?" he whispers.

"At work."

"But he's here..."

"Mm-hm."

He stares at the chest of drawers across the room.

"Why don't you get some sleep now, Robin," Priscilla says gently, adjusting the bed sheets.

"Priscilla..."

"Mm."

"I can't...I can't remember—things..."

"That's because you've been so sick," she says. "When you got out of the hospital you seemed okay. Physically, I mean. That's what your dad said. But then as soon as you got here you came down with your fever." She smiles down at him. "You've been out of it ever since."

"I..." He knows that there are questions he must ask, things he must know: but he cannot find words: and he feels himself dropping away again, sleep pouring over him. Priscilla's image blurs, darkens.

"Am I going to die?" he hears himself asking.

He feels a palm softly on his cheek. "No, Robin," she says. "You're going to be fine. Just fine."

2

Slowly then, over many days, between long dreamless hours of heavy sleep, fragments of light and sound begin to reassemble themselves inside his mind. He remembers straps tightly over his chest and the sensation of rolling movement and blue lights above him whipping by. He sees faces leaning toward him, peering into his eyes, big soft meaty fingers prying at his eyelids. He hears burbling voices, question after question, shouted remarks and instructions. *Look at me.* A sudden stoppage then, and a blue nurse in a blue uniform aiming a blue syringe toward his blue arm....

A violent sickness: his body wrenching and wrenching incredibly, and the voices around him and the ropy blue arms pressing him down like huge snakes, awesome and monstrous. A face, an old man's blue face so close to his own that he could see the pores of his skin and the dark veins in his eyes. Wrenching. Indecipherable voices: laughter, somewhere laughter: evil shining things poking and prodding him: his head strapped down.

After that is a long period of blankness. He seems to recall a white hospital bed; a droning television suspended over him. Urinating into a plastic container. Tubes and tape. Shadowy figures moving around the room. Dim, early-evening light...

Later a different room. Gentle earth tones: unused straps well hidden within the bed frame: meals of watery soup and soggy vegetables served with plastic utensils. "Physical Therapy": light aerobic exercise led by a happily task-mastering black man. "Art Therapy": a frivolous woman in her early twenties with enormous breasts and a voice rather like a twittering parakeet's giving them crayons and construction paper and asking them to draw houses, mountains, "faces that feel like you do." But most of the time spent silently, sitting in a chair out on the big green lawn; or talking with one of several resident doctors. But he does not remember talking much. In fact he cannot recall talking at all. It exists only in bits and pieces: remembered faces and scenes: and they are there only tenuously, they slip away again with astonishing regularity and he is left trying to think of things he knows he remembered once but does no longer. Then at unexpected moments they surface again, or parts of them do, vividly there, sharply living. Light pouring through the limbs of the oak tree on the lawn. The feel of a crayon in his hand and the waxy smell of it. Reaching down and feeling the strap mechanism in the bed frame.

"How are you feeling today, dear?" Aunt Margaret's voice reaches him from a distant place. He opens his eyes.

"I'm okay," he whispers hoarsely.

"Your fever is almost gone."

He nods. She stands there, her hair shorter and grayer than he remembers it, her face fatter, but still recognizably the Aunt Margaret from years before, the eyes of endless concern, the wide mouth and its cluckings of sympathy.

"I'll bring in your breakfast in a little while," she says in her maternal tone.

He nods again and she leaves the room. He pictures briefly the nest of golden cobras her hair had once been, and lying in another bed, her voice in another hall: *Cissy, how could you?*

The pictures fade then and he feels himself floating in a strange grayness. He sees light, then darkness; then light again.

"Priscilla," he says, his voice a rasp.

He is sitting in the chair next to his bed and Priscilla is stripping the sheets away.

"Hm?"

"Where is Koofie?" he says.

"Well—" Priscilla unfolds a fresh sheet and shakes it out onto the mattress—"we're kind of separated right now. She's with her family in Michigan."

He looks at her. "Why?"

"Maybe too much togetherness," she sighs. "I don't know. But we'll get back together. In fact I'm planning on going out to see her in a few months."

"What—what are you...doing?"

"Doing?"

He gestures vaguely. "Life...doing."

She smiles. "Not a heck of a lot, if you want to know the truth. We came back from the trip—you remember, our world trip?"

"No—yes..."

"Well, we came back from *it* flat broke. I called Mom when I was in New York. That was the hardest call I ever had to make in my life." She begins piling the blankets on the bed and straightening them. "I hadn't talked to any of them in ages. Koofie and me paid for the whole trip ourselves, you know. It was strange. Mom sounded so *happy* to hear from me."

"Yes..."

"She told me to come out there and stay with them for a while. But Koofie and me were fighting all the time, about...I don't even know what about."

"Yes."

"We finally decided to separate for a while. I came here, to try to figure things out. Right around the same time I found out about you." She glances at him.

He stares at the window and the pepper tree branches, still now in the windless morning.

"Why'd you do it, Robin?" she asks in a casual tone, picking up a pillow and placing it under her chin, slipping a pillowcase over it.

He looks at her, then at the window again. He sees crayons in his hands. Then blue light and being rolled along a bright blue corridor.

"I don't remember..."

He gets out of the bed occasionally and moves to a chair by the window. Or he puts on a gray bathrobe and opens the door and looks blearily up and down the hallway. In the mornings he can see light pouring through the window in the hall and once he walks to it, stands staring out, remembering the sun bright and blinding and his mother's thumping footsteps rushing to him.

At night he hears footsteps. Hard and flat. Sometimes they pass by his door without slowing; other times they hesitate, then continue on. Sometimes they stop. Sometimes they stop and the door opens slowly and a black shadow stands there, darkness against darkness. Once he opens his eyes to slits and looks toward the figure. A trick of the light casts a soft yellow bar of illumination over the silhouette's two eyes and he can see that they are focused directly on him. The figure stands unmoving for minutes.

He remembers something his Uncle Jasper had said once, lying in a bed in darkness with blankets pulled up to his neck and his voice reduced to a thin whisper. Staring up at the ceiling, his milky and veined eyes wide, his dry lips open and quivering, he had said: *I can remember all the old things.* It is the same for Robin as the days pass and more and more bits and slivers return to him like the glints off a shining diamond. It is the old things, the early ones, which come back most vividly. When he closes his eyes the visions rise before him, super-real, seemingly three-dimensional and alive. He can see his room when he was seven or eight and the baseball magazines in an orderly stack in the corner. He can see Sonya Skyler's face and the cherry blossom paperweight in her tiny hand. He can see his Uncle Jasper's strange, dark room filled with its exotic and indescribable things, can hear his mother's voice, slurred, out in the kitchen with his aunt. But it is not as if he is a passive onlooker toward these scenes: rather it is as if he is again an active participant in them. He hears the sounds and breathes the aromas. He can feel the creepy sensation of running his finger along his uncle's red chest scar. And he can hear the whispered voice behind him: *Kiss your uncle goodbye, honey.*

And the woman in the black dress: and the pearls encircling her neck: he sees her again, hears her softly slurred voice, feels her weight pressing down onto the bed. Feels her fingers at his pajama buttons. Hears her opening the window. Sees them together in a fog-filled morning, the sound of her feet on the wet wood of the pier, his hand in hers, and her voice saying, *Oh Robin, it's a real diamond day.* And later: darkness: his ear pressed to the bathroom wall and the sighs and creakings of bedsprings. Muddy uncertain visions. The knowledge that he, himself, was created out of such a darkness within a darkness: was formed and grew in such a warm lightless place: had felt her heartbeat inextricably bound with his own.

He remembers all the old things. He can feel the material of shirts he once wore and the grain of the wood of school desks at which he once sat; can remember the faded green cloth of the dresses Mrs. Balfour-Ritchie wore when she read stories to them about Noah and Samson; can remember the texture of finger paints sticky on his fingers; can remember the squeak of his tennis shoes on the floor of Mrs. Peterson's classroom. And voices: the librarian Mrs. Klibo's warm European accent and the hissing radiator behind; Uncle Jasper in front of a TV baseball game, crying *We got 'em now!;* and another, never heard, only imagined: a little girl with her arms wrapped around him from behind as they fly down a hill on his bicycle, laughing and shrieking, *Not so fast! Not so fast....!* Sounds, echoes: a refrigerator opening and closing; a heavy, thick-set body dropping into a leather chair; a dish smashing on the floor. Muttered indistinct words. Footsteps...

Sometimes, with Priscilla or Aunt Margaret to help him down the stairs, he will sit for a few minutes in front of the television. At such times the rooms seem almost to whisper to him: familiar tables, chairs, vases, photographs on walls: it is only when he looks across to Priscilla or Aunt Margaret, or at his own ropy and pale forearms, that he sees any evidence that time has in fact been here at all. Or at his father: but his father he sees only sporadically, and usually then in the darkness of the glowing television at night. He recalls that once he had felt sheer terror at being anywhere near the shadowy figure across from him: but now he feels nothing whatever. They rarely speak in anything but monosyllables. The man's eyes never leave the flickering television screen. It seems to Robin that the man has aged. It seems to him that his hair is thinner, an unsullied white now, that his skin is looser and baggier on his face, that his eyes, like his own, have sunk deep into their sockets. But about none of this can he be sure. It seems to him that when the man moves it is with an unfamiliar stoop and listlessness that he cannot connect with the figure of furious energy from before. He remembers his father blocking his path on the stairs, shouting paranoid drunken accusations at him in a high-pitched voice which might have been comical if it hadn't seemed so dangerous. He remembers planning his evenings so that he would not be in the house upon his father's return: arranging it so that he would come back only later, after the thick snoring had begun upstairs. He once felt great emotion about these things, he knows. Now he feels nothing but blankness.

He finds this question of *feeling* an intriguing one. For he feels nothing whatever about anything. He wonders about this. It seems to him that, if he is in fact a living, breathing human being, he should have feelings about something; but if he does, he cannot find them within himself. He views everything now with the objectivity of a machine, passionlessly recording. There was once a time when things were different; but that time is gone now, lost forever. He hears someone's voice, he does not know who or when, say: *You have pretend feelings.* But now, he thinks, he need not even pretend, for there is nothing; and he no longer remembers how it felt to have had anything else.

He does not dream at night, but before he slips into sleep images play in his mind: and he sees the bed of hidden straps; sees his hand holding a crayon and moving it across a piece of children's construction paper, hears a ruthlessly upbeat voice fluttering, *That's very good, Robin, very good!* He sees a group of men and women running around chairs in a childish game. He sees himself sitting in a white wire chair out on the grass and watching figures moving before him, broken by the beams of golden light shining through the oak tree's leaves and limbs.

"Aunt Margaret?" he says one night as the woman helps him into bed.

"Yes, dear?"

His body tingles as the cool blankets surround him. "How long was I...in there?" he asks quietly.

Aunt Margaret adjusts the bed sheets and looks down at him sympathetically.

"Do you mean in the rest home, dear?"

"Yes…"

"About seven months. But then of course you were in the hospital before that."

"For how long?" he whispers.

"Dear, we shouldn't talk about these things. I don't want you to become upset."

"Aunt Margaret, how long?"

She sighs, looking down at him plaintively. He notices wrinkles around her eyes that he does not remember from years before.

"You were in intensive care about a month, dear. And then you were in the...ward. The psychiatric ward. For three months. Almost three months."

He exhales, staring at the ceiling behind the woman.

"Go to sleep now, Robin," she says, brushing her hand gently through his short hair.

"Aunt Margaret?"

"Dear..."

He looks at her. "Where are my things? I mean the things that belonged to me—before..."

She speaks quietly. "In a box in the basement. There isn't much."

"I want to see it." He begins to sit up but the woman pushes him back gently.

"All in good time, Robin," she says.

"Aunt Margaret..."

"Hush, dear. Hush."

He lies back then, weakly resigned, and closes his eyes.

A picture materializes before him: he sees a diamond glittering on a gold band, shafts of light streaming from it, and suddenly there is a pair of round pool-like eyes staring at him in a sea of blackness. He inhales sharply.

"Poor thing," Aunt Margaret says, stroking his cheek.

3

It had taken weeks (Aunt Margaret told him later) to piece it all together. The police had become involved. She carried false identification and for a number of weeks no one knew exactly who she was. Eventually her record was traced back to the state of New Hampshire where it was learned that she had been raised in the state orphanage at Concord, where she had been deposited after the death of her parents in an auto accident when she was three. Her real name was Lilly Brown. The state's record showed her being an exceptionally bright child in her early youth, earning top marks in English and Art and Music; but by the age of ten signs of emotional disturbance had begun to manifest themselves. There were numerous reports of fighting, throwing schoolbooks, screaming, crying, and general disruptiveness. Twice she had been placed in foster homes. In the first, when she was twelve, she had lived with a husband and wife and their three sons. It had lasted seven months before she was returned to the orphanage as "incorrigible and impossible." The second, when she was fourteen, had come to a halt in less than a month. She had been staying with a well-to-do couple and their two daughters in Manchester; several telephone complaints and one letter were represented in the record within the first three weeks of her stay, which had ended abruptly a few days later when, in an hysterical outburst, she had hurled one of the daughters down the stairs, fracturing the girl's wrist.

There followed one sketchily-recorded episode of running away, and a lengthy list of counselors whom she was required to visit. She lived in a state-run halfway house for emotionally disturbed adolescents.

But at the age of fifteen her academic record, which had been dismal for several years, suddenly began to shine: her grades took an inexplicable quantum leap so astonishing that one of her teachers wrote, "This appears to be one of those rare cases in which an exceptionally troubled student has, against all odds, taken it upon herself to succeed where the system has failed." In her junior year she received straight A's, and in her file was found a college recommendation letter from the same teacher. But rather than pursue that course she requested, in her sixteenth year, permission to take a high school equivalency examination. She passed it easily and, on her seventeenth birthday, having received an offer of employment from a local bookbinder's shop, she left.

Thereafter the record was unilluminating. She had lasted half a year at the bookbinder's before resigning suddenly; her whereabouts then became impossible to trace. She was nineteen by the time she registered for courses at the university in northern California using doctored transcripts.

That was the extent of the information the police had been able to gather.

An exhaustive search for any next-of-kin had yielded no results; and since she was of legal age and no longer a resident, the state of New Hampshire had no responsibility toward her. It was therefore up to the state of California to decide what to do with the remains. There were consultations with Mr. Withers who, although he had no legal standing in the matter, nonetheless was the closest thing to a relative that could be found. At last, two weeks after her death (due, according to the official report, to a "massive overdose of phenobarbitals, self-induced"), her body was cremated. Mr. Withers paid for a scattering of the ashes at sea.

⊰⊱

"That's all?" Robin whispers.

"That's all, dear," Aunt Margaret says. "I'm so sorry…Do you want one of your sleeping pills?"

"I'm all right. I don't feel anything."

"Are you sure?"

"I'm sure. I'm all right."

She looks at her lap, picking at her fingers. He studies her graying hair and wide silly mouth.

"I don't understand how some things happen," she says. "Some things I just don't understand at all."

There is a long pause.

"I know I'm a stupid woman," she says quietly, "but things happen sometimes that I think I should understand…and I don't." She looks at him again. "Dear, I'm so sorry," she says again.

"I'm all right, Aunt Margaret. Thank you for…everything."

For a moment he thinks that the woman sitting there, his mother's sister, is going to cry. She looks at him and her face is suffused with pain.

"Aunt Margaret, don't," he says. "I'm okay. Really."

She nods, looking down again.

"Would you like some hot tea?" she says.

"Tea," he says hollowly. He considers for a long moment. "Yes. Yes, tea would be nice."

She nods, standing.

"Let me come with you," he says, moving tentatively to the edge of the bed. "We'll drink it together."

⇌

For a long time he cannot visualize her in his mind, save for momentary glimpses: a pair of eyes in darkness, a small pale hand in his, a lopsided grin and uneven teeth. Though Aunt Margaret shows him numerous photocopied documents, her earlier life remains totally unreal: orphanages, foster homes; the name "Lilly Brown" makes him feel somehow queasy. He reads and re-reads meaningless reports about someone he never knew. He tries to picture the scenes in his mind: tries to connect the fragments he has of her, the eyes, the grin, with a little girl in a car crash, a little girl in a dark Dickens-like orphanage; but the pictures will not come. It reminds him of his father telling him stories about his own youth, about Midwestern farms and Korea and prostitutes: no matter how hard he tried, he recalls, he had not been able to bring any life or reality to them. And no matter how hard he tries he cannot connect the photocopied papers in his hands to anything that had ever been real, human.

It seems to him at times that he should feel some sorrow when he thinks of her: a sense of regret, loss, sentiment, something. But he does not feel a thing. There is nothing left to feel. He is as empty of feeling as a stone.

For it was not, he thinks, really *him* then. It was someone else. Another Robin, another young man with the same physical makeup but a completely different psyche. And he can feel no connection to that other self; they are, it seems to him, utterly separate. The Robin lying in his bed now never knew the strange dark-haired girl who had died. Someone had known her; but it had not been him. If it has been him, he knows, then he would feel something now: human beings, he thinks, have emotions; but he has nothing. Then perhaps somewhere he lost his humanness, he thinks. Perhaps...perhaps it *had* been him, but the "I" that tried to destroy itself with the girl managed only a destruction of the humanness. Not the physical body. And so he walks the earth a zombie, an automaton, not truly human, bereft of emotion or feeling.

I don't feel, a voice says, speaking from some faraway place within himself. *I've stopped. I don't feel anything. I'm not going to feel anything ever again.*

Why? a voice asks.

Because I might die...

4

As he grows stronger Robin and Priscilla begin taking daily walks around town. The skies are steel-gray, winter-cold; he bundles himself carefully into a heavy jacket and wool cap and gloves. At first he grows quickly tired and they must rest in a coffee shop or on a bench halfway through; but gradually he feels strength returning to his muscles and bones like a warm glowing light. Sometimes

Priscilla chats lightly or holds his gloved hand in her own; sometimes they walk thirty or forty minutes without saying a word.

"How're you doing?" Priscilla will ask then. "You okay?"

He will nod, attempt to smile. Each day his body feels a bit better, stronger and more alive.

They visit places that are familiar to him: that he, or rather a lost stranger who went by his name, once visited. The bakery, remodeled but largely the same; the library, almost completely unchanged, with Mrs. Klibo still behind the desk; the pier, with its soft wood and odor of sea-salt. When they stand at the edge and look out into the mist-filled distance Robin can hear the woman's voice talking of diamonds; can hear the sound of her feet on the wood. But he feels nothing. As he stands there, Priscilla's arm wrapped around his, he remembers being here in another time: much later, with the girl with pool-like eyes beside him in the dark. It was a thousand centuries ago, he thinks. He had been shouting, shouting hysterically—about what? He no longer knows. If he ever did. It is lost like smoke in wind, or like tiny flakes dissolving into the sea....

"Did I tell you," Priscilla says one day over tea in a local shop, "that I heard from Cape a while back?"

"No," Robin says. "I don't think so."

She sips from the cup. "Mm-hm. Maybe three, four months ago."

For a moment he cannot quite connect the name with any image or memory; then he visualizes the van, the dirty blankets, the sea.

"How is he?" Robin asks mechanically.

"He lives in L.A. now," she says in her low voice. "He says he's been doing some studio work for people."

"That's good," he says.

"Yeah. He lives with a guy, too. They actually have an apartment and everything." She laughs. "I think he's growing up."

Robin smiles blankly. The memories of Cape are so dim and distant that he can hardly raise anything of them from under the folds and stacks of other images, other voices, sounds and static.

She looks at him. "Does that bother you? I mean, hearing about Cape?"

"No," Robin says. "Not at all."

"You sure?"

"Priscilla, I'm not going to run off and slit my throat or anything. I'm all right."

She looks down, smiling embarrassedly. "Sorry," she says.

"Anyway, I guess I should thank you for spending all this time with me. For helping me so much."

"It's okay," she says. "We're family, aren't we?"

He smirks. "I guess we are."

She looks directly at him. "So you're not going to do anything stupid again, right?"

He feels himself smiling. He looks at her and sees the twelve-year-old at the river, her body glistening in the bright sunlight; sees the young woman with hoops and earrings and bangles looking out over the crystalline vista of Santa Barbara. "Don't know if I can promise that," he says. "Stupidity is my special forte."

She smiles in return. "You know what I mean."

"I know. Don't worry, Priscilla. Please."

"Where would you be if I didn't worry? And my mom? And your dad?"

He looks at the table. "Does my dad worry?"

"Sure he does. He's the one that called us."

Robin frowns; picks up a fork and runs it along the tablecloth, studying the parallel patterns it makes.

"Haven't you noticed?" she says.

"No. He hasn't said anything."

"He can't express himself around you, Robin."

"Why not?"

Priscilla considers. Then she says: "If you want to know my opinion, I think he's afraid of you."

Robin looks up, scoffing. "Afraid of me? Why?"

She scowls. "I think it goes back to what happened to your mom."

Robin studies her.

"I don't have any *evidence* for this," she says, pouring more tea for herself, "but I get the idea that when he's around you he feels…guilty. I mean, you've told me what happened. How could he *not* feel guilty? Especially around you."

"But he shouldn't," Robin says. "It wasn't his fault. It was hers. The whole situation, everything that happened. He just…reacted." He thinks about this. "Maybe if he'd been able to react in a different way…I don't know. But he *couldn't* have." He considers. "He was weak. He *was* weak. But that's not something to be guilty of. It's just a fact."

"But when he looks at you…" She leaves the sentence unfinished.

Robin stares at the fork-tracks in the tablecloth.

"I see what you mean," he says. "But all that was so *long* ago."

"It never goes away, though."

"I thought that it did. Maybe I was wrong."

"C'mon," Priscilla says, "smile. You're looking glum again."

He chuckles. "Please. You've been accusing me of that for ten years now."

"And I've always been right!"

⇌

Sometime later they sit together on his bedroom rug and Robin pulls open a dusty cardboard box they have brought up from the basement.

"Are you sure this isn't going to upset you?" Priscilla asks.

"I'm fine."

He opens the box and looks into it. On the top are some old clothes, neatly stacked. He feels nothing as he looks at them; he brings them out and places them on the floor.

Under the clothes are stacks of papers. He looks through them dully: sees little of any interest. Old school assignments; short stories marked up in Turnham's familiar hand; a few letters, including a rubber-banded collection of Priscilla's postcards.

"Here," Robin says. "Have a look at these."

She grins and takes them in her hand, studying them as Robin looks deeper into the box. He wonders at the absence of any photographs or letters from the girl; he can find nothing whatsoever. It is strange. He remembers that there had been some; but what might have become of them he cannot say. It is all fragments now. Had they destroyed them? Something tweaks his memory at this thought. But surely, he thinks, not *all* of them. And yet as he digs through the musty box he can find nothing. There are a few books at the bottom. Nothing else.

He sighs and sits back against the bed. Priscilla looks up from her postcards.

"Find what you wanted?" she asks.

He shakes his head.

"What are you looking for, anyway?"

"I don't know," he says, thinking about it. "Pictures. Letters. Something to help me remember."

She nods, peering into the box. She reaches into it and brings out a handful of the books, grinning at him. "Look at these million-pounders!" she says. "Dostoevsky. Thomas Wolfe. *Tolstoy*. Yucko. Don't you have any good books?"

"Like what?" he smiles.

"Like something a girl can *lift*." She looks through the volumes. "Hey, here's one that's fairly skinny."

"What is it?"

"It says *The Professor Remembers and Other Stories.*"

He feels an odd sensation pass through him. "Let me see it," he says.

She brings it out, looking at it. "Terrence Llewelyn," she says. "That's funny. Why does that name ring a bell?"

"I've probably talked about him. I used to know him."

She frowns, passes the book to him. "No, I just saw something about him. Just the other day. I'm sure of it."

"I doubt if you saw anything about Terrence Llewelyn anywhere," Robin says. "He's not very well-known."

"No, I *know* I did. In a magazine."

"Really? Maybe he has a new book out."

"I'm positive I saw something." She scowls in thought. "Want me to see if I can find it downstairs?"

He nods. "I'd be interested."

"'Kay."

She stands and leaves the room.

Robin studies the cover of the book, the simple lettering on the dust jacket; then he turns it over and looks at the portrait of young Llewelyn, his dramatically angled face and swept-back black hair. The unordered books behind him: Mansfield, Trollope, Dickens, Kafka. The cashmere sweater tossed over his shoulders. The superior, coolly confident gleam in his eyes.

He opens the book to the flyleaf and reads: *To Robin, Who'll make it. from Lew.* Llewelyn! he thinks. He recalls, dimly, images of a dark and dirty living room and an old man with a cigar in his mouth, unrecognizable from the sharp photograph. As he thinks of it he recalls also his own melancholy disappointment: remembers his naive youthful dreams that somehow people like Llewelyn did not actually live on earth, could not really be *met,* that they existed on some other plane of super-reality untouched by mere mortals. But Llewelyn had been, he recalls, no different from anyone else; it had been an extraordinary thought, then. He remembers the madhouse, just down the hill. Asylum Heights, where all lost souls found themselves—sooner or later.

He remembers too the later disappointment he had felt with Llewelyn's writing: its false, forced emotion that he had never noticed in his younger days. He turns to the table of contents and looks down the list of titles. He recalls most of them. He finds "The Professor Remembers" and turns to it.

As he begins to read he feels an odd sensation course through him. As the remembered words meet his eye and reach into his brain, he has the feeling that he had misjudged Llewelyn. The opening lines, with the professor lying in his bed, seem to him superbly evocative. Llewelyn had employed all the senses, made the reader not only see the room but hear it, smell it, feel it: and simultaneously he set a completely convincing tone of gentle melancholy. The prose rhythm seems to him all but flawless. And as he reads he begins to think that perhaps he had rejected Llewelyn not because of his writing, but because of Llewelyn himself: in the heat of his youthful passion, it seems to him he might have confused the art with the artist: he had found Llewelyn in person to be bombastic, false, a friendly but phony poseur; and so in his disappointment, his frustration, he had ascribed those qualities to the stories themselves. He feels chagrined—he had misjudged everything, entirely: for as his eyes move across the solid black print of the pages he finds himself wrapped once again into the world of the old dying professor. It is vivid and real. He can hear the man's wheezy breath and smell the stale sheets enveloping him. He can hear the children's voices outside.

But before he finishes the story Priscilla's voice breaks in. "Found it!"

He looks up, his own room reassembling itself within his mind. Priscilla comes in with a magazine.

"Only it's not very good news, I'm afraid," she says, looking down at him. "Anyway, here it is."

Robin takes the magazine. His eyes follow Priscilla's pointed finger to a small paragraph at the bottom of the page: in tiny but bold black letters, the heading reads: AUTHOR DIES.

"'Terrence Llewelyn,'" Robin reads aloud in a soft voice, "'American writer of short stories, died Tuesday at a Bridgeport, Connecticut hospital. The official cause of death was given as pancreatic cancer. Llewelyn was known primarily for his early stories published in the 1950's which usually portrayed the solitary lives of lonely people. He is survived by his wife Sheryl. Funeral services are pending.'"

Priscilla tousles his hair. "Now, don't start getting glum," she says.

"I'm not glum." He hands the magazine back to her. "I only met him once, for a couple of hours. And I have a few letters from him." He looks into the box, pushing through the papers. "They must be in here somewhere."

Finally he comes to the familiar envelopes and brings them up. "Here they are." He looks through the small stack, noticing the postmarks. With what unparalleled excitement he had received these letters! He can recall it now, the way his pulse would race and his breath come short when a fresh envelope would appear in his post office box in Virginia.

Virginia...Pictures flash suddenly before his eyes of a big sun, long fields of grass, hard fruit in his hands, and a girl in a baseball cap grinning up at him; her slender naked body tangled in bed sheets in a curtained trailer in a lazy, hot afternoon. The feel of her hair sifting through his fingers and the sound of wind through the grass covering the many graves of her ancestors. It pours over him in an instant, picture after picture, sound upon sound: tapping at his typewriter in the early morning light; the sound of children playing outside; the feel of a water hose in his hand and the sounds of the children being laughingly drenched.

"Robin?"

"What?"

"Are you okay?"

"I'm fine," he says, looking up from the envelopes. "Just remembering some things, that's all."

"What's this?" Priscilla asks, bringing up a brown manila envelope stuffed with papers. "*Drowning*," she reads.

He looks at the envelope. "It's the book I was working on when I saw you in Santa Barbara."

"Really? Can I read it?"

"I don't know," he says. "Let's set it aside. I'll look at it first. I don't remember it very well, but something tells me it's pretty glum."

Priscilla grins, looking into the box again.

Robin's eyes fall to the magazine once more and he stares at Llewelyn's obituary. A line registers in his mind: *He is survived by his wife Sheryl.*

Well I'll be, Robin thinks, seeing in his mind a red-haired girl with hazy eyes and a sheer negligee. Who would have guessed it? Llewelyn had married her. The idea pleases him: as pictures come into his mind of the cluttered kitchen with dog food spilled on the counter he realizes that he had liked her, in her vague way. She must not have left him before the end, he thinks; must have stayed with him. For what? Surely Llewelyn had no estate of any significance.

"Do you see any photos in there?" Robin asks.

"Nope."

Is it possible, then, that old dying Llewelyn and young bleary Sherrie had in fact shared something between them beyond sex and Llewelyn's patronization? He thinks about it. Could they, in their fashion, have loved each other?

Love. The word darts around inside his mind, reverberates in the chambers of his skull. It makes him uneasy and he tries

The Unspoken

to stop thinking about it. He looks at the picture of Llewelyn on the dust jacket of the book. But it is not the Llewelyn who had known Sherrie: the Llewelyn in the photo predates Sherrie's very existence by fifteen years. The two Llewelyns are entirely separate, he thinks; different beings who had existed in different universes.

Robin sighs and watches Priscilla rummaging through the box.

"I guess we won't find anything," he says. "I seem to remember that we destroyed everything anyway...she and I. Everything that...pertained to us. To us together."

Priscilla nods. "You look pale, Robin."

He shakes his head. "I'm all right. I just thought we would find some things. I don't know."

"Want me to pack up this stuff and take it downstairs?"

"No. No, let's leave it here. I'll dig through it all in more detail later."

"Okay." She begins placing the clothing in the box again.

"Funny," Robin says.

"What?"

He looks at her. "I just thought of something. A dream I used to have. I would be floating over this huge glittering ocean and see an island in the distance. And when I floated toward the island I would see a person on it. I didn't know who it was, or even if it was a man or a woman. But I always knew that I was in love with that person, whoever it was. I wanted us to be together forever. I had that dream off and on, every now and then, for years. Since I was a kid. I don't know what made me think of it just now."

"Do you still have it?" she asks.

"No," Robin answers. "I don't have it anymore. I don't dream at all anymore."

5

"You have some mail, dear," Aunt Margaret says.

It is early afternoon. Robin and Priscilla sit watching a movie on television.

"Thank you." He takes the envelope from Aunt Margaret's hand and looks at it: the shape of a card rather than a letter, the address written in elegant calligraphy.

"Who's it from?" Priscilla asks.

"I don't know." He slits it open with his finger and draws out a cream-white folded card, on the cover of which is gold-embossed the letters *R.S.V.P.*

"Looks like you're invited to something," Priscilla says, leaning over and looking over at the card.

"Mm." Robin opens it and reads: *The Pleasure of Your Company and Your Guest's is Kindly Requested at a Banquet in Honor of Our Son, Michael R. Lyon, to be held at the Hollowstone Community Hall*...There follows a date and time.

"Michael R. Lyon?" Priscilla asks. "Who's that?"

Robin stares at the card. "A guy I used to go to high school with."

"Why are they giving a banquet for him?"

"I don't know." He flips the card over absently. "It doesn't say." He pictures the boy with the golden features, the Greek-sculpture body, the fine tenor voice: so perfect as to be nearly a parody of perfection itself. "But Michael Lyon is the kind of guy people give banquets for."

"You're friends with him?"

"I haven't seen him since the day I graduated high school."

"Lyon...isn't there a politician in Oregon called Lyon?"

Robin nods. "Roy Lyon. In the state legislature. Or at least he used to be...I don't know if he is anymore." Robin considers for a moment. "Anyway, this is his son."

"Probably be a big shindig then."

"I bet."

"You going to go?"

He looks at the television screen. "I'm not sure I'm up to it."

"I think it would be good for you," Priscilla says, taking the invitation from him. "See some old friends. Why not? You don't have to stay long. You can take me."

"I don't know."

"C'mon. It'll do you good."

"I don't think so."

"Sure it will." Priscilla turns her head and shouts into the kitchen: "Mom!"

"Yes, dear?" comes the voice in response.

"Help me convince Robin that he should go to this banquet he's been invited to!"

After a moment, Margaret appears again. "You've been invited somewhere?"

"It's a banquet for an old high school friend of his," Priscilla says. "Here he gets this big fancy invitation—see? But he's too glum. I don't think he wants to go."

"I'm not glum," Robin says.

"Why don't you go, dear?" Aunt Margaret says, looking at the invitation. "Take Cissy with you."

"There, see?" Priscilla says, looking at him. She sticks her tongue out.

Robin looks at the floor. "I don't know. I haven't really seen anybody besides you guys since…"

"And it's time you started," Priscilla interrupts.

"I think it's a good idea, dear," Margaret offers.

Robin sighs. "Okay, okay. Maybe I'll try." He looks at Priscilla. "But I don't promise I'll stay long."

Aunt Margaret smiles. It seems to Robin that her eyes are melancholy. "Well, dear," she says, "now that that's settled, would you come into the kitchen? I have something to show you."

"Me?" Robin says.

"Mm-hm."

He stands and the two of them move into the kitchen, leaving Priscilla with the movie.

"Sit down, dear," Aunt Margaret says.

He sits. "What's going on?"

She looks out the window for a moment, then at Robin. "Your father wanted me to give you something."

"What?"

She looks at him a moment longer, her wide mouth frowning, then goes to a drawer and brings out a tiny brown envelope. She brings it back to the table and sits down next to him.

She pushes the envelope toward him gingerly. "Your father... he asked me to give this to you."

"Why didn't he give it to me himself?"

"Dear, I..." Her face is sorrowful and perplexed. "I don't know. He just asked me to give it to you. We thought we should wait until you were strong enough."

"For what?" He opens the envelope.

Onto the table falls a ring: a gold band with golden leaf-clusters surrounding a small diamond in the center.

He exhales. "God..."

The light-rays from the gem bounce and flash and in a rush it comes back to him: the figure sitting next to him on the bed, the darkness, the hiccups, the fingers at his pajama buttons.

He takes the ring in his fingers and gazes at it.

"It was removed," Aunt Margaret says, "before she was...before she was cremated."

Robin nods and rising before him suddenly is another hand, smaller, touching his face and running down his body, her lips and tongue, her dark eyes gazing into his own, her whispered voice in darkness.

"Heather," he says, his voice flat.

"Hey! What's up in here?" Priscilla bounces into the room. "How come you guys up and left me with that dumb movie?"

"Cissy..." Robin notices Margaret's gesture toward him.

"Oh," Priscilla says. "Sorry."

"It's all right," Robin says, sitting up straight and putting the ring back into its envelope. He looks at the two of them. "Just more old stuff. It doesn't matter."

"Are you sure, dear?" Aunt Margaret says.

His eyes move from Margaret to Priscilla and back again. "Come on, you guys. You're both creeping around me like you think I'm going to explode or something."

Priscilla smiles and steps to him, wrapping his head in her arms. "We're just worried about you, you dope," she says.

"You don't have to worry."

He hears hard breathing, gasps, sees a girl's open thighs before him, feels her tiny hands tangled in his hair.

Priscilla lets go of him. "Isn't it time for lunch? Robin, are you hungry?"

Although he is not he says, "Sure," and Priscilla and Aunt Margaret move about in the kitchen, opening the refrigerator and closing it, rattling pans and dishes.

He is on a San Francisco street corner, the sweet smells of flowers and fried food all around, her little body against his, her tongue warm in his mouth.

"Would you like your bread toasted, dear?" Aunt Margaret asks.

Wrapped tightly in a black coat and mittens she scampers across the icy snow crying, *Look at me!* as she flings out her arms for balance and slides on both feet toward him, her breathless laughter filling the air.

"Yes, toasted, please."

"Do you like mustard?" Priscilla asks.

"No, just mayonnaise."

"*Fat,*" Priscilla says. "Yucko."

He fingers the tiny envelope on the table, feels the hard circular shape inside.

Aunt Margaret looks out the window as she places the sandwiches on plates. "I'll never get used to this Wind Point weather," she says. "Fog, just fog all the time. Robin, you should come see us in Runningwater. Clear skies do so much for a person's disposition." She smiles and puts a plate before him.

"My mom would have called this a diamond day," Robin says.

Margaret and Priscilla bring their plates to the table and sit. "That's an expression our father used," Margaret says.

Robin glances at her. "I never knew that."

"Oh, yes." She nods.

"When you were growing up?"

"Mm-hm. When we were children."

Robin stares at his sandwich. He has seen pictures of his long-dead grandparents, but cannot visualize younger versions of his mother and Aunt Margaret: cannot see them as little girls running about, playing. But then, he realizes, he has never really been able to think of Aunt Margaret as his mother's *sister:* she was always just a silly, giddy woman who appeared in his life now and then when he was a child. He has never seen any true connection between them. They are strangers: isolated, lost.

"Anyway," Margaret says, sighing, "it's better not to talk about these things. Cissy, would you pass the pickles, please?"

He remembers that only a few days before his mind had been a nearly blank slate dotted only sporadically by image or sound. Now it is turning to jumble. As he watches television, as he walks in town with Priscilla, a chaotic confusion swirls within him, a mad parade, a barrage. When someone speaks to him he can hardly hear over the figures and voices inside him: Llewelyn and Sherrie and Michael Lyon and his mother as a leaping and laughing little girl and, most of all, most insistent, a pair of small hands and big round eyes and the smell of her and the sound of her whispered voice. They pour over him like wild ribbons of film raining down. He cannot sort any of them out and he feels unfocused, distracted. He will try to blot them out: say to himself: *Be here. Now.* But it works only for a moment; then the pictures and voices take over again.

"Aunt Margaret?" he says when they return from their walk. "Do you know where my wallet is?"

"Why, yes, dear," she says from the hallway. "It's in the kitchen drawer."

"What do you want your wallet for?" Priscilla asks.

"Oh, nothing." He moves to the kitchen. "It's just that I haven't seen it since...you know. Maybe there's a million dollars in it."

"That would be nice. Then you could pay me my back wages."

Robin smiles and opens the drawer next to the refrigerator. He finds it under the telephone book: familiarly curved brown leather.

"Here it is." He does not look inside it; glances instead at Priscilla. "I'm all in. I'm going to take a little nap."

"Okay."

Robin moves up the stairs to his room, closes the door behind him. He glances at his box of things in the corner and then drops onto the bed and unfolds the wallet.

Sixty-two dollars; an old movie stub. He pulls out the clear plastic card-retainer, knowing what he is looking for: bypasses a driver's license (expired), bank teller machine card, gasoline credit card, social security card: then, suddenly bursting into his vision, is the photograph.

It comes back to him. They had meant to destroy everything related to the two of them, and had largely succeeded: no letters remained, no photographs hidden away. He remembers their reasoning: remembers thinking that there was something indecent about other people coming along later and violating what had been theirs alone. Yes, he remembers now. Stacks of photographs, heaps of love-notes had been charred to ashes in the kitchen sink. Everything had to be destroyed. Yes. But—he smiles grimly at the irony—in all their diggings into old boxes and dusty corners, they had neglected the wallet he was carrying in his own back pocket. And she is there now, in the photograph: head tossed back in laughter, the familiar hat, her arms stretched behind her head. It is as if no time has passed at all, as if at any moment she could creep up beside him on the bed and whisper to him and draw him into her. The disparate bits of memory, the eyes, the small hands, suddenly come together into a solid image: and from this single photograph he can see her vividly, in focus, in dozens of other scenes and places and times.

He brings the brown envelope from his pocket and feels the hard ring inside it. Heather, he thinks. He runs the name through his mind, searching for any feeling he can connect to it. No: there is none. He can remember her face and voice and movements, can see her now in the photograph unchanged, can touch the hard ring inside the envelope, but no feeling attaches to any of it. It is interesting in an intellectual way to recreate her like this, almost as an anthropologist would, from a few bits and pieces. But it is nothing he has any feeling about. Especially when he thinks of the new information, the orphanage and foster homes and the odd, unconnected name, Lilly Brown: he realizes then that he does not know her now, but also that he had never known her, never really known a thing about her, and he tries to visualize the new facts, her old life, but the faces of the foster parents appear as mere shadows and the orphanage becomes mixed inside his mind with the set of an old movie of *Oliver Twist*. No, he knows nothing of the endlessly laughing face in the photograph. She is a stranger.

The Unspoken

As he gazes at the image in the photo he wonders if it might have been different if she had told him the truth. He remembers her stories of happy families and loving fathers and mothers and siblings: she had lied, lied from the beginning, but had it made a difference? Would the truth have been any more real? He knows the truth of his mother's younger days and yet they are unreal to him; and his father? The Midwest, Korea? It all seems a mirage. And so what difference, he wonders, would it have made? The past, he thinks, never makes any difference at all. It is dead, smoke in wind, lost.

Perhaps, then, he thinks, there is after all only what he remembers seeking throughout his old, lost lives: the perpetual instant, free of old meaningless baggage. The future is unknowable; the past irretrievable; and thus it is only the moment-to-moment fact of existence, of life, of being in that instant something that is not nothing.

He looks at the photograph, meaningless dead pictures fluttering through his mind. He remembers something Llewelyn had told him, that there is no wisdom, only continuance; no dazzling light of revelation, only wandering, marauding like a shark in the depths. He had not wanted to accept it then; wished in his youthful passion that a way could be found to burst into some new super-reality; but perhaps Llewelyn had been right all along. Perhaps there are no answers at all.

Such thoughts make him weary and he reclines on the bed looking at the photograph, letting the images and sounds dash across his mind. He sees her crooked grin and feels her hands on his bare back and watches as her small breasts bounce with his thrusts and it is all as if he were watching a film in a theater, a film made by someone else with actors he has never met. None of it has any connection to him and he feels nothing about it. It is dead and gone and therefore of no value whatever. Feeling itself is dead, he thinks. Lost. A thick sleep overcomes him.

There is a sharp rap on his door.

His eyes snap open. "Yes?"

"It's dinnertime, Robin."

The voice is his father's. He feels his heart beating and opens his mouth to reply; but no sound comes: and the footsteps proceed heavily down the stairs.

"...I'm coming," he mutters then, to no one.

It is dusk. He had fallen asleep with the photograph on his chest and the ring enfolded in his palm: he puts them away before standing and moving to the bathroom. He splashes water on his face and looks into the mirror: still pale, he sees, eyes still sunken. It occurs to him that save for the eyes themselves—which are big and Siamese-shaped, sky-blue—it is very much the face of his own father, his father as he exists in the old black-and-white photographs in the albums. He presses his palms to his cheeks: the hair, the shape of the head, the jaw line—they are nearly identical. He does not have his father's eyes, nor his hooked nose, but otherwise his face is nearly the same. He had never really noticed before. As a child, he remembers, he had resembled his mother far more: not only the eyes, but the face itself, which had been round and pale like hers. What had happened to that face? he wonders. For it is truly gone now. Now when he looks into the mirror he sees photographs of a man in his thirties with a full head of hair grinning next to an old shiny sports car or with his arm wrapped around a young woman who would later, he knows, grow clumsy and misalign his pajama buttons and—he remembers suddenly—perhaps not be there at all, instead replaced by her darker twin. He looks at his reflection in the mirror, breathing.

Later, downstairs, the four of them eat in near silence. He watches his father only in glances: the man is still in his insurance-office garb, white shirt and tie loose at the neck and slacks.

Priscilla and Margaret carry the conversation. Occasionally he or his father will say something, but never, Robin notices, to each other: not once in a solid hour's conversation do they address one word to the other. Nor do their eyes meet. He considers this and thinks to himself that there is no logical reason that he should be so incapable of speaking to the man: there is nothing to it but opening his mouth and bringing forth sound. And yet the idea strikes a kind of terror in him.

Now this is very interesting, he thinks: a bona-fide *feeling*. A feeling of fear, admittedly, but nonetheless it is a feeling, something he had not been able to discover in thinking about his mother or Heather. It is odd, this feeling, lodged somewhere inside him: an unfamiliar sensation. He had been so utterly lacking in any such thing for so long that he had forgotten what it is like. As he sits there eating, his body begins to seem like a wire being slowly drawn tight: he can feel his heart beating faster, his breath coming quicker. Absurdly, there is something nearly pleasant in these sensations. Not that he is enjoying the fear itself, but the fact of its presence, the fact that it is *there,* is somewhat amazing.

They finish the meal and his father goes upstairs to change. Robin's fear subsides and he desultorily helps with drying the dishes.

Afterwards he and Priscilla bring out the old family photo albums and sit thumbing through them. He can remember these old images: though he finds, strangely, that the events themselves are largely gone from his mind: what he remembers is seeing the pictures themselves in earlier times.

"Hey, look!" Priscilla says, pointing. "Here we are!"

They must be six or seven in the photo, Priscilla still a fat, ugly little girl, Robin himself obviously painfully shy before the camera: they sit together awkwardly on the grass in the front yard, the pepper tree behind them.

"I sure was an ugly kid, wasn't I?" Priscilla says. "Jesus."

"You were a late bloomer," Robin says.

"Late is right. But *you* were cute."

"I don't even remember this. When I think of you as a kid I think of when we ran away together. Remember?"

She smiles. "Sure I do. But we knew each other before that. I remember, even if you don't. I hated you."

"Why?"

"I was jealous of you. You were cute and everybody loved you. It seemed like you had everything."

"I seem to recall that I hated you too. I thought you were obnoxious."

"I'm sure I was!"

It is strange looking at these early photos: himself, his mother's arms wrapped around him, and even a shot of the three of them, himself and his mother and father, all together and grinning before a Christmas tree in the living room. He looks no older than seven: before the rivers of amber and the slurred voices and stains in the rug. It seems not to be connected to him in any way. The woman in the photo is long dead and the other two people have disappeared. It is a picture of ghosts.

They continue turning the pages for many minutes, Robin sometimes sensing a tweaked memory; more often feeling nothing at all. After a while he hears footsteps descending the stairs and he tenses as a shadow falls over the pages from behind. He does not look up; after a moment the shadow moves away and he hears the TV being switched on. He feels the tightness seep out of him then and looks vaguely at the many images in the album. He is interested to realize that when he looks at the pictures of his mother, he can tell—still, a decade later!—exactly what condition she was in when they were taken. In some she is perfectly sober; but in most she is in some stage of disintegration. In a few she is wildly drunk. But, he knows, no one but himself would have any idea of any of this. To Priscilla, he is sure, they are all merely shots of Robin's mother. But he can tell immediately, with every single shot: mostly it is her eyes, but also her smile, the way she is standing: even ten years later the signs and signals are vivid in his mind.

With his father it is more difficult. There are not nearly so many photos of him; and in most, even when he is smiling, his eyes seem to glare at the camera, almost as if to challenge it. The glare masks what might otherwise be telltale signs. But then, he realizes, he had never been so sure with his father: had never studied and scrutinized him the way he had his mother. Not, at least, until later, until high school, when the house became a dangerous place and he needed to be able to read the signs.

And now? he wonders, the pages turning. Since coming back he has not seen his father take a drink, not once; and yet something else has changed. The evil twin is not here but neither, it seems to him, is his father. The silent shadow moving about the house seems to be neither one: for the shadow is older than anyone Robin can remember ever living here, his hair is white and his skin sags, but more crucially there is a flat and uncertain look in his eyes that Robin cannot understand. A tentativeness. Robin has never seen it before. In a way it frightens him. *I Can Insure Your Future,* he thinks. He sees a fish bursting from the turbulent seas, leaping frantically, and hears the man's voice: *You've got one! You've got one!*

He looks at the photographs again. He and his father in bright sunlight, outfitted for tennis. Tennis: bright Sunday mornings: he remembers them suddenly, remembers the simple physical pleasure of banging at a ball with a racket and watching his father's body moving with surprising grace to return it. The court drenched with sun. And later, pleasantly exhausted, the two of them sitting across from each other in an outdoor cafe talking of easy things, sports, school. He remembers it with a sensation of ease, of pleasantness. The darkness was far away then, in those sunny mornings. He had known it would return but it had been gone then, in those moments.

The pages turn. He sees earlier versions of himself growing progressively older. The more recent the photos are, he notices, the less clearly he can remember the incidents they depict: *I can remember all the old things,* a raspy voice says.

Finally they reach the last pages and for a moment Robin is unsure of what he is looking at. He has no recollection of these photos at all. Himself; his father; a woman he vaguely remembers; a huge, sprawling Christmas tree jammed up against the ceiling; and there, in one photo, next to him...

"Robin?" Priscilla says, pointing. "Is that her?"

His heart seems to jump once inside his chest. In the photo they are embracing while grinning toward the camera. Her foot is raised. He looks uncomfortable; she is laughing. He has never seen the photo before; he is sure of it; and a sudden feeling of eerie exhilaration floods into him. For an instant, seeing her in this new unexpected moment, it is as if she is alive again: not simply remembered, as with the familiar photo in his wallet, but actually alive, breathing. He looks up suddenly, thinking she must be here now, in the kitchen or living room.

"Robin?"

"What?" He looks over at Priscilla quickly; remembers. "Oh." He slows his breathing. "Oh, yes, that's her."

"Pretty."

"Yes." He stares at the photo. "She's smaller than I remembered. Funny. I've never seen this picture before."

"Really?"

"I'd forgotten it was even taken. But I remember now. Christmas...a while back. She and I came from my college. We were here a couple of days."

"That's the end of the pictures," Priscilla says, looking at the next page.

"So much for memory lane," Robin smiles, turning back to the photo of himself and Heather again. "I should have this copied. Just to have it."

"Sure."

"I'll do it." He removes the photo from the album and holds it in his hand.

She looks at him. "You're okay, right?"

He gives her a sour look. "I don't know…I keep thinking how easily I could hang myself with that belt around your waist."

She laughs. "Sorry."

"Or that letter-opener on the table there. A perfect dagger to pierce my heart. Or your nail file. All I'd need to do is mosey on over to a friendly light socket…"

"Okay, okay!"

But in truth, he thinks later, it makes little difference. He has fragments of sensation, bits of feeling, but they are jagged and irrelevant; he has not been dead, but he has been near it, and he is unable to see that there is any great overriding reason to prefer one to the other, life over death. He is existing in a state of grayness. True, he is learning to mask it better around Priscilla and Aunt Margaret. But he is the same nonetheless.

It is interesting, however, to study in the privacy of his bedroom the two photographs: the one familiar, the other new: the one from the Florida cafe seems old, frozen, dead, while the new picture of the two of them together is uncannily alive. He studies her dark shirt and the way her arms and hands are wrapped around his waist. He had felt warmth then, he knows. He must have. For a moment he almost senses that he can feel it again.

He studies her face and the creases that have appeared in it because of her grin: for a moment he can smell her hair again, exactly as he must have when she had been standing there: but it vanishes.

He wishes that he could hear her voice. He can reproduce it perfectly inside his mind; but he wishes that his ears could actually receive it again. It would be interesting to hear if it sounded just as he remembers it. But it is lost; he thinks for many minutes, but can recall no time they might have recorded it. Thus he stares at the photographs. He feels nothing toward them but a vague, intellectual interest; no anger, no melancholia. Nothing.

After a time he hears footsteps approaching on the stairs. They ascend slowly, methodically; they reach the hall and come toward him. He feels himself tense.

The footsteps pass by. A door closes. A toilet flushes. The house is silent.

6

As they approach it in the darkness, the community hall in Hollowstone appears to Robin rather like a movie palace of the nineteen-forties on the night of a splashy premiere. Searchlights on the front lawn cross and crisscross the night sky; the building itself is bathed in colored lights; orchestral music pours into the night air from within; men in tuxedoes park cars and escort guests to the door. An image skirts across Robin's mind from *The Great Gatsby*.

"Holy moley," Priscilla says, turning the steering wheel. "Robin, you brought the invitation, right?"

"Mm-hm. And I sent a reply to the R.S.V.P."

"Good. I hope they'll let a couple of bums like us *in*. Do I look all right?"

"You look fine," he says. She does: an attractive cream-colored dress and simple, stylish jewelry.

"I'd better. This is my *only* good dress."

Robin glances down at himself, at the dark blue dress-jacket and pants unworn for years. "I think we're both pretty respectable," he says.

"Do you feel all right?"

"Mm-hm. Fine."

"Okay. Remember, we don't have to stay long if you don't want to. But give it a try."

"I will." He feels a certain sluggishness in his muscles and his mind is rather dull; but he is all right. As they park the car he finds himself thinking about Michael Lyon. He wonders what five years will have done to the boy's appearance: if he will have begun to gain weight or lose hair, if a thickness will have set into his limbs, a pallor come to his previously golden skin. He had looked at himself in the mirror before they left the house and certainly he himself has changed: he looks thin and pale and generally unhealthy. Likely the same has happened even to the ethereal Michael Lyon, he thinks; even to his paramour Kathy Collins…Kathy Lyon now, he supposes. He imagines she will be here. He wonders what other ghosts may be wandering in the halls or lounging around the swimming pool just behind the hall.

They step from the car and Priscilla takes Robin's arm in her own. There is a tremendous crush of people near the entrance.

"Whoever this friend of yours is," Priscilla says, "he must be awful popular!"

"He always was," Robin says, touching the invitation in his jacket pocket. Glancing at Priscilla he says, "You look nice. You really do. Elegant."

She laughs, tossing her hair. "I'm about as elegant as a cow in a field," she says. "But I can fake it once in a while."

Robin smiles. "You're even wearing heels."

"I can *barely* walk on them. I never really learned."

"I'll catch you."

She grins. "You too."

They arrive at the front of the line where, Robin sees, the printed invitations are being checked against a multi-paged list. He feels anticipation running through his dullness: he is growing increasingly curious as to what time will have wrought on the golden Michael Lyon. It would be amusing, he thinks, to see in him the beginnings of a receding hairline or stomach flab. And certainly such things must be beginning to happen: for even Michael Lyon, he knows, exists within time.

Robin nods vaguely to the man standing there looking at the invitations and looks away. He stands there a brief moment, Priscilla's arm pleasantly around his, when he hears his name suddenly shouted: "*Robin!*"

He looks up at the man holding the list and invitation. The man is grinning down at Robin but for a long moment Robin has no idea who he is. The man is dressed in some sort of elegant military uniform, blue and white, and he is large, even beefy; Robin looks up at the face and sees, under the close-cropped hair, a pair of brown eyes and thick lips set in a well-tanned face. Then it strikes him.

"Davy?" he gasps. "*Davy Carp?*"

"One and the same, man!" The big man reaches out and takes Robin's hand in his own, a huge grin on his face. "I didn't know you were coming to this fandango!"

"My God!" Robin says, looking at the handsome young sailor before him. "I didn't recognizes you!"

Davy laughs. "That's the U.S. Navy for you! Listen, man, I've got to get the rest of these people through the line. I'll see you in there, okay?"

"Okay..." They are pushed forward suddenly.

"Friend of yours?" Priscilla asks him.

"Yeah -- an old friend -- he used to be..."

They arrive inside the auditorium. It is dimly lit and filled with milling couples. A small orchestra plays in one corner and the stage at the front has been decked out with streamers and a huge banner reading: *Welcome Michael Lyon.*

"Golly," Priscilla says, "what a layout."

"Yeah."

"Hey," she says, "it looks like the drinks are over there."

They move toward the lengthy bar, covered with white tablecloths. A perky bartender gives Priscilla champagne and Robin a soft drink.

"I wonder what we're celebrating?" Priscilla asks, sipping from her glass and smiling. "Champagne tickles my nose."

"I guess we'll find out soon enough."

"What's through there?" She points to the big rear doors.

"The municipal pool."

"Mm."

Robin looks around at the myriad faces. He does not see anyone he recognizes; but then he thinks again of Davy Carp at the door. Davy Carp! He had not recognized him; but how could he? The man who had stood before him had been muscular and handsome. Where, he wonders, is the boy with the mud-colored eyes who used to stay up late watching *Outer Limits*? Good Lord! The change is unimaginable.

"Robin!" Priscilla says in her slow voice, suddenly grinning. "Let's dance. Do you want to dance?"

"I'm not much of a dancer."

"Come on. Everybody else is." She is right: couples have begun moving gracefully around the center of the auditorium to the sound of the orchestra's slow, romantic violins.

"I don't know," he says.

"Come *on*."

He sighs. "Anna Karenina spent a lot of time dancing...and look what happened to her."

"Who's Anna Karenina?"

"A character in one of those million-pounders."

"And what happened to her?"

"Threw herself in front of a train."

Priscilla laughs and takes him by the hand. "Just for that I'm going to *make* you dance." She takes the drink from his hand and pulls him to the center of the floor, wrapping her arms around him. They rotate slowly, the music soft, facilely romantic.

"See?" she says. "It's not so bad. You do know how to dance."

"Sure," he says in the dim light, "but I figured I wasn't exactly your type."

She smiles.

"Have you talked to Koofie?" he asks. "Lately?"

"I did a few nights ago."

"And?"

"I'll see her soon."

"What does your mom think about all this, anyway?"

"Mom is funny." She rests her head on Robin's chest. "We've never really *talked* about it. I mean as an issue. She's dealt with it really well, though. So has my dad."

"That's good. Unusual, too."

"Uh-huh. Mom always knew anyway. That's the idea I get. I don't mean it was *easy* for them, but they've accepted it. I think."

"Good." He moves slowly to the music, feeling her warm back under his hands. He presses her close to him, enjoying her warmth and the sensation of her arms wrapped around him. For a long moment he forgets entirely about Davy Carp and Michael Lyon and the people moving around them; thinks only of the soft warmth pressed against him. He sees her high above the Santa Barbara vista, the foothills and mountains behind her. He sees the two of them at the river, feels the warm grass underneath them. They are such *living* scenes, he thinks; there is so much life in them, in her and the wind and the hills and the spears of grass. It is strange for him to consider this warmth next to him in places like Africa and India and Asia: she seems still, in a peculiar way, so much the little girl walking along behind him at the river. Not that she looks anything like that girl; not that she talks or moves like her, not really; but there is something else, an essence, which is there still, undiminished by time: something inextinguishably herself. What it is he cannot define. But it is there. And so it is difficult for him to picture her in those unimaginably distant scenes: having been in those places, having done those things, how can she still be recognizably Priscilla Wilder, the girl he remembers from years ago? Shouldn't she have changed completely, become unknowable? And yet here she is: she is herself: and their memories of each other are shared memories of the same events.

It is an odd sensation, thinking about this. Odd but vaguely pleasant. How long has he known her? Since he was six or seven. Periodic visits then, to Wind Point or to Runningwater; the sudden blossoming of their relationship at the river, hours after the disaster; then a long period, years, of nothing but sporadic Christmas cards, until he had seen her again in Santa Barbara. And when he had met her there he knew time had passed, she was a young woman, but still, still there was this sense of her as the same person she had been: within time, yes, but not actually different, not another *self*, as he had so often felt about the face and body people referred to as Robin Withers. And as he thinks about it, the two of them revolving slowly under the colored lights, he pictures the river, the grass, her glistening body, the bottle of Orange Crush spilling: the doe staring at them from across the water: and abruptly, for a vivid instant, he is there again: it is not an unfamiliar little boy long-since lost to time but he, himself, there in the grass, looking out from his own eyes at the doe and at her, at the glittering waters, breathing the sweet marijuana smoke, feeling the warm breeze on his face. The boy's eyes are his again for a wild moment and he inhales sharply, amazed.

"Robin?" Priscilla looks at him.

He shakes his head. "Nothing...it's nothing." He feels a mad exhilaration rushing through him and he grins, blinking rapidly. "Nothing, I...I'm just enjoying this. I really am."

She smiles up at him. "I like that smile," she says. "I haven't seen one of those on you for a long time."

"I..." He presses her to him again. The scene blinks before his eyes: he sees her twelve-year-old face with astonishing clarity: hears her voice: but now, unlike every other time he has ever remembered her, he is not watching her through old eyes but young ones: the eyes he had then, at that time: it is now bright, crystalline, the whole scene, the sounds and atmospheres, the colors and tones, he is inside it, not viewing it across lost time but actually living it again.

He breathes. He has never felt such a sensation before: such a feeling of his memory-images as real things, not mere fading photos of dead ghosts; living, breathing scenes and people and voices. And himself within them. Not someone else, not a lost shadow, but he himself, as he is now, connected, seeing through the same eyes, speaking with the same voice. Many times he has had sudden vivid memories: but always he had pictured them as an observer, looking back over years of ashes and silence. But the river, the doe, Priscilla: for an instant they had been real, tangible. For an instant it had been as if time did not exist at all, as if the perpetual instant were not one moment but all moments, all time.

The orchestra stops playing and there is applause. He looks around himself, holding Priscilla close, sharp bolts of undefinable sensation shooting through him.

"Had enough?"

He looks at her. Then he nods. "Sure, let's…let's take a breather."

They sit in two of the chairs which surround the dance floor and Priscilla retrieves their drinks. At last Robin sees the large man in the military dress uniform coming toward him.

"Man!" Davy says, holding out his hand again.

Robin stands, greeting him, and introduces Priscilla.

"Your cousin?" Davy says, shaking Priscilla's hand. "Robin, I thought you'd gone off and gotten married!"

"Not yet," Robin smiles. He simply cannot believe that the resplendent figure before him is little Davy Carp: the body is bigger, stronger, carries itself with calm authority; even the voice is deeper, confident.

"Well, mine's around here somewhere," Davy says, looking around. "Don't know where she's gotten to."

"You're married?" Robin asks.

"Uh-huh. A year now."

"Well, that's great. Really. Great." Robin tries to smile. "So you're not in the Philippines anymore?"

"Nah. Got myself transferred Stateside. My wife didn't like it there…neither did I, actually."

Robin realizes abruptly that to see Davy Carp's face he must look not down but up. "Davy," he says, "where did you get all this *height?*"

Davy laughs, a resonant, booming laugh. "I had a growth spurt just after I joined the Navy. Put on almost four inches."

"And your build…"

"Comes from working out," he grins. "Courtesy of the U.S. Navy gym."

"My God," Robin says. "You know, I didn't recognize you earlier."

He laughs again. "I know you didn't. Most people from around here don't." His eyes wander from Robin and he calls suddenly, "Linda! Linda?"

In a moment they are joined by a young woman in a delicate taffeta dress. She is, Robin thinks, very beautiful: long auburn hair, green eyes, a fine complexion lightly tanned.

"This is my wife Linda," Davy announces.

Introductions are made. Robin feels a giddy sense of unreality coming over him: Davy Carp, handsome, muscular, well-spoken, with an attractive young wife....

"Hey, Davy," Robin says. "What exactly is this affair for, anyway? I mean, what are we celebrating?"

"Don't you know?" Davy grins. "Our old friend Michael Lyon's entering politics. This is a fund-raiser."

Robin glances at Priscilla. They laugh together.

"I'll have to wish him good luck getting any money out of either of *us*," Robin says. "I don't have a dime to my name. What about you, Priscilla?"

"I guess I could hock my dress," she says.

They all laugh.

"Isn't Lyon a little young to be in politics?" Robin asks.

Davy nods. "But in a year he'll be old enough. He'll have just finished law school and that's when his campaign'll really go into full swing. See, his dad's making a run for the House of Representatives in Washington. It looks like he'll probably get it, so the plan is to get Michael into the same seat in the state legislature his dad has now." He grins. "Like father like son."

"How do you know all this?"

"I've seen him every once in a while. That's how I ended up with the job this evening. I see him with his wife now and then. And hey, speaking of that, you'd better be --"

"David," Linda breaks in, hanging on his arm, "I want to dance. Can we dance?"

He looks at her. "Are you sure you should? In your condition?" He grins at Robin again. "We're going to have a baby Carp."

Congratulations are duly offered.

"Well, all right then, we're going dancing," Davy says, moving with his wife toward the dance floor. "Robin, I'll see you a little later, okay?"

"Sure," Robin says, watching them move off into the circling couples. After a moment he mutters, "Jesus Christ."

"What?"

Robin gestures toward the disappearing couple. "*Him*," he says. "You should have seen him in high school. Nothing like that at all. Little. Scrawny. Maladjusted."

"Really? He looks like somebody who would have been a football star."

"Ha! Davy Carp?" He shakes his head in disbelief. Time has swooped down on Davy all right, he thinks; but instead of draining and destroying him, turning him into a colorless husk, it has made him magnificent. "People made *fun* of Davy Carp in high school."

"So, he gets the last laugh."

"I guess so. On me."

"You stop," she says, squeezing his hand.

They sit again. A peculiar feeling flows over him: half-melancholy, half-euphoria, he cannot make it out. He knows it is connected with time. Something about the figures before him: the reincarnated Davy Carp, the warm touch of Priscilla: they fill him with a strange sensation, a confusion of emotion: not simply fear or terror or dread, something else, something infinitely subtler and more complex, but what it is he cannot define.

There is a commotion and bustle near the entrance of the building and Robin thinks he sees, just for an instant, a glimpse of Michael Lyon entering the hall. He cannot be sure; but he knows he is right when the entire room suddenly explodes into applause and cheering and the lights come up.

"What are we clapping for?" Priscilla asks.

"The guest of honor, I think."

Robin watches. Between the haze of bodies he can see, in sporadic glimpses, Michael Lyon's hand waving greetings and reaching out to people's outstretched arms. The orchestra's lush violins cease; after a moment's pause they flow into a swelling, string-heavy version of "Stars and Stripes Forever." Robin suddenly wants to laugh.

"Come on," Priscilla says dryly. "John Philip Sousa?"

"That's Michael Lyon," Robin grins. "Not even out of law school yet and he's already being inaugurated."

Behind Michael Lyon, Robin sees, are now arriving Roy Lyon and his wife: he recognizes the man from stories on television. The couple is greeted happily enough by the crowd, he notices, but not with the ecstasy Michael Lyon himself receives: the son, he thinks, is already outdistancing the father. He tries to get a good look at Michael Lyon, hoping to see the beginnings of a paunch or a receding hairline, but cannot yet see him well. Surely, he thinks, time cannot have done to him what it has done to Davy Carp: Michael Lyon's magnificence had been such in high school that there could have been no place to go but down. He waits with anticipation for the vision to come into view. As he watches he realizes that there is someone with Michael Lyon: a bright pink dress is moving along with him. Kathy Collins, he thinks. Or Kathy Lyon. Or Kathy Collins-Lyon. Whatever she is called now, he can see already, just from the dress -- he cannot make out her face in the confusion -- that she has kept her exquisite style and grace, her deathless image as a woman destined to be the charming and supportive wife of a state legislator, a senator, a president. He glimpses a bare, creamy arm reaching toward someone's hand and wonders how many Hollowstone High boys' fantasies included that arm.

"It looks like his wife's with him," Robin says. "Kathy Collins. They got engaged on the day we all graduated high school."

The Lyon entourage makes its way slowly toward Robin and Priscilla. The cheering and applause continue. At last, after several minutes (the orchestra is now into "America the Beautiful"), Robin can see him more clearly: the golden hair, the million-dollar smile: and oddly enough, impossible though it is for Robin to believe, Michael Lyon appears to have changed not at all. He looks, for all the world, exactly the same. The same! Robin thinks, aghast. No difference at all! The group comes closer, laughing, shaking hands, and he sees that it is true: they might as well be graduating high school again. He has lost no hair. Gained no weight. His ridiculously graceful stride has not changed a whit.

"What do you think of him?" he asks Priscilla, over the noise.

"Not bad!" Priscilla grins.

Not bad is a massive understatement, Robin knows. The effect -- the smile, the grace, the perfectly tailored suit -- is absolutely electric. Roy Lyon himself, a respected and long-standing state legislator, pales in comparison to his son.

At last Michael Lyon is almost next to Robin and Robin's pulse flutters wildly as he anticipates the moment the young man's eyes will fall on him. He wonders if Michael Lyon even remembers him. He suspects not. How could he, after the years of Yale or Harvard or whatever it is, after years of associating with the rich and great?

But suddenly the eyes move, connect with his own, and the beaming grin seems almost to take on another dimension. "Robin Withers!" he says, taking Robin's hand and shaking it enthusiastically. "Robin! It's fantastic to see you!"

The voice is the same as well: everything is the same. Robin smiles. "Nice to see you, Michael. How are you?"

"I'm great, just great! It's been so long since I've seen you! How have you been?"

"Oh," Robin says, "just fine!"

"That's great! Robin, you've met my wife, haven't you?" He turns away slightly, toward her.

"Well, I remember her from high school --"

"Oh, yes, sure you do! Honey?" He touches the creamy arm. She turns to them.

For one fantastic instant it is as if all the people and sound vanish entirely. For an instant Robin is floating in interstellar space entirely alone, with only the woman's face before him: he cannot believe it: it is impossible: it is absolutely inconceivable: and yet, as she opens her mouth, as the remembered voice floats forth into his consciousness, he knows that it is so.

"Hidee-hi!" Marylou Kirk says.

Michael Lyon interjects: "Marylou, you remember Robin Withers, don't you? From high school?"

She reaches out her hand blithely and Robin shakes it. For a moment he cannot speak. His mouth hangs open.

"Robin Witherson?" Marylou says. "I'm not sure..." Her face takes on a look of pretty puzzlement. Of course, Robin thinks, of course. It's her. It's really her. His mind flashes back to endless hours behind a typewriter, pounding out English papers: and later, a bedroom of cutesy animal posters and a cold, slimy cement prison around himself.

"Sure you do!" Michael Lyon grins. "He was the school's writer. He did a play all by himself once, remember? It was produced and everything. Kind of a Greek thing. Very good."

"Oh, of *course*," she says, beaming blankly at him.

In the moment it takes Michael Lyon to refresh her memory, Robin recovers some semblance of composure. He is thinking again. He closes his mouth.

"Hi, Marylou," he says. "How are you?"

"I'm *wonderful*," she says gaily; and her eyes move from him. In that final moment before her attention is diverted their eyes meet: and she has no idea, he knows, none whatsoever, who he is.

An image flashes into his mind of a hotel sign glowing red in the darkness: VACANCY.

"Michael!" he says, catching him before his attention moves elsewhere.

"What's that?" Michael Lyon leans close to him. "I couldn't hear you!"

"Michael, what happened to Kathy Collins? I thought you married her!"

Michael Lyon grins. "Holy smoke, you have a good memory! No, we called it off. Then I got to know Marylou and let me tell you, it was the greatest thing in my life to discover her. She's like no other woman in the world!"

Robin realizes he is giggling. "No, that's for sure!" he says.

"I'll see you later, Robin! Maybe after the dinner!" And Michael Lyon and wife are swept away.

Robin looks to his left, where Priscilla had been standing a moment before. She is not there; the crowd has pushed them apart. He means to look for her but his body is rifled with giggles. He is not sure why. But there is something funny about Michael Lyon and Miss Goody Two Shoes together: something hilarious: and the giggles bounce and bounce through him as insistently as hiccups. He cannot control them. He pictures her little-girl pigtails and her silly little-girl dresses and hears her little-girl voice within his mind and it seems the funniest thing in the world. He watches them ascend the steps to the stage, all four of them, Michael Lyon and Marylou Kirk (Marylou Lyon? Marylou Kirk-Lyon? the giggles threaten to burst from him), the two elder Lyons, and he sees himself in her bedroom -- himself! Not an earlier, dead incarnation, but himself, sees through his own eyes her passionless body lying on the bed. The giggles begin to grow uncontrollable. Michael Lyon! Married to Marylou Kirk! At last, for once in his life, a thing to which Robin Withers has beaten Michael Lyon! And what, he wonders, what would Michael Lyon think if he knew about his wife's adventures with Robin Withers? What would he say? A tremendous sense of victory overcomes him, of triumph. Michael Lyon may have everything, but he, Robin Withers, has had Michael Lyon's wife….

He pulls away from the crowd, his giggles erupting in loud burbles. He cannot contain himself. He must escape or he will dissolve into helpless laughter in front of everyone. Already people are glancing at him. He moves blindly toward a rear door, pictures pouring over him, remembering how he had thought of Michael Lyon as having the key to fields of sensuality he himself would never have, and yet, unknown at the time, Robin Withers had discovered Michael Lyon's future before him! He sees the girl under him, remembers the sensationless pushing into her, the feel of her dress, her bone-blank eyes staring at him…At last he finds a door and pushes it open, making his way out into the cool darkness and letting loose an uproarious explosion of laughter. He does not think he has ever laughed so hard in his life. He laughs until his stomach grows sore and he falls to his knees.

Finally, after several minutes, the mad laughter subsides to sporadic giggles again and he is able to look around himself. He has found his way behind the building and before him is the municipal swimming pool, glittering in the darkness. Overhead the stars are as bright as knife-points.

The sounds from the gathering within seem distant.

He is alone. The pool, illuminated by two dim safety lights, is very still. He sits against the wall of the building, feels the giggles subside at last.

He realizes suddenly that he is completely exhausted. The laughter has drained him and he sits there unmoving, staring thoughtlessly at the blue waters.

It is then that he notices something. For a long moment he stares toward the glittering pool, his mind free of thought or emotion: a flat blank. Slowly, without conscious effort, he begins to stand up again, his back rubbing hard against the wall. He feels his heart fluttering like a lark inside his chest.

Standing there, directly over the pool, is his mother. She wears a billowy white nightgown and her dark curls tumble to her shoulders. Her feet are bare, suspended inches above the waters.

He stares at her. Her round face is not evanescent as it is within his memory; instead it is harshly real. He can see her skin and her bright siamese eyes, her full lips and strong chin. She is not a vaporous creature of fantasy but his mother, suspended there, herself. He sees her as surely as he does the pool itself. She is there.

"Mom," he whispers.

She looks toward him and smiles. He remembers the smile. It seems, in that moment, as if no time has passed at all: as if she had never gone away: as if it is the most perfectly natural thing in the world that she should be here, now, above the waters.

"Hello, Robin," she says.

He moves toward the pool slowly. He can hear his footsteps as his hard soles scrape across the concrete. He cannot take his eyes off her. The sounds behind him have faded to nothingness and he hears only his footsteps moving toward the gently-waving waters.

He arrives at the edge of the pool. She is but a few feet from him.

"Hi, Mom," he says.

Then, behind her, he sees another figure. This one is smaller, darker, wearing a dark outfit with a blouse unbuttoned to her stomach exposing a streak of pale skin. Her feet are also bare.

"Hi, Robin," she says.

"Hi, Heather," he says.

His eyes move from one to the other and back again.

"Are you ghosts?" he asks finally.

The suspended figures say nothing.

He feels his heart beating. He is standing at the very edge of the pool and can see the depthless blue water before him.

"Are you?" he repeats.

"Robin," his mother says at last, "didn't I tell you I would come back?"

"Yes."

"And Robin," the floating Heather says, "aren't we part of each other? I'm you. Remember?"

"I remember."

There is a pause. He feels their eyes on him.

"What do you want?" he asks.

They stare at him with small smiles on their faces.

"What? What do you want?"

"Come with us, Robin," his mother says.

"Yes," Heather says, "come with us."

He breathes. He feels himself tense.

"Where?" he says.

"To where we are," his mother says.

"Where are you?"

"Come with us, Robin," Heather says.

"Yes," his mother echoes, "come with us."

"I..." He swallows. "What are you? Ghosts? Demons?"

"I'm your mother, Robin," the woman says.

"Are you?"

She looks at him with her crystalline eyes. "Baby," she says, her voice low and soft, "I've missed you so much. So much."

"And Robin," Heather says, "I thought we were going to be together forever. Here. In this place."

"Did you?"

"Come with us, Robin," his mother says.

"Yes," Heather echoes, "come with us."

"How?" he whispers.

Together the two of them open their arms to him.

He stands at the edge of the pool. His legs are weak.

"Come here, baby," his mother whispers. "You've had a nightmare. Come here."

"Come here, baby," Heather whispers. "I've missed you so."

"You've just had a bad dream," his mother whispers. "Everything will be all right. Come here, baby. Let me hold you."

"Let me touch you again, Robin," Heather whispers. "Let me touch you again and feel you inside me. Come here, baby. Please."

"Come here, Robin," his mother whispers. "I love you. We both do."

"We love you, Robin," Heather whispers.

"We love you."

The ends of his feet hang off the concrete into empty space. He looks down at the endless liquid blue beneath him. The reflections of the two women, fragmented, multi-prismed, gaze back at him. He looks up again. They smile with deep caring in their eyes and hold open their arms. He feels himself breathing. He looks down.

"Come to us, baby."

"Come here."

"That's it. Just a step."

"Just a step."

"Come closer…"

There is the sudden *snak* of a door opening behind him. He starts; takes a step back from the pool, looks toward the door.

"Robin?" Priscilla says. "What are you doing?"

"I…" He looks at her face, far away in the darkness. She stands there with one hand on the open door and one against the doorframe. Then his eyes dart back to the pool.

They stand there, the two of them, hovering over the water and smiling.

"I…"

"Why don't you come in?" Priscilla says. "Are you tired? Do you want to go home?"

"I...No..."

"Then c'mon inside. You missed your friend's little speech but it's time to eat now. They've opened up the banquet room. Looks pretty snazzy. Smells good too. Aren't you hungry?"

"I..." He looks at her. Then again at the figures over the pool.

"Robin, we love you so much," his mother whispers.

"Please, Robin," Heather whispers. "Please."

He gazes at their faces, the two of them there suspended in the darkness. Suddenly something threatens to overflow from him, to burst out: he does not know what: his entire life, perhaps, everything that has ever happened to him in the world: he looks into their eyes: he looks: and for one instant all the silences and unspoken images of his life coalesce into one inexpressible moment of perfect clarity.

"Robin?" Priscilla says. "Are you coming?"

He looks for a final time at the beautiful ghosts, suspended like unmoored islands in their nameless darkness. Then he whispers: "Goodbye."

He turns toward Priscilla then and says, "I'm coming...Yes, I'm coming."

7

The old professor lies alone in his bed, his life evaporating slowly away. Pictures waft across his mind of his wife, dead for years, and his son, killed in the war many decades ago; then he sees his mother, his father, hears the sound of his own footsteps running across summer grass in his youth. The sound of laughing children under the window reaches his ears and within his mind the children's voices become mixed with his own voice as a child, with sounds of his own friends' laughter eighty years ago, all of them dead now, and before him rises a vision of himself at five, hair slicked down, ready for school in his little blue suit and short tie and tiny briefcase: then all the visions fragment and dissolve, until all he knows is the sound of the children's laughter, and he feels a joy, an exquisite ecstasy as his mind looses itself from his body and floats, borne up by the voices and laughter, into eternity.

Robin closes the book and places it beside himself on the bed. It is a long moment before the room reassembles itself around him: a moment in which the professor and his final vision fade only slowly, hovering as if suspended in space. At last it dissolves away; and Robin sits there, emotion coursing through him. He looks at the jacket photo of Llewelyn, young, dramatic: remembers the clumsy old man deriding his own work. The two are difficult to connect but there is a connection, a bridge between them. It was the elder Llewelyn whose judgement had been clouded, along with Robin's own; for the story is, he realizes now, exquisite and beautiful. And yet it is also flawed, he knows. He had suspected as much when he had re-read, earlier in the evening, the musty pages of *Drowning* and it had occurred to him that the primary mistake of both might well be the same. And he is right, he knows. *Drowning* has, it seems to him, artistic merit: but its fatal flaw is the same one that mars the otherwise magnificent old professor.

He hears Llewelyn in his mind: *That story is fucked-up.* He had been right. He had been wrong in his cursory dismissal of the story as a whole but he had been right on that point. It *is* flawed; and *Drowning*, while not on Llewelyn's level, shares the flaw. It is clear to him now. He is certain of it.

Both the stories, he thinks, portray death as appealing, desirable; even romantic. The old professor dies in an ecstasy of memory, just the same as Siegel and the cloud and the shore. But it is a lie. He understands it now. His mind flashes across Heather's body gasping in the middle of the desert; his mother charred to ashes, dumped into the sea; Uncle Jasper's brown scar-lines and face crumbling with age and encroaching death; and blue lights passing by above him, his body heaving and wrenching, a bed with hidden straps. At the end, he thinks, at the very end, at the moment the violins fade at last into the deep blue of eternity, there is rebellion. And in that way even Mahler is a lie, the Ninth Symphony and *Das Lied von der Erde*: those gentle, sorrowful fade-outs to oblivion: death is not that way, he knows. He remembers vividly the desert. Pictures pour over him that he had repressed until now: the two of them in the car -- they had decided, they had planned, they were resolved, and yet at the end, when it came to the moment, they had fought back! There had been no gentle lolling into nothingness, no slow dissolution, *ewig, ewig*, not for either of them. She had come with him from the car and tried to walk, to move, to live. In the final moments her body had been rebelling, trying to breathe, to see, to feel. And he had been trying too. At the ultimate moment, he had said -- they both had said -- *no*. All the plans and justifications in the world would not change that fact. Had it been merely fear? he wonders. Simple last-minute fright? No. Fear had been an element, but it was not a fear of death itself: it was a fear of leaving life. A subtle but profound difference. And so Siegel and the old professor, even the lovely ghost Mahler and his *ewig*, are lies. That does not negate their value as art, he thinks, which exists on its own terms, in its own reality. But the attitudes themselves are lies. There is nothing gentle or ecstatic about death. The body always knows this even if the brain forgets, and it will rebel, always rebel, in the face of it.

He closes his eyes. He is not afraid of death, he knows. He is afraid of not having life. He is afraid of the disintegration that will come when life is no longer. That he will continue he knows: that his atoms and molecules will not end but go on, redistributed to a million consciousness and life-forms, lilies and lions and the rays of the sun: this is true: but he himself, as he is now, will cease. This is what frightens him. This is what has caused stark terror to flow through his veins. Not ending, for there is no real ending: what he is will exist forever: but the cessation of what he is now, entering into a different, new intensity, one in which he continues to exist even while Robin Withers ceases forever, this unimaginable synthesis of matter and time is what causes his heart to hammer in his chest. And how it hammers! How it pounds and thunders not like a frightened bird now but like a marvelous stallion in its stall, how it drives pulsing life through his veins and into his fingers and hands and brain! He rebels at the very thought of stoppage, creates tempests of life within him to shout it down. Why had he never listened? Why had he never understood?

Death will come, he knows. It will come as surely as a hellish demon stalking its victim in the darkness. Robin Withers will exist as a thinking, breathing entity for only a fraction of an instant on the scale of infinite cosmic time. But to cut it short, to scatter Robin Withers prematurely to the winds, would be to go against everything his mind and spirit and body tell him. It is not a logical conclusion; but like Siegel, he distrusts logic when it runs counter to everything he feels, every instinct he has. There is a place for intuition. And there is a place for the driving force of life that cannot be analyzed or explicated. In the end he is left with himself sensing and listening to the life-force within him, his own private bit of light against the immense darkness, ultimately as unknowable as eternity itself. But there, flowing within him. He can call it anything, for names do not matter; they are only metaphors. It is the life-force or it is light. It is the spark or the oneness. It is *I*. It is God.

※

Alone, the sun shining a hazy yellow through the mist, he wanders among the Wind Point tombstones. The fog leaves a clammy patina on his face. His hands are buried deep in his pockets; there is a cold wind, stinging to his skin. He watches seagulls swoop and dive in the turbulent air, vanishing as they fly out toward the sea.

He knows no one here, but some of the family names are familiar: Rosselli, Klibo; and the sight of the names brings to his mind the vision of the endless line of stones, an entire family and its history in a smooth geometrical progression in the grass. It had been that way with the Ashers family, he remembers. And he can recall visualizing how April's grave would look when the time came for it, comfortably in its historic place. There had been something pleasant in the idea; to know, if not when he was to die or how, at least where one would end up. But April had not looked at it that way. April had found it ghoulish. And perhaps, he thinks, she had been right, though in a different way: for it was untrue. There was no finality to the long line of graves; they would endure a hundred years or two hundred, perhaps a little longer, until at last there was no one left alive who cared anything about the names on the old stones: and young men, not even dreamed of when the open and receiving earth had first been scooped out, would take new miraculous machines and rip away the useless, decayed wooden crates of vegetal dust. They would build a shopping mall then, or a baseball field, or a launching pad for rockets to sail through interstellar space. And the bones they had dug up, what remained of them, would be summarily heaped into a waste dump or tossed into the sea. The stones themselves, these stolid recorders of lives once lived which he now wanders among and reads, would be smashed to bits and used for walls or roofs or bridges or inconceivable highways to the stars.

There is no permanence here, he thinks, staring at the stones. He looks out toward the fog-filled ocean then, images blinking into his mind of tiny blackened bits floating down through the echoing darkness; dissolving, coming apart, swallowed by huge slick sea-creatures or settling into the watery bottom; dissolving further and still further, always dissolving, becoming one with fish and plankton and sea-plants. Millions of years of dissolutions and redistributions in an endless chain. But even then, he thinks, there is no permanence. He looks up at the hazy light in the sky. He imagines it softening and expanding like a massive yellow jelly, swallowing the sky, engulfing the earth, berserk and blinding heat bursting apart all the graves and highways, all the living and dead, in an instant of cataclysmic oblivion. And the tiniest bits of all of them, everything known and unknown, cast into the infinity of deepest space: to waft in nothingness for a flicker of an instant in endless cosmic time, a million years or two million: until at last the atoms and molecules would be caught in the orbits of other planets circling other stars and sail downward to what awaited them there.

He feels the wind on his face as he looks toward the cherry trees, heavy with blossoms, which line the graveyard. Pictures bounce inside his mind: he sees his father at the other end of the graveyard looking toward him. It is extraordinarily clear, this picture: not dead and still, but vibrant and living, and the boy in the picture is not a remote stranger but himself, he looks out through his own eyes across the grass toward the figure there in the sun. He blinks. Before him then is Cape, the two of them together in the enfolding darkness, shrouded in dirty blankets. He can feel him and smell him and it is he himself who is with Cape, his own eyes, his own sensations. He blinks and is with April in the trailer, feeling her sandy hair in his fingers, hearing her Virginia accent in his ears. He is on the telephone to her and she is shouting at him and crying. He remembers: and he feels a sudden pain, an ache. Should he have asked her forgiveness? Is it possible? Can anyone, finally, ever forgive anyone for anything?

He stares at the blossoming cherry trees across the grass and takes a few steps toward them. As he walks his fingers move in his pockets and he feels the hard round ring in his fingers and the cool stone and rough leaf-clusters. The blossoms overhang the fence and he stands before them, leaning forward to inhale their scent. He hears the foghorn lowing into the sky and the seagulls. What he feels he cannot formulate into words or sentences or a logical progression of ideas: all words seem hopelessly inadequate and void. Love? Forgiveness? Even mourning: for as he fingers the ring in his hand, as he breathes the blossoms which bring to his mind pictures of standing on a San Francisco street-corner with drops of rain splashing on their faces and her tongue warmly wrapped in his, he has no idea of its meaning. And for whom, he wonders, would he mourn? The girl whose pictures even now flash before his eyes (a crooked grin, her small hand in his)? But she had not been real: she had had a false name and false history: Heather Seabright was a lie. There was no Heather Seabright, had never been. If he had loved her he had loved an illusion. Her name was Lilly Brown and she grew up in an orphanage and she had never, not once, allowed herself to be seen by him. Another pang clenches at him. There had been *something* real about her, he knows; he had not lived for so long with a figure of vapor and air; but the reality he knew had been a false one. Lies, he thinks. Lies, endless lies, a life of lies. But why? He thinks about this for minutes, realizing he has never before considered the question: What could have made her reject everything and refuse, always refuse, to admit the truth -- even to him? What could possibly have happened?

And yet as he thinks of it he realizes he will never know: the answers have been scattered into the blue deep for all time. A strange, sick feeling begins to overcome him, to think of ten years passing and twenty and fifty and never knowing, never receiving any answer, remaining always in the silent darkness. Like a shark, he thinks, wandering in the depths. But perhaps it is unreasonable to think of answers, of finality. He thinks of himself and Heather and everyone and everything scattered in veils of dust across space: all answers then, all conclusions, must always be tentative and temporary, for they will wander, all of them, forever through the voiceless halls of infinity, never ceasing, moving always into new lives and dimensions and intensities, striding like giants across space and time.

He fingers the ring in his hand, looking up at the sparkling gray sky. He hears voices inside him, one after another, layer upon layer: and they speak to him, all of them, to him, not to earlier lost versions of himself but directly to him: they are alive within his mind, vivid not as ancient ashes of an irretrievable past but as breathing pieces of an infinite present. They are alive because they are part and parcel of the identity of Robin Withers. All of them are alive, not recaptured but captured for the first time. The voices and pictures flash across his brain, sounds and echoes and movements, and he is one with them, with all of them, expressions and eyes, lights and darkness, rooms and atmospheres. They pour over him and he feels something welling up, threatening to overflow.

He gazes at the hanging blossoms before him and as he looks at them one petal breaks loose and is cast upon the wind. It swoops and swirls and tumbles in the air, does flips and somersaults, dives and rises again. As he watches the petal it seems to him that he has never seen such an exquisitely beautiful thing in his life. And as he watches the petal all the old things flood over him, the old things and the new ones, all the images and cries; for past and present and future are, he knows, merely metaphors for what is really an infinite instant of time without beginning or end. And in the final voyage through eternity, all atoms are the same atoms: all life the same life. Robin Withers will end but in another form he will live forever, one with all matter and energy that are the universe. For *he* is the universe, he knows. He is the universe as surely as the grass or the trees or the soft petal dancing on puffs of air.

He watches the petal. There is still pain, he knows. And fear. And regret. But they are all bits of the same oneness. They are there still because any journey into unknown dimensions will always generate them. But they are no more important than a spear of grass or a floating petal of pink and white. The perpetual instant, he knows, is not to live without those ribbons of time called the past but rather with them, always, and with all other time present and future.

The petal comes to rest in the grass at his feet and he kneels down to it. He touches its tiny pillowy softness and over him pours all the time of his life and suddenly he realizes that he is crying. It pours out of him at first thickly and slowly, in erratic bursts, then begins to flow, heavy sobs wracking his body. He feels the salty water streaming down his cheeks and into his mouth and he hears the sounds he makes, the choked and twisted sounds, and it pours from him in an unstoppable flood, an explosion for all things and all time, for the woman in the white gown whispering of diamond days and the naked girl in the bed saying I'm you, I'm you, for the old man with the red scar over his chest and the tractor-motor voice and the old man in the cluttered study talking of percentages and deals; for the shadow-man lurking on the dark stairs; for the strong body in the dark van and the girl with the baseball cap and sunny smile; for all of them, for Priscilla Wilder and Koofie Mortenson and Aunt Margaret, for Leonard Turnham and Michael Lyon and Marylou Kirk and Kathy Collins and Davy Carp and Melissa Rosselli and Sonya Skyler, for all the living and the dead, but most of all for the blonde boy in the bedroom whose heart pumps in the fright-filled dark: he weeps for all of them, tears neither of sadness nor joy but simply feeling, sensation, emotion: life itself: he crouches in the grass and weeps for them. He weeps.

8

Bulbous clouds lay scattered across the sky overhead. Robin and Priscilla sprawl in the grass beside the drooping pepper tree: Robin watches the sunlight shine in broken yellow beams through the limbs and branches.

"What a lazy Sunday," Priscilla says.

"Mm-hm."

"And clear, too. Pretty."

"It must be the first good day we've had this year, I think."

They lay in silence then, not touching, looking up at the patchy blue sky.

"So," Robin says. "Tomorrow you're going."

"Mm-hm."

"And you'll see Koofie...?"

"In a couple of days. My mom and me will go back to Runningwater. Then I'm going to Las Vegas. That's where we're going to meet."

Robin smiles. "Why Las Vegas?"

"We decided we needed a holiday together. Have some fun."

"Long drive. Big desert."

"I know." Without looking at him she touches his hand. "But I don't plan on staying in it as long as you did."

He chuckles. He feels an enormous calmness within him.

"Are you two going to make it, then?" he asks.

She nods, looking at the sky. "I think so."

"I'll miss you, you know."

She grins. "Anybody would miss a free nurse."

"Seriously."

"Seriously -- I know. And I'll miss you too. Really. What are you going to do?"

"I don't know. I guess I'd better start figuring it out."

"I don't think there's any rush."

"Well --" Robin considers it -- "without you two around, the politics of this house arrangement might become a little more difficult."

"I'm not so sure."

"Mm. You keep saying things like that."

She laughs.

"Priscilla --" He looks over at her again, remembering other grasses, other skies.

"Robin, you don't have to say anything."

"But --"

"You'll just embarrass me. You'll embarrass both of us."

He sighs. "Anyway," he says, "thank you."

"Thank my mom."

"I did. This morning."

They fall into silence again. Two children on bicycles, a boy and a girl, ride by laughing on the street before them.

"Were we ever that young?" Robin asks.

Priscilla chuckles. "Nah."

"It all seems so recent, though. It never used to. It used to feel like those things happened thousands of years ago to some other person. Now they seem like they happened...yesterday." He shrugs.

"Oh?" Priscilla says. "Am I still the ugly little goon I was?"

He looks over at her. She wears a pink shirt and black jeans with no shoes. Her hair is pleasantly unkempt, lying against the grass. Her close-set eyes, sparkling in the sunlight, look toward him. She is very pretty.

"Sure," he says. "You're that little goon. And somebody else too. A lot of somebody elses."

She smiles, rips up a bit of grass and tosses it at him. "You're insulting me."

"I am not."

"Are too."

"Am not."

"Are too. And I don't have to take your fluckin' insults."

Robin laughs. "I'd forgotten about that!" he says. "Your favorite word when you were a kid."

"I'd forgotten about it myself! Until just now."

He tosses a pinch of grass onto her forehead. "So, you see, I was right. That little girl's still in there."

"*Way* down, I hope," she laughs. "Buried very, very deep."

"I don't know. There were things I liked about you then."

"You didn't like me. You were afraid of me. I was a lot tougher than you."

Robin grins, moving close to her and pinning her arms to the grass. "I wonder if you still are?"

"Want to find out?"

"Just try it."

She tries to lift her arms from the grass. Robin holds them fast.

"Think you're smart, don't you?" Priscilla says, straining with effort.

"I don't think. I know."

"You don't know fluck." She lifts her leg and presses her bare foot to his stomach. "I could shove you off like a fly."

"Try it," Robin grins. "I dare you."

She pushes her foot into him and he falls to the side, his grip loosened on her arms. Laughing, she tumbles over onto him and they roll into the soft lower limbs of the pepper tree and Robin can feel the damp peppery mulch under him. She grabs his wrists and straddles him.

"Give?" she says breathlessly.

"Never," he grunts, trying to lift his arms. Then he tries to bounce her off by bucking his pelvis.

"Ho, ho," she grins, "you'll have to do better than that!"

But as she says it he dislodges her sufficiently so that she loses her balance. Her grip is loosened on his right arm and he pushes her down. They roll again, laughing hysterically, in the mulch and soft branches. The smell of the acrid pepper leaves is thick around them. Their struggling embrace is close and tight and Robin watches her face as she giggles, scowling with effort. She looks at him. Their lips press together suddenly.

Their giggles subside and they lay there under the tree, enveloped in its branches.

"Now that wasn't fair," Priscilla smiles.

"I didn't do anything. You did it."

"I didn't do it."

"You did too."

"Did not."

"What a liar you are. A bold-faced liar."

"*You* should talk."

Robin hears the front door open.

"Kids?" Aunt Margaret calls.

"We're under the tree!" Priscilla calls back. "Robin's trying to beat me up!"

"Cissy, would you two like some lemonade before you murder each other?"

"Sure!"

The door closes again and Priscilla moves to extricate herself from their tangle.

"Lemme go," she says.

"You just want to go because I'm winning."

"You were *losing*." She smiles down at him.

"No, sir."

"Yes, sir. It was going to be curtains for you."

She looks down at him, her hands on his shoulders. Then she leans forward and kisses him softly.

"There," she says. "Now can we get out from under this stupid tree?"

They sit out on the lawn in folding chairs, the four of them: Priscilla and Aunt Margaret and Robin and his father. They chat lightly of easy things. Robin glances at the figure beside him: the man wears corderoy slacks and brown sandals and an open-necked white shirt. He seems strangely quiet, but as Robin thinks of it he realizes that his father has been nearly silent ever since his son's return from -- what? Oblivion. Indeed, as he thinks of the many weeks that have passed by, he realizes that he cannot remember more than the most basic monosyllabic utterances coming from the man. It occurs to him that his father looks very old. He thinks of the glowing picture in the office window: *I Can Insure Your Future*: sees the auburn hair, the bright eyes. The man does not look like that now. Now his hair is nearly gone, and what little remains is a stark white. His eyes, when Robin glances at them, seem dull and tired. His skin hangs from his chin and arms.

The man is sitting within five feet of him but it might as well be five miles. He watches the man swallow the lemonade in the glass with an unmistakable listlessness and thinks of sunny Sunday mornings years ago, when they had batted balls to and fro on the tennis court. He cannot imagine doing such a thing with the weary spectre before him now. He remembers also another time, in a restaurant with the man's friends from the harbor, and their two hands clasping together and the man's eyes boring into him like searchlights slicing through a thick fog. And other pictures: a fish bursting from the icy salt water (*You've got one!*); the man blocking his path on the stairs, his voice wildly high-pitched, eyes frantic, crying *My money! My money!* A shadowy figure tearing into his bedroom in the middle of the night and ripping socks and shorts and shirts from his drawers wordlessly, stalking out again....

And he remembers the two of them. It is as bright as sun in his mind: their voices, late at night, stumbling in downstairs, brief grunts of question and answer, the sound of his body dropping into the leather chair, her arm pulling open the refrigerator door. Long silences between the three of them at the dinner table. Silences always: nights of the amber splashing into the rug in the living room, horrendous shouting matches, both their voices unnatural, unreal, and himself -- he, himself -- stopping his ears, closing his eyes. Then silence: perpetual silence: the next morning, silence: no mention of it, no acknowledgement, no words at all. Such silence that he had begun to wonder whether these things really happened or if they were simply figments of his sick, diseased imagination.

Sick. That was it, he knows. The sickness, the madness: that was where it began: the root from which all else sprang. For when they were silent afterward, when they said nothing and acted as if nothing had ever happened, he had begun to know -- to *know* -- that it was *he* who was wrong, not them: not him or her: for the shadow-man was unquestionable, unassailable, and she? She was incapable of lying to him. To pretend that nothing had ever happened, if something *had* happened, would have been a lie: therefore it had been necessarily true that nothing had happened. It had not been them. It was him. He was wrong. He was sick and evil and diseased: it was the only explanation. They were to blame for nothing, either of them. It was he himself, Robin Withers, who was guilty: whose sickness had created all the strange terrors and sentient silences that lurked in the dark house in the cul-de-sac. He was guilty of everything. He was the one with the sick unnatural thoughts and behaviors. They were perfect. They had to be -- yes, he realizes, this is it -- because if they were not, if *she* were not, then there would be nothing left but chaos and madness. And she agreed with the shadow-man; she agreed with her silence that there was nothing wrong with *them*. And so it was he himself. His sickness, his depravity, his guilt. They were entirely innocent of everything because it was necessary for them to be. There had to be, in this conflict, someone right and someone wrong: and since *she* could not be wrong, it was him. Yes.

He looks at the man sitting next to him. They had planted it in him, he realizes: unwittingly, yes, but they had planted it as surely as a seed in the soil. There could be no other conclusion his mind could have come to, not at ten or eleven or twelve years old. Today, yes, today, in this afternoon of broken sunshine with the pleasant company of his cousin and aunt and the pleasant tartness of the icy lemonade in his hand, today he can see differently: can see that it was not his guilt but theirs which had doomed him, made everything all but inevitable. Yes, it is easy now, today. But then? When he had lain in the darkness feeling his heart pumping madly in his chest and listening to the footsteps ascending the stairs?

As Aunt Margaret prattles on about something or other he is suddenly filled with a murderous rage. He feels his hand gripping the arm of the folding chair as if to strangle it. His teeth grind together and sweat pops out of his pores. He closes his eyes for a moment, feeling his pulse inside his skull. He is not sick, he knows; and he is not guilty. Not for that, anyway; not for the dark clouds of silence and the slurred voices in the house in the cul-de-sac. For none of it is he guilty. It was not my fault, he thinks. *It was not my fault.*

He opens his eyes and as he does so he feels the rage begin to dissipate again. He swallows some of the lemonade and looks at the aging man next to him. He wonders why he does not feel angry with him, have the impulse to reach out and choke the life from him. But he does not. And as he thinks about it he realizes that the man sitting there is not guilty either. The man had been weak, and ineffectual, and mistaken; but it had been a situation over which none of them had had control: not himself, not the shadow-man, perhaps not even the woman with the pearls around her neck who talked of floating up to the moon. As horrible as it had been, none of them were truly guilty. There had been no intent, no deliberate malfeasance: and so there could be no guilt...But if there is no guilt, he thinks, there is also no innocence.

"Well," Aunt Margaret says airily, "if everyone is finished, I'll take these glasses in again." She stands and gathers the glasses onto a serving tray.

"I'll help, Mom," Priscilla says, and the two of them move off into the house.

Robin sits unmoving for a long moment, staring at the grass before him. The afternoon seems all at once to be awesomely quiet: there is no sound at all: until at last a light breeze ruffles the branches of the pepper tree.

He looks over at his father. The man sits with his hands covering the arms of the folding chair and his legs straight out before him. There are deep bags under his eyes and pinched, hard skin around them. He is frowning. And suddenly, instinctively, he understands that Priscilla had been right. He looks at his father sitting there tensely in the folding chair and realizes that the man is afraid of him.

He stands up then, moves a few paces to the pepper tree limbs and touches them absently. He can feel the man's eyes following him. He can hear the wind in the branches and blackbirds twittering somewhere above him. They remain like that, neither of them moving in the sunny afternoon.

"How are you feeling, Robin?" his father says at last, staring at the grass.

Robin swallows. "Fine," he says. "I feel fine."

There is a long pause.

"How are you feeling?" Robin asks.

His father shifts in his chair, does not look at him. "I don't feel so well these days," he says. "Maybe I'm getting old."

Robin listens to the wind in the tree.

"It hasn't been easy," Robin offers.

His father scowls and it occurs to Robin how very small the man looks, sitting there.

"No," his father says. "It's something else, though. I cut out the drinking. Doctor told me I had to. But still..."

Robin breathes. He has never once heard his father mention this subject, at least not when sober. He looks at the man's smooth forehead gleaming in the sun and the bright white hair around the back of his head.

"I haven't seen you -- drink," Robin says. "Not since I...since I got back."

The man scowls again, his eyes fixed on the grass. A long moment passes and Robin begins to think that the conversation is over. But just as he is about to turn away and move toward the house the man's voice reaches him again.

"I never thought it was a problem," the man says, not looking up. "I never missed work. I never got a ticket. It wasn't like with your mother."

Robin swallows again, looking at the man in the folding chair. His heart pumps.

"You know something, Robin?" And here his father glances up at him before returning his eyes to the grass. "I've figured out something in the past year."

Robin watches him.

"Maybe you already know it from all those books you're always reading. But it's new to me." He scowls again. "I've figured out what evil is."

Neither of them move.

Finally Robin asks, in a weak voice: "What is it?"

"*Lies.*" The man spits the word out with such venomous disgust that Robin jumps. There is another pause. Then he continues: "Lies. That's it. That's the whole of it." He seems to consider for a long moment. Then: "Where you've got truth you can't have evil. Where you've got..." He does not finish the sentence.

Overhead, patchy clouds cover the sun and uncover it. As Robin looks at the man in the chair he sees him going from light to shadow, shadow to light.

"Dad," he says, "was it really an accident?"

Nearly a full minute passes before the man speaks.

"I don't know," he says finally, in a strange emotionless voice. "I was ahead of her. I was crossing the street. We'd been...shouting. She stood at the corner and I said something like, 'The hell with it, I'm going home.' I was almost to the other side of the street when I heard it, and looked -- looked back."

Robin closes his eyes.

"She was..." His father hesitates. "I don't think it would have been a planned thing...She might have done it impulsively. Or it might have been an accident."

"Did she die right away?" he hears himself asking.

"About an hour later."

Robin exhales slowly. It is a long moment before he opens his eyes again. When he does, he looks at his father in the chair and the man seems to have visibly shrunk: he seems unbelievably small and fragile. The man does not look at him. They are silent.

At last Robin notices that a tiny green pepper leaf has landed in his father's white hair. It clings there, shivering in the light breeze.

Robin makes a step toward the man and reaches out his fingers.

"You've got something in your hair," he says.

The man sits there frozenly, eyes wide, as Robin's fingers pinch the leaf and pull it slowly from the white hair. As his fingers move away he can feel a strand of hair between them, wrapped together with the leaf. The hair has the soft quality of silk. It hovers in the air for an instant, then falls gently back to the man's head.

"What do you think, Robin?" the man asks, his voice tiny and distant as if floating toward him through millions of miles of dark space. "Time to go in?"

Robin's eyes sweep across the grass and the street and the houses. Blackbirds drift gracefully through the air. The pepper tree sighs softly.

"Sure," he says at last. "Time to go in."

Later, when the house is dark again and silent, he moves from his bedroom into the bathroom. He stops the tub and opens the faucets, watching as hot steamy water pours out. He strips off his clothes and stands naked at the sink, brushing his teeth. As the steam fills the bathroom the mirror begins to mist over and as Robin watches his reflection seems to soften and blur and lose detail until the face looking back at him could be almost any age. It could be the face of a twelve-year-old boy or a man in his thirties. He can make out only the blueness of the eyes and small well-formed nose. He can remember, years ago, visualizing a girl's features superimposed over the image; recalls the feeling that, being a boy, he must in some way have profoundly disappointed her. He wanted to be like her, not like him. And yet the loose dangling things between his legs made that in some essential way impossible. He knew that even then, for he recalls with perfectly clarity coming into this bathroom, this very bathroom, here, and her hot wet arms around him and her enormous nipples inches from his face. And then she had stood and the water had poured down her in a melting curtain and he had understood as he gazed at the soaking tuft of hair between her legs his difference, his inadequacy. He had hated himself for it, felt in some inexpressible way that he was responsible. That he had failed her.

And he supposes that in a strange and irrational way he still feels this; and perhaps always will. Logic makes no difference. Reason is ineffectual. For, he knows, his twelve-year-old self is still very much within him: not separate, not dead, but vibrant and living. And every other self at every other age, all of them together and jostling for position, for ascendency. There is no escaping the twelve-year-old, he thinks; he can only attempt to understand him.

He turns to the steam-filled bathtub and turns off the faucets. He looks at the tub and the soap dish and the towel rack, all so familiar to him, so laden with memory. He had half-expected her to appear again in this tub, to open her arms to him in the misty air. But the tub is empty. He steps into it gingerly, tingles shooting up his legs. He settles himself into it and closes his eyes, feeling his inner tensions seeping slowly away.

After a time he becomes aware that it is raining. He can hear the muffled pattering on the roof and the wind pushing against the house. There is a crack of faraway thunder. He listens sleepily, the hot soothing water nearly up to his neck. He feels his heart slowing and his muscles relaxing, all the tensions of the world flowing away into the water.

After a while the sound of the rain fades, diminishing to occasional small dripping sounds. The wind grows still.

Some time later he stands and pulls the plug from the tub. He steps out of the water and pats himself with a fuzzy towel. Then he switches off the bathroom light and moves into his bedroom, switching the light off there too.

He stands naked in the middle of the dark room, running the towel over his body. He places the towel over his closet doorknob and takes up a brush from his bureau, running it a few times through his hair. Then he places the brush down again.

The ring is there on the bureau, glittering in the darkness.

He looks at the ring, his heart beating slowly in his chest. He picks it up.

He moves to his bedroom window and opens it. The pepper tree branches are wet with rain and the odor from the branches and soaked earth below is intoxicating. The air is cold and fresh: he breathes deeply, evenly, aware of each breath's unique sensation. The sky is brilliantly clear. He holds the ring up to the streaming moonlight and watches it glitter and shine.

His attention is diverted then by a sound from the grass below. Peering down through the limbs and branches he sees a little boy standing there, on the lawn, looking up at him.

Their eyes meet; and though Robin stands naked at the window he feels no self-consciousness at the fact. They look at each other for a long moment in the stillness. Then the boy raises his arm and waves at him.

Robin studies the familiar figure below and understands. It is not a gesture of farewell, he knows. It is a greeting. He raises his arm and waves back to the boy.

Then he raises his eyes past the whispering and dripping branches to the star-packed sky above. He thinks that he has never seen so many stars, has never imagined that there could be so many in the universe. As he gazes at the stars they seem to glide toward him. Palms open, ring in hand, he reaches into the glittering sky, life coursing through his veins and all things, all time, the remembered and the forgotten, the spoken and the unspoken, merge within him. His eyes fill with stars.

9

The house is empty now. That which I have not thrown away or sold was packed a few weeks ago into a moving van that has taken the collection to New York; what I shall do with it there I am not sure. It amounted to little, after I had weeded through it as mercilessly as I could: a few boxes and crates, not very much more than I could have hauled in my own car. And so, with all the things gone, I can wander from room to room unimpeded by beds, dressers, lamps. My shoes make hard clicks along the rugless floors. In my own room there is nothing but a pair of window curtains. It seems bigger now, almost cavernous; the distance from the door to the window seems vast; the closet, hanging open, is like an empty mouth. Dust motes and scraps of paper rest in the corners.

In the bathroom the difference is not so noticeable. I have had the water switched off, and the faucets are dry; but otherwise it still looks much the same, clean and shiny, as if it were merely waiting for my mother to come in and drape fresh towels over the rack. Strange that I think always of my mother doing such things, even though I lived in this house for many years without her. But when I stand in this bathroom there is no doubt that what I hear is her soft humming. What I see is her face.

In my parents' room I see nothing, hear nothing. It is only four walls enclosing emptiness. The bed is gone, the dresser, everything that I remember: it belongs now to no one. This, I know, is as it should be -- and as it must be. It is nearly impossible for me to imagine, but the Withers family was not the first to live in this old house; it will not be the last. Other families, other lives will step through these rooms now, living and breathing creatures who will know nothing of anyone named Withers except as a name on a few legal forms. The thought is somehow frightening: but what frightens me, I realize, is not my own leaving here, nor other, unknown life-forms traipsing through these halls. What frightens me is the thought of my own mortality, my own leaving of life which will one day, inexorably, come.

I move from what was once my parents' room into the hallway. I stop at the window there and look out at the January morning, drizzling and bitter cold; think of sunrises, and myself sitting here wondering what it would be like to be blind Oedipus the King. Other children will peer out this window, I know, and just as children did before me, they will think their own thoughts and create their own fantasies. They will not think of Oedipus, and this causes a fleeting melancholy to brush over me; but it should not, I know. For that little boy exists now, here, in this moment; as he will always exist, he and everything else that has pierced the darkness with life. Changed, perhaps, redistributed; but existing, for all time. For time is only a single, endless moment stretching into eternity over which we, the living, stride like giants.

I move downstairs; I sit at my typewriter and begin working at this, my final chapter. As I write, the light overhead suddenly blinks out. They have cut the electricity.

I work now in the soft gray glow coming through the windows.

Of the principals in this story I can now tell you little. I remember hearing a few years ago that my old professor Leonard Turnham had remarried; he is still at the university. I occasionally hear from Davy Carp, who has become a career-man in the service: he is still married and has three or four children. He tells me he is good friends with Lieutenant Governor Lyon and his wife. My Aunt Margaret and Uncle Otto live still in Runningwater; I have thought of detouring to visit them on my way back. And Priscilla called me just a few nights ago.

"Am I going to have to sue you for libel?" she asked. "Or is it slander?"

"Libel," I said. "Slander is what you do with your tongue."

"Oh, God!" she laughed. "That's what somebody'll sue *me* for, then. Are you coming to see us before you head back to the Big Apple?"

"Sure I will. You can read the book."

"You'd better make a copy, in case I get mad and throw it in the fire."

"I'll take precautions."

"How long is it?"

"Long."

"A million-pounder?"

I chuckled. "Something like that."

"I knew it. Oh, well. I'll do my feeble best…"

The others I have lost contact with; they are scattered to the winds. But wherever they have gone, they live still within me: I can see them all with perfect vividness, Cape Barnes and April Ashers, Sonya Skyler, all of them. And I see the others too: Llewelyn and Uncle Jasper, my mother and father: all of them: even a small pale girl with a crooked grin and dark pool-like eyes.

The chronicle is finished now. In a few minutes I will gather up my typewriter and papers, my small bag of groceries, and take them to the car. Then I will step into the house again and make a final check of the downstairs. The house will be completely silent and I will move to the kitchen to close the curtains there for the last time. Then I will move toward the door and loosen the sashes of the front window. The drapes will fall gracefully closed.

I will stand at the door then, looking back into the empty house and listening for any sound. A soft breeze will rise outside and I will hear it passing through the leaves of the pepper tree. I will think of the new lives that will soon be here. Let them come, I will think: let them come—now or later, today or tomorrow.

Arcata, California
Tsabong, Botswana
Quito, Ecuador
Shepherdstown, West Virginia
Washington, D.C.
1987-1992

ABOUT THE AUTHOR

Christopher Conlon has written several critically-acclaimed novels, including the Bram Stoker Award finalists *Midnight on Mourn Street* and *A Matrix of Angels*. His prose and poetry have appeared in such varied periodicals as *Poets & Writers*, *America Magazine*, and *Filmfax*. Conlon's anthology *He Is Legend,* a gathering of original stories celebrating the fantasy writer Richard Matheson, was a selection of the Science Fiction Book Club and a winner of the Bram Stoker Award. Conlon lives in Silver Spring, Maryland. Visit him online at http://christopherconlon.com.

CPSIA information can be obtained
at www.ICGtesting.com
Printed in the USA
LVHW050553170519
618204LV00013B/123/P